Duncan Staff is a leading documentary maker who has produced a number of critically acclaimed and successful programmes. His work has been shown on BBC1, BBC2, Channel 4 and ITV's *World in Action*. He also writes for the national press, principally the *Guardian*.

www.**booksattransworld**.co.uk

THE LOST BOY

The definitive story of the Moors murders
and the search for the final victim

DUNCAN STAFF

BANTAM PRESS

LONDON • TORONTO • SYDNEY • AUCKLAND • JOHANNESBURG

TRANSWORLD PUBLISHERS
61–63 Uxbridge Road, London W5 5SA
a division of The Random House Group Ltd
www.booksattransworld.co.uk

First published in Great Britain
in 2007 by Bantam Press
a division of Transworld Publishers

A CIP catalogue record for this book
is available from the British Library.

ISBNs 9780593056929 (cased)
9780593058534 (tpb)

Addresses for Random House Group Ltd companies outside the UK
can be found at: www.randomhouse.co.uk
The Random House Group Ltd Reg. No. 954009

The Random House Group Ltd makes every effort to ensure that the papers used in its books
are made from trees that have been legally sourced from well-managed and credibly certified
forests. Our paper procurement policy can be found at: www.randomhouse.co.uk/paper.htm

Typeset in 12/15.5pt Times New Roman by
Falcon Oast Graphic Art Ltd.

Printed and bound in Great Britain by
Mackays of Chatham, Chatham, Kent

2 4 6 8 10 9 7 5 3

Freedom and power – power above all.

Fyodor Dostoevsky, *Crime and Punishment* (1866)

Contents

Acknowledgements

I could not have written this book without the support of Keith Bennett's family. In order to do justice to their faith I have drawn upon the help of a large number of people. It is not possible to acknowledge everyone who has helped me, and I apologize to those whose names I have omitted.

I would like to thank my wife, Lucy, for her reading, advice and support; my editor, Simon Thorogood, for his skilful, constructive criticism; and my agent, John Saddler, for finding the right publisher for this book. I have also received invaluable assistance from Professor Malcolm MacCulloch, Professor John Hunter, Professor Bruno Frohlich, Detective Chief Superintendent Geoff Knupfer, Detective Chief Superintendent Ivan Montgomery, Detective Chief Superintendent Barrie Simpson, Detective Superintendent Tony Brett, Detective Sergeant Fiona Robertshaw, Detective Constable Gail Jazmik, Detective Constable Alan Kibble, Detective Constable Andy Meekes, David Astor, Father Michael Teader, Andrew McCooey, Peter Simpson and Trisha Cairns. Finally, I would like to thank a teacher who inspired me, Professor David Blamires of Manchester University.

Introduction

It was a sunny Sunday morning in 1998, Bath's stone lit gold beneath the spring sky. I had my back door open, the newspapers spread out on the breakfast table, a steaming mug of black coffee in my hand. It had been a hard week in London, where I was directing a documentary series for BBC1, and I was looking forward to a day off.

Then, from the basement, came the sound of my office phone ringing. Reluctantly, I got up and ambled down the stairs, half hoping that the answering machine would kick in before I got there. I brushed some toast crumbs off my T-shirt and picked up the receiver.

'Hello, Duncan, it's Myra.'

I paused, startled, then stumbled, 'Hello . . . er, Myra . . . how are you?'

'I'm fine, thank you. I have decided that I will write my story for you.'

'Right . . .'

'A lot of people have asked me to do this, and I have refused.

But I am going to trust you. All I ask is that you are fair.'

I put the phone down and sank back in my chair. Myra Hindley was trying to get out of prison, and her case was due before the Court of Appeal. Months earlier I had written to suggest that she give an account of her role in the Moors murders. If she agreed, I would make a BBC documentary examining the case. My film would test the claim that she was bullied into killing five children by her lover, Ian Brady.

The Moors murderers were sentenced to life in 1966 for killing ten-year-old Lesley Ann Downey, twelve-year-old John Kilbride and seventeen-year-old Edward Evans. The trial judge recommended that Myra Hindley serve twenty-six years. By his reckoning she should have been freed in 1992. But the only person who could issue a licence for her release was the Home Secretary, and no politician wanted to be remembered as 'the man who freed Myra Hindley'.

From the day she was sentenced the families of the murdered children waged a campaign with a single aim: her death behind bars. The mother of Lesley Ann Downey, Ann West, was foremost in ensuring that her raw grief formed a part of every story on the Moors murders. Hindley's supporters, in particular Lord Frank Longford, only poured fuel on the fire by proclaiming, within a few years of her conviction, that she was 'a good girl' who should be released. Like many, he was convinced that she had covered up for Ian Brady out of blind love.

The story was a gift for the newspapers. All it took was a fresh line, a quote from a mother, the iconic arrest photograph, and they had a splash. Uniquely, the power of the Moors murders story never faded. Hindley made things worse for herself by maintaining the lie that she was innocent. Only after she had served twenty years did she finally admit her crimes, and confirm that there were another two children buried on Saddleworth

Moor: sixteen-year-old Pauline Reade and twelve-year-old Keith Bennett.

The tide of public opinion flowed strongly against her. The best she could hope for was that it might ebb enough for a judge to decide in her favour, and overrule the Home Secretary. Hindley saw writing to me, and the film I would make, as a way of saving herself.

I leant forward, stared at the telephone and swore under my breath. I had not really expected her to agree to my proposal. What had, in theory, seemed like a journalistically sound enterprise suddenly seemed fraught with difficulties. I would have to get very close to her to extract the story. Not only would this be distressing, but I ran the risk of being portrayed as a stooge by the tabloids.

The following Friday the first letter arrived. I slit open the envelope, pulled out eight pages of neatly typed words and began reading. The story felt carefully rehearsed but not fictitious; it had a strong, clear voice. I immediately realized that if she continued like this I would be able to make a very powerful documentary. I resolved to apply myself to the task. On the Sunday, I finished breakfast a little earlier than usual.

'Hello, Duncan. Did you get my letter?' She was standing in a corridor. I could hear the echo of footsteps and the rattle of keys in the background.

'Yes, Myra.'

'What did you think?'

'It was very clear, and the depth of the material was about right. It gives me enough detail to examine the credibility of what you are saying.'

'Good. I'll try to continue in the same way. You must let me know if I start rambling.'

'I don't really want to steer you, Myra. If you fail to address an important question I'll repeat it, but that's all.'

'Fair enough.'

We fell into a rhythm. Every week, when I got back from London, there was a letter lying on my desk. I read it straight away, jotted down notes for the Sunday call, and filed it. If not friends, we became familiar. It is impossible to tell your life story, whatever it may be, to a cold and distant stranger.

Things were going well. She described her childhood in Manchester, her teenage years, and the meeting with Ian Brady. But everything changed when she moved on to the murders. I did not find her explanation of how they came about convincing. The descent into violence seemed both inexplicable and horrific.

The words I read at the weekend began intruding into daily life; over time, they even entered my dreams. I began to question my ability to deal with the material in an even-handed manner, to disentangle truth from fiction. I realized that if I was to continue I would need professional help. A former head of Greater Manchester CID, Geoff Knupfer, pointed me in the direction of the forensic psychiatrist who had advised him. Malcolm MacCulloch has expert knowledge of sexually sadistic serial killers in general and the Moors murderers in particular. As the medical director of Park Lane Hospital on Merseyside he recommended Ian Brady's transfer from prison to psychiatric hospital, and spent a number of years treating him. I outlined the situation to him, and he suggested that we meet.

The following week I crossed the Severn bridge to Wales, where MacCulloch was professor of forensic psychiatry at the University of Cardiff. He also, in his spare time, edited *The British Journal of Forensic Psychiatry*. The door was opened by a small, neat man with receding hair and a pair of half-moon glasses.

'Come in, come in. What have you got there then?'

Malcolm MacCulloch did not bother with a lengthy social preamble. He communicated through his manner, as much as his words, that he recognized the journalistic tools I had deployed in pursuit of a story, and understood the situation I now found myself in. His directness, and incisiveness, allowed me to relax and be straightforward. He read through the letters and listened to recordings of my conversations with Myra Hindley.

'Why do you tape your calls?' he asked.

'To be sure I don't miss anything.'

'Very good.'

The professor squatted low over the tape recorder, listened to me laughing at one of her jokes. I shifted uncomfortably in my seat.

'She thinks she's got you,' he said.

'That's one of the reasons I'm here.'

'It's OK. It's all right.' He gave me a conspiratorial smile. 'I've questioned a lot of mass murderers. They have to feel that they are in charge or you get nothing.'

'The question is, am I being manipulated?'

'Of course you are, but you're also getting what you want. The trick is to remain alive to what's going on.'

The professor pulled off his half-moon glasses and held me in his gaze. 'You also have to understand that this is a unique, valuable opportunity to understand these crimes. It's a once-in-a-lifetime opportunity.' He added that he would read all future letters, and help me to frame questions that would get at the truth. 'Pro bono publico – it's in the public interest.'

I travelled back to England with my mind at rest; this was an important job that needed to be done properly. Over the coming days the nightmares faded as I took a more dispassionate view of the material. I also resolved to be more calculating in the way I dealt with Myra Hindley. This was easier said than done, as she retained an unnerving ability to catch me off guard.

'Hello, Duncan, it's Myra.'

'Hello, Myra.'

'Duncan, you have children, don't you?'

'Hmm . . .'

'They can be so mean to one another. The other day my nephew put a pillow on his baby cousin's head. Luckily his mother came in in time. It's just jealousy, isn't it? Do your children get jealous of one another?'

Her anecdote was meant to convey empathy and understanding, but there was too much detail; I felt she was enjoying the story. I went on the offensive.

'Myra, are you going to address the murder of Lesley Ann Downey?'

There was silence, then a sigh. 'I keep trying to do it, but every time I sit down at my typewriter I can't get the words out. I just find it so difficult to deal with. To think that I could have been such a cruel, cruel bastard.'

Over the next few months Myra Hindley consistently failed to explain the circumstances surrounding the murder of the ten-year-old girl. I kept on demanding an answer because this was the case that had sealed her fate more than three decades earlier.

On Thursday, 9 December 1965, Myra Hindley and Ian Brady were led up the stone steps from Hyde police station to the town's magistrates' court for their committal hearing. They faced three justices of the peace who would decide whether the case should go to Crown Court. The magistrates had to consider every piece of evidence against the accused. As proceedings opened, the chairman of the bench made a decision that was devastating to the defence: she rejected an application to hold proceedings in camera. The court's narrow wooden benches were crammed with reporters from around the world. As the evidence unfolded over the next eleven days it was laid before their readers.

Central to the prosecution case was an audiotape hidden in a left-luggage office at Manchester Central station by Ian Brady. Rather than rely on the transcript, the magistrates ordered it to be played. Lesley Ann Downey's mother, Ann West, sat across from Myra Hindley as the magnetic strip was looped up on a machine in the middle of the court, and the clerk set it running.

There were some loud clacking sounds – lighting stands going up and down as Ian Brady moved about, photographing the girl in a series of pornographic poses. Myra Hindley could be heard in the background, closing a window so the neighbours wouldn't hear. Lesley Ann refused to put a gag in her mouth, and begged, 'Please don't hurt me, Mam.' Myra Hindley told her to 'shurrup crying'. The tape seemed to go on for ever. When Lesley Ann did finally fall silent the court echoed to the sound of Bing Crosby's warm voice singing 'The Little Drummer Boy'.

Murderers' and victim's words, seared forever into the most hardened reporters' minds, were repeated the following morning in almost every English language newspaper around the world. From that day on, the idea of being able to find twelve unbiased men and women to sit on a jury lacked all credibility. The Crown Court trial, at Chester Assizes in the spring of 1966, provided the stage for a horrific rehearsal of the crimes rather than a process to determine guilt or innocence.

Professor Malcolm MacCulloch viewed Myra Hindley's failure thirty-three years later to deal with the murder of Lesley Ann Downey as highly significant. 'Her case rests on the argument that she was bullied into abducting the children, and that she did not actually carry out the killings,' he pointed out. 'The tape puts her in the room. As these crimes were systematic, and conformed to a pattern, it is highly likely that she was there during all the murders. This is the point at which her story falls apart, and she knows it. The best she can hope for is that you fail to understand the significance of the omission.'

This argument was to form the conclusion to my documentary. I finished the film, and delivered it to the BBC to await transmission. Although it was a piece of work I could be proud of, there remained a nagging sense of frustration. I might have established that Myra Hindley was lying, but I had not discovered the full truth about the crimes, nor had I explained why they remained part of the fabric of national life. The case also remained open, with a child still missing on Saddleworth Moor.

I had planned to end my working relationship with Myra Hindley once the film was finished, but this felt wrong with so many questions unanswered. The only way to maintain contact was to confront her, face to face, with my conclusions. I spent an uneasy evening in Cambridge before travelling the twenty miles to her prison in Suffolk.

I arrived at a collection of single-storey buildings ranged behind razor wire. But for the sign HMP HIGHPOINT you could have mistaken them for an army barracks. After a short wait in a windswept Nissen hut, a guard waved me through security to a small annexe at the back of the prison. The segregation unit's small visiting room was rectangular and painted glossy beige. In the centre stood a Formica table, on it two vacuum flasks, a plate of biscuits and a small white china bowl for putting used teabags into. I pulled out a chair, faced the door and waited.

A woman's low laugh echoed down the corridor; it was over-loud, an announcement giving me time to prepare myself. I stood up as she shuffled through the door on hospital walking sticks.

'Hello, Duncan.'

'Hello, Myra.'

We held each other's gaze and shook hands. Her eyes were

those of the arrest photograph taken at Hyde police station thirty-four years earlier.

'Would you like some tea?' she asked.

'Yes please.'

She wore an immaculate lilac trouser suit over a loose linen shirt. Her auburn hair was newly dyed, and her nails perfectly manicured. Around her neck hung a thin silver ingot engraved with a cross. She had a confident, worldly air; there was no hint of the empty despair that has gripped every other 'lifer' I've met.

As I sipped my tea, I knew I was about to test our relationship to breaking point.

'Myra, the film is finished. I've laid events out as they happened and allowed your words to speak for themselves. The biggest problem for you is the failure to address the killing of Lesley Ann Downey.'

'Right.' Her eyes bored into me.

'I have included an answerphone message in which you say that you find it too difficult to deal with.'

'Well, at least you've told me,' she said in a flat, emotionless voice, without breaking eye contact.

Before long we parted, agreeing to stay in touch, and to meet again. But I left Highpoint wondering how she would feel when her evasion was laid bare on screen.

In order to get the facts right in my documentary I had carried out research interviews with as many people as possible. Most of them did not appear in the finished film, but they had a decisive effect on its tone and accuracy. No-one made a deeper impression on me than Keith Bennett's younger brother, Alan, who told me about their life together and how it came to an end.

The boys had beds next to each other in a small terraced house at the end of Eston Street in Longsight. The two scrappy white goal lines they painted on the adjoining redbrick wall are still there. It was an enclosed, secure world. But several nights a week the Bennett children left it to spend the night with their grandmother on the other side of the Stockport Road. It gave their mam a break. They usually walked there together, but on Thursday, 18 June 1964, Alan and his sister Maggie had gone on ahead. 'When Keith didn't show up we thought he must have changed his mind and decided to stay with our mam,' Alan said.

Like most working-class families, the Bennetts did not have a telephone. It was only the following morning that Keith's gran called at her daughter Winnie's to ask why he had failed to come round. 'We knew straight away something bad had happened,' Alan told me. 'I didn't know what to do. I just went outside and banged a ball against the wall. I stayed there for hours, kicking away.' The police came round, took his stepfather in for questioning, and dug up the back yard in the search for a body. The Bennett family was plunged into physical as well as emotional chaos.

The children were forgotten among the grief and confusion. Alan retreated into silence. At night he climbed the stairs to the room he shared with Keith and spent hours staring blankly at his empty bed. 'I used to lie there and talk to him. Where are you, Keith? Come back. He was like a presence who was still with me, but physically he'd gone. And that's never changed. He's been with me all these years.'

Alan only found out for certain what had happened to Keith in the mid-eighties. By then, Myra Hindley had broken off all contact with Ian Brady. In revenge, he told a newspaper that there were another two bodies on Saddleworth Moor. His intention was to extinguish any hope of freedom she had. Brady's 'revelation' led to a firestorm of publicity. The police, under severe pressure from the newspapers, reopened the search for Pauline Reade and Keith Bennett. The senior investigating officer, Peter Topping, and his deputy, Geoff Knupfer, visited Myra Hindley at Cookham Wood prison in Rochester. Cornered, she decided to confess. Over three days she gave the detectives a tape-recorded account of her role in the murders. Peter Topping then led a small team of detectives in a long search of Saddleworth Moor. After several months, during which their methods were heavily criticized, they found Pauline Reade's remains in a shallow grave on Hollin Brown Knoll. Shortly afterwards, the Chief Constable of Greater Manchester, James Anderton, told Topping to stop looking for Keith. His remains have never been found.

It took the Bennett family some time to realize that the police would only resume work if they got, as one officer put it to me, an 'X marks the spot'. Alan took charge of the search himself. At weekends he and his brothers combed the moor with a small group of volunteers. Over ten years they dug through every patch of peat, until they hit rock, along the banks of Shiny Brook stream.

Alan, who worked in the stockroom at Argos, was painfully aware that he and his team were amateurs. He compensated for this by tracking down and questioning forensic experts. Most were willing to talk; few could offer practical assistance. An exception was the leading forensic archaeologist Professor John Hunter.

Hunter revolutionized the way in which police forces around the world find murder victims and prosecute their killers. He has researched, in minute detail, how bodies are concealed. Most burials conform to well-established patterns; understanding these can lead detectives to a victim far more quickly than traditional search methods. When Hunter does locate a grave he treats it as a source of evidence. He and an assistant dig slowly using three-and-a-half-inch bricklayer's pointing trowels, rather than spades, looking for signs that might trap the killer. 'It's surprising how often you find a footprint at the bottom! But every cut in the earth tells a story: when the grave was dug, what with, and whether the killer was in a frenzied state of mind or calm.'

When they met, the professor revealed to Alan that it was very rare for a murder victim to be hidden more than twenty metres from a road. A body, even that of a child, is very difficult to carry. But Myra Hindley told the police that Keith was more than half a mile from the A635. 'This means that Keith was almost certainly buried in the place he died,' Hunter reasoned. 'Brady must have chosen a concealed location with exposed peat in which to dig the grave.' Hunter carried out a survey of the moorland; in all, there were around ten areas of 'dead ground' – ground that could not be observed from the road – along the banks of Shiny Brook stream. He made a couple of tentative efforts to narrow the search down further with a police body dog, but what he really needed was manpower to strip off the turf covering all his 'target areas'. There were simply too many of them.

One evening I was sipping tea with Alan Bennett in his bedsit close to Eston Street when he said something that confirmed I could not simply walk away from the 'story' of the Moors murders after transmission of my film. 'There are only two people who can tell us where Keith is buried. Brady's not going to help us, so it can only come from her.' In other words, my relationship with Myra Hindley could be used to extract new information.

The BBC held a preview screening of my documentary, *Myra Hindley*, in a large, crescent-shaped conference room at the front of Television Centre. More than twenty reporters from national newspapers attended. Four or five BBC press officers huddled around me, as much to try to ensure that I said the right thing as to protect me. The Corporation's management was extremely nervous about the film, and the chairman of the board of governors, Sir Christopher Bland, had sent for a copy. As I tried to make an escape, Antonella Lazzeri of the *Sun* intercepted me. I was on my guard as her paper had already run a story headlined MYRA GETS HER OWN FILM. She said, in a quiet voice, as if in confidence, 'I've always thought she should be released myself.' I stared at her, said nothing, and walked off to take a seat at the back of the room. As the projector hummed into life over my right shoulder, I lost myself, concentrating on technical details rather than the content.

When the film finished, I made my way to a chair by the projection screen to answer questions, trying to hide any nervousness I felt.

'Why did you make the film – doesn't it just give her a platform?' asked a *Daily Mirror* reporter.

'You've seen it,' I replied. 'Do you think it gave her a platform?'

He shrugged, and jabbed at his pad with a biro.

'The case has been on the front pages for more than thirty years,' I continued, 'yet in all that time no-one had been able to question her before. As her case for release was coming before the courts it was in the public interest to do so. Where she's refused to answer, or lied, I've included it.'

'All right,' the man from the *Daily Mail* cut in, 'could you pull out the new lines for us?'

The following morning there was nothing in the *Sun*. The paper had decided not to attack me, and it avoids repeating other people's stories. The controller of BBC2, Jane Root, sent me an extravagant bunch of flowers. There was a letter from the chairman of the board of governors saying that his 'trepidation' before watching the film had been 'misplaced'.

That Sunday my office phone rang. I walked slowly down the stairs and lifted the receiver.

'Duncan, it's Myra.'

'Hello, Myra. Did you see the film?'

'Yes.'

'What did you think?'

'It didn't help my cause. But I can't complain. You stuck to the deal.'

I quickly moved the conversation on.

'Myra, you know John Hunter?'

'Yes.'

'Would you be willing to answer some questions about the route you and Ian Brady took with Keith?' MacCulloch had advised me to give her a strong reason to co-operate. I had the follow-up ready. 'It can hardly hurt your case, can it, Myra?'

There was a pause. She read my tactics, but could not argue with the logic.

'All right, I'll do it,' she said.

A few days later I met Professor Hunter in a lecture theatre at Birmingham University. He paced up and down, muttering to himself, as he drew up a list of questions on a whiteboard. 'They have to be simple. Not, "Where is the body?" but, "What could you see, smell, hear?" That way we can narrow down the search area.'

'Sure, but you've got to make the questions direct or she'll think you're playing games and refuse to answer,' I warned him.

'Yes, yes. Well, that's what you're here for.'

We worked together for three hours. He came up with the ideas; I helped shape sentences that might evoke a response.

I sent Hunter's letter off with a handwritten covering note, but there was no reply. The Catholic chaplain of Highpoint, Father Michael Teader, saw her every few days. I called him to ask what was going on. 'I'm afraid she's slipped into a deep depression since her appeal failed,' he said. Father Michael needed little persuasion of the importance of Hunter's endeavour. He told me, 'That boy needs to be found. It's the only way this whole thing is going to retreat into history.' He agreed to try to persuade Myra Hindley to answer Hunter's questions. 'I'm not going to bully her though. That would backfire. I'll wait until she's in the right frame of mind.'

Over the next six months, working with Father Michael, Myra Hindley drew a series of maps. The first of these described the route she and Ian Brady took the night Keith died. It contained many details: 'I climbed up here, flattish; he and Keith went on, I don't know how far; shale bank, buried spade here'. But the map was drawn in black pen on a plain white sheet of paper, with no distance scale, and was very difficult to use on the ground. Professor Hunter's solution was to send her Ordnance Survey maps divided into different coloured zones, for her to draw on. The tortuous process was lengthened by her poor mental health: she kept slipping in and out of depression, and needed much encouragement.

The professor and his assistant, Detective Chief Superintendent Barrie Simpson, the former head of the West Midlands Police murder squad, returned to the moor and used the maps to narrow down the previously identified areas of dead ground. They were assisted by staff and students from the archaeology department at Birmingham University. On a couple of occasions forensic archaeologists on leave from exhuming mass graves in Bosnia came along too. With the help of aerial photographs the archaeologists identified which of the concealed patches of moorland had exposed areas of peat in 1964. They also surveyed the ground using specialist equipment to see if any were deep enough to conceal a body. Hunter's search narrowed down the possible places Keith could be buried to just a few gullies. But, once again, the only way to complete his work was to dig the moorland. He presented his results to the police but, as there was still no 'X marks the spot', they listened politely and took no further action. There was little more Hunter could do.

Myra Hindley's willingness to help Hunter may have been influenced by a recent seismic shift in the legal landscape: the United Kingdom's adoption of the European Convention on Human Rights. The power to decide how long a lifer served could now be taken away from politicians and handed to the judiciary. If this happened, the decision about her future would become legal rather than political. It was the best chance of freedom Myra Hindley had ever had. Helping to find Keith Bennett's body, and closing the case, could only help.

Hindley's legal team, led by Edward Fitzgerald QC, put her case to nine of the country's most senior judges over two weeks in the autumn of 2002. There was a sense of history in the making as distinguished lawyers, many of whom had no direct interest in the proceedings, gathered in committee room nine of the House of Lords to hear the arguments. Fitzgerald was skilful and confident in his submissions. The judges listened carefully as he outlined how the life sentence system should now work. Only when he attempted to deploy an analogy drawn from Wittgenstein's *Tractatus* did Lord Chief Justice Woolf scold him: 'Stick to the point, Mr Fitzgerald.'

While he was deferential in front of the bench, and cautious when he thought there was a reporter nearby, in private Fitzgerald allowed his optimism to shine through. He rang Myra Hindley regularly; 'I'm going to get you out,' he told her. An acknowledgement of the Home Secretary's plight was written on the face of his aptly named counsel, David Pannick QC. Even so, I was surprised when I learned that the then Home Secretary,

David Blunkett, had instructed Greater Manchester Police to see whether they could come up with fresh charges to keep her inside. The chief constable told one of his most trusted detectives, Superintendent Tony Brett, to assemble a team and re-examine the case.

Officially, the Moors murder inquiry had never been closed. But for the past fifteen years there had been just two officers assigned to it. As these were Special Branch 'spooks' and the IRA was active in Manchester, the case was not a priority. In private the detectives acknowledged that their job was to 'manage' the families and members of the public who came forward with suggestions and offers of help. They would act if new information came to light, but they weren't out looking for it.

Brett's team were specialist murder squad officers. He gave each an area of responsibility and told them to become experts in it. DC Dave Warren mapped the moor and carried out an audit of all the searches for bodies; DC Gail Jazmik studied Brady's photographs; DC Andy Meekes read every word that had been written on the case; DS Fiona Robertshaw gathered intelligence; DC Phil Steele checked that nothing was missed. Their purpose was clear: to make sure Myra Hindley was never released. If they found Keith Bennett along the way all well and good, but that was not their primary purpose.

Tony Brett thought he might be able to charge Myra Hindley with the murders she had never been tried for. The statement she had given to his predecessor, Peter Topping, early in 1987 was an unequivocal admission of guilt. The new investigating team met government lawyers but were warned that laying new charges was likely to be ruled an 'abuse of process' because of a decision taken fifteen years earlier. After Myra Hindley confessed, the families of Keith Bennett and Pauline Reade had sought a new trial. The Director of Public Prosecutions had opposed them on the grounds that, as there was no prospect of release, a lengthy court case would be a waste of taxpayers' money. The courts agreed. Tony Brett was told by the government lawyers that this decision could not be reversed. Greater Manchester Police let David Blunkett know the bad news: he was at the mercy of the Law Lords.

The phone call to his office from the Home Office Lifer Unit on Friday, 15 November 2002 must therefore have come as a welcome relief: Myra Hindley was dead. Father Michael Teader asked if I would like to attend the funeral; I declined and watched it on the TV news instead. Cameras crowded the pavement outside Cambridge crematorium. As the coffin was carried in a young blonde woman delivered a carefully rehearsed piece to camera. None of Myra Hindley's family went to her funeral either. It's not that they didn't care – she spoke to her mother every day for news of what was going on 'at home' – but they still live in Manchester under different names, and need anonymity to have any hope of a normal life. Father Michael, who had held her hand as she lay dying, did his best to deliver a dignified service for the six anonymous people who did attend. But the atmosphere was tense.

The week after the funeral a former lover of Myra Hindley's arrived at Father Michael's house to collect her ashes and personal belongings. She drove the remains, which were contained in a plain cardboard box, to a stretch of moor east of Saddleworth. It was a sunny day, and she walked slowly along a high path scattering handfuls of ash into the air as she went. It took half an hour to empty the box.

As she climbed back into her car the woman made a decision: she would release Myra Hindley's papers to me. They comprised part of an unpublished autobiography, thousands of letters and hundreds of photographs taken during the period of the Moors murders. She hoped the documents might contribute to an understanding of the case and help the search for Keith Bennett.

I travelled north with mixed feelings. Even though Hindley was dead I was being sucked back into the world of the Moors murderers. I was shown into a small, dark room at the back of a remote cottage and told to take everything I thought might be relevant. I gathered up the lot, drove home to Somerset and spent the next few months reading and cataloguing what I had been given.

As I studied the documents I realized that they began to explain what made Myra Hindley the woman she was, and the true nature of the relationship between her and Ian Brady. It might now be possible to understand why the Moors murders case had remained open, and a part of the fabric of national life, for so long. I decided to investigate the story they told.

Book One
Manchester

'I am a child of Gorton in Manchester. Infamous, I have become disowned, but I am one of your own.'

Chapter One

Myra Hindley lived the first twenty-three years of her life as a free woman; of these, twenty-two were spent in the tightly packed grid of terraced houses that is Gorton, close to the heart of Manchester. In order to understand the forces that shaped her I began my search there.

I left Manchester city centre and drove east along the Hyde Road, past the Apollo Theatre, a boarded-up Victorian school and a succession of abandoned warehouses. On the passenger seat lay a map marked with my destination. After what must have been two miles I came to a cluster of shops and a Kentucky Fried Chicken outlet. I swung left, opposite Chloe's Beauty and Tanning Centre, and looped round the back of KwikSave, past the Pineapple pub and into Taylor Street. The sight that confronted me was a surprise. The terrace she grew up in had been ripped down and replaced with mock Tudor four-bedroom houses. Each had a carefully trimmed square of grass, a car parking bay out the front and a satellite dish. They looked incongruous, and were surrounded by terraces Myra Hindley would have recognized as the homes of her friends and relations.

Towering over the end of Taylor Street stood a Gothic church with the dimensions of a cathedral. Looking down was a pale stone carving of Christ on the cross. The building was abandoned; a buddleia flowered from a flying buttress; pigeons flapped behind stained glass. In the church's shadow a rusting archway to an abandoned garden bore the name 'Monastery of St Francis'. A brightly coloured, thirty-metre-long hoarding around the perimeter revealed that the building had been acquired by a charitable trust. The top half predicted a proud future; the bottom half bore a legend that summarized Gorton's past: 610, colonized by the Saxons; 1555, families survived Great Famine by eating seeds; 1742, stocks erected opposite the George and Dragon; 1792, Gorton has eight 'boggerts', or evil spirits; 1818, Peterloo Massacre; 1846, Gaol built; 1957, 'Monkeyrama' opens at Belle Vue. There was no mention of Myra Hindley or the fact that this was the place where she took her First Communion.

For the rest of the day I wandered around, trying to make sense of Gorton's geography and falling into conversation with its people. The place had a strong sense of identity but did not feel closed. It was easy to talk to complete strangers. 'Ask people here where they're from and they'll say West Gorton, not Manchester,' an elderly lady sitting on a bench in Sunny Brow Park told me. 'It's like a big village really.' I passed the schools Myra Hindley attended; the railway embankments she played on; the pubs she and Ian Brady drank in. Many of the place names spoke of the countryside: Lower Cat's Knowle, Daisy Bank, Sunnyside, Ryder Brow. I wondered how Gorton had been transformed from pastoral idyll to industrial crucible, and whether this might inform me about the people who lived there.

I sought an answer in Manchester's oldest building, Chetham's College of Music, and library. The building stands in the centre of the city, a few minutes' walk from Victoria station. Its honey-coloured walls lend it the appearance of an Oxford college. Inside, across a neatly trimmed quadrangle, choirs competed with orchestras. I made my way across the imposing space, and down a dark corridor. At the end I came to a small oak door set into a stone wall and hesitated, not sure I had the right place. In the end, reasoning that all I risked was disturbing some-one's work, I tugged on what appeared to be a bell pull. Far above I heard a high ringing and, after a delay of half a minute or more, the sound of leather-soled shoes descending a wooden staircase.

'Can I help?'

'I was hoping to visit the reading room.'

The archivist, a small, smartly dressed woman with long red hair, nodded, turned and led me upstairs.

As we emerged from the dingy staircase I had to squint to adjust to the bright light. Sunshine flooded through leaded windows onto a polished oak table. Beyond it, stretching into the darkness, I could see shelf upon shelf of ancient volumes. In the corner of the room stood a wooden case containing two rows of dusty tethered texts – a 'chained library' donated to the parish of Gorton by Sir Thomas Chetham four hundred years earlier. The contents did not look like easy reading; there seemed to be a lot of Calvin. A sign revealed that until 1974 it had stood in the corner of St James's Protestant Church. This was where Ian Brady and Myra Hindley attended midnight communion.

The archivist informed me, with a hint of pride in her voice, that this was the oldest library in the English-speaking world, and that the table set into an alcove was where Friedrich Engels had researched a book that changed the course of world history: *The Condition of the Working Class in England*. Engels travelled to Manchester for the same reason as thousands of other young men: it was the most vibrant, fastest-growing city in the world. The difference was that Engels, under the cover of working for his father's textile business, came here to study the effect of capitalism on ordinary people. His book, a cornerstone of communist doctrine, had a profound effect on his friend Karl Marx and the shape of his masterwork, *Das Kapital*. It is unmistakably the work of a radical young idealist, and strays into polemic, but it does paint a vivid picture of working-class life during Manchester's formative years: 'Everywhere before the doors refuse and offal; that any sort of pavement lay underneath could not be seen but only felt, here and there, with the feet.' Living conditions in central Manchester were so bad that even Engels, with his vivid powers of description, found it a struggle 'to convey a true impression of the filth, ruin and uninhabitableness, the defiance of all considerations of cleanliness, ventilation, and health which characterize the construction of this single district, containing at least twenty to thirty thousand inhabitants. And such a district exists in the heart of the second city of England, the first manufacturing city of the world. If anyone wishes to see in how little space a human being can move, how little air – and *such* air! – he can breathe, how little of civilization he may share and yet live, it is only necessary to travel hither.'

I spread a large, yellowed map onto the wooden table. The hand-drawn document showed what Gorton looked like in the eighteenth century, before the Industrial Revolution. It was a mass of fields with a few rows of cottages, and a church. The parish, I read, had been reclaimed from the moor and turned to pasture five hundred years earlier. It turned out that one of the poet Byron's ancestors once bought it as 'an investment'. I pulled out a second map, drawn a hundred years later. I stood and stared in wonder at the human endeavour represented by the mass of tiny rectangles that had replaced the fields. It was almost impossible to imagine that this mass of factories and terraces was once the edge of the moor that stretched east, over the Pennines, towards Sheffield.

The Gorton that shaped Myra Hindley had a distinctive set of rhythms. The time people got up, the paths they took to work, the sounds that came from the factories were repeated day in, day out. This imbued its people with common characteristics, and a strong sense of identity. The nature of this identity owed much to the arrival in Manchester of Karl Beyer, a young German from a far humbler background than Engels', in 1834.

The son of a poor weaver from Saxony, the bright young engineer had worked his way through Dresden Polytechnic, existing on just twenty pounds a year. His original plan, laid down by his sponsors, was that he would study the new textile machinery in England and return home with the secrets of its success. But Karl, who soon changed his name to Charles, had no intention of going back to Saxony. He had come to Manchester to make his fortune.

Charles got a job in the drawing office of Sharp Roberts & Company, a firm of textile engineers, and stood out immediately. When the business diversified into the manufacture of steam locomotives Charles was assigned to the new design office. Six years later, at the age of just twenty-five, he was made chief engineer. Over the next ten years he drove the business with bold projects completed on time and on budget. Charles was recognized as one of the brightest engineers in the manufacturing capital of the world, and he expected to be rewarded with a share in the business he had built, not with a wage. His employer, Richard Roberts, saw things differently and refused the young German both a partnership and, it is rumoured, his daughter's hand in marriage.

Charles found a way forward when he met a young railway manager, Richard Peacock, supervising the construction of 'Gorton Tank' to the north of Taylor Street. The vast complex of railway sheds, workshops and lines would bind Gorton to Manchester, transforming it for ever from a village into part of the city. Charles was struck by the ambition and efficiency of the operation, and he closely questioned the Yorkshireman, who turned out to be two years younger than him, about his background. Richard told Charles that he had left Leeds Grammar School at the age of fourteen, seduced by the 'exciting' prospect of working with trains. Within four years he was made superintendent of the Leeds and Selby Railway. He took charge of the larger Manchester and Sheffield line at twenty-one. Richard Peacock, it became clear, was every bit as ambitious as Charles Beyer.

Peacock would visit the design office to place orders with Sharp Roberts, and he and Beyer developed a close relationship. They soon came to realize that a combination of their talents could form the basis of a formidable business, and resolved to set up Beyer Peacock Engineering – 'train builders to the world'. But though the two young men had plenty of ambition, they lacked money. They found a third partner, Henry Robertson, to invest in the business. Although just two years older than Charles, Henry had already amassed a fortune building railways and a famous nineteen-arch bridge over the River Dee at Ruabon in North Wales. He was looking for a new challenge.

The partners bought a field for their new factory across the tracks from Gorton Tank. The trains would be able to roll straight onto the new lines laid by Richard Peacock and, because much of Gorton remained untouched, they could shape it in their image as the business expanded. The new firm's first big order, from the East Indian Railway, was in the bag before a brick had been laid.

This was a significant breakthrough. Beyer was able to poach the best of Sharp Roberts' workforce and guarantee them a future, and he created a design and production process that could deliver high-quality engines faster and more cheaply than his stunned former employer.

The three partners enjoyed their new-found status and wealth. A photograph of 1860 shows Peacock smiling, looking regal in furs and surrounded by packing cases and servants, ready for 'an expedition' to Russia. He was travelling, in style, to sell Beyer Peacock's 'magnificent' trains to yet another new market.

The business challenged, and eventually overtook, the importance of the mills to West Gorton. Former weavers found themselves riveting and hammering engines that helped to power the empire. The work was regular, and for the forgemen there was a perk no mill worker had ever enjoyed: beer to 'quench their thirst'. By the time the owners of Beyer Peacock realized the folly of this practice and offered lemon barley water instead, it had become ingrained. They decided to avoid a confrontation. Men might be getting injured, but the trains were still being built.

Beyer Peacock won orders in South Africa, New South Wales, Caracas and, of course, Manchester. Increasing numbers of men were required for Gorton Foundry, and their families needed houses. The new streets were given names that reflected what Gorton had become. Railway View, later home to Myra Hindley's Auntie Anne, stood so close to the Sheffield and Midland line that the gardens were black with soot and cups shook in their saucers whenever a train went by.

Manchester's reputation as a vibrant, immoral place spread throughout the world. In 1861 seven Belgian monks led by Father Emmanuel Kenners abandoned their monastery in Cornwall and travelled north to establish a 'mission'. Their strategy was simple: they would offer moral encouragement alongside practical help. They bought Bankside cottage, a small house with some land on Gorton Lane, and quickly built a combined school and chapel. Their first mass was held in the new building, amid great excitement, on Christmas Day.

The monks also planned a magnificent church to demonstrate their faith, and determination to stay, to the people of Gorton. Father Kenners hired twenty-four-year-old Edward Welby Pugin – whose father, August, had designed the interior of the Palace of Westminster – to come up with a plan. The High Gothic, cathedral-like building he proposed was both outrageously ambitious and expensive. He told the monks that he wanted to create a church that was 184 feet long, 98 feet wide and 100 feet tall. Light would pour through the stained glass onto a ceiling-high Bath-stone altar designed by his brother Paul, and elaborate, gilded carvings of saints would gaze down on the parishioners as they filed into one of thirteen confessionals that ran from front to back. These were of an ingenious design, with two doors each, so that one penitent could wait in privacy while another unburdened his soul to a priest. Father Michael Teader, Myra Hindley's priest and final confessor, explained the Franciscans' aim to me: 'They were creating a piece of heaven on earth, to lift the people from their surroundings, give them hope.' Because Manchester is flat, Pugin enthused, you would be able to see the church over the roofs of the packed terraces from miles away.

The monks were inspired by the young man's grand vision, but had just £2,500 to spend. They would have to build the church themselves. The job fell to their clerk of works, Brother Patrick Dalton, from County Kerry in south-west Ireland. Over the next eight years he led a gang of volunteers made up of parishioners in his monumental task. First, he ripped down Bankside cottage and replaced it with a friary. Once he had put a roof over his comrades' heads he started work on the church while the other monks fell to work in the parish, opening a soup kitchen for the destitute alongside their school for the poor. Because bricks were expensive and clay was free, Brother Patrick got his gang to build firing kilns in the monastery grounds. While the parishioners worked under the supervision of his deputy, Father Peter Hickey, he fixed a nag to a cart and rode into Manchester. His tall figure, with its closely cropped head, long silver beard and flowing brown robe, stalked the city's construction sites in search of free materials. He relied heavily on a disarming smile and the cross at his waist.

Over the weeks and months St Francis' walls crept higher and higher, first over the terraces of Taylor Street, then over the neighbouring foundry. People across east Manchester stopped and stared in amazement. Until then, the city's grand designs had been wrought to reflect distinctly earthly rather than spiritual values.

Just eight years after starting work Father Patrick nailed the last tile on the roof of the monastery church of St Francis. Every bishop in the country was invited to the grand opening. The rain that lashed priests and parishioners as they arrived only heightened the sense of refuge to be found within its magnificent walls. The bishop of Manchester described it as 'the finest and most beautiful church in the north of England'.

When Myra's great great grandfather, William Lewis, arrived in Gorton the monastery dominated the skyline. He had come to start work as a bricklayer. For years, William resisted the gravitational pull of industrial expansion, but a lack of work finally forced him to leave the small Cheshire town of Warrington. The 1901 census, and Myra Hindley's private papers, reveal that William's circumstances were unusual: his dependants included a wife, Eliza, who was six years older than him, and her young granddaughter Ellen. The bond between the women was unusually strong: both were illegitimate. Eliza and William took the girl in because there was no-one else to look after her. Ellen grew up proud of having survived the challenge of illegitimacy. At the heart of this pride lay a belief in the value of family loyalty. But the Lewis family struggled to make ends meet in Gorton, and Eliza was forced to look for work outside Manchester. She took a job as a maid at Newbury Rectory in Berkshire. Ellen, at the age of just nine, went with her.

The experience had a profound effect on the young girl and it is described in detail in Myra Hindley's autobiography, written in the mid-eighties to try to improve her case for freedom. It is a rambling work that was abandoned when her supporters read it, and judged it unhelpful. 'It was a disaster,' David Astor, the former editor of the *Observer*, told me when I visited him at his house in St John's Wood. He funded Myra Hindley's legal campaign and visited her over more than thirty years. 'There was plenty of accurate detail but it added up to self-justification. Not a single mention of bodies. It went from I-was-a-poor-child-in-Manchester to I'm-in-prison without any mention of what happened in between. I told her not to continue. It would have damaged her case for release.'

'Why did you support her?' I asked.

'Everyone deserves the chance of redemption,' he replied.

Myra Hindley did not make another attempt to tell her story until she wrote to me well over a decade later. Both accounts, although very different, were written in order to help her campaign for freedom. Neither succeeded in this aim, but they do have a real value because, while it may be easy to lie, it is almost impossible to lie consistently. She retold her story from different points in time, with shifts of emphasis and changes in content. Setting these accounts against her police confession and

interviews with those who knew or loved her yields a new understanding of what really happened.

Myra's grandmother, Ellen, had had no experience of wealth
when she moved south to work alongside her own grandmother,
Eliza. The closest she had come was the sight of rich people's
carriages rolling through the dirty streets. Like all children, she
had marvelled at the plumage Richard Peacock's coachmen wore
in their hats. On Sundays he threw coins out of his carriage
window to the running gaggle. But at Newbury Rectory she was
on the inside. She remembered living in the grand old house as a
'golden time', marred only by one incident that gave her 'the
fright of her life' (it is recorded in Myra's autobiography). One
night, as she was drifting off to sleep in her attic bedroom, Ellen
saw 'an apparition' dressed in hunting clothes standing at the
foot of her bed. She jumped up and ran downstairs screaming.
Rather than scold her for being silly, the rector was 'very kind'
and explained that the 'ghost' was a former squire of Newbury
who died in a hunting accident. He came back 'to visit' because
he could not bear to be parted from his home. The rector did not
explain why the ghostly squire preferred the servants' quarters to
the drawing room.

While Ellen was better fed and clothed at the rectory than she
had ever been, she missed the north and returned to Manchester
in her mid-teens. She got a job in the mills, but her pleasure at
being 'home' in West Gorton soon faded. She got up for work
at four in the morning and collapsed, exhausted, into her bed
fifteen hours later. Her boyfriend Pete Burns, an engineers'
labourer, lived two doors down from her on Blair Street. He had
to support his mother as his father, a fish-hawker, had died.
Despite pride in her own background, Ellen did not want to
inflict the stigma of illegitimacy on her own children, so she got

married to Pete Burns, at the age of twenty-one. Ellen concealed her background from the registrar and told him that she was the daughter of Charles Silgram, general labourer. Soon after the wedding Ellen fell pregnant. When her son, Jim, was born she had to keep up the punishing hours in order to survive. She miscarried several times before giving birth to a second child, a beautiful baby girl called Louie.

At the outbreak of war, in 1914, Pete volunteered. He posed for a photograph, stern-faced in his uniform, before embarking for France. Ellen kept it in a frame on the mantelpiece. As the need for weapons grew, Ellen got a job in a TNT factory. The hours weren't as bad as in the mills; the War Ministry might have wanted explosive, but it didn't want tired women making it. There was also the sense of togetherness that came from all the men being away. Then Pete was killed, and Ellen's world fell apart.

After the war, when her wounds had begun to heal, Ellen did find a man willing to 'take on' her children – a coal carter, Bert Maybury. Like Ellen's family, Bert's had come to Manchester from the Cheshire countryside in the 1890s in search of work. They married and set up home at 24 Beasley Street, West Gorton. Many of her comrades from the TNT factory were less fortunate: there was a severe shortage of bachelors in their twenties and thirties. Ellen wanted a large family but she suffered for her dream. She had ten miscarriages and a further three children: Anne, Bert and Myra's mother, Nellie. The trauma of pregnancy was compounded by the death of her eldest daughter, Louie, from a sudden infection. Pete Burns' daughter had been a favourite child. Ellen never really got over his death at the front.

In his history of the monastery, Father Aidan reported that 975 of St Francis' pupils left to fight in the Great War. Of these,

159 never came home. Four old boys were awarded the Distinguished Conduct Medal and nine the Military Medal. The sacrifice of the fallen, and the debt owed to those who had survived, was drummed into succeeding generations of school-boys. They and the monastery that had shaped them were something to be proud of.

Listening to these tales of heroism, young Bob Hindley, whose father worked at the foundry, found something to inspire him. He was not academically gifted but he was good at sport and brave. He left St Francis' school, with his teachers' encouragement, to join the army. Bob found a sense of purpose in the Parachute Regiment and achieved real status. He won the regimental boxing championship and wore the battered nose this cost him as a badge of pride for the rest of his life.

At home on leave, Bob cut a dashing figure. He was pursued by many girls, but one stood out, as much for her strong will as her good looks – an eighteen-year-old machinist called Nellie Maybury. They fell 'head over heels' in love and married. Any notion that the union of two volatile, opinionated characters might lead to trouble was lost in the excitement of the moment. And anyway, Bob was going off to war with the Paras; he might not come back. Seven months after he left, Nellie stopped work to have a child, a daughter she called Myra.

Myra Hindley records in her autobiography that she was born 'an ordinary baby' at Crumpsall Hospital on Thursday, 23 July 1942. The occupants of a very crowded 24 Beasley Street were relieved to discover that she was an easy infant. The tiny terrace stood tucked down a dead end behind Taylor Street. The official tenant was Ellen, long widowed, who now became 'Gran'. Her children Anne and Jim had left home, but Bert remained, with his girlfriend Kath. This type of arrangement was so common, with men away fighting, that landlords could do little about it.

Three weeks after the birth Nellie went to register Myra; the certificate records the baby's father as Private Hindley No. 3853894. Myra told me in a letter that her father was determined she should be baptized a Catholic at St Francis'. But Nellie was suspicious of religion, and only agreed on condition that Myra would not go to a Catholic school. She raged that all the monks taught was the catechism. It was the first time she and Bob had a 'proper' argument. On 16 August 1942, Myra was baptized at the monastery church of St Francis; Kath stood godmother. Bob could not attend, as he was away fighting with the Paras.

The monastery stood next to one of the Luftwaffe's prime targets in Manchester, Beyer Peacock Engineering. When the German bombers came the vaults beneath St Francis provided a shelter for the inhabitants of the surrounding streets. The worst attacks came during December 1940 when incendiaries rained down on West Gorton. There was a tremendous crashing as the boys' and girls' schools in the monastery grounds were hit. Inside St Francis, the priests and parishioners caught their breath as a third device hit the roof high above them. Luckily the tiles held, and the incendiary rolled down and burned itself out in the gutter. Such attacks went on throughout the war. A map taken from an enemy pilot in Holland in 1945 shows Gorton foundry marked out by a thick black line. There is a scale along the bottom and a caption which reveals that it was drawn in October 1939. The crew that used this map was over Manchester on 9 January 1941. The monastery and streets are so tightly packed around Beyer Peacock that it would have been impossible for even the most discriminating bomb aimer to hit his target every time.

Nellie, Ellen, Bert, Kath and Myra did have an 'Anderson' bomb shelter in the back yard but they felt safer in the company of others. If there was time they would run to the communal shelter built at the end of their street by the War Ministry.

Officials paid particular attention to the number and quality of shelters in West Gorton; they wanted its occupants back at work, in the foundry, the following morning, not dead, or mourning loved ones.

Like all families, the occupants of 24 Beasley Street had an 'air-raid routine'. When the sirens sounded Kath and Ellen made straight for the shelter while Bert waited inside the front door. Nellie got Myra out of bed, wrapped her up, and tossed her down the stairs to him. They got quicker and quicker at this, but one night either Nellie misjudged her throw or Bert fumbled the catch, and Myra was dropped. They sprinted to the shelter in a panic, but the baby was fine: she had been saved by landing in a tub of washing. After that, Nellie ran down the stairs holding Myra tightly.

Myra spent the first few years of her life in a world run by women. Her uncle Bert may have resembled a father figure, but he did not carry the financial and moral responsibilities of parenthood. She described him in her autobiography as a gentle figure who loved to play games and never lost his temper.

Because the kitchen ceiling was unsafe, Bert helped Gran hang her long clothes dryer, made of wood and steel, in the front room. It was so close to the front door that adult heads brushed against the damp cotton as they came in and out. This made Myra laugh. Bert, to show his niece what she was missing, would grab her by the arms and toss her high into the air. She'd scream with delight as her blonde curls got lost among the shirts and drawers, before plunging back into her uncle's safe hands.

In 1945, Myra's father returned from the war to his first experience of family life. But the Bob Hindley who came back was very different from the one who had left, newly married, five years earlier. Myra recorded Bob's struggle to adjust to civilian life in various drafts of her autobiography, in her confession to the police, and in her letters to me. With each new version she polished the image of herself as a victim of circumstance. The last, and most refined, account was written to me; by far the most revealing, and unguarded, description of her childhood was to be found in the first version of her autobiography.

Myra's father not only had to get used to family life, he also had to get a job. He ended up at Beyer Peacock, labouring; at least it was a man's world where his physical strength and war record – he served in North Africa, Cyprus and Italy, and the Paras endured some of the heaviest and most prolonged fighting of the war – were appreciated. But stories of glory are not the same as the thing itself, and a bitterness settled over him.

Myra recorded that Bob and Nellie made a stab at happiness when they secured a new house to live in, 'as a family', at 20 Eaton Street. Myra knew something was up when, one morning, her mam climbed out of bed and pulled on a new red dress. At first she accepted, even believed, that 'a move' was the beginning of a bright new future. But as she sat down to breakfast with Bert, Gran, Nellie and Kath for the last time it sank in that the life they had shared at Beasley Street was coming to an end. It did not matter that their new home was just a minute's walk away. She screamed the place down, and blamed her dad for the calamity.

Bob tried to placate his daughter over the next few weeks by taking her out with him. He refused to let Myra cover her blonde curls with a hat as he enjoyed the compliments they attracted. Although Bob could not yet hope to supplant Bert in his daughter's affections, he did begin to earn her trust. They were in town together once, she recorded in her autobiography, when a manager at Lewis's department store, on Piccadilly Gardens, told her she would have to go into the ladies' lavatory alone. Frightened by the 'posh' surroundings and the idea of performing a private act while surrounded by strangers, she burst into tears. Bob insisted that she be allowed to come into the gents' with him. In the face of his determination the manager relented. Myra was proud of the way her dad stuck up for her. On another day out, at Belle Vue, they had a picture taken together. I found it among her papers. Bob holds a chimpanzee in his right arm and Myra in his left. She appears distracted, but he is grinning into the camera with a father's undisguised delight.

Eaton Street was newer than Beasley Street. It had electricity and a tiled fireplace, but that was as far as the improvements went. The house was inundated with cockroaches which scuttled for cover whenever a light was switched on. There were two rooms on the ground floor: the front opened on to the street, the rear on to the yard, and a damp privy. The house was built to such a poor standard that the back bedroom, which was to be Myra's, had been condemned before they moved in. The ceiling leaked and the floorboards were unsafe to walk on. The Hindleys had to share the one remaining bedroom at the front of the house. Myra slept in a single bed next to her parents' double.

Despite this uncomfortable arrangement, and the frequent rows it gave rise to, Nellie got pregnant. A cot was put up in the corner of the bedroom and, on 21 August 1946, Maureen was born. The new baby was quite different from the first, and frequently cried through the night. Myra lay in bed, listened to her wailing and wished that life could go back to how it had been at Gran's. She sensed that things were only going to get worse. Her mam was so tense that she shouted if Myra so much as stood next to, never mind sat in, the only piece of comfortable furniture in the house – 'Dad's chair'.

But Bob rarely spent the evening sitting at home. His way of 'coping' was to get blind drunk, almost every night, at one of the many pubs dotted around West Gorton: the Bessemer (Bessie),

Shakespeare (Shakie), or his favourite, the Steelworks (Steelie). Increasingly often, at around ten o'clock in the evening, a neighbour would burst through the front door shouting that Bob was 'fightin' agen', and that Nellie had best 'come and bring him home'. Bob had been known as a 'hard man' in the army, and needed to be the same as a civilian. To begin with, Nellie pulled him out of the pub, covered in blood and bruises, raging about how 'the other bloke' had come off far worse than him, and dragged him home. She told herself it was 'the war'. Eventually, she tired of this routine. When the door flew open she responded to news of the latest brawl with a shrug, and carried on with whatever she was doing. But Myra's duty remained the same, irrespective of her mam's reaction: to retrieve Bob's jacket. He always took it off before a 'scrap', no matter how drunk he was, so that it wouldn't get ripped. After a fight, the drinkers came to expect the girl with blonde curls. As she ducked into the smoke of the bar a hand would hold the precious jacket out to her.

Professor Malcolm MacCulloch studied the different accounts of Myra Hindley's childhood and asked to see what other material I had.

'He looks a bruiser, doesn't he?'

The professor was stooped over the picture of Bob Hindley, his battered scowl glowering out from beneath a cocked hat, on the benches of the Steelworks. He was not so much looking at the camera as challenging it. The two men either side of him looked like rogues.

'How useful are the details of her early years?' I asked.

'Invaluable. Most of our flaws and strengths are forged before we reach adulthood. The key to understanding her personality lies here.'

Although Myra Hindley wrote several accounts of her childhood, she discussed it openly with just two people: Ian Brady and the woman who replaced him in her affections, Patricia Cairns. Myra met the former Carmelite nun at Holloway prison, where she was a warder, in 1970. Their relationship endured until Myra's death thirty-two years later. But Patricia Cairns was in no way an acolyte of Myra Hindley's. She does not deny Myra's role in the murders or the lies she told about them. And she was instrumental in persuading her to help in the search for Keith Bennett. Whenever Myra was slow to respond to a question from Professor John Hunter, because she was 'depressed' or 'preoccupied', Cairns put her under powerful pressure. This assistance was on strict condition of anonymity. Her importance to Myra Hindley was such that I had to ask her to tell her story for this book. She, perhaps better than anyone, understood Myra because they had talked about every aspect of her life. I explained that it was impossible to fully understand why the Moors murders have remained in the public eye, and unsolved, without hearing from her. After careful consideration she agreed. 'It's time for the truth to come out,' she said.

Myra Hindley and Patricia Cairns had a lot in common. Both women were Mancunian, Catholic and working class with alcoholic fathers. But Cairns says that, while she was also hit regularly, the violence Myra endured was more extreme; it was at the centre of her day-to-day existence. Bob Hindley was the main source of the beatings, but Nellie was far from blameless.

'Her mum was cruel to her when she was little. She didn't protect her and beat her herself. She hit her about the head. I remember Myra telling me that she made her ears bleed.'

'How come there's no mention of Nellie hitting her in the autobiography?' I asked.

'I think when Myra wrote about that time she made excuses

for her mum. She wanted her to be something that she wasn't. She wanted to have a good mum, so she portrayed her as she would have liked her to be.'

It soon became clear to Bob and Nellie that, while they might be physically attracted to each other, they were ill matched. Arguments soon became part of the daily routine. Bob started hitting Nellie and Myra when he got back from the pub. If he had already been in a scrap, or they didn't talk, there was a chance of making it to bed without an argument. But, often as not, one of them would seek out trouble. Nellie goaded Bob about the amount he spent on beer, asking him if there was anything left for food; he rose to the bait, and threatened to hit her. Back and forth they went until the inevitable explosion of violence. Myra said in her letters to me that she and Gran would wait outside as the voices got louder. When her mum started yelping with pain they would open the door and rush in. Gran would hit Bob with a rolled-up copy of the *Manchester Evening News* while Myra grabbed his legs and pummelled them.

The scenes at 20 Eaton Street did not attract the attention of the authorities as domestic violence was part of life. Friday night was known by the kids as 'wife beating night'. The women had different ways of dealing with it. Nellie acted as though it wasn't happening and kept everything 'within doors'. Mrs Harding, who lived across the street, did the opposite. She was married to a small man who worked hard all week and went mad at the end of it. When he hit her she ran into the road and danced around, dodging his drunken punches, until he retreated, exhausted, to sleep it off. Uncle Bert tired of this weekly ritual and tried to cut it short by 'having a word' as Mr Harding returned from the pub. But Mr Harding was not in the mood for listening, and took a swing at him. It was an unwise move as Bert was both far stronger and sober. In his anger, Myra's uncle misjudged the strength of his punch. Mr Harding was knocked out cold and collapsed prone into the gutter. Kath called an ambulance, and sat with her arm round his wife while they waited. Mr Harding made a speedy physical recovery but the sting of humiliation endured. For a while the beating stopped, but the small man 'could not help himself' and soon resumed his former habit. Bert did not intervene again.

The contrast between her father and uncle became increasingly sharp to Myra. She began answering back, and refused to do as she was told. This infuriated Bob. Not only did he have a strong-willed wife who 'griped' at him all the time, but now his daughter was turning out even worse. As the tension rose at Eaton Street the number of fights increased. Violence could swirl out of the calmest of circumstances. Every week they had a bath, taking turns in the tin tub which stood in front of the open fire. Nellie topped it up with hot water from a pan on the stove. At the age of five, Myra was waiting her turn when she spotted Bob's shaving things in front of the mirror on the hearth. Myra smeared shaving soap on her face, stood on tip-toes on the tiled fender and scraped at her smooth skin with a table knife. Bob appeared behind her, asked what she thought she was doing, and cracked her round the head, spraying the mirror with flecks of foam. But Myra refused to cry. Physical punishment was a challenge she squared up to.

'Myra was always a strong character when she was little,' Patricia Cairns told me. 'But they didn't just fight because of their differences. I think there were a lot of similarities between them. They both recognized this and neither of them liked it. And she looked like him, didn't she?'

The thought had never struck me before. I pulled out my laptop and opened pictures of father and daughter. The faces staring out of her arrest photograph and from the bench of the Steelworks are surprisingly similar. I clicked on a file marked 'Maureen: 17'. She had the same heavy jaw and was recognizably from the same family, but her stare was moody rather than combative.

'He never hit Maureen,' Patricia said.

'Why not?'

'She was a lot softer and, frankly, not as intelligent.'

Bob gave Maureen a nickname, Moby. The whole family used it. But Myra was just Myra.

The tension was exacerbated by the fact that six days out of seven a night broken by Maureen's crying was followed by an early morning. The Hindleys' house stood at the end of Eaton Street, next to an alleyway, or 'ginnel', that led to Beyer Peacock's. First, a solitary pair of clogs rang out on the cobbles, followed by the repeated tapping of a long pole on window panes – the 'knocker-up' waking the early shift. It was a ritual repeated across the working-class districts of Manchester. Although the rapping of the pole stirred Myra she was able to roll over, and Maureen usually stayed asleep. But twenty minutes later the tramp, tramp of massed feet bounced off the thin brick walls and into the family's bedroom, waking Maureen. This was the cue for Bob to yell at Nellie about the 'bloody baby', and Nellie to yell at Bob about his 'bloody hangover'. Myra would pretend to be asleep, but there was only so much squabbling she could take. When she did get up the anger was inevitably deflected in her direction. She was told to stop 'slopping about' and look after her sister while her parents struggled into their clothes. At breakfast, Nellie sat and glowered at Bob over her cup of tea until the inevitable, often deliberately misplaced word sparked the first row of the day. If they did appear to be managing a peaceful breakfast Myra would start something off, while Maureen sat there meekly.

Like Myra, Nellie remembered what things had been like during the war and resented her present circumstances. It couldn't go on like this, but rather than leave Bob, she waited until they were alone and made a suggestion: what if Myra went to stay with Gran? Bob did not argue.

Chapter Two

Myra was five years old when she was moved back to her Gran's, and while she was glad to be 'home' again there was a lurking sense of rejection. There had never been any question of Moby being the one to go. Gran, sensing that she needed protection, gave Myra the front bedroom; she would be 'fine', herself, sleeping next to the stove downstairs. It was what she'd done when Bert and Kath lived there. In truth, Ellen saw the new arrangement as 'making the best of a bad job'. She hoped that it might reduce the fighting between Nellie and Bob. There was little shame attached to a girl moving in with her grandmother, even when the parents lived less than a minute's walk away. So many of the houses in West Gorton were over-crowded, and dilapidated, that children were often spread among the extended family. The nature of the Hindleys' problems was far from unique.

Myra's new bedroom was sparse. Standing next to the window was a rickety marble-topped chest of drawers and a straight-backed wooden chair. A grubby door led to a built-in wardrobe.

The floorboards were covered in lino that lifted at the edges, barely disguised by a rag-peg rug. There was an old double bed with a lumpy flock mattress and piles of old coats for blankets. Gran told Myra that the fading jumble was 'cheaper as well as warmer' than blankets. A bolster ran along the base of the head-board, just like in her parents' house, covered in a row of saggy old pillows. There was a fireplace, but it didn't work because it was blocked up with soot.

The back bedroom was empty, but it became part of Myra's small domain. It was completely bare, not even used for junk. All she found when she looked in the built-in wardrobe was a couple of old gas masks. There was no lino in the room to bind the floor-boards together, which tipped up dangerously when you put your weight on them. The rear window looked out over the other houses' yards. At the end of each cobbled rectangle stood a small wooden hut. Myra remembered watching men stagger out to relieve themselves, muzzy with sleep, first thing in the morning and again, sedated by beer, just before bed.

At night, Gran heated bricks in the stove, wrapped them in blankets and put them into the bed to warm it. When the weather got really cold and ice formed on the inside of the window, Myra made a nest in the cupboard and crawled inside, curling round the heated bricks to keep herself warm. Sometimes, Gran let her share her bed downstairs, but not often: Myra wriggled too much.

There is no criticism in anything Myra Hindley wrote of her mother for sending her away. But Patricia Cairns says that resentment at being rejected by Nellie endured long into her imprisonment. The two women discussed it at length, shortly after they fell in love in the early 1970s. 'She always said in public that being sent to live with her gran was a good thing. While she was happy to criticize her father she did not want to upset her mother. In reality, it was the most hurtful thing that could have happened to her. It was the first time in her life that she was made to feel the outsider. That lasted for the rest of her life.'

Gran supplemented her pension by taking in washing from families who did not have the time to do their own, or the money to afford a laundry. The clothes were scrubbed in the sink and boiled in a large tin tub on the stove, the whites with 'dolly blue' bleach added to make them gleam. Between each pair of houses along Beasley Street was fixed a large iron arm. Gran and her neighbour, Hettie Rafferty, shared one. On fine days, the clothes were hoisted up, like sails, using a rope. When the wind blew, the street looked like Nelson's fleet sailing into battle. But if it rained, which was often, the parlour was filled with dripping sheets, shirts and underwear. Gran tested the iron by rubbing it against a bar of laundry soap. When it was hot enough for cotton there was a loud hissing, and green gobbets of soap danced onto the stone below. Myra and Gran scrubbed the floor with brown chalk, and swabbed it down. The front step, and the stones around it, got the same treatment. Nobody was going to take their laundry to be washed in a dirty house. When ready, the clothes were neatly stacked on a dresser behind the front door, and scented with small bunches of lavender. These came from gypsies who sold door to door. Gran never refused to buy for fear of being 'cursed' – unless, that is, she thought they hadn't noticed she was inside.

Gran listened to Valentine Dyall's *Workers' Playtime* as she pressed the cotton. The radio was powered by two large glass accumulator bottles which had to be charged in turn. Myra recalled an occasion when one of the accumulator bottles went. Ellen handed her the discharged glass and a clutch of coins. In order to save time on her way to the radio shop Myra cut across a piece of waste land that separated the back doors of Taylor and Casson Streets. It was covered with bits of broken furniture and discarded bathroom fittings. Unsighted by the large glass bottle she tripped, smashed it, and burned her legs with acid. It took an effort for Gran not to belt her. The accumulator bottle represented a lot of washing.

Despite having sent her to stay at Gran's, Bob insisted that Myra return home for most meals. Breakfast was fine – just a few barked orders to her, Maureen or Mam before he ducked out the door clutching a greaseproof packet of butties. The trouble came at tea time. He'd have had one pint on the way back from work with his mates and would be wanting to get down to the Steelworks for a few more. The 'need of a drink' made him belligerent.

He would tell Myra she should 'stick up' for herself, take rubbish from no-one. He showed her how to throw punches: hooks, jabs, head-shots, gut-shots. Myra recalled Bob's instruction in her autobiography: 'Don't put both hands up! If you can't deflect the first punch with one arm keep the other one ready to protect your stomach.'

West Gorton was so tightly packed with families and kids that friendships and enmities came along in equal measure. Kenny Holden did not like Myra, and found a nasty way of showing it: he walked straight up to her in the street, rested the nails of each hand against her cheeks, and raked them down, leaving behind eight bloody tramlines. Myra burst out crying, and ran into the house. Bob demanded to know who had done it. 'Kenny,' she replied, hoping that he'd march round to Alice Holden's to demand justice. Instead, Myra recorded, he grabbed her by the wrist, opened the door and said, 'Go and punch him, because if you don't I'll leather you. It's either him or you!' Myra heard the bolt slam home behind her. Kenny came down the street towards her, his fingers curled, ready to scratch again. Myra, mindful of Bob's words, threw her left fist at his head. Kenny brought up both hands, leaving his stomach unprotected. She delivered a hard right to the exposed area and, as he doubled up in agony, slammed her left into Kenny's temple. He slumped to the ground, crying. Myra wrote, 'I stood looking down at him triumphantly. At eight years old I'd scored my first victory.' Bob ruffled her hair when she came in for tea. That made her feel good. News of what she'd done to Kenny got around. It didn't do her any harm, just marked her out as someone not to mess with.

I discussed the account of this fight, and Bob's role in it, with Professor Malcolm MacCulloch. He told me that they were key pieces of evidence in trying to understand Myra Hindley. 'The relationship with her father brutalized her,' he commented. 'She was not only used to violence in the home but rewarded for practising it outside. When this happens at a young age it can distort a person's reaction to such situations for life.'

'Hardly an excuse though, is it?' I replied.

'We're not looking for excuses, we're looking for explanations.'

I asked Patricia Cairns whether she agreed with MacCulloch's assessment.

'Yes, absolutely. She was brought up in an aggressive, violent atmosphere. It would have an effect on any child. And she was a strong child . . .'

Increasingly, Myra retreated into her own world. She ate at Gran's whenever she could. Bob and Nellie sometimes let her go – she was 'a right pain' when she was at home, her complaints like a drumbeat. Myra recounted in her autobiography how these confrontations would go.

'I don't like stew and dumpling / fish / hotpot / soup.'

'Eat it or I'll give you a smack.'

She was at her most annoying when she compared Mam's food to Gran's.

'Your rice pudding's not the same. It's not lovely and brown on top like hers.'

'You ungrateful little . . .'

A belt round the head made no difference. Myra was too strong to be bothered, and just sat there staring at Nellie. If Bob wasn't there to give her a hiding, Nellie would try, 'Just wait 'til your father gets home.' If that failed she'd say, 'You not only look like your father. You act like him too.' This infuriated Myra, she admitted in her autobiography, because she knew it was true. She also recognized that her personality was moulded in Bob's image. One letter to her mother from prison reveals that when she had to have plastic surgery following a beating by a fellow inmate, she asked the surgeon to remove all the shared characteristics he could.

Gran's rice pudding was better because she made it in the cast-iron oven on top of the fireplace, rather than on the stove she used for boiling up the washing. There was always a lovely skin on it, which Myra peeled off and ate before mixing in seedless bramble jam. Another of Myra's childhood favourites was steamed prunes. They ate these at the table by the window, looking out on to the street, chatting as they shared their meal. The dark, tasselled table cloth was covered by a smaller white one made of linen. Everything was just so: a tall, thin bottle of sterilized milk, a loaf of 'shop bought' bread, a jar of jam, a quarter-pound of margarine on a saucer, a bottle of HP Sauce and, every now and then, a jar of Camp coffee. Pride of place went to the tin of condensed milk which Myra poured onto her prunes – and, if Gran's back was turned, straight into her mouth.

Nellie thought Gran was far too 'soft', but she was tired of fighting with her wilful daughter. She reached an unspoken compromise: whatever she, Bob and Maureen were eating was accompanied by a 'side' dish of chips which, in reality, were just for Myra. But Nellie couldn't resist a dig. 'If you eat any more chips you'll be called Chippy, just like the Athertons.' Myra ignored her. The family she had referred to were particularly poor and notorious for existing on a diet of almost nothing but deep-fried potatoes.

Myra's triumph over Kenny Holden won her respect from the other Taylor Street kids. Fights, says Patricia Cairns, were a way of establishing a pecking order. 'Like me, she was a tomboy and she stuck up for herself, and for Maureen. If anybody gave them trouble she'd fight. She was always tough. That's how it was on the streets in those days: you either stuck up for yourself or you got picked on. And people were on top of one another in Gorton. There were no gardens. I lived in a working-class area and we had a garden front and back, but there it was all streets and alley-ways. There was no place to hide. We used to call Gorton "town". I went to Mrs Moulton's house, where she grew up, later on. It was grotty.'

Like many children from unhappy families, Myra found a retreat in the world of books. Late in the evenings she retreated to her bedroom in Beasley Street. She sat on the bed, a couple of old cushions propped up on the bolster behind her head, and read. She liked Beatrix Potter and Enid Blyton for the same reason: they were a complete world into which she could escape. She imagined that she was George, the tomboy in the Famous Five. When it got dark, because there was no gaslight upstairs, she had to use a candle. The ability to derive nourishment from literature, to realize that there were other worlds than the one she found herself trapped in, was to prove a common bond with Ian Brady.

*

Opposite the foundry on Gorton Lane stands what was Peacock Street Primary, a brick building painted with murals in bold colours. As I walked towards it I realized that I was looking at self-portraits of children at the 'Buzz pupil referral unit'. Beneath a large planet Saturn, circled with black rings, played a girl with blue hair called Kai, another in a pink top and yellow spotty skirt, and two boys with the Nike 'swoosh' on their jumpers. While the murals were new, the building itself belonged unmistakably to another era. Running up the side of the wall was a heavy cast-iron drainpipe, its dark red shape softened by the contours of eighty years' repainting. The tungsten light shining weakly through the window, mixing with the winter sunset, illuminated a stark classroom.

All the kids from the Taylor Street area came here. Myra's favourite lesson was English. They took it in turns to read out passages from a book. The class sat obediently through Frances Hodgson Burnett's *The Secret Garden*: 'She felt there was no knowing what might happen in a house with a hundred rooms nearly all shut up – a house standing on the edge of a moor.' The book, with its image of beauty hidden in a bleak landscape, captivated Myra. She kept a copy all her life and re-read it at times of stress.

Another favourite was Arthur Ransome's *Swallows and Amazons*. She imagined herself sailing in the Lake District, like the 'posh' children in the book. They had different-sounding names from the Peacock Street kids. Myra enjoyed listening to this book but hated reading it out loud herself. All the boys held their breath when, scanning ahead, they saw their favourite girl's name and fell about laughing as she read out 'Titty'. It didn't matter how often the teacher batted them round the head, they just couldn't help themselves.

After school, Myra mucked about on Gorton Lane with Joyce

Hardy, who lived on Beyer Street, next to Peacock Street. Her friend had a mischievous temperament and short blonde hair that made her look like an urchin. They stood in the doorway of the dry cleaner's and stuck their arms and legs out so that, reflected in the window, they doubled up. If they had the cash they bought sweets from the old-fashioned herbalist's. It sold 'halfpenny Spanish', or real liquorice, pear drops, and lemon drops with sherbet inside. If they were 'rich' they got a glass of sarsaparilla, sat at the high glass counter and watched the traffic go by outside.

The school came up in conversation as I sat having a cup of tea with Alan Bennett. Life was going well for him: he'd escaped the job in the stock-room at Argos and started work as a class-room assistant in Moss Side. It was a rough school, but he felt he was doing something that mattered.

'A strange thing happened . . .' he said.

'What?'

'The local education authority sent me to Peacock Street for a special needs course. One of the people who runs it said, "You'll never guess what. This is where Myra Hindley went to school." '

'What did you say?'

'Nothing. Bit of a conversation stopper, telling them she murdered my brother.'

Myra, emboldened by her triumph over Kenny Holden, did not intend to 'take grief' from anyone. But, over time, some of the boys, like Eddie Hogan, came to imagine that the fight might have been a one-off, or that Kenny was 'soft'. They were look-ing for an excuse to provoke her. Providence granted Eddie his wish when Myra got nits. Gran kept her inside, raked her hair with a steel comb, picked at her scalp until it ached and poured on 'some awful-smelling liquid'. Only when Gran was sure that she had killed all the insects did she allow Myra out. Eddie was waiting, and chanted, 'Nitty Nora, Nitty Nora.' Myra couldn't believe what she was hearing, and stood there while the words sank in.

Suddenly, she leapt at him. They fell to the ground, lashing out at each other and rolling over and over on the cobbles. A crowd of kids gathered round them and began to cheer. Myra's problem was Eddie's weight. When they reached the kerb at the edge of the road, he pinned her down and climbed on top. This was the point at which etiquette demanded one of two outcomes: either she would submit and lose the fight, or she would refuse and they would get to their feet and start all over again. Eddie broke the rules: when Myra refused to give in, instead of letting her go, he punched her in the face. But as Eddie's fist connected his weight shifted, and Myra was able to twist herself free. Once she was on top he was helpless. Her feet and fists flew into him so that he squealed in agony.

Alerted by the commotion, Gran entered the fray. She tried to prise Myra off with one arm and used the other to beat Eddie with a rolled-up copy of the *Manchester Evening News*. Myra enjoyed the exchange that followed, and recorded it in her autobiography.

'Please, missus, it's not me, it's her. She's mad, gerrer off me!'

'Do you submit?' Myra asked him.

'Yes, let me up!'

Eddie scrambled to his feet and shuffled down the street, bent over with pain. Gran retrieved her *Evening News*, bashed Myra on the shoulder, and told her to get in the house. Myra recorded, 'Eddie never called me Nitty Nora again.'

The first draft of Myra Hindley's autobiography contains many detailed descriptions of fights. Later accounts, like the letters she wrote to me, hardly mention them. It was as if she came to understand that these incidents revealed there was a flaw in her long before she met Ian Brady.

While it is clear from the various different accounts of Myra Hindley's childhood that she was tough, it is just as clear that she was not delinquent. One story in her autobiography, vividly related and convincing, describes how she played an important, if legally dubious, economic role in Gran's business.

The laundry business quickly consumed the hundredweight of coal and half-hundredweight of slack (smaller pieces of coal) that Gran bought off the back of the horse-drawn delivery cart each week. Myra made up the deficit. She wandered round the corner to the wash-house and pushed open the door. Steam enveloped her face, and she had to pause, peering into the darkness, while she got used to the change in atmosphere. She made out four or five figures in the large, dark space. A woman in her forties, her dress covered by a cotton 'day coat', stood in the centre stirring a huge boiling vat of clothes; two others stooped over piles of damp cotton at the long wooden draining boards that ran down either side of the room. They wrung out each skirt, shirt, blouse and sock, then carefully spread them on a large drying rack. When this was full they pushed it into a specially heated room off to one side; to the other side Myra could see more women working mangles, and ironing. This was why families were willing to pay Gran to do the work for them. Ignoring the women, Myra made her way towards a pram that stood close to the boiling vat. It was used for transporting dirty clothes. The woman working there turned to her and told her to make sure she washed it down properly before she brought it back. Myra promised that she would.

As she shoved the pram ahead of her down Taylor Street, Myra kept an eye out for the police. If they saw her they would know she was on her way to steal coal off the railway. The train company had nailed up large wooden boards right through Gorton in order to try to stop people breaking in. All they succeeded in doing was creating a new expression: 'going over the boards'. Myra parked the pram next to a hand-sized gap in the fence and scrambled up. She hooked her fingers through whatever holes she could find, braced her feet against the wood and pulled herself up. Out of breath as she dropped over the other side, she lost her balance and tumbled a few feet down the steep embankment. But there was no pain, only pleasure as she felt chunks of coal digging through her cotton dress. They had fallen off the freight wagons as they rounded the bend – large, beautiful chunks of the best-quality coal. Not the gritty slack that other people trudged to the yard for when they had run out. The best, heaviest chunks had rolled to the bottom of the embankment onto the track. She ran up and down the slope, gathering the pieces into an old pillowcase before emptying them, one by one, through the gap in the fence into the pram. She kept listening for trains, and looking out for bobbies. She'd been caught stealing before and been dragged back to Gran's for a telling-off. As it was Gran who had sent her the reprimand was never very severe. On the way back she threw the pillowcase on top of the large pile of coal. That way a passing constable might just think it was slack.

The only adult who showed real signs of concern about Myra's moral development was Auntie Kath, who had never had any children with Bert. On Sundays she took Myra to mass. They met at the junction of Beasley and Bannock Streets, and walked hand in hand towards the monastery. Because of Nellie's hostility towards the Catholic Church there were no plans for Myra to be confirmed, but, like Kath, she still fasted before mass. Myra loved her and wanted to be like her.

Sunday, Myra recorded in her autobiography, was the only time when unfamiliar faces appeared on the streets of Gorton.

People came from all over east Manchester to worship at St Francis'. The ritual of going to mass removed all barriers and people talked easily as they made their way into the cavernous church. At the door, women pulled their scarves tight over their heads and men took off their hats and caps; inside, many paused to pray before a statue of a favourite saint. The 'head of the family' usually put a coin in the collection tray or poor box, with a studied lack of ostentation, before taking his seat. Myra positioned herself at the end of a pew so that she was sprinkled with incense by the passing priest. She didn't understand a word of the mass – it was conducted in Latin – but the ritual offered a soothing escape.

She was ten when she first came back here during the week. There was something about the empty space, with its memories of Sunday, that allowed her to lose herself. The red carpet and gold paint mixed with the afternoon light streaming through the stained glass gave the space a warm glow. She sat at the back and watched the monks, floating in their brown robes, as they came and went through the side door to the monastery. Many fell briefly to their knees in front of the Calvary scene before returning to work.

The woman scrubbing the floor did not look up as Myra made her way between the aisles. She genuflected as she crossed the carpet that ran down the centre of the church, and walked down the side aisle towards the altar of St Anthony. She dropped a penny into the box for a candle and knelt down to place it as close to the saint as possible. As her fingers stretched out they brushed against a small pile of folded papers – petitions to the saint. In her autobiography, Myra described how she read these messages. 'For Catherine, who has pneumonia, that she'll be made well through your prayers.' She refolded each petition and dropped it back in its place before picking up another. 'For Ted, that he might, through your intercession, stop drinking for the sake of his health, and so that we'll have more money for food.'

Myra's affection for the monastery never faded, according to Patricia Cairns. 'Myra had a lot of photos of St Francis'. I went and took them for her on a visit north. It had a wonderful atmosphere with the stained glass and beautiful, beautiful altars. There was no place like it. I used to cycle from Denton to go there.'

After church, on the street, Myra's behaviour remained unchanged; she kept her reputation for being tough. At the bottom of a box of personal effects from her cell I found a small collection of childhood pictures. There was one of her in close-up, grinning, with two bottom teeth missing. It was obviously a cold day as she was wearing an old polo neck beneath a knitted cardigan, and her hair looked like she'd just been playing a rough game. Her head was tipped to one side. She looked self-confident, as if she'd just given the photographer a good ragging.

Beneath this picture were images recording a highlight of Gorton life: the communal trip to the seaside. Two or three times a year the people of Beasley Street, Bannock Street and Taylor Street got together to hire a bus, or 'sharrer', to take them somewhere special – Blackpool, Southport or New Brighton. One trip, recorded in her autobiography, shows that she fitted into these outings like the other children, bowing to the authority of adults.

They were in the sea at New Brighton, being washed back and forth by the surf. The adults, some of them holding bottles of beer, took little notice of what was going on. Until, that is, a boy called Eric, who had polio, lost his footing and went under. When he came up his shorts had disappeared. Eric's mother wrapped the shivering child in her cardigan, but it was no good. He had no pants on; they couldn't go about like that all day. Nellie had a solution – her daughter's knickers. Myra protested at the shame of it, pointing out that Gran wouldn't let her out of the house with snapped knicker elastic 'in case she was run over'. And here they were suggesting she should walk around in nothing but a skirt? Besides, her knickers were wet. But Nellie stood firm. Myra followed Eric round for the rest of the day, trying to ignore the shame of seeing her damp underwear clinging to his wet skin.

Back at school, Myra stood out as one of the brighter children, and at the age of eleven she was chosen to 'have a go' at the eleven plus. The girls sitting for grammar school left Peacock Street in a small group, with their teacher, and caught a bus to Levenshulme High. They were led up a grand staircase to the examination room. Myra was overwhelmed by the strangeness of it all. There were 'real' paintings on the walls; the girls who rushed past them wore smart uniforms, and carried leather satchels. In the examination hall she sat down at a desk covered with blotting paper and got out her ruler, pencil and pen. Then she froze. It was madness to think she could come here. Where would the money for clothes, never mind the bus fare, come from? She failed the paper.

Myra and Nellie fought about where she should go to secondary school. Like all arguments in the Hindley household it raged back and forth. Myra wanted to attend St Francis'; Nellie wanted her to go to a new mixed-faith school. Myra said she wanted to be with her friends; Nellie replied that all the monks taught was the catechism, and a fat lot of good it had done Dad. Bob became involved, said he'd prefer the Catholic school. But Nellie reminded him of the deal they'd made when Myra was baptized a Catholic, and her argument clinched it. Myra was enrolled at Ryder Brow Secondary Modern, on the other side of the Hyde Road, where she would never quite lose the feeling of being an outsider. It was a decision that would affect the rest of her life.

Chapter Three

I walked out of Piccadilly station and headed down the concrete apron that leads to the centre of Manchester. Ahead of me was a tall, overweight man wearing a faded sweatshirt and a pair of baggy tracksuit bottoms. At his side was a similarly dressed boy of about eight. They both carried notebooks, and wore binoculars – trainspotters. But there was something odd about them: they were *leaving* the station with a real sense of purpose, excitement even. Intrigued, I watched where they were going. Five minutes later we were standing next to one another in trainspotting heaven – a shop stuffed with implausible titles like *Diesels of Spain* and *The Great British Traction Engine*. I pretended to be interested while I observed the odd couple.

There was something touching about their absorption, and I had decided to leave them to it when a title caught my eye, *Images of England: Gorton*. I pulled the book off the shelf and looked at the front cover. It showed a sepia-tinted photograph of an extraordinary scene. A terraced street had been closed to traffic, bunting strung across it every few yards, garlands hung above windows and doors. Running down the centre of the road was a long line of kitchen tables jammed end to end, covered in linen and decorated with flower-filled vases. Plates were heaped with carefully cut triangular white sandwiches; biscuits were presented above them on glass stands, covered in crocheted doilies. But the most striking thing was the dense crowd of people staring intently into the lens. The children sat; the parents, some in paper hats, stood behind them. They were impeccably dressed. Everyone looked happy, but there was hardly a smile to be seen. This was a serious endeavour, a demonstration of self-respect, and they wanted it recorded as such. I flipped open the cover: King George V Silver Jubilee party in Henry Street, West Gorton, 1935.

I leafed through the pages – schools, churches, marching bands, the arrival of a new car. Every shot recorded something people had reason to be proud of. Then I came to page 83, Pupils of Ryder Brow in the 1950s. There, carefully captioned, were Myra's friends Jean Hicks and Linda McGurk, and the head boy she fancied, Ronnie Woodcock. At the end of the back row, smiling openly just like everyone else, was a girl in a stripy cardigan, her shoulder-length hair carefully brushed – Myra Hindley. The author must have realized who the girl was but chose to ignore her presence. This story repeated itself across Manchester: there was almost no written record of the city's most infamous daughter.

Myra Hindley described in her autobiography how, soon after starting at Ryder Brow, she began truanting. She used to bully Nellie and Gran into letting her stay at home and writing a letter to the teacher: Myra had a 'bad period', a 'headache', 'the 'flu'. When they refused, she wrote the note herself.

Myra and Pat Jepson, who lived opposite, often walked to

school together. If they were bunking off without consent they waited in Sunny Brow Park before looping back to Beasley Street. Once Mam had gone to work, they sloped off down the ginnel that ran behind Eaton Street and in through the back door for a second breakfast. Myra was confident she knew Mam's habits, knew exactly how long she would have the house to herself. But one day she was frying bacon in the kitchen and Pat was buttering bread in the lounge when there was the sound of feet stopping by the front door and a hand on the knob. Pat was first out the back door; Myra followed in her footsteps, still carrying the pan. She jammed it into the narrow space behind the privy and sprinted down the ginnel. It was only when they got to the road that they realized the person at the door was Gran. If they'd stayed they could have talked their way out of it. As it was, flight was a clear admission of guilt. It was one thing to slope off with permission, quite another to do so without it.

They decided to throw themselves on the mercy of Myra's other grandmother, 'Nanna' Hindley. It was a decision made in the heat of the moment, and one Myra regretted as soon as the door cracked open to reveal the grim countenance that had given birth to her father. Myra's grandmothers could not have been more different. Gran used nothing more than Pears soap on her straight white hair; Nanna's 'styled' curls were dyed a frightening shade of orange. Gran did not wear make-up; Nanna never left the house without her lipstick on. Gran was soft and malleable; Nanna was fearsome and opinionated. But, much to Myra's surprise, she invited the girls in and remained quite calm during the long, detailed confession. She told them to make her a cup of tea, and themselves the second breakfast they'd been denied. Myra glanced round as she cooked. Pat, pale-faced with worry, watched as Nanna took out her pin curls and smeared on lipstick. It was the same shade as her hair. She always looked nice for work on 'The Twister' helter-skelter at Belle Vue, and the married lover Nellie unkindly referred to as her 'fancy man'. Nanna then made the girls wash up and walked them back to Beasley Street.

Pat and Myra didn't exchange a word but they were convinced that Gran would shop them and pack them off to Ryder Brow. But Gran was so astonished to hear Nanna argue leniency for a 'first offence' that she accepted her suggestion: the girls should spend the day cleaning the houses at Eaton and Beasley Streets. But, even as she agreed, Myra could see Gran work out the intended slight: Nanna's house, where she lived alone, was spotless. Nanna departed and, with a cheery wave, told the girls not to do it again. Myra simply resolved never to get caught again.

While the girls worked, Ellen continued with her washing. She had to decide whether to let their parents know what had happened. She turned the handle of the mangle and streams of cold water sprang from the linen into a white basin at her feet. If she told Nellie there would be a row, and Bob would find out. It was easier to let it go; arguments between Myra and Bob almost always turned into full-blown fights. And Gran was not happy about her own daughter's role in this conflict. Too often she had heard Nellie trampling Myra's feelings, transferring the anger she felt at Bob on to her daughter.

But, according to Patricia Cairns, it was difficult for Gran to protect Myra. 'I don't know how much her gran was able to intervene, but she was the only source of kindness to Myra,' she said. 'She was always gentle. Her house was a place of refuge and warmth.'

I was puzzled. 'If her gran was like that, how come Nellie was so violent and malicious towards her?'

'There's no reason for it in her background. Ellen was born out of wedlock, so I have no idea who her father was. Perhaps there's some explanation for it there. I don't know.'

'Do you think that the violence at home affected the way she disciplined Myra?' I asked.

'She was soft. Too soft probably. What Myra needed was a firm guiding hand, and that wasn't there.'

The teachers at school were not fooled by Myra's sick-notes. She remembered how one day, after taking the register, Mr Lloyd-Jones laid down his pencil, leaned back, peered through his thick-rimmed glasses and ordered the class to 'give her a round of applause'. It was the first time she had called out 'present' for five consecutive days. Her truanting had denied her class any chance of victory in the school's attendance competition.

Mr Lloyd-Jones was a patient teacher, but even he found it difficult to endure the quality of Myra's efforts at art, and he expressed his exasperation. Myra replied that while she might not be able to draw, she could write. Taking her at her word, the headmaster got her to keep an 'official' class diary. He noted, with satisfaction, that she concentrated and wrote reasonably well. After a few weeks, worried that the task was becoming boring for her, he suggested that she write a story for a classmate to illustrate. Myra threw herself into the task and, after discarding a couple of ideas, came up with *Adventure at Four Oaks Farm*. The story, which borrowed heavily from Enid Blyton, described how a group of children captured a 'sinister' man who had threatened them in the cellar of a remote farmhouse. A character modelled on George of the Famous Five played a leading role in the adventure. Jean Hicks, the best artist in the class, illustrated it. Mr Lloyd-Jones was delighted; he had it bound 'like a proper book' and put in the school library.

Myra stood out at sport, too. The Ryder Brow rounders team

was well drilled, and it competed successfully against other Manchester schools. Myra acquired the nickname 'Monkey' for the speed with which she once climbed over a fence to retrieve a ball and run out an opponent. Many of the children at Ryder Brow came from the surrounding 1920s estate; their homes were semi-detached, and they had gardens. As Myra walked to school she saw men leaving the houses wearing suits. Even the kids who walked the short distance from West Gorton were mainly Anglican. When they played matches Myra found herself copying her team-mates' superior attitude to kids from 'rough' schools, like Spurley Hay. But she felt uncomfortable doing this, as none of them was poorer than the kids of West Gorton. The pretence increased her feeling of being an 'outsider'.

Bob continued to drink heavily throughout Myra's teenage years, and to batter Nellie. The only time they united was to attack their daughter for her behaviour. Things only got worse as Myra grew bigger and became more able to fight her corner, verbally as well as physically. Once, in the middle of an argument, she used a line she'd learned at school.

'You've only got one bad habit, Dad.'

'Only one? What is it?'

'Breathing.'

Bob was so upset he marched out of the house and slammed the front door. For once, even Nellie was silenced.

Myra hated it when people compared her to Bob, which happened often. It was inevitable, as she had followed in his footsteps by maintaining a reputation as a 'scrapper'. Myra used the excuse of 'defending' other children as a way of getting into fights. Maureen was always being picked on; she lacked the strength, and wit, to look after herself. Myra also 'looked out' for her sister's friend Pauline Reade, the first victim of the Moors murders, and her brother Paul. When someone wanted to prove themselves hard they came looking for Myra Hindley.

Early one New Year, Myra wrote in her autobiography, she was making her way down a ginnel when a voice called out from a back yard. It was a boy called Eric Goodwin asking her to guess what he'd got for Christmas. He was standing there with his hands tucked behind his back. She waited, in silence, knowing he'd tell her anyway. He brought his hands to the front to reveal two pairs of brown leather boxing gloves, their long white laces swaying gently in the breeze. Myra looked at them, then at Eric's legs. One was strong and healthy, the other thin and crippled. Surely he couldn't be serious?

It took Myra a while to tie the laces, which she eventually managed with the help of her teeth. Her hands felt big and clumsy. Eric stood there in a crouch, his fists held up in front of his skinny face. She laughed at him: he looked ridiculous. Eric responded by unleashing a stinging combination that sent Myra careering backwards into the yard wall. Her shoulder bashed against a wash tub balanced on top, and it came crashing down on her head. Stars, she recalled, swirled in front of her eyes, accompanied by the ringing of Eric's laughter. She lay there, careful not to get up before she had collected her senses, then charged at Eric. She rammed him with her shoulder. Her knee crashed into his head as he went down; he had no chance to recover. When she had finished he lay on the floor, whimpering.

She was about to untie the gloves when Albert Goodwin appeared, filling the entrance to the back yard, glaring at her. He asked Myra if she would like to fight someone her own size. She could not refuse, and stood there while he gently unlaced the gloves from his brother's hands and pulled them onto his own. Myra worked out her strategy as she waited. She reckoned she'd got the hang of fighting with gloves on, but she was wrong. Albert did know what he was doing, and he drove her around the back yard at will. He was careful not to finish her off too quickly, and jabbed at her face until she could feel it swelling. When she did finally fall he continued to hit her for a long time after she went still.

Two days later Myra bumped into Albert at the top of Taylor Street. There was only a narrow stretch of pavement as the road was blocked by a large puddle. Albert filled it, and clearly had no intention of moving. Myra's right eye was still puffy from the beating he'd given her. Albert smiled, admiring his handiwork. Without warning, Myra grabbed him by the lapels, tucked her right leg behind his, and tipped him over. She went down on top of him, grabbed his hair and slammed his head into the puddle. Stunned by the cold, wet stone against his skull Albert didn't stand a chance. She continued to hammer his head into the ground until a couple of his mates dragged her off. She knew Gran would be furious with her but she didn't care.

In Myra Hindley's autobiography it is striking how accounts of violence are juxtaposed with stories that illustrate her ability to form close personal relationships. One boy she never fought was Michael Higgins, who lived on Taylor Street. He was two years younger than Myra. The age difference meant that they had never been in the same class, and did not wear the shackles of a shared history. They spent hours together, roaming West Gorton and getting into scrapes. There was no question of romance; they were 'mates'.

Myra and Michael enjoyed swimming, and on summer evenings they went to Mellings Field reservoir. Although in the middle of Gorton the reservoir is surrounded by allotments and tall trees, and the shoreline is ringed by thick green reeds that flower a vibrant yellow in summer. They spent hours mucking about here, either on their own or with friends, secure in the knowledge that they would not be disturbed by adults.

In the city's Central library I flicked through pictures of all Manchester's reservoirs looking for an image of Mellings Field in the 1950s. The mundane municipal title does not do the grand circular building justice. The Central library was built as a symbol of Manchester's wealth and sophistication. Its domed roof and Ionic columns dominate St Peter's Square. Even the magnificent town hall bends around its contours. Its local studies section is the largest and most comprehensive I have seen. At one end of the room stands a line of computers on which members of the public can do picture research. Every photograph in the city's vast collection has been scanned, and many more have been supplied by individuals and local history groups.

I typed in the name of another of Myra and Michael's favourite places: 'Belle Vue'. The screen filled with a list of entries. There was an aerial shot that showed the 'pleasure gardens' lying next to the streets of Gorton – a world of escape that constantly beckoned people as they went about their daily lives. The permanent attractions included a zoo, a wrestling ring, bars, fairground rides and a speedway track. There were also occasional 'spectaculars': amazing fireworks displays and title fights.

Myra and Michael loved the speedway, but did not always have the funds to pay for a ticket. The solution was simple: they would break in through a secret entrance. The more adventurous children of Gorton got to know every ginnel, scrap of waste land and deserted building. They could slip, seemingly invisible, from Far Lane to 'the tank' and back again. It was a world closed to adults by the demands of dignity and respect for the law. Myra and Michael scrambled up the fence, dropped down the railway embankment and crossed the railway line towards the pleasure gardens. As they ducked and weaved their way across Gorton they saw adults taking more conventional routes for a night out.

They did not hang about on the edge of Belle Vue. The trick was to get in quickly, without being spotted. Myra scrambled up the wall, Michael close behind her. She dropped down and rolled a couple of feet, to give him room to land. Without looking around they jumped up and ran into the crowd streaming towards the stands. None of the staff had seen them, and no-one else was bothered.

Before they took their place in the stands, Michael bought a programme; he collected them. The speedway stadium had the feel, and appearance, of a Roman circus: high, banked stands around a circular dirt track full of expectation. The crowd roared as the riders shot out from the side, blipping their throttles theatrically. They lined up by the starting tape in team colours, shoulders hunched to absorb the force of rising handlebars, and blasted into the first corner. As the bikes tipped sideways, spitting dirt from their rear wheels, and as those who had over-done it spilled into the hoardings, the crowd stood as one and roared. Scarves waved and rattles chattered as though the noise would make a difference to the outcome. It was an intoxicating atmosphere.

Myra recorded in her autobiography that she and Michael made use of Nanna Hindley's name to get into the riders' enclosure between races. All she said to the guard at the gate was, 'Kitty Hindley sent me!' It always worked; Kitty was the sort to repay a favour. The riders stood around, sweating and smoking. The bikes made a ticking sound as the engines cooled, and mechanics checked them before the next race. Michael walked up to the riders, holding out his programme and a pen. The men affected indifference to flattery as Myra and Michael made their way round, gathering autographs, before heading back to Taylor Street.

The Hindleys' home life remained uneasy. Fights between

Nellie, Bob and Myra usually ended with one of them storming out, Myra to Beasley Street, Bob to the pub. If one of their preferred escape routes disappeared the pressure might become unbearable. In Myra's mind, the winter of 1954 threatened exactly that.

Gran was upset. Jim, her daughter Louie's widower, had called round for tea. She was pleased to see him, but as she listened to his soft Irish voice her eyes had inevitably been drawn to the large sepia-tinted picture above the mantelpiece. It showed her and Louie in matching dresses and long, flowing brown locks, looking happy and confident. Just a few months after it was taken Louie lay dead, carried away by peritonitis. Gran told Myra that her hair had turned grey 'overnight', and she'd attempted suicide by taking an overdose. Of course she was glad she hadn't died, but Jim just brought it all back to her. Gran's misery was compounded by the fact that she could no longer even see the picture of Louie clearly. Myra told her to go to the doctor. It turned out to be the beginnings of cataracts. She needed an operation, and a date was set for her to go into the eye hospital.

Myra did not know anyone who had had an operation; she did, however, know that there was always a chance of death. As the day of Gran's surgery got closer and closer Myra became increasingly frightened, and fixated by the idea of mortality. What would happen to her if Gran was gone and Beasley Street was no longer there for her? On the day of Gran's admission Myra sat silently through tea and pretended to read one of Bob's Zane Grey cowboy stories. The thought of having to move back permanently to her parents' house was crushing. At bedtime she wandered round to Beasley Street, pushed open the front door, pulled Gran's old black coat off its hook and put it on. Enveloped in her smell, she lay down on the bed, by the extinguished fire, and fell asleep.

The hospital would not let anyone under sixteen onto the wards. But Myra was so unhappy that Nellie agreed to try to smuggle her in. It would do them all good to be together, confirm that things were going to get back to normal. Mam lent Myra some stockings and a pair of shoes with a small heel. She made her comb the tangles out of her hair and put on a light pink shade of lipstick. They caught the number 53 down to Oxford Road. No-one challenged them as they made their way onto the ward. Ellen could not see them approaching as her head was wrapped in bandages. Myra, upset at finding her so helpless, began to weep. A hand reached out and gripped her. Gran told her not to cry, she'd be home soon.

Galvanized by the possibility of loss, Myra set about smartening up Beasley Street for Gran's return. She got hold of a tin of maroon paint to do the woodwork, so that it matched the flowers in the wallpaper, and leaded the black grate until it shone. Auntie Anne and Mam joined in; they hung bunting around the room, and shook out the rag-peg rug. When they had finished they prepared a special tea for Gran's return.

I asked Professor Malcolm MacCulloch what he thought about Myra Hindley's extreme reaction to her gran's illness. He paused before replying: 'There are a lot of mentions of death, or the proximity of death, in her recollections.'

'Is that significant?' I asked.

'It can be the sign of a personality which has been altered by circumstances,' he replied. 'It's certainly not normal.'

'Have you seen it before?'

'In adult serial killers, certainly. But what is special about this material is that it offers an insight into the formation of Myra Hindley's mind as a child. It's quite unprecedented in cases of this kind.'

Myra Hindley mentioned in her autobiography that a frequent

visitor of Gran's was Hettie Rafferty, who lived opposite. The
old woman had a lined face which screwed up 'like an irate
monkey' when she laughed, which was often. A favourite topic
of conversation was their own mortality. It was seen as a matter
of great importance to prepare for death. Even the poorest person
took out 'funeral insurance', paid in weekly instalments, to cover
the cost of a 'proper burial' in consecrated ground. This ensured
a dignified departure and protected relatives from the sudden
expense of a funeral. For some, this cover extended no further
than a wooden box. These families relied on women like Gran
and Hettie to help 'lay out' the deceased in their best clothes. It
was vital to do this properly, as friends and neighbours would
come to say goodbye to the body before the burial. Hettie and
Gran used to tease each other about who would be the first to go,
who would get to lay the other one out. But when a friend
approached death with no funeral insurance it was no laughing
matter.

'Old Pebby', a friend of Ellen's, lay critically ill in the work-
house. His health had been slipping away for years, reducing him
to the occasional labouring job and forcing him to accept
'charity'. A poor, lapsed Catholic, he faced burial in a pauper's
grave. When Ellen went to visit him he whispered, 'If there is a
God, I ask him to forgive me and save my soul from hell.' This
gave Ellen some hope of laying her friend to rest in consecrated
ground. If she could raise the money for a coffin, she could tell
the monks he had repented. The only solution, Gran told Hettie,
was for her to cash in some of her own funeral insurance.

The first thing Myra noticed as she came through the back
door at Beasley Street was the smell of carnations – embalming
fluid. Old Pebby's coffin stood on a couple of chairs under the
front-room window; a beam of light cut across the middle and
illuminated a pair of crossed white hands. Myra stood rooted to

the spot in the doorway. Gran told her not to be 'feart', it was only Old Pebby. Hettie Rafferty was sitting with her. How long was he staying for, asked Myra. Only 'til tomorrow, said Gran; she couldn't leave him 'without a home to be sent off from'. Myra glanced at Gran's bed, just yards from the coffin. Where was she going to sleep? In bed, as usual, replied the old lady. It was not the dead you had to fear but the living. Myra stepped forwards. She noticed how strong Pebby's hands looked. She started as Gran lifted up the hanky covering his face. Myra reached out and touched Pebby's hand. It wasn't cold, as she'd expected, but 'cool and firm'. Gran put the hanky back in place. Myra noticed how still it was. They sat up next to the coffin all evening. When she came back from school the next day Pebby had gone, the chairs were back in their place, and the house smelt normal.

The dark content of this story does not stand out in her autobiography: death keeps reappearing as a theme in her description of everyday events. The decapitated Jack Russell, called Timmy, she found by the railway line; the boy she saw bleed to death after being crushed by a lorry on the Hyde Road; the cat torn in half by two dogs. And the time when she feared she might die herself.

Eddie Hogan did not give Myra any trouble now, and she had come to like him because he had 'nerve'. Myra, Eddie and Michael Higgins had a scam they worked in a corner shop. Myra went in, bought something small and got the shopkeeper chatting while the boys, all innocent smiles, stuffed things into their pockets. Often it was just rubbish, like string or potatoes, which they had to swap or sell. When they got lucky, with sweets, they ate them in secret to prevent awkward questions. Myra recorded that a favourite place was 'over the loco' – Gorton Tank railway yard. She and Michael would climb the boards and wander about among the trains. The risk of it was exciting. They knew the best times to break in without being discovered. But they didn't always get it right.

One day, Michael was in a train driver's cab, playing with the controls, when they were startled by a shout. Two railway workers in blue boiler suits were hurrying towards them. Michael jumped down, they raced towards the boards, scrambled over the top and headed for the allotments. They didn't want the men to get a good look at them. All of a sudden, Myra's leg stopped moving and a searing pain shot up from her ankle. It felt as though her foot had been trapped in a ferocious set of jaws. She lay on the ground and looked at the blood slowly trickling into the teeth of a 'man-trap'. Michael helped Myra to her feet and she tried to stagger on, the iron contraption swinging from her leg, but the pain was too much, and she collapsed. Michael left her and ran off to get help.

Bert and a neighbour, Mr Richards, carried Myra back to Beasley Street. They laid her on the sofa and tried to prise the jaws of the man-trap open. Bert sent Michael for Dr Chadwick; he returned a few minutes later to say that the elderly GP was on his way. Myra lay on the sofa, groaning, and tried not to writhe; every time she moved the teeth sank further into her ankle. Myra later wrote that she asked Michael, 'I'm not going to die, am I?' He replied, 'Course you won't die! You're too young!'

Like the tales of her fighting, almost all of the incidents concerning death were excised from later accounts of Myra's life. But the one story allowed to remain is, probably, the most telling.

As well as baptizing, educating, marrying and burying the people of Gorton, the church organized rituals that brought a sense of occasion and meaning to the passing seasons. The grandest of these were the annual Whit parades. Across Manchester long lines of people, dressed in their finest clothes, walked behind banners that proclaimed the name of their community. St Francis' schoolchildren walked on Whit Friday, the 'scholars' of the monastery on Sunday. The climax was the breathtaking Italian march in the centre of town on a Monday. The women dressed, like marionettes, in layer upon layer of multicoloured petticoats and flared skirts.

The vaults of the North-West film archive, close to Piccadilly coach station, are filled with 8mm images of Whit parades. The dyes have faded, some colours more quickly than others, leaving bright reds and brilliant whites. Young Catholic girls walk in confirmation dresses, each clutching a posy in snowy-gloved hands with a crown of plaited flowers in her hair. The shots are held for a long time, to capture each passing face. The effort that went into putting on, and recording, the parades speaks of real pride.

For weeks beforehand small family groups boarded the bus from Gorton to 'town'. The parents looked nervous and the children excited. From pants and socks to white dresses and grey suits, everything had to be new. Coyne's on Cross Street did the whole lot 'on tick' for a very reasonable rate. Bob Hindley did not go into town with his wife and daughters in the early summer of 1955, but Nellie was still determined to be careful: it would be her name on the hire-purchase agreement. She was delighted with the special offer: a free pleated skirt with each two-piece suit. She bought Myra and Maureen one each. The children were proud of their outfits; the Whit marches were something to be enjoyed rather than sneered at. Michael's mother bought him a new pair of long trousers, a blazer, a tie and a pullover. He had been chosen to take a leading role in the procession.

There were a couple of photographs of Michael among Myra Hindley's possessions. Looking at them, I found it hard to imagine him in his Whit clothes: they were street pictures, showing him the way he was when he played with Myra. In one, a plaid shirt undone almost to the waist; in another, trousers tucked into heavy woollen socks to stop them from getting fouled in his bicycle chain.

Myra watched the 'Franners' parade on a hot Friday in June with her close friends Pat and Barbara Jepson. The smallest girls, at the head of the procession, wore their white confirmation dresses. They were followed by the older boys. Michael walked alongside Eddie, carrying a large embroidered banner. He disappeared as the Children of Mary, League of Mary and a succession of bands marched past. After the parade the girls caught the 109 to Reddish for a 'posh' afternoon tea with the Jepsons' aunt and uncle. They had scones, cream, sandwiches and chocolate biscuits on proper china. On the way back they rode on the rear platform to get some air. They planned to jump off when the bus slowed for the corner with the Bessamer pub.

As the driver applied the brakes a bicycle, being ridden frantically, appeared at the rear platform. It was Wally, a kid from Taylor Street. He drew up behind them and shouted out that Mike was dead, Mike had drowned. Myra jumped off the bus, skidded to a standstill outside the Bessie and grabbed Wally's handlebars. She asked him what he was on about. He told her that after the parade they'd gone for a swim in the Mellings Field reservoir. Halfway across Mike started shouting he'd got cramp. By the time they got to him he'd disappeared underwater.

Myra started to run, down Taylor Street heading for Mount Road; Pat chased after her. They were full from their tea and still in their best Whit clothes, but did not stop. They tore across the playing fields at the back of the reservoir and down the sandy path to the water where they met a crowd of gloomy-looking boys and girls coming in the opposite direction. Michael's body had been found, they said. The ambulance people tried to pump his lungs, give him the kiss of life, but it was no good. They'd taken him away. His mum had gone with him.

Myra climbed onto the crossbar of a friend's bike and sat there, in silence, as it juddered down the track back to Taylor Street. Everywhere she looked there were groups of adults and children, huddled in stunned silence. Pat's mum, 'Chief' Jepson, had taken refuge in her living room. In the stillness of the house Myra sat down and dissolved into tears, rocking back and forth in Chief's arms.

That night she climbed into bed with Gran and dreamed of Michael. She was diving underwater towards him and trying to grab his hair to pull him to the surface, but it was too short. Then she, too, was sinking into the deep, gulping lungfuls of water. She woke to find Gran stroking her head.

Patricia Cairns says that Myra Hindley felt responsible for the death of Michael Higgins. 'She didn't like to talk about it. She felt very distressed about his death and said she was to blame.'

'How could she be?' I asked. 'She'd just gone off for tea.'

'She felt that if she'd been there it wouldn't have happened. She was a very strong swimmer, and would have been able to save him. But she didn't talk about it at length. You know what Myra's like when she's upset. She just pulls the shutters down and blocks everything out. You can't get through. She couldn't cope with what happened to Mike.'

Mrs Higgins gave Myra Michael's speedway programmes and comb. Myra went door to door collecting money for a wreath, wearing a black armband Gran had made from an old coat. The day before the funeral Michael was laid out in the Higginses' front room. Mrs Higgins ushered Myra in and told her to take a look, otherwise she wouldn't be able to accept he was dead. Michael lay there in his altar boy's clothes. In the autobiography Myra goes into great detail about her best friend's appearance:

his lips were slightly parted, and his eyes hadn't been fully closed – Myra could see a thin sliver of blue reflected in the light. Before the coffin lid was fixed in place Mrs Higgins pulled the rosary from Michael's stiff fingers and handed it to Myra.

The monks said a requiem mass for Michael at St Francis'. The coffin was placed in front of the main altar and a choir made up of his schoolmates sang. After the service Myra turned down the offer of a lift to the cemetery with Mrs Higgins and walked with Pat Jepson. She could not face watching the burial and sat, with her back turned, by the canal at the edge of the cemetery. Pat crouched next to her, watched what was going on and commentated in a low whisper: they are at the graveside; his mam has just thrown soil on the coffin; the mourners are moving away; they are filling in the grave.

After the funeral Michael's family and other friends got on with their lives. But Myra remained fixated by grief. She returned every day to sit by the mound of freshly dug earth with a new offering. At first she brought flowers she'd paid for, then flowers she'd nicked from parks and traffic islands. A few weeks after the tragedy Mrs Higgins bumped into her in the cemetery. Michael's mother said she was worried about Myra and suggested they go to church together. It might help.

Attending St Francis' with Mrs Higgins was a way of staying close to Michael. There was comfort to be derived from having his mother kneel next to her as the monks swung incense and intoned Latin in front of the grand Gothic altar. Myra also got fewer comments from people; they seemed to accept her spending hours on her knees in church rather than crouched by a graveside. The only frustration was that she couldn't take Holy Communion. Mrs Higgins suggested she get confirmed.

Her teacher was Father Theodore, who'd gone to school with Bob. They sat in a side room of St Francis' where there were just a few books, a crucifix and a statue of 'Our Lady', and learned the catechism by rote.

'Who made you?'

'God made me.'

Caught up in the excitement of the new, she did not hold up Father Theodore's pronouncements on the sanctity of marriage against her own personal experience. She also did not fully understand the doctrine to which she was swearing allegiance.

Myra chose Therese as her confirmation name. She was anointed by the bishop of Salford. The whole family, including Nellie, came to watch. Auntie Kath sponsored her, and gave her a pocket prayer book as a present. I found it among her belongings, in a frayed white envelope, with a bright picture of Jesus offering benediction on the cover.

Myra did not forget Michael. One evening, she was sitting in the Jepsons' front room listening to music, and watching rain run down the window, when she noticed a shimmering between the thick rivulets of water. It was Michael, sheltering in the fire escape of the Plaza cinema. His wet hair was plastered to his head, he was wearing his old overcoat, and he was staring at her. She ran to the door and pulled it open, but he had gone.

'The obsession with death in her autobiography is quite striking, and very unusual.'

Malcolm MacCulloch put his coffee cup down, pushed the half-moon glasses up so that they rested on his forehead, and clasped his hands.

'In what way?'

'Do you thread stories of death through your entire childhood?'

'Well, no.'

'Exactly! It's a sign of a personality that has been brutalized by personal experience.'

'But what is the significance of an obsession with death?'

'You have to look at the details. There is a constant backdrop of violence here – she experienced it on a daily basis. That led to a distorted personality. The obsession with death is a manifestation of that distortion.'

It does not feel, when reading the earliest version of Myra Hindley's autobiography, as though she had any idea that the frequent, graphic references to death were unusual. The text has no structure, just words poured onto the page from a fast-flowing stream of consciousness. As we know, her supporters, like David Astor, were dismayed by the results and advised her to make changes before suggesting she abandon it altogether. The later version, and the letters to me, are more tightly written, if still self-serving. Incidents that hint at a damaged personality have been cut. An exception, the story of Michael Higgins, was so well known it could not go. The purpose of the more refined versions, of course, was to portray herself as a victim, and Ian Brady as the manipulator.

Chapter Four

When Detective Superintendent Tony Brett was appointed to run the Moors murder inquiry, and told to ensure that Myra Hindley died behind bars, I got a request to meet Greater Manchester Police detectives. This made me nervous. I was willing to do anything that might lead to the recovery of Keith Bennett, but I did not want to become embroiled in a highly charged political dispute. I agreed to meet the detectives with Professor John Hunter and his assistant, the former head of the West Midlands Police murder squad Detective Chief Superintendent Barrie Simpson, who were working with the family of Keith Bennett to try to recover his body. I was questioning Myra Hindley on their behalf.

'They are going to push you, you know.'

Barrie Simpson looked hard at me to make sure his comment had sunk in. We were waiting in Professor John Hunter's office at Birmingham University.

'Great. So what do I do?'

'Be open, but make it clear that you are helping them

because you want Keith Bennett to be found,' replied Simpson.

'But are *they* interested in finding him?' I asked. 'They've hardly done anything for years!'

Hunter stopped battering away at his email and looked round. 'They've got to! The police can't assign a load of officers to keep her inside and ignore the fact that there's still a child missing!'

There was a knock at the door.

I was surprised at the appearance of DC Andy Meekes, DC Dave Warren and DC Gail Jazmik. They looked like bank managers. They were the smartest-looking bunch of detectives I'd ever met. I was to discover that all members of Greater Manchester Police's FMIT (Force Major Incident Team) dress the same way. I wondered whether this was to mark them out as the elite.

'Sorry we're a bit late, the traffic was awful!' exclaimed Jazmik as she brushed raindrops from her brow. They had obviously hurried up the stairs.

The detectives made small talk as they settled round the table and got their notepads out. I noticed that Barrie Simpson took care not to draw attention to his former, very senior, rank. But he did use the same language as them.

'As you know,' said Jazmik, 'we were assigned to the case to see if there is a way of keeping Myra Hindley in prison.'

I was surprised by her openness. It would have been easy to fudge.

Meekes added, in a matter-of-fact way, 'We have read every book on the case, and been through the files. There has never been a better briefed team of officers.'

'And Keith Bennett?' asked Hunter.

'Of course if we can find him we will. It's what we all want,' replied Jazmik.

Hunter nodded and began to describe his work on the case.

Many of the decisions Hunter had taken about how to search for Keith Bennett were founded on a detailed understanding of events and how the Moors murderers were likely to have behaved. This knowledge was based both on published information and what I had learned. The officers were thorough in their questioning; they probed Hunter's logic at every turn. When it became clear that he was relying on a piece of information that had come from me, they tested its quality. The questioning went on all morning. I was grilled on my involvement with Myra Hindley, my motives and my opinions. Did I want her to get out? Who were her friends? Who were my sources? I did my best to help, without betraying any confidences. It was a draining experience.

'The more we know the better we can judge anything new that comes along,' Dave Warren explained as he folded his notepad. 'So you'll make sure you keep us informed of your work, won't you? We all want the same thing, don't we?'

I certainly wanted Keith Bennett to be found, and knew that I had to trust in the detectives' good faith.

When she finished secondary school Myra was offered a place at Didsbury teacher training college. But she'd decided she wanted to 'get on with' her life; she hadn't left one educational institution only to walk straight into another, and spend the rest of her life with kids. She got a job as a typist at Lawrence Scott Electromotors, but had to wait a few weeks, until she was fifteen, before she could start. The three years between leaving school and meeting Ian Brady are described in her autobiography with longing, as though for an opportunity missed. But this description also explains why she was ready to fall into his arms.

Kath 'sorted out' a few weeks' work at a catalogue company in the centre of town. They knew Myra was underage but bent the rules because they were short-staffed. She spent her days packing shoes for sales reps and running errands to buy them muffins or sandwiches. It was a strange environment: wall-to-wall fitted carpets, heating, soft lighting, and cubicles for customers to get changed in. She got £3 a week tax free, ten shillings more than her new job was going to pay. But she was looking forward to leaving. The city centre was far too busy, with so many people on the pavements that you had to weave in and out of them on the way to and from the bus stop.

When she started work at Lawrence Scott's Myra wanted to show that she had grown up, that she was no longer a schoolgirl. They talked about it for weeks in the canteen before Myra finally plucked up the courage – she was going to go blonde. Her friend Margie said she could do it at her flat after work.

Myra rinsed her head under the tap, pulled a towel from round her shoulders and stood up to scrunch her hair dry. An empty L'Oreal bleach bottle lay on the edge of the sink. The face that stared back at her in the mirror looked older, more sexual. She dipped her chin, tilted her head left and right. Margie said her mam was going to kill her; Myra replied that she didn't care.

She went straight round to Eaton Street, walked into the front room without knocking, and stood there with her arms crossed. The silence seemed to go on for ever, then came the inevitable explosion. Dad said she looked like a whore; Mum raged that she wasn't too old for 'a good hiding', stepped forward and belted her round the head. Eventually the fury subsided. Myra had been expecting an order to 'go down the shops for a bottle of tint', but it never came. Perhaps they were so angry it didn't occur to them. Or they realized that now she'd started work, what little control they'd had over her was gone.

Lawrence Scott's was within walking distance of home. The day she came in 'a blonde' there was a noticeable drop in volume as she crossed the shop floor to her office. She enjoyed that. Her boss, Bill Cockburn, laid a handwritten sheet on her desk to type up but didn't say anything about her hair. He was far too much of a 'gentleman'. Myra sat down and started hammering away at the keys of the ancient machine. By the time she crossed the shop floor on the morning toast run the older men had grown accustomed to her new look and managed to disguise any heightened interest. But a couple of the apprentices, who had to move coils of wire and tools so she could pass, couldn't help themselves. They were teased loudly for stealing an extra glance.

The 'association room' at Lawrence Scott's was large, with ranks of table tennis tables for the workers to relax at. There was also a record player with a stack of old favourites. As Myra walked in, 'At the Hop' by Danny and the Juniors was playing. One of the older men, Keith, called over and asked if she'd ever had a go at table tennis. She hesitated; he was obviously just being friendly. If it had been one of the younger boys she would have walked on by. He stood behind her, moved her hand into position and swung it, by the wrist, to serve. Ernie, on the other side of the table, gently returned the ball. She knew that normally he would have smashed such a slow shot.

Myra found that she had a knack for table tennis, and she soon began to beat the men. She recorded in her autobiography that Keith said she had a 'killer serve', and she was asked to join the factory team. They travelled across the city, playing other large companies like Oldham Batteries. Afterwards, they went drinking together. Myra was advised by the older secretaries to have a glass of milk before going to the pub, and to stick to shandies.

Every week Myra paid into a social fund that financed works parties. Her first was at the Levenshulme Palais. She bought a blue woollen dress, matching heels and a bag for the occasion. A

Myra, aged two, in a studio photograph paid for by her auntie Ann.

Myra (*right*), as a bridesmaid at her uncle Bill and auntie Kath's wedding.

Myra, in mismatching layers of winter clothes. By this time she had been sent to live with her gran.

Myra with her first dog, Duke.

Beasley Street, where Myra grew
up with Gran.

Myra's father Bob (*centre*) drank every
day and frequently got into brawls.

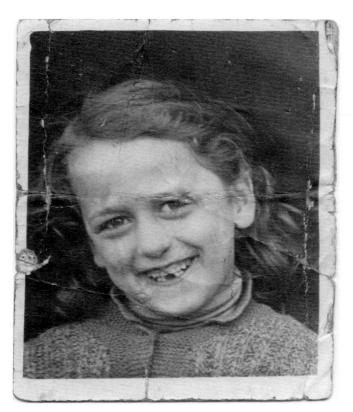

Myra, as she was losing her milk teeth. This is the age at which her father taught her to fight.

Myra and her class at Ryder Brow school. The head teacher, Mr Lloyd-Jones, stands to the left.

Myra, at the back, and friends on
a day out from Gorton.

Ian Brady photographed by a
member of a local camera club
at Millwards Merchandising,
where Ian was a clerk.

St Francis' monastery church, which
Myra stopped attending after she met
Ian. It was abandoned after her arrest
and imprisonment.

The Steelie, where Bob and, later, Ian and Myra drank. (*Manchester Librairies*)

Belle Vue Pleasure Gardens, where Myra first met her secret lover, Norman.

Ian relaxing after work in Gorton.

Sunny Brow Park, where Myra and Ian read about the disappearance of John Kilbride.

Ian had his suits hand-made at Burton's.

Ian's beloved Triumph Tiger Cub.

Myra kept the watch Ian gave her after the killing of Pauline Reade for the rest of her life.

The documentation for the Myra's Morris Mini pickup used to abduct Keith Bennett was also among her papers when she died.

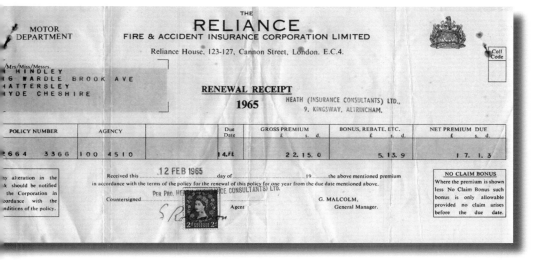

Myra bought a .22 target rifle from a Manchester gunsmith. Ian fantasized about using it for robberies.

bus picked them up at the factory for the short journey there. One of the older women told her to watch out how much she drank; Myra said she'd be fine. But it was a long evening, and everyone was having a good time. She ended up in the arms of a welder called Ray. He had thick blond hair cut in a DA, a wavy lock lying on his forehead and fashionable sideburns. She let him walk her home.

Ray took her for long rides on his motorbike, and on evenings out with his mates. Myra looked good on his arm, but they parted when she refused to have sex with him. She did not want a reputation for being 'loose'. Nor did she intend to end up like her friend Dodo, who got pregnant by a 'flash Ted' called Eric, always moaning about how boring her life had become.

On Friday and Saturday nights Myra and Pat Jepson went to the Ashton Palais, which was 'glamorous', or Chick Hibbert's bar, which was rough. Things often got out of hand between rival gangs, and they fought with motorcycle chains. The bouncers helped the police by turning fire hoses on the scrapping 'bikers' while everyone else fled down the back steps.

Myra took care of her hair. At first she let her mam touch up the roots, but soon decided it would be better to get it done professionally. Every night she washed it and put in rollers. The following morning she lacquered the curls, brushed out the hardness and dressed for work. Her clothes and make-up were immaculate, if a little brash.

One day Myra got home to find Gran in high spirits. They were on the move! Gran told her that Bert and Kath had got a new bungalow in Reddish and had given her the rent book to their place. It had 'all the mod cons!' When Myra walked through the front door of 7 Bannock Street she switched the light on and ignored the cockroaches scuttling for cover. She went from room to room flicking every switch and smiling to herself.

The house not only had electricity, but a tiled fireplace and a hot water geyser. Gran told her she wasn't going to sleep in front of the fire any more; she fancied a room upstairs, felt she deserved it after all these years. Myra agreed. It felt like they'd really gone up in the world. They did not have the money, like their new neighbours, to redecorate the whole house, so they contented themselves with hanging a new, warm red wallpaper with feathers on it in the front room. To finish it off, Kath let them keep the sideboard and drop-leaf table.

Just after they'd moved in, Myra pushed open the front door as she came in from work and heard Gran calling to her; there was something wrong with Billy the budgie. She reached into the cage to lift the bird out, but he was stuck to his perch. His feathers were crunchy to the touch, his eyes darted frantically around the room, and his legs made small tugging motions. Myra understood immediately what had happened: hairspray. He had been entombed since she left the house nine hours earlier. Myra gently prised his legs free, carried him into the kitchen and wiped the brittle covering off with a warm, damp cloth. Gran told her not to worry, at least he was alive. From then on Myra covered the cage with a large cloth before doing her hair.

I discussed with Professor Malcolm MacCulloch the change in Myra's behaviour after she started work. I was struck by how she seemed to calm down, and stopped fighting. 'Yes. But by that time much of her personality had been shaped. She had been taught to deal with violence from others, and to hand it out. These were not lessons she would forget.'

Myra liked Lawrence Scott's. In many ways it was the same as the streets on which she had felt at home as a child. Her life was made up of familiar faces and routines. The difference was that she had money, and did not need to scrap. But after a while she wanted to escape; it wasn't like school, where you could get away with bunking off. She began to feel trapped. Her friend and colleague Margie said that what they needed was a really good holiday. Myra loved the idea, and told her that she'd heard Butlin's at Ayr, in Scotland, was really good.

They got second jobs to help pay for it. After work they caught the bus to the Robertson's jam factory. The first thing Myra noticed as they drew closer was the sharp, thin smell of boiled sugar. Lorries from Kent roared in through the gate packed high with pallets of freshly picked strawberries. The factory needed to work flat out while the fruit was in season, and Myra found herself lining up with what seemed like hundreds of other women in front of a long trough. A supervisor stood at the front of the room and yelled instructions at them: wash your hands, put your apron on, tie up your headscarf. Myra did as she was told, and followed the others into the jam-making hall. Long wooden benches lined a conveyor down the middle of the room. The belt rattled into life, and a line of numbered boxes moved along it. Myra followed the example of the old hands, grabbed one and started plucking the stalks from the tops of the fruit. It was difficult to do quickly without damaging the strawberries, but she soon got the hang of it. In fact, she was pleased to note that she was one of the faster ones. When she finished a box, she wrote her number on the ticket and loaded it back onto the belt.

Supervisors walked up and down the rows making sure that the fruit was being prepared quickly enough, and to the right standard. Their work was checked too as the strawberries made their way into the large, shining steel vats to be boiled with sugar. To her left, Myra heard a sneeze. A supervisor yelled at the woman, told her to get to the washroom, re-scrub, and come back fast. The worker on the receiving end of the order looked shocked, but obediently scrambled for the sink. Every lost minute cost the women money.

At eight o'clock there was a tea break. Myra needed it: her back ached, her fingers were red and raw and she could feel the beginnings of a blister on the tip of her thumb. But as she stood up to take the short walk to the tea urn she noticed that some of the experienced workers stayed sitting at the bench. The trays kept on rolling towards them. One caught her eye and told her that when she was working she was earning. There was plenty of time for rest at home.

The following night Myra stayed on her bench during the break. She made more in piece work at Robertson's over a fortnight than she got in a month at Lawrence Scott's. She opened a post office account with the first week's takings, but was glad when she'd saved enough for the holiday. The work was far too tedious for her to stick at it. Strawberry jam never tasted quite the same again.

Ayr was not the warmest holiday destination, but it was an escape from Gorton. The camp hosts, or 'red coats', provided wall-to-wall entertainment, and when they stopped there was the warm embrace of boys she would never meet again. The freedom from expectation was welcome, as was the absence of prying neighbours, like Mrs Green, who complained to Nellie about the number of boys Myra kissed by her back door in Almond Street.

Most of the 'lads' Myra knew at home had left school and started work. They were having a few wild years before 'settling down' with a family, or being forced to do so by circumstance. She knew that her future probably lay in a relationship with one of them but, having just escaped Bob and Nellie's controlling influence, she did not welcome the prospect. Then she met Johnny; he was different. For the first time, thoughts of escape stirred in her mind.

Next to Gorton Monastery stands a rough patch of land known as Mission Croft. In the 1950s, once a year, the monks allowed travelling Romanies to run a small fair there. They set up camp on Loco Croft, next to the railway line. The painted caravans drew the admiration of children and the suspicions of their parents. Myra made a detour to walk past the slumbering encampment on her way to work. Its world seemed one of unimaginable freedom. In 1957, for a few glorious weeks, it opened up to her.

A beautiful Romany girl called Doreen fell for Jimmy Rafferty, the grandson of Hettie opposite. Although he had a reputation for being wild, Doreen agreed to marry him and moved in. Gypsies, like Johnny, started coming in and out of the houses. With them came a sense of danger and excitement. Johnny had a slim face framed by unfashionably long curly hair, and he wore a white frilly shirt open at the neck. He came to stay at the Raffertys' because he needed to 'lie low' for a few days. Myra hung around, made cups of tea and spent hours listening to his stories. Johnny told Hettie Rafferty he'd like to hang his hat next to the blonde girl's. When the old woman told her this Myra was both excited and embarrassed. No-one she knew spoke like that. Last thing at night, in her bedroom, she wrote Johnny love songs and imagined living in a caravan with him, far away from Gorton. She knew it was an impossible dream but she found it far more enjoyable than facing up to her future.

A few nights after Johnny moved in there was a screeching of tyres. Myra peeped through the curtains and saw two police cars, officers tumbling out of them, in front of the Raffertys. A sergeant hammered at the front door. By the time Jimmy pulled the bolt back Johnny had dropped from a windowsill into the ginnel at the back of the house. The following day Hettie came round to Gran's. Myra asked where he'd gone. Hettie said she didn't know, and didn't care. As far as she was concerned it was 'good riddance to bad rubbish'. Myra was outraged: Johnny wasn't rubbish, he was 'gorgeous'. Hettie said she'd soon learn not to judge a book by its cover.

Myra never saw Johnny again. That summer she started going out with Ronnie Sinclair. They'd known each other since they were twelve; she'd 'belted him one' after he pulled the ribbons in her hair during the Saturday matinee at the Plaza. He asked her to marry him, and they went halves on a second-hand engagement ring. But it felt like a game to her. She could not imagine living with someone who seemed like a boy.

A year after starting at Lawrence Scott's her boss, Bill Cockburn, announced that there were going to be 'cutbacks' on a last in, first out basis. Myra was devastated by the harshness of it but hoped that 'the change' might lead to adventure. Nanna got her and a bunch of friends weekend jobs with the Belle Vue catering department. Myra, Irene, Margie and Pauline worked Saturday nights from five 'til ten on the mobile food trolleys. Myra preferred selling tea to fish and chips as the smell didn't hang about your hair the same way. Either way the time flew by because they were so busy. It was a lot more fun than her new day job in a typing pool.

After a couple of weeks Eugene, the Belle Vue catering manager, said that Myra and Irene were 'wasted' on the food trolleys; would they like to have a go helping out in the German-themed 'beer cellar'? The girls, adhering to Nanna's instructions, tarted themselves up for work the following week. It would be good for tips, and it was important that the policemen who came in for a pint after their shift did not feel obliged to ask questions. The middle-aged barmaid – she looked just like Nanna, thought Myra: mutton dressed as lamb – gave them clear instructions on how to fiddle measures. They must only push the glass up three-quarters of the way, never right to the top. It soon mounted up. The barmaid also reached under the counter and pulled out a couple of packs of cigarettes, tossed them over, and told the girls to keep their mouths shut. Myra knew that by accepting the cigarettes she was entering a world of petty theft, but she didn't care. Every 'punter' who looked like a mug, or drunk, was short-changed by the price of 'a drink'. The girls told one another that it wasn't really criminal. The booze would have cost far more in a pub. The only time the thievery stopped was when the person the other side of the counter was a policeman.

Myra's third job was at Hinchcliffe's. She liked the other girls in the typing pool, Mary and Anita, but their boss was a bully. They sat facing his glass-fronted office, in a line, with their heads down, pummelling their heavy machines from nine 'til five. If they looked up, or started chatting, he would storm out and shout at them. His greatest pleasure lay in finding a mistake in their work. He would sit with his head bent over a large wooden desk and pore over every line, his balding head moving from side to side as he read. They would work away, pretending to ignore him, and wait for the inevitable, triumphant, 'Aha!' He would come out of the door smirking, waving the offending document before him, to humiliate whoever was responsible.

They spent their lunch hours scouring the back pages of the *Manchester Evening News* looking for new jobs. It did not take long before they found something. Wanted: Dictaphone typists. The jobs were at Burlington's Warehouses, a big catalogue company in the city centre. It had to be better than this! Anita was the first to go; she'd only given seven days' notice. The following week Mary and Myra were filled with excitement at the idea of their new adventure together. But on Friday afternoon the phone on Myra's desk rang. It was Anita, in a flap: Burlington's was even worse than Hinchcliffe's. She told Myra that patrols of 'blue caps' marched up and down the lines of typists, terrorizing them. If a girl looked up without good reason or went to the toilet for more than five minutes, her pay was docked. Anita had resigned.

The girls huddled together and discussed what to do. Mary said she was going to take her time. Ken, her fiancé, made good money and she didn't want to get it wrong again. Myra was in a panic: she couldn't afford to be off work. They lapsed into silence, then Mary remembered another advert in the *Evening News*, for a typist at Millwards. She'd worked there for a while; the pay was fair and the boss, Tommy Craig, was a really nice man. Myra sat at her desk, glowered at her boss's downturned head and picked up the phone. Had they filled the job yet? No, was she interested? Did she want to come over now? Myra stood up and, without asking permission, left to catch the bus for an interview.

It did not look promising: a cluster of old buildings tucked round a cobbled yard; two men in blue boiler suits loading barrels onto the back of a flatbed truck. But she liked the atmosphere as she walked into the office. The three men working there seemed relaxed, and there were no raised voices. Tommy sat her down in a side room with a typewriter and a handwritten letter to copy. She sailed through the test, chatted to him for a few minutes, and then he offered her the job. They were about to pack up for the evening, but why didn't she come and meet everyone?

The two men, Myra recalled in a letter to me, slowed the pace of their work as she came in but took care not to stare. She sensed that they didn't want to make her feel uncomfortable. The older one, who was sitting at a desk, stood up and held out his hand. This was Bert; she'd be 'taking quite a lot of dictation from him'. Then Tommy turned to a tall young man standing by a filing cabinet, and said, 'Myra, this is Ian. Ian, this is Myra.'

Book Two

The Moor

'He wanted to carry out the perfect murder, and
I was going to help him.'

Chapter One

'What's in it for me?' asked Malcolm MacCulloch.

'I beg your pardon?' I responded as I perched nervously on the edge of an expensive sofa.

'What's in it for me? It's the one question that precedes every decision.'

The forensic psychiatrist picked up and turned over each new piece of information, examining it for signs of human weakness.

'Why were you given the autobiography?'

'Because my source wanted the truth to come out.'

'Rubbish! Either they're deriving pleasure from influencing events or they're salving a guilty conscience. An altruistic motivation is almost always, at heart, selfish.'

Even though I was an experienced journalist, I found MacCulloch's view of the world reductive. He caught the expression on my face, and his eyebrows rose.

'Don't play naive. It's a truth you apply to get stories. You're good at it.' There was a mocking edge to his voice.

I stayed quiet.

'What you need to do,' he continued in a more placatory tone, 'is work out what the other people around her want and give it to them. You never know what you might find. Never, ever assume that there's nothing else out there.'

A month later I rang MacCulloch to report on progress.

'A church roof,' I said.

'Go on.'

'A friend of hers was wondering whether I might be able to make a contribution towards a new church roof.'

'And what's in it for you?'

'A later draft of the autobiography. It covers the relationship with Ian Brady, the murders and her attempted escape from prison.'

'Does it go further than the letters she wrote to you?'

'I'm told it's six times as long and far more detailed.'

'Good boy.'

I travelled to collect the 'new' draft of Myra Hindley's auto-biography the following week. My source, who asked to remain anonymous, handed over a tattered carrier bag containing four faded cardboard folders. I climbed into my car and pulled out several hundred sheets of closely typed foolscap. They appeared to have been dropped at some stage as the pages were slightly crumpled and out of sequence.

It took me a month to read, and catalogue, the new discovery. The document was written in the late 1980s, after Myra Hindley had finally confessed to her role in the killings. It was invaluable as it helped to explain the formation of her relationship with Ian Brady, the circumstances surrounding the killings, and how the bond between them endured arrest and imprisonment. But there were large gaps in the story, only filled in by the letters she wrote to me more than ten years later. Taken together, the two accounts added significantly to knowledge of the case.

*

The evening following her interview at Millwards, Myra told me in a letter, Ronnie Sinclair was working a night shift. Myra didn't care; she went out with five girlfriends and couldn't stop going on about Ian. She told them he reminded her of Elvis, or Jimmy Dean. The girls were thrilled. They didn't say anything about her being engaged. Perhaps Ian was 'the one'. They only had to look about them to understand the importance of choosing the right husband.

As Myra walked back to Gran's she peered into the cracks of light between net curtains. She glimpsed fragments of people's lives: women knitting, men slumbering, the mess left behind by kids, an old couple sipping tea. Pieced together, they formed a picture of the existence Myra could expect if she married Ronnie. As she crawled under the covers to go to sleep she knew it would not be enough for her.

Patricia Cairns told me that Myra Hindley's instant, powerful attraction to Ian Brady meant there was never any doubt they would form a relationship. 'Once her mind was made up that was it, she would make it happen. She turned her beam on him. It's part of her character.'

'But she couldn't force him to fall in love,' I said.

'Who would have thought that a prison inmate could have achieved the things she did, had the friends she had?' Patricia asked. 'There was a real force of character there. She got me to move south, to live with David Astor, just so that she could see me twice a week in prison! I didn't really have any say in the matter. She wanted it and it happened. I've never come across anything like it.'

Myra described starting work at Millwards in her letters to me. The first morning, she took great care with her appearance. It was important to look good, but not as if she was trying too hard.

Her skirt was tight but not too short; her blouse was fitted but not tarty. When she climbed the back steps to the office she told herself to be friendly but not gushing. Tommy Craig greeted Myra and showed her to her desk. She glanced over at Ian. His head was bent over a ledger; a Capstan Full Strength hung out of the corner of his mouth. She said good morning to him. He did not look up, just twitched his cigarette in acknowledgement and carried on filling in numbers.

Ian's coldness surprised her. She was used to a simple, direct response from men. There was not the slightest sign that he was attracted to her. She continued to glance at him between bursts of typing, noting details: waistcoat and tie; dark hair carefully cut, oiled and combed; shoes buffed mirror black. When he did speak it was in a formal, almost old-fashioned manner. She'd have laughed if he hadn't appeared so serious about it. Her hand tore across the shorthand pad as he rattled out words and figures in a softening Glaswegian accent. When Ian had finished he said, 'Thank you, Miss Hindley,' and went back to the ledgers at his desk.

Myra hoped that given time he would warm to her, and she set about gathering intelligence. She sat at her desk, pretending to work, and studied his conversations with Tommy and Bert. To her dismay, the main topic of discussion seemed to be horses. During the morning break the men spread a copy of the *Racing Post* out on a desk and pored over it, discussing weights, riders and ground conditions. At lunchtime Ian nipped out to put his bets on. If it was a big race – the Gold Cup, the King George VI, or Ascot – Tommy let them listen to the commentary in the bookie's. Otherwise, Ian got the results by ringing up the Tote.

During one of these calls Myra learned that Ian's aloof, controlled exterior was a mask. She could tell from the set of his shoulders that he had lost, and expected disappointment. What followed was an explosion: he hurled the phone down and screamed a string of obscenities. Tommy did not show any surprise at his performance. It seemed that this was part of the office routine. He told Ian to calm down; if he couldn't lose he shouldn't bet. The force of Ian's anger was accentuated by the contrast with his sophisticated appearance. As he raged his accent slipped back towards the Gorbals. But his temper was nothing new to Myra; she had lived with fury all her life.

Tommy and Bert could talk about horses all day, but there was a definite change in atmosphere when Ian came over the intellectual. A glazed look fell over their eyes when he lectured them on his latest discovery – Nietzsche, de Sade, Dostoevsky. Myra realized that Ian wasn't interested in conversation; he was letting his colleagues know that, while he may be employed as a book-keeper, he was above all this. It was a temporary resting place before he went on to better things.

Ian was the first person Myra had met who studied 'proper' books, rather than thrillers or cowboy stories, in order to 'better' himself. The boys she knew had only ever opened a book because a schoolmaster told them to, and had usually accompanied their efforts with ostentatious displays of boredom. Ian's passion for literature was something she understood; she still spent hours reading, seeking refuge in a world created by someone else. But Myra knew from the way he talked that it was different for Ian. He didn't just escape into books, he used them to build a world of his own, a place in which he could live all the time.

Most of the men Myra knew got through life to the beat of an unchanging rhythm: work, bookie's, work, pub, bed and, at the weekends, football. Ian always seemed to be looking for a new tune. Myra smiled to herself when he told Tommy that he'd 'taken up the piano'. Then he replaced Boddington's bitter with red wine – a decision quite incomprehensible to Tommy and Bert. Ian's apparent sophistication, and distance, made Myra want him all the more. In spare moments between typing she recorded her feelings in a small blue diary she kept locked in her desk drawer. The police discovered it in the days following her arrest. It is a record of obsession.

2 August: 'Not sure he likes me.'
11 August: 'Been to Friendship pub, but not with Ian.'

Ian's experimental sartorial touches made him even more attractive: the red and white spotted handkerchief in a tweed jacket pocket; the long leather coat that reached almost to the ground. And all the time a coolness towards Myra. She did not know if he was immune to her or playing some sort of game. She poured her frustration into the diary.

13 August: 'Wonder what misery will be like tomorrow?'
24 August: 'I am in a bad mood because he hasn't spoken to me today.'
30 August: 'Ian and Bert have had a row. Tommy sided with Bert and said Ian loses his temper too soon.'
1 November: 'Months now since Ian and I spoke.'
6 November: 'Ian still not speaking. I called him a big-headed pig.'

I walked down the side of Ryder Brow school to where Millwards' offices once stood. They had been replaced with squat blocks of redbrick flats covered in satellite dishes. The bookie's was still there. I walked inside: formica floor, telly on above the door, sharp-eyed clerk behind a glass screen. He recognized straight away that I hadn't come to gamble. I decided on a direct approach and told him what I was doing. He was different from most of the people I had met in Gorton, relaxed about the past. Perhaps it came from the nature of his job.

'Brady? Oh yeah, I remember him,' he said. 'Awkward sod, never spoke to anyone.'

'Anything in particular make him stand out?'

'Only his betting name.'

'Which was?'

'Gorgonzola.'

'What, like the cheese?' I asked in astonishment.

'That's right.'

I wondered whether he had deliberately chosen an Italian dairy product as his alias or mistaken its name for that of the Gorgon – the snake-haired mythical creature whose glance could turn a man to stone. Perhaps he thought it was funny – Goon humour. The bookie gave me the answer.

'He dropped the "zola" bit after a while, like. Then it was just Gorgon.' He let out a small, dry chuckle.

Myra got hold of Ian's address when he put a bet on the Tote: 18 Westmoreland Street, Longsight. That evening she 'borrowed' Auntie Anne's baby son, Michael, and wheeled him east in his pram, or 'trolley'. There were some posher houses in Longsight – Victorian villas with stucco plasterwork, or mock Tudor façades – but they had seen better days and were now inhabited by working-class families. The spaces in between had been filled in with back-to-back redbrick terraces. The kids playing in the streets looked exactly like those in Gorton. Myra pushed Michael's trolley past the towering windows of the Daisy sewing machine works, down towards the black and white beamed houses on Westmoreland Street. She tried to look casual, in case she bumped into Ian, but her eyes swept over the faces on the Stockport Road hoping to find him. If she got him alone, away from work, he might just ask her out.

Over the next few weeks she came back almost every evening; Auntie Anne was delighted with how helpful she was being. Myra pushed the trolley up and down, past the shops on Hathersage Road, the Victoria Turkish baths, and the end of Eston Street, but there was no sign of Ian. As she passed the pub on the corner of Westmoreland Street she peered in through the windows. He wasn't inside.

On the long walk back to Gorton Myra came up with a plan. She called round to the Hills', and persuaded May to come for a drink in the pub on Ian's street. He was bound to go in there, it would be fun; they might even be able to persuade him to go to Chick Hibbert's, or the Ashton Palais. Myra and May took their time on the way into the pub – he might see them, and decide to follow. They spent hours lingering over their drinks. The locals welcomed the sudden, mysterious appearance of a couple of attractive girls, but Ian never did come in. They kept it up for a couple of weeks before May got bored, and Myra realized she'd have to come up with something else.

After a great deal of thought she resolved to lure him by show-ing that she too was interested in big ideas, that she too wanted to live in a place other than this. She went to Gorton library and prowled up and down the shelves. No good choosing something he knew more about than her. She had to appear an expert. She got to the poetry section, and there was just the thing: *The Collected Works of William Wordsworth*. Myra remembered it from school. She pulled it off the shelf and marched to the front desk.

She sat up in bed that evening, looking for the right poem. 'Daffodils' – far too obvious; 'Lucy' – too soppy and romantic; 'On the Extinction of the Venetian Republic' – too obscure. She

finally settled on an excerpt from *The Prelude*. There was something about it that seemed right for Ian.

At lunchtime the next day Myra positioned herself in a patch
of sunshine by the office door to the yard. Ian was sitting there
playing chess with Dave, an invoice clerk. They seemed to take
for ever between moves, staring in silence at the board.
Eventually Ian glanced up, his eyes scanning the cover of the
book, expecting to find some 'girly rubbish' he could mock. He
was so surprised by what he saw that he seized the bait, and
asked whether Wordsworth was 'any good'. Myra replied that
his poems were 'marvellous', especially the long ones like *The
Prelude*. Ian reached over, took the book from her and read a few
lines. He riffled backwards and forwards through the pages to
assess the worth of the material. As he handed the book back
to her he said it looked interesting, he might get a copy from the
library. Myra told me that she almost 'died from bliss' at his
words.

The ice broken, they started talking. She did not push it
though, waiting a few days before coming in with William
Blake's *Songs of Innocence and Experience*. Again he took it
from her, and read. Ian lingered longer over Blake's clean
rhythms and bold imagery. He asked her what sort of music she
liked. Worried she might say the wrong thing she kept the answer
vague: bit of pop, classical, big band, 'fairly catholic really'. Ian
replied that he didn't like pop; he preferred music that was more
intelligent, that had been properly crafted. He had a tape recorder
to copy things from the library and off the telly. She could
borrow some spools if she liked.

That Saturday, Myra recorded in her autobiography, she put a
deposit down on a Philips machine, just like Ian's. She signed an
agreement to pay it off in weekly instalments, and carried it
home to Gorton. She taped all sorts of things, mucking about

with her friends. I found a police transcript of recordings at the National Records Archive. The conversations were unremarkable; young women bantering, razor-sharp Manchester humour. It was 1961, and the idea of being able to record voices was still novel.

Ian brought tapes into work for her to copy, stuff he said was 'good'. She could often tell where it had come from by the sound quality. There was jazz off the TV and classical music copied from library records. Occasionally, an older man or woman accidentally interrupted the recording, calling from another room or opening the door, and he barked at them to go away. The woman was Scottish, the man Irish. She asked Ian who they were. His mother and stepfather – he shared a house with them.

In Highpoint prison, Father Michael Teader visited Myra Hindley every week to hear her confession and take communion. They met in her 'room' on wing North 4, the segregation, or 'seg', unit for prisoners considered at risk from others. Afterwards they sat together, eating whatever treat he'd brought in, and chatted. She told him what it was that had drawn her to Ian Brady. 'She had never met anyone like him,' Father Michael said. 'He was completely different. Well read, intelligent, with a more sophisticated view of the world than any of the people she had encountered before. He seemed to offer her the chance of escape. It was what she'd looked for in the Catholic Church, and she thought she'd found it in him.'

Myra told Ronnie that their engagement was off. He was distraught, and rang her at work every day to beg for a reconciliation. At first this pleased Myra as it drew attention to her 'single' status. She smiled inwardly when Ian's eyes fell on the white line left by her engagement ring. But then he began to tease her about the calls. He sat across from Myra and laughed when she picked up the phone. She was worried that the disruption might jeopardize her job and decided that the best thing to do was to involve her boss. She told Tommy she couldn't take it any more, would he help? The next time Ronnie rang Tommy took the phone and warned him to stop pestering Myra or they'd have to call the police. He never called her at work again, and stopped mooning about on the corner of Beasley Street. Myra's description of Ronnie, in her letters to me and in her autobiography, was wistful. It was as if writing his name called up images of what might have been: marriage, kids, grandkids.

Where Lawrence Scott's had been large and organized, Millwards was small and informal. There was no 'social fund' for big occasions, and the staff organized parties themselves. They were therefore livelier, bordering on the riotous. Myra Hindley described the most important of these occasions in a letter to me.

As Christmas approached they began dividing up the jobs: sandwich making, baking a fruit cake, bringing in a record player, buying sausage rolls, wine and beer. At lunchtime on the day of the 'do' they piled the feast up on tables in the office and headed out to a pub where they'd booked a room. They talked loudly and drank quickly. Myra did not hang around Ian but kept an eye on what he was up to across the room. He seemed to be sinking pints very fast, even by the standards of the hard-drinking warehousemen, and was uncharacteristically garrulous. At closing time they bundled out of the door and made their way back to the office. The cold air had a sobering effect, and they drew together to keep warm, giggling whenever one of them stumbled.

Things began sedately enough. People had brought in their favourite music and the old record player in the corner of the room was turned up to maximum volume. It belted out distorted hits as the men worked on their courage with beer, and some of the younger women started dancing about. Myra had a sandwich in one hand and a glass of wine in the other as she moved in time to Freddie and the Dreamers. She could feel Ian's eyes on her.

Things moved up a gear when Ron, one of the delivery drivers, crashed through the side door, swaying from side to side in an alarming manner and waving about a large, maroon-coloured bottle with a sailing ship on it. Naval Rum – 80 per cent proof! His thumbs pushed drunkenly at the cork and it flew out with a sharp pop, catching Bert on the shoulder. There was a loud cheer. The booze was almost certainly payment for allowing a couple of extra barrels to 'fall' off the back of his lorry, but nobody cared. Myra was about to swig some neat when her nose, still two inches away from the maroon liquid, filled with fumes. She frowned, trying to focus on the thick rivulets that clung to the side of the glass. Marge, the receptionist, told her to try it with a bit of Coke in. Myra found it went down a lot easier like that. She sat down and smiled as Tommy and a pretty young order clerk from downstairs started shuffling about. They only stayed upright by leaning on each other.

All of a sudden Ian loomed in front of her, rocking backwards and forwards on his heels, and asked if she wanted to dance. Myra wondered if she'd heard right. He didn't ask again, just reached down, put his hands on her forearms and leant back. She rose unsteadily to her feet, too drunk to savour the moment. They moved slowly about the room, occasionally bumping into other couples. Ian was a bad dancer as well as drunk, and he trampled all over her new shoes. There were a couple of glances in their direction, but no disapproval. They were young, single people having a bit of fun.

When the party finally ran out of steam Tommy asked Ian if

he was coming. He had arranged to give him a lift; Myra was meant to be going with Jim and Doris. Ian replied that it was all right, Myra and he needed a bit of air and they were going to walk. They talked about the rum, how strong it was, as they wound down the path through Sunny Brow Park, crossed the small stream and climbed up the other side towards the Hyde Road. The winter sunlight, although weak, hurt her eyes. As they came out of the wrought-iron gate at the top he stopped and turned to her. He asked if she'd meet him that evening for 'a few drinks'. Myra did not hesitate to say yes, even though she was meant to be going out to a sporting club with the girls and they'd already paid for the tickets. She saw Ian onto the bus back to Longsight, then rang Margie, who she knew would be in, to say she couldn't make it, Ian had asked her for 'a date'. Margie, well acquainted with Myra's obsession, replied, 'At last.'

Myra told me in a letter that she pushed open the front door to find Maureen chatting to Gran and her cousin Glenys. She gave the girls some money and told them to go to the chemist's on the corner for a bottle of Yardley's scent and some mascara. They thought nothing of it. Her night out with the girls had been long planned, and it was natural to want to 'be her best'. Myra climbed the stairs to her room, lay on the bed and waited for the ceiling to stop spinning. She didn't notice Moby come into the room with the bottle of Yardley's, and her change. After a couple of hours she went downstairs for a cup of tea and a bacon sandwich. She didn't tell Gran where she was going.

It was dark when she pulled her coat on, and walked to the bus stop where they'd arranged to meet. One bus went by, then another; she thought he'd changed his mind, or had been leading her on. As a third bus appeared she saw a figure crossing the road towards her – Ronnie. She was about to make a run for it when the rear platform pulled level with the stop. Ian was standing there, motioning for her to get on. Myra took his outstretched hand and the bus roared away from Gorton into the night.

The evening passed in a blur; they were both blind drunk. There was none of the edginess and bad temper that usually characterized his behaviour. He spent much of the time doing impressions from *The Goon Show*. When they got back to Gorton Ian walked her home and asked if he could come in. Myra replied no, her gran might still be up. She knew she lacked the will to resist his advances and wasn't going to have him thinking her cheap. If he won her too easily she might lose him. Ian responded by pulling Myra into his arms and crushing his lips against hers. Even through the booze she could feel the pain. It was as though he'd never kissed a girl before. Myra pushed him away and took charge: she held his head in her hands and gently put her lips on his. He relaxed, and seemed to get the hang of it. After a couple of minutes she said he'd better go, someone might see them, and stepped back towards the front door. He stood there, gently swaying in the breeze, and said, 'You don't know how long I've wanted to do this.'

I was struck, reading Myra Hindley's letters to me, by the restlessness that followed her first date with Ian Brady. There was a sense of desperation at the thought that his affection might fade. The exaggerated intensity of her emotions reminded me of her reaction to the death of Michael Higgins. There was no sign, forty years later, that Myra was aware of the unusual strength of her feelings. The days to the New Year of 1962, she wrote, seemed to stretch for ever into the distance.

Ian remained formal at work, careful not to attract the notice of Bert and Tommy, but it was clear from his eyes that he did not intend to discard her. During one lunch break he asked if she'd like to go out with him at the weekend. There was a picture on in town, *King of Kings*, and he thought she might like it. Myra knew about the film; it was a life of Jesus. She thought it kind of him to suggest it as he was an atheist. This time she did reveal to Gran that she was 'seeing' someone from work.

Ian turned up late at the bus stop again, and didn't bother to apologize. She understood that he had done it deliberately, but did not really mind. It was good just to be with him. The cinema was packed. There hadn't been a big-budget, speaking portrayal of Jesus before. Film-makers, wary of upsetting the Church, had kept him as an off-screen character and relied on over-the-shoulder shots or close-ups of 'His' hands. Nicholas Ray's production was a grand epic with a sweeping score by Miklos Rozsa, who'd written the music for *Ben Hur*. It featured Jesus's miracles, and the Sermon on the Mount with hundreds of extras. Myra thought that the lead actor, Jeff Hunter, was 'gorgeous'. She didn't agree with the reviewers who'd said he looked too young. Jesus had been almost exactly the same age as him when he died. The director used grandeur to drive home an unashamedly Christian message. It was a celebration of faith, and Myra loved it. As Jeff Hunter hung on the cross and groaned, 'Father, why have you forsaken me?' tears began to pour down her face.

The cinema lights came up, and she felt Ian's arm slide away from round her shoulder. She described in a letter how he leant back, stared incredulously at her tear-stained face and asked why she was crying. Myra replied that it was a beautiful, moving film. The cinema was filled with the sound of blowing noses. Ian snorted, stood up and announced that he needed a drink.

They went to the Thatched House and stayed until closing time. He picked the film to pieces, argued that the sole function of religion was 'to keep working people in their place'. It was all just man-made lies, mumbo-jumbo; religious people were weak. But Myra still went to St Francis' every week with Kath and could not accept what he was saying. She tried to argue back, pointing out all the good things the church did for the people of Gorton. But he was ready with a trap. Was God good? Yes, she replied. If so, said Ian, how come he had let Michael Higgins drown? What good was there in that? Myra did not have an answer; she had never thought about these things before. The church had been a place to escape to, that was all.

Father Michael Teader discussed the demolition of Myra's faith with her during their weekly meetings. He told me it was built on weak foundations.

'This was pre-Vatican Two.'

'You've lost me,' I replied.

'The mass was in Latin – she didn't understand it. Religious teaching was by rote – she had no arguments to defend it. People were just meant to accept what they were told. If the Church had changed its policy earlier than the Second Vatican Council of 1962 she might have been able to deal with him. As it was, she didn't have a chance.'

Myra's infatuation and the absence of a defendable religious or moral code were a dangerous combination. Ian Brady was pushing at an open door.

They stumbled down Bannock Street arm in arm. She had Ian now and wasn't going to lose him. His arguments about religion did not repel her; in a way they made sense. At least, she reflected, he thought about life rather than simply accepting it like every other person she knew. When they reached Myra's house, she looked over her shoulder to see if anyone was watching and opened the door. The lights were off – Gran was in bed. She took her coat off as Ian slid home the bolt to the front door. Without saying a word he pushed her backwards, towards the living room; she fell to the floor, grabbed his face in her hands and kissed him ferociously. He responded, then gave her a small series of bites down the neck. She groaned at the pain.

Myra Hindley's description of her first sexual encounter with Ian Brady is raw and detailed. It portrays a naive girl stumbling into the arms of a brutal man. While there is no doubt that chance played its part, I did not feel that it explained everything. How many women would agree to see someone again if their first sexual encounter was unpleasant? I asked Malcolm MacCulloch why he thought she had not been repelled.

'She was used to brutal behaviour,' he answered.

'But wouldn't she look for something different in a lover?' I asked.

'No. If you have been treated brutally in childhood and you have a certain sort of temperament, you're going to develop a tough personality. And tough people, as well as having the capacity for sadism, often have masochistic tendencies. Rather than recoil from brutal behaviour, they seek it out.'

Myra did not want Ian to meet Bob and Nellie, but there was no way of preventing it. It was hard enough to hide the smallest secret in Gorton, never mind a relationship. In the end she decided to take him round to Eaton Street. Her parents' reactions were instinctive, and powerful. Bob thought Ian was a 'good lad'. He recognized a strength in him, and they seemed to have the same view of a woman's place. Nellie disliked him on first sight. When he had gone she pulled her daughter to one side. In a letter to me, Myra recalled Nellie's words: 'No good can come of that Ian Brady, you know.' Her mother thought that Ian's attitude to life was sneering and cynical. She also mistrusted his 'airs and graces'.

Patricia Cairns visited Nellie many times. They discussed Ian Brady at length. 'One of the reasons her mother didn't like Brady was that she could see the similarities with Bob. He was a bully.

But there was nothing she could do. The attraction was too powerful.'

Ian stoked Myra's dissatisfaction with life. The further she stood from Gorton the closer she was to him. His outbursts were erratic. He would be behaving quite normally, lovingly even, and then the smallest thing would set him off – like Gran running the water in the kitchen. Why, he demanded, was there just one cold tap in Bob, Nellie and Mo's house? Why could you walk straight off the street into the front room? Didn't she realize it was just luck that had enabled her and Gran to escape from somewhere even worse? They were all trapped. Myra could see what Ian meant: she had always wanted more from life than Gorton had to offer. His rants made her want it even more. This shared resentment came to give them a common purpose, and identity.

May Hill and Pat Jepson noticed the change in Myra, and tried to preserve their friendship. They suggested she bring Ian to the Ashton Palais, or Chick Hibbert's; she told them it wasn't his scene. They tried to get her out when he wasn't there; she told them she wanted to stay at home in case he came round later. Over time, they slipped away from her.

In her letters to me Myra described how Ian changed the way she approached literature, taught her how to use it as a source of inspiration. Where she relaxed into a story, he hunted, looking for ideas he could use. The author had no control over him as he wandered through the pages, pilfering what he wanted. From Harold Robbins' bestseller *The Carpetbaggers* it was the notion that rape, incest and paedophilia were adventures. If the opportunity to perform one of these acts presented itself, a man should take it. The fact that the main character of *The Carpetbaggers*, buccaneering multi-millionaire aviation pioneer Jonas Cord, is drawn as a grotesque completely passed him by. Ian got Myra to work fragments of literature into sex games. Books became fuel to their fantasies.

I found Ian Brady's copy of *The Life and Ideas of the Marquis de Sade* sealed in a see-through plastic wallet at the National Archives in Kew. It had a lurid orange cover in the centre of which was an enlarged reproduction of a dictionary definition: 'sadism (sad/izm), after Count de Sade (1740–1814): abnormal pleasure in cruelty; sadist *n&adj.*'. The book was made public, along with the rest of the trial exhibits and documents, in December 2005. Their release prompted a scramble by newspaper reporters. Details forgotten over the years were hastily plucked out and recycled as 'exclusives'. One correspondent, from a 'respectable' newspaper, even smuggled a trial file out of the archive's reading area and concealed it in a locker in order to confound his rivals. When the fuss had died down I read the documents closely, over a week, in a room with locked-off video cameras. The books discovered by the police range from the perverse, Edwin J. Henri's *Kiss of the Whip*, to the literary, Henry Miller's *Tropic of Cancer*.

But Ian Brady did not just plunder fiction, he stole political ideas as well. They were sitting in the front room at Gran's when he dropped a quarter-inch tape spool onto the spindle, flicked the catch that held it in position and started the machine running. *'Das Deutsche Volk muss glücklich sein zu gewinnen!'* Hitler, he informed her – great, wasn't it? Myra had to admire the sheer passion in the voice, the force of conviction. The roar of the crowd was intoxicating. They sat there, transfixed, until the tape ran out and slapped round and round against the heads of the machine. Ian explained how Hitler had been right about outsiders. Myra did not question his ranting against 'the Jews' or 'blacks'. Instead, she looked around her for evidence to support his views: the Jamaicans in Moss Side who 'sponge off our taxes'; Mr Ziff the Jewish tailor, who ran over her kitten in his big shiny car when he came round for his money. I found a payment book among her papers: 'Ziff: Personal Tailors'. Inside the stained brown card, inscribed in black ink, 'R. Hindley', and what he owed. The amount was never cleared. I wondered why she'd kept it. I supposed it was another reminder of a vanished past, never to be retrieved.

Ian's sadism was not confined to the bedroom; it also manifested itself as bullying at work. Myra's office, which was off to the side, was cold in winter. Even with the door open the warmth from the open fire in the main office died before it reached her. Seeing her shivering in a thick cardigan, Tommy put his head through the door and told her to come through. Myra said she was worried that the noise of her typewriter might put the clerks off. Tommy told her not to be so silly – what did she think he'd bought the new 'silent model' for? But as she worked Myra could see Ian out of the corner of her eye. He kept sighing, shifting his weight from one buttock to the other and dropping his pen on the desk. Eventually, he burst out, 'Christ, Myra, that machine's getting on my nerves. Come to that, so are you.' Tommy and Bert sat there in stunned silence. Myra didn't say a word. She just picked the typewriter up and walked back to her office. As she went she could hear Tommy shouting at Ian. There was no way he could understand what was going on.

Ian introduced her to the ideas of his favourite philosopher, Friedrich Nietzsche. But in philosophy, as in literature and politics, his approach was that of a magpie. If it glistened, he stole it. It was an approach that survived long after his imprisonment. In 2001 Ian Brady published a book, *The Gates of Janus: Serial Killing and its Analysis*. Its pages are filled with references to Ludwig Wittgenstein. For an assessment of its quality I sent a copy to Professor Ray Monk, a leading authority on the Austrian genius. He called me within a day to denounce Brady's references to the philosopher as 'self-aggrandising' and 'pseudo-intellectual'.

I asked Patricia Cairns why Myra did not question such extreme, disjointed views and behaviour. 'What you have to understand about Myra,' she responded, 'is that when she falls in love with somebody, turns her beam on them, she becomes like them.' She paused. 'She must have been getting some pleasure from it as well.'

Ian and Myra retreated further and further from their surroundings, choosing not to play by the rules of a society they scorned. But they used humour as well as radical ideas to mark out the boundaries of their existence. She called him 'Neddy' after a character in *The Goon Show*, and he called her Hess, both the name of Hitler's deputy and that of a famous concert pianist, Dame Myra Hess, who played the great German composers. He failed to recognize, or ignored, Myra Hess's fierce opposition to the Nazis. During the war she gave recitals of Beethoven and Schubert to packed rooms in the National Gallery. The performances were a joint affirmation of Hess's and the audience's belief that Nazi ideology, not German culture, had led to war.

'I suppose they were building a world apart,' I remarked to Patricia Cairns.

She raised a finger, shook her head and responded, 'A world above.'

Chapter Two

Gorton's pubs, many of which have been demolished, are preserved on the computer at Manchester Central library. There are dozens of pictures of the Bessie, the Shakie, the Steelie and the Waggon. Most are long gone, cleared when large parts of the area were knocked down and its people moved to bright new futures on the 'peripheral' estates tacked to the edge of British cities in the 1960s. The Waggon and Horses, however, where Ian and Myra drank after work, is still there, the large mock Tudor façade out of place on the Hyde Road. Perhaps its builder was inspired by the pastoral refuge of Far Lane rolling down the hill behind.

Any such delusion has long since vanished inside. I was greeted by looks of suspicion when I pushed open the bar door; the expressions turned to disgust when I ordered a Diet Coke. Although it was early, many of the regulars looked like they were on their third or fourth pint. But the Waggon is a large space, with dark corners. I walked round the bar and found a table opposite the giant TV screen showing racing from Haydock

Park. The men sitting here were busy with the form, or talking about football. It's the kind of place where, once settled down, you can spend a lot of time without attracting too much attention.

Myra told me in a letter that she and Ian got into the habit of coming here. It was close to his bus stop, and easy for her to cut through the streets and ginnels to Bannock Street. Ian liked talking about current passions and resentments, but resisted divulging the past. When his history did emerge it was in fragments; Myra had to rearrange the pieces to build up a picture of the man she was in love with.

He told her that he had been born in Glasgow's Rottenrow maternity hospital. His mam hadn't been able to look after him so he went to live with the Sloans. Mum, Dad, four kids – they were nice to him. Myra told him that was just like her having to go and live with Gran. The difference was that Myra's start in life, however rough, gave her some sense of identity; Ian's made him feel a complete outsider. The mother who abandoned him, Peggy, was a tearoom waitress; he never mentioned a father. Myra didn't push the point as he was so obviously skirting round it. She suspected that he was illegitimate. When Ian was little Peggy came to visit him most weekends, but later she married and moved south, to Manchester. This was when he started going off the rails, nicking things and hurting animals.

Ian killed his first cat, by throwing it off the top floor of a tenement building, at the age of ten. He told Myra that it screamed all the way down. He'd wanted to see the fear, and he'd enjoyed it. Later, he trapped a cat in a tomb, returning every day to see if it was still alive. But he said Myra needn't worry, he'd grown out of it, come to realize that it was far more satisfying to hurt people because it was on a higher plane. His first experiments involved extreme bullying. He persuaded a group of schoolmates to help tie a boy to a stake and pack newspaper round his feet. They thought Ian was joking when he said he was going to set fire to it. They still couldn't believe it when he got the matches out, and they stood there dumbly as the fire crept about the boy's feet. Only when the 'victim' started screaming did they react. Ian walked away, laughing, as they crawled around swatting at the flames with the arms of their second-hand jackets.

As their relationship developed, Ian revealed his fantasies to Myra. He was sexually inexperienced, but that didn't mean he lacked desire. It's just that what he wanted was hard to get. He started having violent thoughts as a teenage schoolboy. The other lads had these pathetic pornographic cards; Ian had far better pictures in his head. When he read de Sade for the first time it was like looking in the mirror. Myra was the first person he'd been able to tell, and try his fantasies out with.

Ian's words, Myra told me, excited her. His cold indifference to authority, his reasons for holding it in contempt, showed that you could live your life as you pleased. There *was* an alternative to the mundane repetition of your parents' existence.

Professor Malcolm MacCulloch told me that such fantasies are a common feature in the development of sexual sadists. 'Rapists and murderers often act out their fantasies before they commit them,' he said. 'They'll integrate them into other criminal acts – masturbating during a burglary, for example. When they're ready they'll move on to the next stage. The point is that these things develop over time. He had a script; what he needed was someone to help him act it out.'

MacCulloch first worked on Ian Brady's case while a trainee psychiatrist in the 1960s. When Brady developed symptoms of chronic mental illness at Gartree prison in Leicestershire in the mid-1980s, the professor was asked to assess his condition by the Home Office. Over the past twenty years a succession of psychiatrists had recommended his transfer out of the prison system, but the Home Office had consistently refused to act. There was a worry that a move to hospital might make the government of the day look 'soft'.

MacCulloch interviewed Brady at length and concluded that he was suffering from a serious psychosis. The professor's report advocated his immediate transfer from Gartree. 'It's pretty clear he would have died if he'd remained in prison. Some people might say, "So what?" I take the view that it's better for all of us to understand what makes a man do the things he did.' The decision to send him to Ashworth Special Hospital, on Merseyside, was taken by the Prime Minister, Margaret Thatcher. Over the next few years MacCulloch got to know Ian Brady better than any other psychiatrist.

As I sat opposite the professor I wondered what had made Brady open up to him rather than any other doctor. It had to be more than the forensic psychiatrist's ferocious talent for 'working' people – Brady would have seen straight through that. Perhaps it was his contagious enthusiasm for understanding the extreme reaches of human behaviour. I could also see that Brady might have been flattered to be the focus of a sharp intellect.

Ian began stealing soon after he started secondary school, at Shawlands Academy. But he was an indifferent thief and kept getting caught. His law-abiding foster-parents were horrified; they could not understand what caused his behaviour. But they never rejected him. Although this made no difference to Ian's fate, it was an act of kindness he never forgot. Even after he had been imprisoned for decades he remained vulnerable to mention of the Sloans.

When he left school Ian worked as a butcher's assistant, but the pay was lousy and the urge to steal uncontrollable. In 1954, when he was seventeen, a Glasgow Sessions magistrate gave him a choice: go live with your mother in Manchester or go to gaol. He chose Manchester, and caught the train south. His natural mother, Peggy, met him at Victoria station.

She and her husband, an Irish fruit merchant called Pat Brady, lived in a small house in Moss Side. Ian moved into their second bedroom, took his stepfather's surname and accepted the offer of a job as a fruit porter at Smithfield Market. Apart from drinking too much, and complaining continually about the number of Jamaican immigrants on the streets of Moss Side, he seemed to have 'straightened himself out'. But Ian had been stealing for too long to stop just because he had moved south. He got away with the robberies he carried out, Glasgow style, on businesses and private homes, but he was not so lucky at work. The Bradys were mortified when he was caught trying to smuggle a sack full of stolen lead seals through the gates of Smithfield Market.

On remand, Ian did a spell in the dingy Victorian warren of Strangeways prison. No other gaol in the country dominates the surrounding city in quite the same way. Its tall red spire looms over the prisoners as a reminder of their failings, and over the inhabitants of Manchester as a deterrent. It is a place that speaks of retribution rather than rehabilitation. On the first day of October 1955, just a year after arriving in Manchester, he was taken from Strangeways to the city's magistrates' court for trial. Ian's lawyer did not have a lot to work with, and his client was surly and unprepossessing. As he stood in the dock awaiting the verdict, Ian told Myra, he tossed a coin in his head. If it landed heads – not guilty – he'd go straight; if it landed tails – guilty – he'd remain a criminal. The magistrate looked up. 'Ian Brady, I find you guilty as charged.'

Because he was under eighteen Ian was sent to Borstal for 'training' rather than prison. Myra told me that he was a diligent student, but not of the subjects the magistrate who sentenced him had in mind. The only difference between the people in Borstal and those in prison was their age. Ian met accomplished thieves who had worked with professional gangs. They told him how to do bigger jobs, how to avoid getting caught so often, and where to find 'fences' for the things he'd knocked off. For the first time he made friends, petty criminals Dougie Woods and Gilbert Deare. It was the happiest time of his life so far.

Ian was released on 14 November 1957 and returned to Moss Side. He tried labouring, but hated it. He got a job in a brewery, but was fired. He decided the only way out was to 'better' himself, went to Longsight library and took out a set of manuals on book-keeping. He astonished the Bradys by spending hours in his room swotting over ledgers until he felt sure he could excel at interview.

He bought the *Manchester Evening News* in search of a job 'with prospects', and a set of clothes to look the part. The first few companies didn't want to know: what good was a clerk who'd done time for theft? But in February 1958, just three months after getting out of Borstal, he got an interview at Millwards Merchandising, a wholesale chemical company based at Ryder Brow in Gorton. Ian was in luck: the boss, Tommy, was a Scot. He took a liking to the smartly dressed young man and decided that he deserved a 'second chance'. He gave him a job at £12 a week and told him he could begin work on the Monday.

The following month the Bradys moved to a larger house at 18 Westmoreland Street in Longsight. The shots in Manchester Central library show two lines of Victorian villas facing each other across a cobbled street. Children stand about staring at the camera; they are clearly not used to posing for pictures. There is a sign at the end of the road: DESIGNATED PLAY STREET. It is a portrait from a distant, more innocent time.

Ian almost always returned to Westmoreland Street after work, before heading back into Gorton. His mother still cooked and washed for him, and his darkroom was there. When he was sure of his ground with Myra, he suggested taking some pornographic pictures; not ordinary stuff, but the kind of thing de Sade might have approved of. He bit her before he fucked her, he bit her as he fucked her, and he bit her again afterwards. Her body was covered in small oval eruptions of burst blood vessels. The whisky dulled the pain but did not block it completely. Only when he was sure that the marks would show up in a black and white picture did he pick up his camera. He snapped away with the twin-lens reflex, twelve shots a roll, until he had what he wanted. He taped the film up, tucked it into his jacket pocket and staggered outside to catch the bus back to Longsight.

Ian often failed to appear, and was slow to tell Myra where he'd been. It came out later, much of it at trial: the Rembrandt pub in the city centre, Canal Street, round the back of Central station. The sorts of places 'respectable' types – lawyers, teachers, policemen – went for sex with each other, and with rent-boys. To them it was a shared secret; to him it was just another experience that fuelled his contempt for the 'hypocrisy' of ordinary life. Patricia Cairns says that Myra Hindley knew about these sexual adventures. 'Myra accepted that. If it was what he wanted, he could do it. After all, it was just sex. He needed her on a far deeper level.'

Malcolm MacCulloch peered at one of the photographs showing Myra Hindley, fully clothed, crouched down on a picnic blanket, staring up at the camera – a pose at once submissive and suggestive. 'This relationship is very strong,' he commented.

'She is happy in a sexually sadistic relationship; he has found someone who can help to realize his fantasies. It is a very unfortunate concatenation of circumstances.'

Myra Hindley and Ian Brady soon began to turn fantasies about violence into reality. In its court reports the *Manchester Evening News* regularly featured cases of animal cruelty and always printed the address of the person who'd been convicted; sometimes there was a photo too. Myra and Ian read these stories with a shared sense of outrage. Now that he had decided to hurt people, Ian had come to feel a powerful affinity with animals. This, and a shared contempt for those they considered beneath them, lay at the heart of his and Myra's relationship. They decided to punish the perpetrators. It became a ritual: they would choose a victim out of the paper, go round to their home, and give them 'what they deserved'. Sometimes it was a brick through the window. If the opportunity presented itself and they were able to follow them somewhere quiet, Ian gave them a beating. One night they stalked a man in his local all evening just so that Ian could 'get him'. The joint endeavour of the enterprise, and its secrecy, made them feel as one.

I am sure that Myra Hindley included this story in her letters to me in order to demonstrate that she *did* love animals, that not everything she and Ian did was bad. But read in conjunction with her autobiography and other private papers, it simply reinforces the impression of a flawed character falling into a fatal alliance.

Ian, fed up with catching the bus back to Longsight, saw an advert for the Triumph Tiger Cub motorcycle – 'Fabulous Little Four Stroke'. It showed a smart, slim man in a tweed jacket, leather helmet and gauntlets chatting confidently to a pretty blonde girl in a chunky-knit sweater with her hands in her pockets. The flawless landscape was rural, autumnal. It was just

£150. He put down a deposit on the model with a tall windscreen. It opened up their world. At weekends, and in the evenings, they travelled on the bike out into the hills of Cheshire and the Peak District. There is a shot of Myra sitting side-saddle in a twin-set in front of a cottage. Brady taught her how to use his twin-lens reflex, and there are endless images of him on the bike, grinning, looking dapper. One day, climbing the long, winding hill out of Greenfield, they came round a bend and there it was – Saddleworth Moor. Its magnificence captured their imagination. They returned week after week until they knew every stream, hill and gully. From the granite of Greystones to the grit stone at Hollin Brown Knoll, they made the moor their own. At its heart lay an enclosed bowl of heather and grass on the banks of Shiny Brook. They put wine in the stream to chill while they explored and, after a picnic, had sex in the cotton grass.

It was on the moor, Myra Hindley told me, that Ian Brady finally revealed his great secret: he was a bastard. She'd long guessed it, and tried to console him: her gran was illegitimate, as was her gran before her. But they both knew that while generations of Hindley women had overcome their difficulties with the help of their families, Ian's mother had cast him adrift.

The moor was a place of solace and fascination to Ian. He named the rocks that dotted it. An outcrop from where he could survey the Shiny Brook valley became 'Eagle's Head' after Hitler's Eagle's Nest. Greystones was his Stonehenge. He set up the camera to take a shot there. They sat on a great slab of granite wearing leather motorcycle helmets, and he put his hands round her neck as if strangling her. He released the shutter by squeezing a vacuum bulb, as she grinned at him.

'Landscapes seem to have had a special meaning for him,' Malcolm MacCulloch told me.

'They have an effect on lots of people,' I replied.

'No, no. From an early age. He suffered some sort of attack, had a vision in Scotland when he was a teenager. They had a pantheistic, almost religious significance.'

The professor said that on a trip out of Glasgow with his adoptive family Ian had fallen into a trance at the sight of mountains. It had taken the Sloans several minutes to bring him round. A decade later, Ian became so attached to the rocks, boulders, valleys and streams of Saddleworth Moor, Myra told me, that he imagined they were talking to him. This sense of belonging made him feel secure in his separation from 'normal' life.

Ian told Myra that he did not intend to spend the rest of his days as a stock-clerk at Millwards. He'd learned lessons in Borstal and planned to apply them; he had contacts; he knew how to get rid of stuff. They rode to Bradford on his bike to try to track down Gilbert Deare, with whom he'd been locked up, to see if he wanted to help on 'a job'. Myra knocked on the door, pretending to be an old girlfriend, but he wasn't there. Ian told her they'd have to go it alone. She pointed out that he'd never done a big robbery before – they were bound to get caught! She was right to be concerned. Years later the police revealed to her that Ian and Gilbert Deare had once attempted a hold-up with knives. It had gone wrong, and they'd fled empty-handed, narrowly avoiding capture. But Ian was adamant. He told Myra that one way to avoid getting caught was to 'hit' the people who carried money to and from banks and businesses – the messengers. They were alone and unarmed. He got her to stand around on street corners, tracking movements, working out the best time to attack. The softest target seemed to be an electricity showroom on the Hyde Road. He fantasized about hurting the messengers, but she thought he would never go through with it. Then his mind seemed to wander, to go in search of bigger things.

A key moment in the development of Ian Brady's fantasies was his discovery of the book *Compulsion* by Meyer Levin. He devoured the text, then handed it to Myra and demanded she do the same. I found a copy for sale on the internet. When it arrived, a few days later, I tore open the brown paper packaging. The cover featured two smartly dressed young men, who bore more than a passing resemblance to Ian Brady, scowling out of a blood-red cover. The blurb at the bottom of the page boasted, 'Bestselling novel of the most cold-blooded crime of the Century.' Set in the centre of the back page were the words, '*You know why we did it? Because we damn well felt like doing it!*'

When she'd finished the book Myra told Ian it seemed like 'a rubbish thriller'. Why had he wanted her to read it? Having studied my copy, I had no doubt about Ian Brady's motives, and I found it hard to believe that Myra had any either. *Compulsion* is not a 'rubbish thriller'. It is a non-fiction novel written by a liberal, politically motivated former newspaper reporter. Levin's book deals with the murder of a Chicago schoolboy, Robert Franks, by two wealthy, good-looking young men, Nathan F. Leopold and Richard A. Loeb. Their only motive was to commit 'the perfect murder'. The killers picked their victim up in a hired car, beat him to death with a chisel, burned his face, hands and genitals with hydrochloric acid, and hid him in a drainage pipe before trying to secure a ransom. Levin's purpose in writing the book was to examine how the protagonists' background and psychological make-up contributed to their actions. In many ways, his work prepared the ground for Truman Capote's *In Cold Blood* and Norman Mailer's *The Executioner's Song*.

Ian told Myra that he couldn't believe the mistakes Leopold and Loeb had made. They bungled the pick-up and were seen by people who knew them; they beat Franks to death in the car so there was blood everywhere; then they hid him in a drainage pipe but left a foot sticking out. Finally – silly buggers – they rang the victim's father to try to extract a ransom. The way to commit the perfect murder was to plan it properly. You had to make sure that the body was never discovered. Ian laid it all out for her. She would help him pick up a child, wearing a disguise; they would then drive to the moor where he would rape, kill and bury it. Everything would be carefully prepared: the grave, the body disposal plan, the clean-up afterwards. Nothing would be left to chance. There was no way they would be caught. He was going to commit the perfect murder, and she was going to help him.

This is the point at which most people, however infatuated, would have reached the limit of their endurance. Her agreement to participate in sado-masochism and fantasies about robberies can, at a stretch, be explained away by the force of her infatuation; child murder cannot. But rather than flee the relationship with Ian, or try to talk him out of the perfect murder, she allowed things to continue. I wondered whether he would have been able to proceed without this tacit approval.

Myra was a useless driver; she failed her driving test three times. Ben Boyce, a grocer who had 'a soft spot' for her, occasionally lent her his Ford Prefect van to practise in after work. It was a big, black old thing and Myra never had it long enough to master the controls, never mind navigate the traffic with any skill. But in July 1963 Ben bought a new van and offered to let her drive the old one all the time, in return for help with deliveries.

Ian and Myra drove round east Manchester in the van and parked up watching children. They did not attract any attention; they just looked like a 'courting couple' getting away from the prying eyes of their parents, or neighbours. Ian liked to pick out an imaginary victim and describe what he'd do with 'it'. But these trips were about more than feeding sexual fantasy: he was working out the details of a successful abduction, and how to avoid the errors that Leopold and Loeb had made.

When he could get away with it, Ian took photos. I found an envelope crammed with negatives of boys playing football behind the railings of Ryder Brow school. There was something odd about how the pictures had been shot, so I went back to see what he had done. As I lined the pictures up with the railings I realized that they were all taken quite low down. At first I thought he must have knelt. But I could see no reason for doing this – it messed up the shot. Then I worked it out: he'd fired the shutter from the passenger seat as Myra tracked her old school's perimeter in the Ford Prefect. The distance between shots was determined by the speed with which he was able to wind the crank of the camera. 'These photographs are part of the rehearsal,' Malcolm MacCulloch said as he laid the images out side by side on the polished wood of his dining-room table. 'He is planning what to do, and at the same time transferring the script in his head to her. But she is not fighting it. She is a willing participant. People have features to their personality which are brought out by circumstances. I think that Brady's knowledge, attitude, personality and what he wanted to do had this effect of bringing out the cruel, determined streak in Myra Hindley.'

The idea of 'the perfect murder' became part of their sex life. They talked through the abduction, what they would say to a child to persuade it to get into the van. As time went on what had seemed a fantastic idea became a possibility, but Myra still needed a final push. In a series of letters, she told me how Ian Brady finally persuaded her to help him turn fantasy into reality.

One day she woke up on the settee, at around one p.m., with a shocking hangover. Gran was standing over her, going on about the state she was in. Her clothes were unbuttoned and twisted awkwardly around her body. Myra couldn't remember what had happened the night before. She was a regular heavy drinker but usually knew when to stop. Embarrassed, she struggled into fresh clothes, had a wash and drank a cup of tea, but she still felt awful. Through the front window she saw her neighbour John Booth's bike leaning against the kerb opposite. Myra staggered outside and asked his mother if she could borrow it. A few minutes later she was careering down the road on the bike, the wind in her hair, blowing away the hangover. On and on she went, for mile after mile, factories and terraces going by in a blur. But her reflexes still weren't quite right. At Crown Point, in Denton, she lost concentration and slammed into the back of a bus at a red light. The traffic queued down the road as she picked herself up off the floor and sought refuge on the kerb. Why was she feeling so groggy?

Ian supplied the answer a few hours later: he'd drugged her with Gran's sleeping tablets. It took a while for the meaning of the words to penetrate her hangover. What the hell had he done that for? Ian was quite calm: he was going to commit the perfect murder, and she had to help him.

Myra kept her head down at work the following morning. She was barely able to type. She loved Ian, and the world they had built together, but the drugging worried her. She could live with sadism, enjoy it even, but, as she stated in a letter to me, she did not want to end up as his victim. When five o'clock came round she accepted his offer of a lift to the top of her road on the bike. Then she climbed off and walked the last few yards home, without glancing over her shoulder.

Myra knew he would not come round that evening, so she went to visit May Hill. It was ages since they'd seen each other, but it did not take long to fall back into the conversation of old friends. May confided in Myra that her boyfriend had given her the push for refusing sex; Myra admitted that she was fed up with Ian. They decided to drown their sorrows at the bar of the Steelie. The girls drank heavily, and as they walked home alcohol set the truth in motion. May said that no-one liked Ian, and Myra was getting a shocking reputation by sleeping with him. May's words, Myra told me, played on her fears, and she decided to write a letter to be given to the police in the event of her disappearance. Sitting at the Hills' kitchen table, she scrawled out instructions on where they would find her body: close to the lay-by on Saddleworth Moor, probably by the rocks. She shielded her words from May and made her promise not to deliver the letter unless 'something happened'. They rolled back the Hills' sofa and tucked the envelope beneath the carpet. If not an insurance policy, it at least ensured that Ian would not get away with killing her.

The following Saturday Ian came round again. As Myra put a fresh pot of tea down on the coffee table she saw him fishing in his pocket. He pulled out a small folder, drew the table up to the couch, and began spreading out photographs – shots of her, naked, close up, in a series of pornographic poses. Newspaper had been spread on the floor to hide the rug. Where you could see her face, Myra told me, she had a 'stupid drunken expression' on her face. She had no memory of posing for them. He told her that he'd taken them while she was out cold; she would do what he wanted. The teapot stood steaming between them in the ensuing silence. After a short while Ian scooped up the pictures, slipped them back into his pocket and walked out of the door. When he had gone Myra walked briskly round to the Hills', hammered on the door and asked May to get the envelope for her.

Myra's decision to retrieve the letter did not fit with the case she was building in her letters to me that she was bullied into taking part in the murders. If she had truly been terrified, surely she would have left the letter there, or gone straight to the police? Rather, it suggested that she realized he would not kill her, and she made a conscious decision to go along with his plan for the perfect murder. I asked Professor MacCulloch for his opinion. 'I find the idea that she was frightened into taking part in the murders unconvincing,' he said. 'I accept that there's a balance here but, on balance, the attraction of the relationship, and what's going on, is more powerful than being abused. She doesn't have a normal reaction to that sort of behaviour. Besides, she must have realized that he needed her to pick up a child.'

Myra did describe other attempts at 'escape' in her letters to me. She applied for a job with the NAAFI in Germany, went for an interview in London and was accepted. But when she got back to Manchester Ian was waiting for her at Piccadilly station. Myra told me that he took her home, threatened her family, and anally raped her. But still she stayed with him.

In her autobiography Myra described how, far from fleeing Ian, she allowed him to further 'educate' her about his background and motivation. He told her she should see where he came from. Ever since the day of his banishment by a Scottish magistrate he had made regular trips back 'home'. They loaded up the van with food and headed north. Because Myra did not have a driver's licence they stuck to the back roads; there were far fewer police there than on the motorways. In Glasgow, Ian directed her towards the Gorbals. The tenement he had grown up in was all but derelict. Most families, like the Sloans, had been moved out. Ian walked about in his long coat, a light-meter round his neck and camera in his hands, and recorded the places where he'd grown up. Myra followed him as he walked into one of the blocks and ran up the steps, two at a time, like a boy coming in from school. He leant backwards out of the staircase window and called up, in a mock child's voice, pretending to be 'Sloany' the misfit again. Myra collapsed laughing. On the way back to the van they glanced through the door of a pub. The first thing Myra noticed was the sawdust on the floor, and the spittoons, but she retreated under the force of the drinkers' suspicious expressions. Ian told her that they did not like women in pubs. He also warned her to keep her mouth shut as her accent would not go down well.

From the Gorbals, they followed a bus out to Pollock. The Sloans had moved here in the hope of a better life when Ian was still a boy. They parked the van at the top of the road and sat watching the small house he had grown up in. It was identical to all the others. After a few minutes Ian grew restless, told her he was worried about being observed. He jumped out of the car and strode towards a low block of flats opposite. They climbed the stairwell to the third floor and continued to watch the Sloans' house from there. Myra tried to imagine Ian playing down there with childhood friends.

They were disturbed by a young boy coming up the stairs. He gave them a wide berth and knocked on the door of the flat opposite their look-out. A girl answered; Myra guessed she was about twenty. When the door had closed, Myra could feel her eye on them, through the spyhole. Five minutes later the door cracked open. What the fucking hell did they want? Myra was taken aback by the girl's venom. Ian turned, said they weren't bothering her. The girl spat back that they 'fucking were'. Ian's jaw clenched tight, and his cheekbones seemed to stand out. Myra thought he was going to slap her, but he simply turned and walked down the stairs. In her autobiography, Myra recalled his words as they walked back to the van: 'I'd never hurt one of my own.'

They sat outside the Sloans' for hours. Ian sent Myra out for fish and chips; he stayed hidden in case anyone recognized him. Just as she returned, Ian's stepsister, May, emerged from the front door of the house. Ian pulled Myra's head down so that it obscured his face until May had passed. She did not notice him, bought her chips and walked briskly home, pulling the door to behind her.

Myra asked Ian why he didn't just go in. He did not reply, just sat there staring straight ahead. They spent that night sleeping in the van, outside the Sloans' front door, wrapped in their coats. In the morning, stiff with cold, they drove to the public wash-house at Glasgow Central station for a bath. As she lay soaking in the hot water Myra decided to put a couple of blankets in the back of the van for future excursions.

The trip to Scotland helped Myra to understand Ian's hunger to 'rise above' the 'confines' of the working class. Committing the perfect murder was a way of asserting his superiority. But she was still not quite ready to help him. Nevertheless, he insisted that she go out looking for a victim. Myra described in a letter to me how she drove round and round Gorton. She looked at kids and imagined telling them she'd lost something, taking them up to the moor and handing them over to die. Ian knew that every time she went out there was a chance he would get to fulfil his ambition. Everything else was in place. His frustration grew every time a victim failed to materialize. When Myra returned empty-handed yet again he wanted to know what the hell had happened this time. Her excuse was lame: there were too many people about. He grabbed her round the neck and slapped her repeatedly, told her that he'd been watching on his bike and she'd bottled it. He released her and slammed out of the door.

Myra, as her letters to me reveal, was not the only one affected by her sexually sadistic relationship with Ian Brady. One morning Myra stood over Gran in her work clothes, shaking her by the shoulder. She was fast asleep. A fresh cup of tea stood steaming on the bedside table. No matter how hard Myra shook, Ellen did not move. She ran round to Eaton Street to get Nellie, then down the road to Dr Chadwick's. The doctor prodded Ellen and listened to her chest before announcing that there was nothing wrong. Did she use sleeping tablets? Myra held the packet out to him, and blanched. Dr Chadwick nodded understandingly; the old dear had got in a muddle and taken one too many, that was all. But an image from the previous evening had come into Myra's mind: Ian making a cup of tea and taking it up to Gran. He'd doped her too.

Myra rang in sick and stayed at home to look after Gran. That evening she heard the Tiger Cub come down the street and pull up. She struggled to control her temper as she waited for Ian to come inside. He was quite calm, and did not bother to deny what he'd done. He told her that he'd had no choice, as she kept backing out. He knew it was difficult, but she'd enjoyed the fantasy so she'd enjoy the reality. They both would. Besides, all she had to do was hand them over. The rest could stay up here, he added, tapping the side of his head.

Myra recorded in a letter to me that she knew he was right. Every time she climbed behind the wheel of the black van she was a step closer to 'doing it'. Her account of this period is filled with foreboding. There is the sense of an actor rehearsing his part, over and over, in the certain knowledge that he will eventually take to the stage.

Chapter Three

On a warm summer's evening I walked down Taylor Street, turned right opposite the Steelworks and, a minute later, left into Froxmer Street – the site of the first abduction. The low sun shone through a willow and danced on the wall of Gorton Foundry. I turned and looked back in the direction Myra Hindley would have come. There was Peacock Street Primary. It seemed extraordinary that they set out to abduct someone so close to home. Perhaps it added to the excitement, the feeling that they had a secret no-one else was party to.

The account of the first abduction, in Myra Hindley's letters to me, is extraordinary in its detail. It was just after eight on Friday, 12 July 1963. Myra's stomach fluttered as she signalled left by Beyer Peacock. She had watched the pretty girl in a party dress turn into Froxmer Street and knew she was alone. She glanced in her rearview mirror. Ian flashed the Tiger Cub's headlights on and off, on and off, then roared past the van to the end of Froxmer Street. The bike disappeared out of sight, but Myra listened for the engine note and heard it die as he cut the ignition.

She pulled the van to the side, leant over, rolled down the window and asked the girl where she was going. Pauline Reade, whom Myra had known since she was little, turned and smiled in recognition. A dance at Openshaw. She'd fixed up to go with Pat Cummings, but she'd had to cancel. Yes, thanks, a lift would be great.

Myra could see Ian parked up on his bike in an alley next to the Vulcan pub at the end of Froxmer Street. As the van rolled past him Myra asked Pauline if she'd mind a small detour to look for a glove she'd lost near Greenfield; it had been a present from her boyfriend. She'd drop Pauline back at the dance after. No problem, said Pauline.

Myra Hindley's senses were so sharpened that every one of this evening's experiences etched itself into her memory. Each word, sound and smell read as though it had been lived and committed to paper the same day. 'The clarity of her recollections is very striking, and important,' Malcolm MacCulloch told me. 'It means that the omissions are likely to be obvious, and significant.'

Myra glanced across as she steered the heavy old van down the A635. Pauline had on white gloves, a pastel blue coat over a pink dress and white high-heeled shoes. She was wearing only a little make-up and her hair had been newly curled. Her perfume was light and fragrant. It reminded Myra of her own – June, by Saville. She stuck carefully to the speed limit as they drove through the outskirts of Manchester, Stalybridge and Greenfield. The Tiger Cub's headlight bobbed up and down in her wing mirror. To pass the time, Myra told Pauline how Ben's new van had broken down and she had agreed to help him tow it when they got back to Gorton. It was 'only fair', as he'd let her borrow this one. Pauline asked Myra where her boyfriend was. Oh, he'd had to go off on an emergency, she replied. He'd join them later if he could.

The light was failing when they turned the corner to the moor, and they sat in silence for a few moments. Then Pauline asked if Myra was all right – she was gripping the steering wheel ever so tight. Myra flexed her fingers, flashed a smile and explained that she was still getting used to driving the big old van.

Ian had counted all the buttons on their clothing before they went out. His shirt, jacket and trousers; her blouse, skirt and coat. Every number had been written down on a piece of paper to be checked off when they got home. He'd also listed all the things they would need to do afterwards: burn shoes, cut up clothing, wash spade. Myra knew exactly where to park when they got to the moor and what to say so that their stories fitted together. Unlike their inspiration, Leopold and Loeb, they had left nothing to chance.

They reached the lay-by; the Tiger Cub stood at its edge, concealed between a couple of large rocks. Myra feigned surprise as she greeted Ian. He 'suggested' that she park round the corner while he and Pauline started looking for the lost glove. The light was disappearing fast now. Myra glanced in the rearview mirror as she pulled onto the road and saw Ian leading Pauline onto Hollin Brown Knoll. She was having trouble walking in her white high-heeled shoes. He had taken her arm to lend her support.

It was almost dark when Myra pulled the Ford into the smaller lay-by, two wheels on the verge, two on the tarmac. She sat staring at the moor and noticed a couple of ditches that had been dug for new gas pipes. Other than a soft wind drumming against the slab-sided van, it was quiet. She was almost certain that Ian was raping Pauline.

After twenty minutes there was a scrabbling sound. Ian slid back down the hill to the van. He banged on the window and gestured for her to get out. Myra walked at his side, careful not to twist her ankle. Even though it was dark Ian knew exactly where he was going, and he guided her round the newly dug ditches. The first things to emerge from the darkness were Pauline's white gloves and shoes, caught in the moonlight as the cloud broke in the black night sky. Myra asked whether he'd raped her. Of course he had, said Ian matter-of-factly. He told Myra to wait while he went and got the spade.

Myra stared down at the body. Pauline's clothing had been pulled up and blood was seeping from a deep wound in her neck. She was surprised: Ian had said he was going to strangle the victim. She heard him coming back. He grumbled about not having been able to find the spade easily in the dark, jumped off a rock and landed next to her. The peat juddered with the impact of his weight. He told her to get back in the van. As she walked off Myra noticed, with dismay, that his clothes were covered in blood. This part of the moor was completely exposed in daylight. At night-time car headlights cut through the darkness, their drivers' eyes locked on the road in front. Myra knew that Ian would enjoy the fact that 'normal' life was hurrying by with no idea of the horror he was perpetrating.

When Ian got back to the van he carefully wrapped the spade in a plastic sack and the knife in cloths before stowing them. He told Myra to head back to the other lay-by. She bungled the three-point turn and had to repeatedly back up and down between the verges before the van was finally facing the right way. Ian swore at every missed gear and stamp on the brake. When they reached the bike they pulled a couple of planks out of the back of the van to make a ramp and pushed the Tiger Cub inside. It was a tricky manoeuvre but they had practised it in daylight. As she climbed behind the wheel Myra asked Ian the time. Ten thirty, he replied.

They sat in silence as the van rattled back down the hill to

Manchester. On the edge of the city, Ian said, 'If you'd shown any signs of backing out you'd have ended up in the same hole as her.'

'I know,' Myra replied.

As they passed the foundry they saw Joan Reade with her son Paul, looking for Pauline. Myra stared straight ahead and pretended not to notice their obvious distress.

Gran had banked up the fire to keep the front room warm. Ian carried the knife and spade in through the back door and locked them in a cupboard. Then he reminded Myra about Ben's van. Myra swore; she was exhausted and did not feel up to pretending that everything was normal. But Ian insisted; they mustn't draw attention to themselves by changing their behaviour. He buttoned up his overcoat, to hide the blood on his shirt, and pushed her out of the door.

At Ben's house Myra saw, through a crack in the curtains, that he was fast asleep in front of the fire. She knocked. It was a couple of minutes before he came to the front door, yawning. Rather than put the job off 'til the morning, as Myra had hoped, he pulled on his shoes. She apologized for being late, said that they'd stopped in Whaley Bridge and hadn't been able to get the van going again afterwards. Ben said not to worry, the old banger was always doing that, it could happen any time. Ian chatted away to the grocer as they drove, and helped him hitch a rope to his broken-down van so that Myra could tow it back to Gorton. Ben tapped the roof of her Ford and climbed behind the wheel of his vehicle. Myra started the engine and let out the clutch. The first time she used too few revs and stalled; the second, she pulled away so fast the rope almost snapped. Ben got out and walked up to her open window. Would she like him to drive? Ian jabbed Myra in the ribs; they hadn't cleaned the back out yet. No, no, it would be fine. She was just a bit tired.

When they got home Myra filled a bucket with hot, soapy water in the kitchen and carried it out to Ian. He washed every inch of the van and wiped the surfaces down with strips of sacking stolen from work. They moved quietly so that the neighbours wouldn't hear, and spoke to each other in a low whisper. Myra hissed at him, demanding to know why he was washing the tyres. He replied that he didn't want to leave behind a single fingerprint. Leopold and Loeb's car had been full of 'forensic'; the only way to be sure was to wash everything down. Myra shone a torch over the surfaces as he worked. He was methodical, turning small circles with the cloth, obliterating every trace of Pauline and the moor.

Back inside, Ian laid out his list and spread a large plastic sheet on the floor in front of the fire. Myra came out of the kitchen, pulling on a pair of washing-up gloves. She told me in a letter that he snapped at her, 'What do you need those for? Don't be so fucking squeamish. It's only earth.'

She replied, 'I'm not having grave-dirt under my fingernails!' He slapped her, sat down and started cutting his clothes into strips. They hissed lightly as he laid them on the coal. Myra half-filled the sink with soap powder and scrubbed the spade clean, even though there was no blood on it, and he'd wiped most of the dirt off on the rough tussock-grass. Myra asked Ian what they should do about her clothes. The plan had been for her to stay in the van, but she had walked across the moor and stood next to the body. He said she hadn't touched anything so she'd be fine if she sponged off any flecks of peat and wiped her shoes.

Ian pressed on the handle of the knife, trying to snap it off. But it was too well made and the steel rivets clung stubbornly to the wood. In the end he gave up and threw the whole thing in the fire. He told her that the heat would burn off any blood; they'd have to get rid of the blade in the morning. Myra vigorously scrubbed the bottom of the cupboard where the knife and spade had been. It was 4.30 in the morning by the time they had finished. Myra crept upstairs, swallowed a couple of Gran's Nembutal and pulled on clean underwear and a dressing gown. She and Ian fell asleep next to each other in front of the fire.

Myra woke with a start at 6.45, rousing Ian, who swore. He noticed his black coat lying over the arm of a chair, caught in the light fingering its way through the lace curtains. The collar was coated in blood. Worried that Gran might wake up, he carried it straight to the sink and sponged off as much of it as he could. Then Myra put the kettle on while Ian retrieved the burnt knife from the fireplace and wrapped it in pages pulled from the *Manchester Evening News*. After breakfast they headed into town in search of a dry cleaner's. He told her to book the coat in under the name of the US president, Kennedy, while he sat round the corner with the bike engine running. When she'd done that she climbed on the back of the bike and they headed out along the Stockport Road. They were going to dump the knife far away from home and Saddleworth Moor.

After twenty minutes, while they were still in Manchester, Ian pulled up by a newsagent's. He called over his shoulder, as he kicked out the sidestand, that he was just going to get some fags. Myra waited for him on the pillion. A short while later Ian emerged holding a packet of Capstan Full Strength, and handed Myra a Crunchie bar. She slipped it into her pocket for later. Ian did not climb straight back onto the bike, as she expected, but stood there looking down at her with a lop-sided smile on his face. He asked, why didn't she eat it now? Was she put off by the fact that he'd bought it with the four half-crowns in Pauline's pocket?

Myra growled at him through gritted teeth. He'd drummed the law into her: you could still get hanged for treason, killing a policeman, and murder in the furtherance of theft. She ordered him to go back up to the moor and replace the money. Ian looked at her as though she were mad. Who was going to find out? It was the perfect murder. Myra snapped at him. He was going to do it, and she was going to watch. It didn't matter how angry he got, she wasn't going to swing from the gallows for his pride. He pulled a Capstan out, lit it, pushed his foot down hard on the starter, kicked the engine into life and roared off down the Stockport Road.

Ian picked a quiet lane and rode slowly up it until they came to a suitable place. There was a river on the other side and some children were skipping stones on the water. They leant the bike up and wandered casually past the kids looking for somewhere quiet. After a few minutes they were on their own. Ian glanced downstream, checked no-one was watching, and threw a few stones to test the depth of the water. Satisfied, he pulled the package out from under his jacket, unfurled the newspaper and tossed the knife into the stream. The blackened blade sank quickly out of sight. He lobbed a couple of large rocks after it, in the hope that they might rest on the burnt steel, pinning it to the bottom of the stream. Myra sat on her haunches and watched the sunlight catch on the water. He snapped her out of it, told her it was time to go. They walked back to the bike, pausing briefly by a wall so that he could set fire to the newspaper he'd wrapped the knife in.

Myra denied to me that Pauline was targeted as a victim, even though she'd known her all her life: 'all the victims were in the wrong place at the wrong time – it could have been anybody that was "chosen".' The random selection of targets was part of Ian's plan as it gave the police fewer leads to follow; Leopold and Loeb were caught because there were too many connections to their victim. In that sense, the choice of someone so close to home was a mistake. It was an error, I reflected, that would have driven most people to distraction, yet Myra was able to keep functioning.

Malcolm MacCulloch took a sip from a glass of water, and picked up his notes.

'Her reaction is abnormal. This is one of the most horrendous things that can happen to anybody. A person of a more nervous disposition, or with less fortitude, would disintegrate. They would become distressed, anxious, develop post-traumatic stress disorder. There is no evidence of any of this.'

'How does that further our understanding?' I asked.

'There are lots of people with tough personalities who do great and brave things – save nations, get the VC. Under other circumstances they might be labelled abhorrent psychopaths. It's really a question of who you meet.'

Myra stood on Hollin Brown Knoll and watched Ian scatter the half-crowns. He didn't drop them on the grave, but around it. When he was satisfied with their position he crouched down and pushed them into crevices in the peat. The coins would not lead anyone to Pauline's body, but if the police did somehow discover her they would also find the money. Myra looked on approvingly. Then she noticed something on Ian's hand, and asked him what it was. A plastic glove, he replied; he'd wiped the coins clean before scattering them. Had she forgotten? This was the perfect murder. No-one was going to catch them.

When Myra and Ian got back to Gorton the living room was packed, and noisy: Gran, Mam, Maureen and cousin Glenys were sitting there chattering about Pauline's disappearance. Amos Reade had been on the phone to the police several times during the night, but they had only come in the morning. 'Young girls often go missing, sir,' they told him. Now they were questioning poor Amos and talking about dredging the canal and reservoirs. What did Myra think? asked Nellie. Ian smiled. He had warned her to act normally, told her this was bound to happen. Oh, she hardly knew the girl, Myra replied. Pauline was Maureen's friend really, wasn't she? Maureen agreed, then recalled, wistfully, that David had gone out with her for a while. Myra turned up her nose at the mention of Maureen's new boyfriend, David Smith. He was a thug with a long list of convictions for violence.

That night, after a meal with his mother, Ian came round. On the doorstep he pulled a bottle of Drambuie from under his leather coat, to 'celebrate'. Myra, already half cut on wine, smiled and stood back to let him in. They talked late into the night, and went over the killing again and again. Ian, Myra told me in a letter, was ecstatic. He'd finally done it, after all these years – the perfect murder. He reached over, pulled Myra to him, and stroked her hair. Warmth flooded through her and she lay there, breathing deeply, staring into the flames. They soon fell asleep, and Myra did not suffer any nightmares.

The following week, for her twenty-first birthday, Ben gave her the van. He could no longer afford to keep three vehicles on the road. The tax and insurance had only two weeks left, and it needed an MOT. Ian bought a tin of white gloss and they spent a weekend painting the interior, front and back – it was certain to get rid of any 'forensic' that might be left. When they'd finished Ian said he'd like to get the outside resprayed as well. The electricity board lettering still showed through, made it too memorable.

Ian's twenty-first birthday present to her, eleven days after Pauline died, was a gold-plated Ingersoll wristwatch. I found it among her possessions in its original crocodile-skin-effect brown cardboard box. The receipt was neatly folded underneath a red plastic plinth. A rusting staple held it to the twelve-month guarantee.

Those days and weeks after the murder of Pauline Reade were Myra Hindley's last opportunity to run. The version of events she presented to me – that Ian Brady forced her into the killings – might just have worked. She'd probably have done a few years for being an accessory. Her decision to stay with Ian, sleep with him, wear the watch he gave her, meant that there was no turning back.

Chapter Four

Gran snapped at her: she'd been caught. Myra's heart gave a lurch, but she tried to keep her face expressionless. A policeman had been round earlier about the tax on her van. Gran had told her to get it sorted but it was always Ian this, Ian that. Myra hid her relief.

The *Manchester Evening News* and *Gorton and Openshaw Reporter* were still full of Pauline Reade's disappearance. The police dragged the canal and the reservoirs. There were house-to-house enquiries; Maureen's boyfriend, David Smith, was interviewed twice. Ian questioned Mo closely about what they'd asked. Did they have any theories? Did they suspect anyone?

Myra and Ian returned to the moor many times. Seeing Pauline's grave, Myra wrote in her autobiography, made Ian calm, reminded him that he really had committed the perfect murder. There is a photograph of him, wearing a dark suit and glasses, standing on the rocks of Hollin Brown Knoll; another of her grinning in a long woollen coat, a transistor radio at her feet. She noted that the song playing on the radio was 'My Guy' by

Mary Wells. They were in front of Pauline's grave. Myra's clear recollection of posing by the grave, and the gleeful expression on her face, did not seem to me to be the actions of someone who was living in fear; rather, they suggested that she was complicit in savouring the murder. 'That is the sort of thing that happens with sadists,' Professor MacCulloch told me. The photographs were spread out on his dining-room table. 'They review what they've done. Either they remember it in fantasy, and that reinforces them, or they have souvenirs – body parts, hair, pictures – through which they're able to relive what happened.'

Ian printed the pictures of Pauline's grave in his darkroom at Westmoreland Street. The negatives were large 6cm × 6cm professional quality medium-format images. He took great care to make sure that they were processed and washed correctly. Rather than make enlargements he produced 'contact prints'. By the red glow of a safe-light he pressed the negative straight onto photographic paper, then exposed it for twenty seconds to the white light of the enlarger. It was a fast way of working, and it meant that the resulting pictures were the right size to stick straight into his new tartan-covered picture album.

Myra avoided passing by the Reades' house in case she bumped into Pauline's mum, Joan. They had often walked to work together when she was at Lawrence Scott's. She did once encounter Pauline's dad, Amos. He looked drawn, was staring into nothingness, and did not see her. His daughter's disappearance was the main topic of conversation at work. There was a wild rumour that Pauline had run off to Australia with a man from the fair because she was pregnant and couldn't face telling her strict Catholic mother. Complete rubbish, Myra said. Pauline was far too reliable a girl for that; she'd known her all her life. Myra told me in a letter that she coped by walling herself in and operating on a different plane from everyone around her. It was the same strategy she'd used to cope with the violence at home when she was a child. Only this time she was not alone. The shared secret of the perfect murder made her feel even closer to Ian.

Gran waited up with Myra for the police night patrol to come round about the tax disc. Ian had told her to act normally and gone back to Longsight to keep out of the way. Somehow, Gran's nervousness made it easier for Myra to detach herself; when the knock of leather on wood finally came she was quite prepared. The sergeant said that he wouldn't have booked her as she'd never been in trouble with the law before, but now it had to go ahead. The probationary constable at his side, who had written the ticket, shifted uncomfortably. Myra complained that the van did have a disc in the window – Ben had lent her one. That was the other problem, the sergeant explained: because there was a third party, and deception, involved they'd really have to charge her. Gran, listening to everything from the kitchen, was horrified. She went round all the neighbours telling them it was 'just a traffic offence'.

Myra decided the best thing to do was to come clean with Tommy Craig. She didn't want her boss to hear about it from someone else and think that she might have something to hide. He told her not to worry. It was just a 'misdemeanour' and she'd probably get no more than a caution. A week later the papers arrived summoning her and Ben to appear at Manchester Magistrates' Court.

She heard the thunk-thunk of the Norton's engine coming down Bannock Street long before she saw it. It was a sound, Myra noted, quite different from the phut-phut of Ian's little Tiger Cub. Rising over the top of the engine note was another noise: the chatter of a shortwave radio. Myra and Gran watched from behind the net curtain as the policeman dismounted and strode up to the front door, unbuckling his helmet. Gran hovered, demanding to know what she'd done this time. Nothing, replied Myra, irritably, it was probably just about the van. She stood in the darkness behind the front door and waited for the knock.

When the door swung open, light flooded in and there stood 'the tallest, best-looking man' Myra had ever seen. The officer, who introduced himself as PC Norman Sutton, had heard about her 'spot of bother' and wondered whether she intended to keep the van. A friend of his had a refrigerator business and needed something just like it. Gran scuttled across the road to the neighbours to let them know that Myra wasn't 'in trouble' again. Myra asked PC Sutton if he'd like a cup of tea. It was clear from his behaviour that he liked her. She told him he could have the van, but Norman insisted on giving her £25 for it. He said, with a sly smile, that he couldn't hand over the cash on duty; how about meeting up one evening for a drink so that they could settle the deal? Myra agreed. Gran came back and stood fidgeting in the doorway. The noise of that radio was a bit unsettling; was there any chance the constable might be able to turn it down? Norman took the hint, stood up and said he'd see Myra next Wednesday. Gran did not say anything. Meeting a different man from Ian Brady might do Myra 'a bit of good'.

Ian and Myra were having a picnic in a field when she told him about the van. The sound that came out of him astonished her: it started as a low hoot and dissolved into hysterical laughter. He lay on his back in the grass, the beer bottle in his right hand shaking with the power of his convulsions. They'd used a van to commit the perfect murder, and she'd sold it to a policeman! Myra had to admit it was funny.

After the murder of Pauline Reade, Ian's 'absences' became more frequent, and more lengthy. He spent hours out on his bike in the evenings, cruising round Manchester. His thirst for killing slaked, he needed new 'experiences'. Myra sat in and waited for the sound of the Tiger Cub turning into Bannock Street, the engine cutting before it rolled to a standstill outside number 7. Even when he wasn't physically there she was with him.

In order to pass the long evenings, Myra enrolled for night-school classes back at Ryder Brow: English on a Wednesday, Maths on a Friday. Miss Webb, the English teacher, appeared amused to see such a diligent truant walking back through the school gates. Once she'd set the class a task she slipped into the desk next to Myra. She said she was surprised to see her there; English had been her best subject. Myra could probably teach it better than she did! Wouldn't it be better to catch up on the subjects she'd bunked off from? Myra replied that she liked English and wanted to get even better at it. The teacher nodded, stood up and resumed the lesson.

After class, Miss Webb told Myra what had become of the other girls in her year – this one was a nurse at the Manchester Royal Infirmary, that one a secretary. There was one surprise among them, a police officer. Myra's ears pricked up. That sounded interesting, she was meeting a constable for a drink later on. Well, said Miss Webb, if Myra ever wanted to join the police force she should let her know. A lady friend was an inspector at Mill Street station. She'd be happy to recommend her.

Norman was waiting outside, standing next to his 650cc bike. If anything, he looked even better out of uniform – grown up and fashionable. They walked in the opposite direction to West Gorton in search of a 'discreet' pub where no-one would recognize Myra. As they sat down with a rum and Coke for her and a pint for him, Norman said he'd known her right away. What did he mean? Myra asked. The policeman replied that he'd been a regular at Belle Vue when she was a barmaid. Myra fished in her memory, trying to remember him. It had all been a blur, the faces just 'punters', not people. Norman added that May, the manageress, was his mam. Myra gasped in astonishment. Her old boss and the pleasure gardens belonged to a different time.

Norman gave Myra the money for the van and took her home on his bike. The house was dark: Gran was in bed and Ian was out, prowling about. Myra had no idea whether he was going to appear that night. She agreed to let Norman come in, but said that if Ian showed up he'd have to pretend he'd just popped round with the cash for the van, and leave. Myra put the small TV light on and went into the kitchen to make a cup of tea. Norman sat down and stroked her dog, Lassie. He asked if she was serious about Ian. Myra replied that she was. The only problem was that Ian had said he would never get married, or have kids. Myra set the tea things down on the small table, stirred the pot and poured. Norman eased the dog off the settee and pulled her to him. They kissed; it was long, slow and gentle. Myra wanted him; he was a new 'experience'. If Ian could have them, why couldn't she? They arranged to meet again after her next night-school class.

In the early 1960s the police were not as remote as they are today. People were in and out of the station; the front desk even provided change for people to feed the gas and electricity meters, which both discouraged the 'fixing' of coin slots and meant that officers had day-to-day contact with the community they policed. Myra felt relaxed, she told me in a letter, about going to Mill Street station for an interview. She'd talked over the prospect of training as a policewoman with Norman, who'd agreed it was a good idea. It might give them a future together. The inspector gave her a grilling on her past, but it was easy to deal with: she just blocked out the memory of Pauline's death. It was a convincing performance, and she was passed fit for training. The business with the van wouldn't be a problem, they said – none of us was perfect! Myra was handed the paperwork to complete a formal application to join the force and she trotted down the station steps and into the cool autumn air clutching the forms.

When she got back to Bannock Street Ian was waiting for her. At first, he was shocked at what she'd done. But as he thought about it his enthusiasm grew, and he encouraged her to join the police. Just like selling the van to Norman, the idea heightened the excitement of having committed the perfect murder. Ian demanded to know if she was sleeping with 'the policeman'. Myra refused to answer. He said, casually, that he might just kill him. That night Ian and Myra made love, and he bit her hard on the shoulder from behind.

Ian was now disappearing for as many nights as he was around. Myra saw more and more of Norman. They went dancing at the Levenshulme Palais, for rides on his bike, and for drinks in pubs. Then they made love. It was quite different from the sex she had with Ian. But Myra knew the relationship was temporary – Ian only allowed it to carry on because it amused him. She still belonged to him.

Myra Hindley only ever told the story of her relationship with Norman in her letters to me. I believe that she included it in order to try to show that she was looking for a means of escape, that she would have been 'normal' if she'd never met Ian. But as I read it I suspected that the policeman got caught in a game between them: he became a means of heightening their sense of danger and excitement.

I tracked down Norman Sutton to a nursing home on the out-skirts of Blackpool. His name was 'kept out of the papers' by his sympathetic colleagues after the arrest of the Moors murderers. The *Sun* newspaper sniffed him out years later and put the story on the front page. It revealed that he was divorced and living in Bolton. Norman had refused to comment to the paper but was captured on the end of a long lens peering round a doorway. He looked frightened. Myra Hindley read the piece in her cell, and cut it out; it was there when she died. In a letter to me she wrote, 'I hoped he hadn't suffered from the press exposé . . . I do still treasure him in my heart.'

As we walked down the antiseptic corridor to Norman's room the nursing home sister told me that he had ME. 'He's not in a good way, but he'll see you.'

Norman Sutton was lying on the bed in blue and white striped cotton pyjamas, hacking into a screwed-up handkerchief. The small space was dimly lit with a bedside light. He gave me a baleful, suspicious look as I came in. At first, he denied having a relationship with Myra Hindley. Then I told him what she had written.

'Oh Jesus!' he said.

As he shifted in the bed I could see that his frame, now racked by illness, had been that of a strong man.

'I just want to check the story.'

'All right. It's true. Brady was a complete maniac. He came round when I was there, having a cup of tea. The bastard started screaming at me. He wanted to kill me.'

'But you were a policeman.'

'I was married when I met Myra, and couldn't do anything. It ruined me when it came out. I ended up leaving the force. I've got nothing, nothing.'

Before I left, Norman asked whether I could spare some cash for cigarettes.

One Friday evening Ian and Myra packed up and headed north, to Scotland, for a break. It was to become part of their routine between murders. Away from Manchester, they relaxed. Ian led Myra across the hills around Loch Lomond, and they took a trip across the lake on a paddle steamer. Everything was recorded with Ian's camera: him leaning against the rail of the ship; her with a transistor radio round her neck. They listened to *The Goon Show* sitting by the lake shore. Their conversations were shot through with black humour. Ian was particularly pleased with a picture of Myra sitting on a monument painted with the words 'Maggie Well burnt as a witch in 1776'. She stared, inscrutable, straight into the lens. Ian printed the pictures and stuck them into the tartan album alongside the ones of Pauline Reade's grave.

As requested, I had regular conversations with Greater Manchester Police detectives to inform them about what I had found in the new material, and what Professor Malcolm MacCulloch thought of it. As a result, they decided to do more work on Ian Brady's photographs.

DC Gail Jazmik handed me a reproduction of the tartan album. We were sitting in a corner of the headquarters' canteen. 'All the meeting rooms are booked,' Jazmik had explained. She wanted to know whether any of the pictures I had been given might lead to the grave of Keith Bennett. 'Do you have any photographs that aren't in this album?'

A group of secretaries at the next table were shouting about how drunk they'd got the night before. I screened them out and studied the heavy black pages. There were four to six monochrome pictures per side. At first sight, the album could have belonged to anyone. The moorland scenes were interspersed with snapshots of dogs, friends and family; Nellie and Bob Hindley glued in alongside shots of Ian's mother and the Sloans in Glasgow. There was also a shot of a kilted soldier playing the bagpipes. The only hint of mystery lay in the strange way in which the images were arranged. Technically superb pictures were interspersed with the kind of thing a good photographer would discard as soon as it emerged from the developer: Bob Hindley's blurred back shuffling through a doorway; Ian, over-exposed, holding a tiny baby. The absence of an emotional narrative was also striking; this was no complete world the photographer was trying to present. Where there was humour or warmth it showed up the colder, unsmiling pictures for what they were.

'There are a few pictures that don't seem to be here,' I said.

I handed DC Jazmik a stack of compact discs with thumbnail images on the back. She held them close to her glasses and stared intently, scribbling notes when she came across any she didn't recognize.

'I can see three we haven't got. Would you mind doing us some prints?'

'No problem.'

I ran off three landscapes for her. There was nothing that appeared to point to a grave, but at least the police could be sure that they had all the evidence available if there were further developments.

Myra finally passed her driving test on 7 November 1963, at her fourth attempt. The following Sunday she and Ian were sitting watching *Sunday Night at the London Palladium* when Ian turned to her and said he wanted to 'do another one'.

Myra wasn't really paying attention and asked, 'Another what?'

'Another murder. What did you think I meant?'

She could not believe what she was hearing. He'd wanted to commit the perfect murder, and had achieved it. Why did he want to do another? Ian replied that he just did.

Myra met Norman after her night-school class, made love to

him, and told him it was over. He asked her why, said he didn't understand what she saw in Ian. She told him that it was impossible to put into words. The ending of this relationship freed Myra to concentrate once again on helping to realize Ian's desires.

Chapter Five

'What I'm looking for are patterns, repetition,' Malcolm MacCulloch said. 'He was systematic in the way he operated. By understanding this we can untangle his crimes. It may even, one day, contribute to the case being closed.'

'You mean, something may have been missed?'

'Exactly. But then that's hardly surprising as this material has not been available before.'

Myra recorded in her autobiography that the only way Millwards' warehouse foreman, George Clitherow, could hold Ian's attention was to talk about guns. He was an expert. Small-bore, large-bore, Webley, Smith and Wesson – George seemed to know it all. What's more, he was president of Cheadle gun club. Ian was careful, though, not to make his interest in weapons too obvious. If George picked up on it and invited him along to shoot, he'd have to refuse. There was no way he could get a firearms certificate with his criminal record. Myra, however, was a different matter. Ian told her to 'work on' George and get an invitation to Cheadle.

When the offer came, Myra did her best to look surprised. After work, Ian rode her into town to apply for a firearms certificate. The police at Bootle Street station were not bothered by the traffic offences on her record. Not exactly Al Capone, is it, love?

The following weekend, Myra found herself flat on her stomach, eye clamped to a sight, loosing off .22 rounds at a target. Not bad, said George. She wasn't much of a shot but he seemed to like her enthusiasm. Myra sensed that he was surprised at her interest, and by the fact that Ian allowed her to spend the weekend like this. He asked her whether she'd like to come for a drink after.

Myra took great care to be sociable. She had instructions to get to know people, to find out where they got their guns from. Firearms were expensive; there was bound to be a black market. She finally secured an 'off-ticket' pistol from a mate of George's for £5. She also bought a target rifle, legally, from a gunsmith's in town for £10.14s. It came with a certificate stamped 'to be used on approved ranges only'.

Myra and Ian rode across the moor to a lay-by at the head of Hoe Grain stream. They needed privacy to shoot the gun. Ian, Myra told me, was like a small child as they made their way deep onto the moor, skipping over the rough landscape with excitement. They had to cross and re-cross the rapid water, swollen with winter rainfall, as they made their way to the confluence with Shiny Brook, and turned right. The rifle, in a canvas bag, was slung over Ian's shoulder with a leather cartridge belt Myra had stolen from the gun club. After twenty minutes they arrived at a stone sheep pen, in the middle of a large, secluded clearing. Ian turned and held out his right hand, shaking it impatiently. Myra started to hand him empty tins – she'd been collecting them all week – and he lined them up on the wet, grey rock. Ian grinned at her, got the gun out of its case, and walked twenty paces back in the direction they'd come. Myra went with him: he'd never fired a gun before. She'd had to show him how to clean, load and handle it.

The loud crack of the pistol was followed by silence. The bullet buried itself deep in the peat; a second ricocheted off rock; then he found his target. They stayed there for two hours while Ian blasted away at the tins. He only stopped when all the bullets had gone. It was relaxing; Myra took pleasure in his childish satisfaction. When they had finished they gathered up the bullet-riddled tins and spent cartridge cases.

I found endless pictures of Myra and Ian posing with the guns. The shots of her are carefully posed, pin-sharp; those of him are often blurred. She did not have his knack for bracing the camera against her body, to keep it steady at slow shutter speeds. Myra's face is expressionless in the pictures with guns, picking out some imaginary target with a hunter's eye. Ian is grinning in some, scowling in others. The most alarming shows him wearing a leather helmet and his long black coat, pointing the rifle barrel straight at the lens.

Myra was angry, but hiding it well. The man at Warren's Autos, next to Piccadilly station, had told her she couldn't hire a car with the pink slip of paper that said she'd passed her test; she needed a full licence. Ian would be furious. They had worked out all the details of the next killing and planned it for the following afternoon. Myra's licence arrived a few days later. She went straight back to Warren's Autos to reserve a car for the weekend. The man behind the counter said he was sorry but they only hired with a week's notice. Myra bit her lip and reserved a car for the following Saturday, 23 November. Ian was beside himself with impatience, but he agreed that she'd done the right thing, sticking with the plan, staying calm.

On the morning of the 23rd, Ian gave Myra a present, Gene Pitney's 'Twenty-four Hours from Tulsa'. They listened to it as she got ready to leave for Warren's Autos. The American's trembling falsetto echoed round the kitchen; the words were about not coming home any more. It was a grim play on the fate of their next victim. Myra groaned inwardly when she saw the Ford Anglia washed and ready on the forecourt. The bright white lettering of the number plate, 9275 ND, matched the rest of the car. It would show every speck of peat. Ian exploded when she picked him up, at eleven a.m., on the corner of Westmoreland Street. He raged that the thickest plod would be able to see exactly where they'd been. Myra fought back: what was she supposed to do, wait another week? How would he have taken that? Ian eventually calmed down and accepted she was right.

In order to create an alibi they drove south to Staffordshire and took photographs of themselves against a jagged line of rocks, Ian slim and formal in his old-fashioned clothes, Myra looking staid – a secretary on her day off. When they were done they headed north to Huddersfield, stopping off for a coffee and a Danish. Myra couldn't finish hers. Ian grabbed the sugary pastry, wolfed it down and told her it was time to go shopping. The hardware shop had everything she wanted: a roll of thin cord, a small kitchen knife with a serrated edge, and a spade. She was wearing a black wig she'd bought in Lewis's on Piccadilly Gardens, and a headscarf to hold it in place. She tried to act as normally as possible when she paid, to blend into the background. Ian was waiting for her round the corner in the Anglia. He got out as she walked up to the car and swiftly opened the boot, which was lined with black plastic. She carefully laid her new purchases alongside the freshly cleaned rifle and a torch.

Myra pulled away slowly and drove round the small town looking at all the cinemas. Ian chanted to himself in the passenger seat: hadn't seen it, no good, hadn't seen it, no good. Then they found what they were looking for, and Ian laughed. *From Russia with Love*. They'd gone to that last week. If they needed an alibi for the evening they were in there watching it.

Ashton-under-Lyne is a small town on the edge of Manchester. It has a strong sense of community, and feels gentler than the city. In its centre, surrounded by robust municipal buildings, stands the market. Bright canvas canopies protect shoppers from the rain sweeping in off the surrounding moor. When Myra and Ian arrived it was dark, but the stalls were still lit up. There were lots of kids hanging about, scrounging and mucking about. Ian was irritated when Myra told him that she needed the toilet. She told him it would affect her concentration if she couldn't go. He growled something about behaving inconspicuously. A group of women was gossiping in the toilet block; they did not look at Myra as she came in. She caught her reflection in a mirror and noticed that the wig needed re-clipping. Turning her face from the women, she backed into a cubicle to sort it out. As she washed her hands she checked it, gave a small nod of satisfaction, then walked out into the night to meet Ian.

He'd 'seen one', buying left-over food. Could she remember the script? Myra nodded and walked alongside him as they made their way down the back of a line of stalls. John Kilbride was sitting on a wall eating a bag of broken biscuits. Ian and Myra walked past him, arm in arm, scanning the area for witnesses. When they were satisfied the coast was clear, she turned and delivered her opening line.

'You're out late for such a young boy, aren't you?'

Ian picked up the cue. 'We've got kids, and we'd be worried if they were out like you, with it getting dark.'

Myra smiled reassuringly and offered the young boy a lift home. He agreed, stuffed what was left of the bag of biscuits into his jacket pocket, jumped down off the wall and walked with them to the white car. Myra asked him his name. He said he was called John Kilbride, but people called him Jack. He told them that he lived nearby, on Smallshaw Lane.

Ian hung back a few paces as they walked to the car. When they reached it he dived into the back seat, feigning innocent enthusiasm, and told John to get in the front. Myra slid behind the steering wheel, leaned across and locked the passenger door. She asked John if he'd like an adult treat, a bottle of sherry. The boy responded with enthusiasm. It was all so easy. As they pulled away, Myra looked in the mirror and saw Ian checking over his shoulder. She told the boy that they'd have to go home to get it for him. They lived in Greenfield, was that all right? John nodded. He did not suspect anything.

In a letter to me, Myra recalled Ian's words as they came into the village on the edge of the moor: 'Now that we're almost home, why don't we drive up to where we picnicked this afternoon and get that pair of gloves you left? I've just remembered them.' He told John that they were a present for their wedding anniversary and had a sentimental value. The boy was untroubled, staring out of the window, enjoying the ride. Ian had already chosen where he was going to be raped and buried.

When they got to the lay-by Ian asked John to help him, got the torch out of the boot, and walked off down a shallow incline onto the moor. A half moon lit their way. After a couple of minutes Myra drove off down towards Greenfield. She got the rifle out of the boot and laid it on the floor, next to a bag of bullets. She sat there fidgeting and glancing at her watch every couple of minutes. Ian had said she'd be less conspicuous there. If anyone 'suspicious' came up the hill she was to follow and, if necessary, shoot them.

At eight o'clock she headed back to the lay-by, flashed her lights twice and pulled in. Almost immediately there was an answering flash from the moor. As she opened the boot she noticed that, as well as the spade, Ian was holding a shoe. He told her that it must have come off while he was raping the boy; he'd only noticed it while filling in the grave. Myra asked if he'd hurt John. Ian replied, no more than he had to. The point was to rape, kill and bury – it was the ultimate thing. He wasn't interested in hurting. Myra replied that he hurt her during sex. That was different, said Ian, he wasn't doing the 'ultimate thing' to her. Then he changed the subject, complaining that the knife she'd bought was too blunt. He'd had to strangle the boy with string.

Back in Gorton, they fell to cleaning up. Everything had been planned so carefully that, even though it was only the second time they'd done it, it felt almost routine. Ian cut up his clothes and shoes and burned them alongside John's in the fireplace. He threw the small knife on top and wiped down the spade before putting it in the cupboard with the gun. The one 'improvement' lay in how they cleaned the car. Ian had covered almost every surface in plastic sheeting. Rolling this up and wiping down the surfaces was far faster than washing down every inch of carpet and upholstery. He and Myra threw buckets of hot, soapy water over the wheels and white paintwork. 'He was unusually forensically aware,' Geoff Knupfer, the former head of Greater Manchester CID, told me. 'Remember, this was the 1960s, and most people did not know about these things. The level of planning was quite extraordinary.'

When they had finished, Myra drank off a bottle of wine in one; Ian followed suit. The third bottle went down more slowly, and was followed by whisky chasers. Myra was still drunk when she dropped the Anglia back at Warren's Autos at nine the following morning. *Another* hangover, Gran shouted at her as she came in. Myra had to stop drinking so much; she was only twenty-one but looked old and haggard! Her mam and the Hills were right, that Ian Brady was no good. Myra told Gran to stop lecturing her. The old lady fell silent, handed her a cup of tea and some aspirin and encouraged her to go to bed.

It is clear from Myra's letters to me, and the different drafts of her autobiography, that the relationship with her family had lost all meaning. She went through the motions, did the least that was expected of her, but there was no longer any real emotional connection. Gran, Nellie and Maureen knew that there was something wrong, and that Ian was 'the cause'. But they had been unable to exercise any control over her as a child. Now that she was an adult they had no chance.

Myra and Ian read about John Kilbride's disappearance the following afternoon, as they sat on a bench in Sunny Brow Park, in the *Gorton and Openshaw Reporter*. The police were doing house-to-house enquiries, and they had sniffer dogs out. She gazed out over the lake, remembered playing there as a kid. Ian read from the paper: John Kilbride lived at 262 Smallshaw Lane; he went to St Damian's Church School; his father was from Ireland – they were all Catholics, breeding like animals. Myra ignored the jibe, but he continued: that was two fewer Catholics in the world today. Myra couldn't take any more. Her head was throbbing from the hangover, and she told him to shut up.

The talk about John Kilbride's disappearance was incessant. Myra, glad that it was busy at work, kept her head down and muttered noncommittally whenever anyone mentioned it. Gradually, as had happened after Pauline's disappearance, the story faded from the front pages then stopped appearing altogether. There was simply nothing new to write.

In a letter to me, Myra related how, soon after the killing of John Kilbride, she and Ian were sitting on the sofa in front of *Sunday Night at the London Palladium*. Bruce Forsyth's camp voice filled the room: 'I'm in charge!' Ian leant across to her and asked, 'What do you think I get out of doing what we've done?' Myra replied immediately that it was about being in charge, having the power of life and death. Ian smiled, said good, she knew where he was coming from. It was the same for her, wasn't it? I felt sure that Myra told me this story in order to explain Ian's motivation and how driven he alone was. But I found it unconvincing. She must also have been caught up in the feeling of power, and superiority, to continue helping him.

A few days later Ian told her to wrap up warm, they were going for a ride on the Tiger Cub. When he turned onto the Ashton Old Road she banged him frantically on the arm. The bike wobbled a little, but he ignored her. They sat on Smallshaw Lane, opposite the Kilbrides' house, for what seemed like an eternity. A small girl came to the gate and peered up and down the road. She didn't give them a second glance.

A couple of weeks later they went back to the moor. Ian took a picture of Myra squatting down, peering at the ground, holding her new dog Puppet wrapped inside her coat. She was on the grave of John Kilbride. They talked about killing, agreed that it put them 'in charge' and freed them from 'the confines of the working class'.

Professor MacCulloch put his notes down. 'They used very similar methods in both murders. They rehearsed each killing and took pictures on, or by, the graves afterwards. This could be a system.'

*

On New Year's Eve, 1963, Ian and Myra rode back up to the moor on the Tiger Cub. In her autobiography Myra recalled that he parked up in the lay-by next to John Kilbride's grave, held his whisky bottle to the full moon and said, 'To John!'

Chapter Six

'Duncan, these negs are absolutely filthy.'
Tim, the manager of Redcliffe Photographic Laboratories in Bristol, had to clean each of the images by hand. His cotton-gloved fingers were stained nicotine brown. He stared at them and grimaced.

'I've already had to throw one pair away!'

He pulled his gloves off and handed me a set of prints.

'I was on my own here last night. These really disturbed me.'

He was pointing to the shots of boys in football kit at Ryder Brow.

Ian Brady developed the pictures of John Kilbride's grave in his makeshift darkroom. He laid a towel over the crack below the door, to stop light leaking in, and tacked a heavy piece of material over the window. Then he turned out the light. He was careful not to crease the film as he transferred it from its roll to a developing spool. It was a relief to be able to slide it into a tank, fasten the lid and turn the light back on. Then the comforting smell of chemicals: ten minutes for the developer; thirty seconds stop bath; four minutes fixer; twenty-minute rinse, just to be sure. He pulled down the material blocking out the light and a low evening sun angled into the room. Large square negatives dripped onto the floor. The one of Myra and Puppet was well exposed and sharp.

Outside his window, between Westmoreland Street and the Daisy Works, ran a path. Several nights a week Keith Bennett, his brother Alan and his sister Maggie walked along it on the way to their grandmother's house. They spent the night there while their mother Winnie went out. Sometimes they walked close by Myra's van, parked up, waiting for Ian. She'd bought an Austin, kept it for a couple of months, and traded it in for a brand-new Mini pick-up.

Myra told me in a letter that on the evening of 18 June 1964 she drew up into her usual place, glanced around for any witnesses, and calmly pulled on the black wig. She felt at one with Ian; they stood on one side of a chasm that divided them from the rest of the world. They had stowed mementos of their killings in a suitcase at a left-luggage office. That morning he'd given her Roy Orbison's 'It's Over'.

Ian walked swiftly up to the Mini, climbed into the back and they drove off. Keith had just turned off Stockport Road, where his mother left him on her way to 'the bingo', and was walking towards his grandmother's house. Myra said that the instant she saw him she knew that Ian was going to tap on the glass for her to stop. She pulled over, wound down the window and asked if he'd mind giving them a hand with some boxes. It was so easy, Myra thought. They trusted her just because she was a woman.

Now that Ian had found he preferred children, he wanted time with them. He led Keith more than a mile from the road to the confluence of Shiny Brook and Hoe Grain streams. It was their 'special place' where they came to shoot, picnic and have sex.

I followed Professor John Hunter down Hoe Grain. The moor at Shiny Brook is a constantly shifting world. Each change of light and tilt of the wind makes it feel different. The only constant is the fast babbling of water. The noise rises and falls with the rain, but never stops.

'It's a long way from the road, John.'

'Yes. But the better you know the terrain the easier it is to move across it. Even if you are leading someone who has never been here before.'

Myra followed Ian and Keith. She thought that the boy looked like a lamb going to the slaughter. Ian knew exactly where he was going; he had chosen the spot carefully and hidden a spade there. As they got close he motioned to Myra to climb the plateau that rises above Hoe Grain and Shiny Brook. She sat down there with her back to the stream and listened to the echo of the wind in the grass and the fast-running water. Off to her right she could see the tall, Stonehenge-like shape of Greystones.

After half an hour a high whistle pierced the sounds of the moor. She looked down and saw Ian waving for her to join him. They made their way back up Hoe Grain towards the car. On the way they buried the spade in the shale of the steep left-hand bank.

It was late when they got back to Gorton. They had to be at work the next day, so there wasn't much time to clean the car out. Ian wiped it down and burned their shale-scarred shoes. His had specks of blood on them. The last thing he threw on the fire was the thin cord he'd used to strangle Keith.

Myra dropped him back at Westmoreland Street, the twin-lens reflex hanging inside his coat. He'd taken a photograph and wanted to develop the film. The negative he pulled off the developing spool showed Keith lying in the peat. But Ian was disappointed, he later told Myra: the picture was out of focus. He showed it to her, and said he was going to burn it.

'There are pictures of her in this area,' John Hunter said.

'Yes,' I replied, 'they all show her on Shiny Brook. The two most easily identifiable are by the waterfall. There's one of her at the top and one at the bottom. The question is, are they significant?'

Hunter looked down at the fast-flowing stream. 'We don't know if they're markers, so I have decided to concentrate my search on gullies where Brady would have had complete cover to do what he wanted.'

It is only because Keith Bennett has never been found that his murder stands out from the others. Indeed, the most striking thing about the way Myra described it to me in her letters was the brevity of the account, and the language used. It was as if the routine was so well worn by now that its finer points no longer needed explanation. She was locked into the relationship with Ian Brady, mechanically going through the motions. It was just another murder.

Chapter Seven

While Nellie Hindley's dislike of Ian Brady was based on intuition, the loathing of her other daughter's fiancé, David Smith, was grounded in hard fact. Although only seventeen he already had a long criminal record: one stabbing, at the age of eleven, and three further counts of actual bodily harm. When David and Maureen got married at All Saints register office on 15 August 1964, she refused to attend. Ian and Myra stayed away too. He thought it best not to attract attention by being seen to approve of Smith. But Myra, as she related in a letter to me, wanted to avoid a rift. She arranged a day trip to the Lakes and a celebratory meal at a 'nice' hotel, with wine. Things they had never experienced before.

Myra drove, and Maureen sat next to her; Ian and David squatted in the back with bottles of wine. She looked in the mirror and could tell that they were getting very drunk. They were telling each other about the things they hated, crimes they had done time for. By the time the Mini pulled up outside the hotel the two men could hardly stand. She began to fear that admitting Smith to their world had been a mistake.

Myra and Maureen had grown closer with the passing of the years and the fading of their parents' divisive influence. On the way back to Manchester they talked about the future. Mo wanted to know why Myra didn't marry Ian; she replied that she didn't need a ring on her finger or a piece of paper to feel secure. Myra knew that Ian's love for her would never die. Maureen said she didn't feel that way at all. She was sure that now she and David were married he would 'settle down' and stop looking at other women. Myra tried not to show her feelings. She doubted that David Smith would be able to stay out of prison, never mind settle down.

Myra, Ian, David and Maureen saw more and more of one another. The routine never seemed to change: they all got blind drunk before 'the girls' retired to bed and 'the boys' slumped in armchairs, rambling away into the small hours. David confided that he beat Maureen; Ian told David that he hit Myra too, it was nothing to be ashamed of. He gave him a copy of de Sade's *Justine* to read. But there was a difference between the sisters' situations. Where Myra was a willing participant in a sexually sadistic relationship, Maureen was a victim. She was not hardened to violence and had no idea how to cope. Myra's mistrust of David Smith turned to dislike. She recorded in her autobiography how his violent behaviour led her to seek revenge.

One evening there was a hammering at the door. Myra pulled it open to see David standing there, dripping with rain. She demanded to know what he was after. He said that Maureen had run out on him, and was in hiding; Myra must know where she was. David's words gave Myra an idea, and she softened her tone. Moby had gone to Blackpool, she was on her way to see her, did he want to come? David swallowed, tried not to look too surprised, and nodded his head.

The Mini's small windscreen wipers lashed back and forth as the rain kept on coming, streaking down the glass and making it almost impossible to drive. Myra stayed silent: to do anything else would have aroused David's suspicion. When she thought he'd drifted off to sleep she kicked her heel hard against the base of the footwell. What was that knocking? she asked loudly, as though alarmed. David jerked to attention. Myra pulled down the left-hand indicator stalk and turned onto the hard shoulder. She told him to get out and listen by the front wheel while she revved the engine. David, still thinking about Maureen, did not see the trap. The instant he stepped onto the hard shoulder Myra floored the accelerator and roared off. She glanced over her shoulder and saw him, dumbstruck and soaking, staring after her.

In September 1964 a letter fell through the door at Bannock Street: a notice of compulsory purchase by the council. The Corporation of Manchester was demolishing many of Gorton's oldest streets and moving their occupants to large new overspill estates on the fringe of the city. It was the latest fashion in 'town planning'. Myra and Gran were allocated a brand-new, pre-fabricated concrete house on the Hattersley estate. Gran was nervous. She was leaving almost all her friends behind. Her anxiety was eased only slightly by the news that the Hills – John, Maggie, May, Winnie and two married daughters with children – had all been allocated houses just across the road. Nellie helped Myra to get the house ready, installing a new cooker and curtains, before she and Gran moved in. Myra kept telling Gran that it would be like a home from home: she'd be able to bring Mam from Gorton to see her in the car. But Ellen knew things would never be the same, and fell into long silences. These were all but impenetrable when Ian was around.

Then Myra suggested that he move in; it would be 'a help with the bills'. It took a couple of trips to move all of Ian's stuff. Besides all of his photographic equipment there were the suits he'd had hand-made at Burton's to transport. He wasn't going to have them crushed, even if they were made from the latest creaseproof polyester. Life at Wardlebrook Avenue settled into an uneasy rhythm. Ian and Gran made an effort to be civil to each other but there was no warmth there. She saw the change he had wrought in Myra, and did not like it.

Forty years on, Hattersley is a desolate place. Manchester's social problems, removed from the centre of the city, have been accentuated by isolation. I went there the day after the community centre was burnt down. Many of the shops were boarded up, and the one newsagent open had a special offer on three-litre bottles of White Lightning cider. The small plastic signs on the lamp-posts, KILL YOUR SPEED NOT A CHILD, seemed like a tasteless joke. As I walked past the gap where number 16 stood until the council pulled it down, a shaven-headed, bare-chested man tumbled out of number 15 spitting four-letter words.

But Myra told me in a letter that she loved this place when it was new. For the first time in her life she had an 'upstairs bath-room'. The best thing was that you could see the countryside from Wardlebrook Avenue, imagine yourself in it. The hills above Hattersley are fringed with heather – the beginning of the moorland. Myra and Ian were out in the van all the time, explor-ing with their dogs Puppet and Lassie. It was a friendly road, and they worked hard to 'fit in'. Some people disapproved of them for 'living in sin', others were won over and allowed their children to go on 'excursions' with the young couple.

'They used to go out of their way to be friendly,' Carol Waterhouse, who was ten when Myra and Ian moved in next door, told me. 'I first met Myra when she came round to borrow an onion. That tells you how poor we were.' Ian and Myra offered their neighbours generous hospitality. 'My brother David and I used to wash the car out for money and sweets. They seemed so sophisticated. They drank wine. Well, for a working-class person like my mam to be invited in and offered wine was quite something. It just didn't happen.'

Most of the children from Hattersley who accompanied Ian and Myra on 'outings' to the moor remained anonymous. But Patti Hodges was later dragged into the glare of public scrutiny for one simple, horrific reason: she was taken to picnic by the grave of John Kilbride, at Hollin Brown Knoll. And Patti, as Myra Hindley revealed in her autobiography, was not alone. Carol and David Waterhouse were taken to the Shiny Brook area, where Keith Bennett died. When I spoke to Carol it turned out that the police had not been back with her since it was confirmed, in the mid-1980s, that Keith was a victim of the Moors murderers. I asked whether she would be willing to return with Professor John Hunter and his assistant, the former head of the West Midlands Police murder squad, Barrie Simpson.

Carol was nervous, but Barrie put her at ease, giving her time and allowing her to lead the way from the lay-by at the edge of the A635 onto the moor. As she picked her way over the rough tussock grass, Carol said, 'I'm looking for broad, yellow stones you can walk up the middle of the stream on.' She led Barrie, John and me down Hoe Grain to the confluence with Shiny Brook and turned right, towards the Wessenden Head reservoir. Nothing quite matched the picture in her memory. There were yellow stones, but it would have been impossible to navigate them, whatever the water level. She turned and headed back up Shiny Brook.

'How did they behave towards you?' asked Barrie.

'They were adults, but not like parents. That's what made them so attractive. She was quiet, he was chatty. He kept his sunglasses on all the time. We had a great day. This is it!'

We were heading upstream, towards the waterfall where Myra posed for two pictures.

'You can walk up the centre of the stream on the rocks. David and I stood in the middle and Ian took photographs. We all had a picnic together on the bank.'

'Can you remember exactly where?' asked Barrie.

'No, I'm afraid not. It's so long ago . . .'

Myra told me in a letter that Patti Hodges spent most of Christmas Eve 1964 with her and Ian in the lay-by at Hollin Brown Knoll. They got home in the small hours, shivering from the cold, and dropped Patti home. While Myra was banking up the fire in the front room, Ian made an announcement: he wanted to 'do another one'. They'd get the victim from a fairground he'd seen advertised on a booze run to the new Tesco at Newton Heath. He added that this time he wanted to bring 'it' back to the house so that he could take photographs. He could sell them.

The recklessness of the idea, and the speed with which Ian wanted to proceed with the murder, alarmed Myra. She felt that he was getting careless. She tried to dissuade him, but he would not be moved. At breakfast on Boxing Day, Ian gave Myra a copy of 'Girl Don't Come' by Sandie Shaw. It was the one part of their ritual he chose not to abandon. The song was about tears filling eyes, hurting inside, wanting to die.

They went over the final details of the killing in snatched conversations, making sure that Gran didn't overhear. He said they'd do the same as before: get 'it', a girl, to help carry some boxes back to the car, then make off without attracting any attention. Myra was surprised that he wanted a girl.

Myra drove Gran round to spend the day with relatives. Ian stayed at home to rig his camera lights in the upstairs bedroom. He hid his reel-to-reel tape recorder, microphone attached, under the sheet of the divan bed. When Myra got back they headed for the new Tesco and bought just too much shopping to carry comfortably.

In Myra's letters to me, the story of the fourth murder ended abruptly at this point, with the words, 'Thank God I'm out of space. That murder is the one which haunts me most. I'll try and write again over the weekend. Best wishes, Myra.' But she never did write about the killing of Lesley Ann Downey, or explain it to me in one of our regular telephone conversations. It was the case that led to her conviction and directly implicated her in an act of unspeakable cruelty. She did, however, talk about it to the police when she gave them a confession in early 1987.

The Stones' 'Little Red Rooster' was playing as they staggered between the rides at the fairground with their boxes of food and drink. Myra dropped her shopping next to a girl who appeared to be on her own. The girl bent down to help, told her that she was called Lesley Ann, and said she was ten. She called Myra Mam and Ian Dad. They had no trouble getting her into the car.

At Wardlebrook Avenue, Ian took the girl upstairs while Myra locked the dogs in the kitchen. She heard a scream and ran upstairs. He was trying to pull her coat off.

'Please, Dad, no!'

'Shut up!' Myra didn't realize Ian had already set the tape recorder running. She was worried people would hear, shut the window and switched on Radio Luxembourg to cover the noise.

After raping Lesley Ann, Ian strangled her, wrapped her in a bed sheet and put her in the back of the Mini. Myra glanced out of the window to check the weather. It was snowing, so she rang the AA. They told her only to travel if it was absolutely essential. Ian swore, furious at having to change the plan. They'd have to get Gran to stay the night at the relatives' house.

The following day they drove to the moor. Ian ran onto Hollin Brown Knoll with Lesley Ann slung over his shoulder. As Myra watched him she thought of the hours they had spent practising this routine – her hanging limp, like a corpse, while he learned how to move over the rough ground. He came back for the spade and buried the child in a shallow grave, sweeping a dusting of snow over the top to disguise it.

The photographs Ian took of the girl were far too strong to sell, never mind put in the album. Myra told me in a letter that she begged him to burn them. He refused, put the pictures in a suitcase, along with the tape recording, and stowed them under the bed. A few days later they went back to the moor and Ian took shots of Myra standing by the grave. Innocuous 'snaps' that would not stand out from the others in the tartan album.

'I'm struck by the consistent themes,' Malcolm MacCulloch said. 'Here is another murder that was carried out in a systematic, sadistic manner. Once again the burial location appears to have been selected beforehand, and recorded afterwards.'

'What does he get from the pictures?' I asked.

'He is reminded of the fact that he has committed the perfect murder, and that the bodies remain undiscovered. They are his possessions.'

Ian put a lock on the spare bedroom door after the murder of Lesley Ann. He used it to store his 'personal' things – mementos of the murders. Occasionally he'd get something out and show it to Myra. Ian tried to make the evidence less incriminating by hiding key parts of it outside the house. As well as the left-luggage office, he had taken to using a disused filing cabinet at Millwards. The coded body disposal plans hidden there would mean nothing without the names and photographs of the victims.

Four months after the murder of Lesley Ann Downey, David and Maureen's baby, Angela Dawn, was rushed to hospital and died. David and Maureen, their marriage already under strain, slipped into despair. Myra thought it might be better if they moved from Gorton to Hattersley, and helped to sort out a flat in Underwood Court, two minutes' walk away. Ian was delighted. He and David spent hours together in the upstairs bedroom, drinking and talking. Maureen told Myra that she was baffled by the books David was bringing home: *The Carpetbaggers*, *Kiss of the Whip*. He sat for hours in the front room copying out long extracts about child rape and sadism.

One night, Ian suggested that they all drive up to the moor together – it was a full moon, it would be beautiful. He told Myra to park in the lay-by where they had 'toasted' John Kilbride, then turned to David and suggested going for a walk as there was a fantastic moonlit view of the reservoir. David clambered out of the car and followed him a short distance onto the moor where they paused, in silence, to drink in the atmosphere. They were standing on the grave of John Kilbride.

Chapter Eight

Myra Hindley's old Olivetti typewriter broke while she was writing to me. I said I'd try to get it mended, and we arranged for a handover to take place at David Astor's house in St John's Wood. I sat with a coffee, chatting to his wife Bridget, while we waited for an unnamed courier to arrive.

After a short while Pat Hepburn, David Astor's secretary, put her head round the door. 'She's here. Could you go outside?'

I stood on the pavement and waited. On the other side of the road a short, dark-haired woman was bent over, rummaging in a car boot. She pulled out a black bin-liner, strode across, thrust it at me and turned without saying a word. I stood staring after her, wondering who she was – prison warder, lover, friend?

When I got back to my office I split the bin-liner open. The smell of Myra Hindley's prison cell escaped into the room – roll-ups and detergent. The Olivetti turned out to be broken beyond repair. I supplied a new machine, on long-term loan, and had it delivered.

Myra called me the following weekend.

'There's a problem, Duncan.'

'What, Myra?'

'They won't let me have the typewriter until it's been tested for safety by an electrician.'

'Oh no!' I groaned.

'Don't worry, I'll find a way round it,' she replied. 'And, Duncan?'

'Yes?'

'About this loan. You can have the machine back when I get out.'

I heard her laughter bouncing off the walls of the prison corridor.

The following week a tape arrived. I loaded it into my cassette machine and pressed play. She was speaking in a whisper, and had Radio 4 on in the background so that no-one would discover her recording how Edward Evans came to die. Every now and then the story was punctuated by the sound of her dragging on a roll-up.

There was a knock at the front door, Myra began. It was David Smith, standing there clutching a letter from the council, looking sorry for himself. David told Myra it was an eviction notice; he and Mo had to be out by next Saturday. He'd used her sister's name to try to evoke sympathy. He wanted cash. Myra told him it was no good: she was broke, so was Ian. There was nothing they could do. But then Ian appeared at her shoulder and told David to come in. The men climbed the stairs to the spare bedroom. Myra dropped onto the settee and listened to the radio, fidgeting. She didn't trust Smith.

When Ian came downstairs, Myra recalled, he announced, 'We're going to roll a queer!' She had never heard the expression before, though it hardly needed explanation. She was deeply worried at Ian's recklessness. It had been safe when there was just the two of them. Myra understood that while she was in love with Ian, David Smith was in awe of him, and she did not feel that their bond was strong enough.

On 5 October 1965, David and Ian came down from the upstairs bedroom with two suitcases. Ian told Myra that he wanted her to take them to Central station. Didn't want anything incriminating in the house, did they? Myra demanded to know what was in them. Ian glared at her; she was showing him up in front of David Smith. He told her not to be so stupid. In the past Myra had trusted Ian to manage the evidence: keep what he wanted, destroy the rest. But now that Smith was involved she felt things were getting out of control. Ian was making mistakes, like Leopold and Loeb had done. Myra wanted to believe that there was a way of preserving what they had.

When they got home, Ian took Myra's mother-of-pearl prayer book out of the bottom drawer of the dresser. It was her confirmation present from Bert and Kath. He slowly turned the book over. It had a latch and lock to keep it shut – a symbol of virginity. Ian smiled, pulled the left-luggage ticket from his pocket and tucked it down the spine before replacing the book on the shelf. Myra told Ian that she was worried about Smith: he knew too much, they couldn't trust him. In that case, asked Ian, should he kill him? It would be easy. Myra said no, it would upset Maureen too much.

The following morning they were sitting down to breakfast when Ian held a flat, rectangular brown bag out to her. 'Here you go, girl.' She looked at him. 'It's All Over Now Baby Blue' by Joan Baez. The song bothered Myra; it wasn't just the words about the dead left behind, but the reference to the vagabond rapping at the door, in the clothes she once wore. Ian was teasing her about the involvement of David Smith.

Myra worried as they drove into town. She did not want their world to end. Her mind was jerked back to the present when a dog ran out into the road, its owners looking on helplessly. The car ahead of them hit it. Myra braked, opened the door and jumped out. Ian ran after her. She found the animal whimpering in an alleyway and gently felt it all over for injury. The breathless owners finally caught up with them. She offered to take the dog to the vet – it was no trouble. Ian looked down. The couple said no, he'd be fine, thanks anyway.

Myra parked the car outside Central station. Ian got out, slammed the door and walked off to find a victim. Myra noticed the assurance in his stride. Again, he knew exactly where he was going. Myra lost herself in thought about Smith. Maybe Ian should kill him once this was over. It would be for the best.

She was startled by a sharp rapping on the car window next to her head. A policeman stood there, motioning for her to wind it down. He told her she was parked on double yellow lines, she'd have to move. Myra apologized, and explained that she was waiting for her boyfriend. The officer replied that he was going to walk round the Theatre Royal block. If she was still here when he got back he'd have to book her.

A couple of minutes later Ian appeared with a slim, dark-haired teenager. He introduced Myra as his sister. The boy said he was called Eddie, Eddie Evans. He told them he was an apprentice and had just been to see Manchester United play Helsinki. Eddie had meant to go with his mate, Jeff, but he'd had to stay in to mind his sick mother.

At home, Ian opened a bottle of wine while Myra let the dogs out. They had planned this, to create a relaxing atmosphere. Eddie settled into his chair, and Ian motioned at Myra to go and get her brother-in-law. David answered the buzzer immediately and told Myra to come up. Maureen was in bed. David quickly pulled on his shoes and jacket. As he walked out of the door he picked up his heavy dog-walking stick. On the tape, Myra recorded that she asked David why he was taking it. He replied that he always did so at night. She replied, 'You're in the frame, you are.'

Myra told David to wait outside; she would signal for him to knock on the door by flashing a light. He did not have to wait long. Ian opened the door, greeted David, and asked him if he'd come for the miniature wine bottles. The men stepped inside; Myra went off to feed the dogs. Her hand was turning the can opener when there was a loud crashing and the sound of a chair flying across the living room. Myra looked through the serving hatch and saw Ian grappling with Edward Evans. She ran into the hall to find David standing by the front door. She shouted at him that they were fighting – he should go and help! Gran's voice quavered down the stairs, demanding to know what was going on. Nothing, replied Myra, she'd just knocked something over. Myra stood and guarded the bottom of the stairs as the scuffling subsided. It was replaced by the rhythmic thunk of Ian's axe going home.

When the house finally fell silent, Myra went into the front room. She had never seen such a mess: the walls were covered with blood. Ian stood there with the axe in his hand, hopping on one leg – he'd sprained his ankle. Edward Evans was too heavy for David to carry to the car on his own. They wrapped the body up in plastic sheeting and put it in the spare bedroom. David said he would come back the following evening with his dead daughter's pram to shift it. It took them hours to clean up all the blood. They did not finish until three in the morning.

Just a few hours later Myra got up to make Gran a cup of tea. When she came down Ian was sitting on the couch, with his sprained ankle up, writing a letter to Tommy Craig to say that he would not be in that day. He looked up sharply at the sound of a knock on the back door. Myra opened it to a bread delivery man wearing a white jacket with Sunblest on the pocket.

'You've got the wrong house, we have Mother's Pride,' she said.

'I'm a police officer. Is the man of the house in?'

Myra realized immediately that David had shopped them. Superintendent Bob Talbot walked into the room to find Ian sitting, with his foot up, in the front room. Uniformed officers swarmed through the house. Talbot demanded the key to the back bedroom.

'I've no idea where it is,' said Myra.

'Give him the key,' said Ian.

Had Ian Brady been content with committing the perfect murder he would probably have got away with it. But, perhaps inevitably, turning fantasy into reality gave him a thirst for more, and Myra's complicity made it possible for him to keep on killing. But repetition bred boredom, and the only way to re-invigorate himself was to take ever greater risks. Ian and Myra may have been cleverer than Leopold and Loeb, but in the end it was the same thing that brought them down: hubris. Their defiance of the gods was far from over.

Book Three
Prison

'Dear Mam . . . keep all the photos for us, <u>for reasons,</u>
the one of dogs, scenery etc . . .'

Chapter One

The last thing I lifted out of the car boot and carried down to my office was a clutch of bulging supermarket carrier bags. I moved carefully as the plastic was so old it had begun to break down; it felt tissue thin. I laid the bags on my desk and looked round. Every available surface was covered with Myra Hindley's personal effects. In order to get at what mattered I was going to have to sort through a lot of detritus.

'She was a hoarder,' Father Michael Teader told me. 'She lived in prison but longed to be outside. Every scrap of paper or small gift was a connection with the real world.'

I pulled the lid off a faded Quality Street tin. It was filled to the rim with old 45s – Joan Armatrading, Tim Hardin, Joan Baez. At the bottom of a Tesco bag, rattling around among dozens of old cassette tapes, was an old pair of large-framed eighties-style reading glasses. In another carrier were fifteen-year-old Christmas cards from people she had never met, but whose words had moved her in some way. Many were religious and contained quotations from the Bible, or poems full of hope.

There was a card from 1990 with a picture of a cartoon cat hanging upside down. The inscription read, 'Hang on! You're almost there! This year is the beginning of a new decade – it will be a time for you.' Something about the way the card was signed, with smiley faces, made me think that it had come from a lover.

Balanced on top of my photocopier were box upon box of legal documents – a record of every twist and turn in an increasingly desperate campaign for freedom. Tucked inside a sheaf of papers to her solicitor was a letter, written in an uneven hand, begging for information about the whereabouts of Keith Bennett. It was written by the missing ten-year-old's stepfather, Jimmy Johnson. 'All the bodies of the victims have been found except our son, Keith . . . please help us, Myra.'

I reached inside an old Woolworth's bag and pulled out a thick wad of paper covered in small, neat handwriting. The pages had darkened with age but the words were clearly legible. I was astonished at the contents. In my hands were the letters Myra Hindley had written to her mother over a period of thirty-six years in gaol. The change in paper size marked the passing of the decades: black-lined, folded A5 sheets in the 1960s and 1970s; blue-lined, flat A6 sheets in the 1980s and 1990s. The prison paper seemed to get cheaper with the passing of the years, but the heading on the letters never changed: M. Hindley, 964055.

I started reading, and did little other work for the next three weeks. I discovered that the letters from Myra to Nellie have the value of a diary. The contours of a story appear fixed when captured from a single point in time; set that same story alongside a day-by-day record and the way it has been shaped emerges. Each shift in loyalty, change in circumstance is laid bare.

'Almost every one of these letters contains an instruction for it to be destroyed,' said Malcolm MacCulloch. He was skimming through the four bound volumes I had made for him. The professor ran his finger down the page, using the index to skip straight to key events. 'How did you get hold of them?'

'Nellie ignored Myra's instructions,' I replied. 'They have been passed on in case they are of any use in resolving the case.'

MacCulloch paused, then said, 'So at the time Myra Hindley wrote her autobiography, and the letters to you, she had no idea that her own, contemporaneous account still existed?'

'No.'

'Excellent, excellent.'

Records locked in a vault beneath Greater Manchester Police headquarters explain why officers did not arrest Myra straight away. They had a body, a prime suspect and a witness. It was difficult to know what to make of the rest of Smith's story – robberies, guns, bodies on the moor. Given his history of violence they were certainly not going to take it at face value. He might even have killed Evans himself.

Myra Hindley's arrest, interrogation and prosecution are also recorded in her autobiography. When the police cuffed Ian to take him to the station, she demanded to go too. The reality of the situation hadn't sunk in. The officer in charge, Superintendent Bob Talbot, agreed; he had 'a few questions' for her anyway. Then Myra remembered Ellen. She said she was going to have to get one of the neighbours to look after her, and asked if she could tell them she'd 'run someone over'. The bewildered policeman agreed, so Myra scooped Gran up and took her round to the Hills'. Neither Maggie nor May believed the story about an accident: her Mini was parked, undamaged, on Wardlebrook Avenue. And there were far too many police around for that.

In the back of the panda car, on the way to the station, Myra remembered Ian's words: 'Say nothing.' Puppet rocked back and forth on her lap as she stared out of the window. The strategy held up until she was in an interview room, facing Constable Philomena Campion. I found a verbatim record of this conversation, and all the police interviews, at the National Records Archive.

'This morning the body of a man was found at your house. Who is that person?'

'I don't know, and I am not saying anything. Ask Ian. My story is the same as Ian's.'

'What is the story of last night?'

Myra told the policewoman that they had bought some wine and been for a picnic at Glossop. The officer let her go on, then gently steered her back to events at Wardlebrook Avenue.

'All I'm saying is I didn't do it and Ian didn't do it. We are involved in something we did not do. We never left each other, we never do. What happened last night was an accident and it should never have happened.'

Philomena Campion softened her approach to try to get Myra to open up. 'It is in your interests to tell the truth of what did happen,' she said.

The police were suspicious of Myra's sullen defensiveness. But it was possible that her behaviour was born out of loyalty to Ian, rather than guilt. In order to weaken her resolve they left her 'to stew' for a few hours.

Meanwhile, the forensic team worked its way slowly through the house at Wardlebrook Avenue, taking samples: carpet, cigarette butts, dog hair. One officer was given the job of lacing up and playing every one of the tapes they found with the two Philips machines: a recording of *The Goon Show*, a speech by Winston Churchill, a man, woman and child talking. Superintendent Talbot flicked slowly through the pages of a tartan-covered photograph album. Days out. Family snaps, endless shots of dogs – it looked innocent enough, almost too innocent. The house was full of photographic equipment: an enlarger, safe-lamps, rows of chemicals, stacks of trays, 149 negatives, 170 prints. There might just be a connection to the killing here, he thought. He clapped the album shut, and tucked it under his arm.

In the afternoon, eight hours after the discovery of Edward Evans, a Home Office pathologist climbed the narrow stairs to the spare bedroom at Wardlebrook Avenue. Charles St Hill found the body trussed up in plastic sheeting, just as Ian had left it. The doctor gingerly lifted up the three books on the victim's head: *Tales of Horror, Among Women Only (La Dolce Vita – Love and Sensation in Post-war Italy)* and a children's book, *The Road Ahead*. He cut the string holding the polythene wrapping in place, and carefully removed it. Superintendent Bob Talbot and Chief Superintendent Arthur Benfield watched in silence. The unease they'd felt at the sight of the books only increased when the doctor pointed out a ligature round the victim's neck. It looked as though it had been put there *after* the fatal blows to the skull. The scene bore the hallmarks of ritual, not a spontaneous killing after a fight.

Ian sat there, calm and in control, when Arthur Benfield came in. The policeman had never seen anyone arrested on suspicion of murder behave that way. The transcript of the interview shows that he was determined to find out why.

'Inside the wallet are several pieces of paper on which are written certain words and abbreviations. Would you care to tell me what they mean?'

'Yes,' replied Ian. 'That was the plan for the disposal of Eddie. We planned that after it had happened. We sat up doing it.'

'What does "Det" mean?' asked Benfield.

'Details,' Ian replied.

'Stn?'

'Stationery.'

'Hat?'

'Hatchet.'

On and on Ian went, so confident that he might have been in charge of the interview. He laid everything on Smith, trying to protect Myra.

The hours dragged by as Myra waited to see Ian; she needed to get instructions, it had all been so rushed. Just before nine p.m. the policewoman assigned to her, Philomena Campion, came back with Dr Ellis, the police surgeon. She told Myra the doctor had come to take some 'samples': nail clippings, saliva, blood, hair and pubic hair. Pubic hair? Myra was outraged, but the police constable stood firm and she had to relent.

When the doctor left they let Nellie and Bert in; the hope was that they might 'bring her to her senses'. The police gave the family a few minutes, then had another go at breaking Myra's resolve. Arthur Benfield, with Philomena Campion at his side, used a firm, fatherly approach.

'Do you wish to say anything to me about what happened last night?' he asked.

'No, not until you let me see Ian first.'

'He's been charged and will be up in court in the morning.'

Myra refused to respond. They decided to let her go. There was no evidence that she had helped to kill Evans.

Myra told me, on tape, that Bert took her back to Reddish for the night. He and Kath questioned her closely about what had happened and were not satisfied by the answers. They tried to persuade her to 'come clean', to look after her own interests, but she wouldn't listen. The following morning she left the bungalow to return to the police station with something approaching a sense of relief.

Myra was desperate to see Ian, and she hovered in the court doorway hoping to catch his eye as he was led in. He appeared from the cells below, with a policeman on each arm. When their eyes met he turned to the officer at his side and asked whether he and Myra could share solicitors – he'd thought she was going to be charged too. The policeman recorded the slip and passed it on to his boss.

Ian was charged, and remanded to Risley. Myra was pulled straight back in for questioning by Arthur Benfield. She was furious that she hadn't been able to see Ian, get the story straight. They'd planned all the other murders so carefully. If only it hadn't been for David Smith.

'Ian and I didn't do it, and I didn't do it,' she blurted out, then sat there, square-jawed, staring at the superintendent and ignoring Constable Campion.

'Well, who did?' he asked.

'I am saying nothing else until I have seen Ian's solicitor.'

Frustrated, and mystified, the police again decided to let her go. Myra agreed to come back on Monday, after she'd seen Robert Fitzpatrick, Ian's solicitor.

On the Saturday morning, Myra told me in a letter, she and her mother carried a large bag of washing to the launderette opposite Millwards. While Nellie stuffed clothes into a machine, Myra crossed the road to work. Tommy wasn't in yet, but the office fire was burning in the grate; Myra realized that the cleaner must have been in. She walked quickly through the main building to the store at the back. This was where the records to the orders were kept – Ian's domain. She riffled through the files until she found what she wanted – the body disposal plans.

Myra knew it was only a matter of time before she was arrested. They were bound to find the ticket to the left-luggage locker. Why the hell had he hidden it down the back of her confirmation prayer book? One by one she fed the papers into the fire, made sure that they crumpled in the heat and turned to ash. Mesmerized by the flickering light, she wondered if she would have to go to prison for long. When Tommy arrived Myra asked him to sack her. He refused, said he was sure that whatever had happened was nothing to do with her and the typing job would be kept open until everything had been 'sorted out'. What about Ian? Myra asked. That was a different matter, replied Tommy. He'd have to go.

On Monday, 11 October 1965, Myra got off the bus in Stalybridge, crossed the street to the police station and reported to the desk sergeant. She performed each action mechanically, her mind incapable of turning itself from Ian. His solicitor, Robert Fitzpatrick, was waiting for her. The interview was halting; she did not know what to say, did not have her instructions. She told the baffled lawyer that she agreed with whatever Ian had said. Afterwards they took her back to Hyde and hurled questions at her. She sat there in stony silence, refusing to answer. Superintendent Benfield told her they had all the evidence they needed. There was Evans's body, Smith's confession, and she and Ian hadn't been as clever with the clean-up as they thought. There was a blood-stained cigarette butt in front of the fireplace, blood splatter on her shoes. How was she going to explain that? Why didn't she help herself by telling the truth? At three o'clock, WPC Campion and Superintendent Benfield watched in exasperated silence as DS Carr read out the inevitable words: 'Myra Hindley, I am charging you with being an accessory after the fact in the murder of Edward Evans.'

Myra's first ever letter to me recorded the events which followed. They took her out of the room and led her down the grand stone steps at the centre of the police station, one WPC on each arm, a plainclothes detective walking ahead. He pushed open a pair of swing doors and led the group down another staircase. Stone turned to concrete, daylight to tungsten. Instead of offices they were now passing cells. The corridor was so narrow that the officers had to bunch together as they pushed Myra along. Then the detective stopped, turned to his left and kicked open a reinforced wooden door. They led her to a chair in the middle of the room and pushed her down. Myra told me that she thought she was going to be interrogated, and clenched her teeth defiantly in expectation of a slap. Instead, there was a blinding flash of light – a police photographer had captured her image. On the way back up the stairs, Myra wrote, the WPC holding her left arm leant towards her. 'Come on, love. If you stick up for him you'll go down for ever. He's a man; he probably made you do it . . .'

Re-reading this letter, I reflected on why Myra chose to begin her story with the taking of her arrest photograph. It is clear that she recognized the power of the picture, and all that it symbolized. She needed to demolish this image in order to convince people that she was bullied into the killings by Ian Brady, and win her freedom. If only she'd known it was coming, she was saying, she'd have struck a different pose and the world might have seen her as she really was.

The red and white brickwork of what was once Hyde's municipal heart – a combined town hall, magistrates' court and police station – looms over the market place. It is a decaying symbol of Victorian rectitude. I told the caretaker what I was doing and he let me into the derelict area once inhabited by Cheshire Constabulary, deep beneath the building, where Myra Hindley and Ian Brady were held.

'Why is it like this?' I asked.

'The council don't know what to do with it. Been this way for years.'

A string of sixty-watt bulbs led the way down below ground through narrow, dusty corridors, pale orange in the tungsten light. The paint on cell doors had peeled and cracked; their name-plates were empty. I pushed one open. The walls were covered in grubby white tiles, and cobwebs breathed in and out at the barred windows. The cells had stood empty for years, a monument to Manchester's shame. From the abandoned monastery of St Francis to the clumsy omission of Myra Hindley's name from picture captions, it was the same. No-one quite knew how to deal with the legacy of the Moors murders. It was painful to admit that they had happened, but impossible to consign them to history for the case was still alive: a mother still yearned to bury her missing son, and refused to fade away until she had done so.

Detective Chief Inspector Joe Mounsey, police records show, was troubled by Ian Brady's negatives. Why had he kept them all? The ones of Myra and him posing in front of the Mini were easy enough, but what about the empty stretches of moor? David Smith's words about there being 'other bodies' washed into his mind and would not recede. Lying on the desk was a notebook that PC Roy Dean had found at Wardlebrook Avenue. It was full of scrawls, doodles and names: 'John Birch, Frank Wilson, Alec Guineas, *John Kilbride* . . .' There was also a receipt for the hire of a white Ford Anglia on 23 November 1963, the day the twelve-year-old boy had disappeared from Ashton market. Mounsey called the photographic officer, Ray Gelder, and asked him to print up the negatives, see if he could find out where they had been taken.

In her autobiography, Myra recorded that she and Ian travelled in different cars to Risley. They may have been separated, but there was a sense of relief in knowing that they were going to the same place. Ian had given her a look at the remand hearing that told her to keep quiet – they only had the one body. The connection between them felt unbreakable; if anything, what was happening strengthened it.

The officer on reception demanded to know her religion. Myra took a while to reply: none. The officer sighed and wrote 'C of E' in the ledger. Did she have any birthmarks? No. What was that behind her right ear then? Myra apologized, she'd forgotten it was there. Did she have any false teeth? Myra asked if the officer was joking – she was only twenty-three! They had to ask, came the weary reply. People often took them out to hide fag stumps in their gums.

They put Myra in a room on the hospital wing, away from the other prisoners. The next morning she woke early, instantly aware of where she was, and stared at the prison uniform draped across the back of the chair: two grey skirts, two brown blouses, thick lisle stockings with a seam, baggy knickers, a suspender belt and a bra. She was desperate to go to the toilet but couldn't face the humiliation of the chamberpot under the bed.

Myra got dressed and fiddled with the stockings, trying to get the seams straight, while she waited for breakfast. Eventually, the cell door cracked open and an officer handed her a small brown envelope. It was very thin, and had no stamp on it. Myra turned her back on the guard, slipped her nail under the flap, and tore it open. It was Ian's 'reception' letter – every prisoner was allowed one on their first day. She read it over and over, smudging the black ink with her tears. He wrote that she'd be out in no time, but he was going to get life. It was not something he could face – three months in Strangeways had been enough – and she'd have to be brave *like Emmy*. The last two words chilled her heart. The actress Emmy Sonnemann was married to Hitler's deputy,

Hermann Goering. On 15 October 1946, rather than be hanged – the Allies had refused him permission to be shot – the head of the Luftwaffe crushed a cyanide capsule between his teeth. Emmy was released from Straubing prison in March 1946 and lived on until 1973. 'My influence will pall,' Ian wrote, 'and you can begin a new life.' But Myra knew that she could never let him go. He ended the letter 'I love you.' It was the first time he had openly expressed the sentiment.

Myra asked the governor for an 'inter-prison' visit before their next court appearance, in three days' time. She whiled the hours away acquiring the skills that women at Risley taught one another: how to use cigarettes as currency, forge a cheque and carry out an abortion.

Myra described that first 'visit' with Ian in her autobiography. She walked into the room, and he smiled at the sight of her in prison clothes. He was wearing a smart three-piece suit. She just sat there, drinking in the sight of him. They were separated by a sheet of glass, and a guard stood at each of their shoulders. Didn't she know, he asked, that there was no need to wear prison clothes as she hadn't been convicted? Myra replied that she did, but she wanted to preserve her smart clothes for court; they'd only get messed up doing the prison cleaning. They made small talk and tried to appear relaxed so that the guards would get bored and start thinking about what they were having for tea or what was on the telly. Ian told her she'd go mad if all she did was talk to the other women. She had to keep her mind outside; she should order books from the prison library. Suddenly, he asked if she'd got the luggage ticket. The guards looked as though they had drifted off. No, whispered Myra, she hadn't been able to get back in the house. Ian's face barely registered an expression – he did not want to attract the guards' attention. She told him that she had been able to get the stuff at Millwards though. He nodded to show his pleasure, and swiftly changed the subject.

Detectives hadn't found the ticket yet, but they had been told by David Smith that Ian and Myra hid evidence at a left-luggage office. British Transport Police went through Manchester's stations looking for a locker containing two cases – one brown, one blue. On Friday, 15 October, they tracked them down at Manchester Central. The contents confirmed Joe Mounsey's suspicions: the killing of Edward Evans was not a one-off.

The brown case contained nine pictures of Lesley Ann Downey, naked, with a scarf tied around her mouth. Her limbs had been arranged in a succession of pornographic poses; the negatives were in a halibut liver oil tin. There were also two tape spools. Police records show that the red leader on one was damaged; Superintendent Bob Talbot watched as a technician replaced it with new, yellow, tape and laced it up. Ian's voice boomed out, 'This is Green track one.' Music filled the room. 'This is Green track two'– a recording of *The Goon Show*. 'This is Green track three' – a commentary by the BBC announcer Freddie Grisewood. 'This is Green track four':

CHILD: (*screaming*) Don't, Mum – ah!
WOMAN: Shut up!
CHILD: Please, God, help me. Ah. Please. Oh.
WOMAN: (*whispering*) Come on.
       (*Footsteps.*)
WOMAN: (*whispering*) Shut up.

The recording was just thirteen minutes long, but the officers in the room never forgot it.

Professor Malcolm MacCulloch asked to hear the tape when he was treating Ian Brady and working with the police to find Pauline Reade and Keith Bennett in the mid-1980s. 'There's no element on that tape which betrayed any sympathy towards a little girl who was plainly in great fear,' he said. 'No sympathy whatsoever. It's brusque, aggressive, commanding, tough, impatient. It's very distressing to listen to.'

The tape galvanized the police into action. A team of officers worked its way down Wardlebrook Avenue questioning every man, woman and child. They all said the same thing: he was a bit aloof, she was friendly, great with kids. Then officers knocked on the door of number 12, and Elsie Hodges answered. Oh yes, her Patti was always out with Ian and Myra. Detectives interviewed the small, frightened girl. Her witness statement explains that the first 'outings' with Myra were to pick up Ian from Longsight. They waited for him in the van down a little side street just off the Stockport Road. Myra had told her she didn't like to go in because Mrs Brady kept her chatting for too long. After a couple of weeks Myra suggested a trip to the moors. Patti thought it was a great idea.

The police were already digging on the Moors, acting on Ian Brady's 'landscapes' and David Smith's claim that there were bodies buried in the peat. The *Manchester Evening News* splashed the story under the headline POLICE IN MYSTERY DIG ON MOORS. Myra heard the news on the canteen radio. But the police team was at Woodhead Pass, eight miles from Saddleworth.

When DC Clegg and WPC Slater drove Patti out of Manchester on the A635 she told them that she, Ian and Myra went to Saddleworth, not Woodhead. They climbed out of Greenfield, up the steep hill and round the left-hand bend that took them onto the moor. That was it! The little girl was quite sure. That lay-by was where they'd parked, by the road sign warning of a dangerous bend ahead. The landscape matched the pictures in the tartan album.

*

The taxi driver, Myra recorded in her autobiography, was silent all the way from Risley to Hyde. On the outskirts of town the prison officer sitting next to her turned and suggested she pull her scarf up over her hair. Myra was startled. Why on earth should she do that? There may well be photographers, said the officer; the case had been getting a lot of attention. Silently, Myra pulled the material up and over her head. As the driver swung sharply left through the back entrance of Hyde Magistrates' Court and the flash bulbs exploded, she ducked and stared at her feet.

Ian squeezed her hand as they sat in the dock. The remand hearing was short, the atmosphere low key. They both pleaded not guilty, and the magistrate ordered them to be held for another seven days. The proceedings hardly seemed to matter to Myra. She was looking forward to seeing Ian afterwards with Mr Fitzpatrick.

Robert Fitzpatrick was a partner in a local solicitor's practice, more used to divorce and conveyancing than murder. The lawyer met them after the hearing, in Hyde police station canteen; officers were moving about on the other side of the serving hatch. He told them that they couldn't possibly have joint legal visits; it was unusual enough to have the same solicitor! They had to, Myra said. Mr Fitzpatrick insisted: they would need different defences. Ian told him that they wanted the same defence. Reluctantly, the solicitor agreed. When the meeting was over he slid down the bench to allow them a few minutes alone together.

In her autobiography Myra recalled the words she spoke to Ian. 'I love you!' she said. 'I've always loved you and wanted to tell you so much that I did. You told me you loved me in your letter. I can actually say it to you now. I love you.' Ian, she wrote, replied, 'I love you too.'

*

Police records show that the search party arrived on Saddleworth Moor at 9.30 a.m. on 16 October 1965. An aerial photograph shows how Detective Chief Inspector Mounsey and Detective Inspector Mattin spread their men out: one party to the left of the A635, one to the right. The officers hacked at the peat all morning, slowly working their way further onto the moor. They tested the ground ahead of them by jabbing in long sticks, 'tamping rods', and smelling them for signs of corruption. The work was slow and frustrating. After lunch, Joe Mounsey decided that he and Norman Mattin should return to Manchester. Detective Sergeant Eckersley could always send for him if they found anything.

The day's searching was drawing to a close, just before four p.m., when Constable Bob Spiers wandered a little deeper onto the moor to relieve himself. As he stood there he spotted something sticking out of the ground – bone. Sergeant Eckersley ordered his men to dig out a small test pit before sending for Joe Mounsey. No, he told him when he arrived, it definitely wasn't a sheep.

Lesley Ann Downey's exhumation was carried out under the supervision of the pathologist, Professor Poulson. The body was buried so close to the surface that half of it had decomposed, and part of the forearm was missing. Wild animals, probably. The operation was recorded by photographic officer Ray Gelder. Every now and then he was called forward to take a picture. He worked with the rapid skill that comes from years of experience, but his mind kept wandering. There was something about the photographs Joe Mounsey had given him. He moved away from the burial party until it was framed by the landscape, with the hills in the background, and took a series of pictures. He was standing in the same place Ian had stood to take his 'landscapes'.

*

Myra walked into the interview room. Chief Superintendent Arthur Benfield sat behind a large table, the two cases open in front of him. His fatherly manner, police records show, had gone. 'What is this?' he asked, tossing the black wig on the table. Myra remained silent. 'And this?' A photograph of Lesley Ann Downey. And this, and this, and this, and this, and this? Benfield scattered the contents of the cases in front of Myra, who remained silent.

'Please, Mam, no!'

Myra's head jerked up. They were playing the tape. She listened in silence. Thirteen minutes later the machine stopped. Benfield fired questions at her but she just sat there shaking her head, saying nothing.

As I read through the police accounts of the interviews, and her own recollections, I was amazed at Myra Hindley's resilience. It's one thing to live a lie, quite another to maintain it under skilled and determined interrogation. 'It's the same toughness that made it possible for her to carry out the crimes in the first place,' Malcolm MacCulloch told me. 'It is very, very unusual.'

The paper rocked to and fro in the developing tray, under the glow of a red safe-light. Detective Constable Peter Mascheder watched intently as chemical reacted with silver halide. Myra Hindley, clutching Puppet in her arms, slowly appeared. The officer used tongs to drag the paper first into the stop bath, then the fixer. He had to force himself to leave it long enough. Two minutes later he held the dripping sheet in his hands. Ray Gelder had been right about the neg: she was staring at the ground instead of the dog. He plunged the sheet into the washer and went to find Joe Mounsey.

*

Ian sat with his head bowed as the tape played; DCI Haigh was taking notes, Chief Superintendent Benfield and Superintendent Talbot were watching. Police records contain a transcript of the ensuing conversation.

'You know the tape,' said Superintendent Benfield. 'The voices appear to be those of yourself and Myra, and, I believe, that of Lesley Ann Downey, whose photograph you admit taking.'

Ian replied, 'She didn't give the name of Downey, it was something else.'

The officers were stunned by the coldness of his reaction. In order to try to jolt him, Benfield threw the dead girl's shoes and socks onto the table.

'Look at these photographs. Do you agree that the shoes and socks on the photographs are similar to these?'

It didn't work. Ian continued to deny all involvement. He'd 'only' taken the pictures, not killed the girl.

At eleven a.m. on Thursday, 21 October, Peter Mascheder faced north on Saddleworth Moor and held the photograph of Myra and Puppet in the air, trying to line it up with the hills behind. Joe Mounsey stared intently at him. Mascheder nodded – this was it. Even the rocks at Myra's feet were in the same place.

Detective Inspector John Chaddock of the West Riding Constabulary walked up to the two men. His witness statement records what followed. Mounsey told him to look at the stones and at the picture. His meaning was clear. Chaddock leant forward and put the tip of a probe between two of the stones; he pushed the rod into the peat, then withdrew it. The stench of decomposing flesh was unmistakable. The officers fell to the ground and scraped at the bare peat. Nine inches down they discovered a boy's black shoe and, beneath it, a foot. They had found the body of John Kilbride.

Superintendent Bob Talbot stood in the front room at Wardlebrook Avenue. The boots Myra had worn on the grave of John Kilbride lay bagged up by his feet. In his hands was a white prayer book – an odd discovery among the sexually sadistic material Ian had used to fuel his fantasies. He flipped the gold catch and read the inscription: 'To Myra, from Auntie Kath and Uncle Bert, 16th November, 1958.' It was a souvenir of her first Holy Communion. He feathered the pages and held the book up to the window so that the light spilled down the spine. There was something there. Talbot banged the book against the palm of his hand, dislodging a tightly rolled piece of paper. He unrolled it: British Railways Board left-luggage ticket No. 74843. The depositor had chosen not to fill out his name.

Ian and Myra's court appearances, she recorded in her auto-biography, soon turned from administrative routine into public theatre. The roar of the crowd crashed against the walls of Hyde Magistrates' Court. Mostly, the competing cries of 'Hang them!' 'Bitch!' and 'Bastard!' drowned one another out. But the occasional voice made its way through, bounced off the wood panels of the courtroom and echoed down the corridors of the police station. Everyone was on edge – everyone, that is, apart from Ian and Myra. They were completely unmoved as the magistrate remanded them for another week.

Their solicitor, Robert Fitzpatrick, tried to talk strategy with them in the police canteen afterwards, but he had difficulty concentrating. The people beyond the walls were his people and they might find it hard to understand why he continued to represent Ian and Myra. It was no great surprise when one of the uniformed officers on escort duty interrupted to say that they needed to go – it was getting far too dangerous.

Myra sat up and peered through the window of the Black Maria as it pulled out of the back gates. Fists hammered on the sides of the van. Ian smiled at her as she slumped back down, blowing her cheeks out. It was then that she realized something was up: the van had turned the wrong way for Risley. A wave of indignation built in her as the vehicle was driven to the outskirts of Ashton. A few minutes later it roared through the gates of the police station.

It had obviously been carefully planned. They were led to separate interview rooms as soon as they arrived. Waiting for Myra were Detective Inspector Mattin and Detective Chief Inspector Jack Tyrell. The police transcript of the interview shows that they wanted to know about the photographs.

'What were you looking at?' asked Tyrell.

'I was looking at the snow or the dog,' replied Myra.

'Who chose the place where you would kneel?'

'No-one. We just took a photograph where we felt like it.'

Myra was sweating heavily. The officers thought it was nerves, but she had Ian's letters stuffed down the back of her skirt, underneath a heavy mohair coat. There was no way she was going to leave them in the cell.

They went on and on, showing her the photographs only she and Ian knew had been taken in front of Pauline Reade's grave. They also showed her the pictures taken around the grave of Lesley Ann Downey. But Myra wound the detectives up, deliberately misunderstanding the simplest of questions, playing stupid about where the shots had been taken or who had taken them. It was exasperating, but the policemen refused to rise to the bait.

'This photograph is taken very close to the grave of Lesley

Ann Downey,' said Tyrell, 'and the spot you are looking at there is the grave of John Kilbride.'

'As far as I am concerned they are two normal photographs that I have had taken,' said Myra.

'It would appear,' Tyrell pressed on, 'that you and Brady took delight in taking photographs of graves.'

Myra broke off, told them she was thirsty. They agreed to get her some tea. She drank three or four cups. For five and a half hours the detectives went over the same ground, but Myra did not give an inch. At 6.30, in exasperation, they left the room.

Twenty minutes later Detective Chief Inspector Joe Mounsey came in. He had been getting the same thing from Ian all afternoon, and he looked furious. He slammed down the picture of her kneeling on the grave, then slammed another of the boy's exhumed body on top, then another, and another. Myra told me, on tape, that she shouted, 'Take them away. I'm not looking at them.' Mounsey raged at her, pacing up and down, bellowing, 'Come to me little children and suffer.' It made no difference. He didn't break her.

The following day, Myra told me, the police changed tactics. Mam, Bert and Kath were allowed to see her. The police still hoped that they might get her to 'see sense'. Bert reminded her that she was quite normal until she met Ian; it was bound to be all right, if only she'd tell the truth! Myra refused. One by one her relatives broke down and sobbed, clinging onto her. Then the police escorted David Smith across the back of the room and out of a door. Her manner hardened. She'd had enough of this – she was going to stand by Ian! The police, watching from a distance, saw her reaction. They led her back downstairs to a cell.

Detectives suspected that she and Ian had also killed Keith Bennett and Pauline Reade. But there was no proof, so they abandoned the search for their bodies. They had all the evidence they needed to ensure that the Moors murderers would get life.

Robert Fitzpatrick was let in by the custody sergeant. He said he had some bad news for Myra. The police had asked a vet to knock out her dog, Puppet, in order to age him, but he'd failed to come round. What did he mean? asked Myra. Her dog was dead, replied the solicitor warily. Myra screamed that the police were murderers, they'd rot in hell for this. Her next letter home to Nellie was filled with bitter recriminations and an aching sense of loss. Myra remained firmly locked into the world she shared with Ian; Puppet was an important part of that world, so she mourned his death. The outrage at the killing of five children meant nothing, so she ignored it.

Chapter Two

Nellie kept all of her daughter's letters from prison. She carried them about from house to house until, in old age, she decided they were too much of a risk and had them stored away for safe-keeping. The change in tone over the years is striking, but the strength of Myra Hindley's voice never diminishes.

She did not write to her mother immediately. The first letter was dated 5 November 1965 – thirty days after the death of Edward Evans. Myra told Nellie that she wanted to look her best for the committal. 'If you could send to the station a decent pair of high heels, I'd feel a lot better than I do in these mules. I feel like a tramp in your clothes (only because they don't fit me properly).' There was not the slightest hint of remorse, or even mention of the crimes she stood accused of. There was furious criticism of the police for killing her dog: 'I feel as though my heart's been torn to pieces. I don't think anything else could hurt me more than this has. The only consolation is that some moron might have got hold of Puppet and hurt him.'

Myra told Nellie to retrieve Puppet's neck-tag and store it with the rest of her and Ian's possessions. 'This letter will probably be censored,' she concluded. 'If you should write at all, <u>do not mention anything regarding the cases</u>.'

Ian came into the visiting room. They exchanged letters every day. Myra still carried hers wherever she went. It wasn't just a question of security, they made her feel closer to Ian. She dropped the bundle onto the table, ran her eyes up and down his body, and sat down next to a woman prison officer. In her autobiography she recalled teasing him about his prison uniform, a kind of 'hairy jerkin suit'. She said he looked gorgeous. He replied that she didn't look so good herself in those lisle stockings and shoes – like Minnie Mouse! Humour had found room in their relationship again. They were able to relax, safe in the knowledge that they could see each other several times a week: at Risley, during meetings with their solicitor, and at court. They had insisted on their rights: all unconvicted, cohabiting prisoners were allowed to see each other. There was no reason, they argued, for them to be treated differently.

As usual, they shifted through apparently mundane topics of conversation in order to bore the guards. They spoke about trips they'd taken, films they'd seen. The 'screws' didn't know what else had happened on those days. Ian told her that it might be an idea to get her mam to look after *all* the snaps. He did not know that the police had seized every picture and were going through them, looking for evidence of other missing bodies. Oh yes, said Myra. It would be a way of remembering the good old times, wouldn't it?

Myra wrote home: 'Dear Mam . . . keep all the photos for us, <u>for reasons</u>, the ones of dogs, scenery etc.'

*

Ian was captivated by dramatic landscapes.

Ian in a photograph that Myra said marked the grave of Pauline Reade.

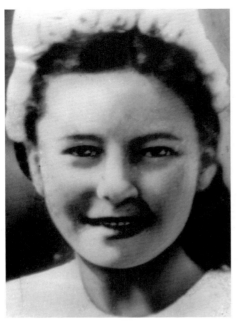

Pauline Reade. Disappeared 12 July 1963, aged sixteen; body recovered 1 July 1987.

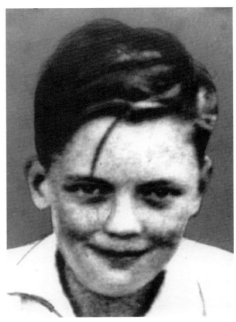

John Kilbride. Disappeared 23 November 1963, aged twelve; body recovered 21 October 1965.

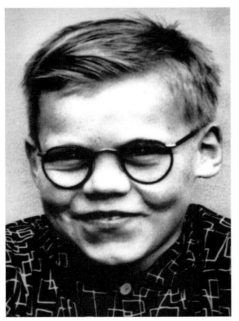

Keith Bennett. Disappeared 16 June 1964, aged twelve; still missing.

Lesley Ann Downey. Disappeared 26 December 1964, aged ten; body recovered 16 October 1965. (*Rex Features*)

Edward Evans. Disappeared 6 October 1965, aged seventeen; body recovered 7 October 1965. (*Rex Features*)

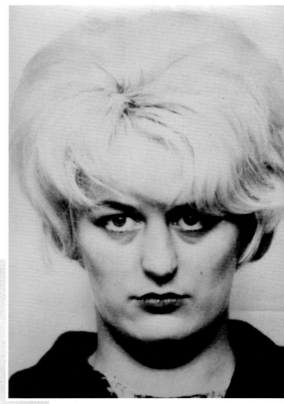

Myra Hindley. Arrested 11 October 1965.

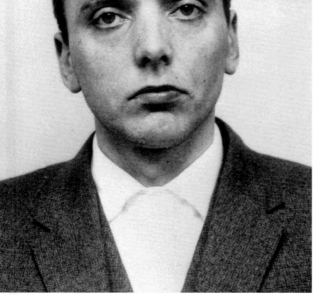

Ian Brady. Arrested 7 October 1965. (*Empics*)

Police search the moor, using rods to probe the ground, after Myra and Ian's arrest.

A furious relative is restrained as the Moors murderers arrive at court.

Scores of ordinary people queue to see the accused.

A special dock was constructed at Chester Assizes to protect the defendants from attack.

Ann West (*right*), mother of Lesley Ann Downey, at Lesley's funeral (*above*).

Myra, photographed using the camera of her lover Trisha Cairns, shortly before her failed escape attempt from Holloway prison. Myra and Trisha planned to work as missionaries in South America.

Below left Myra poses in front of a copy of *Papillon* – the story of a prisoner's amazing escape.

Below right Myra in 'graduation pose' after receiving an Open University degree in the humanities.

Myra and Trisha made impressions of Holloway's keys in Camay soap and plaster of Paris. The teapot, PG Tips box and clock were used to hide the escape kit. (*TNA UK*)

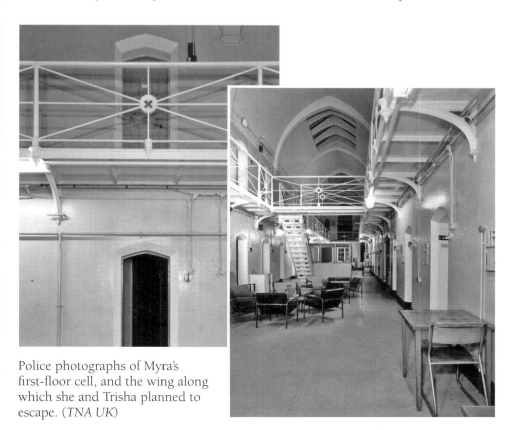

Police photographs of Myra's first-floor cell, and the wing along which she and Trisha planned to escape. (*TNA UK*)

Above Alan Bennett (*left*) and Professor John Hunter (*second right*), searching for Keith's body.

Above right Alan Bennett and the former head of West Midlands murder squad, Barrie Simpson, pause for a cigarette.

Peter Topping's team abandoned the search for Keith Bennett two months after the discovery of Pauline Reade.

The Bennett brothers: left to right, Alan, Ian and Keith, shortly before Keith's murder.

Malcolm MacCulloch held the letter out to me, waving it. 'It looks like there *are* marker photographs for all the missing bodies,' he said.

'How can you be sure about that?

MacCulloch shrugged. 'There was very little that was spontaneous or accidental about the way these crimes were carried out. If he retained reminders of one killing he is likely to have retained reminders of all of them. And remember, three of the victims had been recovered by this point – they were no longer perfect murders. He knew this and would have wanted mementos for the undiscovered bodies. That's why he wanted the photos!'

Myra did as Ian had suggested, and visited the prison library. The prison governor accompanied her. As Myra's eyes flicked up and down the shelves she noticed that many of the titles were religious, and complained. The governor responded that religion helped people to cope in here; it might not do her any harm to give it a go. Myra resisted the temptation to answer back, and walked between the sparsely stacked shelves. She found a copy of *Catch 22*, which had just come out, and Spike Milligan's *Puckoon*, which would remind her of Ian. She wrote an analysis of each book in her letters to him. From the beginning they made sure that they had things in common, something to talk about besides the murders.

In the front of the Black Maria there was a meshed window between the prisoners' and driver's compartments. Myra leant forward, hooked her fingers through the wire and looked ahead: Hyde Magistrates' Court came into view. Both she and Ian had newly trimmed hair, and Nellie had sorted out her clothes for her. It was pouring down, and the water drummed against the small, rectangular window, obscuring the view. But Myra could make people out, queuing three deep: press, photographers and ordinary women with rollers in their hair. She could not believe how many there were. She had avoided the papers, looked inwards, concentrated on Ian, and did not understand the true strength of public opinion.

I ordered the BBC news film on the case. It arrived in a couple of battered cans from the Windmill Road store in west London. Inside were twenty or so small, taped-up rolls of cellulose. I found an abandoned Steenbeck editing machine to view them on. But as I tried to load each clip it snapped. The edits had dried out over four decades. I went in search of help. 'This is going to take a while,' said Rex, the telecine operator, who was an old-school BBC craftsman. He painstakingly replaced every single edit before transferring the material to tape.

The pictures showed a surprising number of children clustered outside the court before the start of the committal. There was a sequence of Lesley Ann Downey's uncle attacking a Mini, sent out as a decoy by the police, imagining Myra Hindley to be inside. The camera was battered from side to side by still photographers fighting to capture the moment.

Myra and Ian were represented by junior counsel at the committal: Philip Curtis for her, David Lloyd-Jones for him. The defence opened proceedings by asking for the whole case to be heard in camera. The magistrates, two men and a woman, replied that they would hear the opening speeches in private before making a decision on the rest of the case. Myra and Ian smiled to each other as court ushers pushed disappointed members of the public and anxious journalists out of the door. But their happiness was short-lived: the prosecution won the day, and the 'hordes' were re-admitted.

David Smith, Myra recorded in her autobiography, was the first witness against them. Myra reached out and squeezed Ian's hand. They needed each other now. They would stand or fall together. A curious calm settled over her. She and Ian sat and stared, without once lowering their gaze, as the 'traitor' took the oath. Myra could feel Ian's anger as David gave his version of events. But to the rest of the world he looked aloof, doodling absent-mindedly on a pad, like a bored clerk at work. He never lost control in court. Myra took his lead, but struggled when Maureen stood up to say that her sister had gone off children once she met Ian. What about the hours Myra had spent caring for the Smiths' baby, Angela Dawn? The tears she'd shed when she died? In a letter home, Myra railed against her sister and David Smith. 'Did you read the lies Maureen told in court, about me hating babies and children? She wouldn't look at me in the dock, Mam. She couldn't. She kept her face turned away.' Myra went on, bitterly, that she knew the couple had sold their story to a newspaper. 'I noticed she was wearing a new coat and boots, and that Smith had a new watch on and a new overcoat and suit. I suppose he's had an advance on his dirt money.'

One by one, relatives of the dead children stood up to give evidence. Myra and Ian stared them down: Mrs Evans, bent double with grief; Mrs Kilbride, who cried as she talked about John. Then came Ann West, the mother of Lesley Ann Downey, who screamed across the court, 'How can you look at me after what you've done?' On and on she went, her voice filled with loathing, hurling insults at Myra, calling her a tramp. Myra recalled in her autobiography that she turned to Ian and said, 'I'm not a tramp!' 'No, I know you're not,' he replied.

Ian and Myra drew closer and closer together. She did not allow herself to feel any emotion in the face of the relatives' grief; he was completely unmoved by it. Committing the perfect murder, he'd told her, was an existential exercise. It was proof of their ability to reject an 'ordinary' life.

Myra maintained the fiction of innocence to Nellie and begged her not to believe all the things she read in the press. The reporters were being misled by the number of prosecution witnesses – eighty, can you imagine! Her lawyers would work on the defence once the committal was over. What Myra did not understand was that there was no possible defence against the tape of Lesley Ann Downey. By the time the child's words had stopped echoing round the courtroom she and Ian stood condemned in the eyes of the world. There was not a man or woman in the country who would acquit them.

On Thursday, the weather was so bad that the van couldn't make it back to Risley. Myra and Ian spent the night in the police cells, deep beneath the court. She was unable to sleep, and sat with a blanket pulled round her, shivering through the small hours on the board bed. In the morning the officer on duty refused to bring her make-up bag. Then she was given a cup of tea with salt in it. She kicked it over, and called the station commander, Chief Inspector Wills, to complain. Her only friend in the world was Ian. Myra wrote to Nellie, 'Nothing matters in the World as long as Ian is all right. If you'd drop [him] a short note and a box of Maltesers, I'd be glad. He says he doesn't want anything sending in, even from his mam, but I know he'll be glad you sent them.'

Years later, in her confession to the police and in her letters to me, Myra Hindley said she was 'under Ian Brady's spell' throughout the trial. This implies, if not resistance, at least a degree of passivity. I found this difficult to reconcile with the police record of her behaviour during her interrogation and committal. And a story in her unpublished autobiography shows she remained actively involved in the enjoyment of sadistic sexual fantasies even while on remand for child murder.

Just before Christmas their solicitor, Robert Fitzpatrick, came to Risley. He gave her a book of poems by Wordsworth. It brought back happy memories of meeting Ian and trips they had taken to the Lake District. Ian got a volume of Ovid. He seemed pleased, and tucked the slim book into his jacket pocket. While Mr Fitzpatrick's head was down, getting out his papers, Ian slipped Myra a notebook. It was filled with stories about harming children, written in a secret code. He also handed her a slip of paper on which he'd written the key. When she got back to her cell she began copying these 'messages' into an exercise book. She disguised them as verse and interspersed them with real poems. When decoded, one read, 'Why don't you throw acid on Brett?' Brett was the younger brother of Lesley Ann Downey; acid was what the killers in *Compulsion*, Leopold and Loeb, used to burn the body of their victim. The messages made her feel that they were still as one.

There were seven exercise books among her belongings. The pages had discoloured with age but the poems, written in blue biro, were clear. I recognized Housman, Tennyson and Wordsworth, but wasn't sure about 'A. C.' Clough and Charlotte Mew ('Moorland Night'). Inside one I found a fragment of one of Brady's letters, a violent invocation to love. It looked like fantasy, but it was difficult to be sure. I called Greater Manchester Police and told them what I had found.

DC Gail Jazmik and DS Fiona Robertshaw sat opposite me in a dingy BBC office on Whiteladies Road in Bristol. Lists pinned to a noticeboard showed that the last occupant had been a personnel officer. The notebooks were scattered on the desk in front of them. DS Robertshaw read in a flat Manchester accent, 'Moorland night, moorland night. Perhaps you will give back one day what you have taken.' The officers split the books into two piles and continued to read, only speaking to each other when they found something unusual or had finished a volume. As Fiona Robertshaw read, the lines on her forehead deepened. When she had finished she looked up.

'I want someone, an expert, to go through all of this to assess it,' she said.

'Right.'

'Would you let us borrow these to get them checked?'

'Of course.'

The police asked a cryptologist, supplied by GCHQ, to examine the notebooks for new evidence. The message came back: it was going to take him a while.

Ian and Myra were determined to spend their time inside well. They began by improving their knowledge of Shakespeare. She got *Richard III* from the library and gave him a copy of Richard Armour's *Twisted Tales from Shakespeare*, a comic history of the bard and his work – Goon-type humour. They wove quotations in and out of the coded letters. Myra sent Ian Richard's opening soliloquy. The first lines – 'Now is the winter of our discontent / Made glorious summer by this son of York' – were intended as a play on their situation. Myra felt that the latter part of the speech accurately described Ian's place in the world:

> 'Why, I, in this weak piping time of peace,
> Have no delight to pass away the time,
> Unless to spy my shadow in the sun,
> And descant on mine own deformity.
> And therefore, since I cannot prove a lover
> To entertain these fair well-spoken days,
> I am determined to prove a villain,
> And hate the idle pleasures of these days.'

Ian enjoyed the letter, and responded with Edmund's words from *King Lear*:

> 'I grow, I prosper:
> Now, gods, stand up for bastards.'

Myra dug out a memory to share in his resentment. Just before she went to secondary school, Bob and Nellie were arguing about whether she should go to 'The Franners' or Ryder Brow. Her father invited his old school friend, Father Roderick, round to work on his wife. Myra recalled that the monk sat there, over a steaming cup of tea, and lectured that because Nellie and Bob had got married in a register office rather than a church those two poor little girls were nothing but bastards. Bob may have sought Father Roderick's help, but he was not going to stand for that. He bundled the monk out of the front door and only stopped short of hitting him because he was 'a man of the cloth'. Myra ran round to Gran's to tell her that she was a bastard just like her, and her mother before her. They were all outsiders!

Towards Christmas, Myra sat on her bed to write home to Nellie. She had to be careful, her autobiography records, not to touch the red-hot radiator with her feet. She asked her mother to 'take care' of all the things left at Wardlebrook Avenue, to move them to Ian's mum's as quickly as possible. She said that 'Mr F.' was writing to the Attorney General to demand the return of anything that was not an exhibit. This included the tartan album, and almost every picture in it.

On Christmas Eve, Myra told Nellie, Ian's mother brought a meal in. They shared a roast chicken, turkey sandwiches and half a bottle of Sandeman's port wine. Ian ate heartily. It was the happiest time since their arrest – almost like being at home again.

In the run-up to the trial, Myra's family sought to rekindle her faith, hoping to break the bond with Ian. Auntie Kath, who had encouraged her to get confirmed, sent a 'holy' picture. On the back she wrote, 'Pray for me and I'll pray for you.' Myra told Nellie in a letter, 'I suppose she means well, but it means nothing to me.'

The Home Office paid for a psychiatrist, Dr de Ville Mather, to come and see Myra. Her lawyers said she should co-operate, and she did as she was told, but refused to give him any detail. The information he extracted would only be used by the prosecution. The doctor asked her what music she listened to, what books she read. Her taste was catholic, she replied, there was nothing he could learn from it. She viewed him with contempt. The defence then sent their own psychiatrist. She liked him, and things were going very well. Then he remarked that she was really very well read and articulate. Myra snapped, what, for a murderess? No, no, the doctor replied, it was intended as a compliment! Myra calmed down, and explained that she just didn't like being taken for a working-class idiot. The psychiatrist – Myra forgot which – suggested an EEG to pick up abnormalities in the brain. Myra declined.

Myra was still worried about how she'd look in court. She told Nellie in a letter that the governor of Risley had refused to let her get her roots done. 'I'll have to appear at the trial looking terrible with streaky, lifeless hair.' Her counsel complained to the authorities. Grudgingly, they relented.

Myra read in the *News of the World* about the changes to Chester Assizes for the trial: microphones, speakers, fitted carpets and security screens to protect her and Ian from assassination. It was reported that the Lord Chief Justice wanted to hear the case himself but was unable to leave London.

For the trial, Myra was given her grey striped suit and two

blouses, one yellow, one blue. She washed them, ironed the suit, and polished her shoes. The black high-heels belonged to Nellie and were size 5; Myra took a 7, so they were agony when she pulled them on. She'd have to slip them off in the dock. The hairdresser came in to set and bleach her hair one last time. Myra was relieved to find that she did not give her a hard time, just chatted away as if she were working on her at a salon in Gorton.

The Sunday before the trial she wrote to Nellie. 'This is just a few lines before the "off" in case I don't have any time during the week to drop you a line. I had my hair done on Saturday. It looks so nice that I'm sorry that I'm all dressed up and nowhere to go (joke).'

Chapter Three

Ian and Myra clasped hands as they entered the darkness. The corridor, two prison officers to the front and two to the back, was a refuge from the courtroom. For five years they had been alone in their secret world. Now, Myra wrote in a letter to Nellie, lawyers were turning it over, in the company of 'scabrous' journalists, for strangers to judge. But they still had their love, and their secrets.

Mr Fitzpatrick was waiting for them in an oak-panelled meeting room. A stack of pictures lay on the table before him. Myra told Nellie that their solicitor had arranged a special viewing of all the photographs seized by the police so that they could pick out those pictures that were 'special' to them.

I asked Malcolm MacCulloch about the significance of this meeting. 'If I'm right about the existence of more markers, Brady would have derived enormous satisfaction from his superior knowledge.' He paused. 'And so, as his disciple, would she. The marker photographs tie her into the sadistic sexual enjoyment of the crimes more than any other piece of evidence.

The tape recording of Lesley Ann Downey showed cruelty; this is the celebration of cruelty.'

Ian and Myra ignored most of the pictures, selecting just a few. Mr Fitzpatrick said he'd do his best to get these back after the trial, whatever happened. Myra's letters to Nellie reveal that she and Ian knew they were going down. The question was, for how long? Their lawyers' strategy was to sow doubt in the jury's minds about one or two of the charges. There was no hope of an acquittal.

The junior counsel who had represented them at the committal were replaced by senior QCs; Myra recorded in her auto-biography that she was surprised to hear them called 'silks' as she'd never heard the term before. Ian's case was led by the highly experienced lawyer and Liberal MP Edwin Hoosen; Myra's brief was Godfrey Heilpern, who had achieved silk six years earlier at the age of just thirty-five. Opposing them, in a highly unusual move, was the Attorney General himself, Sir Frederick Elwyn Jones QC, MP. The judge, Mr Fenton-Atkinson, had overseen war crimes trials at Nuremberg. He spoke in a conversational voice, with natural authority. When he addressed the jury, the barristers in the pit below him stopped shuffling their papers in order to hear what he said. I found his notes on a large, buff sheet of cartridge paper at the National Records Archive. The words are carefully chosen, well ordered, and set down in an immaculate copperplate – the work of some-one used to being in total control of their surroundings.

The judge, trial records show, was outraged when he dis-covered that David Smith, the principal prosecution witness, had done a deal with a newspaper. Not only did he stand to earn £1,000 in the event of a conviction, he and Maureen were being put up at a sumptuous hotel in Chester. Everywhere the couple went they were chaperoned by reporters. Mr Fenton-Atkinson challenged David Smith in court to reveal the name of the paper.

'Come on, you know the name. Tell it to us.' The judge leant forward, glaring at the mute and stubborn witness.

'I don't know if the newspaper would wish me to do that,' Smith replied, infuriating Mr Fenton-Atkinson still further.

'They may have some questions to answer about this. Who are they?'

The judge kept on pushing, but to no avail. David Smith had never had the chance to make so much money, and he wasn't going to squander it. Only his importance to the case saved him from being charged with contempt of court. Nevertheless, the judge demanded an immediate investigation by the Attorney General. 'It sounds to me like a gross interference with the course of justice,' he said.

It is illegal to take photographs in English courts, but the temptation proved too much for one snapper who, somehow, smuggled a camera in. The photograph appeared in newspapers around the world. I found it in the *Toronto Star*; it is still forbidden to publish it in Britain. The picture shows Myra and Ian standing beside each other in the centre of an imposing, oak-panelled room, facing the judge. George I and William III stare down on the proceedings. Ranged in front of the dock are lines of defence and prosecution lawyers. At the back of the court, wedged in on tiered, horseshoe-shaped benches, are members of the public, press and relatives. The most striking thing about the defendants is their sense of strength and togetherness.

'This is where the picture was taken from.' The manager of Chester Court, Mark White, was standing in an ornate wooden gallery just yards from the judge's chair. I marvelled at the photographer's nerve. 'The thing is, it's not a press gallery. This is where guests of the court – dignitaries – would have sat.'

'You mean, a photographer got someone to take the picture for him?' I asked.

226

'Must have done,' he replied.

The defendants sat dressed as if for work at Millwards: Ian, sober in made-to-measure Burton's terylene, and Myra, prim in her grey wool suit. Every few days she changed her hair. At the beginning of the trial it had a lilac tint, by the end it was ash blonde. She wore make-up too – Ponds' Angel Face, shade Golden Rose. She'd asked Nellie to get a bottle for her. They listened attentively to the evidence and wrote notes with rapid, composed efficiency. Every now and then one of them tore off a sheet and handed it forward to a lawyer. Ian emerged three times to give evidence. Myra twice.

Myra recorded in her autobiography that they sustained themselves through shared love and shared secrets, some serious, some silly. One day Myra smuggled a Quality Street Easter egg from Nellie out of Risley. She and Ian sat scoffing it in the back of the van on the way to Chester. They both felt sick by the time they reached the sandstone city walls. Myra ended up flushing most of it down the court toilets.

Ian's calm, undisguised arrogance did not endear him to the jury. Neither did his pedantry. The court transcript records that, ten days in, the Attorney General cross-examined him for the second time.

'You admit it was you that killed Evans?'

'I admit that I hit Evans with the axe.'

'Are you suggesting that you did not kill him?'

'No. Somebody else has.'

'Who?'

'The pathologist said it was accelerated by strangulation.'

'The questioning of the pathologist by your own counsel was to the effect that Evans was dead or dying when the ligature was applied, was it not?'

'Yes.'

'And that was the conclusion of the pathologist.'

'Yes, eventually.'

'You killed Evans – there is no qualifying that, is there?'

'I hit Evans with the axe. If he died from axe blows, I killed him.'

Obsessed with the details of his crimes, Ian Brady demonstrated no understanding of their meaning. When Myra took the stand, on the eleventh day, she tied herself to him.

'Could you tell us, Miss Hindley, what were your feelings for Ian Brady?'

'I became very fond of him. I loved him. I still do love him.'

Godfrey Heilpern asked whether she shared Brady's beliefs on religion.

'Yes,' she replied.

'On politics?'

'Yes.'

'On sex?'

'Yes.'

'On people in general?'

'Yes.'

'The same literary tastes?' the lawyer concluded.

'Not quite . . . I didn't have any enjoyment from pornography.'

Her replies, rapped out as a staccato 'yes' or 'no' in a flat Gorton accent, made her appear hard and calculating, as though she were reluctant to elaborate for fear of betraying a secret. She had agreed with Ian that he would 'do the talking'. Any chance there may have been of winning the jury round evaporated long before the tape was played.

Myra had heard that recording twice now, studied the transcript, and constructed a story to fit. When Lesley Ann was being undressed Myra was 'downstairs'; when the girl was being forced to kneel, naked, in an attitude of prayer, she was 'looking out the window'; when she was being strangled, Myra was 'running a bath'. She was asked, under cross-examination, why she told the girl to 'shut up' and said she'd 'get a slap' if she didn't. Myra agreed this was 'unforgivable' and 'cruel'. But words of contrition, uttered alongside obvious lies, rang hollow.

Myra did not deal with any of this in her letters to Nellie. Her loyalty to Ian forbade it. 'He's not concerned about his future, just mine. It's the same with me: I'm not interested in my future, just him. However, we'll have to wait and see what happens. I believe in one thing, though, that no matter how black things look, some day we can begin again together. I know what we've done and what we haven't done. You know too, no matter what happens.'

But as the trial wore on, shorn of credibility, Myra wrote less and less. She and Ian stuck rigidly to their strategy of lying. They had two aims: to protect their secrets, and to get her a shorter sentence than him. Patricia Cairns told me that they were already planning for the future. 'The idea was that she would do a few years and be released. She would go to places, experience things and let him know what they were like. He would live his life through her until, after many years, he was released.'

Recalled to the witness box on the twelfth day of the trial, Ian did all he could to play down the significance of the photographs. It wasn't a system, as the police alleged, simply a coincidence that there were 'landscape shots' in the vicinity of the two graves. What's more, the police pictures taken to match his own were completely inaccurate. The trial transcript shows that the judge struggled to take in what he was saying.

'You are saying they are not exactly the same spot?'

The court was looking at two photographs of Lesley Ann Downey's grave: one taken by Ian, the other by Detective Constable Ray Gelder.

Ian remained quite calm. 'I am just going on what I can see. There is boulders all over this and there is no boulders at all on that. This is sandy and this is dark.'

The Attorney General cut in. 'You know it is the identical spot. You know it was a deliberately taken photograph of the grave of Lesley Ann Downey, do you not?'

'No,' Ian replied.

'And a number of photographs similarly taken. We will see them before the end of the cross-examination. Those are photographs of this cemetery of your making on the moorland, are they not?'

'Those photographs are snapshots,' Ian replied, as though mystified by the suggestion that he had recorded where the bodies lay buried.

The cross-examination moved on. The purpose of the trial was to establish the defendants' guilt or innocence, not to prove that there was a system for recording where bodies were buried. Nor was its aim to establish what had happened to the other missing children. Everyone knew about Pauline Reade and Keith Bennett, but their names were not mentioned by the prosecution. Keith's mother, Winnie Johnson, sat watching in the public gallery; she was sure they had killed her son. Detective Chief Inspector Mounsey came up to her, teased her for being cross with him, said he understood, and that they would find her son's body. Winnie recalled the meeting with regret in her voice. 'He was the only one who seemed bothered. Soon afterwards he died, and I'm still waiting.'

In his summing-up, Mr Fenton-Atkinson drew attention to a slip made by Brady in the witness box. When asked what happened after he finished photographing Lesley Ann Downey, he'd replied, 'We all got dressed and went downstairs.' The judge told the jury, 'This, possibly, casts a flood of light on the nature of the activities that were going on.'

Rather than crumble as the verdict and sentencing drew near, Ian and Myra's relationship hardened under the force of opprobrium. Myra found a poem in the prison library she hoped might sustain Ian as he faced up to years of separation from her, Wordsworth's *Tintern Abbey*.

> Five years have past; five summers, with the length
> Of five long winters; and again I hear
> These waters, rolling from their mountain springs
> With a soft inland murmur. Once again
> Do I behold these steep and lofty cliffs,
> That on a wild and secluded scene impress
> Thoughts of more deep seclusion; and connect
> The landscape with the quiet of the sky.

In their hearts, neither of them had left the moor. They could not accept that they would never go back.

On the final morning of the trial, sitting in the back of the prison van, Myra scrawled a note to Nellie. 'I don't know what the verdict will be yet but I do know that I will be convicted of something, like harbouring Ian after he and Smith killed Evans. Once you know what the verdicts and sentences are you must not let them affect your life as they will mine. I've just started crying and don't want anyone to see me.'

Myra stood shoulder to shoulder with Ian to hear the verdict. The clerk of the court asked the foreman of the jury whether she had murdered Edward Evans: 'Guilty.' Lesley Ann Downey: 'Guilty.' A feeling of numbness spread through her. She hardly heard the words 'not guilty' to the murder of John Kilbride, and 'guilty' to harbouring Brady after the boy's death. Ian was found guilty of all three murders. The clerk asked him whether he had anything to say. 'No,' he replied, 'except the revolvers were bought in June '64.' Rather than plead innocence, Ian had pointed out a mistake made by the prosecution.

'And you, Myra Hindley?'

'No.'

The judge turned to pass sentence. His words indicate regret at the abolition of hanging.

'Ian Brady, these were three calculated, cruel, cold-blooded murders. In your case I pass the only sentences which the law now allows, which is three concurrent sentences of life imprisonment. Put him down.'

As Ian was led below, the judge shifted his gaze to Myra.

'In your case, Hindley, you have been found guilty of two equally horrible murders, and in the third as an accessory after the fact. On the murders the sentence is two concurrent sentences of life imprisonment. And on the charge of being an accessory after the fact to the death of Kilbride, a concurrent sentence of seven years' imprisonment. Put her down.'

Chapter Four

The cubicle was three feet across, three feet deep and six feet high. There was a slatted wooden bench to sit on; it vibrated in time with the van's large diesel engine. Myra was heading south, towards London. She told Nellie that she could not bear the thought of Ian being carried away, in the opposite direction, to Durham.

The prison gates showed black through the small rectangular window behind her head; a great stone griffin loomed out of the brickwork. The van slowed, and she heard a door slam as a warder came round the back to let her out. Myra emerged, squinting, into the light. The redbrick walls of Holloway towered above her. Each narrow wing, isolated in the middle of a large gravel yard, stretched cell upon cell into the sky. Where Risley had offered the hope, however remote, of freedom, this place looked like the end of the road.

Myra was led into a room beside the gate where she was told to strip, put on a blue dressing gown and sit in a curtained cubicle. A few minutes later the nurse came and checked her over for nits and any obvious diseases. A prison officer handed over a small pile of clothes: black shoes, grey skirt, grey cardigan. Which colour blouse would she like? There were three to choose from: blue and white, pink and white or green and white. Myra went with the blue. The rhythm of the admission was faster than at Risley. It was a huge place, used to turning prisoners round fast.

The reception officer told Myra that she was on E-wing, maximum security, and pointed at a bundle of bedding for her to pick up. She was led through the railings and across the court-yard. Myra read recognition in the eyes of the women she passed. Some glanced away immediately, others stared with open curiosity or contempt. There would be no hiding here.

In her cell, Myra threw herself onto the cot and stared at the ceiling. Light reflected down off the magnolia paint. It really wasn't too depressing. She thought of Ian and imagined holding him again. Other prisoners were given 'conjugal rights'; they would get the same, wouldn't they?

I asked Patricia Cairns, who left her convent in Salford for life as a prison officer, what the atmosphere on Myra's wing was like. 'It was quiet. They put Myra there to make up the numbers rather than because she was an immediate risk. There were a couple of child killers, a pair of Russian spies, and Bunty Gee, who was in for treason. They all got on OK. They had to – they were in for long stretches.'

Ian and Myra worked at their love. They wrote to one another every day and started the same German course, exchanging hints and comparing marks. It was a link back to what had mattered during the killings, and a way of preserving their relationship for the future. Myra was a more diligent student: she sat her O level before Ian and got an A grade. He wrote to tell her he was proud.

Ian and Myra were furious when their respective governors

refused them permission for inter-prison visits. They took it in turns to bombard the Home Secretary with 'petitions'. These were declined with metronomic efficiency. In desperation, Myra asked Nellie to lobby on her behalf. 'Now, you remember I drafted a letter for you, some weeks ago. For you to copy, more or less, and send to the HO? I want you to look it up and take points from it, and write to Lord Stonham, the Home Office, SW1, and tell him I've asked you to confirm that Neddy and I lived together for over 4 years.'

Ian continued to assure Myra that she would be out in a few years. It would make sense to start saving now so there was 'something to fall back on'. Once again, she had to turn to Nellie for assistance. 'Take out a policy for half a crown a week. It's not much but it'll mount up over time.' Nellie did as she was asked. The man from the United and Friendly called at her house. The policy document, grand and reassuring, offered Myra hope of a future. It's hard to tell, looking at it, when the payments stopped.

Myra wrote to Nellie every week, and on the back of each letter she added a page in bold capitals to Gran. The fiction, dreamt up to 'protect' her, that Myra was 'living in Scotland' had long evaporated. But Ellen never cut her granddaughter off. Instead, she offered unquestioning love, and knitted her clothes – a cardigan, a jumper, a scarf. Myra's letters to her harked back to a simpler time when they'd lived alone together.

Although Holloway was housed in Victorian buildings, its morals were those of sixties London. Myra had never seen women holding hands before, or kissing. Some had ragged-out pages from porn mags on their walls. At night, lovers in different wings called to one another through the bars. A film crew from the BBC's *Everyman* series came to make a documentary about Holloway. They recorded a prison officer walking past Myra's cell. As I watched the film I marvelled at the free access the director had been given. There were open displays of physical affection between inmates; prison officers looked on and made no attempt to stop filming. Myra saw the documentary at a special screening for inmates in the prison gym the week before transmission.

She described all this to Ian as an observer, not yet part of the place. He sent her new messages, in their secret code, about harming children. Sadistic sex was still the fire that burned at the heart of their relationship, and it needed fuel to survive. The descriptions weren't explicit; the slightest allusion to a shared secret was often enough to recall an experience. There were a lot of references to photographs.

They continued to share the same solicitor, Robert Fitzpatrick. The lawyer from Hyde served them as he would any other client. He worked doggedly to recover their negatives and the tartan album. Myra wrote to let Nellie know how his campaign was going. As the months dragged by this commentary increased in urgency; the pictures were very important to her and Ian. 'The material he had in his head was losing its power,' Professor Malcolm MacCulloch explained. 'The fantasies that sadists like Ian Brady use tend to lose strength over time so they escalate the content of what they're fantasizing. They're being more violent, more obscene or distressing to their victims in fantasy. The request for pictures is driven by the fact that he has remembered material which is important to him, which will reinvigorate him.'

Just before Christmas, a letter arrived from Ian. He had a cold, and was confined to bed. She thought back to Risley, where they had been able to celebrate together and share half a bottle of port wine. There was no alcohol in here. Ian's mother, Peggy, tried to make up for this by sending her chocolate liqueurs – whisky, rum, cherry brandy.

Ian told Myra that she must agree to see the police, who had booked a visit for 27 January 1967. They wanted to ask her about the other missing children. The detectives had allowed Myra enough time to 'cool down' – a common strategy. Myra wrote to Nellie to say she was only agreeing to the visit so that it would look good on her prison record. 'Once the police have been, I'm not going to see them again. They can leave us alone for the rest of our sentence, and I'll tell them that when they come. Remember the record you brought down one week, "It's All Over Now Baby Blue?" Can you get me another copy of it some time and keep it for me?' I read these last words with astonishment. The Joan Baez record had been Ian's gift to her on the morning of Edward Evans's murder. Her request for a new copy suggests that she was still caught up in reliving, and savouring, the murders with Ian.

In 1968 the Attorney General finally gave in and agreed to hand over the pictures. Robert Fitzpatrick delivered the tartan album, and negatives, to Nellie for safe keeping. There were around 200 images. Ian was very clear about which ones he wanted. 'I told Neddy you were having those 3 of me developed, and he's pleased, for he feels you will get them done quicker than his mam. Post them direct to him, right away. Put his number 605217 HMP Old Evet Durham.' Myra told Nellie that once she'd done this the rest of the pictures could be destroyed. Just a week later Myra wrote again. 'Have you sent the slides to Neddy yet?' But Nellie had stalled; it seemed as though she'd suspected what the pictures were. Time after time Myra's letters sidled up to the issue with chatty descriptions of prison life before the inevitable question about the slides.

Professor Malcolm MacCulloch was clear about the reason for Ian Brady's persistence. 'The only reason I can think of is that they portray, or remind him of, burial sites. He wants them so he can relive the murders, and enjoy possession of the bodies.'

'So,' I said, 'the letters between them might tell us which pictures he was after, and where the last body is buried.'

'They might do. But remember, Myra Hindley and Ian Brady were very, very good at this.'

Two weeks after this conversation I was sitting opposite Superintendent Tony Brett in his sparse office at Leigh police station.

'We have asked the Home Office to pull all the letters between Myra Hindley and Ian Brady for us,' the detective told me. 'They were copied and are held at a store in Staffordshire.'

'How hopeful are you?'

'If the letters can be decoded we might get the information we need to find the final missing body. At the very least they'll tell us more about the way they operated. That may help us in the long run. It's got to be done.'

Over time, Myra's questions to Nellie about life 'at home' became more detailed. Have you been re-housed yet? How is little Mikie (a nephew)? Tell me about the kids in their Whit clothes. Her references to Ian became more desperate. 'I've been in prison for three years now, Mam, and haven't seen Neddy for two and a half of them, which I think is awful, thinking how many other prisoners have been granted this privilege.' It was as if the rope to one anchor was slipping through her fingers, and she was grasping at another.

Lord Longford came to see her for the first time in 1968. She asked him to lobby the Home Office for inter-prison visits with Ian. Incredibly, the serving cabinet member agreed. Myra's solicitor in later years, Andrew McCooey, says that Longford agreed to help her out of religious conviction rather than because he believed her claims of innocence.

'Frank was extremely sharp,' McCooey told me. 'He was alive

to what was going on but believed that no-one was beyond redemption – not even Myra Hindley.'

Lord Longford told Myra about his conversion to Catholicism and suggested she try praying. She wrote to Nellie, 'I doubt I'll "see the light" again, but who knows?'

Myra's tastes altered along with her friends. In prison she had the time to read, and study, in a way that would not have been possible had she remained free. 'I hate Radio 1,' she wrote. 'The third programme has all the best classical music, study and good plays and poetry readings.'

For all these superficial changes, Myra remained bound to Ian by their shared secret. But then his demands for the slides became threatening, and in her letters home she stopped calling him Neddy. 'He keeps asking why he hasn't received them yet. In his last letter he said he'll have to send someone round for them.' Slowly, the bonds were being broken.

Chapter Five

The first six hundred pages of Myra Hindley's autobiography were delivered, in instalments, to the house of her most trusted supporter, David Astor, in the mid-eighties. They were checked for spelling mistakes, typed up and numbered by his secretary, Pat Hepburn. The former editor of the *Observer* newspaper read the completed pages with a growing feeling of dismay. 'I tried to suggest changes, persuade her to be more honest, but she just couldn't do it.' In the end, of course, Astor told her to abandon the project and ordered Pat Hepburn to destroy the handwritten original manuscript. But Myra Hindley kept a complete copy of her work, and several years before she died it was parcelled up and sent out of prison for safe keeping. She didn't want it to fall into the hands of a tabloid newspaper.

When I pulled the last section out of its brown manila envelope I found, at the back, a handwritten addition of more than two hundred pages. The words were laid down with a passion and honesty missing from the earlier chapters. Myra was able to achieve this tone because she was no longer writing about the murders. It was the story of a love affair that Ian Brady viewed as a supreme act of betrayal.

In 1970, Myra's friend and fellow inmate Carole O'Callaghan returned from a visit to the dentist in a state of high excitement – she'd just seen Myra's type! Myra did not get over-excited as Carole was always picking out potential lovers for her. Just what, she asked, made Carole think she knew what her type was? No, no, came the breathless reply, this one was really lovely. Her name was Trish Cairns – she was an officer!

Around this time, the prison governor, Dorothy Wing, decided that keeping the inmates of E-wing – child killers, spies, traitors – locked up together with no outside contact was a bad idea. It would be better to integrate them, mix them with a better class of criminal, in the hope of rehabilitation. It was the first time, Myra recorded in her autobiography, that she had left E-wing in four years. Her group of women were sitting on a bench in the prison 'centre', outside the canteen, waiting to be called in for their pay. The other inmates, many of them short-termers, treated them circumspectly. Carole O'Callaghan and Myra Hindley did not look like the sort to mess with.

They were waiting for F-wing to finish, watching people they had never seen before, when the door to A-wing opened and a lithe, brown-haired young officer emerged. As soon as she saw her Myra knew she was the one. She felt Carole tense up with mirth at her side. 'There she is!' she said in a loud stage whisper as the officer passed within a few feet of them. The women either side of them collapsed in a heap of giggles. Myra wrote that the officer turned and stared, and 'something happened' deep inside Myra. Just like with Ian, it was love at first sight.

Myra's cell faced the main gate. She took to standing on her bed when the warders changed shifts, at 7.45, 12.15, 1.30, 5.15 and 9.15, in the hope of catching a glimpse of her. The young officer always walked briskly, and looked happy. Myra and Carole talked about nothing but how attractive she was, and what she could do to meet her. In the end, it happened by chance.

Myra felt a rising sense of excitement. She had not been into a library since 1965. Heads turned as she and five other E-wing inmates passed by. She was walking beside her 'special' friend, Alice. They ignored the glances thrown in their direction by the other prisoners. Acknowledging them would have eroded respect, and invited trouble. The E-wing escort chose a key from the ring at her waist, slid it into the gate and pulled. The heavy iron door swung open to reveal the object of Myra's desires.

The escorting officer, Myra noted in her autobiography, laid a hand on her head and said, 'This one's Cat A.'

'I know,' replied the officer. She turned, and led the group inside.

Over three decades later, Patricia Cairns's recollection of this meeting remained bright in her mind. 'She stood out, straight-backed and calm, not like the others. They were chatting away. She would think that was beneath her. She was very dignified. And she was very bonny in those days as well.'

'What was she wearing?' I asked.

She laughed. 'They were allowed their own clothes by this stage. She was wearing black trousers, a turquoise and black blouse that came down to six inches above her knees, and a cardigan.'

Patricia Cairns recognized Myra's name but said she had very little idea of her crimes. During the Moors murders trial she was living in an enclosed Carmelite convent in Salford. By the time a crisis of faith prompted her to leave, Myra and Ian were behind bars. Her first job was at a borstal, Bulwood Hall. She had just started work at Holloway when she met Myra.

There was a limit to the number of prisoners allowed into the library. As one left, another came in. When Alice's turn arrived, Myra tried it on. She was teaching her friend to read; could they go in together to choose some books she'd like? Patricia gave Myra an 'old-fashioned' look and let her in. Myra scooped up a few titles for teaching and got lost in finding books for herself. Even though the library was small – it was in a cell – it offered a wider choice of reading material than she had seen for years. She became so absorbed that she almost forgot about Trisha. She was pulled back to the present by the officer's voice at her shoulder: they'd better go back to the wing or they'd think she'd lost her. Myra apologized, took the books to the front of the room, and had them stamped. She was reading with a purpose other than entertainment. There were rumours that male lifers were to be allowed to study for an Open University degree, and she wanted to do the same.

Back on the wing, Myra was distracted from her books by thoughts of Trisha. She was attractive. More than that, there seemed to be a warmth about her. But there was no point even thinking about it: Myra was an inmate, Trisha Cairns a warder.

It was several days before they met again. Trisha stood stern-faced in the doorway: what was that girl doing in her bed? Alice lay sprawled across the mattress watching Myra, naked after a bath, apply 'intimate' body lotion. Myra looked up and replied that where she came from, when you were on top of the bedspread you were on, not in, the bed. The officer did not back down: she was from the same place, and she said the girl was in the bed. In order to avoid a fight, Alice pulled herself up and ambled over to the wash stand. She did her best to imbue the act of brushing her teeth with insolence. Myra held the officer's gaze and asked her where she was from. Crown Point, Denton came the reply. Myra smiled – the place next to the sewage works? The officer ignored the dig, and said that she knew Gorton

Monastery. She'd taught Sunday School there when she was a nun. A bell rang. The officer said goodnight, pulled the door to, and turned the key. Myra lay back on her bed. A nun?

The following week Trisha was on reception. She noticed in the prison records that Myra's friend Alice had been transferred to Styal prison. Trisha's duty, as third officer, was to escort women to their wings. Most of the runs back and forth did not go near the area for 'high-risk' inmates – E-wing had the smallest population. But the inmate on reception duty that evening was a neighbour of Myra's.

At the end of her shift, Trisha walked the woman back and stood in the corridor, waiting while she went to get some water for the night. She had the feeling of being watched through a spy-hole. Nothing unusual in that – prisoners didn't have much to do. It was less common, however, for them to start banging on the door. She heard Carole's voice, demanding that she open up. Trisha hesitated and asked, impatiently, what she wanted. There was every reason to be suspicious. Carole said she had something for her – it was from Myra. Trisha glanced quickly up and down the corridor, pulled at her keys and opened the door. Carole was standing there, holding out a letter in her right hand. Trisha took it, stuffed it into her uniform pocket, and went back to her duties. Myra watched through the bars of her cell as Trisha made her way out of the wing. In the letter she'd told Trisha how much she loved her, and spent hours watching the prison gate just so that she could see her come and go. As she peered into the darkness Carole boomed, with mock sonority, 'It is consummated!' Myra ignored her, and lay back on her bunk.

That night was hell for Myra. If Trisha reported her she'd be up before the governor and was certain to be punished, but even worse was the possibility of rejection. Ian's spell had been broken; she wanted someone else, someone who would make her happy now. From her letters, and her autobiography, it is clear that this was a turning point for Myra. She had come to realize that she was never going to see Ian again. Unlike him, she could no longer find nourishment in the crimes of the past. She needed new experiences, and love, in the present.

Where was everyone? asked Trisha the next day. The E-wing duty officer, Stevenson, looked up from her book and replied that they'd all gone to see a film in the hall – except Myra. Oh, said Trisha, she'd come in to practise her table tennis for the prison tournament. Stevenson said she'd go and find Myra, see if she fancied a game.

Myra was in the ironing room. She didn't recognize Trisha at first, dressed carefully in jeans, an olive green suede jacket and matching Chelsea boots. She felt suddenly awkward in her black bell-bottoms and nylon housecoat – a more fashionable version of Gran's. She considered changing, but didn't want to be seen to be trying too hard. When Stevenson left them Trisha thrust out a record-shaped package at Myra. She took it, tore off the paper and read the title: Rachmaninov's 'Rhapsody on a Theme of Paganini'. They walked down to the music room and sat in silence as notes filled the air. Trisha passed her a card showing Dalí's *Christ of St John on the Cross*. On the back were the words 'The feeling is mutual.'

Myra was the happiest she had been for years.

They were interrupted when the door swung open and Carole walked in. A look of glee spread over her face. Oh sorry! Had she interrupted something? Myra cut her off and asked if she wanted to join them for a game of table tennis.

Myra and Trisha discovered that they had more in common than working-class, Catholic, Manchester backgrounds. Like Myra, Trisha came from a home dominated by a violent, hard-drinking father. She had entered the Carmelite convent in Salford to escape home as well as to dedicate her life to God. They worked out that they must have attended mass at the monastery together. Myra still went there for a year after she met Ian. In Myra's letters home now there were no more expressions of frustration at not being allowed to see Ian, no more complaints about the small number of letters she received, and fewer requests for information about life 'at home'. She seemed, for the moment at least, to have found something to keep her genuinely happy inside.

One night, Myra heard a knocking on her cell door. She got up off her bed and there was a rose bud, wet with dew, in the centre of the spy-hole. She took it, and found Trisha staring at her. Myra seized the initiative and told her to put her ear to the spy-hole. Trisha did as she was told. In her autobiography, Myra recorded that she whispered, 'I love you!' The spy-hole fell shut and Myra wondered if she'd gone too far. She banged on the door. 'Are you there? Did you hear me?'

'Yes, I heard. And I love you too. It's hopeless, but I can't help it.'

I found it hard to understand how anyone could fall in love with a person convicted of multiple child murder. Trisha Cairns explained that it was both because she was living in an enclosed order during Myra and Ian's trial, and that the nature of prison life meant people's crimes were rarely discussed. Inmates were taken at face value. What's more, Trisha told me, Myra did not rush to discuss her past. 'She told me after a few months. I was upset when I found out it was children. But it was beyond my control by then. I was just in love with her.'

Security at Holloway was lax, and it did not take long for them to work out a way of meeting every day. They set up arrangements using a warder's trusty, or 'red-band', called Pat to carry their letters. There was no shortage of private places: the craft room, where Myra 'worked' on a large tapestry; the prison chapel, where she practised piano; the room in the tower, where she made tea for the prison officers; even her cell on E-wing, where Trisha 'dropped in' to visit colleagues. They got even more time together when Trisha was made Myra's legal aid officer. But it never felt like enough. 'Some people like the risk of situations like that,' Patricia Cairns told me, 'but it wasn't like that. I found it very worrying. But my feelings were so strong it was beyond my control. It was overpowering.'

The relationship gave Myra a reason to cut off all ties with her 'one-time God'. Patricia Cairns said that she began to dread getting Ian Brady's letters and having to fake love in her replies. 'She had been struggling to reply to his letters for about a month before we met. His grip was loosening and her world view had broadened. Do you know that she used to get 150 Christmas cards a year – peers of the realm, religious leaders, prison inspectors, artists? How many people can you say that about? But she needed a push to get rid of him. I was a sort of replacement.'

Although Myra Hindley was physically attracted to Patricia Cairns, the relationship went far beyond sex. She had enjoyed other physical affairs, but none had threatened her bond with Ian. Myra recorded in her unpublished autobiography that Trisha was the love of her life; she had 'led her by the hand out of the wasteland'.

As her love for Trisha deepened, so the letters to Nellie, demanding that she supply the pictures to Ian, became increasingly urgent. 'Ian's going on about slides and photos again . . . he thinks of little else . . . you promised to write and let me know about the slides and photos . . . he'll keep on for years . . . I'm so sick of the whole thing . . . don't make things difficult for me, love . . . I'm sorry (in more ways than one) to have to mention the slides and photos yet again . . . <u>post</u> the things . . . try to do this for me, love, and let me know when it's been done.' But Nellie refused to send the pictures. Finally, on 11 May 1972, Myra wrote the words that finally changed her mother's mind: 'I have decided to bring our relationship (mine and Ian's) to a close.' Nellie sent a total of five pictures to Ian Brady. After that, the letters home from Myra, although still frequent, were no longer edgy.

Professor Malcolm MacCulloch told me that supplying the pictures was the only hope Myra had of achieving a clean break. 'She's spent all these years together with Ian Brady, corresponding about what they've done. She knows he has got to have closure. If she's going to cast him aside he has got to have what he needs. That's why things happened in the order that they did.'

Myra sat down to write her final letter to Ian. The words did not come easily, even though she was clear about the decision and had committed herself to Trisha. They had shared so much. She forced herself to go on, posted the letter, and waited for the reply.

'He was furious,' Patricia Cairns told me. 'He was blazing that she should reject him.'

'Do you think he realized that you had replaced him?' I asked.

She paused before replying. 'He must have picked up signs in her letters. It's hard to fake emotion convincingly.'

Ian Brady refused to accept that the relationship was over. He no longer had someone to share his secrets, a lover who might one day be free to send back sounds and smells from the outside world to sustain him. In the end, the social skills which he needed Myra for during the murders carried her away from him. Myra asked the governor to return all of his letters unopened, then demonstrated to Trisha that there would be no turning back. 'She burned all his correspondence,' Patricia Cairns told me. 'At the bottom of E-wing there was a gate on the left-hand side that led out to a brazier for inmates. I helped her. It took a few weeks.'

The prison governor, Dorothy Wing, was impressed with Myra's decision to cut off Ian Brady. It seemed as though there might be some hope of rehabilitation. She took a keen personal interest in the development of her prisoners. When she felt they were 'ready' to be reintroduced to the outside world she took them on trips: up the river to Kew; down the river to Greenwich; a day out at Crufts; an evening at the Royal Tournament. It was against all the rules, but she was a determined maverick.

Mrs Wing lived in a house by the prison gates with her cairn terrier Piper. On Tuesday, 12 September 1972, she was finishing off her early-afternoon cup of tea when the small dog began to whine. He needed to go for a walk. 'I suppose if it hadn't been for him wagging his tail at me, this might not have happened,' she later told the *Daily Mail*. She decided to take Myra out with her. They were gone for two hours. It was the first time Myra had felt grass and smelt fresh air since 1965. The papers were tipped off, and reporters only missed them coming back through the prison gates by a few minutes. The story headed the evening news and was splashed on the front pages of the tabloids the following morning. The Home Secretary, Robert Carr, issued an official rebuke: there were to be no more of Mrs Wing's excursions. That weekend Myra wrote home to Nellie, 'I spent the two most enjoyable hours for many years, and certainly the quickest two. I'll tell you all about it when I see you. I feel terribly sorry for all the publicity the governor has had to contend with today, and that such a kind and thoughtful gesture has been abused.'

I visited the newspaper library at Colindale to see if I could learn why the story had gained such momentum. Every page of national newspaper print is stored here, most of it on microfiche. The first roll I loaded onto the viewer gave me the answer: Lord Longford. The former cabinet minister had begun a campaign for Myra to be paroled; he said she was 'a good girl, and a devout Catholic'. The 'walk in the park' was seen as evidence of her being prepared for release. Neither the families of the victims nor the newspapers were willing to countenance this possibility, however. The former Chief Constable of Lancashire, Bill Palfrey, told the *Daily Mail*, 'I think some of our do-gooders are living in cloud cuckoo land. I have always believed in the death penalty and I would have said this was a case where it should have been imposed.' Myra did not understand that, by allowing Lord Longford to campaign on her behalf, she was fanning the flames of controversy. Her judgement was impaired by a desperate desire for freedom, for a life outside with the woman she loved.

Myra and Patricia's relationship continued for the next three years. A former assistant governor of E-wing, who did not want to be named, told me that it was an open secret among the prison management. There was a lot of sympathy for the pair: many of the officers were gay and involved in relationships either with one another or with inmates. But Myra found the situation deeply frustrating. She wanted a complete life with Trisha. The snatched moments they shared together over more than three years began to feel like footholds on an impossibly steep climb.

It was as she was contemplating the abyss beneath that a friend, Maxine Croft, came up with a solution: why didn't they escape? What was she on about? demanded Myra. Maxine was in for fraud; she'd been caught carrying a large sum of used notes in Holland. Myra liked her, but thought she was dippy. That's what I would do in your position, explained Maxine. You'll die in here otherwise. The idea began to take hold in Myra's mind.

But where would they go? she asked. Abroad, replied Maxine. She could get hold of passports, visas, cash. Some people on the outside owed her one. She had taken the drop for the fraud and had refused to grass up the other members of her gang. It was a mad idea, but it nagged away at Myra. It seemed like the only chance she and Trisha had of living together. The more she thought about freedom, the more impossible the idea of a life without it felt.

'She just came out with it,' Patricia Cairns told me. ' "I want to escape." "So do I," I replied. "No, I mean it," she said. "I'm going to be stuck in this place until I die. I want you to think about it." ' At first, Trisha Cairns said, the idea seemed like pure fantasy.

'But she was depressed at the time. What I did was to keep her going. I had no intention of springing her. In my mind I was pretending to go along with it.'

Myra, however, was determined to go through with the escape and went over the details again and again. Over time, it slowly became real. They would flee over Holloway's perimeter wall using a ladder, drive to Heathrow in a hired car and take the 'very convenient' eleven p.m. flight to Rio. Once there they would book themselves into a hotel and make enquiries about missionary work. Myra began to make practical arrangements, and asked Maxine for help. 'I was annoyed because involving Maxine made it real,' Trisha said. 'It had turned from a fantasy I was happy to go along with into a reality.'

Maxine and Trisha met in a small office off the warders' rest room to press the master key to the prison into a bar of Camay soap. They'd never done anything like it before, and bodged the job. The only thing for it was to try again the following evening with plaster of Paris. Maxine had agreed with the forger that the package containing the impressions would be 'dropped' in a left-luggage office at Euston station. The locker slip would be sent, for collection, to a garage in Kilburn. A few days later, Trisha caught the tube to Euston to meet Maxine, who was on day-release.

'It went wrong because the IRA were active at the time and they'd closed the left-luggage office.'

'Because of the letter bomber Shane Paul O'Doherty?' I asked.

'That's the one!' A flash of anger showed in her eye.

'I interviewed him once.'

'Well, give him a punch from me next time you see him!'

Maxine and Trisha discussed what to do, and decided to post the package to the garage direct. They walked down the hill to the post office opposite King's Cross. Maxine, who was on her way to meet her girlfriend, also a prison officer, promised to call the forger. Trisha made the mistake of taking her at her word.

The garage owner, George, did not know what to make of the package when it arrived. He was worried: the IRA bombs seemed to be everywhere; one had even injured the Home Secretary, Reggie Maudling. George asked the customer he was serving what he thought. The man bent down, felt the weight of the parcel and ripped it open. Inside were the impressions of Holloway prison's master keys and a note. The man asked George who this Maxine was. It turned out that he was an off-duty detective inspector.

The following day Myra walked into her cell to find Maxine sitting on the bunk, white as a sheet: Scotland Yard were coming to see her that afternoon! Myra got a message to Trisha, who was on escort duty at Croydon Crown Court, asking to meet her in the chapel that evening. But the net was closing in. When Trisha tried the chapel door from the officers' side, she found it had been security locked. Maxine must have started talking. Myra told her, through the door, to get rid of all the incriminating evidence in her flat.

Trisha rushed to Earls Court and cleared everything out: the luggage she'd bought for their escape, the literature from the Brazilian Embassy, and all the letters Myra had written to her over the past three years. She'd just finished when, at ten p.m., the police arrived to search her flat. They missed it the first time, but when they came back the following day detectives found Myra's new driving licence. Trisha had completely forgotten about it.

Maxine told the police that Trisha had threatened to get some 'heavies' she knew to hurt her mother unless she helped organize the escape. Trisha was charged with 'conspiring with persons unknown to effect the escape of a prisoner', and bailed. The other officers had a whip-round to help raise the £2,000 she needed for a bond. The police questioned Myra before charging her too. Civilian workmen arrived to change the prison locks. This had a profound effect on Myra, and a deep depression began to set in.

The only good thing about being back in court was that Myra got to see Trisha, but the case did not go well for either of them. What's more, they had to see Maxine every day. Maxine's co-operation with the police earned her some reprieve. The judge, Mr Melford Stephenson, said that he felt sorry for the way she'd been manipulated and sentenced her to eighteen months (this was later quashed on appeal). He was a good deal less sympathetic towards Trisha, describing her piety as 'brittle', and gave her six years. An escorting officer tried to stop Myra as she reached out across the dock for Trisha. 'I almost crushed her hand as I held it for the last time.'

The attempt at escape shows that Myra Hindley was desperate for freedom from the moment her relationship with Ian Brady ended. And that the feelings she had for the woman who replaced him, Patricia Cairns, were overwhelming. Once again, she was blinded by the force of her emotions.

Ian Brady, Professor Malcolm MacCulloch told me, watched every twist and turn of the court case from his prison cell.

'Her disloyalty devastated him,' he said.

'But they hadn't seen one another for years,' I replied.

'He called her "my girl" to the day she died. And she was.'

'How do you mean?' I asked.

'He always had a hold over her. Her failure to admit to their surviving secrets meant he could reveal them, and damage her, whenever he liked. She was trapped by her lies.'

And Ian Brady would get his revenge. It was only a matter of time.

Chapter Six

Myra's despair at the loss of Trisha was alleviated by a piece of good news: she was to be allowed to study for an Open University degree. Books were a way of reaching out beyond the walls of Holloway. She told Nellie in a letter home, 'I'll be the first woman in prison to do it, right from scratch. So to speak. It'll be nice to make "history" in a more pleasant way.' A BBC news reporter did a stand-up outside the prison about the lifers' degree scheme. It was all about Myra; no-one was interested in the men, even if they were murderers. The implication was that the decision offered her a glint of freedom.

Myra worked hard and tried to smother her distress at losing Trisha. But prisoners transferred from Styal prison, where Trisha was being held, brought news. Most of the inmates were kind to her – it was a good job she'd been well liked as an officer – but the staff were harsh. She was being kept in 'Bleak House', the punishment block, just because of who she was. The only way to communicate with other inmates was through the pipes running along the back of the cell wall. The prisoner in the adjoining cell was a woman she'd guarded at Bulwood Hall Borstal. Months later came the news that Trisha had been moved to the block for short-term prisoners – the worst place to be for a long-term inmate, let alone Myra Hindley's girlfriend. Anyone who wanted to show that they were 'hard' could have a go at her, safe in the knowledge that they'd soon be beyond reach.

'Did you hear from Myra?' I asked Trisha Cairns.

'I hardly got any news. She did send me letters, got them smuggled through. I read them then destroyed them straight away. It was dangerous though, and we used a code right from the start.'

The authorities refused to allow the women to write openly to each other, and it became increasingly dangerous to use couriers: there was always the risk that a letter might be sold and end up in the *Sun*. Trisha Cairns served four years and one week. When she was finally released the former lovers were denied permission to see one another.

Myra was faithful to Trisha during the initial pain of separation, but she knew that they had very little prospect of ever being together again. It was only a matter of time before she took another sexual partner. Trisha was just going to have to get used to it.

'Weren't you jealous of Myra having other relationships?' I asked.

Trisha replied, without faltering, 'She couldn't have coped without someone else by then. It's a question of depth anyway – what we had endured.'

Myra increasingly turned to her family for emotional support. One by one they came to see her in Holloway, relatives like Nanna Hindley, who had wanted nothing to do with her while she was loyal to Ian Brady. Myra's happiest moment came when, after years of beatings from her hard-drinking husband, Maureen finally left David Smith. Mo wrote to Holloway begging for reconciliation. In her reply, Myra said that the letter had brought forth 'sweet tears of joy', and she enclosed a precious 'V.O.' (visiting order).

A month later, Myra was sitting at a table in the visiting area, waiting for Maureen. She watched her come in, glance anxiously round and walk forwards – straight past her table. Myra caught her arm.

'Moby, it's me!'

Maureen gasped, and put her hand over her mouth. She hadn't recognized her sister with brown hair. She looked so different! Myra had stopped using any dye, had had it cut straight across her shoulders, just like Joan Baez.

Each new reconciliation and visit was recorded with delight in letters home. These documents are a record of Myra Hindley's shifting feelings. Shortly after her capture, and while she remained in love with Ian Brady, she was cool and manipulative. When she fell in love with Patricia Cairns her tone softened but remained full of confidence. Now that 'the love of her life' had gone from her day-to-day existence there was a needy, almost desperate tone. Her focus settled on Manchester. She hated it when the members of her family forgot about her. In the middle of February 1975 she wrote to Nellie: 'I haven't heard anything from home for ages. If I wasn't so worried and anxious I'd feel very annoyed . . . no visit and no letter.'

When a letter did eventually arrive the wait for the next one seemed interminable, and Myra often became depressed. 'Do try to drop me a line occasionally, mam, it makes such a difference to life in here to receive letters regularly. I've been in prison 10 years this year, as you know, and things don't get any better. I'm weary of it all, and often wish it would just quietly end, with no bother.'

Myra's reaction to Nellie's letters and visits was euphoric. She allowed herself to imagine what things would be like when she was released, able again to play a part in life outside. I found repeated descriptions in Myra's letters home of how she would care for Nellie, and make things up to her. 'I'm living for the day when I'll be able to look after you.' It seemed as though she could not survive without at least the flickering hope of freedom. The candle might spit and gutter, but if it went out completely she would no longer be able to survive.

Lord Frank Longford continued to see Myra regularly. He was pleased that she had maintained her faith, and introduced her to David Astor. Sir John Trevelyan, the Chief Inspector of Prisons, also became a friend, as did his daughter Sarah Boyle, a young GP who had recently returned from Australia.

'I wasn't really aware how sensitive the case was because I'd been living abroad,' she told me.

'How did you come to see her?'

'The people visiting her, including my father, were predominantly older men, or members of her family. It was felt that it would be good for her to have contact with someone her own age who had a life outside.'

As Myra was allowed just a handful of visits a month, most friendships had to be sustained by writing. The volume of correspondence was huge. She only kept the letters that moved her or were relevant to her campaign for freedom; the rest were burned to prevent them being sold to newspapers by unscrupulous warders. Nevertheless, it took me several weeks to sort through a mound of boxes stuffed with carrier bags, containing carefully labelled envelopes.

Her two most enduring correspondents were David Astor and Frank Longford, but there was a marked difference in the tone and content of their letters. Longford wrote on whatever material fell to hand – House of Lords paper, that of charities he chaired; Astor always used the same restrained, cream-coloured personal stationery. Where Longford was passionate, ungrammatical and campaigning in tone, Astor's carefully formed words spoke of a more politically astute mind. Myra was encouraged to apply for parole. The decision to pursue her freedom ensured that she stayed in the papers. Ann West, the mother of Lesley Ann Downey, accused her supporters of being 'dirty old men'. Myra was enraged by the ensuing banner headlines and attacked the 'vulturous, scabrous pigs' who wrote them. 'Why can't they leave me alone?' she asked Nellie.

I was driving across the rolling Wiltshire Downs, heading for London. On the passenger seat next to me was a package that had arrived in the morning post. I reached over, pulled out a cassette box, flipped it open and slipped the tape into the stereo. I thought there must be some mistake as a clear, pitch-perfect voice filled the car with the words of Joan Baez's 'Prison Trilogy' – the story of three criminals mistreated by the penal system. It was several seconds before I realized that this was Myra Hindley's winning entry to the 1976 Koestler Prize, an arts competition for prisoners. The song ended on a lilting refrain about razing all prisons to the ground.

I pulled in, rewound the tape and listened again as I read the accompanying judges' notes, scrawled in a spidery hand. 'Very well put across – with some sensitive touches which gave it a strange beauty. Words and tuning excellent.' They did not understand, or ignored, Myra's calculated choice of a song that portrayed the criminal as a victim. I ejected the tape, pulled back onto the road and accelerated away.

*

Every prisoner who came through the gates of Holloway knew it as 'Myra Hindley's nick'. She could feel their eyes on her. Most people just wanted to do their time in peace – get on and get out; there was nothing to be gained by trouble – but not everyone was capable of such rational detachment.

Josie O'Dwyer, a striking young woman who dressed like a man, had a volatile temper. She got on with the child killer Mary Bell but deeply disliked Myra Hindley. Antipathy turned to violence on the tenth anniversary of the Moors murders trial when the *News of the World* re-examined the case in detail. Trisha Cairns told me that the governor had been warned, and she told the warders on E-wing to cut the feature out. But, somehow, it 'found' its way to Josie.

She came at Myra on the landing, grabbed her hair, kicked her in the face, stamped on her leg and tried to heave her body over the railings onto the concrete floor twenty feet below. Blood gushed from her split skin, but Myra did not offer any resistance; she just hung limply on to the metalwork as the blows rained down. Her close friend Janie Jones, recognizing that her life was in danger, leapt onto Josie, grabbed the hand that was holding Myra's hair and stamped on her foot. Josie let go, and Myra slumped to the ground, moaning. Her nose was smashed and the cartilage in her knee torn.

Myra spent six weeks in the prison hospital wing. Her injuries were beyond Holloway's medical staff, and specialists had to be brought in. After careful assessment she was spirited out of the prison for a series of operations. Despite severe warnings from the governor, a warder leaked the story to the *Sun*.

Myra wrote a letter to Nellie from her hospital bed on 12 December 1976, cancelling their Christmas visit. She did not want her niece, Sharon, to see the state she was in. The torn knee cartilage had been removed and her nose rebuilt. 'The centre of my nose wasn't just knocked right, as it appeared to have been, but the whole nose was twisted in all directions. So first the surgeon put it back in the centre, then he took out "the hump" (my request) which we all have (our family, I mean).' The distinctive shape of her nose, the deep shadow it cast, is central to the power of her arrest photograph. It was a trait directly inherited from Bob Hindley. She told Nellie the surgery had left her with 'huge black eyes, but I'll be better soon'.

The decision was taken that she'd be better off in Durham prison. She had been at Holloway for eleven years and had fallen deeply in love there. Despite what had happened, and the knowledge that she'd always be at risk among so many short-termers, leaving was a wrench.

Myra's supporters, Frank Longford and David Astor, wanted the parole board to consider her for release. Their campaign stirred the interest of the BBC's *Brass Tacks* current affairs programme, which was based in Manchester. Shortly after the move to Durham Myra got a letter: would she help to arrange a televised debate on her case for freedom? The idea was to have four people arguing for her, and four against. In the end, Myra was seduced by the BBC producer's promise to examine the 'role of the press'. In a letter to Nellie she stated that the programme would 'ascertain how much "decision makers" are influenced by public opinion (which is prostituted by the press). The producer has made it clear that the showing of the programme will necessarily depend on my willingness.'

The BBC library tape shows an earnest presenter in a flared suit. The camera jerks around the bare studio in a self-conscious display of 'gritty' realism. Maureen sits in silhouette, an outline of beehive hair and dark glasses projected against the studio wall. Janie Jones and Sarah Boyle argue calmly on Myra's behalf, but struggle to defeat the simple argument that she murdered three children and should not be released after serving little more than a decade. Maureen, her fag-roughened Gorton voice tense with nervousness, sounds aggressive. She loses a slanging match with Ann West, who bellows, 'It was Myra Hindley's voice on that tape, not Ian Brady's. And my daughter was begging for her life!'

Myra heard the parole decision on the radio. Merlyn Rees, the Home Secretary, told the House of Commons that her case had been rejected and would not be reconsidered for another three years. 'I just couldn't believe that the decision could be so savage and callous,' she told Nellie. 'I feel spiritually battered and shattered, but I'll pull myself together because we have to keep each other going. As long as you're alive and waiting for me out there, I'll struggle along somehow.'

Myra got ever closer to Nellie; a continual stream of mundane detail sustained her. Were her workmates kind? Which shops did she go to? When her mother replied that a street had been re-developed or a cinema closed, it became harder to remember where she was from. She got Nellie to tell her what the new buildings looked like, and where they stood in relation to the old ones. Gorton was the only place she had known, and she needed it, 'otherwise I'll die in here'.

But it wasn't only Nellie who mattered to Myra. Each member of her family represented a tie to the outside world, to where she came from, to what she was. One message delivered to her by the prison chaplain – Mo was ill and had been taken in for 'some tests' – provoked near panic. She sent Mo a get well card, and Nellie a fiver so that she could afford the bus fare to and from the hospital. But before either letter could arrive, tragedy struck. The governor called Myra in to ask whether she wanted to go and say goodbye to her sister, but she arrived at the hospital half an hour after they switched the life-support off.

No-one had thought to tell Maureen's husband, Bill, that Myra was on the way. A few days later, she wrote to Nellie, 'It's the worst pain I've ever felt . . . but it must be worse for you.' Mo's death made Myra question her faith, but she concluded, 'If we have no faith in God, how can we take comfort knowing that Maureen is in heaven with God?'

In the agony of loss, Myra Hindley poured out page after grief-riven page to Nellie. The letters stood in stark contrast to those she had written immediately after her arrest. I travelled to Cardiff to discuss them with Malcolm MacCulloch.

'Do you think Maureen's death made her reflect on the suffering she'd inflicted on others?' I asked him.

He leaned back in his chair and looked out of the window at the garden before replying, 'She did not think of it in those terms. She retained the immunity to violence that allowed her to carry out the crimes in the first place.'

With Maureen gone, Nellie became more dependent on Myra. She was always complaining about how little money there was. Myra asked Lord Longford and David Astor for help – they were rich men – but she could go begging only so often. It was not worth jeopardizing the friendship she had with them, and losing their support. These relationships had a profound effect on Myra's world view, according to her friend and regular visitor Dr Sarah Boyle. 'Her friendships were windows on the world!' she exclaimed. I looked quizzically at her. 'They allowed her to look outside. Gave her intellectual stimulation.'

Another form of escape was Myra's Open University degree course. I found her essays, carefully folded, in their original brown envelopes. They looked as though they had been taken out and re-read several times. In March 1981 she wrote nine neat pages of comment on the banquet scene in *Macbeth*: 'This is the point in the play, so to speak, when his past catches up with him and he is faced not merely with Banquo's ghost, but with all the consequences of his past actions.' There are ticks and encouraging comments on every page. At the end the tutor has circled a large A and written, 'Very good indeed. A pleasure to read.'

Myra's efforts to escape her past only encouraged newspapers to pursue it. In July 1982, a reporter working for the *Sunday Times*, Linda Melvern, called round to see her mother. There was an unpaid gas bill on the table, and the journalist offered to help. Nellie, who was desperate, agreed, and let her take the tartan album. When she discovered what had happened, Myra was apoplectic with rage. 'She'll keep that album over my dead body, and for her claims that she paid you for it – that'll go on the score sheet too, the— just as well I can't swear.' Losing control of the tartan album made Myra feel deeply insecure. The more people who saw it, the greater the risk that it would give up its secrets. She had yet to admit to any of the murders she'd been convicted of, let alone reveal that there were any more victims buried on Saddleworth Moor.

The following year life became easier for Myra with her transfer to Cookham Wood prison at Rochester, in Kent. The regime was gentler, and the buildings newer. But her letters to Nellie remained full of longing for home.

I asked Malcolm MacCulloch what he thought her state of mind was at this time. 'She needed to get out,' he replied. 'The relationship with her family had replaced the obsession with Brady, and she wanted to go home. She thought that the best way of achieving that was to stick to the plan she'd made with Brady: stay silent. The trouble was, he knew the plan and wanted revenge for her betrayal.'

Ian Brady had developed a relationship with the chief reporter of *Today* newspaper, Fred Harrison, and started feeding him lines designed to damage Myra Hindley. Once he was sure of his man, Brady handed him a scoop: there were another two children buried on Saddleworth Moor.

Chapter Seven

Myra was desperate. Her only hope lay in undermining the story. She wrote a letter to the *Observer*, David Astor's old paper. To her relief, they printed it in full. I found a draft, written in blue biro, complete with crossings-out and underlinings, among a bundle of legal documents. 'Ever since I broke off contact with Ian Brady, 13 years ago,' she wrote, 'he has been implying that he could implicate me in "other matters". I have always denied this. If he does have information about other killings then I wish he would tell what he knows to the police, and not just to journalists and psychiatrists, to end the speculation.' But the damage was done. Four days later the Home Secretary announced that the parole board would not reconsider her case for another five years. It looked as though the decision had been influenced by Brady's 'revelations', but Myra still thought that confirming his story would make matters worse.

Friends like Sarah Boyle risked ridicule by remaining loyal to her. 'My husband, Jimmy, said she was lying. I got very cross with him because I felt he was being unjust and cynical.' But

Jimmy Boyle knew about criminals: he had been Scotland's most feared gangster. He met Sarah, who was a prison psychiatrist, at Barlinnie Gaol's special unit. He was doing life for the murder of a rival, Babs MacKinchie. Jimmy arrived at the unit as the most feared and uncontrollable prisoner in the Scottish prison system. He had led riots and dirty protests, and had even demolished part of a prison wing. Then an artist in residence handed him something that was to change his life – a chisel. Jimmy found that he could sculpt, very well. On his release he became a celebrated artist and wrote an autobiography, *A Sense of Freedom*.

Jimmy and Sarah visited Myra in prison. I was astonished to read, in a letter to Nellie, that they asked Myra to be godmother to their first child, Susie. Today, Sarah Boyle lives in a large Georgian house in the prosperous Inverleith area of Edinburgh. The garden is full of Jimmy's sculptures, but he has moved to France.

'Jimmy said she should tell the truth, that it had worked for him. She said, "I am, Jimmy, I am."'

'What did he reply?'

'"Come off it, hen! I've been there." But she stuck to her guns, and I believed her.'

Trapped by lies, Myra Hindley tried to make her story ring true through repetition. In a letter to Nellie she wrote, 'Two friends of mine went to read the trial transcripts. One of them, who has known me for fifteen years, said she's absolutely stunned that I was convicted on no evidence at all, while it's obvious Smith set me up so he wouldn't go down with Brady.'

But Brady's claim wouldn't go away. The families of the missing children demanded the reopening of the case. They were supported by the parents of the victims who had been found. Both were sure that exposing the full horror of the crimes would ensure Myra Hindley's death behind bars. The police issued a statement saying that the case had never been closed. The families' response, Myra told Nellie, was furious: 'Mrs pain in the neck West got back on her band-wagon and threatened to dig up the moor herself if the police didn't. She seems to feed on such publicity with a somewhat masochistic compulsion.'

The details of the murders were repeatedly reprinted in every national newspaper. Myra railed to Nellie, 'What on earth is amiss when they have to start scraping the bottom of a twenty-year-old barrel for news when there is so much happening out there? Anyway, my precious one, for your sake more than mine, I hope they don't print any garbage. I hate them. God forgive me, but I do.'

Myra's exaggerated indignation reminded me of the words she had written to Nellie while on remand at Risley in 1965. It was the same tactic: denying an allegation in the hope that it would never be proven. The increasingly desperate tone of Myra's protestations suggest that Nellie might have voiced the same thought. But Myra's resolve began to weaken when she got the news that Fred Harrison was writing a book.

The police were compelled to revisit the case. The head of Greater Manchester CID, Superintendent Peter Topping, and his deputy, DI Geoff Knupfer, went to see Myra Hindley on the off chance that she might help. 'We were there on a flyer, really,' Knupfer told me. 'We didn't expect her to give us anything.' The detectives told her that there had been 'a lot of pressure' since Brady's revelations for them to reactivate the investigation into the disappearance of Pauline Reade and Keith Bennett. At last, Myra decided to abandon the strategy she had maintained for the past twenty years and agreed to help. The police moved quickly in case she changed her mind, but Myra had finally realized that the best way out of the current situation, and to make people forget that she had lied for so long, was to help find the missing bodies. However, according to Patricia Cairns, there is no doubt that given the choice she would have kept silent about the murders of Pauline Reade and Keith Bennett. 'She only came clean because she had to. She needed to get in first. She wanted to stop him taking control. She told me that the effort of going through with it nearly killed her.'

Myra was determined that any help she gave should improve her chances of release rather than damage her image still further. She knew how sensitive the Home Office was to the demands of public opinion. There was no mention to the police of a system for recording where bodies were buried, or her role in creating it. She did, however, agree to return to the moor to try to find the missing children. The police blocked the A635 and threw a cordon of armed officers round the moor. Myra was told that she'd be going in by helicopter, with a bodyguard. She was advised to wear a pair of cords, a couple of pairs of socks, and two thick sweaters.

The deputy governor came to see Myra the night before with some 'news'. She wasn't going to like this, but there would be two prison officers going along as escorts and she'd have to be cuffed to one of them, 'for her own safety', at all times. Myra was furious, and demanded to know who was behind the decision. 'Head office,' came the answer – probably a government minister. 'The idiot' who made the decision had clearly never set foot on Saddleworth Moor; she could see herself and the escort floundering from tussock to tussock, slipping hand in hand down peat crevices.

They woke Myra at four in the morning and introduced her to her bodyguard, Detective Inspector Roy Rainford. The firearms officer had arrived with a selection of different-sized wellingtons, waterproof trousers, balaclavas and bulletproof vests for her and the prison officers. He told them they had to keep their balaclavas pulled down at all times. The police wanted to make it as difficult as possible for the press, or an assassin, to pick Myra out. Myra told the officer that she wasn't worried, whatever happened happened. The policeman gave her a look which said that he was worried, it was his job. Once they were dressed, Myra was handcuffed to 'Speedy', the junior of the two prison officers.

They sat three abreast on the back seat and waited for the prison gates to open. Roy Rainford told them to duck their heads, and the car accelerated at high speed towards the waiting helicopter. There was just one photographer's car, a Jaguar, waiting outside the gate. The Metropolitan Police helicopter was surrounded by armed officers. Myra and 'Speedy' went up the steps crabwise, their arms twisting in the cuffs, and settled down in the back of the machine. In her confusion, Myra put the earmuffs on back to front; Rainford turned round, gently lifted them off her head and put them back the right way round. Myra felt comfortable with him. The helicopter lifted off and slipped over the green fields of Kent towards Saddleworth Moor. Myra noticed that 'Speedy', who hated flying, had gone very pale. The officer lit a cigarette to calm her nerves, and handed one to Myra. A convoy on the ground followed the helicopter north, in case of emergency; police records show that they had checked out the accident facilities in every hospital along the route. They stopped twice to refuel, the second time just twenty miles from their destination.

Before long the moor appeared through the clouds, covered in patches of snow. They were so high up that it appeared featureless – not the beautiful landscape Myra had known so intimately. Still, she felt a thrill of excitement to be returning to a place that lived on inside her. The winds were so strong that the pilot had to circle several times before bringing the machine down.

On the ground they were led across the uneven turf to the police command centre. Myra held her wrist up to her solicitor, Michael Fisher, in exasperation. Could he do something about the handcuffs? What about calling the lifer unit at the Home Office? A man who had been watching stepped forward and introduced himself as Commander John Metcalfe, the Home Office liaison officer. He said he knew about the order and it couldn't be changed. Peter Topping, who'd been up all night, took the commander into an adjoining room for 'a chat'. When they came back, the cuffs were removed.

Myra told Topping that their best chance lay in starting at the lay-by where she and Ian Brady parked the night Keith Bennett died. But the whole operation was considered so risky that every detail had been worked out beforehand, and the superintendent was reluctant to change his plan. They drove her down a water board track to where Shiny Brook poured into the reservoir. It was a route she had never taken before.

Topping's decision, which he later admitted was a mistake, is understandable. He was under severe pressure. A junior Home Office minister, David Mellor, had given away what they were doing on Radio 4's *Today* programme. His revelation robbed the police of the element of surprise over the press. It was only a matter of time before hired helicopters carrying photographers with long lenses appeared in the sky above them.

The walk up Shiny Brook from the water board track is treacherous, especially in wet weather. At the start you have to climb over large boulders to join a narrow path above the roaring water – one slip, and you're in. Further up, where Myra and Ian shot guns, the stream cuts back and forth across the valley floor. The only way to make your way up is to jump across the water. It is difficult for a fit person, never mind a sedentary, middle-aged life-sentence prisoner.

It was not long before the press helicopters arrived. The police machine held position in the sky above, trying to give the search party some cover, but every so often one of the newspapers' helicopters broke through and the police had to form a protective circle around Myra. What if it was a man with a gun rather than a camera? In the distance, a helicopter touched down and two journalists sprang out. They were pursued across the moor by police officers. Another photographer was discovered, shivering and close to hypothermia, in a bush. He was in no state to take a picture. John Kilbride's father, Pat, walked up to a police roadblock brandishing a kitchen knife. As he was escorted by a couple of reporters, the police suspected he'd been put up to it and turned him back gently rather than arrest him. He repeated the scene, over a pint, in front of the cameras a short while later. 'You see what I've got here? I'd like to fucking kill her!' he bellowed. I watched the BBC library tape with discomfort: the journalists in the background looked far too eager for this display of grief.

Myra struggled to orientate herself. She was looking for a gully close to the waterfall, but was confused by the direction from which they had approached Shiny Brook. The snow on the ground didn't help. One after the other the two dog handlers accompanying the party fell into the stream. Then 'Speedy' twisted her knee. Peter Topping called for a stretcher to carry her off the moor, but the ground was so rough that first the front, then the rear stretcher bearer stumbled, dumping 'Speedy' among the tussocks.

After lunch, Topping agreed to approach Shiny Brook from the lay-by. But by then Myra was hobbling on a strapped ankle, sleet had begun to fall, and the press helicopters had returned. She was doing her best to find the right gully, but did not make any mention of marker photographs. After reading her account of this visit I found it hard to accept that Myra had forgotten about the pictures. It seemed more likely that she did not mention them because they tied her directly to the murder of Keith Bennett, and its subsequent celebration. This could only worsen her chances of release.

Back at Cookham Wood Myra spent all night sitting up with her 'very close friend' Noreen, from New Zealand. They agreed that the 'hate-inciting gutter press' might leave her alone if she managed to find the missing children. But she hadn't formally admitted to taking part in their murders yet. Her manoeuvring was getting in the way of the truth.

Over the next eight weeks Myra turned the story over and over in her mind, and in February 1987 she finally agreed to give Peter Topping a formal confession. The details were worked out with the help of a former prison governor, and clergyman, Peter Timms. It was agreed that he would attend to support her. The confession was tape-recorded over three days at Cookham Wood. Her solicitor, Michael Fisher, read a statement from Myra to the press outside, saying that she had made the decision to 'tell the truth' in response to a letter from the mother of Keith Bennett, Winnie Johnson. Again, it is hard to accept this as the driving force behind her decision as there had been many heart-rending letters over the years. The difference now was that Myra had been cornered by Ian Brady.

During the interview Topping asked Myra a direct question: did Ian Brady use photographs to mark graves? As far as she knew, came the reply, he didn't. The police officers felt that every word she uttered was carefully chosen, the desire for freedom at the forefront of her mind.

'She was always in the other room, or over the hill,' Geoff Knupfer said. 'She was never there when things happened.'

'Did you feel that she was shaping her story?' I asked him.

'Definitely. She never told a direct lie, and was always very helpful, but there was no doubt that she had an agenda.'

Many of Myra's friends cut her off when they realized she had been lying to them about her role in the murders. They had accepted her promise that she was innocent. 'It was a betrayal,' Sarah Boyle told me. 'I felt devastated by it. It was very, very difficult because I had trusted what she'd told me and I'd put my own name and reputation on the line to support her, as had many other people.' Her friend from Holloway Janie Jones was also outraged at the deception, and spent the next year writing a book, *The Devil and Miss Jones*. Myra could live with this, but she was devastated when Maureen's husband Bill cut off all contact with her niece, Sharon. She kept dozens of pictures of the little girl and wrote to her every week. 'I cannot bear it,' Myra told Nellie, 'but I thank God your feelings towards me haven't changed.'

Peter Topping rang Myra at the end of each day's digging to tell her what his men had done, in the hope of unlocking some hidden memory. He was dispirited when he called Cookham Wood late on the evening of 7 July. Frustrated by a lack of progress, the press, lacking anything to report, had turned on him. On the table lay a copy of the *Manchester Evening News*: STOP THIS FARCE NOW.

The detective told her they were looking on Hollin Brown Knoll. Geoff Knupfer sat and watched the conversation. He didn't expect anything to come of it, but you never could tell. 'He asked her what she could see from the graveside. It was a chance thing. She said, "Nothing, except the body, and the dark outline of the hills against the sky." We knew we were on to something straight away.' There was only one place on the knoll where you could see the distant Pennine ridge. The following day Topping and his team found the grave of Pauline Reade. 'I have to admit,' Knupfer told me, with a gentle smile, 'that we took a certain amount of pleasure from the apology in the *Manchester Evening News*.'

Chapter Eight

Myra told me that she watched the funeral on the news. The service was held at the monastery church in Gorton. Joan Reade, driven half-mad by the agony of unresolved grief, scattered soil on the coffin as it was lowered into the ground. Topping and his team stood around, looking awkward. Frank Longford gave an interview to demand Myra's release as she had 'done the right thing'.

A few days later Topping went to see Myra at Cookham Wood. He wanted her to help find the body of Keith Bennett. She still did not tell him that she and Ian had taken marker photographs of his grave. Had Topping been able to read the first draft of her autobiography, written two years earlier, he would have found a clue, for there Myra described an incident that occurred before any of the murders. She and Ian had been to midnight mass at St James's Protestant Church in Gorton. He staggered out of the front door, took a swig from a whisky bottle and relieved himself on a grave. 'Little did I realize then that his graves would be marked by photographs and not headstones,' Myra wrote.

After Topping's investigation she completed another draft of the autobiography. Here she admitted being less than frank with the detective superintendent and his deputy, Geoff Knupfer, during an interview. The policemen produced pictures of her and Ian standing, grinning, on the rocks at Hollin Brown Knoll. Myra wanted to help, to take the credit for finding the missing children, but did not want to admit the depth of her complicity as this would undermine her case for release. In the autobiography she wrote, 'I wanted them to know, without saying in so many words, which grave was in which area.' So she was not completely open about the meaning of the pictures, even though 'they were taken to indicate there was a grave'. Instead, she suggested Topping get the pictures blown up – her way of saying that they mattered. The enlargement would reveal the expiry date on the tax disc, April 1964, by which time two children were dead, John Kilbride and Pauline Reade. As the picture was clearly not of John Kilbride's grave, 'it had to be marking the location of Pauline Reade's grave, which, in turn, meant that Keith Bennett's grave was in the Hoe Grain/Shiny Brook area [where similar "landscapes" were taken]'. But at the time Topping and Knupfer had no chance of working out what she meant. Nevertheless, Geoff Knupfer did go through the tartan album in a fruitless search for clues. He also looked at his predecessors' claims about a system.

'There was some mention of a system at the original trial,' Knupfer told me. 'But we felt it was all pretty tenuous stuff. The only picture you could be sure about was John Kilbride's.'

In the second draft of her autobiography Myra Hindley writes in detail about the pictures taken at Shiny Brook. 'We visited this place several times before Keith Bennett was taken there, and often packed a picnic lunch, cooling a bottle of wine in the stream on top of what I called the plateau of the moor,' Myra wrote. There are some pictures of her standing by the waterfall, others of her with Carol and David Waterhouse from Wardlebrook Avenue. 'The police on the original case returned the slides after about 18 months. Ian had them in prison, where he had permission to view them through a hand-size projector.'

I took the autobiography to Birmingham University, and sipped bad instant coffee while Professor John Hunter and his assistant, Barrie Simpson, read it from cover to cover. When Simpson had finished he re-read the passages dealing with marker pictures. The former head of the West Midlands Police murder squad was emphatic: 'This is it. This is the confirmation that they marked Keith's grave, and they took him to Shiny Brook. The police have got to act on this.'

Several weeks later, in the basement of a small west London independent production company's premises, DC Gail Jazmik and DS Fiona Robertshaw read the newly discovered text. I was cutting a film for Channel 4 along the corridor, and popped in to see them every couple of hours. At the end of the day they got to the section about marker photographs.

'Can I take a copy of these pages?' Fiona Robertshaw asked, pinching four sheets between her fingers.

'Of course.'

Topping decided to take Myra back to the moor. Not only had she helped to find Pauline, but she had also confessed to her role in the killings. This time they would be able to openly discuss burial sites, not 'places of interest to Ian Brady'. But first Topping had to persuade the Home Office, which had taken a battering from the press over the last visit and was anxious to avoid a repeat. Topping got his way, and he smuggled Myra onto the moor at 5.40 one morning without any journalists spotting her. But the reason for the reporters' failure also hampered the search: mist. Even officers who had spent months searching Hoe Grain struggled to work out where they were. Myra could not be certain about any locations.

Ian Brady observed events closely from his cell at Ashworth Special Hospital. His former psychiatrist, Malcolm MacCulloch, told me that he was worried about losing control. 'So, almost as a retaliation, in order to recoup power and omnipotence about what had happened, he assisted as well and Peter Topping was able to go and speak to him.' Topping decided to accept Ian Brady's offer of 'help' and got the Home Secretary's permission to take him to Saddleworth. Brady appeared confident of success, and strode so fast over the tussock grass that Topping had to grab hold of his arm for support. But when they reached Eagle's Head rock, which has a clear view of a vast expanse of moorland, he acted confused. It was all different. Topping asked what he meant. Brady replied, improbably, that the rock sheep pens had moved.

I pored over Topping's notes at Greater Manchester Police headquarters. They state that two days after the visit to the moor he went to Ashworth Special Hospital. Brady got out the pictures procured by Myra. Surprised, Topping asked why Brady was showing them to him. Brady replied, only so that he could see how the landscape had changed. A few days later Topping rang Brady: there was no other meaning to those pictures, was there? Oh no, came the reply, of course not! Brady knew that Myra had not admitted to helping mark all the graves, that it conflicted with her story and her campaign for freedom.

I pointed the notes out to DC Gail Jazmik. The blood drained from her face.

Professor Malcolm MacCulloch smiled wryly when I asked him about Ian Brady's return to the moor.

'It is possible that Ian Brady was on the moor and checked the site without letting on. So he has got his last body still in place, and I think that would be entirely consistent with what we know [about him].'

'And would it be very important for him to have that control?' I asked.

'Yes, absolutely. The final control is the possession of the body.'

'He's the winner?'

'Yes. "I know you don't know, you want to know, and I'm not going to tell you."'

The press had been friendly since the discovery of Pauline Reade, but it was only a matter of time before they turned again. Peter Topping and Geoff Knupfer decided to call off the search for Keith Bennett. 'We'd done everything we could,' Knupfer told me. 'There was no way forward.'

Shortly afterwards a letter bearing a Manchester postmark arrived for Myra. The handwriting looked like Winnie Johnson's. She slit the envelope open and began to read. 'Dear Ms Hindley, My name is Alan Bennett, Keith's brother . . .' Myra understood now why the letters she had received from 'Mrs Johnson' had sounded so calm, while her public statements were filled with anger. The letter asked whether she might be willing to help. Myra wrote back and invited Alan to correspond with her.

In his next letter Alan told her that he had begun to search Saddleworth Moor with his brothers, and a team of volunteers. He said his family felt as though they had been abandoned by the authorities. When he called Peter Topping, who had left the police to write a book based on Myra Hindley's taped confession, he was told to speak to his 'publicity agent'. He later discovered that Topping's team had kept no record of their search.

At first, Alan and Myra's exchanges were cautious. She half expected her letters to appear in the *Sun*, but it never happened. Finally, she asked him to come and see her. He hesitated before deciding that she was his only hope. 'It was a very difficult thing to go through,' Alan told me. 'But what choice did I have? There was no other way of finding Keith. I wrote to Brady as well. At first it seemed as if he wanted to help. But I soon realized that he was just playing games.'

'How do you mean?'

'Look at this letter here.' Alan held out a sheet of paper covered in neat blue copperplate. 'He says that trying to tell me where Keith's grave is would be like "describing colours to a blind man". He's getting off on it.'

Myra's decision to 'co-operate' with the police had not improved her prospects of release. An opportunity to stem the flow of negative headlines arose in 1989 when she was told that she'd passed her Open University degree. The certificate was awarded to her at a specially arranged ceremony. It was one of the proudest days of her life. David Astor rang up his former picture editor on the *Observer* for advice on how to get photographs of the ceremony into all the nationals. The answer was simple: the Camera Press agency, 'totally reliable and very efficient'.

David Astor and his wife cropped the pictures themselves, to exclude 'irrelevant figures', before handing them over. The result, he wrote to Myra, was not all that he had hoped for: 'They interpreted the issue of the pictures as the launch of a new campaign to get you out. I think they would have said this whatever we did.' Reading Astor's words I could not help but feel that, however crudely expressed, the tabloids had understood the situation correctly. The following year, her parole application was turned down.

Five Home Secretaries in succession ruled that Myra Hindley should die behind bars. She was certain that this was because her face was never out of the papers, and raged about them in letters home to Nellie. At Durham it had been: 'Myra and Rose West in Love'; at Cookham Wood the governor allowed inmates to have a go on a pony to maintain their awareness of the outside world. The *Sun* front page: 'Trot in Hell'. Then she was moved to Highpoint in Suffolk, or 'Hi-de-Highpoint': a 'holiday camp' with 'luxury rooms'. Her arrest photograph stared out of every new story.

In order to try to lower the temperature, Myra even cut off Frank Longford, refusing to send him invitations to visit. In a letter to me she wrote: 'It is a task even beyond Hercules to gag Frank Longford . . . if the dangerous dogs act was still in force I'd take it upon myself to muzzle him.'

Alan Bennett asked Myra whether she might consider hypnotherapy as a way of unlocking the 'secret' of where Keith lay buried. He had a doctor, Una Maguire, lined up to do the work. Myra agreed; the Home Office dithered. Only after a lengthy campaign, behind closed doors, did they finally relent. But before going ahead Myra 'sought medical advice' and wrote to tell Alan that her doctors had advised her it was 'unsafe'. Knowing Myra, I could not imagine her ever going through with hypnotherapy. She was such a controlled figure that letting go would have been extremely difficult. Especially as she might have revealed the true depth of her complicity.

But Myra knew that the case would stay in the public eye as long as it remained unsolved. In 1998 she decided to have one last go, without incriminating herself, at telling the police where the final missing victim of the Moors murders lay buried. She sent Alan Bennett a visiting order to come and see her at Highpoint prison.

As they sat in the segregation block's small beige meeting room she agreed to meet detectives, with him, to go through the police copy of the tartan album. 'You never know, I might remember something.'

As Alan walked out of the prison gate a smartly dressed man crossed the car park towards him.

'Hello, Mr Bennett. Dick Saxty of the *Sun*.'

Alan refused to speak to him, and failed to see the photographer on the other side of the road. He was on the front page the following day: 'Evil Myra murdered his little brother . . . yet he's gone to jail to give her a *hug*.'

Undeterred, Alan met the police, and they agreed to the visit. Myra wrote to Sarah Boyle to tell her about it. 'She said she was looking forward to it,' Sarah said. 'She seemed ready to help.' Myra also called me to ask whether I could advise Alan Bennett on how to deal with the press. The plan was for him to come in with the detectives. She seemed optimistic: 'I have seen the pictures before, but I am hopeful. It's definitely worth doing.'

Alan and I met at his bedsit in Longsight and roughed out a statement. It explained that he was visiting Myra Hindley so that he could find, and bury, his murdered brother. But two days before the visit was to take place Alan got a call from Sergeant Alan Kibble to cancel – Superintendent Montgomery had a 'family crisis'. A few days later Myra Hindley was rushed to West Suffolk Hospital after suffering a cerebral aneurysm. To Alan Bennett's dismay, the visit was never rearranged. 'I suspect now they were worried about the press. The focus was always on her getting out, and I think someone warned them off. They were so paranoid they even suggested I shave my beard off to avoid being recognized.' Alan stared through the net curtains, towards the school he and Keith had attended. The campaign to keep

Myra Hindley behind bars had also hindered the search for Keith Bennett.

It took Myra Hindley six months to recover from the operation to save her life, and the deep depression it precipitated. She cut off contact with Alan and passed a message through her priest, Michael Teader, to say that she 'couldn't cope' with seeing him any longer.

Chapter Nine

I laid the magazine down. Myra Hindley's arrest photograph
was splashed across the cover of *The New Statesman* above
the words LORD CHIEF JUSTICE GIVES HINDLEY HOPE OF FREEDOM.
Lord Woolf, Britain's most senior judge, had spoken about the
adoption of the European Convention on Human Rights. He
believed that judges would now take over the Home Secretary's
role in deciding how long lifers should serve.

Woolf was due to hear Myra Hindley's case in the House of
Lords towards the end of 2002. It seemed as though Myra's
strategy of withholding the whole truth might be about to pay
off. David Astor called me to say that he had begun planning
what would happen when she got out. There was a convent in
New York that had agreed to take her, and Myra had accepted;
all they had to do was 'get the tabloids off her back'. Did I think
a press conference might do the trick? I told him that I didn't
think so.

There was a leaflet about the convent among her papers. It
spoke of a reflective life and showed nuns at prayer. Tucked

inside were photographs of the building where they lived, a white 1930s stucco-fronted house near the sea. It stood on a large plot surrounded by similar buildings, and looked in good order. I struggled to imagine her there, and asked Patricia Cairns how deep she thought Myra's faith really was. 'I never sensed it was 100 per cent genuine,' she replied, 'but I don't know. She returned to the faith to please me, and even when we were separated she kept it up. But she read the spiritual works of a number of people like the Dalai Lama and Khalil Gibran. I'd say she was spiritual but not religious.'

The *Sun* found out about the plan – MYRA TO BE NUN. The sisters took fright and David Astor had to start all over again. He asked Terry Waite, the Archbishop of Canterbury's former special envoy to the Middle East, to help. The court case was approaching rapidly and they did not have much time.

During the House of Lords hearing her advocate, Edward Fitzgerald, called Myra every evening to tell her how things were going. The Law Lords were giving him a hard time, but he thought he was winning the argument. I watched the hearing from the public benches a couple of metres behind Fitzgerald. The feeling among the spectating lawyers seemed to be that his optimism was well founded. The judgment was due in the New Year.

I was about to go into a meeting in London on Friday, 15 November 2002 when my mobile rang.

'Duncan, it's Gail Jazmik. The boss asked me to let you know she's been taken ill.'

'Is it serious?'

'Yes.'

Father Michael Teader sat by Myra's side as the ambulance rushed her the ten miles to Bury St Edmunds Hospital. The doctors said there was nothing they could do. Father Michael summoned a nun, Sister Bridget, who was close to Myra. He thought she would want her there.

'Yeah, won't be long now, she's on the way out,' the uniformed policewoman barked into her radio.

'Do you mind!' snapped Sister Bridget. She was holding Myra's hand; Father Michael held the other.

Myra Hindley slipped away at lunchtime, taking all that she knew with her.

Chapter Ten

'Duncan, we've heard back from the cryptologist about the letters and notebooks.'

Superintendent Tony Brett sat with his back to the window, staring at me. To his right were DC Gail Jazmik and DS Fiona Robertshaw. Their faces remained impassive as he spoke. The press officer, DC Andy Meekes, flicked nervously at his notepad with a pen. Brett did not sound like a man with good news.

'There is a code,' he said.

'What does it say?'

'That's the problem. The messages are unclear to anyone other than Myra Hindley and Ian Brady.'

'In what way?'

'If I were to say to you, remember the day we went to Blackpool? It sounds innocuous, but if that were the day we had killed someone you'd know instantly what I meant.'

The police faced a difficult situation. Myra Hindley had taken the secret to her grave, and Ian Brady was clearly not going to help.

'We're going to do his room, see if we can find the pictures, and see if they are markers.'

'When?' I asked him.

'We need to speak to our lawyers. You can be sure that Brady will take legal action. Everything's got to be watertight.'

I felt a sense of excitement as I walked out of Leigh police station imagining detectives pushing their way into Brady's room at Ashworth Special Hospital and seizing the pictures that show where Keith Bennett is buried. His family would, at last, be able to lay him to rest.

I called Alan, and he invited me round to his bedsit for a cup of tea.

'It's great news,' he said. 'For years there has been no progress, and now this.'

We sat in silence for a couple of minutes. Suddenly, Alan stubbed out his roll-up and stood up.

'I've got something I want you to hear.'

He walked over to the large stereo system next to the window and slipped a cassette into the tape deck. From the speakers emerged the sound of a middle-aged lady speaking, and the giggling of excited children. Then a high, clear voice filled the room. It was several moments before I realized that I was listening to Keith Bennett singing 'Jerusalem'.

> And did the countenance Divine
> Shine forth upon our clouded hills?
> And was Jerusalem builded here
> Among these dark Satanic Mills?

As the hymn ended, Blake's words were replaced with the applause of proud adults.

Alan clicked off the tape.

'My Auntie Kath recorded that the Christmas before he died. Towards the end of each year, I drive up to the moor, park up, and listen to it. It makes me feel close to him.'

Brett told me that he intended to carry out a search within days. But three weeks after the meeting at Leigh there was still no news. He called me as I was walking, in the rain, up to Birmingham New Street station.

'Duncan, there's a problem.' He sounded angry.

'What?'

'Treasury Counsel says because Brady can't be charged with the murder of Keith Bennett we can't have a warrant to search his cell.'

Only recently, of course, had Greater Manchester Police sought to charge Myra Hindley with the murders for which she had never been tried. Treasury Counsel, the government's legal service, would not proceed with this attempt to keep her behind bars because of an earlier court decision. The families of Pauline Reade and Keith Bennett had demanded a new trial in the mid-eighties. The Director of Public Prosecutions refused then on the grounds that it would be a waste of taxpayers' money. To try to reverse that decision would have been ruled an 'abuse of process' – and the same applied to Brady now. After being denied permission to raid Brady's cell Tony Brett did hire a firm that analyses images for the security services to study his photographs. But they ran up against the same problem as GCHQ: the coded messages in the pictures were too oblique. There was nothing that said 'X marks the spot'. I realized that Greater Manchester Police would definitely not resume a search of the moor without information that pinpointed the exact location of Keith Bennett's grave.

The family of Keith Bennett and forensic archaeologists

working on the case were exasperated by the police's insistence on precise information. 'I just don't agree with their strategy,' Professor John Hunter told me. He remained determined to find Keith Bennett and was certain that the body lay buried by Shiny Brook. 'They know which area he's in and should get on and clear it. It's politics: they took a battering from the press last time they searched and don't want the same again.'

I returned to Saddleworth Moor for a final time and took the path to Shiny Brook. It was a grey day, and Professor Malcolm MacCulloch's words seemed to hang in the wind: 'Final control is possession of the body. "I know you don't know, you want to know, and I'm not going to tell you." '

I now understood that the struggle over Myra Hindley's freedom had obscured the truth. In order to try to present a favourable image and win release she failed to admit complicity in recording the murders; and in order to respond to the demands of public opinion successive Home Secretaries focused on keeping her inside rather than on the needs of justice. Manchester's most senior detective was only assigned to the case, after fifteen years of inactivity, to make sure Myra Hindley died behind bars rather than to find Keith Bennett. By playing to the gallery, Myra Hindley and the forces of law and order unwittingly conspired to hand Ian Brady what he wanted – the perfect murder.

I climbed back into my car to drive home, and tried to put out of my mind the stretch of windblown cotton grass where Keith Bennett still lies.

Conclusion

It should not have been necessary for me to write this book. The forces of law and order, rather than a journalist, should have discovered the truth behind the Moors murders. I firmly believe that, had they been told to go looking, detectives would have found much of the material that has fallen into my hands over the past few years. Why does this matter? After all, Myra Hindley is dead and Ian Brady will never be free. The answer is that a family remains trapped by suffering, a great city continues to live under a dark shadow, and Ian Brady still has his perfect murder. It is a matter of national shame.

On Thursday, 7 October 1965, Superintendent Bob Talbot's knock on the back door at 16 Wardlebrook Avenue set in motion the mechanism that deals with all major crime. The police investigate, a case is put before a court and the guilty are, more often than not, convicted. The recovery of the bodies of Lesley Ann Downey and John Kilbride was necessary to this process. There was evidence directly linking the accused to their disappearance: a tape, photographs, and Ian Brady's notebook.

Although Keith Bennett and Pauline Reade were also believed to be victims they did not need to be found in order to secure a conviction.

The legal system functioned as it is meant to. A well-constructed prosecution case, and the offensive behaviour of the accused, ensured guilty verdicts. There were glimpses in court of what lay behind the killings: references to de Sade, Hitler, pornography, and a system for marking where bodies lay buried. It was clear that Myra Hindley had been 'normal' before she met Ian Brady – the judge said so – and that something had turned her from a 'good Catholic girl' into a 'monster'. But these facts only emerged as the defence and prosecution vied with each other to establish guilt or innocence. Neither side was interested in cause, in what had brought them all to Court Number 2, Chester Assizes.

It was only thirty-six years later, with the death of Myra Hindley and the discovery of her private papers, that an explanation for the Moors murders emerged. In large part, this account is told from Myra's point of view. But that is its strength, as it leads us to an understanding of the woman and her actions. The account is far too comprehensive, and full of detail, to be the work of an outright liar. It stands up to comparison with contemporaneous sources. Where there is deception, it is by omission.

There may be even more to be learned about the Moors murders, but what has emerged over the past few years is of real value. We now know, as Professor Malcolm MacCulloch said, that the murders were the result of an appalling 'concatenation of circumstances'. A young woman with a tough personality, taught to hand out and receive violence from an early age, became obsessed with a sexually sadistic psychopath. They found common cause in their dislocation from the working class and set out to establish their superiority through murder. Myra told me that she and Ian Brady were 'separated by a chasm from the rest of the world'. On their side of this divide they built a home, and in that home they kept their possessions – the perfect murders. The killings were what defined them; they were something to be treasured and remembered. Ian Brady's marker pictures and the tartan album were an affirmation, and celebration, of what they had achieved together. When Judge Fenton-Atkinson sentenced them to life he may have glimpsed these facts, but they did not really concern him. What mattered was that Ian Brady and Myra Hindley had killed, and must pay the price.

The year after she was sent to Holloway prison the police did interview Myra Hindley to see if she'd 'cooled off' and might tell them the truth. What they found was a woman still in love with her accomplice and, although physically separated, still as one with him. The officers returned north to Manchester and the case, although still open, was put back on the shelf. The Moors murderers were behind bars – what else was there to do? I wonder what photographic officer Ray Gelder, who first suspected there was a system for marking bodies, must have thought when he learned that the tartan album had been returned to the Moors murderers. Almost every police officer was sure that there were more bodies.

During the first five years of their imprisonment, we now know, Myra Hindley and Ian Brady exchanged sexually sadistic fantasies. They wrote to each other incessantly, in a secret code, about the photographs in the tartan album. The Prison Service meticulously copied all of these letters and put them into storage. But it was only when I pointed out their contents to Greater Manchester Police that GCHQ was called in to try to decode them. No-one had thought to do so before because the job of the

Prison Service was to keep the Moors murderers behind bars, not to try to close the case.

It is now clear, from Myra Hindley's papers, that a fundamental shift took place when she fell in love with Patricia Cairns. The bond with Ian Brady was broken and she became desperate for her freedom. In retrospect, this may have offered an opportunity to get at the truth. An adviser to Greater Manchester Police in the 1980s, and professor of forensic archaeology at the Smithsonian Institution in Washington, Bruno Frohlich, told me how the authorities in the United States might have approached the situation. 'We cut deals,' he said. 'You give us the body, we'll consider your request for freedom. It works.' But there was no question of talking to Myra Hindley at this stage, never mind cutting a deal. It wasn't worth the political cost for any Home Secretary to be seen to engage with her. The overriding priority was to keep her behind bars.

Myra Hindley, in her desperation to be released, did not mention either Keith Bennett or Pauline Reade during the first twenty years of her sentence. Only when the case was revisited following Ian Brady's revelation that there were another two bodies on Saddleworth Moor did she agree to talk to the officer in charge of the inquiry, Superintendent Peter Topping. But we have now learned that this co-operation was partial, her words hemmed in by the need not to say anything that might harm her chances of release. It was a vague description of the view from Pauline Reade's graveside – 'the dark outline of the hills against the sky' – that led to the recovery of the teenager's body.

During the subsequent search for Keith Bennett, Myra Hindley did hint at the existence of a photographic marker system to Peter Topping, but her words were so convoluted as to be meaningless. The superintendent's work was further hampered by the debate surrounding her campaign for freedom, the press hectoring on the one hand, politicians grandstanding on the other. The interests of the Bennett family were not at the forefront of reporters' or government ministers' minds.

The decision to abandon the search for Keith Bennett left his family quite alone. In desperation they spent a decade digging over miles of moorland. Alan Bennett contacted both Ian Brady and Myra Hindley for help. Brady taunted him, Hindley appeared to co-operate. But, once again, her help was partial. Although she had described the existence of a marker system in her unpublished autobiography, she did not disclose its existence to Alan. Instead, she offered to look at Ian Brady's photographs, with the police, 'in case' she 'remembered something'.

What could have proved a decisive meeting never took place. When Alan Bennett was snapped by a *Sun* photographer outside Highpoint prison, the newspaper's front page the next day lambasted him for going to see her, portrayed him as a fool. 'It's just a story to them,' he told me, 'but it's our life.' Alan believes that a consequence of the paper's action was to frighten the police off. It reminded them of the hammering they had taken from the press during the search in the mid-eighties.

Myra Hindley was deeply frustrated by the police's decision. I believe that she wanted to help find the body, but needed to do so without incriminating herself further. She sent a series of maps, through me, to the forensic archaeologist Professor John Hunter. But these drawings were vague, always lacking enough detail to lead to the body. She could not put herself by the grave-side in case it compromised her case for release.

After the failure of John Hunter's search, Myra Hindley focused on her legal campaign and took her case for freedom to the highest court in the land, the House of Lords. Frightened that she might succeed, the Home Secretary, David Blunkett, ordered Greater Manchester Police to assign a team of officers to the case. Again, Detective Superintendent Tony Brett's brief was not to find Keith Bennett. But Brett was a Mancunian, and he responded the way most Mancunians in his situation would: 'If we can find Keith Bennett, we will.' But after spending months trying to work out which of the pictures in the tartan album might be the marker, no 'X marks the spot' had materialized so no full-scale search was started. The police have now fed all the new information into a review of the case by Bramshill Police Academy.

There is a sharp divide between experts who have worked on the case. The police, and the Home Office, want certainty before conducting another search. Professor John Hunter, who works for police forces all over the world, says that such certainty cannot be found. The peat of Saddleworth Moor, he explains, lies like a blanket on top of the underlying rock. Over time, that blanket slips. A photograph in the tartan album that would have provided pinpoint accuracy forty years ago might now be several metres out. The professor says that the only answer is for the area around Shiny Brook to be cleared. But this action would need to be taken in the knowledge that it might fail, and that's a risk the authorities are not prepared to take.

Alan Bennett has waited patiently since a new police team was assigned to the case, hoping that a fresh search might be sanctioned. But it seems, once again, that the work will be left to him and his family. As I was writing this conclusion, a text message came through from him: 'Going to see the police and if nothing happens hope to start digging again.'

It is wrong, over forty years after his murder, that Keith Bennett's family are left to scrabble for his remains in the peat of Saddleworth Moor. Greater Manchester Police, and the Home Office, can be forgiven for their failure to see through the Moors murderers' lies, but they could not be forgiven for inaction now that they know the truth. Do they really want Ian Brady to retain possession of the perfect murder?

Index

Praise for *Weyward*

'Alive, vivid and gripping'
ABIGAIL DEAN

'Humming with a sly, exhilarating magic'
BRIDGET COLLINS

'A generational tale of female resilience'
GUARDIAN

'A much-heralded epic'
OBSERVER

'Totally unique'
GILLIAN MCALLISTER

'Utterly absorbing'
ABI DARÉ

'Fierce and moving . . . magnificent'
ROSIE ANDREWS

'A stunning debut'
LUCY CLARKE

'An entertaining read'
THE TIMES

'Leaves you keen to turn the page and find out more'
INDEPENDENT

'Fabulous'
PRIMA

WEYWARD

Emilia Hart is a British-Australian writer. She was born in Sydney and studied English Literature and Law at the University of New South Wales before working as a lawyer in Sydney and London. Emilia is a graduate of Curtis Brown Creative's Three Month Online Novel Writing Course and was Highly Commended in the 2021 Caledonia Novel Award. Her short fiction has been published in Australia and the UK. She lives in London.

WEYWARD

EMILIA HART

b

THE BOROUGH PRESS

The Borough Press
An imprint of HarperCollins*Publishers* Ltd
1 London Bridge Street
London SE1 9GF

www.harpercollins.co.uk

Harper*Publishers*
Macken House,
39/40 Mayor Street Upper,
Dublin 1
D01 C9W8

This paperback edition published 2024
1

First published by HarperCollins*Publishers* 2023

ISBN: 978-0-00-849912-9

Set in Meridien by Palimpsest Book Production Ltd,
Falkirk, Stirlingshire

Printed and bound in the UK using 100% renewable electricity
at CPI Group (UK) Ltd

For my family

The Weyward Sisters, hand in hand,
Posters of the sea and land,
Thus do go, about, about,
Thrice to thine, thrice to mine,
And thrice again to make up nine.
Peace, the charm's wound up.

Macbeth

'Weyward' is used in the First Folio edition of *Macbeth*.
In later versions, 'Weyward' was replaced by 'Weird'.

PART ONE

PROLOGUE

ALTHA

1619

Ten days they'd held me there. Ten days, with only the stink of my own flesh for company. Not even a rat graced me with its presence. There was nothing to attract it; they had brought me no food. Only ale.

Footsteps. Then, the wrench of metal on metal as the bolt was drawn back. The light hurt my eyes. For a moment, the men in the doorway shimmered as if they were not of this world and had come to take me away from it.

The prosecutor's men.

They had come to take me to trial.

1

KATE

Kate is staring into the mirror when she hears it.

The key, scraping in the lock.

Her fingers shake as she hurries to fix her make-up, dark threads of mascara spidering onto her lower lids.

In the yellow light, she watches her pulse jump at her throat, beneath the necklace he gave her for their last anniversary. The chain is silver and thick, cold against her skin. She doesn't wear it during the day, when he's at work.

The front door clicks shut. The slap of his shoes on the floorboards. Wine, gurgling into a glass.

Panic flutters in her, like a bird. She takes a deep breath, touches the ribbon of scar on her left arm. Smiles one last time into the bathroom mirror. She can't let him see that anything is different. That anything is wrong.

Simon leans against the kitchen counter, wine glass in hand. Her blood pounds at the sight. The long, dark lines of him in his suit, the cut of his cheekbones. His golden hair.

He watches her walk towards him in the dress she knows

he likes. Stiff fabric, taut across her hips. Red. The same colour as her underwear. Lace, with little bows. As if Kate herself is something to be unwrapped, to be torn open.

She looks for clues. His tie is gone, three buttons of his shirt open to reveal fine curls. The whites of his eyes glow pink. He hands her a glass of wine and she catches the alcohol on his breath, sweet and pungent. Perspiration beads her back, under her arms.

The wine is chardonnay, usually her favourite. But now the smell turns her stomach, makes her think of rot. She presses the glass to her lips without taking a sip.

'Hi, babe,' she says in a bright voice, polished just for him. 'How was work?'

But the words catch in her throat.

His eyes narrow. He moves quickly, despite the alcohol: his fingers digging into the soft flesh of her bicep.

'Where did you go today?'

She knows better than to twist out of his grasp, though every cell of her wants to. Instead, she places her hand on his chest.

'Nowhere,' she says, trying to keep her voice steady. 'I've been home all day.' She'd been careful to leave her iPhone at the flat when she walked to the pharmacy, to take only cash with her. She smiles, leans in to kiss him.

His cheek is rough with stubble. Another smell mingles with the alcohol, something heady and floral. Perfume, maybe. It wouldn't be the first time. A tiny flare of hope in her gut. It could work to her advantage, if there's someone else.

But she's miscalculated. He shifts away from her and then—
'Liar.'

Kate barely hears the word as Simon's hand connects with her cheek, the pain dizzying like a bright light. At the edges of her vision, the colours of the room slide together: the gold-lit floorboards, the white leather couch, the kaleidoscope of the London skyline through the window.

A distant crashing sound: she has dropped her glass of wine.

She grips the counter, her breath coming out of her in ragged bursts, blood pulsing in her cheek. Simon is putting on his coat, picking up his keys from the dining table.

'Stay here,' he says. 'I'll know if you don't.'

His shoes ring out across the floorboards. The door slams. She doesn't move until she hears the creak of the lift down the shaft.

He's gone.

The floor glitters with broken glass. Wine hangs sour in the air.

A copper taste in her mouth brings her back to herself. Her lip is bleeding, caught against her teeth by the force of his hand.

Something switches in her brain. *I'll know if you don't.*

It hadn't been enough, leaving her phone at home. He's found another way. Another way to track her. She remembers how the doorman eyed her in the lobby: had Simon slipped him a wad of crisp notes to spy on her? Her blood freezes at the thought.

If he finds out where she went – what she did – earlier today, who knows what else he might do. Install cameras, take away her keys.

And all her plans will come to nothing. She'll never get out.

But no. She's ready enough, isn't she?

If she leaves now, she could get there by morning. The drive will take seven hours. She's plotted it carefully on her second phone, the one he doesn't know about. Tracing the blue line on the screen, curling up the country like a ribbon. She's practically memorised it.

Yes, she'll go now. She *has* to go now. Before he returns, before she loses her nerve.

She retrieves the Motorola from its hiding place, an envelope taped to the back of her bedside table. Takes a hold-all from the top shelf of the wardrobe, fills it with clothes. From the en-suite, she grabs her toiletries, the box she hid in the cupboard earlier that day.

Quickly, she changes out of her red dress into dark jeans and a tight pink top. Her fingers tremble as she unclasps the necklace. She leaves it on the bed, coiled like a noose. Next to her iPhone with its gold case: the one Simon pays for, knows the passcode to. The one he can track.

She rummages through the jewellery box on her bedside table, fingers closing around the gold bee-shaped brooch she's had since childhood. She pockets it and pauses, looking around the bedroom: the cream duvet and curtains, the sharp angles of the Scandi-style furniture. There should be other things to pack, shouldn't there? She had loads of stuff, once – piles and piles of dog-eared books, art prints, mugs. Now, everything belongs to him.

In the lift, adrenalin crackles in her blood. What if he comes back, intercepts her as she's leaving? She presses the button for the basement garage but the lift jerks to a stop at the ground floor, the doors creaking open. Her heart pounds. The doorman's broad back is turned: he's talking to another resident. Barely breathing, Kate presses herself small into the lift, exhaling only when no one else appears and the doors judder shut.

In the garage, she unlocks the Honda, which she bought before they met and is registered in her name. He can't – surely – ask the police to put a call out if she's driving her own car? She's watched enough crime shows. *Left of her own volition*, they'll say.

Volition is a nice word. It makes her think of flying.

She turns the key in the ignition, then taps her great-aunt's address into Google Maps. For months, she's repeated the words in her head like a mantra.

Weyward Cottage, Crows Beck. Cumbria.

2

VIOLET

1942

Violet hated Graham. She absolutely loathed him. Why did he get to study interesting things all day, like science and Latin and someone called Pythagoras, while she was supposed to be content sticking needles through a canvas? The worst part, she reflected as her wool skirt itched against her legs, was that he got to do all this in *trousers*.

She ran down the main staircase as quietly as she could, to avoid the wrath of Father, who thoroughly disapproved of female exertion (and, it often seemed, of Violet). She stifled a giggle at the sound of Graham puffing behind her. Even in her stuffy clothes she could outrun him easily.

And to think that only last night he'd boasted about wanting to go to war! Pigs had a greater chance of flying. And anyway, he was only fifteen – a year younger than Violet – and therefore far too young. It was for the best, really. Nearly all the men in the village had gone, and half of them had died (or so Violet had overheard), along with the butler, the footman, and *both* the under-gardeners.

Besides, Graham was her brother. She didn't want him to *die*. She supposed.

'Give it here!' Graham hissed.

Turning around, she saw that his round face was pink with effort and fury. He was angry because she'd stolen his Latin workbook and told him that he'd declined all his feminine nouns incorrectly.

'Shan't,' she hissed back, clutching the workbook to her chest. 'You don't deserve it. You've put *amor* instead of *arbor*, for heaven's sake.'

At the bottom of the staircase, she scowled at one of the many portraits of Father that hung in the hall, then turned left, weaving through the wood-panelled corridors before bursting into the kitchens.

'What are ye playing at?' barked Mrs Kirkby, gripping a meat cleaver in one hand and the pearly carcass of a rabbit in the other. 'Could've chopped me finger off!'

'Sorry!' Violet shouted as she wrenched open the French windows, Graham panting behind her. They ran through the kitchen gardens, heady with the scent of mint and rosemary, and then they were in her favourite place in the world: the grounds. She turned around and grinned at Graham. Now that they were outside, he had no chance of catching up with her if she didn't want him to. He opened his mouth and sneezed. He had terrible hay fever.

'Aw,' she said. 'Do you need a hanky?'

'Shut *up*,' he said, reaching for the book. She skipped neatly away. He stood there for a moment, heaving. It was a particularly warm day: a layer of gauzy cloud had trapped the heat and stiffened the air. Sweat trickled in Violet's armpits, and the skirt itched dreadfully, but she no longer cared.

She had reached her special tree: a silver beech that Dinsdale, the gardener, said was hundreds of years old. Violet could hear it humming with life behind her: the weevils searching for its cool sap; the ladybirds trembling on its leaves; the damselflies, moths and finches flitting through its branches. She held out her hand and a damselfly came to rest on her palm, its wings glittering in the sunlight. Golden warmth spread through her.

'Ugh,' said Graham, who had finally caught her up. 'How can you let that *thing* touch you like that? Squash it!'

'I'm not going to *squash* it, Graham,' said Violet. 'It has as much right to exist as you or I do. And look, it's so pretty. The wings are rather like crystals, don't you think?'

'You're . . . not normal,' said Graham, backing away. 'With your insect obsession. Father doesn't think so, either.'

'I don't care a fig what Father thinks,' Violet lied. 'And I certainly don't care what *you* think, though judging by your workbook, you should spend less time thinking about my *insect obsession* and more time thinking about Latin nouns.'

He lumbered forward, nostrils flaring. Before he could make it within five paces of her, she flung the book at him – a little harder than she intended – and swung herself into the tree.

Graham swore and turned back towards the Hall, muttering.

She felt a pang of guilt as she watched the angry retreat of his back. Things hadn't always been like this between them. Once, Graham had been her constant shadow. She remembered the way he used to crawl into her bed in the nursery to hide from a nightmare or a thunderstorm, burrowing against her until his breath was loud in her ears. They'd had all sorts of japes – ripping across the grounds until their knees were black with mud, marvelling at the tiny silver fish in the beck, the red-breasted flutter of a robin.

Until that awful summer's day – a day not unlike this one, in fact, with the same honey-coloured light on the hills and the trees. She remembered the two of them lying on the grass behind the beech tree, breathing in meadow thistle and dandelions. She had been eight, Graham only seven. There were bees somewhere – calling out to her, beckoning. She had wandered over to the tree and found the hive, hanging from a branch like a nugget of gold. The bees glimmering, circling. She drew closer, stretched out her arms and grinned as she felt them land, the tickle of their tiny legs against her skin.

She had turned to Graham, laughing at the wonder that shone from his face.

'Can I've a go?' he'd said, eyes wide.

She hadn't known what would happen, she'd sobbed to her father later, as his cane flashed through the air towards her. She didn't hear what he said, didn't see the dark fury of his face. She saw only Graham, screaming as Nanny Metcalfe rushed him inside, the stings on his arm glowing pink. Father's cane split her palm open, and Violet felt it was less than she deserved.

After that, Father sent Graham to boarding school. Now, he only came home for holidays, and grew more and more unfamiliar. She knew, deep down, that she shouldn't taunt him so. She was only doing it because as much as she couldn't forgive herself for the day of the bees, she couldn't forgive Graham, either.

He'd made her different.

Violet shook the memory away and looked at her wristwatch. It was only 3 p.m. She had finished her lessons for the day – or rather, her governess, Miss Poole, had admitted defeat. Hoping she wouldn't be missed for at least another hour, Violet climbed higher, enjoying the rough warmth of bark under her palms.

In the hollow between two branches, she found the hairy seed of a beech nut. It would be perfect for her collection – the windowsill of her bedroom was lined with such treasures: the gold spiral of a snail's shell, the silken remains of a butterfly's cocoon. Grinning, she stowed the beech nut in the pocket of her skirt and kept climbing.

Soon she was high enough to see the whole of Orton Hall, which with its sprawling stone buildings rather reminded her of a majestic spider, lurking on the hillside. Higher still, and she could see the village, Crows Beck, on the other side of the fells. It was beautiful. But something about it made her feel sad. It was like looking out over a prison. A green, beautiful prison, with birdsong and damselflies and the glowing, amber waters of the beck, but a prison nonetheless.

For Violet had never left Orton Hall. She'd never even been to Crows Beck.

'But *why* can't I go?' She used to ask Nanny Metcalfe when she was younger, as the nurse set off for her Sunday walks with Mrs Kirkby.

'You know the rule,' Nanny Metcalfe would murmur, a glint of pity in her eyes. 'Your father's orders.'

But, as Violet reflected, knowing a rule was not the same as understanding it. For years, she assumed the village was rife with danger – she imagined pick-pockets and cut-throats lurking behind thatched cottages. (This only enhanced its allure.)

Last year, she'd badgered Graham into giving her details. 'I don't know what you're getting so worked up about,' he'd grimaced. 'The village is dull as anything – there isn't even a pub!' Sometimes, Violet wondered whether Father wasn't trying to protect her from the village. Whether it was, in fact, the other way around.

In any case, her seclusion would soon come to an end – of sorts. In two years, when she turned eighteen, Father planned to throw a big party for her 'coming out'. Then – he hoped – she would catch the eye of some eligible young man, a lord-to-be, perhaps, and swap this prison for another one.

'You'll soon meet some dashing gentleman who'll whisk you off your feet,' Nanny Metcalfe was always saying.

Violet didn't want to be whisked. What she actually wanted was to see the world, the way Father had when he was a young man. She had found all sorts of geography books and atlases in the library – books about the Orient, full of steaming rainforests and moths the size of dinner plates ('ghastly things', according to Father), and about Africa, where scorpions glittered like jewels in the sand.

Yes, one day she would leave Orton Hall and travel the world – as a scientist.

A biologist, she hoped, or maybe an entomologist? Something to do with animals, anyway, which in her experience were far preferable to humans. Nanny Metcalfe often spoke of the terrible fright Violet had given her when she was little: she had walked into the nursery one night to find a weasel, of all things, in Violet's cot.

'I screamed blue murder,' Nanny Metcalfe would say, 'but there you were, right as rain, and that weasel curled up next to you, purring like a kitten.'

It was just as well that Father never learned of this incident. As far as he was concerned, animals belonged on one's plate or mounted on one's wall. The only exception to this rule was Cecil, his Rhodesian ridgeback: a fearsome beast he had beaten into viciousness over the years. Violet was forever rescuing all manner of small creatures from his slobbering jaws. Most recently, a jumping spider that now resided in a hatbox under her bed, lined with an old petticoat. She had named him – or her, it was rather hard to tell – Goldie, for the colourful stripes on his legs.

Nanny Metcalfe was sworn to secrecy.

Though there were lots of things Nanny Metcalfe hadn't told *her* either, Violet reflected later, as she dressed for dinner. After she'd changed into a soft linen frock – the offending wool skirt discarded on the floor – she turned to the looking glass. Her eyes were deep and dark, quite unlike Father and Graham's watery blue ones. Violet thought her face quite strange-looking, what with the unsightly red mole on her forehead, but she was proud of those eyes. And of her hair, which was dark too, with an opalescent sheen not unlike the feathers of the crows that lived in the trees surrounding the Hall.

'Do I look like my mother?' Violet had been asking for as long as she could remember. There were no pictures of her mother. All she had of her was an old necklace with a dented oval pendant. The pendant had a *W* engraved on it, and she asked anyone who'd listen if her mother's name had been Winifred or Wilhelmina. ('Was she called Wallis?' she asked Father once, having seen the name on the front page of his newspaper. He sent a bewildered Violet to her room without any dinner.)

Nanny Metcalfe was just as unhelpful.

'Can't quite recall your ma,' she'd say. 'I was not long arrived when she passed.'

'They met at the May Day Festival in 1925,' Mrs Kirkby would offer, nodding sagely. 'She were the May Queen, being so pretty. They were very much in love. But don't ask your father about it again, or you'll get a right whipping.'

These crumbs of information were hardly satisfactory. As a child, Violet wanted to know so much more – where did her parents marry? Did her mother wear a veil, a flower crown (she pictured white stars of hawthorn, to match a delicate lace dress)? And did Father blink away tears as he promised to have and to hold, until death did them part?

In the absence of any real facts, Violet clung to this image until she became certain that it had really happened. Yes – her father *had* loved her mother desperately, and death *had* done them part (she had a shadowy idea that her mother had died giving birth to Graham). *That* was why he couldn't bear to talk about it.

But occasionally, something would blur the image in Violet's head, like a ripple disturbing the surface of a pond.

One night, when she was twelve, she'd been foraging for jam and bread in the pantry when Nanny Metcalfe and Mrs Kirkby walked into the kitchens with the newly employed Miss Poole.

She'd heard the scraping of chairs on stone and the great creak of the ancient kitchen table as they sat down, then the pop and clink of Mrs Kirkby opening a bottle of sherry and filling their glasses. Violet had frozen mid-chew.

'How are you finding it so far, dear?' Nanny Metcalfe had asked Miss Poole.

'Well – Lord knows I'm trying, but she seems such a difficult child,' Miss Poole had said. 'I spend half the day looking for her as she tears around the grounds, getting grass stains all over her clothes. And she – she . . .'

Here, Miss Poole took an audibly deep breath.

'She *talks* to the animals! Even the insects!'

There was a pause.

'I suppose you think I'm ridiculous,' Miss Poole had said.

'Oh no, dear,' said Mrs Kirkby. 'Well, we'd be the first to tell you that there's something different about the child. She's quite . . . how did you put it, Ruth?'

'Uncanny,' Nanny Metcalfe said.

'No wonder,' Mrs Kirkby continued, 'what with the mother, being how she was.'

'The mother?' Miss Poole asked. 'She died, didn't she?'

'Yes. Awful business,' said Nanny Metcalfe. 'Just after I arrived. Didn't have much chance to know her before that, though.'

'She were a local lass,' Mrs Kirkby said. 'From Crows Beck way. The master's parents would've been furious . . . but they'd passed, just the month before the wedding. His older brother, too. Coach accident, it was. Very sudden.'

There was a sharp intake of breath from Miss Poole.

'What – and they still went ahead with the wedding? Was Lady Ayres . . . in the family way?'

Mrs Kirkby made a noncommittal noise before continuing.

'He was very taken with her, I'll say that much. At first, anyway. A rare beauty, she were. And so much like the young lady, not just in looks.'

'How do you mean?'

Another pause.

'Well, she were – what Ruth said. Uncanny. Strange.'

3

ALTHA

The men took me from the gaol through the village square. I tried to twist my body away, to hide my face, but one of them pinned my arms behind my back and pushed me forward. My hair swung in front of me, as loose and soiled as a whore's.

I looked at the ground, to avoid the stares of the villagers. I felt their eyes on my body as if they were hands. Shame throbbed in my cheeks.

My stomach turned at the smell of bread and I realised that we were walking past the bakers' stall. I wondered if the bakers, the Dinsdales, were watching. Just last winter I had nursed their daughter back from fever. I wondered who else bore witness, who else was happy to leave me to this fate. I wondered if Grace was there, or if she was already in Lancaster.

They bundled me into the cart as easily as if I weighed nothing. The mule was a poor beast – it looked almost as starved as I was, its ribs jutting out beneath its dull coat. I wanted to reach out and touch it, to feel the beat of its blood beneath its skin, but I didn't dare.

As we set off, one of the men gave me a sip of water and a heel of stale bread. I crumbled it into my mouth with my fingers, before leaning over the side of the cart to vomit it up. The shorter man laughed, his breath rancid in my face. I lay back against the seat and tilted my head so that I could look out at the passing countryside.

We were on the road that runs alongside the beck. My eyes were still weak, and the beck was just a blur of sunlight and water. But I could hear its music and smell its clean, iron scent.

The same beck that curves bright around my cottage. Where my mother had pointed out the minnows shooting out from under pebbles, the tight buds of angelica growing along the banks.

A dark shadow passed over me, and I thought I heard the beat of wings. The sound reminded me of my mother's crow. Of that night, under the oak tree.

The memory turned in me like a knife.

My last thought before I drifted into darkness was that I was glad Jennet Weyward did not live to see her daughter thus.

I lost count of the number of times the sun rose and fell in the sky before we reached Lancaster. I had never been to such a place; had never even left the valley. The smell of a thousand people and animals was so strong that I narrowed my eyes to squint, in case I could see it hanging in the air. And the sound. Loud enough that I couldn't hear a single note of birdsong.

I sat up in the cart to look around. There were so many people: men, women and children thronged the streets, the women hitching up their skirts as they stepped over mounds of horse dung. A man cooked chestnuts over a fire; the smell of their golden flesh made me dizzy. It was a bright afternoon but I was shivering. I looked down at my fingernails: they were blue.

We stopped outside a great stone building. I knew without needing to ask that it was the castle, where they held the assizes. It had the look of a place where lives were weighed up.

They pulled me from the cart and took me in, shutting the doors behind me so that I was swallowed whole.

The courtroom was like nothing I'd ever seen before. The sun flared through the windows, lighting on stone pillars that reminded me of trees curving towards the sky. But such beauty did nowt to quell my fear.

The two judges were seated on a high bench, as if they were heavenly beings, rather than meat and bone like the rest of us. They put me in mind of two fat beetles, with their black gowns, fur-trimmed mantles and curious dark caps. To the side sat the jury. Twelve men. They did not look me in the eye – none bar a square-jawed man, with a kink in his nose. His eyes were soft – with pity, perhaps. I could not bear the sight of it. I turned my face away.

The prosecuting magistrate entered the room. He was a tall man, and above his sober gown, his face had the raw, pitted sign of the pox. I gripped the wooden seat of the dock to steady myself as he took his place across from me. His eyes were pale blue, like a jackdaw's, but cold.

One of the judges looked at me.

'Altha Weyward,' he began, frowning as though my name might sully his mouth. 'You stand accused of practising the wicked and devilish arts called witchcraft, and by said witchcraft, feloniously causing the death of John Milburn. How do you plead?'

I wet my lips. My tongue seemed to have swollen and I worried that I would choke on the words before I got them out. But when I spoke, my voice was clear.

'Not guilty,' I said.

4

KATE

Kate's stomach is still oily with fear, even though she's on the A66 now, near enough to Crows Beck. Just over 200 miles from London. 200 miles from him.

She's driven through the night. She's used to getting by without much sleep, but even so, she's surprised at how alert she is, the fatigue only beginning to show itself now in a cottony feeling behind her eyeballs, a thudding at her temples. She switches on the radio, for voices, company.

A jaunty pop song fills the silence, and she grimaces before switching it off.

She winds down the car window. The dawn air floods in, clean and grassy, with a tang of dung. So different to the damp, sulphuric smell of the city. Unfamiliar.

It's been over twenty years since she was last in Crows Beck, where her great-aunt lived. Her grandfather's sister – Kate barely remembers her – died last August, leaving her entire estate to Kate. Though estate seems the wrong word for the small cottage. Barely bigger than two rooms, if she remembers correctly.

Outside, the rising sun turns the hills pink. Her phone tells her that she's five minutes away from Crows Beck. *Five minutes away from sleep*, she thinks. *Five minutes away from safety.*

She turns off the main road down a lane thick with trees. In the distance, she sees turrets gleam in the morning light. Could this be the Hall, she wonders, where her family once had their seat? Her grandfather and his sister grew up there – but then they were disinherited. She doesn't know why. And now, there's no one left to ask.

The turrets disappear, and then she glimpses something else. Something that makes her heart thud sharply in her chest.

A row of animals – rats, she thinks, or maybe moles – strung up on a fence, tied by their tails. The car rolls on and they slip mercifully from view. Just some harmless Cumbrian custom. She shudders and shakes her head, but she can't forget the image. The little bodies, twisting in the breeze.

The cottage is slung low to the ground, like an anxious animal. The stone walls are blurred with age, ivy-covered. Ornate letters carved into the lintel spell its name: *Weyward*. A strange name for a house. The familiar word with the odd spelling, as if it's been twisted away from itself.

The front door looks done-in, the dark green paint peeling from the bottom in ribbons. The old-fashioned lock is large and cobwebbed. She fumbles for the keys in her handbag. The jangling sound cuts through the morning quiet and something rustles in the shrubbery next to the house, making her jump. Kate hasn't set foot inside since she was a child – way back, when her father was still alive. Her memories of the cottage – and her great-aunt – are dim, shadowy. Still, she's surprised by the fear in her gut. It's just a house, after all. And she's got nowhere else to go.

She takes a breath, goes inside.

The hallway is narrow and low-ceilinged. A cloud of dust

rises from the floor with each step, as if in greeting. The walls are lined with pale green wallpaper, almost hidden by framed sketches of insects and animals. She flinches at a particularly lifelike rendition of a giant hornet. Her great-aunt had been an entomologist. Kate can't quite see the appeal, herself – she's not exactly fond of insects, or anything that flies. Not anymore.

She finds, at the back of the house, a threadbare living room, a wall of which comprises the kitchen. Blackened copper pots and twists of dried herbs hang above a range that looks centuries old. The furniture is handsome but weathered: a buckling green sofa, an oak table surrounded by a motley of mismatched chairs. Above a crumbling fireplace, the mantelpiece is littered with strange artefacts: a withered husk of honeycomb; the jewelled wings of a butterfly, preserved in glass. One corner of the ceiling is shrouded in cobwebs so thick they look intentionally cultivated.

She fills the rusted kettle with water and puts it on the hob while she searches through the cupboards for supplies. Behind tinned beans and jars of pale, pickled mysteries, she finds some teabags and an unopened packet of chocolate bourbons. She eats over the sink, looking out of the window to the bottom of the garden, where the beck glints gold in the dawn. The kettle sings. Clutching her mug of tea, she tracks back up the corridor to the bedroom, floorboards creaking underfoot.

The ceiling is even lower here than in the rest of the house: Kate needs to stoop. Through the window she can see the hills that ring the valley, dappled by clouds. The room is crowded with bookcases and furniture. A four-poster bed, piled high with ancient cushions. It occurs to her that this is probably the bed her great-aunt died in. She passed away in her sleep, the solicitor said – found by a local girl the next day. Briefly, she wonders if the bedding has been changed since, considers sleeping on the sagging sofa in the other room. But fatigue pulls at her, and she collapses on top of the covers.

When she wakes, she is confused by the unfamiliar shapes in the room. For a moment, she thinks she is back in the sterile bedroom of their London flat: that any minute Simon will be on top of her, inside her . . . then she remembers. Her pulse settles. The windows are blue with dusk. She checks the time on the Motorola: 6.33 p.m.

She thinks, with an acid wave of fear, of the iPhone she left behind. He could be looking through it right now . . . but she'd had no choice. And anyway, he'll find nothing he hasn't already seen before.

She isn't sure when he started monitoring her phone. Perhaps he's been doing it for years, without her realising. He'd always known the passcode, and she offered it up to him to inspect whenever he asked. But even so, last year, he'd become convinced she was having an affair.

'You're meeting someone, aren't you?' he'd snarled as he took her from behind, his fingers tight in her hair. 'At the fucking *library*.'

At first, she thought he'd hired a private investigator to follow her, but that didn't make sense. Because then he would know that she wasn't meeting anyone – she just went to the library to read, to escape into other people's imaginations. Often, she reread books she'd loved as a child, their familiarity a balm – *Grimms' Fairy Tales*, *The Chronicles of Narnia*, and her favourite, *The Secret Garden*. Sometimes, she would close her eyes and find herself not in bed with Simon, but among the tangled plants at Misselthwaite Manor, watching roses nod in the breeze.

Perhaps that was what he really had a problem with. That he could control her body, but not her mind.

Then there were other signs – like the row they'd had before Christmas. He knew, somehow, that she'd been looking at flights to Toronto, to see her mother. She realised that he'd installed spyware on her iPhone, something that allowed him to track not only her whereabouts, but her search history, her emails and texts. So when the solicitor called her last August about the cottage – her inheritance – she'd deleted the call log from her history and resolved to somehow get a second phone. A secret phone, that Simon would never know about.

It had taken her weeks to scrounge enough cash – Simon gave her an allowance, but she was only supposed to spend this on make-up and lingerie – to buy the Motorola. Only then had she been able to start planning. She'd had the solicitor deliver the keys to a PO box in Islington. Began hiding her allowance in the lining of her handbag, depositing it weekly into the bank account she'd opened in secret.

Even then, she wasn't sure whether she'd go through with it, whether she deserved it. Freedom.

Until Simon announced that he wanted a child. He was expecting a lucrative promotion at work – starting a family was the natural next step.

'You're not getting any younger,' he'd said. And then, with a sneer, 'Besides, it's not as if you have anything better to do.'

A chill had spread through her as she listened to him speak. It was one thing for *her* to endure this – to endure him. Spittle flying in her face, the burn of his hand against her skin. The ceaseless, brutal nights.

But a child?

She couldn't – wouldn't – be responsible for that.

For a while, she'd kept taking contraception, hiding the sheath of pink tablets inside a balled-up sock in her bedside table. Until Simon found it. He made her watch as he popped each pill from its blister pack, one by one, before flushing them down the toilet.

After that, it became more difficult. Waiting until he had fallen asleep to slip from the bed, crouching silent in the bathroom over the blue glow of her secret phone, she researched the old methods. The ones he wouldn't suspect. Lemon juice, which she stored in an old perfume bottle. The sting of it was almost pleasurable; it left her feeling clean. Pure.

As she planned her escape, greeting the monthly petals of blood in her underwear with relief, his rule tightened. He interrogated her endlessly about her daily movements and activities: had she taken a detour, spoken to anyone else, when she collected his shirts from the dry cleaner? Had she flirted with the man who delivered their groceries? He even monitored what she ate, stocking the kitchen with kale and supplements, as if she were a prize ewe being fattened up for lambing.

It didn't stop him from hurting her, though – from twisting her hair around his knuckles, from biting her breasts. She doubted he wanted a baby for its own sake. His need to possess her had grown so insatiable that it was no longer enough to mark her body on the outside.

Swelling her womb with his seed would be the ultimate form of dominance. The ultimate control.

And so she found a grim satisfaction in watching a green swirl of kale disappear down the toilet, the same way her birth control pills had. In smiling slyly at a delivery man. But these small acts of rebellion were dangerous. He tried to catch her in a deceit, laying verbal traps as deftly as if he were a lawyer questioning a witness in court.

'You said you would collect the dry cleaning at 2 p.m.,' he'd say, his breath hot on her face. 'But the receipt is time-stamped for 3 p.m. Why did you lie to me?'

Sometimes his cross-examinations lasted an hour, some-times even longer.

Lately, he'd threatened to confiscate her keys, declaring that she couldn't be trusted during the long hours when she was alone in the gleaming prison of their flat.

The net was closing. And a baby would bind her to him forever.

Which was why yesterday, the future – with its distant promise of freedom – seemed to drain away as she huddled in the bathroom, watching dye spread across a pregnancy test. The tiles were cold against her skin. The whirr of a fly batting itself against the window mingled with her own ragged breaths to form an unreal music. 'This can't be happening,' she said out loud. There was no one to answer.

Twenty minutes later, she ripped a second test from its packaging, but the result was the same.

Positive.

Don't think about that now, she tells herself. But she still can't believe it – the whole drive up, she itched to pull over and open the cardboard box she'd stowed in her bag, just to check that she hadn't imagined those two blurred lines.

She had tried so hard. But in the end, none of it mattered. He had got his way.

Nausea roils in her, furs the roof of her mouth. She shivers, swallows. Tries to focus on the here and now. She's safe. That's all that matters. Safe, but freezing. She heads for the other room, wondering if the fireplace is functional. There's a stack of firewood next to it, and a box of matches on the mantelpiece. The first match refuses to light. So does the second. Even though she's hundreds of miles away from him, his voice is loud in her head: *Pathetic. Can't do anything right.* Her fingers tremble, but she tries again. She grins at the sight of the small blue flame, the orange sparks.

The sparks grow into flames, and Kate stretches out her hands to warm them, before thick smoke billows into the room. Chest heaving, she grabs the kettle from the range and flings water on top of the fire. Once it is out, her insides grow cold. Perhaps the voice is right. Perhaps she *is* pathetic.

But she's come this far, hasn't she? She can do this. Rationally, she knows, now that her breathing has slowed, that something must be blocking the chimney. A fire poker leans against the fireplace. Perfect. On all fours, eyes stinging from smoke, she shoves the poker up the chimney and feels it connect with something, something soft . . .

She screams when the dark bundle tumbles down, screams again when she sees it's the body of a bird. Ash quivers on feathers the colour of petrol. A crow. The bright bead of its eye follows her as she recoils. She doesn't like birds, with their flapping wings and sharp beaks. Has avoided them since childhood. For a moment, she resents her great-aunt for having lived in – of all the places on God's green earth – *Crows Beck*.

But this crow is dead. It can't hurt her. She needs a bag, some newspaper or something, to dispose of it. She's almost out of the door when she feels a shiver of movement in the room. Turning, she watches in horror as the bird takes flight, risen like some sort of corvine Lazarus. Kate opens the window and frantically brandishes the poker at the crow until it flies out. She slams the window shut and runs from the room. The sound of its beak tapping on the windowpane follows her down the corridor.

5

VIOLET

Violet straightened her green dress as she followed Father and Cecil out of the dining room. She'd barely been able to eat a thing, and not just because Mrs Kirkby had made rabbit pie (she had tried not to think of silky ears and delicate pink noses as she chewed). Father had asked her to accompany him to the drawing room after dinner. The drawing room – furnished in oppressive dark tartans – was where Father enjoyed his postprandial glass of port and silence, observed by the stuffed head of an ibex that hung over the chimney-piece. Women were forbidden (apart from Mrs Kirkby, who had lit an unseasonable fire in the grate).

'Close the door,' Father said once they were inside. As she swung the door shut, Violet saw Graham glower at her from the corridor. *He* had never been invited to the drawing room. Though perhaps that was a good thing. Violet turned back to Father and saw that his face had taken on the ashen hue that usually signalled grave displeasure. Her stomach flipped.

Father stalked over to the drinks trolley, where crystal decanters sparkled in the firelight. He poured himself a generous glass of port before sinking into an armchair. The leather squeaked as he crossed his legs. He did not invite her to sit down (though the only other chair in the room, an austere wing-back, was rather too close to the fire – and Cecil – to be inviting).

'Violet,' Father said, crinkling his nose as though her name offended him in some way.

'Yes, Father?' Violet hated how thin her voice sounded. She swallowed, wondering what she had done wrong. He normally only bothered to discipline her when Graham was around. Otherwise, she largely escaped his notice. For the second time that day, she thought of the incident with the bees and winced.

He leaned over to stoke the fire violently, so that it spat pale ash onto the richly patterned Turkey carpet. Cecil yelped, then began to growl in Violet's direction, deducing that she must be the cause of his master's displeasure. A vein jumped at Father's temple. He was silent for so long that Violet was beginning to wonder whether she could just creep out of the drawing room without him noticing.

'We need to discuss your behaviour,' he said, finally.

Her cheeks grew hot with panic.

'My behaviour?'

'Yes,' Father said. 'Miss Poole tells me that you have been . . . *climbing trees*.' He spoke the last two words slowly and clearly, as if he couldn't quite believe what he was saying. 'Apparently, you ripped your skirt. I'm told it is . . . ruined.'

He stared into the fire, frowning.

Violet twisted her hands, which were by now slick with sweat. She hadn't even noticed the tear – snaking the full length of the wool skirt – until Nanny Metcalfe had collected it for the wash. The skirt was ancient, anyway, and far too long, with horridly prissy pleats. Secretly, she was glad to be rid of it.

'I'm . . . I'm sorry, Father.'

His frown deepened, creasing his forehead. Violet looked to the window, forgetting that the black-out curtains were drawn. A fly buffeted its tiny body against the fabric in desperate search of the outside world. The whirr of its wings filled Violet's ears and she didn't hear what Father said next.

'What?' she said.

'*"I beg your pardon, Father."*'

'I beg your pardon, Father?' she repeated, still watching the fly.

'I was saying that you have one last chance to conduct yourself appropriately, as befits my daughter. Your cousin Frederick is coming to stay with us next month, on leave from the front.' He paused and Violet braced herself for a sermon.

Father often talked about his time fighting in the Great War. Every November he made Graham polish his medals in preparation for Armistice Day, when he had the entire household gather in the first sitting room for the minute of silence. Afterwards, he gave a repetitive speech about valour and sacrifice that seemed to get longer every year.

'Knows nowt about real fighting,' Violet had heard Dinsdale, the gardener, mutter to Mrs Kirkby once after a particularly long address. 'Spent most of his time in the officers' mess with a bottle of port, I'd wager.' Father had seemed almost gleeful when war was again declared in 1939. He had immediately commanded that Graham and Violet set about gathering conkers from the horse chestnut trees that lined the drive. Apparently, the round seeds, glossy as rubies, were bound to be indispensable in the production of the bombs that would explode all over Germany and 'send the Boche to kingdom come'. Graham collected hundreds of the things, but Violet couldn't bear to think of the beautiful seeds coming to such a grisly end. She secretly buried them in the garden, hoping that they would grow anew. Fortunately, Father soon lost enthusiasm for the war – kept from enlisting by a gammy knee and 'duties to the estate' – and forgot all about this assignment.

But there was no martial sermon tonight. 'I expect you to be on your best behaviour around Frederick,' Father continued instead. Violet thought this was all very odd. She couldn't remember ever hearing about a cousin called Frederick – or any cousin at all, for that matter. Father never spoke of any relations – not even his parents and older brother, who had died in an accident before she was born. This subject too was forbidden – she had once received three stinging raps on the hand for asking about it. 'Consider it . . . a test. If you fail to conduct yourself appropriately during his visit, then . . . I'll have no choice but to send you away. For your own good.'

'Away?'

'To finishing school. You'll need to learn to behave properly if you're to have any chance of making a match. If you can't show me that you're capable of comporting yourself like the young lady you are, there are several institutions that may be suitable for the task. And where none of this gallivanting around outdoors, collecting grubby leaves and twigs like some sort of *savage* will be permitted.' He lowered his voice. 'Perhaps they can stop you from turning out like . . . *her*.'

'Her?' Violet's heart fluttered. Did he mean her mother?

But Father ignored her question. 'That's all,' he said, looking up at her for the first time. 'Good night.'

There was a strange expression on his face. As if he were looking at her but seeing someone else.

Violet waited until she was safely alone in her bedroom before she let the tears fall. She wept quietly as she changed into her nightdress and got into bed. After a while, she tried to steady her breathing, but it was no good. The air in her little room tasted stale, and – not for the first time – she had the feeling that she was as out of place in the Hall as a fish would be in the clouds. She longed for the sturdy embrace of the beech tree, for the night breeze on her skin.

The snippet of conversation she'd overheard when she was younger rang in her ears.

So much like the young lady, not just in looks.

Had her mother been like this, too? Had nature pulled at her heart the same way it pulled at Violet's now?

And what could possibly be so wrong with that?

Sighing, she kicked off the coverlet. After turning out the lamp, she crept over to the window, pushed aside the horrid black-out curtain and opened the sash.

The moon shone like a pearl in the dusky sky, lighting up the cragged hills. There was a gentle wind, and Violet heard the trees shift and murmur. She closed her eyes, listening to the hoot of an owl, the flap of a bat's wings, a badger rustling on the way to its burrow.

This was home. Not the Hall, with its dingy corridors and endless tartan and the threat of Father hulking around every corner.

But if she were sent away . . . she might never see any of it again. The owls, the bats, the badgers. The old beech that she loved, and its village of insects.

Instead, she'd be cloistered indoors, and forced to learn all manner of useless conversational skills and rules of etiquette. All so that Father could offer her up to some grizzled old baron or another – as if she were something to be bartered with for favours.

Or something to be rid of.

But no – he *wouldn't* send her away. She wouldn't let him. When she left Orton Hall – she imagined herself moving deftly through a jungle; brushing against ferns dripping with beetles – it would be on her own terms. Not Father's, nor anyone else's.

She'd be here, she vowed to herself, not at some horrible finishing school, when winter came to take the leaves from the trees. She would even stay inside, if that was what it took. Just until the visit from the dullard relative was over. That would show Father how well behaved she could be.

6

KATE

Kate burrows under the duvet to muffle the *clink* of beak on glass, waiting for the crow to give up its assault on the window. She takes deep, shuddering breaths, gagging on the musty scent of the bedding. Eventually, the sound fades, and she imagines that she can hear the cut of wings through air as the crow flies away. Her breathing settles, the thrum of her pulse slows.

She lifts her head and looks about the room: the stooped ceiling, the green-painted walls that are almost convex with age, closing in. Framed photographs stare down at her, along with sketches – all of animals, insects, birds. One image looks three-dimensional; sculptural, almost: a tawny snake, gleaming beneath its glass frame. Struck by its russet glimmer, she takes a closer look. It isn't a snake at all, she sees, but the preserved body of a centipede: shining wetly in thick segments, caught forever in glass.

She shudders as she reads aloud the curling script on the frame, the words strange as a spell.

'*Scolopendra gigantea.*'

The thick silence makes her dizzy. Sick, almost, with the

unfamiliar feeling of freedom. It sits uneasily, like rough cloth against her skin. It needs adjusting to.

This is the longest she's gone without speaking to Simon since they met six years ago, when she was twenty-three. Thinking of that first night makes something in her stomach hurt. She can see herself clearly: impossibly young and shy, standing with her friends in a pub in London. Though she wonders now if 'friends' was ever the right word for the women she met at university. She never managed to match her speech to the cadence of theirs, never quite correctly timed a joke or a laugh. It's a feeling she's had since childhood: that she is somehow separate, closed off from everyone else.

The feeling of separateness had been particularly strong that night, because her mother had just moved to Canada with her new husband, leaving Kate all alone. It was no more than she deserved, but it still hurt. She remembers looking down into her pint glass, full of the heavy, sour ale she pretended to like, trying to think of an excuse for leaving early.

She'd looked up, with the idea of heading to the toilets for a reprieve, when she'd seen him. It was his posture she'd first admired. The easy, leonine grace with which he leaned against the bar as he surveyed the room. Flushing with surprise and pleasure, she had realised that he was looking at her. A deep, primal part of her had recognised something in his slow, sensuous smile when their eyes met. Had known what would happen, even then.

There's a rushing sensation inside her skull, and Kate shuts her eyes.

She breathes deeply and listens. If she were in the flat, she'd be able to hear traffic, the laughter of the post-work crowd drinking outside the pub on the corner, a plane rumbling overhead. The double glazing on their trendy

Hoxton high-rise was no match for the soundscape of London, for the hum of eight million lives.

But here there are no cars, no planes roaring overhead, no distant drone from a neighbour's television. Here there is just . . . silence. She can't tell if she likes it or finds it eerie. If she strains, she thinks she can hear the distant babble of the beck, vegetation rustling with the local nightlife. Caterpillars, stoats, owls. Though of course that isn't possible. She draws back the faded curtains from the window and sees that it is securely shut. There's no way her hearing is that good. She's imagining things, like she used to as a child. 'Come down from those clouds,' her parents used to say, catching her in one of her reveries. 'And while you're here, do your homework!'

But she never listened.

No matter where they were, she was always letting things distract her . . . a worm, glimmering pink in the sand at the playground; a squirrel, streaking up a tree on Hampstead Heath. The birds, nesting in the eaves of their house.

If only she'd listened.

She was nine the day it happened. Her father was walking her to school – a summer morning; hazy with heat. They took their usual route, a road shaded with lush oak trees, their leaves dappling the light green. Her father held her hand as they approached the pedestrian crossing, reminding her to look both ways, to pay special attention to the blind corner on the left, where the road curved away in a sharp bend.

They were halfway across the road when a bird call tugged her back, pulling at some strange, secret part of her. A crow, she thought, from its husky caw – she had already learned to recognise most of the birds that sang in her parents' garden, and crows were her favourite. There was something intelligent – almost human – about their sly voices and dark, luminous eyes.

Kate turned, scanning the trees that lined the road behind them. And there it was: a velvet flash of black, shocking against the lurid green and blue of the June day. A crow, just as she'd thought. Pulling her hand free of her father's, she ran towards it, watching as it took flight.

A shadow fell across the road. There was a distant roar, and then a monster – the kind that she pretended she was too old to believe in, with red scales and silver teeth – appeared around the corner, bearing down on her.

Her father reached her just in time. He shoved her, hard, onto the grassy verge. There was a sound like paper ripping, like the air tearing in two. She watched, stunned, as the monster ploughed into him.

Slow, then fast, he fell.

Later, when the emergency services had arrived – two ambulances and a police car, a convoy of death – Kate saw something gold on the tarmac.

It was her bee brooch, the one she always carried in her pocket. It must have fallen out when her father shoved her away, saving her from the monster – the monster that she now knew was really just a car, with chipped red paint and a rusted grille. She looked around and saw the driver, a thin-shouldered man, sobbing in the back of one of the ambulances.

A stretcher bearing something black and shiny was being loaded into the other ambulance. It took her a moment to realise that the thing on the stretcher was her father; that she would never again see his smile, the crinkles around his eyes. He was gone.

I killed my father, she thought. *I am the monster.*

She picked up the brooch and turned it over in her hand. There were ugly gaps like missing teeth where it had lost some of its crystals. One wing was dented.

She put it back in her pocket as a reminder of what she had done.

From that day on, she kept away from the squirrels and the worms, from the forest and the gardens. Birds in particular were to be avoided. Nature – and the glow of fascination it had always sparked in her – was too dangerous.

She was too dangerous.

As her fascination turned to fear, she stayed inside, putting herself behind glass. Just like her great-aunt's framed centipede. And she didn't let anyone in.

Until she met Simon.

In the cottage, she chokes down tears. Her throat feels parched and narrow. She can't remember when she last had a drink: she needs some water, something. Vodka would be better, but her aunt's spirits collection – crammed into the kitchen cupboard along with jars of instant coffee and Ovaltine – hasn't yielded anything so pedestrian, only unfamiliar words curled on yellowed labels: *arak, slivovitz, soju*. Languages Kate doesn't even recognise. And anyway – she's not sure it's a good idea. She remembers the chardonnay, with its stink of rot. The decision she has to make, about the baby, sits heavy inside her.

The shadowy shapes of the kitchen loom out at her in the second before she switches on the light. She averts her eyes from the pale rope of cobwebs hanging from the ceiling and turns to the chipped enamel sink.

Taking a mug from the rack on the windowsill, her knuckles brush against something: a jam jar full of feathers. White and delicate, tawny red. The largest is glossy and black – almost blue with iridescence. Looking closer, she sees that it is speckled with white, as though it has been dipped in snow. Just like the crow from the fireplace, which, she realises now, was flecked not with ash but with similar white marks. Perhaps it is some sort of disease that afflicts the crows around here? The thought spikes the hairs on the back of her neck. She turns on the tap, gulps the water down as if it could cleanse her, from the inside out.

Afterwards, she takes a moment to look out of the window. She can see the moon clearly, so full that she can make out the dips and ridges of its craters. It casts its yellow light on the ramshackle garden, landing on the leaves of the plants, on the branches of the oaks and sycamores. She is looking at the trees, wondering how old they are, when she sees them . . . move.

She can feel her heart beating in her ears. Her breathing grows shallow, the panic washing over her like a tide. Then, as she watches, dark shapes – hundreds of them, it seems – rise from the trees in unison, as if pulled by a puppeteer's string. Silhouetted against the moon.

Birds.

7

ALTHA

The guards took me down a cramped stone staircase to the dungeon. If the castle had swallowed me, now it had me in its bowels; for here it was even darker than where they'd held me in the village.

My gut churned between hunger and sickness, thirst clawing at my throat. My heart hammered at the sight of the heavy wooden door. I was already so weak. I did not know how much longer I would last.

But they gave me provisions, this time, before they locked me away – a thin blanket, a pot and a pitcher of water. And an old hunk of bread, which I ate slowly, biting off tiny amounts and chewing until the saliva flooded my mouth.

I only took note of my surroundings once I had eaten my fill, my shrunken stomach cramping. They had given me no candle, but there was a small grate set high in the wall, letting in the last embers of the day.

The stone walls felt cold to the touch, and when I took my fingers away, they were damp. A dripping sound came from somewhere, echoing like a warning.

The straw beneath my feet was sodden, mouldering; the

sweet rot mingling with the reek of old piss. There was another smell, too. I thought of all who had been held there before me, growing pale as mushrooms in the dark, awaiting their fate. It was their fear I could smell, as if it had bled into the air, seeped into the stone.

The fear hummed within me, gave me strength for what I had to do.

I pulled up my shift so that my belly met with the chill air. Then, gritting my teeth I began to scratch; fingernails tearing at the tiny bauble of flesh below my ribcage. Below my heart.

Just when I was sure that I could bear the pain no longer, I felt flesh come away, then the thick wetness of blood, its sweet tang filling the air. I wished that I had honey, or some thyme, to make a poultice for the wound; instead, I made do with some water from the pitcher. When I had cleaned it as best I could, I lay down and drew the blanket over me. The straw did little against the stone floor, and my bones rang with the cold.

Only then did I allow myself to think of home: my little rooms, neat and bright with jars and vials; the moths that danced round my candles at night. And outside, my garden. My heart ached at the thought of my plants and flowers, my dear nanny goat who kept me in milk and comfort, the sycamore that sheltered me with its boughs. For the first time since they'd torn me from my pallet, I let myself sob. I wondered if I would die of the loneliness, before they had the chance to hang me. But at that moment, something brushed my skin, as delicate as a kiss. It was a spider, its legs and pincers blue with moonlight. My new friend crawled into the hollow between my neck and shoulder, clinging to my hair. I thanked it for its presence, which did more to lift my spirit than even the bread and water.

As I watched a moonbeam dance through the grate, I

wondered who would give testimony against me the next
day. Then I thought of Grace.

I was sure I would never sleep. But it seemed the thought
had barely left my mind when I was woken by the creak of
the door swinging open. The spider scuttled away at the burn
of torchlight, and my heart lurched at the sight of a man in
Lancaster livery. Court would begin shortly, he said. I was to
make myself presentable.

He gave me a kirtle, spun of rough cloth and smelling of
sweat. I did not like to think who had worn it before me,
where they were now. I winced at the feel of the cloth against
my wound, but when the man returned, I was glad that I
had on a proper dress, even if it was crudely made. I wished
I had a cap, or something to neaten my hair with, for it hung
about my face in rags. Adding to my shame.

My mother always taught me that cleanliness commands
respect, and that respect was worth more than all the king's
gold – to us, especially, seeing as we often had little of either.
We had washed every week. No smell of curdled sweat hung
around the Weyward women, not even in high summer.
Instead, we smelled of lavender, for protection. I wished I
had some lavender now. But all I had were my wits, dulled
as they were by lack of proper food and sleep.

The man shackled me for the short walk from the dungeon
to the courtroom. I stopped myself from flinching at the shock
of the cold metal on my skin, and held my head high as we
walked up the stairs and into the courtroom.

The prosecutor rose from his seat and walked towards the
bench, where the judges sat. His footsteps on the boards
drove fear into my heart, and I shook in the awful silence
before his speech.

Still, I was unprepared for the horror of his words. His
pale eyes burned as he denounced me as a dangerous,

malicious witch, in thrall to Satan himself. I had, he said, engaged in the most hellish practice of witchcraft and sorcery, to take the life of Master John Milburn, him being an innocent and God-fearing yeoman. His voice grew louder as he spoke, until it rang like a death knell in my skull.

He turned and spat the closing words at me. 'I have confidence', he said, 'that the gentlemen of this jury of life and death shall find you as you are. Guilty.'

And then, to the court:

'I call the first examinate to give evidence against the accused.'

The blood rushed in my ears when I saw who the guards escorted to the box.

Grace Milburn.

8

VIOLET

Violet was on her best behaviour.

All week, she had been focused and diligent in her lessons. Miss Poole was thrilled that she had finally grasped the French pluperfect tense and said that her drawing of a vase of irises was *exquisite*. Violet thought that the blue flowers looked like corpses, with their wilting heads and drooping leaves. Miss Poole had picked them. Violet didn't believe in picking flowers, in snapping their stems for no reason other than to look at them. But she kept her mouth shut and drew their likeness as best she could.

She even made some crooked progress on the silk slip that Miss Poole insisted she sew for her 'trousseau'. (She couldn't for the life of her think why such a thing was necessary. Nanny Metcalfe was the only person who had ever seen her in her 'combinations' – as the nursemaid rather archaically called them – and Violet intended for matters to stay that way.)

Determined to avoid the purgatory of finishing school, she had stayed inside for two weeks now. Two weeks since she had felt the kiss of an insect's wings against her skin. Two weeks since she'd climbed her beloved beech, since she'd

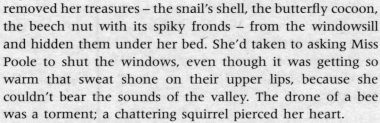

removed her treasures – the snail's shell, the butterfly cocoon, the beech nut with its spiky fronds – from the windowsill and hidden them under her bed. She'd taken to asking Miss Poole to shut the windows, even though it was getting so warm that sweat shone on their upper lips, because she couldn't bear the sounds of the valley. The drone of a bee was a torment; a chattering squirrel pierced her heart.

But gradually, the sounds faded away. She was glad of it.

Even Goldie seemed to lose interest in her. Normally, she could hear the faint *click* of his legs as he climbed out of the hatbox and scuttled about the room at night – sometimes she even woke to find him nestled safe in her hair – but now there was just silence. She worried that he'd died but couldn't bring herself to look.

Most days, when she wasn't attending to what Miss Poole dubbed her 'improvements', Violet lay on her bed with the curtains drawn, sweating in the dark heat. Mrs Kirkby began bringing trays to her room: first, elaborate fruit pies and cakes, towering with cream, and when those went untouched, bowls of bland nursery food. Nanny Metcalfe even came in one afternoon and asked if she wouldn't like her to read aloud, something she hadn't done since Violet was small.

'There was that book of tales you loved,' she said. 'Brothers Slim, or summat—'

'Grimm. The Brothers Grimm,' Violet said. She had loved them, it was true, even if Nanny Metcalfe had pronounced half the words wrong. 'I'm much too old for that now, Nanny.' She turned to face the wall. She could see a chink of golden light on the floral wallpaper.

She heard the rustle of Nanny Metcalfe's dress as she bent over Violet's bed.

'Do you need—'

'Can you draw the curtains more closely together, please, Nanny?' she asked, cutting the nurse's questions off.

'All right, Miss Violet,' she said. 'If you're sure.'

Violet bit her lip. She just had to get through this visit from Father's relative. She had to show him that he didn't need to send her away to some stuffy old school. Then she could go outside again. Until then, all she needed was to be left alone.

That evening, as Violet drifted between sleep and wakefulness, she heard Nanny Metcalfe and Mrs Kirkby muttering outside her door. Mrs Kirkby had come to collect another tray of uneaten food.

'I've never seen a person take to their bed like this, without being ill,' Nanny Metcalfe said. 'But there's nowt wrong with her that I can find. No fever, no rash . . .'

'I have,' said Mrs Kirkby. 'The late mistress took to her bed, not long before the end.'

'Why? Nerves?'

'That's what Doctor Radcliffe said. The master had him come out, the first time, on condition of secrecy.'

'Could he say what triggered it?'

'He didn't need to. We all knew the reason. Especially after what happened next.'

Perhaps they can stop you from turning out like her.

The next afternoon, while Violet sat limp in the schoolroom, embroidering with Miss Poole, Nanny Metcalfe burst through the door.

'The Master wants Miss Violet to take the air,' she said.

Miss Poole looked at the clock, a frown accentuating her reptilian features.

'But we've only just started our needlepoint lesson,' she said.

'Master's orders,' said Nanny Metcalfe.

'I'd rather stay inside,' said Violet, looking down at her

fingers on the canvas. Her hands, like the rest of her, had grown pale from lack of sun. Her fingernails were speckled and thin, as if they might peel away. Could you die, Violet wondered, from longing?

'Well, Violet, if your father wants you to, perhaps you should,' said Miss Poole. 'But you can continue with your needlepoint after dinner. I'm so very pleased with your enthusiasm. Where has *this* Violet been hiding?'

Nanny Metcalfe offered Violet her arm as they made their way around the grounds. The gardens were bright with flowers – blue spikes of hyacinth, fleshy whorls of rhododendrons – so bright that she averted her eyes and looked down at her feet in their leather brogues.

'Isn't it lovely to be outside, listening to the birds?' Nanny Metcalfe said.

'Yes,' she said. 'Lovely.'

But she couldn't hear the birds. In fact, she could barely hear anything at all, other than Nanny Metcalfe's voice. It was as if her ears were wrapped in wool.

A butterfly passed them. Out of habit, Violet lifted her hand, but instead of coming to rest on her palm, it flew on, like she wasn't even there.

'Your father would like you to take your tea downstairs this evening, in the dining room with himself and Graham,' said Nanny Metcalfe.

'Very well,' said Violet faintly, watching the butterfly until it was no more than a white flash in the corner of her vision.

'Nanny,' she said, pausing as she tried to word the question that had worried at her for days. 'Was there something wrong with my mother?'

'Your mother? Don't know where that's come from. Violet, I've said it before and I'll say it again: I barely knew her ladyship, rest her soul.'

But Violet saw that Nanny Metcalfe's cheeks had reddened.

'And . . . what about me? Is there something wrong with me?'

'Here, pet,' Nanny Metcalfe said, turning to look at her. 'Wherever would you get an idea like that?'

'Just something Father said. And I'm not allowed in the village, but Graham is. And – until this cousin – no one has ever come to call.'

People were always calling on each other in novels, Violet had learned. And it wasn't as if there was a shortage of nearby families of similar status, who might be disposed to friendship. Why, Baron Seymour lived only 30 miles from Orton Hall *and* had a son and a daughter of equivalent ages to Graham and Violet. She had once looked them up in Father's battered copy of *Burke's Peerage*.

'Och, your father's just overprotective, that's all. Don't you pay him any mind. Here, we'd better be getting back so you can have your bath.' Her words made Violet feel very small, as if she were six instead of sixteen.

Violet didn't brush her hair before supper, and wore her least favourite dress, an ill-fitting orange gingham. She knew it made her look sallow and drawn, but she didn't care.

Mrs Kirkby set a shrunken joint of roast mutton on the table. Violet hated mutton, though she knew from Father's lectures that they were rather lucky to have it at all. Still, she tried not to picture the gentle, cloud-soft sheep that had given its life for their meal.

She looked at her plate. The meat was grey and lumpish, the sort of thing Father would never have eaten before the war. Watery blood leaked from its flesh, staining her potatoes pink. She felt as if she might be sick.

She put her knife and fork down, before realising that Father was watching her. A fleck of gravy quivered at the corner of his frown.

'Eat up, girl,' he said. 'Follow your brother's example.'

Graham, whose plate was already nearly empty, flushed. Father helped himself to more gravy.

'You will recall,' he began, 'that your cousin Frederick is coming to stay with us tomorrow. He's an officer in the Eighth Army, taking leave from the fighting in Tobruk. Do you know where Tobruk is, Graham?'

'No, Father,' said Graham.

'It's in Libya,' said Father between mouthfuls. Violet could see strings of meat in his teeth when he talked. The urge to vomit returned. She trained her eyes on the painting hanging on the wall behind him – the portrait of some long-dead viscount, looking on imperiously from the eighteenth century.

'Godforsaken place,' Father continued. 'Full of savages.' He shook his head. Violet flinched as she felt something brush against her leg. Pretending to drop her napkin, she peered under the table in time to see Father deliver Cecil a swift kick to the rump. 'Those wops haven't a clue what they're doing out there. They couldn't govern a sandbar.'

The maid, Penny, began clearing the plates to make room for pudding. Eton mess, a favourite of Father's, who never lost an opportunity to remind Graham that he had expected him to follow in his Etonian footsteps. (Graham had not got into Eton. He was on summer break from Harrow.)

'Your cousin', said Father, 'is risking his life every day, fighting for his country. I expect you to treat him with the utmost respect when he arrives. Is that clear, children?'

'Yes, Father,' said Graham.

'Yes,' she said.

'Violet,' Father said, 'you will not hide in your bedroom. Such laziness disrespects the soldiers fighting hard for King and country and is unbecoming of a woman. I expect you to maintain a cheerful presence around the Hall and be gracious towards your cousin. Understood?'

'Yes,' she said.

'You will recall what we discussed,' he said.

'Yes, Father.'

After supper, Violet finished her needlepoint lesson with Miss Poole. When they were done, she sat for a while, looking longingly out of the window. It was very bright for seven o'clock. Normally, she'd spend an evening like this outdoors, sitting under her beech tree with a book, perhaps; or down by the beck, sketching the frothy white plumes of angelica that grew there.

But with her voluntary confinement still in effect, there was not much for Violet to do other than to go up to bed. On her way to the staircase, she passed the library. Perhaps she would try to read in her room. She went inside, and from the very bottom shelf in the corner, she picked up a book with a red leather jacket, the front cover embossed with gold script: *Children's and Household Tales* by The Brothers Grimm.

She tucked it under one arm and continued upstairs to her bedroom, where she saw there was a little glass jar on her coverlet, glinting in the evening sun. Something was moving inside it.

It was a damselfly. Whoever had put it there had poked holes in the lid of the jar. A note had been fastened to the lid with a green ribbon tied in a clumsy bow. Violet opened the note and saw that it was from Graham.

Dear Violet, he had written in neat, Harrovian script. *Get well soon. Best wishes, your brother Graham.* She smiled to herself. It was like something the old Graham would have done.

She opened the jar, hoping the insect would come to rest on her hand. Instead, it flew towards the window, fast, like it was afraid of her. It seemed to Violet to make barely a sound. She opened the window to let it out, quickly shutting it again. The fleeting happiness brought by Graham's gift evaporated.

She drew the black-out curtains, blocking out the view of the pink setting sun, turned on the bedside lamp and got into bed.

Dust fell from the pages when she opened them, at random, at the story of 'The Robber Bridegroom'.

It was a grisly story – much grislier than she had remembered. A man was so desperate to marry off his daughter that he had her betrothed to a murderer. The only saving grace was that the girl managed to outsmart him, with the help of an old witch. In the end, the bridegroom was put to death, along with his band of robbers. Serves them right, she thought.

Abandoning the book, she took off her necklace, reaching over to put it on the bedside cabinet. She sighed at the clink and rustle of it slipping onto the floor. Violet peered over the edge of the bed but couldn't see its gold glint; perhaps it had rolled underneath. Cursing, she climbed out from the covers and crouched on the floor, groping for the necklace. Her fingers came away empty, grimed with dust. Had it fallen behind the cabinet, somehow? She should have been paying closer attention. A chill gripped her heart at the thought of losing the necklace. It was true – as Nanny Metcalfe had commented more than once – that it was ugly; misshapen and blackened with age. But it was all she had of her mother.

Violet grunted with effort as she moved the cabinet, wincing at the sound of it scraping across the floorboards. Her pulse slowed when she spotted the necklace, the links of its chain threaded through with great ropes of dust. She couldn't recall the last time her room had been properly cleaned: Penny, the maid, only seemed to give it a cursory mop once a week. Guilt tugged at her stomach. She knew Penny was a little afraid of her, ever since Violet had convinced her to peer into Goldie's hatbox. She'd only wanted to show Penny the pretty gold stripes on his legs. She couldn't have known that the maid – who, it transpired, had a horror of spiders – would faint clean away.

Violet bent down to retrieve the necklace and was just about to move the cabinet back again when she noticed something. There was a letter, scratched into the white paint of the wainscoting, half hidden by a spool of fluff. It was a *W* – the same letter engraved on the pendant she gripped in her hand. Gently brushing away the dust, she uncovered more letters, which looked as if they had been painstakingly etched with a pin, or – she shuddered – a fingernail. Together, the letters formed a word which was somehow familiar, like a long-lost friend, though she had no recollection of ever seeing it before.

Weyward.

9

KATE

Kate grabs her bag and runs to the car.

In the rear-view mirror, she sees that the birds – crows, she thinks – are still ascending, higher than the bone-yellow moon, the night shimmering with their cries.

'Don't look, don't look,' she says to herself, her breath misting in the chill air of the car. Her palms are slippery with sweat and she wipes them on her jeans so that she can turn the key in the ignition. The engine jolts into life and she reverses onto the road, heart pounding.

There are no streetlights, and she flicks on the high beams as she speeds down the winding lanes. Her breathing is shallow, her fingers tense as claws on the steering wheel. She half expects the headlights to reveal something menacing and otherworldly lurking around each corner.

She makes it to the slip road. If she keeps driving, she could be back in London by morning. But then, where would she go? Back to the flat? Staring down the barrel of the motorway, she remembers what happened the first time.

The first time she tried to leave.

*

It had been soon after they'd started living together. Another argument about her job in children's publishing – he'd wanted her to quit, said she couldn't deal with the stress. She'd had a panic attack at work, during the weekly acquisition meeting. Simon had picked her up and brought her home, then sat across from her in their living room with its glittering view, haloed by the sun like some terrible angel. His words crashed over her – she couldn't cope, he didn't have time to deal with this, there was no point in her working when he earned so much. It was a useless job, anyway – what was the value in a bunch of women nattering about made-up stories for children? Besides, she obviously wasn't very good at it – after all, she barely brought home a quarter of his salary.

It was this last statement that did it – that sparked some forgotten fire in her. And so she looked him in the eye and said what she hadn't been able to tell the kindly colleagues who'd brought her tissues and a cup of tea, as she'd recovered at her desk.

Work wasn't the problem; Simon was. His face darkened. For a moment he was still, and Kate's breath caught in her throat. Without a word, he threw his cup of coffee at her. She turned her face away just in time, but the boiling liquid splashed her left arm, leaving a pink line of scalded skin.

It was the first time he had hurt her. Later, it would scar.

That night, he'd begged her not to go as she'd packed her things, telling her he was sorry, it would never happen again, he couldn't live without her. She had wavered, even then.

But when the taxi arrived, she got in. It was the thing to do, wasn't it? She was, supposedly, an educated, self-respecting woman. She couldn't possibly stay.

The hotel – in Camden, she remembered; it had been all she'd been able to find (and afford) at such short notice – had been cold, with the musty stink of mice. The room overlooked the street and the window shook with every car that drove past. She lay sleepless until morning, watching the ceiling glow with the passing headlights, her phone vibrating with pleading texts, the burn on her arm throbbing.

She'd called in sick to work the next morning, spent the day wandering the markets, staring into the oily depths of the canal. Searching for resolve.

By the second night, she'd decided to leave him. But then came the voicemail.

'Kate,' he'd said, voice heavy with tears. 'I am so, so sorry that we fought. Please, come back. I can't live without you – I can't . . . I need you, Kate. Please. I – I've taken some pills . . .'

And just like that, her resolve evaporated. She couldn't do it. She couldn't let someone else die.

She phoned 999. As soon as she knew the paramedics were on their way, she called a taxi. On the drive back, she stared blankly out of the window as the neat terraced houses, gleaming dark in the rain, gave way to the images from her childhood nightmares. Black wings, beating the air. The tarmac glossy with blood.

I am the monster.

What if she was too late?

The yellow ambulance was parked on their street by the time she got there. She'd barely been able to breathe in the lift, had hated it for delaying her as it cranked slowly up the building.

The front door of their flat was open. Simon sat on the couch in his pyjamas, flanked by two female paramedics, pill bottles glinting on the coffee table in front of them. Unopened. Ice formed in her gut.

He hadn't taken them at all. He'd lied.

She stared. He looked up at her and the tears fell freely down his face.

'I'm so sorry, Kate,' he said, shoulders shaking. 'I was just . . . I was so scared that you would never come back.'

The paramedics didn't notice the blistered skin on Kate's arm. She walked them to the front door, promising she'd call 999 again if Simon displayed any more signs of suicidal ideation, agreeing not to leave him alone, to follow up on a referral to the local psychology team. Then she shut the door behind them carefully.

Simon got off the couch and walked towards her, until she felt his breath on the back of her neck. Together, they listened to the lift going down the shaft.

'I'm so sorry that I left,' said Kate, without turning around. 'Please promise me you'll never hurt yourself or do anything stupid again.'

Stupid.

She knew as soon as the word left her mouth that she'd made a mistake.

'Stupid?' Simon asked, keeping his voice low. He gripped the back of her neck tightly, before shoving her against the wall.

She resigned from the publishing house the next day. Surrendering not just her pay cheque and her sense of self, but her strongest link to the outside world. To the women who had made her feel valued, intelligent – like she was more than just his girlfriend, his plaything.

Kate switches off the indicator. She thinks of the cells knitting together inside her and is hit with a wave of nausea. If she goes back . . . if he finds out about the baby . . . he'll never let her leave.

She turns the car around.

The next morning, Kate walks to the village for supplies.

The early spring air is cool against her skin, with a smell of damp leaves and things growing. Kate shuts the front door and swallows burst from the old oak in the front garden. She flinches, then watches them pinwheel through the blue sky while she collects herself. The village is just 2 miles away. The walk will be invigorating, she tells herself. Maybe she'll even enjoy it.

She sets off down the lane, which is bordered by hedgerows fringed with unfamiliar white flowers that remind her of seafoam. There's the squawk of a crow, and her heart quickens. She looks up, craning her neck until she grows dizzy. Nothing. Just branches patterning an empty sky, their tiny green leaves quivering in the breeze. She walks on, passing an old farmhouse with a sunken roof. Sheep bleat in the surrounding fields.

Crows Beck looks as though it's barely changed for centuries: the only signs of modernisation are a BT phone box and a bus shelter. She passes the green, with its ancient well and another stone structure, a small hut with a heavy iron door. Perhaps it was the village jail, once upon a time. She shudders at the thought of being confined in such a small space, doom closing in.

Beyond the green is a cobbled square, hemmed in by buildings – a mishmash of stone and timber, some hunched beneath jutting Tudor gables. A few of them are shops: there's a greengrocer and a butcher, a post office. A medical centre, too. In the distance she sees the spire of the church, glowing red in the sun.

She hesitates in front of the greengrocer. Nerves jostle in her stomach: she hasn't been grocery shopping alone since . . . she can't remember when. Simon had arranged for their food to be delivered by a high-end grocery supplier on Sunday evenings. She tries to calm her rapid breathing with the thought that this time, she can buy anything she likes.

The trestle tables out the front of the shop heave with fresh produce. Rows and rows of apples, the air thick with their woody scent. Carrots, half hidden beneath great green fronds, pale mounds of cabbages.

Inside, the only other customer is a woman – middle-aged and flame-haired, a pink sweater clashing luridly. Kate smiles as she shuffles past her, stifles a cough at the strong smell of patchouli oil. She smiles back and Kate turns quickly, scrutinising a box of cereal. She is relieved when the woman leaves the shop, singing out a cheery goodbye to the cashier.

Kate pulls things from the shelves: bread, butter, coffee. She looks down at her basket. Automatically, she has selected Simon's favourite brand of coffee. She puts it back on the shelf, swaps it for another.

She mumbles hello to the raw-boned cashier. This, she knows, is an interaction she can't avoid.

'Not seen you here before,' the woman says as she scans the jar of instant coffee. Kate sees that there is a single hair sprouting from her chin, and suddenly doesn't know where to look. Her skin prickles. She feels horribly conscious of what she's wearing: her top and trousers too tight, too revealing. Simon had liked her to be on display like this. Exposed.

'Um – I've just moved,' says Kate. 'From London.'

The woman frowns, so Kate explains that she's inherited a cottage from a relative. 'Oh, you mean Weyward Cottage? Violet Ayres' place?'

'Yes – I'm her great-niece.'

'Didn't know she had any family living,' the cashier says. 'Thought all the Ayreses and Weywards were gone. Save the old viscount of course, losing his marbles up at the big house.'

'Not me,' says Kate, offering a tight smile. 'I'm an Ayres. Sorry – Weywards, did you say? I didn't realise it was a family name. I thought it was just the name of the cottage.'

'It was, and an old one, too,' she says, inspecting the carton of milk. 'Went back centuries, that name did.'

The cashier seems to think the Ayreses and the Weywards are related in some way. She must have it wrong. Aunt Violet had been an Ayres, too, and born in Orton Hall. She would have bought Weyward Cottage after she left home. After she'd been disowned.

'Card or cash?'

'Cash.' Kate feels the woman's eyes on her as she pulls notes from a hole in the lining of her handbag. Again, she has the feeling of being exposed. She flushes, wondering if it's obvious. That she's running away from something. Someone.

'You'll be all right, pet,' says the cashier now, as if she has seen Kate's thoughts through her skull. She hands over the change. 'It's in your blood, after all.'

Walking back to the cottage, Kate wonders what she meant.

Kate looks everywhere for Violet's papers, for some connection to the Weywards. In the drawers of the bedside table, inside the cavernous wardrobe. There, she pauses for a moment, inhaling the scent of mothballs and lavender. Her great-aunt's clothes are odd; the sort of things one might find in a charity shop – kaftans, linen tunics, a beaded cape with the gunmetal sheen of a beetle's shell. Chunky necklaces cascade down the inside of the door, clinking against an age-spotted mirror.

She can't stop looking at the cape, at the way it catches the light. Tentatively she brushes it with her fingertips, the glass beads cool against her skin. She plucks it from its hanger and slips it around her shoulders. In the mirror she looks different: the cape's dark glitter brings out something in her eyes, a hardness she doesn't recognise.

Shame flushes her cheeks. She's acting like a child playing dress-up. She takes off the cape, hurriedly shoving it back on its hanger. Shutting the wardrobe doors, she catches another glimpse of herself in the mirror. There she is: clad in the clothes he has chosen. Her hair, bleached and perfectly layered, just the way he likes. The woman with the hardness in her eyes is gone.

She looks under Aunt Violet's bed. Battered hatboxes yield sketchbooks, their mottled pages filled with annotated drawings of butterflies, beetles and – she grimaces – tarantulas. A heavy, square object wrapped in muslin turns out not to be a photo album, as she suspected, but a crumbling flank of stone. Turning it over, she sees the striated red imprint of a scorpion.

A folder pokes out from under one of the boxes. Grunting, she yanks it free.

The cover is faded and furred with dust, but the papers inside are neatly ordered: bank statements; utility bills. There are several old passports, their yellowed pages crowded with stamps. She flips through one from the 1960s, recording visits to Costa Rica, Nepal, Morocco.

There's something familiar about the sepia-coloured photograph on the first page; about the young woman with dark waves of hair and wide-spaced eyes, the smudge of a birthmark on her forehead. She's never seen any pictures of her great-aunt as a young woman before, and she shivers as she places the feeling of recognition. In the picture, Aunt Violet looks like . . . her. Kate.

10

ALTHA

Grace looked very young and small on the witness stand. Her skin was pale under her cap, her brown eyes wide. In that moment, I found it hard to believe that she was a grown woman of one and twenty.

It seemed like barely any time had passed since we were girls, chasing each other through the sunlight. The summer when we were thirteen was sharp in my memory as I looked at her.

It had been a hot summer: the hottest in decades, my mother said. We had roamed all over the village and splashed through the beck, and, once we tired of that, stolen away to the cooler air of the fells. There we'd found slopes and crags wreathed with heather and mist. We'd climbed so high that Grace said she could see all the way to France. I remember laughing, telling Grace that France was very far away, and across the sea, besides. One day, we'd go and look for it, I said. Together.

At that moment, an osprey screamed overhead. I looked up to watch it fly, the sun tipping its wings with silver. Grace took my hand in hers, and a feeling of lightness spread through me, as though I too was soaring through the clouds.

Even then, some of the villagers feared our touch, as if my mother and I carried some pestilence, some plague. But Grace was never afraid. She knew – then, at least – that I would never bring her harm.

On our way down, I lost my boot to a bog. I remember being so nervous about telling my mother that I barely said a word to Grace as we walked back. She wouldn't understand, I thought. A yeoman's daughter, she'd had new boots every twelvemonth. My mother had sold cheese and damson jam from dawn till dusk, and tended each sick villager who came to our door to pay the cobbler to repair mine.

But Grace had come in with me, when we'd got to the cottage, and had told my mother it was her fault the boot had been lost to the mud. She'd insisted on giving me her spare pair.

I'd worn them for years after, until they pinched my toes purple. I'd been saving them, thinking I'd give them to my own daughter one day.

There was another reason that this summer, of our thirteenth year, was so strong in my mind when I looked at her across the courtroom. It was the last of our friendship.

And the last of my innocence.

In the autumn, as the leaves fell from the beech trees, Grace's mother fell sick.

My mother woke me well before dawn, candlelight chasing shadows from her face.

'Grace is coming here. Something is wrong,' she told me.

'How do you know?' I asked.

She said nothing, but stroked the crow that perched on her shoulder, its feathers sparkling with rain.

It was the scarlatina, Grace said, as she sat at our table not long after, still trying to catch her breath. She'd run the whole 2 miles from the Metcalfe farm. Her mother had lain, pink-cheeked and sweating, in her bed for three days and two nights, she said. When she was awake, which was rare, she cried out for her long-dead babies.

Grace told us that her father had called for the doctor, who'd said that the patient had too much blood in her body. All that blood was boiling her from the inside out. I watched my mother's face, her mouth set in a grim line, as Grace went on. The doctor had put leeches on her mother, Grace said, only it wasn't helping. The leeches were growing fatter while she grew weaker.

My mother stood. I watched as she filled her basket with clean cloths, and jars of honey and elderberry tincture.

'Altha, fetch our cloaks,' she said. 'We must make haste, girls. If the physician keeps bleeding her, I fear she will not last the night.'

The moon was obscured by cloud and drizzle, so that I could barely see as we walked. My mother strode on determined, gripping my hand tight. I could hear Grace breathing hard next to me.

In the darkness and the wet, I could not see my mother's crow, but I knew that she flew on ahead through the trees, and that this gave my mother strength.

We were halfway there when the rain grew heavier. Water dripped from my hood into my eyes. In the rush to leave I had forgotten my gloves, and my hands were numb with cold. It seemed like an age until I saw the squat, sunken shape of the Metcalfe farmhouse in the distance, the windows yellow with candlelight.

We found William Metcalfe slumped over his wife's sickbed. There was no sign of the physician. The bedchamber was filled with candles, a score of them at least: more than my mother and I used in a month.

'Mama does not care for the dark,' Grace whispered.

In the bed, Grace's mother looked like she was asleep. Only, it was no kind of sleep that I had ever seen before.

Anna Metcalfe's chest rose and fell rapidly under her night-gown. In the leaping candlelight, I could see her eyelids flickering with movement. Then her eyes opened and she half rose from the bed, screaming and tearing at a leech at her temple, before sinking back down again.

'Holy Mary, Mother of God,' William Metcalfe murmured over his wife's crumpled form, 'pray for us sinners . . .'

He turned suddenly, having heard us come in at that moment. I saw he clutched a string of crimson beads to his lips: these he quickly stowed in the pouch of his breeches.

'What the devil are you doing here?' he asked. He looked hollowed out by exhaustion, his face almost as pale as his wife's.

'I brought them, Papa,' said Grace. 'Goodwife Weyward can help. She knows things . . .'

'Naive child,' he spat. 'Those things she knows won't save your mother. They'll condemn her soul. Is that what you want for her?'

'Please, William. Be reasonable,' said my mother in a tight voice. 'You can see that the leeches are just making her worse. Your wife is frightened and in pain. She needs cool cloths, and honey and elderberry, to soothe her.'

As she spoke, Anna let out a moan. Grace began to cry.

'Please, Papa, please,' she said.

William Metcalfe looked at his wife, then at his daughter. A vein throbbed at his temple.

'Aye,' he said. 'But you must stop if I say so. And if she dies, it will be on your head.'

My mother nodded. She set about removing the leeches from Anna's skin, asked Grace to fetch a jug of water and a cup. When these arrived, she knelt by the bedside and tried to get Anna to drink, but the liquid just dribbled down her chin. She laid a damp cloth over her forehead. Anna muttered, and I saw her fists clenching and unclenching beneath the bedclothes.

I sat down next to my mother.

'Will you try the elderberry tincture?' I asked.

'She is very far gone,' my mother said, keeping her voice low. 'I am not sure she will be able to take it in. We may be too late.'

She took the small bottle of purple liquid from her basket and un-stoppered it. She held the dropper over Anna's mouth and squeezed. A dark splash fell on her lips, staining them.

As I watched, Anna's whole body began to shake. Her eyes opened, flashing white. Foam collected at the corners of her mouth.

'Anna!' William rushed forward, pushing us out of the way. He tried to hold his wife's body still. I turned around and saw Grace standing in the far corner of the room, her hands over her mouth.

'Grace, do not watch,' I said, crossing the room. I put my hands over her eyes. 'Do not watch,' I said again, my lips so close to her face that I could smell the sweetness of her skin.

The room was filled with the terrible sounds of the bedframe shaking, of William Metcalfe saying his wife's name over and over.

Then it grew quiet.

I did not need to turn around to know that Anna Metcalfe was dead.

'Why did you not save her?' I asked my mother as we walked home. It was still raining. Cold mud seeped into my boots. The boots that Grace had given me.

'I tried,' my mother said. 'She was too weak. If Grace had come to us sooner . . .'

We did not speak for the rest of the journey home. Once we arrived, my mother started the fire. Then we sat looking into the flames for hours, my mother with her crow at her shoulder, until the rain eased and we could hear the birds singing outside.

In the days that followed, I longed for Grace; longed to hold her close and comfort her for her loss. But my mother kept me inside, away from the square, the fields. Where I might hear the rumours that tore like flames through the village. It did not matter: I could guess at them, from the pale set of my mother's face, the dark rings under her eyes. Later, I learned William Metcalfe had forbade his daughter from seeing me.

We did not speak again for seven years.

11

VIOLET

Violet woke the next day exhausted from lack of sleep. But she got straight out of bed, even though it was a Saturday, and she had no lessons.

She couldn't get her discovery out of her head. That strange word, scratched into the wainscoting behind her bedside cabinet. Weyward.

She touched the gold pendant that hung from her neck, tracing her fingers over the *W*. What if the initial didn't stand for her mother's first name, as she'd thought for all these years? What if it stood for her *last* name, before she married Father and became Lady Ayres?

Longing swelled in Violet's ribcage. She was struck with a sudden desire to push the cabinet aside again and run her fingers over the etchings, to feel something her mother might have touched. But why would her mother have put her own name there? Had she meant for Violet to discover it one day?

She threw back the covers, but quickly drew them up again when Mrs Kirkby knocked on her door with a tray of tea and porridge.

The housekeeper had a distracted look clouding her broad

features, and a faint, meaty aroma. Her knuckles were dusted white with flour, and there was a dark smear of what looked to be gravy across her apron.

Violet supposed she was busy preparing for the impending arrival of this mysterious cousin Frederick. Violet imagined Mrs Kirkby rather had her work cut out for her, given that they never had guests at Orton Hall. Perhaps she could catch her off guard.

'Mrs Kirkby,' she said in between sips of tea, taking care to keep her tone indifferent. 'What was my mother's last name?'

'Big questions for so early in the morning, pet,' said Mrs Kirkby, stooping to inspect a stain on the coverlet. 'Is this chocolate? I'll have to get Penny to put it in to soak.'

Violet frowned. She had the distinct impression that Mrs Kirkby was reluctant to look her in the eye.

'Was it Weyward?'

Mrs Kirkby stiffened. She was still for a moment, then hurriedly removed the tray from Violet's lap, even though she'd yet to finish her porridge.

'Can't recall,' she huffed. 'But it doesn't do to go ferreting around in the past, Violet. Plenty of children don't have mothers. Still more don't have mothers *or* fathers. You should count yourself lucky and leave it at that.'

'Of course, Mrs Kirkby,' Violet said, quickly formulating a plan. 'I say – speaking of fathers, do you know what mine has planned for the day?'

'He left early this morning', she said, 'to meet your young cousin off his train at Lancaster.'

This was excellent news. But she had to hurry, or she would miss her chance.

Violet dressed quickly. She was quite sure that Mrs Kirkby had been lying when she said she couldn't recall if Weyward had been her mother's last name. What was less certain was how it had come to be scratched onto the wainscoting of Violet's bedroom.

She crept down the main staircase to the second floor. It was a brilliant day outside, and the multicoloured light flooding in through the stained-glass window made the Hall look ethereal.

As she turned down the corridor, she passed Graham, carrying an algebra textbook with a look of despair. She remembered the gift he had left for her.

'Um – thank you for the present,' she said quietly. It occurred to her that it must have been quite an ordeal for him to coax the damselfly into a jar, given his fear of insects. The bees shimmered in her mind.

'That's all right,' he said. 'Do you feel better now? You look a bit more – normal. Well – normal for you, anyway.'

He pulled a face and she laughed.

'Yes, thanks.'

'That's good,' he said. 'Well, ah – better get on with this.' He motioned to the textbook and sighed.

'Graham, wait,' she said. 'Um – you wouldn't be a brick and do me a favour, would you?'

She saw him hesitate. It had been a long time since she'd asked him for a favour.

'Of course,' he said.

'Father's gone to get cousin whatshisname from Lancaster,' she said.

'Ah,' said Graham, rolling his eyes. 'The feted Frederick.'

'Anyway, I've got to look for something in Father's study,' she said, hoping she could trust him. 'Could you tell me if he comes back?'

Graham's ginger eyebrows shot up.

'Father's study? Why on earth would you go in there? He'll skin you alive if he finds out,' he said.

'I know,' she said. 'Which is why I need you to be my

lookout. You can have my share of pudding for a week if you say yes.'

Violet watched Graham mull it over, hoping that the lure of extra custard would be too great for him to resist.

'Fine,' he said. 'I'll knock on the door three times, as a signal. But if you renege on the pudding promise, I'll tell Father.'

'Deal,' she said.

She turned towards the study.

'Are you going to tell me what it is you're looking for?'

'The fewer people know,' said Violet, adopting a low voice, 'the better.'

Graham rolled his eyes again and kept walking.

Violet felt a rush of nerves as she came upon the study. Normally, Cecil could be found growling at the threshold, as if he were Cerberus guarding the entrance to the underworld. Thank heavens he had gone with Father to Lancaster.

She pushed open the heavy door. Violet tended to avoid the study – and not just because of Cecil. This was where Father had caned her after the incident with the bees.

The room was no less unsettling now that she was older. It looked as if it belonged to a different era. A different *season*, even – Father had the curtains pulled, and the air felt chilly and stale. She turned on the light, flinching as she made eye contact with the painting that hung behind the desk. It was yet another portrait of Father, and so realistically done – even down to the gleam of his bald pate – that for a moment she thought that he had been there all along, waiting to catch her out.

Pulse thudding, she crept inside, inhaling the scent of pipe tobacco. There had to be some record of her mother in here. How could a person have lived and died in a house yet leave only a necklace and a scratch of letters behind? It was as if Father had scrubbed her from the face of the earth.

She scanned the shelves, with their ancient spines labelled in faded blue ink. Ledgers. Dozens of them. She pulled out one marked *1925* and flipped through it. Could there be something in here about the May Day Festival where her parents had met? But no – it was just pages and pages of numbers, transcribed in Father's cramped, terse hand (it took skill, Violet thought, to make even your handwriting look angry). She slammed the ledger shut in frustration.

She looked around the room. Father's mahogany desk hulked beneath his portrait. Strange objects littered the surface. Some of them were interesting – like the faded globe that showed the countries of the British Empire in delicate pink – but others gave her the willies. Especially the yellowed ivory tusk mounted in brass, which spanned almost the entire length of the desk. It conjured images of Babar and Celeste, heroes of her favourite childhood books (which, like all the other nursery volumes, had originally been given to Graham) tuskless and bleeding.

It made her feel sad for another reason. As a child, Violet had assumed that Father's 'curios' (as he called them) were signs that he shared her love of the natural world. But it was when Father was telling her and Graham the story of how he came to possess the tusk – on the same hunting trip to Southern Rhodesia that he'd acquired Cecil, skinny and cowering as a puppy – that she realised how wrong she was. Father didn't care that elephants formed close-knit, matriarchal groups; that they mourned their dead like humans. Nor did he consider that the elephant he had killed – for the mere sake of an ornament on his desk – would have been bewildered by fear and pain at the moment of its death.

For Father, the tusk – and everything else in the Hall like it – was just a trophy. These noble creatures weren't to be studied or venerated, but conquered.

They would never understand each other.

But there wasn't time to dwell on such things now, she told herself. After all, she had a mission to accomplish.

She was sure that the desk drawer would be locked but – to her delight – it slid open easily.

Violet rifled through the contents quickly. Father's leather writing-case, with the Ayres insignia (an osprey, picked out in gold); an old pocket watch with a broken face; letters from the bank, his pipe . . . she was just beginning to think that Father hadn't bothered locking his desk because it held nothing important when she saw the feather.

It was large enough to have come from a crow, Violet thought. Or perhaps a jackdaw?

Carefully, she took it from the drawer. It was black as obsidian, shimmering blue where it caught the light. She saw that it was streaked with white – or rather with queer absences of colour, like an unfinished painting. The feather appeared to have come loose from a soft wad of material. On closer inspection, Violet saw that it was a handkerchief, fashioned from a delicate linen that had been eaten away by moths. There was a monogram in the corner of the handkerchief, the letters *E.W.* picked out in bottle-green silk.

Violet's heart fluttered in her chest. *E.W.*

W for Weyward?

Underneath the layer of dust, Violet detected the faintest whiff of something light and floral coming from the handkerchief. Lavender. It was barely there, the ghost of a scent, but it was enough. The memories instantly flooded her brain, as if she had tapped into a hidden spring. The feeling of warm arms around her, a thick, fragrant curtain of hair tickling her face. The low melody of a lullaby, the sound of a heart beating next to her ear.

The feather, the handkerchief.

They were her mother's.

And Father had been keeping them in his desk drawer, as if they were something important. Special.

The old fantasy of her parents' wedding day hovered before her. Father looking almost handsome, in a morning suit of soft grey. Her mother – Violet imagined a woman with a heart-shaped face and a dark river of hair – smiling as she took his hand. Their faces golden with sunshine; petals swirling overhead.

Violet sometimes wondered if Father was capable of loving anything – apart from hunting, and the Empire – but she also knew that he had defied tradition and his dead parents' wishes to marry her mother. And he had held on to these keepsakes, things that reminded him of her, for all these years. She imagined him sitting at his desk, pressing the handkerchief to his nose the way Violet was doing now.

Could she have misunderstood, that night in the study? *Perhaps they can stop you from turning out like her.* The very words had seemed to drip with hatred.

But perhaps she'd been wrong, confused somehow? Her heart leaped at the thought. Perhaps he *had* loved her mother, very much. And then she had died.

Violet began to feel almost sorry for him.

She wasn't sure how long she stood there with the little bundle in her hand, but after a while she became aware of something strange.

She could *hear*. Properly, this time. It was as if the heavy curtains, the thick glass of the window and the ancient stone walls had fallen away. She could hear the beat of a sparrow's wings as it took flight from a sycamore. The throaty yell of a buzzard, calling to its mate as it circled in the sky. A field mouse, chittering as it foraged in the bushes beneath the window.

Violet stared at the items in her hand in wonder. Then, there were three knocks: Graham's signal. How could Father be back already? Violet looked at her watch: it had just gone ten o'clock. He must have set off earlier than she'd realised.

She wanted to take the feather and the handkerchief with her, but what if Father noticed they were missing? Then he would know she had been inside his study. Perhaps – her heart thudded with the thought, with what she was about to do – he wouldn't miss the feather. She could just keep it, for a little while, and put it back later. After all, Father had had it all to himself for years and years . . .

'Violet?' Graham hissed through the door. 'Are you in there? He's back! Hurry!'

Her blood humming with excitement, Violet put the hand-kerchief back in the drawer, then shoved the feather into the pocket of her dress. She shut the door of Father's study quietly and crept back up the stairs.

As a test, Violet crouched on the floor and pulled the hatbox out from underneath her bed.

The inside of the box was filmy with spider silk. Goldie was alive and well, and judging from the dead flies and ants that speckled his lair, possessed of his usual appetite. He reared up on his legs and blinked his eight beady eyes at her, before leaping into the air in a tawny flash. He came to rest on Violet's shoulder, and she smiled as he nestled against her. Warmth unfurled in her chest, fizzing through her veins.

It was like taking off a blindfold. She hadn't realised how deadened to the world she had become – now, her nerves seemed to bristle with electricity. Colours looked brighter than they had before – through her window, the outside world flared with sunshine – and the *click* of Goldie's pincers was miraculous to her ears.

She was herself again.

*

Violet smoothed her hair and clothes, checking in the looking glass that she was presentable before going downstairs. She remembered what Father had said after supper last night. He expected her to be a *cheerful, gracious presence* around her cousin Frederick. Eugh.

As she walked down the stairs, she heard Father talking loudly in the entrance hall. A boorish laugh echoed through the house. It was so loud that Violet heard the family of blue tits that lived in the roof chirrup in fright. She disliked cousin Frederick already.

When she reached the hall, she saw that the owner of the boorish laugh was a straight-backed young man in a sand-coloured uniform. He smiled when she drew near, revealing white, even teeth. Below his officer's cap, his eyes were green. Her favourite colour. Father, who had just finished telling some dull story, clapped him on the back. Graham stood awkwardly off to one side, looking as if he didn't know what to do with his hands.

'Frederick,' said Father, 'I'd like to introduce you to my daughter, your cousin. Miss Violet Elizabeth Ayres.'

'Hello,' said Frederick, extending his hand towards her. 'How do you do?'

'Hello,' said Violet. His hand felt warm and callused. Close up, he smelled of a spicy sort of cologne. She wasn't sure why, but she felt suddenly light-headed. Was this, she wondered, a normal response to the young adult male? She had never known any apart from Graham, and the second under-gardener, Neil – a buck-toothed, wan-faced lad who had perished at the Battle of Boulogne.

'Violet,' said Father. 'Have you forgotten your manners?'

'Sorry,' she said. 'How do you do?'

Frederick grinned.

Father rang for Penny, who flushed and almost forgot to

curtsey when she saw Frederick. Father asked Penny to show Frederick to his room. Dinner would be at eight, he said.

'Don't be late,' said Father, looking at Violet.

Violet wore her favourite dress to dinner – green serge with a full skirt and a Peter Pan collar. It had no pockets, so she had stowed the feather safely between the yellowed pages of the Brothers Grimm. She sat across from Frederick and stole glances at him. She was heady with looking – at the sharp line of his jaw; the square, golden hands with their dark smattering of hair across the knuckles. He was so unlike Father – whose own hands recalled joints of gammon – that he might have been a different species. He repelled and fascinated her in equal measure.

She was trying to work out the exact shade of his eyes – the same colour as the enchanter's nightshade that grew beneath the beech tree, she decided – when he turned his gaze to her. She flinched.

'How are your parents, Frederick?' Father was asking. Apparently, Frederick's father was Father's younger brother Charles – whom Violet and Graham had never met. It seemed, from the familiarity with which they spoke to each other, that Father and Frederick had kept up a rather involved written correspondence for many years. Knowing this made Violet feel a little smaller in her chair. Why hadn't Father wanted her to meet her only cousin until now? She thought again of the lack of callers, the prohibition on leaving the estate.

'As well as can be expected, I suppose,' said Frederick. 'Mother's nerves are still a bit frayed, after the Blitz. I keep telling them to leave London – too many reminders – but they won't hear of it. I'll go down and see them, before I head back. But I wanted to get some country air first.'

'Did you grow up in London?' Violet asked, finding her

voice. The prospect horrified her. Everything she knew of London came from newspaper articles and Dickens. In her mind, it was soot-choked and sunless, with no animals except mangy foxes foraging in alleyways. 'What was it like?'

'Well, I spent most of the year at school,' said Frederick. 'Eton, of course.' Graham stiffened and looked at his plate. 'But it's a wonderful city. Full of life and colour. Or, it was, before the war.'

'But . . . are there any trees?' Violet asked. 'I couldn't imagine living without *trees*.'

Frederick laughed and took a sip of wine. The bright green flash of his gaze landed on her again, like sunlight in a forest.

'Oh, yes,' he said. 'In fact, my parents live in Richmond, just next to the park. Have you heard of it?'

'No,' said Violet.

'It's beautiful. Over two thousand acres of woodland, just on the outskirts of London. You even see deer there, sometimes.'

'Have you thought about what you'd like to do once the war ends, Frederick?' Father interrupted.

'Well, I was planning to move back to London, and rent somewhere for a while; maybe in Kensington – if it's still standing, that is . . . my allowance would cover it. I thought I might write a book, about the war. But now . . .'

'Yes! Didn't you have a title? *Torment in Tobruk*? You mentioned it in your last letter. Sounded like stirring stuff. You've changed your mind?'

'Well. I'm not sure yet,' Frederick began. 'I thought of going to medical school, perhaps. One sees things, in a war . . . so much death.' He is watching Violet. 'But miracles, too. Chaps brought back from the brink. In a field hospital, doctors are like . . . God.'

There was an awkward pause. Father cleared his throat.

'I think what I am trying to say', Frederick added quickly,

'is that I just would like to contribute somehow, when all this is over, to making people's lives better.'

'A noble aspiration,' said Father, nodding his approval.

'So, would you get to see inside a body?' Violet asked. 'Learn how it works? If you went to medical school, I mean.'

'Violet,' Father frowned. 'Hardly appropriate table conversation from a young lady.'

Frederick laughed.

'I don't mind, Uncle,' he said. 'The young lady is right, anyway. To become a doctor, I'd first need to be acquainted with how the human body works. Intimately acquainted.'

He was still watching her.

12

KATE

Kate holds her breath as she dials the number.

Beams of afternoon sunshine pour into the bedroom, catching dust motes. Out of the window, she can see the mountains that ring the valley, purple and distant.

The phone is still ringing. Canada is – she tries to think – five hours behind, so it will be midday there. Her mother will be busy, at her job as a medical receptionist. Perhaps she won't answer. Kate almost wills it.

Don't pick up.

'Hello?'

Her heart sinks.

'Hi, Mum, it's me.'

'Kate? Oh, thank God.' Her mother's voice is urgent, harried. She can hear the trill of office phones in the background, faint conversation. 'Hold on a second.'

A door opens, shuts.

'Sorry, just had to find somewhere quieter. Where are you calling from? What's going on?'

'I've got a new phone.'

'Jesus, Kate, I've been going out of my mind. Simon phoned

me about an hour ago. He said you'd taken off, left your phone behind.'

Guilt pulls at her.

'Sorry, I should have called earlier. But listen, I'm fine. I just . . . had to get away.'

She pauses. Blood rushes in her ears. Part of Kate does want to tell her the truth. About Simon, about the baby. But she can't seem to shape the words in her mouth; to force them through her lips. To break the glass.

He abused me.

She has already caused her mother so much pain. Even the sound of her voice brings it back – those long days after the accident, when her mother barely left her parents' bedroom. Coming home from school and finding her grey-faced and sobbing, the bed strewn with her father's clothes.

'They still smell like him,' she had said, before disappearing back into her grief. In that moment, Kate wished she had never been born.

Years later, when her mother married Keith, a Canadian doctor, she had asked Kate to move with them to Toronto. They could start again, she'd said. Together.

Kate had said no, insisted that she wanted to stay in England for university. But really, she just didn't want to ruin her mother's second chance at happiness. Their infrequent conversations – eventually dwindling from weekly to monthly – felt stilted, awkward. It was for the best, Kate told herself. Her mother was better off without her.

'Away from what?' her mother is asking now. 'Please, Kate – I'm your mum. Just tell me what's going on.'

He abused me.

'It's – complicated. It just . . . wasn't working. So I wanted to get away for a bit.'

'Right. OK, darling.' Kate hears the resignation in her voice. 'So where have you gone, then? Are you staying with a friend?'

'No – do you remember Dad's Aunt Violet? The one who lived up in Cumbria, near Orton Hall?'

'Oh, yes, vaguely. A bit eccentric, I always thought . . . I didn't know you'd become close.'

'We weren't,' says Kate. 'Close, I mean. She's – dead, actually. She died last year, left me her house. I guess she didn't have any other family.'

'You never told me that.' She hears the wound in her mother's voice. 'I should have stayed in touch with her, your dad would have liked that.'

Kate's insides clench with guilt. This is why it's better that they don't speak. She has hurt her mother again, like she always does.

'Sorry, Mum . . . I should have said something.'

'It's OK. Anyway, how long are you planning to stay up there? You can always come here, you know. Or – maybe I could come there?'

'You don't have to do that,' Kate says quickly. 'It's OK. I'm OK. Anyway – sorry again, about Aunt Violet. I should go, Mum. I'll call you in a few days, OK?'

'OK, darling.'

'Wait – Mum?'

'Yes?'

'Don't tell him. Simon. Don't tell him where I am. Please.'

She hangs up quickly, cutting off her mother's questions.

Tears blur her vision. She gropes blindly for the box of tissues on the bedside table – perched precariously atop a towering stack of *New Scientist* magazines – and knocks it over. Items topple onto the floor.

'Fuck,' she says, bending down to pick them up. She needs to pull herself together.

Something else has been knocked to the ground – an enamel jewellery box, patterned with butterflies. Its contents are splayed out on the floorboards, glowing in the sun.

Mismatched earrings, a couple of rusted rings, a dirty necklace with a battered-looking pendant. Flustered, she puts them back in the box, tidies the surface of the bedside table.

There's a photograph of her grandfather, Graham, behind the stack of magazines. Younger than she's ever seen him: his hair still red, wisps of it lifting in a breeze. He died when she was six and her memories of him are shadowy, fragmented. He used to read to her – *Grimms' Fairy Tales*, mainly, the rich resonance of his voice transporting her into another world.

Though now, as she looks at the photograph, another memory flickers at the edge of her brain. His funeral, here in Crows Beck.

Gripping her mother's hand, looking up at the clouds that hung low in the sky. Thinking that it was going to rain. The graveyard was all moss and stone and trees, full of birds and insects, and Kate remembers it being *loud*. So loud she'd barely been able to hear the vicar talking.

Afterwards, she and her parents had gone back to Weyward Cottage for afternoon tea. The only other time she has set foot inside the house. The only time she met Aunt Violet.

She has a vague impression of green. The green door, the green wallpaper inside the house, Aunt Violet wearing an odd, flowing outfit. She remembers the smell of her perfume – lavender, the scent that still lingers in the bedroom. She tries to conjure more details but she can't; the memory is too hazy, as though its edges are frayed.

Really, she'd half forgotten that she *had* a great-aunt, until the call from the solicitor.

Not for the first time, she wonders why Violet left her cottage to a great-niece she hadn't seen for over twenty years.

'You're her only living relative,' the solicitor had said when she'd asked him that same question, his northern accent gravelly on the phone. But this sparked more questions than it answered. For instance: why had her great-aunt never contacted her while she was still alive?

Later, Kate decides to explore the garden, while it's still light.

It is overgrown and heavy with the scent of plants she doesn't recognise. Green, furred leaves brush her shoes, trailing silvery lines of sap. Ferns rustle in the breeze.

She hesitates when she comes to the ancient sycamore tree, remembering the crows from her first night. She looks skyward, at the reaching branches, red with the setting sun. The tree must be hundreds of years old. She imagines it standing sentinel for generations, keeping the little cottage safe in its shadow. She reaches out her hand and presses her palm against the bark.

It feels warm. Alive.

The air shifts. Suddenly, she wants to go back inside. There's something about the garden that feels crowded, over-whelming. It's as if there is no longer any barrier between the outside world and her nerves.

She reminds herself she is safe. She won't go back inside. Not yet.

She walks deeper into the garden, listening to the hum of insects, water running over pebbles. The beck glimmers below. She climbs down to its banks, holding the twisted roots of the sycamore to steady herself. The water is so clear that she can see tiny fish, their little bodies shimmering in the light. An insect hovers nearby. She can't remember what it's called: smaller than a dragonfly, with delicate mother-of-pearl wings. It skims the surface of the beck. She stays like that for a long time, listening to the birds, the water, the insects. She shuts her eyes, opening them again when she feels something brush her hand. The dragonfly-like creature with the iridescent wings. The word swims up from the depths of her brain: a damselfly.

Tears well in her eyes, surprising her.

She was fascinated by insects, as a child. She remembers begging her mother to spare the moths that fluttered out from wardrobes, the gauzy spider's webs that clung to the ceiling. She'd collected vividly illustrated books about them. About birds, too. She would hide under the covers reading, in the small, silent hours of the morning while her parents slept in the next room. It hurts now, to think of that little girl, her innocent wonder: torch in hand, turning the glossy pages and marvelling at the wild and wonderful creatures. Butterflies with eyes on their wings, parrots in candy-coloured plumage.

After her father died, Kate had collected the books into a shiny, colourful stack and put them on the pavement outside the house. She'd woken in the night, heart swollen with regret, and crept outside to retrieve them. But they were already gone.

Kate took this to be a sign, confirmation of what she already knew. It was too dangerous for her to be around the insects, animals and birds she loved. She'd already caused her father's death. What if she hurt her mother, too?

She kept her other books – *Grimms' Fairy Tales; The Secret Garden* – the stories that became a salve during those long nights when the only sign of life from her mother's bedroom was the neon glow of the television under the door. Fiction became a friend as well as a safe harbour; a cocoon to protect her from the outside world and its dangers. She could read about Robin Redbreast but she must avoid at all costs the robins that tittered in the back garden.

And she kept the brooch, tucked safe in her pocket through compulsory netball matches, exams, even her first kiss. As if it were a good luck charm rather than a reminder of what she'd done, who she was. A monster.

The brooch is worn now, the gold dull and black with age.

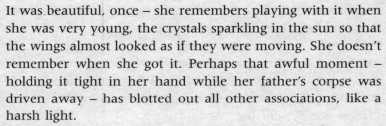

It was beautiful, once – she remembers playing with it when she was very young, the crystals sparkling in the sun so that the wings almost looked as if they were moving. She doesn't remember when she got it. Perhaps that awful moment – holding it tight in her hand while her father's corpse was driven away – has blotted out all other associations, like a harsh light.

Kate shivers. It's getting colder, the warmth leaving with the sun. She stands up, looks around. Then she notices something.

A wooden cross, weathered and green with lichen, is nestled among the roots of the sycamore.

There is no name, no date. But, leaning closer, she sees the faint outline of jagged letters. *RIP.*

The sun has disappeared behind dark clouds, and her skin smarts with the first pinpricks of rain.

As she stands before the cross, the garden seems to swell with sound. Her skin feels raw and open, like a new-born animal's. There's a feeling, in her stomach and in her veins, of something wanting to get in. Or wanting to get out.

She runs, then; the strange, grasping plants leaving smears of red and green on her clothes. She shuts the door behind her, drawing the curtains on the windows so that she can't see the garden, the sycamore tree. The cross. The green-mottled wood, the way that it juts out from the roots of the sycamore.

It couldn't be a person's grave, could it? The cottage is so old, after all . . . she remembers what the cashier said. *Went back centuries.* Could it be one of the Weywards?

She'd hoped to learn more in Aunt Violet's papers. But the folder she found under the bed contained nothing earlier than 1942, and nothing about the cottage itself, or anyone who might have lived there before Aunt Violet.

Then she remembers that there's an attic. She saw a

trapdoor, didn't she? Set into the ceiling of the corridor. Perhaps there'll be something up there.

The top rung of the ladder creaks as Kate steps on it. God knows how old it is: she found it rusting against the back of the house, half covered in creeping ivy. Ignoring the ladder's protest, she pushes the trapdoor open.

Aunt Violet's attic is enormous – big enough that she can almost stand up. She switches on the torch on her phone, and the dark shapes take form.

Shelves line the walls, sparkling with insects, preserved in specimen jars. The space is dominated by a hulking bureau. Even under the torchlight, it looks scratched and very old, possibly even older than the furniture in the rest of the cottage. There are two drawers.

She opens the first drawer of the bureau. It's empty. Then tries the second, which is locked.

She feels around in the recesses of the first drawer again, just in case she's missed something, some clue. She breathes in sharply as her fingers connect with a package. Pulling it out, she sees that it is wrapped in fraying cloth. She won't open it here, in the dark, she decides. Something skitters on the roof and her heart rises into her throat.

She lowers herself down into the yellow oblong of light, the package tight in her hand, its dust working itself into the tread of her skin.

She'll start the fire, make a cup of tea, turn on as many lights as possible. Then she'll look at it. Strange, that the other drawer would be locked. Almost as if Aunt Violet was hiding something.

13

ALTHA

I watched as Grace swore on the Bible, to tell the whole truth and nothing but. The prosecutor rose from his seat and walked slowly towards her. I could see her eyes searching for mine.

I wanted to look away, to hide my face in my hands and curl myself up small, but I couldn't. There were too many people watching. I was Lancaster's greatest attraction. In the gallery, men pointed me out to their wives; mothers shushed their grubby children. There was a low and constant hiss. *Witch,* I heard them say. *Hang the witch.*

The prosecutor began.

'Please state your full name for the court,' he said.

'Grace Charlotte Milburn,' she said, too quietly. So quietly that he had to ask her to repeat herself.

'And where do you reside, Mistress Milburn?'

'Milburn Farm, near Crows Beck,' she said.

'And who did you live there with?'

'My husband. John Milburn.'

'And do you have any children?'

She paused. One hand went to her waist: she wore a kirtle

of dark grey wool, thick enough to hide her shape. I willed her not to look at me.

'No.'

'Could you tell the court what is raised at Milburn Farm? Crops, or livestock?'

'Livestock,' she said.

'Which animals?'

'Cows,' she whispered. 'Dairy cows.'

'And how did your husband come by Milburn Farm?'

'He inherited it, sir. From his father.'

'So he lived there from birth.'

'Yes.'

One of the judges cleared his throat. The prosecutor looked up at him.

'Bear with me, your honour, this has relevance to the charges laid upon the accused.'

The judge nodded. 'You may continue.'

The prosecutor turned back towards Grace.

'Mistress Milburn. Would you say that your husband was familiar with cows? With the patterns and habits of these beasts?'

She hesitated.

'Yes, of course, sir. Dairy farming was in his blood.'

'And the particular cows at the farm were familiar with him?'

'He took them from byre to field and back every day, sir.'

'I see. Thank you, Mistress Milburn. Now, mistress, could you describe for the court the events of New Year's Day, in this, the year of our Lord 1619?'

'Yes, sir. I woke up, at dawn as usual, sir, to feed the chickens and put the pottage on. John had already got up, to milk the cows and then take them from the byre.'

'And was John alone in doing this, or did he have assistance?'

'He had help, sir. The Kirkby lad comes to help – came to help – John on Tuesdays and Thursdays.'

'And this was a Thursday?'

'Yes.'

'What happened next?'

'I was getting ready to get water from the well, to wash the clothes, sir. I had picked up the basin and I was looking out of the window. I wanted to see how thick the snow was, sir, to see if I needed my gloves.'

'And what did you see, Mistress Milburn, when you were looking out of the window?'

'I saw the cows, sir, coming out of the byre and into the field, and John and the Kirkby lad.'

'And how did the cows seem to you?' Did they seem – agitated? Aggressive, in any way?'

'No, sir,' she said.

I knew what was coming next. I felt giddy with dread, as if I might swoon. I was grateful that no one could see my shackled hands, how they shone with sweat. I wiped them on the skirt of my dress.

'Please, go on, Mistress Milburn.'

'Well, I had been looking at the window, but then I dropped my basin, sir. It made an almighty clang, loud enough that God himself could've heard, I thought. I bent down to pick it up. While I was crouched on the floor, there was sound from outside, like thunder. I thought maybe a storm was coming. Then I heard the Kirkby lad yelling.'

'Yelling? What was he saying?'

'Nothing that made much sense, at first. Just sounds, like. But then he started saying my husband's name, over and over again.'

'What did you do next?'

My heart drummed in my ears. The edges of my vision grew hazy. I wished for some water. I wished that none of this had ever happened. That I was safe in childhood, climbing trees with Grace. Pointing out the finches, the shining beetles; her laughing wonder in my ears.

'I went outside, sir.'

'And what did you see?'

'The cows were all scattered in the field. Some of them had heaving flanks, wild eyes, as if they'd been running. The Kirkby lad was still yelling, bent over something on the ground. At first I couldn't see John. But then I saw that he . . . my John . . . he was the thing on the ground.'

Grace's voice grew thick with tears. She took a handkerchief and wiped her eyes. The gallery murmured with sympathy. I felt their eyes on me; heard the hiss again. Witch. Whore.

'And can you describe to the court your husband's condition at this point, Mistress Milburn?'

'He was – he was not recognisable as himself, sir.' She paused and licked her lips, steadied herself.

'In what manner?'

'His arms and legs were all twisted, sir. And his face. It . . . weren't there no more.'

A memory rose up, like vomit in my throat. That face, bruised and pulped as damson jam. The teeth gone. One eye split and oozing.

'My John was dead, sir. He was gone.'

Her voice broke on the last word. She cried prettily, the head bowed in its white cap, the slight shoulders hunched with pain.

She had the courtroom rapt. In the gallery, men comforted their wives who wiped away tears in sympathy. To the jurors, she presented a perfect picture of grief. Even the judges looked softened.

The prosecutor – mindful of this, no doubt – went on gently.

'Could you tell me what happened next, please, Mistress Milburn?'

'It was then that I saw her, running towards me from the trees.'

'Who?' he asked.

'Altha,' she said softly.

'Please, Mistress Milburn, would you point her out to the courtroom.'

She looked at me, raising one hand slowly. Even from where I was sitting, I saw the delicate fingers were shaking. She pointed at me.

The gallery erupted.

One of the judges called for order. Gradually, the shouts fell away.

The prosecutor continued.

'Were you surprised to see Altha Weyward running towards you?' he asked.

'It was all a blur, sir. I can't remember what I felt when I saw her. I was – overcome.'

'But it would have been an unusual occurrence, I assume, to see the accused by your field, not so long after daybreak?'

'Not so unusual, sir. She is known for taking early walks.'

'So you had seen her before, then? Taking walks of a morning, near your farm?'

'Yes, sir.'

'Regularly?'

'I wouldn't call it regular, sir.' I saw Grace's tongue dart out to moisten her lips. 'But once or twice I'd seen her, yes.'

The prosecutor frowned.

'Would you continue, please, Mistress Milburn. What happened after you saw the accused running towards you?'

'She rushed towards me, sir. She asked me what had happened. I can't remember what I said all too well, sir. I was just so – shocked, you see. But I remember, she took off her cloak and threw it over his body, and then she bade the Kirkby lad to fetch the physician, Doctor Smythson. She took me inside to wait.'

'And when did the doctor and the Kirkby boy arrive?'

'Not long after, sir.'

'Did the doctor say anything to you?'

'Just told me what I already knew, sir. My John were gone. There were no bringing him back.'

The little head bowed again. The shoulders quivered.

'Thank you, Mistress Milburn. I can see that having to relive this grave tragedy has been wearing on your spirits. I thank you for your courage and assistance in this matter. I have only a few more questions to ask before I can release you.'

He paced back and forth before the bar, before speaking again.

'Mistress Milburn, how long have you known the accused, Altha Weyward?'

'All my life, sir. Same as with most others in the village.'

'And what has been the nature of your relationship with her, during your acquaintance?'

'We were – friends, sir. As children, that is.'

'But no longer?'

'No, sir. Not since we were thirteen, sir.'

'And what happened, when you and the accused were thirteen, that caused the friendship to abate, Mistress Milburn?'

'To – what, sir?'

'To end. What caused the friendship to end?'

Grace looked at her hands.

'My mother fell ill, sir. With the scarlatina.'

'And what did that have to do with the accused?'

'She and her mother—'

'Jennet Weyward?'

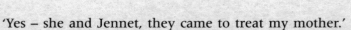

'Yes – she and Jennet, they came to treat my mother.'

'And could you tell the court, please, the outcome of that treatment?'

Grace looked at me before she spoke, so quietly that I had to strain to hear her.

'My mother died, sir.'

14

VIOLET

Violet was looking for something to wear.

Father had said that they were going to go clay pigeon shooting with Frederick after breakfast. Violet wasn't fond of shooting. She'd never shoot *real* pigeons, of course (even Father knew better than to ask her to do that), but she still didn't like the way that the gunshots startled the birds in the trees. Besides, she always worried that a bullet intended for a clay pigeon would find a real one instead. She loved wood pigeons, with their pretty plumage and gentle songs. She could hear them now, cheering the morning.

She wondered if Frederick liked birds and animals as much as she did. The thought of Frederick – the heat of his eyes on her – made her stomach flip. She both dreaded and longed to see him. The previous year, she had read about magnetic fields in one of Graham's schoolbooks, and it seemed to Violet that Frederick had his own such field; that it pulled at her like a tide.

She could speak to him today. Over breakfast or while they were shooting. But would *he* want to talk to her? She may have been sixteen, but Violet still felt – and, worse, looked

– like a child. She frowned at the looking glass. She had put on a scratchy tweed skirt and jacket, with her stiff brogues. The jacket and skirt were slightly too large for her (Nanny Metcalfe ordered everything a size too big, promising that Violet would 'grow into it'), which made her seem even smaller than she was.

Her hair fell past her shoulders in shiny dark waves. She wished she knew how to put it into an elegant chignon – or even pin curls, like the modern-looking women who smiled from the advertisements in Father's newspapers – but the best she could manage was a clumsy plait. She could have passed for twelve.

Before giving up and going downstairs, she made sure her mother's necklace was tucked securely beneath her blouse. Father didn't even know she still had the necklace. He'd made Nanny Metcalfe confiscate it when Violet was six (fortunately, the nursemaid had taken pity on her sobbing charge and returned it). Had it pained him to see it, she wondered now?

She had almost put the feather in her pocket again but thought better of it. What if Father saw? It was too risky. Instead, she'd briefly pressed it to her nose, inhaling its dark, oily scent, the sweet hint of lavender, before tucking it back into its hiding place inside the Brothers Grimm.

Violet still hadn't figured out why that word – Weyward – had been scratched into the wainscoting. She'd stayed up until almost one in the morning hunting for more clues in her room, but had found nothing apart from dust and a scattering of mouse droppings. If Weyward was her mother's last name, and if she really *had* been the one to score it into the paint, Violet couldn't for the life of her work out why. Could the room have once belonged to her mother? Violet assumed she would have shared Father's room . . . though the thought of a woman in that draughty, tartan-draped space was somehow wrong, like a robin singing out of season.

Violet had slept in the nursery while her mother was alive, and had been too young for her to remember now what her current room was used for back then. She could still recall the ache she'd felt when she was moved from the nursery, just after the incident with the bees. She had missed its enormous sash windows and the gentle rhythms of Graham snoring at night. Her new room was the smallest in the Hall, with walls painted a greasy yellow that reminded her of fried kippers.

Over time, though, it had become as familiar to her as part of her own body, with its slanting ceiling, chipped enamel washstand and frayed curtains (these, too, were yellow). She'd thought that she knew every inch of it. She couldn't quite believe it had been keeping secrets from her for all these years. It felt almost like a betrayal.

Perhaps she could ask one of the servants about her room? But then she remembered the way that Mrs Kirkby had evaded her question about her mother's last name. They were keeping something from her.

Violet felt sure of it.

Mrs Kirkby had outdone herself for breakfast: the serving table was piled high with an almost pre-war quantity of food – silver dishes of baked beans, scrambled eggs, kidneys and even bacon. (She had an awful feeling that the latter had been procured from one of their sows, a fleshy-nosed, clever animal that she'd taught to respond to the name Jemima.)

From the way *The Times* was folded at his usual chair, Violet could tell that Father had already had his breakfast. Graham was nowhere to be seen: she'd never known him to rise before 9 a.m. (much to Father's consternation).

Frederick was sitting at the table. He wasn't wearing his uniform today; instead, he'd donned casual trousers and a pale shirt, which made his dark hair and green eyes stand out. The first three buttons of the shirt were undone, and Violet flushed to see tiny curls of hair on his chest. She filled her plate with beans and eggs – leaving the kidneys and bacon well alone – and sat down opposite him.

'Good morning,' she said, looking at her plate.

'Good morning, Violet,' he said. She heard the grin in his voice and looked up. She smiled at him shyly. 'Did you sleep well?'

'Um – very well, thanks,' she said. She had barely slept at all; instead she'd stared at the ceiling, listening to the rustle of bats in the attic and thinking about her mother.

They ate in silence for a while, Violet taking care to eat very neatly. Eventually Frederick put down his knife and fork.

'Your father tells me you're to come clay pigeon shooting with us today,' he said. 'I expect you're jolly sharp with a rifle, country girl like you.'

She quickly wiped away any stray bean sauce from her mouth before answering him.

'Oh – not really, actually,' she said. 'I don't much like the idea of killing things.'

Her cheeks burned as she realised what she'd said.

'Sorry,' she said. 'I didn't mean that you—'

'That I kill things?' He leaned back in his chair. 'Well, it's part of the job description, really. What I signed up for.'

Violet looked down at the smears of bean and egg on her plate. The colours seemed very lurid on the white Wedgwood (Penny had laid out the best breakfast service in honour of Frederick's presence). She wasn't sure she wanted to eat any more. When she looked up, he was watching her, waiting.

'Yes, of course,' she said, the words rushing out. 'You're defending your country.' She opened her mouth again, then bit her lip.

'Go on,' he said. 'Ask what you wanted to ask. I don't bite.'

'Well, I suppose I just wondered whether you had . . . whether you had actually ever killed anyone.'

He laughed.

'You know, you do seem *much* younger than sixteen,' he said. 'But in answer to your question – yes, I have. More than one.' He stopped. There was a new, dark look in his eyes when he continued.

'You can't imagine what it's like. The Libyan heat sticking to you, day in, day out. Nothing but sand and rock for miles. Not a bit of green. All day, crawling in the dust, shooting and being shot at. Men dying around you. You realise, when you see a person die, that there's nothing *special* about humans. We're just flesh and blood and organs, no different to the pig that gave us this bacon.

'So, all day, dust, death, everywhere. I went to sleep each night with dust in my mouth and the smell of blood in my nose. Even here – I'm still finding dust on me. Under my nails, in my hair, caked into the soles of my shoes. And I can still smell the blood. All so that some English girl, sitting pretty in her father's manor house, can ask me if I ever *killed anyone*.'

He stopped talking. The sun was streaming through the windows onto the back of Violet's neck. She felt prickly and hot. She was so stupid. What had possessed her to ask him a question like that? No wonder he'd got upset. She didn't dare look at him. She kept her eyes on her hands, knotted in her lap. Then, fighting back tears, she looked to the ceiling.

She heard a sigh and then the clatter of china as he picked up his cup of tea and put it down again.

'Ah, listen. I've been a brute. Sorry, Violet. Still tired from the journey, I expect.'

She had opened her mouth to say something when Father

walked into the dining room, wearing his tweeds and cap
and carrying his rifle bag, Cecil snarling behind him.

'Good morning,' he said, beaming at them. 'Marvellous to
see you two getting along so well!'

It was a beautiful day outside, and Violet hoped that Frederick
would brighten at the sight of the valley. As Frederick and
Father instructed Graham on how to throw the clay pigeons
in high arcs, she sat on the lawn and looked out at the soft
green hills. A bee buzzed nearby, hopping from dandelion to
dandelion. She thought of poor Frederick stuck in Libya,
without so much as a scrap of green or anything nice to look
at. Seeing all those horrible things. Having to *do* all those
horrible things.

She tried to imagine killing another person. She had no
sense of what a battlefield really looked like: would you be
able to see the person you'd shot? Would you have to . . .
watch them die?

Violet had seen animals die. The weasel she'd kept as a
pet when she was small; a rose-breasted bullfinch grievously
injured by Cecil. She had watched the light go from their
eyes; their little bodies slacken. She had felt how afraid they
were, of whatever came after: the dark unknown, yawning
ahead. Violet couldn't imagine condemning another human
being to that fate.

But poor Frederick had been given no choice.

They were ready to start shooting now, Father first. She
hung back and watched Graham, who was sweating and
puffing already, throw the clay pigeons high in the air.
Blackbirds flew from the trees at the first shot. Father missed.

'Throw them higher, boy!' he yelled to Graham.

Frederick stepped forward to take his shot. He lifted the
rifle as easily as if it were an extension of his body. The clay
pigeon shattered, shards drifting to the ground like snow.

Father clapped Frederick on the back. They talked for a while – Violet couldn't hear what they were saying – before Frederick walked over to her.

'Your father wants you to have a go,' he said. 'Come on, I'll show you – it's easier than it looks.'

Violet didn't say anything. She'd never shot the rifle before – normally Father just let her sit on the grass and watch.

He handed her the rifle and stepped behind her.

'Put it on your shoulder, that's it,' he said.

The rifle was impossibly heavy; Violet's arms shook with the effort of lifting it. The metal felt cool under her hands, and slightly damp from Frederick's sweat. Out of the corner of her eye, she saw Graham watching.

'I'll help you,' she heard Frederick say behind her, so close that his breath tickled her ear.

'Here,' he said. 'Like this.'

Frederick put his hands on her waist. When the gun went off, Violet fell backwards into his arms.

15

KATE

Kate takes a long sip of tea before she opens the package. There is a sweet, cloying scent as she unwraps the cloth, which is spotted white with mould. Inside, a stack of letters. The ink has faded to a dull brown, and the paper is creased and yellowed. The date on the first letter reads 20 July 1925.

My darling Lizzie,

I have not slept this week for thoughts of you.

Outside, the world is bright and green with summer, and even young Rainham has a spring in his step. But I cannot bear the long days. In fact, I hate them. I hate each and every day that stands between now and when I shall see you again.

I cannot settle to anything – even hunting brings me no comfort. All I can do is mope about, like a man tormented.

I long for you to come and join me, here at the Hall. I truly believe, my darling, that you will be happy here – much happier than in that dank little cottage. As I write this, I am looking out through my study window at the gardens. The roses are in bloom and their delicate beauty is unmatched in this world, other than by your face.

Trust me when I say this, for I have seen the world. The world, and every specimen of woman it contains. Oriental girls with coal-black hair and obsidian eyes. African princesses, their swan necks looped with gold. So many faces I have seen and admired.

But none compare to yours.

Oh, your face. I dream of it each night. Your ivory skin. Your lips, as red as fresh-spilled blood. Those dark, wild eyes. Each night I fall deeper into dreams, like a man drowning.

I must have you.

My darling. I have spoken to the vicar and he can perform the ceremony in two weeks' time. But we must ensure that everything is in order before we can proceed, as we discussed. My parents and my brother are due to return from Carlisle on Thursday. I expect them home by sundown.

We are closer than ever, now. You must not falter but be brave, for the sake of our union. For our future. It is as Macbeth said:

'Who could refrain, that had a heart to love, and in that heart courage to make love known?'

I enclose, as a symbol of our promise, a gift. It is a handkerchief. I sent to Lancaster for it, demanded only the finest quality for my love. My bride.

I count the days until you are mine.

Yours forever

Rupert

Who are Rupert and Elizabeth? Previous inhabitants of the cottage, perhaps. But, no – Rupert had written of 'the Hall'. Did he mean Orton Hall – her family's old seat?

Could they be related?

She searches through the other letters, hunting for more

details. Rupert writes of first setting eyes on Elizabeth at a May Day Festival in the village. He had – in his words – been 'transfixed by her ivory skin and raven locks'.

Some of the letters are about arrangements to meet – always at dawn or dusk, where the lovers won't be seen. There's a dark undercurrent to Rupert's words, as though danger stalks the couple; their stars conspiring against them. What did Elizabeth need such courage to face?

She can't figure it out. Nor can she confirm the identities of the correspondents – Rupert never signs his last name, and there are no further references to the Hall.

Sadness wells up in her. Something in Rupert's tone reminds her of early texts from Simon.

I can't stop thinking about you, he'd texted, after their third date. *I feel like I'm sixteen again.*

He had taken her to a little sushi place in Shoreditch. She had felt out of place among the other female diners, with their sleek hair and expensive jewellery. She had agonised over what to wear, texting pictures of different outfit options to her university friends. She'd wanted to wear something simple, a plain navy dress she'd had for years, but one of the girls, Becky, had talked her into borrowing a slinky red top. It was so low-cut that it exposed a mole on her breastbone, a dark pink smudge she'd hated since childhood.

She had felt incredibly self-conscious as she walked into the restaurant and scanned the tables, looking for Simon. He stood up when he saw her and smiled, his perfect teeth dazzling. Later, she'd convinced herself that she imagined it, but at the time she thought that a hush fell over the room, as the other diners looked between her and Simon and thought: *Her? Really?*

But Simon had poured her a glass of wine and smiled at her again, in that slow, sensuous way he had. Gradually, her nerves had fallen away, replaced by butterflies of excitement.

They had talked about everything, the conversation flowing as easily as the wine that Simon poured into her glass, until quickly they'd had one bottle, then two.

They'd talked about their families – Simon was an only child, just like her. He wasn't really in touch with his parents, he'd admitted – there'd been some kind of argument, when he was younger. Later, she'd realise he wasn't in contact with most people from his childhood, or from university. He had a talent for moving on and starting over, extricating himself as seamlessly as a snake shedding its skin.

But she didn't know any of this that night, as she looked into his eyes – so blue – and opened herself up to him in a way she couldn't remember doing with anyone before. The glass wall she'd built around herself was disintegrating – she could almost see it happening; the fragments winking in the light like tiny mirrors.

Really, it was just that the glass wall was being replaced with another kind of cage. One that Simon spun from charm and flattery, as binding and delicate as spider silk.

Now, she wonders if she'd known this, even then. Perhaps it had been part of the allure – the thought that, after all those exhausting years of locking herself away, here was someone who could do it for her.

Their jobs couldn't have been more different – he seemed to relish the challenge of private equity, telling her of the electric thrill when he acquired a floundering company. It was like hunting, he said, but instead of shooting deer or foxes he was seizing assets and balance sheets, stripping a company of its deadweight like flesh from a carcass.

His world – with its own set of bewildering rules and jargon – couldn't have been more foreign to her. And yet he'd listened attentively as she'd gushed about her job in children's publishing. About the thrill of reading manuscripts, of immersing herself in a story that no one else had yet experienced. She'd even told him how reading had been such a comfort – a life raft, really – after her father's death.

'I love your passion,' he'd said, placing his hand on hers, the fine hairs of his arm gold in the candlelight. And then, with a tenderness that made tears prick her eyes, 'Your father would be very proud of you.'

Other images from that night haunt her, too. Simon helping her into a taxi, asking her to his for a nightcap. Sinking down into his soft leather couch, brain muddled from too much wine . . .

'You're so much prettier when you smile,' he'd said, as she laughed at one of his jokes. He had leaned over, brushed the hair from her face and kissed her for the first time. He touched her gently at first, as if she were a wild animal he might spook away. Then the kiss deepened, and his fingers were firm on her jaw.

I must have you.

It was romantic, she told herself the next morning, the way he undid her trousers, pulled down her underwear, pushed himself inside her. The strength of his need.

In the early days of their relationship, she returned to that memory again and again, smoothing its rough edges into a lie she almost believed. It would be years before she remembered the word she had whispered, mind and body dulled by alcohol, as his face blurred over hers.

Wait.

Suddenly, she can't bear the sight of the letters anymore. She folds them up and puts them aside.

She clutches her mug of tea tightly, letting it warm her hands. Outside, it is raining in earnest now; the windows are jewelled with it. She can't see the garden, but she thinks she can hear the branches of the sycamore, scraping across the roof in the wind.

Nausea grips her stomach. The only sign of the baby, other

than a new heaviness to her breasts. She wonders if it is normal, this feeling that her guts are pushing up into her throat, if it indicates how far along she is. Almost two months since her last period, since the familiar twist of pain in her womb, the smear of blood on her underwear. Always the colour of silt, of soil, on the first day. Looking more like something from the earth than from her own body.

Simon didn't care for blood, unless he'd been the one to draw it. He collected the bruises that bloomed across her skin as if they were trophies, fingering them with pride. But her menstrual blood flowed from her body with its own rhythm, one that he didn't care for and couldn't control. He hated the feel of it, slimy and fibrous. The smell. Like an animal, he said. Or something dead. So, Kate had one week a month when her body was her own.

And now she is sharing it.

She pictures the clump of cells, clinging to her insides. Even now, splitting and reforming, growing. Into their child.

Will it be a boy, she wonders, and grow up to be like Simon? Or a girl, and grow up to be like her?

She isn't sure what would be worse.

16

ALTHA

It had been strange, seeing Grace again. Strange to think of how we'd started off together, side by side, and had ended up with a courtroom yawning between us. She in her neat gown and me in my shackles. A prisoner.

The dungeons were silent, but for a distant wail that might have been the wind, or the souls of those already condemned. I searched for the spider, looking under the matted straw, and my heart ached at the thought that it had gone, had left me to my fate. But just as I had given up hope, and curled myself into a ball on the ground, I felt it brush against my earlobe. I wished I could see it: the glitter of its eyes and pincers, but the night was too dark, with not even a sliver of moonlight coming through the grate. So dark that I felt as if I were in my grave already.

If I were to have a grave, that was. I didn't know what happened to witches after they were hanged. I wondered whether anyone buried them. Whether anyone would bury me.

I wanted to be buried. If I must depart this life, I thought, let me live on in the soil: let me feed the earthworms, nourish the roots of the trees, like my mother and her mother before her.

Really, it wasn't death I feared. It was dying. The process of it; the pain. Death had always sounded so peaceful, when it was spoken of in church: a gathering of lambs to the bosom, a return to the kingdom. But I had seen it too many times to believe that. The sweep of the reaper's shadow over an old man, a woman, a child. The face contorting, the limbs flailing, the desperate gasp for air. There was no peace in any death I had seen. I would find no peace in mine.

When I did sleep, I saw the noose, tight around my neck. I saw the breath choked out of me in a white vapour. I saw my body, twisting in the breeze.

They had finished with Grace, it seemed. But I saw her there in the gallery when they took me into the dock the next morning. As of course one would expect. What woman would not want to know the fate of her husband's accused murderer?

We rose when the judges entered the courtroom. I saw one of them look at me, eyes narrowed, as if I were the rot at the centre of the apple, a canker to be cut away.

The prosecutor called the physician, Doctor Smythson, to the stand. As I knew he would.

They had brought him to see me, at the village gaol. Before they brought me to Lancaster. Though I was mad with hunger and exhaustion, I had not yielded to their questions. They asked if I had ever attended a witches' sabbath, had ever suckled a familiar or lain with a beast. If I had given myself to Satan, as his bride.

If I had killed John Milburn.

No, I said, though my throat was caked with thirst and my stomach groaned with want. No. It took all my strength to force the word from my body. To protest my innocence.

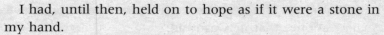

I had, until then, held on to hope as if it were a stone in my hand.

But when they brought Doctor Smythson to the gaol I feared it was over.

Now, I watched him take his oath on the Bible. He was an old man, and his veins made red patterns on his cheeks. That'll be the drink, my mother would say, if she were here. He'd indulged in it as much as he'd prescribed it. Though that was by far his least dangerous method of treatment. As I looked at him, I remembered Grace's mother, Anna Metcalfe: her milk-white face, the colour sucked out of her by leeches.

The prosecutor began his questioning.

'Doctor Smythson, you recall the events of New Year's Day, in this, the year of our Lord 1619?'

'Yes.'

'Are you able to relate them for the court?'

The physician spoke with confidence. He was a man, after all. He had no reason to think he would not be believed.

'I began the day at dawn, as is my custom. I'd been up late, the night before, with a patient. The family had given me some eggs. I remember I ate them with my wife that morning. We had not long broken our fast when there was a hammering at the door.'

'Who was at the door?'

'It was Daniel Kirkby.'

'And what did Daniel Kirkby want?'

'I remember thinking he looked very pale. At first I thought he might have taken ill himself but then he told me there'd been some sort of incident, at the Milburn farm. Involving John Milburn. From his face, I knew it was not good. I collected my coat and my bag and set off to the farm with the boy.'

'And what did you find when you got there?'

'Milburn was on the ground. His injuries were very grave. I knew at once that he was dead.'

'Can you describe those injuries to the court, please, Doctor?'

'A large portion of the skull had been crushed. One eye was badly damaged. The bones of the neck had been broken, as had those of the arms and legs.'

'And what, in your opinion, would have caused the injuries, Doctor?'

'Trampling by animals. Daniel Kirkby told me that Master Milburn had been stampeded by his cows.'

'Thank you. And have you ever seen such injuries, in your career as a physician?'

'I have. I am regularly called upon to attend the aftermath of farm accidents, which are common in these parts.'

The prosecutor frowned, as if the physician had not given him the answer he wanted.

'Are you able to tell the court what happened next, after you viewed Master Milburn's body?'

'I went inside the farmhouse, to speak to the widow.'

'And was she alone?'

'No. She was with the accused, Altha Weyward.'

'Can you describe for the court the demeanour of the widow, Grace Milburn, and that of the accused, Altha Weyward?'

'Mistress Milburn looked very pale and shaken, as you would expect.'

The prosecutor nodded, paused.

'Are you able to tell the court', he said, 'your opinion of Altha Weyward?'

'My opinion? In what respect?'

'To put it another way. Are you able to tell the court the nature of your acquaintance with her, over the years?'

'I would say that she – and her mother before her – has been something of a nuisance.'

'A nuisance?'

'On several occasions, I've had reports that she's attended to villagers, patients who were already under my regimen.'

'Are you able to provide an example, sir?'

The physician paused.

'Not two months ago, I was treating a patient for fever. Baker's daughter, girl of ten. She had an imbalance of humours: too much of the sanguine. This led to an excess of heat in the body, hence the fever. As a consequence, she needed to be bled.'

'Go on.'

'I administered the treatment. Advised that the leeches should remain for one night and one day. When I returned the next day, the parents had removed the leeches prematurely.'

'Did they say why?'

'They'd had a visit from Altha Weyward in the night. She'd recommended the girl take quantities of broth instead.'

'And how did the child fare?'

'She lived. Fortunately, the leeches had been left on for long enough that most of the excess humour was removed.'

'And has this sort of thing happened before?'

'Several times before. There was a very similar case when the accused was still a child. She and her mother treated a patient of mine suffering scarlatina. John Milburn's late mother-in-law, actually. Anna Metcalfe. Sadly, Mistress Metcalfe passed away.'

'In your opinion, what caused her death?'

'The accused's mother. Whether through malice or not, I cannot say.'

'And, in your view,' said the prosecutor, 'what role did the accused play in Mistress Metcalfe's death?'

'I could not say for certain,' the physician replied. 'She was but a child at the time.'

I could hear the hum of whispers again. I looked at Grace, sitting at the back of the gallery. She was too far away for me to make out her expression.

'Doctor Smythson,' the prosecutor continued, 'are you familiar with the characteristics of witches, as laid out by His Royal Highness in his work, Daemonologie?'

'Of course, sir. I am familiar with the work.'

'Are you aware', said the prosecutor, 'of whether Altha and Jennet Weyward possessed animal familiars? Familiars', he spat, turning to face the court, 'are evidence of a witch's pact with the devil. They invite these monstrous imps – who wear the likeness of God's own creatures – to suckle at their bosom. Thus they sustain Satan himself with their milk.'

At this question my heart hammered in my chest, so loud that I wondered that the prosecutor himself could not hear it. Doctor Smythson had never been inside the cottage.

But so many others had. So many others might have seen the crow that perched, dark and sleek on my mother's shoulder, the bees and damselflies I wore in my hair when I was small.

Had someone told him?

The courtroom was still, all eyes trained on Doctor Smythson for his answer. The physician shifted in his seat; mopped his brow with a white handkerchief.

'No, sir,' he said, finally. 'I have not seen such a thing.'

Relief flooded my veins, sweet and heady. But the very next moment, a cold dread took its place. For I knew what question would follow.

The prosecutor paused.

'Very well,' he said. 'And have you, in the course of your acquaintance with the accused, had the opportunity to examine her for a witch's mark? An unnatural teat, from which she may give suck to the devil and his servants?'

'Yes, sir. I made the examination at Crows Beck gaol, in

the presence of your men. The mark is on her ribcage, below the heart.'

'Your honours,' said the prosecutor. 'I would like to ask the court's permission to make an exhibit of the accused's body, to demonstrate that she shows the witch's mark.'

The stouter judge spoke: 'Your request is granted.'

One of the guards strode towards me. I was hauled, still shackled, to the boards in front of the jury. I stood queasy with fear, until I felt harsh fingers tug at the bindings of my gown before pulling it over my head.

I quivered in my filthy shift, shamed that all and sundry could see me thus. Then the fingers were back, and the shift was gone. My skin met with the clammy air. The gallery roared, and I shut my eyes. The prosecutor circled my body, looking at my exposed flesh the way a farmer looks at his cattle.

I would have prayed, if I had believed in God.

'Doctor,' called the prosecutor, 'can you point out the mark?'

'I can no longer see it,' said Doctor Smythson, his features furrowed. 'Alas – what I took to be the witch's mark in the dim of the gaol appears to be but a sore. A flea bite, perhaps. Or some sort of pox.'

The prosecutor stood still for a moment, his cold eyes blazing with fury. Rage gave his scarred cheeks a purple hue.

'Very well,' he said, after a time. 'You may clothe her.'

17

VIOLET

Violet fancied that she could still smell Frederick's cologne in her hair from when he had caught her in his arms.

Father had given them an odd look, as if he had come upon Frederick borrowing something of his without permission. Then the look passed, like a cloud going over the sun, and he had merely nodded at them. The shooting had wrapped up fairly quickly after that, with Frederick declaring that his shoulder ached ('thanks to Jerry') and suggesting an afternoon nap before a walk through the grounds.

Violet decided she would walk next to Frederick. She would show him all of her favourite spots in the grounds, including the beech tree. Perhaps he'd like to climb it with her? She caught herself. She was being ridiculous. She must be *ladylike*. Father would have a fit if she climbed a tree in front of a guest. Anyway, she didn't want Frederick to think she was . . . well, a child.

In the afternoon, when the sun had dipped in the sky to cast long shadows over the valley, she made her way downstairs to meet the others. Father and Graham hadn't come down yet, but Frederick was waiting in the entrance hall. He looked up as she walked down the stairs, and the feel of his eyes on her body made her giddy. A wave of heat rose up her neck. He extended a hand as she approached the bottom step, as if he were helping her down from a horse-drawn carriage in a romance novel.

'M'lady,' he said, kissing her hand. The brush of his lips against her skin was like an electric shock. She couldn't tell if she liked it or not.

'Aha,' Father's voice boomed down the stairs. Violet looked up to see a reluctant Graham trailing him. 'Raring to go, I see.'

Outside, the valley was hazy with the afternoon sun. Midges shimmered in the sweet-smelling air.

'Ugh,' said Frederick, swatting at his face. 'Don't care much for midges, I must say. Not quite sure there's any point to them, the blasted things.'

'Oh, but there is,' Violet said, excitedly. 'A point to them, I mean. They're a very important food source for toads and swallows, actually. You could say the whole valley depends on them, in the summer. And I think they're rather pretty – they look a bit like fairy dust, in this light, don't you think?'

Fairy dust? She chided herself. She was trying to seem grown up in front of Frederick. She hadn't got off to a very good start.

'Hmm. I'm not sure I'd go that far,' he said, frowning. 'Though they're a damn sight better than Libyan mosquitoes. If I have to be bitten to death by insects, I'd rather they were bloody English ones.'

Violet flushed at the swear word. Father hadn't heard: he was walking ahead with Graham, Cecil loping alongside. The occasional burst of their conversation floated back to them and it sounded to Violet as though Graham was getting a lecture about his shooting.

'Terribly sorry,' said Frederick. 'Not used to keeping fine company these days.'

'Are there no girls in Libya?'

'None such as yourself,' Frederick said. Violet flushed again. They walked in silence for a while. They were approaching the beech tree now. It looked rather majestic, Violet thought, with the sun dappling the green leaves and painting the branches gold. She waited for Frederick to comment on it, but he didn't. They walked on.

'I say,' she began, 'how is it that we're cousins, and yet we have never met before?'

'Oh, but we have,' said Frederick. 'I came to visit with my parents when I was a child. Though I expect you won't remember – you couldn't have been more than a toddler, then.'

'Well, why did you come only the once?' Violet asked. 'I'd have loved to have a cousin around, growing up. It's just me and Graham, and we . . . aren't close, not anymore. Then, when he goes to school, I'm all alone.'

'It's all a bit fuzzy, to be honest,' said Frederick. 'But – and I don't want to offend you – I think it was something to do with your mother.'

'My mother? I barely remember her.'

'You look like her,' said Frederick. 'She had the same dark hair. She was sort of – curious. Spoke like the servants. Mummy told me she was a local girl, from the village. Daddy was a bit put out by the whole thing, I think. Kept saying his parents would never have allowed it, if they'd been alive. Anyway. Sorry, I don't want to offend you any more than I have already today.'

'No – please,' said Violet, grasping at his words. 'Please, tell me more about her. Father never tells us anything. You said she was curious? What did you mean?'

'Well, she . . . wasn't quite well, I don't think. For one, she was always going around with this ratty old bird on her shoulder. Some sort of raven – or maybe it was a crow, I don't remember, but it was obviously diseased: there were these ghastly white streaks on its feathers. Anyway, she called it . . . what was it? Oh yes – *Morg*. Odd name. Mummy was rather scandalised.'

Here, Frederick paused and looked over at Violet. She kept her face neutral – afraid that if he could see the effect his words were having on her, he would stop.

A crow with white streaks. Could the feather she found have belonged to Morg? Violet's heart sang. *Her mother*. So she had loved animals too – just as Violet had suspected.

'She couldn't take meals with us,' Frederick continued. 'She'd start off but then she'd begin to make strange comments, out of nowhere . . . "I'll tell them," she'd say, as if it were a threat. None of us had the faintest idea what she was on about, though perhaps she didn't either, the poor thing. Anyway, your father would have to take her back to her room. Then she'd be ranting and raving, shouting . . . often, he had no choice but to lock her in.'

Violet started. 'Lock her in?'

'It was for her own safety, you see,' said Frederick. 'Just until the doctor came. She was – a danger to herself. And the baby.'

Violet shivered.

She had never met a mad person. She had an image of a waifish figure draped in white, speaking gibberish, like Ophelia from *Hamlet*.

Perhaps *this* was why Father never spoke of her mother? Because he didn't want Violet to know that she had been mad. Perhaps he was trying to protect her memory. She frowned, then turned to Frederick again.

'Well – can you tell me anything else about her? Was she . . . was she kind?'

Frederick snorted.

'Not to me. Though she didn't like me much – that was

evident. I used to catch her staring at me and muttering to herself. And – well, the visit ended rather abruptly.'

'What happened?'

'One night, I found a toad in my bed. A live one. I remember touching it with my foot. It was cold and slimy. Horrible,' he shuddered at the memory. 'They probably heard me scream back in London. Anyway, then Mummy came, and saw the toad . . . and she got it into her head that your mother had put it there. She was hysterical. Your father kept telling her to calm down, that it had to be one of the servants – that your mother had been in her room the whole evening, with the door bolted, but both my parents got quite worked up really. They packed the car – we had a little green Bentley, I remember, new that year – and we left in the middle of the night.'

'Oh,' said Violet.

'On the way home, my mother kept saying your father hadn't been right in the head since the Great War . . . then our grandparents and Uncle Edward dying in that horrible accident . . . And then my father said . . .' He paused to flick a midge from his shoulder.

'What did your father say?' Violet asked, scarcely breathing.

'That Uncle Rupert had been bewitched.'

She didn't know whether or not to believe Frederick's story. She couldn't imagine why he would lie. And yet . . . it was hard to believe the horrible things he had said about her mother. It was awful to think of her mother ranting and raving, needing to be locked in a room – and, worst of all, being unkind to Frederick. Perhaps she hadn't meant to scare him with the toad? Violet wouldn't particularly mind finding a toad in her bed. In fact, she was rather fond of them.

But then she remembered Father's words.

Perhaps they can stop you from turning out like her.

Was that why she had this sick, wrong feeling in her stomach?

The air was growing colder now. Violet could hear crickets, calling for their mates. She looked at Frederick, walking next to her. In the dim light, his dark features and long strides made her think of a panther.

They hadn't spoken for a few minutes. Violet wondered if he thought she was 'curious' too, like her mother. She would need to take care that he didn't catch her staring at him. She wished he would say something. He hadn't commented on the beauty of the sun setting slowly over the valley at all, even though it had put more colours in the sky than she knew the names for.

'Do you hear that?' she asked. 'It's such a lovely sound.'

'What is?'

'The crickets.'

'Oh. Yes, I suppose it is.' She heard his laugh, rich and deep.

'What's so funny?' she asked.

'You're an unusual girl. First the midges, now the crickets . . . never known a girl – or a chap, for that matter – to be so fond of insects.'

'I just find them so very interesting,' she said. 'Beautiful, too. It's sad, though – they have such short lives. For instance, did you know that the mayfly only lives for one day?'

She had seen a swarm of mayflies, once, down at the beck. A great, glittering cloud of them, pulsing above the surface of the water. They looked to Violet as if they were dancing – she had been quite disturbed when she learned from Dinsdale, the gardener, that they had in fact been *mating*. Now, her cheeks flushed at the image. Would Frederick be able to tell she was having such unseemly thoughts? She wished she hadn't brought them up.

'Imagine', she continued, anxious to change the subject, 'having only one day left on Earth. I don't think I'd be able to decide between catching a train to London to see the Natural History Museum, or . . . lounging by the beck all day. One last afternoon with the birds, the insects and the flowers . . .'

'I know what I would do,' said Frederick. They were passing by a briar bush now. Violet realised that she didn't know where Father and Graham had got to: perhaps they were already back at the house. The sound of Father lecturing Graham ('You must *aim* the rifle, boy') had long since faded.

'And what would that be, Frederick?' she asked, blushing at the sound of his name on her lips. A strange, quivery feeling bubbled inside her.

He laughed and moved closer: his arm brushed hers and her heart juddered.

'I'll show you, but only if you close your eyes.'

Violet did as she was told. Suddenly, there was a hand on her waist, large and rough through the fabric of her skirt. Opening her eyes a fraction, she saw that the pink glimmer of dusk was blocked out by Frederick's face in front of hers. She could feel his breath tickling her nose. It felt hot and smelled of coffee and something else, a sour note that made Violet think – oddly, unseasonably – of Christmas pudding. Violet tried to remember the word for the thing that Mrs Kirkby soaked the pudding in before setting it alight, but then—

He was kissing her. Or, Violet supposed that was what he was doing. She knew that people kissed, from reading books ('to smooth that rough touch with a tender kiss' – that was Shakespeare, wasn't it?) and because she had once seen Penny kissing Neil, the ill-fated under-gardener. They had been pressed up against the stable, clinging onto each other as if they were drowning. It had looked rather unpleasant.

Violet was surprised that she was still thinking so much, even though her lips had been completely enveloped in his (rather wet) ones. She was finding it quite difficult to breathe. She wasn't sure *how* she was supposed to breathe, with her mouth covered by his (the taste of his mouth was very adult, as though he had seen things, been to places she couldn't comprehend . . . again she was reminded of Christmas pudding, why was that?).

She was breathing through her nose now, Violet wondered if he could hear it, if she sounded like a cow . . . Her brain was a whirlpool. She thought of drowning, again. He was kissing her more fiercely now, pressing her against the briar bush; she felt twigs poking into her back and her hair – she would have to get them out before Father saw . . . Then he did something that made her almost stop thinking. He pushed something wet and slimy into her mouth – Violet thought of the toad – and she realised it was his tongue. She sputtered, and he pulled away. She took a deep breath, gulping at the clean evening air.

'Sorry,' he said. 'Got rather carried away there.' He reached out a hand and traced the chain of her necklace with one finger.

She shivered. It was almost nicer than the kiss.

'Best be getting back for dinner,' he said. 'We should do this again, though – same time tomorrow evening?'

She nodded, struck dumb. He turned to go, heading towards the Hall, which, with its yellow windows and high turrets looked to Violet like a scene from a book – a ship on a stormy sea, perhaps. She stayed for a while, waiting for her breathing to slow and picking out the twigs from her hair. As she walked back to the Hall (she tripped a couple of times, still reeling from the feel of his mouth on hers) she wondered if she looked changed, if anyone would be able to tell what had happened just by glancing at her. She certainly felt different. Her heart was beating as hard in her chest as if she had been running.

It wasn't until she shut her bedroom door and her racing mind had settled that something Frederick had said, before he had kissed her so suddenly, returned to her.

She was a danger to herself. And the baby.

Violet had always believed that her mother died giving birth to Graham.

But Frederick had made it sound as though he had already been born.

18

KATE

Kate has been at the cottage for three weeks now. It's late spring, and the year is ripening. It rained last night – hard enough that she feared the roof would buckle – but today the sky is low and blue, the air hot. Hot and thick to match her blood, which seems, in these last weeks, to have slowed its pace through her veins.

On the walk into the village this morning, she passes another row of moles, tied by their tails to a rusted gate. Flies hover about them, flitting between their damp fur and the clumps of dog violet that grow alongside the road. She's learned that it's a local tradition – the cashier at the greengrocer looked bemused when Kate shyly asked about it, explained that was how the mole-catcher proved his worth. But the shrivelled bodies still feel like a warning, especially for her.

By the time she reaches the medical centre, her shirt is sticky with exertion and anxiety. She was instructed to arrive with a full bladder, and her lower abdomen is tight and painful, straining against the waistband of her skirt. She checks her watch: ten past nine. She's five minutes early.

Perhaps she won't go in. Perhaps she'll turn and walk back to the cottage without even knocking on the door, the same way she repeatedly dialled the number and hung up before anyone could answer. She did this five times before her nerve held and she managed to speak to the receptionist, to actually book this appointment.

She looks around her. This early, the square is empty and quiet, save for a cow's distant lowing. There is no one to see her go in. She looks down at her feet, watching ants serpentine across the cobbles.

Taking a breath, Kate opens the door and is hit by the smell of disinfectant. The waiting room is cold and whitewashed, the plastic chairs and tired noticeboard a stark contrast to the building's Tudor exterior. The space is dominated by a large desk, behind which a woman sits tapping away at a computer. The muffled sounds of conversation come from behind a heavy door: the consulting room, according to a gleaming brass plate.

'Name?' asks the receptionist, a thin woman with a vulpine face.

'Kate,' she says. 'Kate Ayres.'

The receptionist's eyebrows lift as she looks at Kate properly for the first time.

'The niece,' she says. It isn't a question.

'Um – yes. Did you know my great-aunt? Violet?'

But the woman is looking back at her computer screen.

'If you could take a seat, please. The doctor will be with you in a minute.'

Kate sits heavily on one of the plastic chairs. She wishes she had some water; her stomach roils, and there is a strange taste in her mouth. Metallic, like blood, or even dirt. She's been waking up with it. It reminds her of something, a childhood memory that she can't quite hold on to.

The door of the consulting room opens.

'Miss Ayres?'

The doctor is male – in his late sixties, perhaps; weathered cheeks shaded by white stubble. A stethoscope around his neck. Panic bubbles up in her.

She'd asked for a female doctor, hadn't she? Yes – she's sure of it. The receptionist – likely the same woman staring at her now – had assured her that there would be a female doctor. 'Dr Collins is only available Tuesdays and Thursdays,' she'd said on the phone. 'So you'll have to come in on one of those days if you want to see a woman, otherwise it's Dr Radcliffe.'

'Ah – sorry,' she says now as she rises from the seat, wincing at the feel of her thighs unsticking from the plastic. 'I think I was booked in to see Dr Collins?'

'Couldn't make it in,' says the male doctor, gesturing for her to follow him into the consulting room. 'Sick child. Always the way with that one, I'm afraid.'

She hesitates. Part of her wants to leave; to ask for an appointment with the female doctor another day. But she's here now. And she's not sure she trusts herself to come back.

She follows the doctor into the consulting room.

The gel is cold on her skin. Dr Radcliffe has already drawn volumes of blood from her arm, prodding and sticking her like a laboratory specimen.

'Just relax,' he says, running the ultrasound wand over her stomach. He moves closer and she smells his breath, stale with coffee. 'Your husband couldn't make it?'

She has an image of Simon's face over hers, his hand resting on the base of her throat as he moves inside her. His cells travelling up into her body, ready to tether her to him forever.

'I'm not married,' she says, blinking the memory away.

'Your boyfriend, then. He didn't want to come?' There is

a strange whooshing sound in the room, almost like the beating of wings.

'No, I don't . . . what's that noise?'

The doctor smiles, pressing the wand harder into her stomach.

'That', he says, 'is the heartbeat. Your baby's heartbeat.'

There is a plummeting sensation inside her.

'Heartbeat? I thought it was . . . too early for that.'

'Hmm, you're between ten and twelve weeks along, I'd say. Here, take a look.'

He gestures to the blinking monitor, where her womb undulates in grey and white. For a moment she can't make sense of the image, it's like static. Then she sees it: a pearly glimmer, pupa-shaped, almost. The foetus.

Her mouth is so dry that it's hard to get the words out.

'Can you tell it . . . the baby's sex?'

The doctor chuckles.

'A bit too soon for that, I'm afraid. You'll have to come back in a few weeks.'

There is something else she wanted – planned – to ask. But now, with the doctor's liver-flecked hands on her stomach, the room filled with the sound of the baby's heartbeat, it feels . . . impossible.

The question shrivels inside her.

The doctor looks at her strangely, as if he has read her thoughts.

'All done,' he says abruptly, handing her a piece of paper towel. 'You can clean yourself up.'

He is silent as he enters information on a computer, carefully labels the ruby-red vials of her blood.

'You look a bit like her,' he says after a while. 'Your great-aunt, I mean. Violet. Similar sort of eyes – just the hair that's different. Hers was dark when she was younger.'

'It's dyed.'

'You'll have to stop doing that. Bad for the baby.' He goes back to his labelling.

'Did you treat her, then? My aunt.'

The doctor pauses, fiddles with the stethoscope around his neck.

'Once or twice, when Dr Collins wasn't in – she was her patient, really. Only in recent years, though. Before that I think she went to a surgery out of town – she only started coming here when my father died. The first Dr Radcliffe. He started the practice.'

Finished with his labelling, the doctor gets up to usher her out of the consulting room.

'See Mrs Dinsdale on your way out, please, so you can book in for the next appointment. We'll want you back in eight weeks.'

Back in the waiting room, Kate looks at the noticeboard again, at the pamphlets on display at the receptionist's desk. But there's none of the information she is looking for.

'Will you book in for the next appointment today?' asks the receptionist.

'Um. Actually, I was wondering', Kate lowers her voice, glancing over at an elderly woman in the waiting room, 'if you have any information about . . . termination services.'

The receptionist slides a leaflet across the counter, her eyes narrowed.

'Thank you,' says Kate. She pauses. She wants to leave, to get away from the woman's cold stare, but her bladder is tugging at her painfully. 'Is there a toilet I can use?'

A nod at the corridor to the left.

She washes her hands, grimacing at the chemical smell of the soap. As she cups water from the tap and drinks, snatches of conversation from the waiting room float back to her.

'Did she ask for what I think she did?' An unfamiliar voice – the elderly female patient.

Kate freezes. She doesn't want to hear this. Her cheeks sting with shame.

'Can't say I'm surprised,' the receptionist is saying. 'Being from that family.'

'Who is she?'

'That's Violet's great-niece.'

'Really?' says the old woman. 'Didn't know Violet had any family, save for himself up at the big house. Though not sure he counts for much.'

'I wonder if she has it, too.'

'They all do, don't they? That Weyward lot. Ever since the first one.'

Then the receptionist says something else – a word so unexpected that Kate is sure she must have misheard.

Witch.

Outside, Kate takes deep, gulping breaths. Her brain feels disordered, fogged.

She can still hear it; the strange thrumming of her baby's heartbeat. The way it filled the room. It was hard to believe that it had come from her own body. It sounded like something from the sky – a bird taking to the air. Or something not of this world at all.

It is 2 a.m. but Kate is awake, watching bats flutter past the window, dark against a pale slice of moon.

Her thoughts feel scattered, panicked – flitting away from her as though they, too, have wings. She rests a hand on her stomach, feeling the smooth heat of her own flesh. It seems impossible that, even now, the larval creature she saw onscreen floats inside her. Growing into a child.

Those things the women were saying about her family – they made it sound as though Kate was carrying some sort of faulty gene, an error code lurking in her cells, plotting her demise. Like the crow she found in the fireplace with the strange white pattern across its glossy feathers – a sign of leucism, she'd read, a genetic trait handed down over generations.

She remembers what the greengrocer said, about the viscount. How he'd lost his marbles.

Perhaps they were referring to some kind of mental health issue, running in the family? That wouldn't surprise her. All those panic attacks she'd experienced over the years – the clawing in her chest, her throat tightening.

The feeling of something trying to get out.

After another hour of trying and failing to sleep, she gives up, pushing the bedcovers aside.

Switching on the light, she drags the hatboxes out from under the bed. There has to be something in here – something she missed the first time she looked.

Again, she rifles through the folder with its faded, dusty cover. But there's nothing – nothing she hasn't already seen before. Not a single mention of the Weywards.

Sighing in frustration, she picks up Violet's old passport and opens it to the photo page, staring into the dark eyes that are so like Kate's own. There's a determination there that Kate didn't notice before – the firm set of the mouth, the jut of the chin. As if Violet has fought something and won. She would never have ended up like Kate: soft and malleable, yielding as easily to Simon's fingers as if she were clay.

Suddenly she wishes her great-aunt were still alive, that she could talk to her. That she could talk to someone. Anyone.

She is about to put the passport back when a slip of yellowed paper falls out of it.

It's a birth certificate. Violet's birth certificate.

Name: Violet Elizabeth Ayres
Date of Birth: 5 February 1926

Place of Birth: Orton Hall, near Crows Beck, Cumbria, England
Father's occupation: Peer
Father's name: Rupert William Ayres, Ninth Viscount Kendall
Mother's name: Elizabeth Ayres, nee Weyward

She remembers the letters. Rupert and Elizabeth – they are Violet's parents; Kate's great-grandparents.

Which means that Kate – Kate is a Weyward.

When she does sleep, Kate has the same nightmare that haunted her throughout her childhood – her father's large hand over her small one; the dark shadow of the crow in the trees. Wings thrashing the air; the shriek of rubber on tarmac. The wet thump of her father's body hitting the ground.

Except that at the cottage, the dream is longer – the flapping of wings morphing into the gallop of her baby's heartbeat. She sees the foetus: growing and growing, like a moon rising into the sky. Growing into a child. But not a boy, blond and blue-eyed like Simon. A girl, with dark hair, dark eyes. A child that looks like Aunt Violet. That looks like Kate.

A Weyward child.

In the morning, she takes the crumpled brochure from the bedside table and unfurls it. But she doesn't dial the number. She can't bring herself to. Every time she picks up the phone, she remembers the sound of the baby's heartbeat, remembers the way it looked inside her, glimmering like a pearl. Remembers that dream-child, with hair and eyes the colour of jet, of richest earth.

She is still for a moment, thinking of what Simon would do if he knew she was pregnant. How he would treat their child.

Things will be different, this time. *She* will be different. She will be strong.

She remembers the way she appeared in the mirror, when she tried on Aunt Violet's cape. That dark glitter in her eyes. For a second, she felt almost powerful.

She will keep her baby, her Weyward child. She knows, somehow, that she is carrying a girl.

She will keep her safe.

19

ALTHA

Even though they'd let me dress, I felt the pressure of a hundred eyes on my flesh as if I were still unclothed. The men stared with hunger, like I was a sweetmeat they wanted to devour. All except the man with the pitying eyes, who turned his gaze away.

After a time, I could not look at them: not the public sitting in the gallery, nor the judges, the prosecutor, or the doctor. Grace, in her white cap. I had wanted to bring the spider from the dungeons, a friend amidst foes. But I knew it was not safe, that it would only darken the cloud of suspicion that hung over me. Now, a sparkle caught my eye, and I saw that the spider had followed me, that it was spinning its web in the corner of the dock. Tears filled my eyes as I watched its legs dance over the shimmering strands of silk. I wished I could shrink myself as small, and scuttle away from this place.

I was born with the mole. The one I had scratched away, my first night in the castle. I should have thought to do it sooner, before they brought Doctor Smythson to the gaol, back in Crows Beck. But my wits were deadened, from lack

of food and light, from resisting the questions of the prose-
cutors' men. And it was a gamble, in any case: the wound
is crusting over now; weeping and angry. Doctor Smythson
might have seen it for what it was.

The witch's mark, they call it. Or the devil's. It serves as
instant proof of guilt.

My mother had one too, in near enough the same place.
'Matching,' she used to say. 'As befits a mother and
daughter.'

It wasn't the only thing we'd had in common. Everyone
said I was the spit of her, with my oval face and shocking
dark hair.

I used to be proud of this, especially after she first died. I
would stare at my reflection on the surface of the beck,
desperate for a trace of her in my features. The rippling water
blurred my face so that it was just a pale moon. I imagined
it was my mother, looking at me through the veil that sep-
arates this world from the next.

I wondered what she'd make of it. Of her only daughter,
stripped naked in a courtroom, while men roamed their eyes
over her. Searching for a sign that she had sold her soul to
the devil.

What did they know of souls, these men who sat on bolsters
all day, clothed in finery, and saw fit to condemn a woman
to death?

I do not profess to know much of souls, myself. I am not
a learned woman, other than in the ways my mother handed
down to me, as her mother handed down to her. But I know
goodness, evil, light and dark.

And I know the devil.

I have seen him. I have seen his mark. His real mark.

I have seen these things. And so has Grace.

*

I dreamed of him, sometimes, in the dungeon. The devil. The form he takes when he appears.

I also dreamed of Grace.

Most of all, I dreamed of my mother, on that final night. Her last in this world. Her dry fingers in mine. The little rasping sounds of her breath, her skin so pale I could see the blue-green veins beneath it, like a network of rivers. Her parting words. 'Remember your promise,' she said. She has been gone these last three years, but the memory of her in her sickbed was as strong as if I had just lost her.

Time seemed changed by the trial. Whereas before, my days had been broken up by little rituals and milestones – milking the goat of a morning; picking berries in the afternoon; readying tonics for the sick in the evening – now there was just court and sleep. Fear and dreams.

The day after he questioned Doctor Smythson, the prosecutor called the Kirkby lad. Daniel.

We'd attended his birth, my mother and I. I couldn't have been more than six years old, had only seen animals birthed. Lambs in blue cauls. Kittens with milky eyes. Birds, hatching pink and scrawny. I had felt their fear, coming into the world with all its unknowns. Its dangers.

I did not know birthing babies was something humans did, too. I took my own existence for granted, and it was only after watching Daniel's mother push him out of her body that I learned my mother had made me with a man and pulled me from her like a root from the earth. I never found out who the man was. She refused to tell me. 'That is not our way,' she'd said. She hadn't known her own father either, she told me later.

As a babe, Daniel Kirkby had screamed so loud that I'd covered my ears. But in court he spoke with a quiet voice. He was solemn and wide-eyed when he took the oath. I saw him look towards me, then away, like a horse flinching from the whip. He feared me. My mother would have been sad to know this, having assured his safe passage into the world.

'How long have you worked at the Milburn farm, Daniel?'

'Just since last winter, sir.'

'And what was the nature of the work you undertook?'

'Just helping, like. Whatever the master needed. Milking the cows, when Mistress Milburn could not.'

His cheeks coloured, at her name on his lips. His eyes flickered, roaming the gallery. I wondered if he was seeking her face.

'And were you working this past New Year's Day, in the year of our Lord 1619?'

'Yes, sir.'

'Please could you tell the court the events of that day, as you can best recall them.'

'I got up early, sir, when it was still dark. It's a long walk from ours to the Milburn farm so I set off in good time like I always did.'

'And when you got there?'

'Everything was normal, sir. Same as before. I met John – Master Milburn – round the back, outside the byre.'

'And did he seem well to you?'

'He seemed in good health, sir. John were always hale. I never known him to be ill or have funny turns, not while I worked there.'

'And what happened after you arrived?'

'We milked the cows, then freed them from the byre, so they would go out to the field.'

'And how did the cows seem to you? Were they placid, docile? Or aggressive?'

'They were less keen than usual to get outside into the field, sir. It was a very cold morning. But they were calm.'

'Did you ever know them to be aggressive in any way, while you worked for Milburn?'

'No, sir.'

'I see. So, you and Master Milburn were out in the field, having just released the cows from the byre. Are you able to tell the court what happened next?'

'I was looking back to the byre, sir, thinking I ought to go and shut the gate. Then I heard the cows . . . they weren't making no sound I'd ever heard an animal make before. They was almost – shrieking, like. There was a bird – a crow, I think – swooping down from the sky. They were spooked by it, sir. Their eyes were back in their heads, their mouths were frothing. John was trying to calm them. He loved them, you see, those cows. Didn't want them to be scared.'

At this the boy's voice broke. I saw his Adam's apple quiver as he gulped away tears. He was fifteen, a man. It would not do to cry, not in court, wearing the finest wool he was ever like to wear, seeing that his master got justice.

A brave little lad. I could see it was important to him, the getting of justice. I knew the value of it, myself.

I wondered what he'd known, while he worked there. I knew Grace would have fed him, those mornings. She'd have fed the both of them, would have ladled steaming pottage into their bowls when they came in from seeing to the cows. The three of them would have sat round the table together, Grace looking down into her bowl, John looking at Daniel, wondering if he'd ever have his own boy to help him take the cows to the field.

I saw the muscles work in Daniel's jaw as he gritted his teeth to continue his tale.

'But the cows couldn't be calmed, no matter what John did. They dug at the ground with their hooves, eyes rolling, as if they were about to charge. Like they were bulls. And they did charge. They charged straight at John.'

He paused. The air in the courtroom grew taut as a skin drum.

'It was loud, with the cows' hooves thundering and John

shouting . . . He fell and I couldn't see him no more. The shouts turned to screams.'

I looked at Grace. Her head was still bowed. I saw some in the gallery watching her as Daniel Kirkby continued with his testimony.

'John became quiet. Then the cows stopped. As if nothing had ever happened. As if . . . as if . . .'

He turned his head to look at me. I could see in his face that he did not want to look at me, that he was forcing himself. But he kept his eyes on me while he spoke.

'As if a spell had been broken.'

Gasps and cries rent the air. I didn't look at the gallery. I watched the spider, still spinning its web.

I didn't need to see the prosecutor to know the look he had on his face. I could hear the pleasure in his voice.

'Thank you, Master Kirkby. You have been very brave. Your king and our heavenly Father will be grateful for your service. I hope not to take up too much more of your time. Please could you tell the court what you saw next?'

'I saw the master's injuries, sir. They were . . . I still see them now, when I shut my eyes. I pray I never see anything like them again. Then Mistress Milburn came running out the door of the farmhouse. She kept asking what had happened, repeating herself again and again. Then I saw there was someone running towards us. It were the accused, Altha Weyward. She were yelling out the mistress's name. She flung her cloak on the master's body – for the sake of decency, she said – and told me to fetch Doctor Smythson from the village. I ran and did what she said, sir.'

'Thank you, son. And was that the first time you saw the accused that day? You didn't see her – or anyone else, besides the Milburns – before the incident occurred? Did you see her muttering an incantation, inciting the cows to stampede their master?'

'No, sir. I didn't see her before then, that day. But I had a funny feeling that morning, before it happened, when we was taking the cows out to the field.'

'And what was that?'

'I had a feeling of eyes on me. As if someone were watching, from the trees.'

PART TWO

20

VIOLET

Violet studied her reflection as she dressed for dinner. She tried to work out if she looked different now that she had been kissed. But she was still the same old Violet – with maybe a new touch of redness around her mouth. She put a hand to her face. The skin there felt tender and sore, as if it had been scraped by sandpaper. She wondered if anyone else would notice.

She picked a stray twig out of her hair and combed it. The dark strands shimmered in the low light of the room, making her think of her mother.

She had the same dark hair.

Violet was reminded of the conversation she'd overheard between the servants when she was younger. What was the word Nanny Metcalfe had used for her mother? *Uncanny*.

What on earth did that mean? Her stomach churned as the awful image came back to her: her mother, wild and pale, trapped in a room. Mad.

Perhaps that was why everyone lied about what had happened to her. Although, when she came to think of it, Violet couldn't remember anyone ever *telling* her that her mother had died giving birth to Graham. Instead, Nanny Metcalfe and Mrs Kirkby had said things like 'Your brother survived, thanks to Jesus' and 'The doctor did his best'.

Violet's fingers went to the pendant around her neck, the way they often did when she was worried, tracing the delicate *W*. Her head was beginning to ache: there was a tightness to her forehead and a thudding at her temple. She was still very thirsty after the kiss (how was it that something so wet could make one so parched?) and a little faint.

She had the queer feeling that she was looking at something so closely that she could not yet make out its full shape. Frederick's words echoed in her mind.

Your father would have to take her back to her room . . . Lock her in.

The gong rang for dinner, reverberating through the house like a call to battle. She looked in the mirror one last time, trying to ignore the throbbing in her skull. She was wearing the green dress again, same as last night. Suddenly, she noticed how short it was: her knees were perilously close to exposure. She couldn't decide if she looked like a child or a strumpet ('strumpet' was the word Violet had heard Mrs Kirkby use to describe Penny after she'd kissed the under-gardener).

Violet tried to see the dining room through Frederick's eyes. It was a rather grand room, and in the candlelight the slight grubbiness that had set in since the start of the war was barely noticeable. The space was dominated by an enormous mahogany dining table that Father referred to – inexplicably – as the 'Queen Anne'. (Had Queen Anne sat at it, Violet wondered?) Long-dead Ayreses looked out from the gilt frames on the walls with a melancholy air, as if they regretted not being able to sample whatever meal was being served. A stuffed peacock – which Violet had secretly nicknamed Percy – perched atop a Georgian sideboard, once-glorious tail feathers hanging limp to the floor.

This evening, Mrs Kirkby served a roast pheasant which Father had shot a few days prior. Violet could see the bullet hole in the pheasant's neck, a dark smudge in the golden flesh. The sick feeling in her stomach returned. As she cut into her serving, she was horribly aware of poor Percy watching from the other side of the room. One day, when Violet was grown up and had become a biologist (or a botanist, or an entomologist), she would eat only vegetables.

There seemed to be little chance that Frederick shared such dietary aspirations, Violet noted as he tucked into his roast pheasant with relish. There was a hungry look to him, she thought, as he surveyed the things in the dining room: the Queen Anne, the musty old portraits, her. It didn't go away, even though he'd eaten rather a lot of pheasant already.

Father and Frederick were having a long conversation about the war. Violet was distracted, haunted by what Frederick had said about her mother, until Graham kicked her under the table. She set her mouth into a prim smile and tried to focus on what Father was saying.

'Can't say I'm a huge fan of General Eisenhower,' he said. 'Do we really need all this help from the Yanks?' He spat the last word out violently, as if he were still smarting from American independence.

'We need all the help we can get, Uncle,' Frederick said. 'Unless you want the Hun sitting here eating pheasant with your daughter. He'd make short work of both, I expect.'

The wave of heat again. Violet wasn't exactly sure what Frederick meant, but she thought unaccountably of the pulsing swarm of mayflies; the roughness of Frederick's mouth on hers. Next to her, Graham was watching Father, his eyebrows raised.

But Father hadn't heard: Mrs Kirkby had come to ask if they were ready for the pudding. Violet saw a flash of gold out of the corner of her eye. It looked as though Frederick had put something in his drink. They were drinking claret, like they always did at dinner. It was watered down, so that Graham and Violet could 'get a taste for it'. There was the Christmassy smell again. Violet remembered the word for the substance Mrs Kirkby had deployed to make the Christmas pudding go up in blue flames. *Brandy*. That was it. It lived in a beautiful crystal decanter on Father's drinks trolley. Violet had never seen anyone drink it – Father preferred port after dinner.

She looked at Frederick more closely. There was a glassiness to his eyes, she saw, and his fingers shook when he reached for his claret.

Was he drunk? In the same way that she'd read about kissing long before she'd actually kissed someone, her reference points for drunkenness also came from literature – Falstaff being 'drunk out of his five senses' at the start of *The Merry Wives of Windsor*. She'd read rather a lot of Shakespeare – not that Father knew this, of course (he hadn't noticed that his *Complete Works* had been missing from its rightful place in the library for the past two years).

Frederick was now attacking the pudding – a rather pale spotted dick, doled out generously by Mrs Kirkby – so the retention of at least one of his senses wasn't in doubt. Violet looked down at her bowl. The pudding glistened with fat. She ate the thin custard around it instead. Her headache was gathering strength, like a summer storm. 'Good heavens,' Father said. 'Suet! Mrs Kirkby must have been saving some up.'

Violet couldn't remember Father commenting on Mrs Kirkby's cooking before the war. She suspected that Father's war (against a scarcity of his favourite port, a shipment of which had been bombed crossing the Atlantic) was rather different to Frederick's.

Violet wondered if Frederick was thinking this too, from

the forceful way he clasped his goblet (part of a set given to the First Viscount by Elizabeth I, or so Father claimed).

'Delicious,' he said, attacking the spotted dick once more. 'Don't think I've had pudding that didn't come from a tin since 1939. My compliments to Mrs Kirkby.'

The conversation returned to the war. Frederick was telling Father about the sort of guns his regiment used ('Howitzers for tanks and Colts for close range') and Violet let her thoughts drift again as Mrs Kirkby came to take away the plates. She could still hear the crickets chirping outside. Actually, it sounded like just one cricket – which made Violet feel rather sorry for it. Perhaps something had happened to its mate. Or perhaps there had never been a mate at all.

She wondered what it would be like, to live out one's days alone, without having someone to love and be loved by. She thought of the Virgin Queen again, the illustrious donor of the goblets. She had never married, of course. Perhaps no one would ever marry Violet, either. Father would be most put out by that. Miss Poole, too – Violet imagined her bemoaning the waste of a perfectly good trousseau.

Violet had never much liked the idea of being married. She would have been quite happy to pursue her ambitions alone, like Elizabeth I – though Violet's ambitions were rather more prosaic than victory against the Spanish and conversion of the nation to Anglicanism.

She thought, with powerful longing, of the giant moths and scorpions from Father's atlases. She pictured herself bending to stroke a scorpion's glittering head, the desert heat pressing against her skin . . . perhaps discovering a new species, being the first to decipher the secrets of its cells . . .

Might it be possible to have both things? Love *and* insects? Perhaps Frederick would fall in love with her, and then, once they were married, would be quite happy for her to become a world-travelling scientist. But even as these thoughts made her feel warm and light inside, doubt rolled in like a dark cloud.

She remembered the way that her heart had punched in her chest while Frederick kissed her. There was that feeling again, of being pulled by a tide. Her lungs tightened. She hadn't expected that love – if this was what she felt – to be so similar to fear.

Truthfully, she wasn't sure that anyone had ever loved her in her life, apart from Graham perhaps, in an irritable sort of way. Violet supposed that her mother must have loved her, but other than the faint memories triggered by the discovery of the handkerchief and feather – now somewhat tarnished by Frederick's story – it was impossible to imagine what this might have felt like.

It was hard to tell if Father loved her. Often, it seemed that all he cared about was whether or not he could mould her into something pretty and agreeable, a present to be given away to some other man.

Though Violet wondered if there wasn't another layer to her father's feelings about his daughter – sometimes, she thought she could see regret cloud his face when he looked at her. Perhaps it was because – according to Frederick, anyway – she looked so much like her mother.

Now, Father was pouring three glasses of port to take into the drawing room. Graham was staring at the third glass with an expression of mingled terror and pride.

She cleared her throat. Father looked up at her and frowned.

'Violet,' he said, looking at her and then the grandfather clock opposite the door. 'It's late. You should be getting to bed.'

It was half past eight. Shafts of pink light patterned the staircase as Violet made her way back to her bedroom. As she passed the window on the second floor, she realised that she could no longer hear the chirp of the solitary cricket. Perhaps it had given up.

21

KATE

As the days grow warmer, Kate opens the windows and the doors, so that the cottage is filled with the scent of the garden. Sometimes, she sits for hours on Aunt Violet's sofa, enjoying the sun on her skin as she reads. The fresh air helps with the nausea that still pulses in her gut, and she finds the distant murmur of the beck soothing. Outside, the other-worldly plants look almost beautiful, the ragged stems curling towards the sky. She rests one hand on her stomach, thinking of her daughter, blooming inside.

Violet's bookshelves burst with tomes on science – insects, botany, even astronomy. One of them – a guide to local insect life called *Secrets of the Valley* – seems to have been written by Violet herself. Kate was relieved to find some fiction, too – even a few volumes of poetry.

Most of the novels are by female authors – Daphne du Maurier, Angela Carter, Virginia Woolf. In the last month, she has read *Rebecca*, *The Bloody Chamber*, *Orlando*. It's been a long time since she's derived such pleasure from it, from the stories spun of other people's dreams. Those last days at the library, before she left Simon, had felt furtive, dangerous: she'd flinched at the tick of the clock on the wall, at every shadow that fell over the page. She had thought, for a while, that she'd lost the magic of it: the ability to immerse herself in another time, another place. It had felt like forgetting to breathe.

But she needn't have worried. Now, worlds, characters, even sentences linger – burning like beacons in her brain. Reminding her that she's not alone.

She's just finished a slim novel called *Lolly Willowes* by Sylvia Townsend Warner, about a spinster who moves to the countryside to take up witchcraft. A stamp on the flyleaf reads *Kirkby's Books and Gifts, Crows Beck*. The bookshop next to the church. There is a handwritten message next to the stamp:

Made me think of you! Emily x

Looking through Violet's collection, Kate sees that some of the others bear the same stamp. There are no other books about witches – although she does find a collection of Sylvia Plath's poetry, dog-eared at a poem called 'Witch Burning'. Two lines have been circled in pencil:

Mother of beetles, only unclench your hand:
I'll fly through the candle's mouth like a singeless moth

She remembers what she'd overheard the receptionist hiss at the medical centre. That one of the Weywards had been a witch.

Kirkby's Books and Gifts is a red-brick building attached to the village church, St Mary's. Small and squat, it nestles close to the church, as if trying to hide behind it. A bell chimes as Kate opens the door, welcomed by the comforting smell of dust and old leather bindings. Original floorboards are almost hidden by brightly coloured Turkish rugs, dusted here and there with glimmering strands of what seems to be cat hair.

'Hello,' calls a voice, its owner hidden by a maze of book-shelves. Kate peers around a sparsely populated shelf labelled

'St Mary's History' and sees a woman in her fifties, standing behind a desk stacked high with new releases. The woman is wearing a sweet, woody perfume – patchouli oil. In her arms she cradles an enormous orange cat, which swats at the glasses that dangle from a chain around her neck.

'Get off,' she says to the cat, who meows and leaps to the floor. And, to Kate: 'Can I help you?'

There is something familiar about her, about the way her eyes crinkle as she smiles. The greying auburn curls. Kate flushes when she realises: it's the same woman she saw at the greengrocer, all those weeks ago.

Could this be Emily?

'Are you all right, love?' the woman asks, when Kate doesn't answer.

'Yes, sorry.' She wipes her sweaty palms on her trousers. 'My name's Kate . . . Kate Ayres. I'm looking for Emily?'

'Oh!' The woman's smile widens. Kate is embarrassed to see a sheen of emotion in her eyes. 'Violet's great-niece. I should have known – you have her eyes. I'm Emily – your great-aunt and I were friends. I'm so sorry for your loss. She was a wonderful woman.'

'Oh, it's OK.' She colours. 'I mean – I didn't really know her. I didn't even know she had died until her solicitor contacted me – she left me her house.'

'We should get together sometime,' Emily says brightly. 'Me and Mike – that's my husband – live out at Oakfield Farm. We'd love to have you round. Then I can tell you all about her.'

'Oh,' Kate falters. 'That's really kind. Maybe I could let you know?'

'Of course.'

There is a pause, and she feels Emily's eyes on her. She wishes, suddenly, that she was wearing something else: her T-shirt is cut too low, and her jeans stick uncomfortably to her thighs. Even her hair feels wrong. She lifts a self-conscious hand to the coarse, bleached strands of it.

'Anyway, is there anything else I can help you with?' Emily asks. 'Book recommendations?'

'Actually,' she says, 'I was wondering if you had anything on local history. Or if . . .' She pauses, nerves ticking in her stomach. 'You could tell me about the Weywards?'

'Ah,' Emily grins. 'Heard the rumours already, then?'

Kate thinks of the receptionist at the doctor's surgery, the word she had spat from her mouth as though it was something rotten.

Witch.

'Something like that, yeah.'

'The villagers do like to gossip. Well . . . the story goes that a Weyward was tried as a witch, back in the 1600s.'

She thinks of the cross under the sycamore tree. Those carved letters. *RIP*.

'Really? What happened to her?'

'I don't know the details I'm afraid, pet. But there was a lot of that going on around here then, sadly. Women being accused left, right and centre.'

'Did Aunt Violet ever talk about them? About the Weywards?'

Emily pauses, frowns. She fiddles with the chain of her glasses, so that the lenses blink in the light.

'She didn't like to talk about her family much. I got the impression it was too painful. Something to do with leaving Orton Hall.'

Kate thinks of the turrets she passed on the drive up, gilded by the dawn.

'Anyway,' Emily blinks and turns to look up at the clock, which is shaped like a cat's face. One of its whiskers – the shorter one – hovers close to 5. 'I'll be closing up soon, I'm afraid, pet. Do come back another time, though, let me know how you get on. And the offer stands.'

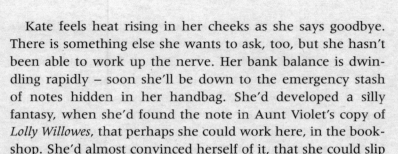

Kate feels heat rising in her cheeks as she says goodbye. There is something else she wants to ask, too, but she hasn't been able to work up the nerve. Her bank balance is dwindling rapidly – soon she'll be down to the emergency stash of notes hidden in her handbag. She'd developed a silly fantasy, when she'd found the note in Aunt Violet's copy of *Lolly Willowes*, that perhaps she could work here, in the bookshop. She'd almost convinced herself of it, that she could slip on that old professional persona the way one would a coat.

But now that she's standing here, her skin prickles with self-doubt. She hasn't worked for years – not since Simon made her quit, after she tried to leave him the first time. Her memories of work seem so distant that they might have happened to someone else. Even at the time, she'd known the job wouldn't last. She didn't deserve it.

It was a silly fantasy. Nothing more.

Not ready to face the walk back to the cottage, Kate tries the front door of the church. It's locked. But the gate of the little graveyard is open, swinging on its hinges. She looks behind her to see if anyone is watching, and then slips inside.

The graveyard is bordered by high stone walls, green with moss and lichen. Ancient trees line the walls, their branches threatening to brush against the tops of the headstones.

She has been here before, she realises with a start. Of course. Her grandfather's funeral. She remembers the other mourners, black as crows in their sombre raincoats, the drone of the priest. And the *noise*.

There is a rustle of movement. She looks up: a dark shadow flits from one tree branch to another, and her heart jolts. She runs her fingers over the reassuring shape of the brooch in her pocket as she walks through the graveyard.

The headstones are a motley of different ages: some of them are new, sparkling granite, surrounded by tiny terracotta pots of bright flowers. Others are so worn by time and weather that the inscriptions are barely readable. She sees the same names again and again: *Kirkby, Metcalfe, Dinsdale, Ridgeway*. As if the same cast of actors has been brought out to play each generation of villagers.

She weaves her way through the lanes of headstones in search of her family. At first, she makes towards a gloomy-looking mausoleum in the centre of the graveyard. It is ornately carved from marble; topped by a cross and a crouching bird of prey. But the marble is stained green with age, half covered by some creeping plant. The little door, set into the centre of the tomb, is padlocked shut – to keep something in or out, she isn't sure. There is a sad bouquet of wilted lavender at the entrance. Kate, seeing a little card attached with mouldering ribbon, crouches down to get a look, but the writing is blurred, illegible.

Eventually, she finds her relatives in the far corner, protected from the elements by the heavy boughs of a large elm. Graham, her grandfather, and Violet, his sister. Side by side, beneath a starry quilt of wildflowers. She crouches down next to the headstones to read their inscriptions. Graham is described as a loving husband and father. A loyal brother. There is a quote from Proverbs 17:17 – *A friend loves at all times, and a brother is born for a time of adversity*.

Violet's headstone – a hunk of granite, still in its natural shape – is simpler. There is just her name, Violet Elizabeth Ayres, and the dates of her birth and death. And something else – faint, inscribed so delicately that she doesn't notice it straight away.

The letter *W*.

W for Weyward? There is something familiar about the look of it. A hot breeze blows through the graveyard, rustling the leaves of the trees.

She stays like that for a while, looking at Violet's headstone. Her great-aunt had left explicit instructions for it, according to the solicitor. She wonders who attended her funeral: she hadn't been able to go without rousing Simon's suspicion. Kate feels an ache of regret at not being there. She'll come back another day, she decides, with some flowers. Violet would have liked that, she's sure.

She gets to her feet and decides to see if she can find any Weyward graves. She wanders up and down the graveyard a few times, but sees none, though some of the headstones are blank from age. Perhaps a woman accused of witchcraft wouldn't have been buried in a church graveyard. It is – what's the word for it again? – *hallowed ground*. But surely, if the family does go back centuries, other Weywards must have lived and died in Crows Beck? If not in the graveyard, then where could they be buried?

A vague unease fills her as she thinks of the weathered cross under the sycamore tree. Could it – surely it *doesn't* – mark a human burial site?

She distracts herself by taking the scenic route home, the path that follows the beck, which is the colour of burnt sugar in the afternoon light. She looks at the clumps of vegetation on the banks: ferns, nettle, a plant she doesn't know the name of with tiny buds of white flowers.

Something makes her look up at the sky: there is a dark shape against the pink clouds. A crow.

Later, Kate opens Aunt Violet's jewellery box.

In the dim light, she sees that the necklace is tangled. She lifts it out gently. She sits down on the bed, switching on the bedside lamp to take a closer look. She wonders how old the necklace is. It looks at least a century old, if not older: the gold is dull and tarnished. It feels cool in her palm, reassuring.

The engraving on the oval pendant is dark with grime and dust, but it is unmistakeable: the same *W* that is carved onto Violet's headstone.

22

ALTHA

I feared that they all believed the Kirkby boy. The men and women in the gallery, but also the judges and the jurors, who were the ones that mattered.

They believed that I'd been there, that I had set John's own cows on him, as if I were some great puppeteer. As if I were God himself.

While I sat in the dock, still watching the spider, I thought back to that morning, the morning that John died. I'd woken with the light, as I always did. I looked out of the window and saw the sky was still pink and new. I remember I thought of beginnings, as I dressed and put on my boots. Then I set off on my walk. I always took a walk at that time, in the weeks leading up to the new year. It had become my habit.

It had been very cold that day, and I had walked through great banks of snow which soaked my boots and the hem of my dress. My breath was like crystals in front of me. The valley was always at its most beautiful in the morning. I remember thinking that it was as if it had been made so on purpose, to remind us to keep living.

The cows looked almost majestic in the field: the gold dawn

turning their flanks amber. The power in those flanks as they
ran towards him; the muscle rippling. As if they were different
animals entirely, and had spent their days chewing cud, biding
their time until this moment of glory. The sharp cries of the
crow reeling above had mingled with the men's shouts. I
could feel the ground shake with their hooves from where
I stood, under the trees at the edge of the field.

It was over quickly. The cows returned to their former
selves, with only the white roll of an eye, the heave of a
flank, to show what had gone before. And the body. John's
body.

I saw Grace come out of the farmhouse. I gathered up my
skirts and ran, the winter air sharp in my lungs. As I ran, I
unfastened my cloak, so that I could cover the body. I didn't
want her to see. The limbs like broken tools, the pulped face.
I knew then that I would see that face, again and again, until
I took my last breath.

They are dismissing the Kirkby boy now. His Adam's apple
quivers as he walks down the aisle of the court, stiff in his
new clothes. He has done his master proud. On the way
home – I imagine – he will go over each detail of the trial
until it is polished and sparkling, ready to show to his parents,
the other villagers. The prosecutor's questions. The ancient
stone of Lancaster Castle; the soaring rafters of the courtroom.
Grace, pretty in her white cap. And in the dock: Altha, the
witch.

Witch. The word slithers from the mouth like a serpent,
drips from the tongue as thick and black as tar. We never
thought of ourselves as witches, my mother and I. For this
was a word invented by men, a word that brings power to
those who speak it, not those it describes. A word that builds
gallows and pyres, turns breathing women into corpses.

No. It was not a word we ever used.

I did not know, for a long time, what my mother thought

of our gifts. But I knew what was expected of me, from a young child. She named me Altha, after all. Not Alice, meaning noble woman, nor Agnes, lamb of God. Altha. Healer.

She taught me how to heal. And she taught me other things, too.

'They say that the first woman was born of man, Altha,' she said to me once when I was a child, for this was what we had heard the rector say in church that Sunday. 'That she came from his rib. But you must remember, my girl, that this is a lie.'

It was not that long after we'd attended Daniel Kirkby's birth that she told me this. 'Now you know the truth. Man is born of woman. Not the other way round.' I asked her why Reverend Goode would lie about something like that.

'It comes from the Bible,' she told me. 'So the rector isn't the first to tell that lie. As for the reason: it is my belief that people lie when they are afraid.'

I was confused.

'But what could Reverend Goode be afraid of?'

My mother smiled. 'Us,' she said. 'Women.'

But she was wrong. We were the ones who should have been afraid.

I sensed it in my marrow, much as my mother tried to shield me from it. There were strange happenings, in the years before she died. Long days and nights when she would be gone, having begged a horse from whichever family was in debt for our services. She would leave under cover of darkness, her crow flying ahead, its feathers stippled by moonlight. She would not tell me where she was going, only that if anyone were to ask, I was to say she was visiting relatives in Lancashire.

I knew that was not the truth, though. For we had no other relatives. Only each other.

One night, the autumn Grace's mother died, a couple came

to our door. The air was chill with the threat of winter and I remember that the woman held a babe to her breast; though it was swaddled in many layers, its tiny fist was blue.

My mother set her face tight, and I had the impression she did not want to admit them to the cottage. But she could not leave them out in such conditions, especially with the babe in such a state. She bade me put a pot on the fire, and spoke to them in hushed tones, but even so there was no escaping their conversation in our little cottage.

The couple had travelled from a place called Clitheroe, in the south, and had walked for many days and nights. It was no wonder they looked as they did: their faces haggard, and the babe half starved when out of his swaddling clothes, for his mother's milk had dried up. They were heading to Scotland, they said, and thence across the seas to Ireland, where no one would know them.

The woman was a healer – though not in the way my mother was. She made the occasional poultice, that was all. But they feared this would not matter: two families had been rounded up, they said, near Pendle Hill, and tried for witchcraft. Nearly all of them had been hanged.

What names, my mother asked.

The Devices, they said. And the Whittles. More besides.

These names were unfamiliar to me, but my mother's face blanched at their mention.

Things changed, after that.

The prosecutor called a second witness that day.

Reverend Goode himself. His black cassock flowed behind him as he walked towards the stand. It made me think of a bat's wings, and without thinking I smiled. Then, I heard the hum of voices rise in the gallery and remembered I was being watched. I kept my face still. I looked for the spider, but it was gone. Only its web remained, glinting and delicate. I wondered if it was an omen, if the spider could sense what was to come.

The rector took the oath. A thin man, his face was pale and pinched from years of sermons.

'Reverend,' said the prosecutor, 'would you be so good as to tell the court where you preach?'

'Certainly,' said Reverend Goode. 'I am the rector of St Mary's church, Crows Beck.'

'And how long have you held this post?'

'It will be thirty years this August.'

'And in that time, have you been familiar with the Weyward family?'

'Yes – though I am not sure that "family" is the proper term.'

'What do you mean, Reverend?'

'While I've been there, it has been just the two of them. The accused and her mother. Now only Altha remains, since Jennet passed some years ago.'

'Has there never been a male member of the household?'

'None that I have been acquainted with. It appears that the girl was born out of wedlock.'

'And did the Weywards attend services, Reverend?'

Reverend Goode paused.

'Yes,' he said. 'They came every Sunday, even in winter.'

'And has the accused kept up her attendance, since her mother's death?'

'Yes,' said Reverend Goode. 'For this, at least, I cannot fault her.'

I hated slinking into the back of the church, feeling the other villages shrink away if I took the same pew. But I knew I had to go, as my mother and I had always done, to avoid being dragged before the church courts.

At Reverend Goode's last words, the prosecutor looked like a cat who'd been handed a dish of cream.

'"For this at least", Reverend? What can you fault her on?'

'One hears things, in a small village,' he said. 'Like her mother, Altha tends the sick. Sometimes she has favourable results. She's nursed quite a few villagers back to health in her time.'

'"Sometimes" she has good results? What of the other times?'

'Sometimes the patient has died.'

I remembered the last death I'd witnessed, before John's. Ben Bainbridge's father, Jeremiah. He'd passed ninety winters: had been the oldest person in Crows Beck for two score years. His mind had died long before, leaving only his body behind. His eyes were blue and clouded, and I remember looking into them as I sat by his deathbed, wondering what he was seeing in the world beyond this life. He had said his wife's name with his last breath, his body shuddering like leaves in the wind. Old age, it was. And nothing more. There was nowt I could do but ease the pain of his lingering.

They could not pin that death on me. Not that one.

There had been others, too. Times when the patient's skin was so blanched with approaching death that I knew I could do little. The Merrywether woman, who'd died in childbed, her blood lapping at my wrists, the babe a mere knot of still flesh. These ones had been past my help.

I expected the rector to produce a litany of these deaths. But he did not. After all, he had stood at their gravesides and told their families that their loved one's passing was part of God's plan. It would not do well for him to say, now, having taken his sacred oath, that God had planned for them to be murdered by a witch.

'They did die, sometimes,' he went on. 'Though death awaits us all, along with reunification with our Father in Heaven, if we have lived well.'

I felt the gallery grow restless. They were not here for a

sermon. Someone coughed, another giggled. I saw one judge lean close to another, to murmur something.

The rector had the prosecutor in a bind, now. But he needed the church to stand with him, on the matter of witchcraft.

He paced.

'Thank you, Reverend. And thank you for the great service you have done to your country and king, in coming forward to report this crime. For it was you, was it not, who wrote to me, informing me there was suspicion of a witch in Crows Beck? And that it was suspected that this witch had had a hand in the death of John Milburn?'

'Yes,' said the rector slowly. 'It was.'

'Reverend,' said the prosecutor. 'Did you see the body of John Milburn?'

'I did. He was injured most grievously.'

'And did you bring the accused to his corpse, to see if it bled anew at her touch?'

'No, sir.'

'But, Reverend, would this not have been conclusive proof of murder? Why was this not done?'

'Master Milburn had already been buried, sir, by the time suspicion fell upon the accused. It was his widow's wish that he be laid to rest quickly, the sooner he could be reunited with his maker.'

'Thank you for that explanation. And could you tell the court how it was that suspicion did fall on the accused? What caused you to make the report?'

'Someone in the parish spoke to me of their concerns. They were certain that an innocent life had been taken, through a wicked contract with the devil. They wanted to do their duty, by their Lord and maker.'

'And who was that person?'

Reverend Goode took his time in telling the court who

had brought suspicion on my name. Who had consigned me to sit on the cold, hard seat of the dock by day and dream of death by night.

'It was the deceased's father-in-law,' he said finally. 'William Metcalfe.'

The courtroom grew loud, the whispers from the gallery like the drone of a hundred insects.

The prosecutor was finished with Reverend Goode. He climbed down from the stand slowly, and I saw his age in his faltering movements. The intimidating figure I remembered from childhood was diminished. Soon he too would start his journey from this world to the next. I wondered what he would find there.

I was taken back to the dungeons. Night had already fallen for me.

23

VIOLET

Frederick didn't come down for breakfast the next morning.

Violet was beginning to feel quite worried about him, until he emerged at luncheon, looking pale and green. He barely touched his food, taking only a delicate bite of Mrs Kirkby's leftover rabbit pie before crossing his knife and fork on his plate.

'They finished off that whole bottle of port last night,' Graham whispered to her, as they filed out of the dining room. A rough note in Graham's voice told Violet he was jealous. 'Actually, I think *he* had more of it than Father did.'

'Don't be so quick to judge,' Violet hissed. 'He's fighting a *war*. I imagine it's been utterly exhausting. I should think he's earned a glass or two of port.'

They hung back and watched Father and Frederick go on ahead. Father had his hand resting on Frederick's shoulder ('Good thing too, or he'd fall over,' said Graham) and was pointing out various items of furniture in the entrance hall, as if he were some sort of sales merchant.

'That', said Father, motioning to a rather hulking side table, 'is an original Jacobean. 'Worth at least a thousand pounds. It was commissioned by our ancestor, the Third Viscount, in 1619. James I was on the throne then – though you knew that already, I expect, with your interest in history.' Father beamed, and Graham rolled his eyes.

'Strange fellow, King James,' said Frederick. 'Rather fancied himself a bit of a witch-hunter. He wrote a book about it, did you know?'

Father's face darkened, and he moved away from Frederick before continuing the tour as if he hadn't heard.

'This clock', he said, gesturing to an ornate gold carriage clock carved with cherubs, 'was my mother's, given to her by her aunt, the Duchess of Kent, for her twenty-first birthday . . .'

'Never told me any of that,' Graham muttered. 'Anyone would think *he* was the son and heir.'

Later, as they played bowls on the lawn outside, Violet thought that Frederick must have forgotten his suggestion that they take a walk that evening. He had barely looked at her all day. Perhaps he had forgotten about the kiss, too. Or perhaps – worse – he regretted it. Maybe it hadn't been a very good kiss; maybe she'd done it wrong.

She was doing a terrible job of the lawn bowls. It was very warm, and her hairline was damp with sweat. Though she wasn't the only one – dark stains had appeared on Father's shirt, and Graham's face had flushed to match his hair. Even Cecil was subdued: curled up beneath the rhodo-dendrons, pink tongue lolling from his mouth. He looked almost sweet.

Only Frederick seemed unbothered by the heat – she supposed he had got used to it, in Libya – and had perked up considerably since luncheon. He rolled his ball so that it hit the jack with a *plink* and grinned, white teeth flashing in his tanned face. She would have thought he looked perfectly at ease, if she hadn't noticed that his hand kept straying to the pocket of his trousers and patting something hidden there, as if it were a talisman.

'I'm going to go and ask Mrs Kirkby for some lemonade,' she said.

'Rather you than me,' said Graham, watching his ball veer away from the jack and into a rose bush. Graham was afraid of all the servants, but especially Mrs Kirkby, who had recently caught him divesting a roast chicken of its legs. She had ardently vowed to box his ears if he ever set foot inside her kitchen again.

'I'll come with you,' said Frederick. 'You might need help carrying the glasses.'

Violet's stomach lurched.

'Thank you,' she said, barely pausing to wait for him as she made her way to the house. Conscious of his eyes on her, Violet moved stiffly, as if she had forgotten the correct way of walking.

He caught up with her as they entered the cool of the house. She thought how quiet it was, in the entrance hall. Although the doors had been flung open to let in the summer air, she couldn't even hear the bees buzzing outside. Frederick took a step closer to her. Blood rushed in her ears.

'I'm looking forward to our walk later,' he said softly.

So he *had* remembered. Her pulse flared as he moved closer. Why was there this awful thrumming sensation in her veins? Sweat prickled in her armpits. She was merely excited at the prospect of asking him more questions about her mother, she told herself. That was why her heart was thudding. Suddenly, she worried that he would kiss her again. Did she – should she – *want* him to?

There was the sound of a door opening and closing and Frederick sprang back. They looked up to see Miss Poole at the top of the stairs, carrying a stack of French textbooks that Violet supposed she would have the joy of wading through at some point in the future.

'Good afternoon,' said Miss Poole, curtseying as though Frederick were King George rather than her employer's nephew.

'How do you do,' he said.

'We're just off to the kitchens for some lemonade,' Violet said, but Miss Poole merely nodded, her eyes still trained on Frederick.

'I hope you enjoy your stay,' she said to Frederick.

'I'm sure I will,' he said, looking at Violet.

The lemonade was watery and sour from lack of sugar ('Anyone would think there wasn't a *war* on,' Mrs Kirkby had hissed, once Frederick was out of earshot).

When Father wasn't looking (Graham's lawn bowl technique required significant refinement), Frederick produced a golden flask from his pocket. Without asking, he unscrewed the cap and poured a generous amount of amber liquid into her glass.

'Is that—?'

'Brandy. Have you never had it? How innocent you are,' he said. Something in his smile reminded her of the hungry way he had looked at the dining-room furnishings the night before.

'Drink up, quick,' he said. 'Before your father sees. I don't want him thinking I'm a bad influence.'

The brandy was like fire going down her throat. She coughed, and Frederick roared with laughter.

Father made his way over to them, having given up his attempts to tell Graham how to aim his ball so that it hit the jack rather than Dinsdale's roses.

'What's so funny, Freddie?' he asked. It stung to hear the nickname on her father's lips. Father never called Violet and Graham anything other than – well, Violet and Graham.

'Your daughter is a very amusing young woman,' said Frederick.

After a while, Father seemed to tire of lawn bowls, and instead had Mrs Kirkby – who looked very disgruntled to have been torn away from the dinner preparations yet again – set folding chairs up on the lawn.

'The cheek of 'em,' she could be heard muttering as she walked away. 'Where they think their meals come from, I don't know . . . magicked up by fairies . . .'

'I'm afraid we're rather short on the ground with staff,' Father told Frederick apologetically. 'My butler went down on the HMS *Barham*.'

'Poor old Rainham,' said Violet, who had always liked the butler, a whiskery man with a penchant for colourful waistcoats. She'd once seen him carry a mouse – which had narrowly escaped Cecil's grasp – out into the garden, as delicately as if it were made of glass. It was very strange to think that he would never return to Orton Hall. His coat still hung on the hook at the servants' entrance as if he had merely gone for a stroll around the grounds.

Violet watched as Frederick drained the rest of his lemonade, before looking down into the empty glass. She saw his hand brush the pocket of his trousers and wished that Father hadn't mentioned the war.

The canvas of the chair creaked as she settled back into it. She considered fetching a book to read, but the brandy had made her mind heavy and slow. The sun was lovely and warm on her face and the world was a pleasant, green-gold blur. Both Graham and Father had fallen asleep and were snoring almost in unison. Violet thought she might just close her eyes for a moment. She heard the rasp of Frederick dragging his chair closer to hers. She shifted onto her side and opened one eye to see him watching her with that same hungry look. There was a hot, liquid feeling in her stomach.

She could hear a faint buzzing sound – a mayfly, she thought, or perhaps a midge.

'Ow.' Violet sat up straight in her chair, her cheek throbbing with a sudden pain. Graham muttered in his sleep, but Father snored on, undisturbed. She pressed her fingers to her face: she could already feel the skin growing hot. Alarm flickered in her gut.

'Are you all right?' Frederick asked, leaning closer to her.

'Yes – thanks. Something bit me. A midge, I think.'

'Ah. Damned things. I expect you're used to that, around here.'

'Actually, I've never been bitten by one before.'

He studied her for a moment. Opened his mouth, closed it again.

'I say – it's gone rather red,' he said. 'I think you need something cold on it.'

She watched as he came closer. He picked up his lemonade glass and pressed it to her cheek, the cool shock of it blotting out the pain.

'There,' he said softly. She could feel his breath, the rough edges of his fingertips.

They stayed like that for a moment, Violet's heart drumming furiously in her ears.

'Thank you,' she said finally, and he took the glass away.

'This'll sort you out,' he said, pulling the flask from his pocket and handing it over to her. Fingers shaking, she unscrewed the cap and lifted the flask to her lips. The brandy burned as much as before, but this time she didn't cough. She pictured it, a fireball glowing down her oesophagus. Dutch courage, they called it in books, didn't they? She had a strange, portentous feeling that bravery would be required for whatever was going to happen next.

'Better?' he asked.

'Better.'

'Do you know what,' he said. 'I think a walk could be just the ticket. Take the edge off the shock. What do you say? I'll protect you from the midges.'

'You're right,' she said. 'Just the ticket.'

She rose unsteadily, as if she were on the sloping deck of a ship. Frederick offered her his arm. She looked at Father and Graham, both of whom continued to snore. Graham would be disturbed to learn how much he looked like Father when he slept.

'We'll let these two catch up on their beauty sleep,' said Frederick, steering her away.

24

KATE

Kate was right.

She *is* having a girl. The female GP, Dr Collins, confirmed it today, at her twenty-week scan. She gave Kate a printout of the sonogram: her daughter, cocooned safe inside her womb, iridescent fingers curled into fists.

'She looks like a fighter, this one,' Dr Collins said.

Now, Kate sits on Aunt Violet's bed, caressing the photograph. The window is open and outside, a wood pigeon coos, the gentle notes carrying on the breeze. There's something she needs to do.

Her mother answers on the second ring.

'Kate?'

Her voice is muffled, concern driving away traces of sleep. What time is it there? The early hours of the morning. She should have checked. She is forgetting things, these days – lying down for a nap after putting on the kettle, waking with a start to its anguished whine. The tiredness makes her feel as if her bones have been sucked of their marrow.

'Are you OK? You haven't been returning my calls.'

'I know,' she says. 'Sorry – I've been a bit distracted. Settling in, you know.'

Her mother sighs into the phone.

'I've been so worried about you. I wish you'd tell me what's going on.'

The saliva leaves her mouth.

'I need to . . .'

'Need to what?'

Her pulse beats a frenzied rhythm in her ears. She can't do it.

'I need to ask you something. About Dad's family.'

'What is it?'

'Do you know who lives in Orton Hall now? Someone in the village said something about a viscount, but I don't know if he's related to us.'

'Hmm. I think your father said he was a distant relative. There was that scandal, the disinheritance – but I don't really remember the details.'

'So you don't know why they were disinherited? What the scandal actually was?'

'No, love. I'm sorry. I'm not even sure your father knew.'

'That's OK. Um – one more thing . . .' She pauses, licks her lips. 'Did Dad ever say anything about one of his ancestors being accused of witchcraft?'

'Witchcraft? No. Who told you that?'

'Just something I overheard,' she says. 'They seem to have had some funny ideas about Aunt Violet around here.'

'Well, she was a bit of a strange woman,' her mother says, but Kate can hear the smile in her voice.

Kate looks around her, at Violet's things. The shelves of books, the framed centipede glimmering on the wall. She thinks of the cape in the wardrobe, the dark glitter of its beads. Violet wouldn't be afraid, the way Kate is now.

She would tell the truth.

'Actually, Mum, I do have to tell you something.' She takes a breath. The next words, when they leave her mouth, sound as if they've been spoken by someone else. 'I'm pregnant.'

'Oh my God.' For a moment there is silence. 'Does Simon know?'

'No.'

'OK, that's good. And have you . . . decided what you're going to do?'

She knows about Simon, Kate realises. *She's always known.*

The pain in her mother's voice sends a jolt of nausea to her gut. Sun flares bright through the window, blinding her. *She knows.*

For a moment, she thinks she might be sick. Her eyes sting.

But she won't cry. Not today. She looks down at the sonogram, grips it tighter in her hand.

'I'm having it. Her. It's a girl, I found out today.'

'A girl! Kate!'

She can hear her mother crying into the phone.

'Mum? Are you OK?'

'Sorry,' her mother says. 'I just – I wish we hadn't left, Kate. I should have stayed. And then maybe you wouldn't have met him . . . I should have been there.'

'Mum. It's OK. It's not your fault.'

But it's too late, the words are tumbling from her mother's mouth, as if she can undo the years of silence between them. 'No, I knew something wasn't right. Quitting your job, losing touch with your friends . . . it was like you were becoming someone else. But he was always in the room, whenever we spoke on the phone . . . and then I didn't know if he was reading your messages, your emails . . . I didn't know what to do.'

Kate can't bear this, her mother's guilt. It burns, like acid on her skin. She remembers the night she met Simon. The way she'd been pulled towards him, a moth kissing a flame.

Can't her mother see? It is no one's fault but her own.

'There was nothing you could have done, Mum.'

'I'm your mother,' she says. 'I sensed it. I should have found a way.'

For a moment, neither of them speak. The line crackles with distance.

'But I am happy,' her mother says eventually, in a soft voice. 'About the baby. As long as it's what you want.'

Kate touches the photograph, tracing the bright bulb of her daughter's shape.

'It's what I want.'

After they say goodbye, Kate takes her wallet out of her handbag. She wants to put the sonogram picture inside it, to keep it safe.

Now, it holds a Polaroid of her and Simon. Taken on holiday, in Venice. They are holding ice cream cones on the Ponte di Rialto. It had been a hot day: she remembers the fetid stink of the canal, the blisters that had formed on her feet from hours of walking. She looks happy in the picture – they both do. He has a smudge of ice cream on his lip.

The following day, he had yelled at her in the middle of St Mark's Square. She can't remember why. Probably he didn't like something she'd said, or a particular way that she had looked at him. Later, in the hotel, he had hit her during sex, so hard that blood blisters formed on her thigh.

She crumples the Polaroid in her hand, then rips it to tiny shreds. They float to the floor, like snow.

The next day, Kate frowns as she walks. She zips up her rain-jacket: the day is muggy but overcast, the clouds swollen purple. It begins to spit. Already, the hedgerows glisten with water, tiny drops quivering like crystals on the wildflowers. Some she recognises: frothy white pignut; the golden bells of cow wheat. She has been learning the names from a great botanical tome of Aunt Violet's.

She has to cross the fells to get to Orton Hall. The ground becomes steeper as she leaves the familiar comfort of the hedged paths for open fields. The grey sky suddenly seems both enormous and far too close.

Her calves burn, her trainers slipping on the rocky trail. Her heart beats dizzyingly fast and her mouth feels dry. She's never much liked heights, or wide open spaces. She touches the bee brooch for reassurance, and then, on impulse, takes it from the pocket of her jeans and pins it to her lapel like an amulet.

At the crest of the hill, she pauses, doubled over and panting for breath. She can see a dark pocket of woods ahead, next to an old railway line. According to the blurry map on the Motorola, Orton Hall is just behind the trees.

She reaches the bottom of the hill with relief. Drystone walls rise on either side of her, the flint green with age and moss. Raindrops begin to fall in earnest as she enters the woods. The trees are tight and claustrophobic, and she can barely see the sky for the branches overhead. The winding trail is uneven and overgrown: greenery rustles as she walks, and a pale rabbit streaks away into the undergrowth.

The downpour grows heavier, and soon the leaves and tree trunks are shining wet. Kate pulls up her hood. She looks at her phone: she should be nearing the edge of the woods now. She walks a little faster. Something about the woods makes her feel uneasy: the cloying scent of damp earth, the snap of twigs around her. A shape flickers at the edge of her vision, shadow-black, a shiver of wings against leaves.

She turns around, scans the twisted canopy overhead. There is nothing, other than a brown and orange butterfly quivering on a leaf. She takes a deep, steadying breath and keeps walking.

The woods are so thick that she doesn't see Orton Hall until she is almost out of them. It rises up before her so suddenly that she gasps. She was not expecting this. She wonders if Emily was wrong about someone living here – the whole place looks as if it's been abandoned for years. Its stone is dull and faded, with great craters where the render has worn away. Thick ropes of ivy climb the turrets. Movement flutters on the roof, and she sees that the gutters are lined with birds' nests. As she approaches, she can't shake the feeling that she is being watched – but that could just be the huge, dark windows, staring down at her like eyes.

She walks through the weed-choked gardens to get to the imposing front door. There is no doorbell. She clangs the heavy iron knocker and waits.

Nothing. Kate shuffles her feet. The stone is slick with a patina of old leaves, the balustrades fissured with cracks. The whole place has an air of neglect, sadness, and she has just decided to leave when she hears the scrape and click of a bolt being drawn back. The door creaks open slowly, until she and a wispy old man in a tartan dressing gown are staring at each other in mutual surprise. The viscount. It's got to be him.

'Yes?' says the man in a thin, reedy voice. 'What do you want?' His eyes narrow behind the clouded lenses of his glasses, and for a moment Kate can't think what to say.

'Hi,' she begins. 'I hope I haven't disturbed you – um – my name is Kate. I've just moved in around the corner. I'm doing some research into my family history, and I think some of my relatives used to live here . . .'

She trails off awkwardly. The man blinks and for a moment she wonders if he hasn't heard her, if he could be deaf. The whites of his green eyes are yellow, the lids pink and hairless.

He opens the door wider, and then turns, disappearing into the fathomless dark of the house. It takes her a while to realise that he means for her to come inside.

She watches the ragged hem of his dressing gown lick away from his feet as she follows him into a dim entrance hall. The only source of light comes from a dusty-looking lamp on a large side table. In its yellow pool, she can see that the table is stacked high with mail: old, gnawed-looking envelopes at the bottom, and plastic covered brochures at the top. The stack of mail rustles as they walk past, and Kate notices that the curling envelopes are covered with a strange, glittering film, like tiny particles of broken glass.

The other furniture in the room is covered in ragged dust sheets, as is a large painting on the wall, above a cavernous fireplace. Something glints on the mantelpiece, and Kate sees that it is an old carriage clock, swathed in cobwebs. Its hands are stopped; frozen forever at six o'clock.

Kate wonders how on earth the man can see as she follows him up a sweeping staircase. The large windows over the staircase are dark with filth, and only let in a chink of light here and there. Kate squints to see the little man bobbing up the steps in front of her. For a moment, she stumbles and grips the banister, feeling grit under her palm. Peering at her hand, she sees it is the same glittering substance that covered the mail. It is not dust, she realises with horror. Her palm is coated with the crystal flakes of wings. Insect wings.

With a jolt, Kate realises that she has lost sight of him. There's the creak of a door opening somewhere. She reaches the top of the staircase, and, following the sound, turns left down the corridor.

There is a slender chink of orange light ahead, and her eyes adjust to make out the form of the old man standing outside a slightly open door, waiting for her. When she is a few paces away, he enters the room and she follows. As she crosses the threshold, fear leaps in her veins, for what she sees unsettles her even more than the rest of the house.

There are no wings to be found in this room, which would

have been impressive, once. The space is dominated by a beautiful mahogany desk. A floor-to-ceiling window, largely hidden by rotting curtains, takes up much of the wall behind the desk. The rest of it is covered by a dark portrait of a bald man with an angry expression.

The desk itself is crowded with strange trinkets: mirrored boxes, an old compass. A globe, half of its sphere rotted away. Most startling is an elephant's enormous tusk, which she initially takes to be a human bone, yellow in the dull light.

There is a sour stink of flesh, and Kate quickly averts her eyes from a sort of nest in the corner of the room, made from blankets, rags, and even items of clothing. There's another smell, too: over-sweet and chemical, abrasive in her nostrils. Insect repellent. A hurricane lamp – of the kind she's only ever seen in old films, or antique shops – burns on the floor, giving the room its gauzy glow. Empty tins glint orange in the lamplight. He has been living here, she realises. In this one room.

'They can't – couldn't – get in,' the little man says, as if he has read her thoughts. 'I made sure.'

He gestures to the door, and Kate turns to see a roll of fabric nailed to it, another stretched across its hinges. Turning back, she realises suddenly why the room is so dark: behind the frayed, rotted curtains, the windows have been boarded up.

The little man sits down at the desk, slowly lowering himself into a high-backed chair, its leather streaked with mould.

'Please,' he says, gesturing to a small chair in front of the desk. Kate sits, and dust rises around her. She stifles a cough.

'What did you say your name was?' the man asks. Kate finds the contrast between his cut-glass accent and shabby appearance jarring – unsettling, even. She notices that his hands are shaking, that his gaze flickers repeatedly to the edges of the room. He's looking for them, she realises. The insects. The skin on the nape of her neck prickles.

'Kate,' she says, her unease growing. She wants to leave, to get away from this little man with his vacant stare and animal smell. 'Kate Ayres.' He leans forward, the papery skin of his forehead furrowed.

'Did you say *Ayres*?'

'Yes, my grandfather was Graham Ayres,' she explains. 'I think he used to live here, as a child. With his sister, Violet. Do you – are we . . . related?'

Kate isn't sure if she's imagining things, but his hands seem to shake harder at the mention of her great-aunt, the bony knuckles whitening.

'There were so many of them.' He licks his lips, which are pale and cracked. His voice is so quiet that it takes her a moment to understand the words. He is looking past her, now, his eyes glazed with distance. 'And then the swarm . . .'

What is he talking about?

'The swarm?'

'The male taking the female . . . and then the eggs, every-where . . . covering every surface . . .'

Doubt nags at her. This man – whoever he is – clearly isn't well. The way he is talking, the way he is *living* – he needs help, rather than to be pestered with questions. He seems . . . traumatised.

But just as she rises in her chair, making to leave, his gaze fixes on her with a startling clarity.

'You had some questions for me?'

Perhaps he is more lucid than she thought. Really, she knows, she should leave – but she's walked all the way here, over the dizzying fells and through the woods. Surely there would be no harm in asking a question or two . . .

She takes a deep breath, trying not to think about the staleness of the air.

'I was wondering, actually – if you could tell me anything about my grandfather and his sister? They've both passed away, and so I don't have anyone to ask. My father is dead, too – and I . . . well, I was hoping you might be able to tell me a bit about them.'

The man shakes his head vigorously, as if trying to dislodge her words from his ears.

'Terribly sorry,' he says. 'Memory isn't what it was.'

Kate looks around the room. There are shelves stacked with old books, the spines cracked and dusty.

'Oh,' she says, hearing the disappointment in her voice. 'What about records? Would you have any I could look at? Family trees, birth certificates, that sort of thing? Letters?'

The man shakes his head again.

'Those are all farm records, tax ledgers,' he says, seeing her look at the shelves. 'Wouldn't be of help to you, I'm afraid. Everything else . . . gone. The insects . . .' He trembles.

'Oh. That's OK.' Kate sits quietly for a moment. She feels a twinge of pity for him, all alone in this decrepit house, with only dead bugs and old ledgers for company. 'What happened? With the insects, I mean. That must have been awful. I'm not such a fan of bugs, myself. Did you have to get an exterminator?'

The man's eyes become dark pools as he fixes them upon the space above Kate's head. When he speaks, even his voice has changed; the accent that sounded cold and hard moments ago is now tremulous, uncertain.

'I must give thanks,' he says, his voice barely louder than a whisper. 'The Lord answered my prayers. Last August, they all began to die – the sweetest sound, it was, their little bodies falling to the floor. Like rain on parched earth. It was then that I knew . . . she had released me at last.'

'Sorry – what do you mean? Who had released you?'

She takes a deep breath as she waits for him to answer – the air is rank in her mouth. How can he stand it? She unzips her jacket, to alleviate the feeling of being choked.

Suddenly, the man jolts in his chair. He is staring at her, she realises.

'Oh dear,' she says, standing hurriedly. 'Um – sir? Are you all right?'

He lifts his hand and points. Kate sees that his fingers are shaking again. The nails are yellow and curved, their undersides coated with grime.

'Where', he says, his breath coming in little ragged bursts, 'did you get that?'

For a moment, Kate thinks he is pointing at Aunt Violet's old necklace, which she'd almost forgotten she was wearing. But then she realises: he means the brooch, in the shape of a bee.

'This?' she says, touching it. 'Sorry – it looks quite real, doesn't it? It's silly, really; I've carried it around since I was a child . . .'

The man rises out of the chair, his small frame trembling.

'Get. Out.' The eyes are wide, the lips snarled away to reveal pale, desiccated gums.

'OK,' says Kate, zipping up her jacket. 'I'm so sorry for disturbing you. Really.'

Kate fumbles her way down the corridor and the stairs, wincing at the crunch of the wings beneath her shoes. Shutting the heavy front door behind her, she gulps in the air, fresh with the scent of rain. It is coming down in sheets and she begins to run, forcing herself to look straight ahead. The leaves of the trees whisper in the downpour and she wishes she'd brought headphones to block out the eerie noise. The fell seems even steeper on the way back: the wind buffets her, knocking the hood from her head. Water runs into her eyes, so that the valley is a blur of green and grey.

Fear turns to frustration as she finally reaches the cottage. She is no closer to knowing anything about her family. No closer to knowing why Violet and Graham were disinherited, no closer to knowing what – or who – is buried in Violet's garden.

Kate sighs as she shuts the front door behind her. She turns on the shower, desperate to scrub away the memory and the grime of the house, with its blanket of tiny, broken wings. The dank, animal stench of the study. While she waits for the water to heat, she unpins her brooch, then holds it up to the light. The viscount must be very traumatised indeed to have had such a reaction to a mere replica of an insect.

She remembers the way his eyes danced from side to side, as if he were searching for movement in the corners of the room. She can still taste the acrid stink of insect repellent on her tongue.

If she closes her eyes, she can picture it.

The air shimmering with thousands of beating wings, the sound droning through the walls of the house, the little man cowering in his fetid nest inside the study . . . and then, the briefest moment of stillness, silence . . . before the rain of tiny bodies.

She had released me at last.

Once the bathroom fills with steam from the heat of the shower, Kate begins to undress. Unbuttoning her shirt, she shivers as her fingers brush against a pale, glimmering wing.

The words from 'Witch Burning' come back to her.

Mother of beetles.

Who had released him? And from what?

25

ALTHA

In the dungeons, I wished for parchment and ink. These words were already forming in my head, you see, and I wanted to set them down while I still could. So that something remained of me, after they cut my body down from the rope. Something other than the cottage, which would hold my things – things that belonged to my mother, and her mother before her – until someone came to clear them away.

But I had no parchment and ink then, of course – and even if they'd given me some, I'd have had no light to see my letters. My mother had taught me to read and write. She considered it as important a skill as knowing which herbs brought relief from which ailments. She taught me the alphabet just as she taught me the uses for marshmallow and foxglove. Just as she taught me the other things, of which I cannot yet speak.

Having no way of writing, back in the dungeons, I ordered things in my head. I was practising, almost, in case what Reverend Goode said about the next life was true and I would soon see my mother again.

My mother. Her death weighed heavily upon me still, for she was another one of my failings.

Not long after the couple from Clitheroe came to see us, my mother began to change. One night, as the moon rose outside – it was a young moon, I remember, just a pale scratch in the sky – she told me to put on my cloak. Then she took the crow, placing her gently in a covered basket. I asked her what she was doing, for we had raised the bird from a hatchling, just as we had its mother, both of whom carried the sign. She did not answer me, only had me follow her into the night. She did not speak until we came upon the oak trees that bordered one of the farms – the Milburn farm, where one day Grace would live, though I did not know this then. I was thinking of her that night, of how we used to climb those trees together, their gnarled branches cradling us. The memory sat heavily in my heart.

My mother knelt before the largest oak tree and coaxed the crow from its basket. No sooner was it on the ground than it took to the air, the moon catching on its feathers. It flew back to its usual spot on my mother's shoulder, but she pressed her cheek against its beak and shut her eyes, murmuring something that I could not hear. The crow gave an anguished cry, but it flew away to the upper branches of the oak, which were thronged black with its kind.

We walked back to the cottage. In the darkness, I could not see my mother's face, but from the sharp, shuddering sounds of her breath I knew that she wept.

She bade me stay indoors, after that, only leaving the cottage for church and for walks when darkness fell over the land. I began to prefer the winter months to the endless summer days, though I was hungry by this time. We had less coin, now, and would have gone without meat if not for the kindness of the Bainbridges. My mother refused to take on new work; she would only see to those she trusted.

'It isn't safe,' she said, her eyes shining large and frightened in her skull.

As the months went on, turning into years, she looked less and less like my mother. She grew thinner. Curled into herself, like a plant missing the sun. Her cheeks lost their bloom and her skin was tight on her bones. Still, we only left the cottage for church services. The villagers stared at us as we crossed the nave, my mother leaning against me, the two of us hobbling like some monstrous creature.

Some of them said we were cursed. For what we had done to Anna Metcalfe.

'We should go outside,' I said, when my mother did not rise from her pallet for five days. 'You need to feel the air, to listen to the wind in the trees. To hear birdsong.'

For I had begun to suspect that nature, to us, was as much a life force as the very air we breathed. Without it, I feared my mother would die.

Sometimes, in my darkest moments, I wonder if she herself knew this – if she had decided that she would rather face that great, yawning unknown than continue our existence in the shadows.

'No,' she said that day, her eyes blacker than I had ever seen them. She gripped my arm, her nails sharp on my flesh. 'It isn't safe.'

It was the sweating sickness that took her, in the end. Three years after my first blood. She had directed her treatment from her own sickbed, telling me which roots to crush, which herbs to apply, even when she could barely lift her head from the pallet. I did everything she asked of me, but soon she was more asleep than awake, the bedclothes damp around her as she murmured my name. I was frightened of her, her yellow face in the candlelight.

'Remember your promise,' she said, her body arching with pain. 'You cannot break it.'

One morning, as dawn split the sky, she grew still. Then I knew she was gone. I thought of how she had named me. Altha. Healer. I had let her down.

I thought a lot of Grace, after my mother passed. She was the only other person I had ever loved. Now I had lost both of them.

Grace was married by then. William Metcalfe had arranged for his daughter to marry another yeoman – a dairy farmer, like himself. Grace had already played the role of farmer's wife since her mother passed, no doubt. I imagine she thought herself ready for marriage.

John Milburn was well thought of in the village. And handsome, too. They looked well together, at the wedding: she pale and pretty, and he with his dark hair shot with gold.

I wasn't invited, of course. But I found a place to watch, in a shaded lane where I could see the entrance of the church while remaining in shadow. It was a summer morning. The villagers threw wildflower petals over the couple as they crossed the nave. Grace had hawthorn flowers woven into her red hair. Pain closed my throat as I remembered the flower chains we'd made as girls. She'd loved to pretend at marriage, then – describing the face of her future husband as though she could conjure him with speech alone. I had been quiet in those moments. If I hoped for a future with anyone, it was with her.

She looked happy, hand in hand with her husband. Perhaps she was, then. Or perhaps I was standing too far away. A great many things look different from a distance. Truth is like ugliness: you need to be close to see it.

I would explain all of this to my mother when I saw her in the life that follows this one, I decided in the dungeon that night. I would tell her the ugliness. The truth.

The next day, the prosecutor called William Metcalfe. The years had not been kind to the man who walked down the aisle to take the box. Time and grief had made deep crags in his face. His hair hung in strings over his forehead. I felt his eyes on me when he took the oath, the hatred in his gaze like a brand on my skin.

The prosecutor smoothed his robes before he began the questioning. I wondered if this was the last witness. His last chance to prove my guilt.

'Master Metcalfe,' he said. 'Could you tell the court who first made this charge of witchcraft against the accused?'

'I did.'

'Why?'

'Because she killed my son-in-law, sir.'

'Were you a witness to your son-in-law's death, Master Metcalfe?'

'No.'

'Then how can you be so sure of the accused's guilt?'

'Because of what happened before.'

'What happened before?'

'She killed my wife.'

I looked for Grace in the gallery. I wished the white cap would turn so that I could see her face. So that I could see some small sign that she didn't still believe her father, after all these years. After everything.

'Master Metcalfe, are you able to tell the court about your wife's death, and the accused's involvement in it?'

When Metcalfe spoke again, his voice had changed. The fire had gone out of it, the words cracking with pain.

'My wife – Anna – she fell ill with scarlatina. It were eight years ago. Grace were only thirteen. Doctor Smythson came out and applied some leeches. But my Anna didn't get better. I would have sent for the doctor again, but one night Grace slipped away. She returned with the accused and her mother. She was . . . friendly with the accused, at that age.'

He stopped. I didn't want to look at him. I looked about

the courtroom for something else to focus on. Nothing remained of the spider's web in the dock. I wondered if someone had brushed it away.

A fly hovered above the gallery. I kept my eyes on it as William Metcalfe continued.

'Altha's mother – Jennet – she was known around Crows Beck for her healing skills, at that time. And seeing as the girls were close . . . well, you can see why Grace saw fit to fetch them. She were only trying to save her mother. The first thing Jennet did when she arrived was pull the leeches off my Anna. Then she promised me she could save her. But she gave her something, some noxious draught, and then my Anna . . .'

Metcalfe paused, shuddering. His hand went to his throat, and I recalled the string of beads I had seen clutched in his fist the night his wife died. Only later had I realised they were rosary beads; that Grace's family were papists.

I remembered the fear in his eyes when we came upon him at prayer. Perhaps he had worried that we would expose him. Or perhaps I was searching for another reason for his hatred of my mother and me, when the truth was simple: he believed us murderers.

'My Anna shook all over,' he continued. 'It were . . . unspeakable. And then she was gone. Jennet had killed her.'

'And where was the accused, in all of this? Was she near your wife when she passed?'

'No. She were standing with my daughter. But . . . I know she helped her mother. And even if she didn't, you just have to look at her to see she's the spit of Jennet.' The fire returned to his voice as he continued, growing louder and louder. 'The spit of her. In image and in manner too – it has been passed down, this rot, like a contagion, from mother to daughter . . . They're not like other women. Living without a man – it's unnatural. I wager that the mother took the devil for a lover, to beget a child . . . and now that child has done his will. You must cut her out, like bad flesh from meat! You must hang her!'

The gallery had been shocked into silence by Metcalfe's claims. A child born of the devil. I wished to scrub myself all over, to scrub away time with my skin and return to a place where I had never heard those words spoken about my mother and myself.

Metcalfe had stopped yelling. He was slumped forward in the stand, shoulders heaving with keening sobs, the likes of which I have never heard from a man before.

A guard came to lead him away. Just as he reached the doors, he turned back towards me.

'Damn you! I hope you rot in Hell like your whore of a mother!'

The heavy doors closed and he was gone.

I had striven to show no emotion through the trial, but to hear my mother spoken of thus was too much. My eyes burned with the salt of the tears that ran down my face. Whispers rose in the courtroom. From the corner of my eye I saw that they were pointing at me, at my tears.

I put my face in my hands and cried. I kept my face hidden as the prosecutor spoke. It was clear from the testimony of Grace Milburn, Daniel Kirkby and William Metcalfe that I was the devil's whore, he said, who had used my evil influence to goad innocent animals into trampling their master to death. I must be cut from society like a canker, he said, scoured from the earth like rot from wood. I had robbed my community of a good and honest man. I had robbed a woman of her loving husband. Her protector.

At this I raised my head and looked at him, staring until my eyes burned. I did not hide my face in my hands again.

26

VIOLET

'So,' said Frederick. 'Where are you taking me? Somewhere with shade, I hope – I'm absolutely roasting.'

They were walking in the meadow at the very edge of the grounds. It was hilly, and at its crest they could see the green landscape below. Violet felt strangely light, as though her bones had filled with air. The sun was hot on the back of her neck. She should have brought a hat. Nanny Metcalfe would give her a telling-off if she got sunburnt.

'There's the wood, down by the old railway line,' she said, pointing to a dark seam of trees running through the fields. Technically that was public land, not part of the grounds, and she didn't think Father would like it if she went there. But he couldn't really object if she were chaperoned, she reasoned. Especially not if she were chaperoned by Frederick. Freddie.

The lemonade suddenly seemed like a long time ago.

'I'm parched,' she said. She shut her eyes. Frederick was half carrying her to the woods now, her arm draped over his shoulders. Her body felt very heavy but Frederick walked on steadily, as if she weighed nothing. She felt the cool metal

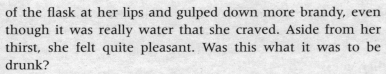

of the flask at her lips and gulped down more brandy, even though it was really water that she craved. Aside from her thirst, she felt quite pleasant. Was this what it was to be drunk?

She could smell the rich, damp scent of the wood. She opened her eyes. The sun was dappled by the trees, which were ancient and packed closely together. Frederick reached down and plucked a primrose flower, before putting it behind her ear. She didn't know how to tell him that she didn't believe in picking flowers. A butterfly took flight from a branch, orange circles on its wings like eyes.

'Scotch argus,' she murmured.

'What?'

'The butterfly. That's what it's called.'

Everything was growing dimmer. Violet opened her eyes and saw that they had come to a clearing in the woods, thickly carpeted by foxglove and dog's mercury. Through the trees, Violet saw blue irises and thought of Miss Poole. She wondered how long they had been away from the Hall. Perhaps someone would come and look for them.

Frederick was laying her down on the ground. She must be very drunk, she thought. Perhaps she had become too heavy for him to carry, and he was going to go back to the Hall for help. Father would be furious. Perhaps they could just leave her out here. She wouldn't mind. It was so pretty. She could hear a bird singing – a redstart.

Frederick was still there. She wondered why he hadn't set off for the Hall yet. He was getting down on the ground next to her – maybe he didn't feel well either? She could smell him – rich cologne, mingled with an animal scent of sweat. It was overpowering. The bite on her cheek was stinging rather painfully.

He was on top of her. She wanted to ask him what he was doing but her tongue was too clumsy to form the words, and then he was covering her mouth with his. He was very heavy; her lungs burned from lack of air. She tried to put her hands on his shoulders, to push him off, but they were pinned by her sides.

Violet felt his hand on her thigh, under her skirt, and then he was forcing her stockings down. She heard them tear. They were silk; the only pair she had. He moved her legs apart and for a moment she was freed from his weight as he unbuckled his belt and undid his trousers. She gulped at the air, tried to speak, but then he was upon her again, his hand on her mouth, and there was a bright, searing pain between her legs. She felt the ground dig into her back harder as he moved, again and again. Still the pain continued, as if he were opening a wound inside her.

She could taste sweat and dirt on his hand. Her eyes watered. She looked up and tried to count the green leaves that filtered the sunlight but there were too many and she lost track of them. After a while – it felt like an entire lifespan, the years stretching on and mercilessly on, but afterwards she realised it couldn't have been more than five minutes – he cried out and grew still. It – whatever horrible thing it was – had ended.

Frederick rolled over onto his back, panting.

She could feel something wet trickling out of her. She put her hand between her legs and when she looked at it, it was sticky with blood and something else – something white, like the mucus from a snail.

The redstart was singing again, as if nothing had happened.

'We'd better get back,' he said. 'I say, you do look a bit of a fright. We'll tell your father that you had a tumble, shall we? Good thing your cousin was there to help you up.'

She lay for a moment, winded, watching him push through the trees. Slowly, she pulled up her stockings – she could hardly bear to touch her own skin – and crawled to her feet.

Something glimmered in the greenery: looking down, she saw that her pendant appeared to be cracked into two halves, like rusted wings. It was this, rather than anything else, that brought the first hot pricks of tears to her eyes.

Her mother's necklace. He had broken it.

It looked like a smaller piece of the pendant had snapped off and fallen onto the ground. Picking it up, she realised it was a tiny key with jagged edges. It dawned on her that her mother's necklace wasn't a pendant at all, but a locket; with a hinge so small that she had never noticed it. The key shone brighter than the battered locket, as if it had not seen daylight for many years.

As Violet made her way through the woods, listening to the strange sound of her own breathing, she gripped the key tightly in her palm. Distantly, she wondered if her mother had been the last person to touch it. Even that thought gave her no comfort.

The deckchairs had been put away and Father and Graham had gone inside by the time they got back. The entrance hall was filled with the smell of whatever Mrs Kirkby was cooking for supper – some kind of roast meat. It turned Violet's stomach.

'I think I'll go and lie down before dinner,' she said. Her brain felt like it was swimming, and her speech sounded slurred and thick.

'Good idea,' said Frederick. 'Shattered, myself. You've rather worn me out. I trust you enjoyed yourself?'

She made for the stairs, swallowing the bile that coursed up her throat. The colours from the stained-glass windows, backlit by the afternoon sun, were impossibly bright, streaking the parquetry as though with blood. Her head thudded and she gripped the handrail for support. The staircase seemed longer and steeper than usual, as if the Hall had turned into some nightmarish inverse of itself.

Once she was in the safety of her bedroom, she tried to wash away the strange, sticky substance at the old enamel washstand. Then, she changed into her nightgown. She bundled her soiled underwear and ripped stockings into a ball and hid them between the mattress and the bedframe. She thought of the silk slip she'd made for her trousseau, intended for her wedding night – useless, now.

Before she got into bed, she took the feather – Morg's feather, as she thought of it – from its hiding place between the pages of the Brothers Grimm. She placed it gently on her pillow, next to her mother's locket and the tiny key. She stared at them, the blue-black of the feather blurring into gold as her vision swam with tears.

When the gong rang for dinner, she squeezed her eyes shut. The room seemed to be shifting, like a carousel at a fair. She must have slept, because the next thing she knew, Nanny Metcalfe was calling her name, holding a tray of tea and toast.

'Sorry,' she said, sitting up and quickly sweeping her treasures under the coverlet. 'I don't feel at all well.'

'The heat,' said Nanny Metcalfe. 'I'd say you've gone and given yourself sunstroke. Should've had your hat on. Lots of water and a bit of food, followed by a good long sleep, and you'll be right as rain in the morning.'

Violet nodded weakly.

'Frederick was asking after you,' said Nanny Metcalfe. 'Came down to the servants' sitting room, after he'd had his supper. Wanted to know if I'd look in on you. Nice young chap, isn't he?'

'Yes,' Violet said. 'Very nice.' She could still smell the sour tang of his sweat.

'What's that you've got in your hair?' Nanny Metcalfe reached out and pulled something from behind Violet's ear. It was the primrose flower that Frederick had given her.

'Very pretty,' said Nanny Metcalfe. 'But be careful you don't ruin the sheets with such things. Flowers leave stains, you know.'

She slept without dreaming, and when she woke with the birds, her whole body felt stiff and painful.

She dressed slowly. In the mirror, she looked pale and sallow, as if she were an invalid in a book. She almost wished that she were an invalid (was there a way of becoming one?) and could stay in her room for the rest of the day. Then she would never have to see Frederick again.

The dining room was rich with the smell of breakfast. Father was hidden behind *The Times* ('*Kentucky* sunk near Malta' the front page blared) and Graham was forking food into his mouth over a Dickens novel. Scrambled eggs congealed in their dish, a lurid yellow. A plate of bacon rashers (the last remains of Jemima, Violet thought grimly) looked like flayed skin.

Frederick wasn't there. Gradually, the hammering in her heart slowed.

She sat shakily at the table.

'Nice walk with Freddie yesterday?' said Father from behind his newspaper. Violet flinched.

'Yes, thank you,' she said, because what else could she say? Even if she knew the words for what had happened, Father could never know. He would think it was her fault somehow, she knew. Perhaps it had been her fault? *I trust you enjoyed yourself?* He must have thought she wanted him to do it. She thought she might be sick. How could she face him?

'He's gone back to London, by the way,' said Father. 'Took the early train this morning. Ran him down to the station myself. He said to tell you goodbye, Violet.'

'Oh,' she said, not knowing what she should feel – relief?

Sadness? She remembered the primrose flower, with its crushed petals.

'A fine young man,' Father said. 'Rather reminds me of myself, at that age. I do hope he makes it through the war.'

Graham rolled his eyes at her. She tried to smile at him, but her cheeks felt as though they were made of India rubber.

'What happened to you?' Graham asked her. For a moment she thought that he could see – that everyone could see – the shameful memory that lay coiled inside her, like something rotting.

'Nothing,' she said quickly.

'I mean, what happened to your face? There's a big red mark on it.'

'Oh.' She had forgotten all about the bite. 'Something got me – a midge, I think.'

Father turned a page of his newspaper, apparently uninterested.

'Ha,' said Graham. 'But they never sting you! Whereas I can never get the bloody things off me. Maybe they got sick of me and thought they'd sample something new.'

'Language, Graham,' said Father.

'Who knows,' said Violet. 'Maybe they did.'

27

KATE

Two hundred pounds.

Kate counts again, just to be sure. Her bank account is empty, so she's down to her last clump of notes, still hidden in the lining of her handbag. She needs to make this last, until she finds a job. Several times, now, she has walked past Kirkby's Books and Gifts in the village. But she couldn't bring herself to go in.

But she has to do *something* . . . there is food to buy, and utility bills to pay – fat brown envelopes have begun to appear through Aunt Violet's letterbox, the most recent marked 'URGENT' in angry red letters.

Later, a book in Aunt Violet's collection catches her eye: *The British Gardener*.

Looking out of the kitchen window at the garden, she feels a twinge of doubt. It is so overgrown, and filled with the oddest of plants: great green trumpets reach skyward, vying for space with hairy stems, purple buds nodding on their leaves. She's not sure she's up to this. But a baby needs nutrients, vitamins. From vegetables, green things, like the ones that crowd Aunt Violet's garden.

And so she has to try.

It is a hot day, almost midsummer. In the bedroom, she peels off her jeans and top – both of which are starting to become uncomfortably tight – in favour of a pair of canvas dungarees she finds in the wardrobe. She dons one of Aunt Violet's hats – a straw behemoth with a tawny feather tucked into the band. In the cupboard under the sink there are gardening gloves, and leaning against the back of the house, a spade.

With *The British Gardener* tucked under her arm, she takes a deep breath and ventures outside.

She touches the smooth shape of the brooch in her pocket, reflecting that she's breaking the only rule she's ever set for herself. But it's hard to feel threatened by the plants and flowers golden with the sun; the clean gurgle of the beck. She even enjoys listening to the birds – wishes she could identify each species from its song, the way she used to when she was a child.

A caw, throaty and almost human, sends a cold needle down her spine.

She looks up. Her heart beats a little faster when she sees the crow, observing her from the highest branch of the syca-more. For a moment she is still, fearing that sudden movements will bring a rain of claws and feathers. But the bird just shifts on the branch, the sun coating its wings with an oil-slick sheen.

Blinking away the memories, she resists the urge to touch the brooch in her pocket. Focus. She must focus on the task at hand.

Guided by the pictures in Aunt Violet's gardening book, she learns that the green trumpets are rhubarb; the hairy-stemmed plant wild carrot. These, she digs from the ground, marvelling at the delicate stems of the rhubarb, the pale, gnarled carrots. She can make soups, salads. Hunger gnaws at her; the craving for food borne from the earth so intense she is almost giddy with it. She looks down at the carrot she grips in her hand. Part of her wants to eat it now – to suck the soil from it, feel the freshness burst into her mouth as she crunches down, hard. She needs this, she realises. The baby needs this.

She breathes deeply, places the carrot into her basket.

There are herbs, too, she sees: sage, rosemary, mint. These she also collects. She leaves behind other strange plants that don't seem to feature in the book: under the sycamore tree she finds a long-stemmed bush with yellow buds, like clusters of tiny stars.

After a while, she has an urge to remove the gloves, to feel the soil against her skin. She pushes her fingers deep into the earth, relishing its softness. The smell of it is intoxicating: its mineral tang reminds her of the taste that still coats her tongue when she wakes every morning.

She feels something brush against the scar on her forearm. Turning, she sees it is a damselfly: the same insect she saw down by the beck, when she first arrived. It trembles there for a moment; then, as she watches, it flutters to her stomach.

There is a surge inside her – a fizzing warmth in her gut, her veins. Rising into her oesophagus.

For a moment she thinks it's morning sickness; worries she might vomit, faint. She bends over, on her hands and knees in the dirt, lets the blood rush to her head.

She feels a tickling sensation against her hand, different to the silky touch of soil. Looking down, she sees the pink glimmer of a worm – and then another, and another. As she watches, spellbound, other insects emerge from the earth, glowing like jewels in the summer sun. The copper glint of a beetle's shell. The pale, segmented bodies of larvae. There is a buzzing in her ears, and she's not sure if it's from the roar of her pulse or the bees that have begun to circle nearby.

They're getting closer. It's as if something – as if *Kate* – is drawing them to her. A beetle climbs her wrist, a worm brushes against the bare skin of her knee, a bee lands on her earlobe. She is gasping, now, overwhelmed by the heat that blooms in her chest, surges up her throat. Her vision blurs like snow, then goes dark.

When she wakes, the day is cooler, the sun hidden behind clouds. Her mouth tastes of earth, and her body, sprawled on the ground, feels heavy, wrung out. Hazily, she watches the crow take flight from the sycamore, wings blotting out the sun. Blades of grass itch against her skin, and she flinches, remembering the insects. She scrambles to her feet, brushing the dirt from her clothes, fingers searching for the creatures that surely crawl over her neck, in her hair.

But there is nothing.

Looking down, she sees that the earth is still: just an empty, velvet mound where she has dug up the soil. No worms, no beetles, no larvae. She can't even hear any bees.

Did she imagine it? Hallucinate?

But something catches at the edge of her vision – a glitter of wings. The damselfly she saw earlier, before she blacked out. She watches as it flits towards the sycamore, dancing over the gnarled trunk, the little wooden cross, before disappearing from view.

Then she knows. She didn't imagine it. It was real.

A memory hovers, clouded and uncertain, like something seen from a distance. Early childhood. Sun on her face, the brush of wings on her palm, that feeling in her chest . . . She squeezes her eyes shut, tries to pull it closer, but she can't bring it into focus. Somehow, though, she is left with the odd sense that this has happened before.

The villagers' gossip echoes in her mind. One word, ringing louder than the rest.

Witch.

She has to know the truth.

About the Weywards. About herself.

The next day, Kate sets off to Lancaster. The drive reminds her of the night she left London. The road snaking through the hills, stretching endlessly out before her. She feels the familiar rise of fear in her gullet as she speeds along with the other cars. Her blood beats hard in her veins. Her blood, but the baby's blood too – the Weyward blood – and the thought makes her feel stronger, grip the steering wheel hard, determined. She can do this.

She's never been to Lancaster before. It's quaint and pretty, with its neat white buildings and cobblestones. But something about the throng of crowds – she is almost swallowed up by a gaggle of tourists – unsettles her. There's a sharp taste in her mouth, a sour coating that she recognises as the precursor to an anxiety attack. She's surprised to feel relief when she catches sight of the River Lune flashing silver in the distance, the hazy mountains beyond.

She finds the council office easily enough: a large, imposing building hulking on the city's main street.

Inside, the air is crisp and still, and Kate gathers herself together, joins a winding queue to speak to the man at the desk. Her appointment is at 2 p.m. She'd thought the Cumbria County Council Archives might hold some information, but the curt woman she'd spoken to on the phone explained that Lancashire Council holds the records of local witch trials, given the trials took place at Lancaster Castle.

Eventually, she is ushered to another waiting room, and then summoned to a cubicle, where she takes a seat opposite a thin, middle-aged man, shoulders dusted with dandruff.

A manila folder rests on the desk in front of him. Nerves flicker at the thought of what might be inside. She shuts her eyes briefly, thinking of how much she spent on petrol to get here . . . *Please, let it be worth it. Let him have found some-thing.*

The man offers a perfunctory greeting before detailing the results. She watches as his tongue flicks out to moisten his lips before he talks, like a frog catching flies.

'I've only found four records about a Weyward,' he explains. 'Three of them I had to pull from the Cumbrian archives. Let's start with those, shall we?'

He opens the file, takes out two documents.

'Both of these records concern an Elizabeth Ayres, nee Weyward.'

Kate nods.

'Yes – my great-grandmother, I think.'

'We have a record here of her marriage to a Rupert Ayres in August 1925.'

Kate nods again. She knows this already.

'And a death certificate. From September 1927.'

She leans across the table, heart pounding.

'What does it say? How did she die?'

'The cause of death is quite vague – "shock and blood loss", it says. Childbirth, perhaps? Quite common in those days, of course, though unusual that it hasn't been explicitly refer-enced. The certificate was made out by a Doctor Radcliffe, place of death listed as Orton Hall, near Crows Beck.'

'I think my grandfather was born that year. Maybe she died giving birth to him?'

Something else the man said snags in her brain.

Doctor Radcliffe.

With a start, she thinks of the doctor in the village, who performed her first ultrasound. His liver-flecked hands, cold on her skin. He'd mentioned inheriting the practice from his father, hadn't he?

How strange, to think that his father might have been present for Elizabeth's death. For her own grandfather's birth.

Though she supposes that is the way of small villages – of rural life. She remembers the weathered headstones in the graveyard. The same names, again and again. And yet not a single Weyward. If it weren't for the cottage, it would be easy to imagine they'd never existed; that they were merely the stuff of local legend.

She turns her attention back to the man across from her. How is it that he has only found four records? Can that really be all there is?

'Next, we have a death certificate for an Elinor Weyward. Died aged sixty-three, in 1938. Liver cancer. Given a pauper's funeral.'

'A pauper's funeral? What does that mean?'

The man frowned. 'It means that there was no one to cover funeral expenses. She would have been buried in an unmarked grave.'

Kate feels a throb of pain that this woman – her relative – had been so neglected in death. And yet she'd had family living just a few miles away, at Orton Hall.

The man takes the last sheet of paper from his file. She notices that the skin of his hands is moist, with a pearlescent webbing between the fingers. Again, she thinks of frogs.

'This last one is much older,' he explains. 'One result for the surname Weyward in the records of the assizes for the Northern Circuit, from 1619. An Altha Weyward, aged twenty-one, indicted for witchcraft and tried at Lancaster Castle.'

Her heart jumps. Prickles sweep her skin, like the tracings of phantom insects.

So the rumours are true.

'Was she found guilty?' she asks, her mouth dry. 'Executed?'

The man frowns.

'I'm afraid we don't have that information,' he says. 'We only have the record of the indictment – not the outcome of the trial. Sorry not to be of more help.'

'Do you know', Kate begins, thinking of the cross under the sycamore tree, 'where she would have been buried? If . . . if she had been executed, I mean.'

'Again . . . that's not something we know. There aren't records. At least, not anymore.'

'And – there's really nothing else? No other records of the Weywards between 1619 and 1925? For three hundred years?'

The man shakes his head. 'Nothing I could find. But official registration of births, deaths and marriages only began in 1837. And a lot of parish records haven't survived. So it was quite easy to fall through the cracks – especially if you were from a poorer family.'

Kate thanks him, trying to ward off the disappointment that spreads through her. She's not sure what she expected, really. That it would be easy to draw her family's history from the murk of the past, the way she'd somehow drawn insects from the soil. That doing so would help her understand herself.

But at least she isn't leaving empty-handed.

On her way out of the building, she turns the fragment over and over in her mind, as if it is some precious heirloom.

Altha Weyward. Aged 21. 1619. Tried for witchcraft.

Altha. A strange name. Soft and yet powerful. Like an incantation.

On the drive home, the afternoon sun settles pink on the hills. The landscape is so ancient – the sweeping meadows, the rocky crags. The slate-coloured tarns. Altha Weyward – whoever she was – would have looked out at these same hills, once.

Kate has an image of a young woman, wan-faced in the dawn, dragged to a pyre, or gallows . . . She shudders, pushes it from her mind.

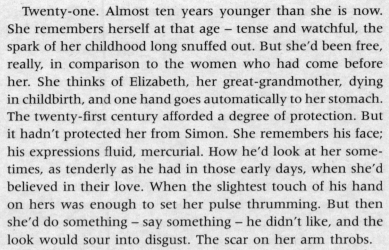

Twenty-one. Almost ten years younger than she is now. She remembers herself at that age – tense and watchful, the spark of her childhood long snuffed out. But she'd been free, really, in comparison to the women who had come before her. She thinks of Elizabeth, her great-grandmother, dying in childbirth, and one hand goes automatically to her stomach. The twenty-first century afforded a degree of protection. But it hadn't protected her from Simon. She remembers his face; his expressions fluid, mercurial. How he'd look at her sometimes, as tenderly as he had in those early days, when she'd believed in their love. When the slightest touch of his hand on hers was enough to set her pulse thrumming. But then she'd do something – say something – he didn't like, and the look would sour into disgust. The scar on her arm throbs.

All those years. Caught in a brutal dance, with steps she never knew how to follow.

Perhaps things haven't changed so much, after all.

It was quite easy to fall through the cracks, the man at the archives had said. But wasn't it also possible that Kate's ancestors – the Weywards – had wanted to hide, given what had happened to Altha? After all, it was Elizabeth's marriage to Rupert that had earned her a place in the record books. A relationship with a man.

I must have you.

Kate knows better than anyone how dangerous men can be.

The thought sparks fury in her. She's not sure if it's a new feeling, or if it was always there, smothered by fear. But now it burns bright in her blood. Fury. For herself. And for the women that came before.

Things will be different for her daughter. She'll make sure of it.

And that means she has to be brave.

*

It is 3 p.m. Kate doesn't have long until Kirkby's Books and Gifts closes for the day.

She stands in Aunt Violet's chilly bathroom, looking at herself in the mirror. Sunlight falls across her body, washed green by the creeping ivy on the outside of the cottage.

It's been a long time since she looked at herself properly. For years, she hasn't been able to bear the sight of her own nakedness. All of those evenings, moulding her flesh into whichever lingerie Simon wanted her to wear. Lying back and letting him arrange her limbs how he liked. She had become a vessel. Nothing more.

Perhaps this was why she had hated the idea of being pregnant before, when she still lived with him. She already felt like a means to an end.

But. She hadn't known it would be like this.

Now, in the mirror, Kate assesses herself. The strong lines of her limbs, the new spread of her hips. Her belly, with its growing curve. Her breasts amaze her – the darkening of the nipples, the veins that glow blue and bright beneath her skin. The mole on her breastbone has darkened, too: ruby deepening to crimson.

Even her skin is different – it is smoother, thicker. As if she is armoured.

Armoured and ready, to protect her daughter.

The force of it – this love that surges in her veins – shocks her. As does the searing clarity that she will do anything, whatever is necessary, to keep her child safe.

Unbidden, the day of the accident flashes in her mind. Her father's hand on her shoulder, rough and desperate, pushing her out of the way of the oncoming car. Had he felt this way, too?

She blinks the memory away, refocuses her gaze on the woman in the mirror. A woman she can barely recognise as herself.

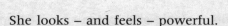

She looks – and feels – powerful.

There's only one thing she wants to change.

Aunt Violet's kitchen scissors are next to the sink. Kate lifts them to her head and begins to snip, smiling as coils of bleached, brassy hair fall to the ground. By the time she is finished, only the roots remain, bristling from her scalp like a dark halo.

She dresses before she leaves.

Not in her old clothes, the things that Simon chose for her. Those, she leaves behind.

Instead, she dons a pair of Violet's linen trousers, and a loose tunic of green silk, embroidered with a delicate pattern of leaves. Last, the straw hat with the feather. The walk to the village is peaceful, and she tests her growing knowledge of the local plant life – there, by the side of the road curl green fronds of stinging nettle; from the hedgerows peer creamy spouts of meadowsweet. Silver flashes amongst the green: the silky strands of old man's beard. She breathes deeply, inhaling the scent.

She is passing under the oaks when she feels a dark shape fall across her body, hears a guttural cry. But there is no needle of ice, this time. Instead, a whisper of the feeling she'd had in the garden, when the insects had brushed against her skin, returns. Movement in her chest, like the unfurling of wings.

Come on, she tells herself. *You can do this*.

She keeps walking.

Emily slumps forward over the counter, flanked by stacks of books. Her greying curls quiver as she scribbles in a ledger. A ceiling fan putters, ruffling the pages of the books.

'Hello,' Emily looks up at the sound of the door chime. 'How can I—'

For a moment, she looks a little pale, before she recovers herself and smiles.

'Kate! Sorry,' she says. 'It's just that – I didn't realise before, how much you look like her. Like Violet. How are you getting on?'

'I'm good, thank you. Actually, I was wondering', says Kate, the confidence of her tone surprising her, 'if you needed an assistant.'

28

ALTHA

That night in the dungeon was the longest of my life. The next day, I knew, the jurors would decide my fate. I knew that I would be hanged – that evening, or the following day. They would take me to the moor. One of the guards told me. I comforted myself with this, with the thought that at least then I'd see the sky, hear the birds. One last time. I wondered if anyone would come to watch – whether there would be a crowd, thronging below the scaffold, hungry for the sight of my body twisting on a rope. Satan's bride dispatched back to Hell.

Perhaps they would be right to hang me.

I thought of the promise I had made to my mother. The promise I had broken. I had failed to live up to her name for me. I had not been able to save her. For this, and the broken promise, guilt weighted my heart like an anchor.

But to be hanged for the death of John Milburn . . . that was a different matter.

I do not know if I slept at all that night. Images appeared before me, looming in the dim of the cell. My mother's face, her features bloated by death. A crow, black wings cutting the sky. Anna Metcalfe writhing on her deathbed. And John Milburn, or what had remained of him. His ruined face, dark and wet as spoiled fruit.

When they unlocked my door the next day, I felt as if I had already begun my passage from this world into the next. I seemed to be seeing everything through a haze.

Shadows haunted the edges of my vision. The veil was lifting, I thought. The veil between this world and the next. Soon I would be with my mother. I hoped she would understand what I had done, and why.

There seemed to be more people in the gallery than ever: as they led me to the dock, the courtroom swelled with jeers and booing. I looked at the faces of the judges, set into heavy creases of thought. The jurors, blank-eyed in their dark garb. Only the juror with the square jaw looked me in the eye. I was not proud, this time: I searched his face, hungry for some clue as to what would become of me. Then he looked away and a chill took hold of my heart. Perhaps he did not want to look upon a woman condemned.

I sought Grace in the crowd. Her cap shone white, pristine. She was sitting with her father, her head bowed. I willed her to turn, so that I could see her face – the face that haunted my dreams – one last time. But she did not.

One of the judges spoke.

'The accused, Altha Weyward, has been charged with murdering Mr John Milburn by witchcraft. The alleged crime took place on 1 January, in the year of our Lord 1619.

'Witchcraft is a grave scourge on this land, and our king, His Royal Highness King James, has charged us with fighting against its insidious evil. We must be wary of it in all aspects of our lives. The devil has long fingers and a loud voice, which reaches us all with sweet entreaties.

'As we know, our womenfolk in particular are at great risk

from the devil's temptation, being weak in both mind and spirit. We must protect them from this evil influence, and where we find it has already taken root, tear it from the earth.

'We have heard the evidence against the accused. It has been established that Master Milburn was trampled to death by his cows. Neither witness to John Milburn's death has given evidence to suggest that the accused uttered any incantation to compel the animals to behave in this manner.

'Indeed, Daniel Kirkby described how a crow tormented the animals and drove them into a frenzy. We know that crows are common in this part of the land, and that they can be violent in their interactions with other animals and humans alike.

'The accused was not brought to touch the corpse; and thus we cannot know if it would have bled at her touch. The court, aided by the good Doctor Smythson, has examined the accused's body for the witch's mark.

'None was found.

'Having heard this evidence, I ask the gentlemen of the jury to deliver their verdict, bearing in mind their duty to God and their consciences.'

A hush fell over the court as the foreman stood. My breath caught in my chest. It did not matter what the judge had said. I could see the gallows. Could feel the noose rough against my neck. I thought of all the other women who had been put to death before me, the fate my mother had tried to shield me from. The women of North Berwick. Of Pendle Hill. Soon I would join them. I was sure of it.

'Of the charge of murder by witchcraft,' he said, 'we find the accused . . . not guilty.'

Then, I was floating. Dreaming. I could hear the condemnation from the gallery, but it seemed to be sounding from miles away. My body was weightless, as though I were in water. I looked for Grace. Next to her, William Metcalfe had his head in his hands. So he did not see it. He did not see Grace look at me. He did not see the expression on her face.

29

VIOLET

Violet spent the weeks after Frederick departed in her room.

'Lovesick,' she heard Nanny Metcalfe say to Graham one morning, who had come to ask if she'd seen his biology textbook.

'Over *whom*?' she heard him hiss. Then, louder, for her benefit: 'Bloody hell, Violet, not you too.'

Later that day, he'd pushed a note under her door that read:

Forget about the old git. You're as bad as Father, pining for his lapdog!

Violet didn't write back.

She had decided that it would be easier to forget about what had happened in the woods if she never spoke of it to anyone. But it wasn't. At night, she dreamed of Frederick, forcing his way inside her while the trees loomed overheard, spinning in circles. It was as if he had left a spore of himself in her brain, which was now multiplying and spreading through her neurons. She felt *infected*. She remembered the sticky substance he had left dribbling out of her.

This was the thing she wanted to forget most of all.

Whenever she thought of it, something tugged at her brain, threatening to form a connection. It – the sticky thing – had reminded her of a word she had read in Graham's biology textbook. *Spermatophore*. It was the substance that male insects used to fertilise the eggs of female insects. She refused to think about it further. She couldn't bring herself to find the section of the textbook that covered it: she had hidden it under her mattress, along with the soiled underwear and stockings.

Most of the time, Violet lay cocooned in blankets, quite cold although it was past midsummer by now. She didn't feel right in her body – the room continued to spin even when she wasn't having nightmares, and there was a heaviness to her limbs, as if her bones had been threaded through with lead. She had a constant urge to bathe, to slough off the tainted skin in hope of finding a new, clean layer beneath.

She could still hear properly: starlings in the morning, the chirp of crickets in the evening. But there was a new edge of pain to these sounds, one that she hadn't noticed before: an owlet in search of its mother, a bat lamenting its broken wing, a bee in its death throes.

Sometimes, it all seemed too much to bear, suffering weighting the air like gravity, pressing down on her skin. It was as if the sparkle had gone from life, as if the apple had withered and rotted.

At first, she managed to draw comfort from her mother's things. The silky, speckled strands of Morg's feather, the locket with the delicate *W*, the tiny key that had lain hidden inside it for years. But what was the key *for*? There were no longer any locked rooms in the Hall. She began to wonder if Frederick had lied about her mother – about that white-faced, desperate woman, needing to be locked away. She could almost believe that he had made it up, if it weren't for the word scratched into the wainscoting. Weyward.

Crouching next to it one night, when the Hall was silent save for the mice that rustled in the walls, she wondered whether her mother had used the key to gouge those letters into the paint. She couldn't bear to think of her like that. Instead, she tried desperately to conjure up the memories that had been triggered by the handkerchief: the scent of lavender, the dark fall of hair, the warm embrace . . . sometimes she even thought she could remember Morg, appraising her with a beady, glittering eye . . .

She didn't even know where her mother was buried. When she was younger, she had spent long afternoons carefully examining the crooked headstones in the grounds, next to the old chapel they no longer used. She had knelt in cold soil, gently brushing away green threads of lichen, to no avail. The graves all belonged to long-dead Ayreses; even the most recently departed had been in the ground for a century.

Perhaps she was buried in the village graveyard. That was where she had been from, wasn't it? Violet thought about running away, running to Crows Beck and looking for her mother's grave. But what would that solve? She would still be dead.

And Violet would still be alone. Alone with what had happened, that day in the woods.

There was only one way to escape Frederick's pollution of her mind, her body. Her very cells.

Violet wasn't sure she believed in Heaven or Hell (though she doubted they'd let her into the former, after Frederick had sullied her so). She was a lover of science, after all. She knew that when she died, her body would be broken down by worms and other insects, and then she'd provide nutrients for the life-sustaining plants above ground. She thought of her beech tree. She'd rather like to be buried under it, to give it sustenance. And while the tree fed from her, she would feel . . . nothing. Oblivion. She imagined the nothingness, as heavy and dark as a blanket, or the night sky. Her mind and body would cease to exist, along with the spores Frederick had left behind. She would be free.

She spent the long days planning. She settled on dusk, her favourite time of the day, when the sky was the colour of violets – her namesake – and the crickets sang. She would leave with the light.

In the summer, as far north as they were, the days stretched on until almost midnight, which meant that everyone was asleep at the time she had chosen. She put on her favourite green dress and brushed her hair in front of the looking glass one last time. The bite on her cheek had faded to a silvery pink semicircle, like a crescent moon.

Her bedroom was amber and gold with the sun setting through the windows. Violet opened them and looked out, savouring the last sight of her valley. She could see the wood from here, a dark scar on the soft green hills. She looked down. She was very high up – about ten metres, she thought. She wondered who would find her in the morning. She imagined her body, crumpled like the petals of the primrose flower. Violet had left a note on the window seat, asking to be buried under the beech tree.

She climbed up onto the windowsill and felt the cool evening air on her face. Breathed it in deeply, one last time. Just as she prepared to propel herself forward into that empty horizon, she felt something brush her hand. It was a damselfly, its diaphanous wings golden with the sun. Just like the one that Graham had given her, all those weeks ago.

There was a knocking on the door, and then Graham – whom Violet had thought was asleep – burst in.

'Honestly, Violet, you can't keep taking my things without ask— Jesus, what the devil are you doing up there? One wrong move and you'd be splattered all over the garden.'

'Sorry,' said Violet, scrambling down from the windowsill and scrunching the note into her pocket. 'Was just – looking out at the view. You can see the railway line from here, did you know?' Graham loved trains.

'No, Violet, despite living in this house all my life I did not know that the second-floor windows offered views of the Carlisle to Lancaster line. Honestly, what's got into you lately? Thought I was going to have to put another damned insect in a jar for you.' He shuddered. She looked down at her hand, but the damselfly was gone.

'I'm fine. Just – rather tired.'

'*Please* tell me you're not heartbroken over bloody *cousin Frederick*. Or I suppose he's probably Freddie to you, isn't he? *Darling* Freddie. What did you talk about on your walks together? More rubbish about his hunting prowess? I must say, I wouldn't have expected you to fall for such a crashing bore.'

'It's nothing to do with Frederick,' said Violet, too quickly.

Graham looked at her for a moment, raising one pale red eyebrow.

'If you say so. Glad to see the back of *darling Freddie*, myself. Reminded me of a chap in the year above at Harrow. Similar air of arrogance. Expelled last autumn for getting a girl pregnant. One of the professor's daughters. She had the baby in a convent, poor thing.'

'Really,' Violet said, feigning disinterest. *Spermatophore*, she thought. 'How awful for her.'

'Indeed,' said Graham. 'Anyway, you've got to be careful of chaps like that. He didn't try anything with you, did he? That day we played lawn bowls – Father and I fell asleep and when we woke up you were both gone. Father seemed quite pleased about it, actually.'

'Nothing happened,' said Violet. 'We just went for a walk. I showed him the woods.'

'Hmm. So long as that's *all* you showed him. Look – anyway, it's really late. I was waiting for Nanny Metcalfe to give up her post so that I could come and get my biology book back. You do have it, don't you? I'm supposed to have wrapped my head around the subphyla of anthropods by the end of the summer. Running out of time.'

'Arthropods, you mean. The ones with exoskeletons.'

'Ugh. Yes, those. Well – anyway, can I have it back?'

Violet thought of the book, wedged under her mattress along with her bloodied undergarments.

'Lost it. Sorry.'

'*Lost* it? How the blooming hell do you lose a *textbook*?'

'Dropped it in the beck.'

'Can you imagine the look on the science master's face when I tell him that? Sorry, sir, don't have my textbook – my feckless sister *dropped it in a stream*. Well, that is just capital, thank you Violet. Now I'll have to send off for another one. It'll probably arrive after I'm back at bloody Harrow. Thanks *a lot*.' He left, slamming the door behind him.

Once the sound of Graham's footsteps had faded down the corridor, Violet tried to think what to do about the note. She couldn't very well burn it. Nanny Metcalfe was bound to smell smoke – she had the nose of a bloodhound – and then there would be questions. And, anyway, she hadn't completely decided whether or not she would still need it. But then she thought of the damselfly and her stomach ached with guilt over Graham. Could she really leave him all alone with Father?

She retrieved the Brothers Grimm book from next to her bed, opening it to stash the note inside. Before she fell asleep, she thought of her mother again. If Violet died, she would never learn the truth. She carefully placed Morg's feather next to her face on the pillow, hoping she would dream of her mother. Instead, she dreamed of Frederick, of what had happened in the woods. In the dream, she looked down at her pale body and saw the flesh of her stomach darken, felt it give way under her fingers. Mayflies swarmed around her, wings glistening as they ducked and weaved in their endless, brutal dance.

She woke the next morning to the strong smell of kippers wafting from a tray borne by Nanny Metcalfe.

'Get these down you,' she said. 'Nanny's orders.' The fish was yellow and puckered, like the carcass she had once seen of a slow-worm, mummified in the summer heat.

She struggled to sit up and took the tray. Her stomach churned and she shuddered at the memory of the dream.

'Are you all right, Violet?' Nanny asked.

'Fine, thank you,' she said, bringing a forkful of fish to her mouth. She chewed slowly, and even after she swallowed, the gelatinous sensation lingered on her tongue and on the roof of her mouth.

She managed one more mouthful. Then, the roiling in her stomach intensified, and the room shifted again. She felt a gathering inside her, something pushing up from her stomach and into her oesophagus, the acid sweet in her mouth.

She vomited. Again, and again.

Afterwards, when Nanny Metcalfe had sponged the flecks of vomit from her mouth and helped her change into a clean nightgown, they sat in silence for a while. A crow screamed outside. Violet could see it through the window, a black comma in the blue sky.

Eventually, Nanny Metcalfe spoke.

'I think we'd better call the doctor,' she said.

30

KATE

Time passes more quickly, now that Kate's days are filled by her shifts at the bookshop.

She finds the work soothing – sorting through the boxes of donations, stamping them with the label gun. Mostly, the shop sells Mills & Boon novels ('Beggars can't be choosers,' Emily says); though occasionally Kate will unearth a first edition Austen or Alcott. These are displayed in the window, so that their gilt-embossed covers spark in the sun.

She and her boss settle into a comfortable routine, the older woman often bringing her cups of tea and plates of biscuits, chattering easily about her husband Mike, about growing up in Crows Beck. Emily is impressed by Kate's affinity with her ginger tomcat, Toffee, who – she swears – despises all humans (Emily's own hands are often patterned with scratches from his eager ministrations).

She is due in December. Kate hopes for snow for the birth. Often, alone in the cottage, she tests names out loud, tasting them on her tongue. Holly, perhaps – a nod to the season. Or maybe Robyn. Though nothing feels quite right, yet.

It is early autumn when she feels the first kick. She is out in the garden, pulling up clumps of tansy from beneath the sycamore – quite a poisonous plant, she's learned, despite its bright yellow flowers – and listening to the trees murmur in the wind. She gasps at a sudden fluttering movement inside her womb – a liquid feeling that makes her think of quicksilver, or the pale minnows darting in the beck.

Her daughter.

By November, her skin is stretched tight as a drum over her stomach. None of her old clothes fit – she raids Aunt Violet's wardrobe for loose smocks and tunics; draping herself in pashmina shawls and a battered mackintosh. As it has grown, her hair has become unruly – she'd forgotten its tendency to curl, in all those years of expensive hair treatments. The back is a sort of mullet, now, but Kate doesn't care. She doesn't even brush it, these days – just lets it fall in dark waves to her ears.

Simon wouldn't recognise her.

'Are you in touch with him?' asks Emily. 'The baby's father, I mean.'

Kate has invited her over for Bonfire Night; they have built a small pyre in the centre of the garden and sit in front of it on camp chairs, gripping mugs of hot chocolate. Kate breathes deeply, savouring the scent of woodsmoke. Above them, the sky is thick with stars.

'No,' she says. 'I haven't spoken to him for months. It's . . . better that way. For the baby. He . . . isn't a good person.'

Emily nods. She reaches over, squeezes Kate's hand.

'I'm here, you know,' she says, taking her hand away. 'If you ever want to talk about anything, you just say the word.'

'Thank you.'

Kate's throat narrows. She stares into the fire, watching sparks dance gold into the night. For a while, neither of the women speak. The only sounds are the hiss and crack of the flames and, somewhere, an owl.

She wonders if Emily has guessed the truth. It could be obvious, she supposes, from the way that she flinches when her phone rings, her refusal to talk about her old life in London. About why she left.

But she can't bring herself to say the words. Not yet. She doesn't want to risk the delicate threads of their friendship. It's been so long since she's spent time with another woman. She hasn't seen her university friends for years.

The last time was the wedding she and Simon went to, in Oxfordshire. Five years ago now, not long after she'd left her job. Her friend Becky was getting married. She remembers the dress she wore – that Simon picked out for her – pink, the colour of broken flesh, the colour of the scar on her arm. Gold heels she couldn't walk in. She'd sat across from Simon at the reception, laughed too loudly at the feeble jokes of the man next to her. It was an open bar; Simon was drunk. But he was watching. He was always watching. One of her friends saw him push her into the taxi before the speeches, the practised way his hand gripped the back of her neck. He wouldn't let her take their calls, afterwards. In the end, her friends had stopped trying.

'I wish Violet were still here,' Emily says eventually. 'She'd be gutted to be missing this. To be missing you.'

'What was she like?'

'Sorry,' Emily shuffles her chair closer to the fire. 'I always forget you didn't really know her, you remind me of her so much. She was . . . odd. In the best way. I used to think that she had no fear – the things she did when she was younger! She climbed to Mount Everest base camp once, she told me. To make a study of the Himalayan jumping spider. Crazy woman.' She shakes her head, laughing. 'You have her spirit.'

'I wish,' Kate grins.

'You do. It takes strength what you've done, starting again. She had to do the same.'

They fall into silence.

'She never told you what happened? My mum said she was disinherited, that there was some sort of scandal.'

'No. Like I said . . . I think it was too painful for her. So your mum had no idea what it was? This scandal?'

'No. My dad might have known, but he died when I was a kid.'

'Oh, I'm sorry.'

'It's OK.' She has been thinking of the accident more and more lately, her perception of it shifting now that she carries a child of her own. A child she would do anything to protect. Even if that meant sacrificing herself, the way her father had done.

Sometimes, lately, she can almost believe that maybe – just maybe – it wasn't her fault. That she isn't a monster after all. But then she'll remember – the blood, slick and glossy on the road. The bee brooch, forever tarnished, in her hand.

'I had a baby, once, you know,' Emily says softly, in a strange echo of her thoughts. Looking over at her, Kate sees tears shine in her eyes. 'Stillborn. She'd be about your age, if she'd lived.'

'I'm so sorry.'

'It's all right. We all have our cross to bear.'

After Emily leaves, Kate sits for a while, watching the fire.

As she stares into the leaping orange flames, resolve hardens in her. She won't repeat the mistakes of the past. Things will be different, this time. *She* is different. And she is never going back to him.

She fetches her hold-all from the bedroom, struggling slightly under its weight.

In the garden, she unzips it, pulling out clothes – the clothes she used to wear, for Simon. The skin-tight jeans, the clingy tops. Even the lingerie she'd been wearing when she left: red lace, a diamante heart quivering between the cups of the bra. She throws the lumpy shape of them onto the fire, watching as the flames burn brighter. An effigy of the past, melting away. Shreds of lace float into the air, like petals.

She stands for a while, watching. One hand resting on her belly, where her daughter swims safe inside.

December.

The days begin white and glittering with snow – on the roof, the branches of the sycamore, where a robin has taken up residence. It reminds Kate of Robin Redbreast from *The Secret Garden* – for so many years, her only safe portal to the natural world. Only now does she truly understand her favourite passage, memorised since childhood:

'*Everything is made out of magic, leaves and trees, flowers and birds, badgers and foxes and squirrels and people. So it must be all around us.*'

Often, before she leaves for work, she stands outside to watch the sun catch on the white-frosted plants, searching for the robin's red breast. A spot of colour against the stark morning. Sometimes, while she watches it flutter, she feels a tugging inside her womb; as if her daughter is responding to its song, anxious to breach the membrane between her mother's body and the outside world.

The robin is not alone in the garden. Starlings skip over the snow, the winter sun varnishing their necks. At the front of the cottage, fieldfares – distinctive with their tawny feathers – chatter in the hedgerows. And of course, crows. So many that they form their own dark canopy of the sycamore, hooded figures watching. One bears the same white markings on its feathers as the crow that startled her in the fireplace when she arrived at the cottage. She is growing braver – testing herself each day by moving closer and closer to the tree. This morning, she presses her palm against its ice-crusted bark, and warmth swells in her chest.

Later, Kate is at the bookshop, thinking about this and

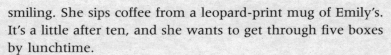

smiling. She sips coffee from a leopard-print mug of Emily's. It's a little after ten, and she wants to get through five boxes by lunchtime.

It's been seven months since she left. Sometimes she feels as if she's always lived in Weyward Cottage; always had this routine of waking with the sun, then either spending time in the garden or walking leisurely into the village for her shifts at the bookshop. Even some of the locals seem to be starting to accept her. According to Emily, they treat her with the same slightly baffled acceptance they reserved for Aunt Violet.

Other times, it's harder to forget what happened.

Her phone rang last night at 2 a.m., its blue flare jolting her gut. A number she didn't recognise. She knows it wasn't him calling. It's impossible: he doesn't know about the Motorola; doesn't have the number for it. But it doesn't stop her from running through scenarios in her mind as she sorts through boxes of books, worry ticking inside her.

Thank God he doesn't know about the baby.

'Oh, Kate?' Emily walks into the storeroom, a welcome interruption. She crouches next to a stack of weathered-looking boxes under the window. 'Someone dropped this off yesterday . . . I think you might find it interesting.' She grunts as she lifts a box from the top of the pile and plonks it down in front of Kate.

'What is it?'

'Take a look,' says Emily, beaming at her. 'You can keep what's inside, of course. Yours by right, really.'

At first, Kate thinks she has misread the label, scrawled hastily over the top of the box in pen. She checks again, but there is no mistaking it.

Orton Hall.

31

ALTHA

Outside the castle, it was a bright day. The light seared my eyes so that the streets and buildings of Lancaster looked white as pearls. For a moment I wondered whether they had actually hanged me, whether this was Heaven. Or Hell.

I staggered towards the road out of the town, keeping my head bent in case anyone should recognise me. Everywhere, I jostled through crowds, the warm press of bodies making me sweat and panic.

'Have you heard the news?' One woman said to another. 'Queen Anne has died!'

A man shouted; another woman uttered a prayer for the queen's soul. The babble of voices rose in pitch, and the crowd pushed and heaved. My thoughts swam. In a wild moment, I had the thought that it should have been me who died, that there had been some great error, my life saved instead of hers.

My heart froze at the feel of a rough hand on my shoulder. I turned, fearing it was someone from the gallery, come to right the jury's wrongs, to set me back on the path to death.

But it was one of the jurors. The square-jawed man with the pitying eyes.

I saw for the first time the richness of his clothing: both his cape and doublet were embroidered with silver thread. Standing in front of him in my crude gown, I felt every bit the pauper I was.

For a while, neither of us spoke as the crowd flowed around us.

'My wife,' he said eventually, slowly, as if it pained him to speak the words. 'She nearly died in childbed, delivering our son. A wise woman in our village saved both their lives. Beatrice, she was called. I said nothing, when they accused her. She was hanged.'

He took a velvet pouch from his breeches and pressed it into my hands, before melting away into the throng.

I looked inside the pouch and saw gold coins. I understood, then, that I had this man – or the woman who saved his family – to thank for my life.

On the road, I found a pedlar travelling by donkey and cart. He would take me back to my village, he said, for one of the gold coins. I should have been wary of him, a strange man in the dark, but I reasoned that even if he killed me it would be a quick death compared to the long one I faced on the road, without food or shelter.

The pedlar gave me some ale and a sweetmeat. Then he put me in his cart, amongst his wares, which were soft shawls and blankets. Nestled among them, I felt almost as if I too were an exotic ware from some distant land, spun from foreign cloth. I tried to stay awake but the blankets were warm and comfortable and the motion of the cart gentle and rocking, as I imagined the ocean to be.

When I woke next, we were half a mile from Crows Beck.

*

I knew when I saw the gate swinging on its hinges that the villagers had been at the cottage. Those who broke bread with William Metcalfe, who mourned John Milburn.

The shutters had been torn from the window, and lay in a splintered, ruined heap.

The front door was dented, the lock broken. Inside, shards of glass sparkled on the floor like fallen stars, and I had to be careful where I stepped. The smell of herbs and fruit hung rotten in the air and I realised they had broken my precious jars of salves and tinctures.

I lay down on my pallet, which was slashed so that tufts of straw poked through. I slept. When I woke at dawn it was to a sea of broken things.

It took me the better part of two days to put the cottage to rights. Mercifully, they had left my dear goat unharmed, though my absence meant that her ribs now showed clearly through her hide and, when I put my hand to her, she bleated in fear. 'All will be well,' I murmured as I led her inside, though I was not at all sure that it would.

One of the chickens had died, but the other had lived. I could still have eggs for my breakfast, and milk from the goat. I made nettle soup and dandelion tea from the plants in the garden. They hadn't got to the vegetable plot, either, so I pulled beets and carrots from the earth and ate and pickled them. They were small, misshapen things, hard with frost and forced from the soil before their time.

I broke up one of the chairs and used this for firewood. The cottage was very cold, with the shutters gone from the windows, and I ripped one of Mother's old gowns in two and used it to block the draught from getting in.

When I had done all this, I was ready.

I took down the parchment, quill and inkhorn from the hiding place in the attic, thankful that it had not been discovered.

Then I sat at the table and began to write.

I have been writing for three days and three nights now, pausing only to make fires and food, and to check on the animals. I do not want to sleep until I have finished.

They could come back, you see. The villagers. They could drag me through the village square, in protest against the verdict, and hang me themselves. Or they could find another crime to accuse me of.

So I must write what has happened while I still breathe. Perhaps I will go away from here, when I have finished. I do not yet know. The thought of travelling on the open road frightens me. And I cannot bear to leave the cottage behind. I wish I were a snail, and the cottage my shell that I carried with me everywhere. Then I would be safe.

It is hard to write the next part of my story. So hard that, even though it happened first – before I was arrested, tried and acquitted – I come to write it last. My heart has shrunk away from it until now.

But I promised to set things down as they happened and this I will do. The act of it brings me comfort. Perhaps if someone reads this, if someone speaks my name after my body has rotted in the earth, I will live on.

I am trying to think of where the beginning is. Who decides where things begin and end? I do not know if time moves in a straight line, or a circle. Here, the years do not pass so much as loop back on themselves: winter becomes spring becomes summer becomes autumn becomes winter again. Sometimes I think that all of time is happening at once. So you could say that this story begins now, as I sit down to write it, or you could say that it began when the first Weyward woman was born, so many moons ago.

Or you could say it began a twelvemonth ago today.

Last winter was a cold one, stretching its fingers well into spring. On this particular night early in 1618, there was a storm, and so when I heard the pounding, I thought it was only the wind at the door. But the goat, who I keep near me in the winter months, looked up with eyes of liquid fear.

A high female voice called my name.

When you have grown up with someone, as close as sisters, you come to know her voice even better than your own. Even if you have not heard it call your name for seven years.

So I knew before I opened the door and saw her, standing there with shadows ringing her eyes, that it was Grace.

32

VIOLET

The doctor's hands were cold on Violet's abdomen.

'Hmm,' he said. Violet could see white specks of dandruff clinging to his brilliantined hair. He turned to Nanny Metcalfe, who hovered next to Violet like an anxious moth, her hands wrung red.

'Are her menses regular?' he asked.

Menses? Whatever were those? Violet wondered if the doctor had meant her *mens*, Latin for mind. Well, that certainly wasn't regular. Far from it. For instance, although she knew that it was the doctor who was touching her, not Frederick, and that she was lying comfortable and safe in her bed rather than in the woods, her heart fluttered in her throat. The smell of brandy and crushed flowers returned and she fought the impulse to retch. She wanted desperately for the doctor to take his hands away, for him to stop poking and prodding at her stomach. It was taking all her willpower not to scream.

'Oh, yes,' said Nanny Metcalfe, flushing. 'Always on the fifteenth, like clockwork.'

Violet thought of the clots and clumps of blood that came out of her every month, accompanied by days of cramping pain. So that was what he meant. She'd never heard the medical term for it before – Nanny Metcalfe always referred to it as *her curse*. It had barely occurred to Violet that it was something that happened to other girls, too. Last month was the first time it had let her alone in years. She hadn't missed it one bit.

Nanny Metcalfe was frowning at her.

'She didn't ask me for any rags last month, mind,' she was saying to the doctor. Violet wished they would stop talking about her as if she weren't lying right there. Her cheeks grew hot at the mention of these private subjects to a complete stranger.

'Hmm,' said the doctor again. There was more prodding, and then he asked a question so bizarre that Violet thought she must have misheard.

'Is she intact?'

Violet thought of the pictures from Father's newspaper, of soldiers wounded in the war, arms ending at elbows or legs ending at the knee.

'As far as I know, Doctor,' said Nanny Metcalfe. There was a slight quaver to her voice, as if she were afraid.

Then, without warning, the doctor had slid his fingers between her legs, to that place that had felt like a bruise since the day in the woods. She winced from pain and shock.

'She is not,' he said, looking at her with mild disgust. Nanny Metcalfe gasped, clapping her hands to her mouth. Violet felt cold shame spreading through her. Somehow, he had known exactly what had happened between her and Frederick, almost as if he had looked inside her brain.

The doctor had her urinate into a humiliatingly clear vial, which he held up to the light and inspected briefly before putting it in the pocket of his jacket. Violet turned her face away.

'I'll telephone in a few days with the results,' he said.

Nanny Metcalfe nodded, barely able to force out a 'Good day, Doctor,' as he went down the stairs. They sat together in silence as they listened to Father's study door opening, a low murmur of conversation, followed by the heavy clink of the front door and the sputter of the doctor's motor car.

A moment of stillness hung in the air, like a raindrop threatening to fall from a leaf. Then there was a great crash, and the sound of glass breaking. A high-pitched whine from Cecil. Later, Nanny Metcalfe would report that Father was so angry that he had swept the Jacobean side table in the hall clear of its ornaments in one fluid movement.

'What have you done?' said Nanny Metcalfe, who had still not explained to Violet what was happening. But she didn't need to, not really. Violet thought of the word that had lingered on the edge of her consciousness for weeks, no matter how hard she tried not to think about it. *Spermatophore*.

Violet barely slept, for fear of dreaming about the woods. About Frederick. She passed the days between the doctor's visit and his telephone call in fog, halfway between sleep and wakefulness. She tried her hardest not to succumb to her drooping eyelids and heavy limbs, but often she found herself in a terrifying kaleidoscope of dreams: Frederick on top of her, under a tree-veined sky; her stomach distended and dark, rotting from the inside out. Mayflies, pulsing all around.

Not even Morg's feather brought her any solace.

Graham and the servants had been told that she was ill again, with the same 'condition of the nerves' that had kept her bedbound earlier. Only Father and Nanny Metcalfe knew the truth.

When the telephone rang, five days after the doctor's visit, Violet lay under the coverlet and waited for Nanny Metcalfe to come and tell her the news. But the footsteps that sounded up the stairs and down the corridor were too heavy to belong to Nanny Metcalfe.

Father opened the door. Violet sat up in bed, wondering

if her appearance would shock him. He had not been to see her in weeks, and she had lost a lot of weight from the constant vomiting. Her bones felt sharp in her face; her eyes were shadowed by lack of sleep. Perhaps he would ask her how she was feeling.

He looked at her for a moment with an expression of distaste, as though she were a piece of spoiled food on his plate.

'I have spoken to Doctor Radcliffe,' he said, his voice chill with fury. 'He has informed me that you are with child, and have been for several weeks.'

Violet's pulse flickered. She thought she might faint.

'What do you have to say for yourself?' he asked, taking a step closer. The anger made his face larger and redder, so that his blue eyes almost disappeared. A blood vessel on his cheek was swollen and purple, like a fattened slug. Violet wondered if it would burst.

'Nothing,' she said softly.

'Nothing? *Nothing?* Who do you think you are, the bloody Virgin Mary?'

She had never heard him speak like this before.

'No,' she said.

'Who is the father?' he asked, though surely he must have known all along. For whom else could it be? She remembered what Graham had said, about when he and Father had woken from their nap that day to find Violet and Frederick gone. *Father seemed quite pleased.*

'Cousin Frederick,' she said.

He turned on his heel and slammed her bedroom door behind him, sending dust motes flying. For a moment they hung suspended in the shaft of sunlight from the window, reminding Violet of the midges she had seen with Frederick, the day he had kissed her. She had thought they looked like fairy dust.

What a child she had been.

*

That day, Nanny Metcalfe came into her bedroom with a large, worn-looking suitcase that Violet had never seen before. She had never been anywhere, had never had need of a suitcase. Without looking at her, Nanny Metcalfe began piling things into it.

'Am I going somewhere?' Violet asked, though she wasn't particularly interested. Everything had felt muted and colourless since the doctor's visit. She knew that she was heading inexorably towards something, something terrible, and there was little point in resisting. She thought of the dreams, the flesh of her stomach dark and soft beneath her fingers. Rotten.

'Your father will explain,' said Nanny Metcalfe. 'The others think you're going to a sanatorium in Windermere, for your nerves. You're not to tell them different.'

Violet added nothing to the suitcase, apart from Morg's feather, which she wrapped carefully in an old scarf. Everything else – her books, her green dress, her sketching things – she left behind. She didn't even take Goldie the spider – Nanny Metcalfe had agreed to release him into the garden when Father wasn't looking.

Graham and the other servants were lined up in the hall to say farewell. Nanny Metcalfe had dressed her in one of Father's old trench coats and a wide-brimmed hat, to hide the weight she'd lost and the shadows in her face. Violet felt like a scarecrow, and she saw Graham blanch when she appeared on the staircase.

Miss Poole and Mrs Kirkby said goodbye and told her to get well soon. Graham said nothing, watching in shocked silence as Father took her by the elbow and marched her out of the front door to where his Daimler waited in the drive. Violet had never been in Father's motor car before. The chrome green exterior reminded her of the shiny casing of a pupa. Perhaps she would emerge from it a butterfly and fly away, miles and miles away, to a place where she would be safe and free. One could dream.

There was a lingering smell of cologne. It occurred to Violet that the last occupant of the passenger seat, where she was sitting now, must have been Frederick. The thought of it made her want to open the door and hurl herself out onto the road. Instead she just looked out of the window, at Orton Hall disappearing behind them.

'Where are we going?' Violet asked. Father didn't answer. Rain began to splatter on the roof of the car in fat, loud drops. Father turned a dial and mechanical arms unfolded themselves across the windscreen to wipe the rain away. For a while, there was no sound in the car but their rhythmic scraping.

They drove through the gates, rising up on either side of the car like omens. Violet wondered if she would feel something when she left the estate, having spent her whole life inside its bounds, but she felt nothing. Father cleared his throat.

'I have written to Frederick,' he said, keeping his eyes on the road. 'I have told him of your condition and asked him to marry you.'

Violet watched a bird rise and fall with the wind. Father's words seemed to come from a place very far away. She wondered if she hadn't imagined them; if she hadn't imagined everything that had happened since the afternoon they had played bowls on the lawn. Perhaps she was still asleep in her canvas chair, the sun warm on her face and the brandy warm in her belly. *Wake up*, she thought.

'Marry me?' she said. 'Why?' What had any of this to do with marriage, she wondered. She had thought that couples wed when they were in love. There had been nothing of love that afternoon in the woods.

'It is the decent thing,' he said. 'For the child. And for the family.'

The child. The spore that was growing in her stomach, feeding from her like a parasite. She hadn't thought of it as a child.

'But I don't want to marry him,' she said softly. Father ignored her, looking ahead at the road.

'I *won't* marry him,' she said, louder this time. Still he ignored her.

Outside, the sky grew dark and knotted with clouds. There was a storm coming, she could feel it on her skin. She watched the sudden glow of lightning. The rain grew heavier, blurring the window so that she could barely see out of it. Then, the car slowed and juddered before coming to a halt. She tried to remember how long they had been driving. Less than ten minutes, she thought – surely that wasn't long enough to get to Windermere?

Father opened his door and Violet breathed in the fragrant smell of wet earth. He collected her case from the trunk and then opened the door for her to get out. She drew her coat around her and pulled the brim of her hat down against the rain. Squinting ahead, she could see a low, squat cottage, overgrown with vegetation, the stone dull and wet. The windows were cobwebbed and dark.

Father rummaged for the keys in his overcoat. Now that they were closer, Violet saw that there were letters carved into the stone above the door. *Weyward.*

She rubbed the rain from her eyes, in case she was seeing things. But there it was. It looked like it had been carved a very long time ago: the first slant of the *W* was faint, and the other letters were green with lichen.

'Father? Where are we?'

He ignored her.

Violet was gripped by the sudden fear that Frederick would be in the cottage, waiting for her . . . but when Father unlocked the heavy green door and she saw the dim corridor beyond, it was clear that there was no one there.

Father lit a match, piercing the blackness.

Inside, the dark rooms had a sunken look, as if they were trying to disappear into the earth. The ceiling was so low that Father, who was not a tall man, had to stoop.

There were only two rooms: the largest one, at the back of the cottage, had an ancient-looking stove and a cavernous fireplace. The other, two single beds and a battered old bureau. There was a scrabbling sound in the roof: mice, Violet thought. At least she wouldn't be totally alone.

'You will stay here until Frederick next has leave and can return for the ceremony,' said Father. 'I'll come to check on you every few days with provisions. For now, you'll find some tins and a dozen or so eggs in the kitchen. Perhaps the solitude will help you reflect on your sins.'

Her cheeks burned as the memory of the woods came back to her.

Father was still talking.

'I have been foolhardy,' he said. 'I should have known. You are your mother's daughter, after all.' He turned away, as though he could no longer bear the sight of her.

'My mother? Please – where are we? What is this place?' Violet asked as he walked towards the door. He stood at its threshold, his hand on the doorknob, and for a while she thought he would simply leave without responding.

'It belonged to her, actually,' he said. 'Your mother.' He slammed the door behind him, so hard that the little house shook.

PART THREE

33

KATE

Kate stares at the writing on the box for a long time.

Orton Hall.

The cardboard is mildewed and lifting at the edges. One side looks as though it has been eaten by something. She remembers the glittering remains of the insects at Orton Hall and shudders. She isn't sure she can even bring herself to touch the cardboard, but she is conscious of Emily watching her, eyes bright with anticipation.

She takes a deep breath. Then she opens the box.

Dust clouds the air, catching in her throat. She coughs as she peers inside.

All the books are very old, and some are in better condition than others. She pulls out a copy of *An Encyclopaedia of Gardening*. Its green cover is faded and swirled with mould. She shakes it, and crushed insect wings fall out, glimmering like pearls in the light.

'Ugh,' says Emily, reeling backwards. 'That'll be the infestation Mike mentioned. He's been up at the Hall, helping to clear it out. He thought I might want the books. The viscount's been moved to a care home, over in Beckside. He was in quite a state, apparently. Poor man. Hold on – I'll get a dustpan.'

Emily bustles out of the storeroom, and Kate pulls the next book out of the box.

It's a rather dense-looking tome titled *Introduction to Biology*. One of the pages is folded down, and Kate shudders at the unsettlingly graphic diagrams of insect reproduction.

There are some fiction titles, too: a dog-eared copy of *The Adventures of Sherlock Holmes. The Complete Works of Shakespeare.* She wonders who they belonged to. If they could have belonged to Graham or Violet.

There's one last book in there. Kate fishes it out. It is very handsome – it looks as though it could be more valuable than all the others. She should tell Emily, she knows; ask her what sort of price it could fetch. But for some reason she doesn't want anyone else to see it. She wants to keep it for herself.

She runs her fingers over the front cover. The book is bound in soft red leather, the title embossed in gilt:

Children's and Household Tales
The Brothers Grimm

The Brothers Grimm. She'd had her own copy as a child, she remembers – though her newer edition had been titled *Grimms' Fairy Tales*. Some of the stories, she recalls, had been rather frightening, the characters – no matter how innocent and pure – meeting grisly ends. Hansel and Gretel, eaten by a witch. Good preparation for the real world, she supposes.

Could the book be a first edition? She opens it, looking for a publication date on the first page.

A crumple of yellowed paper falls onto her lap. Unfurling it, she sees it's a handwritten letter, but before she has time to read it, Emily opens the storeroom door, dustpan and broom in hand.

She slips the letter into the pocket of her jacket before Emily can see.

Toffee creeps in, climbing over her, his claws digging into her legs. He settles into her lap and begins purring. The baby kicks in response.

'I think she likes you,' she says to the cat.

'And he's smitten with the pair of you,' Emily laughs. Her feathered earrings quiver as she bends down to sweep up the wings. 'I can only get him to purr by leaving the room. What have you got there?'

'Fairy tales,' says Kate quietly. 'I wonder if it belonged to Violet,' Emily says. 'Though it's odd, isn't it – that she didn't take her things with her, when she moved out of the Big House.'

'Yes,' Kate says, struggling to reconcile what she knows of Aunt Violet – her love of green dresses, the insect drawings, the strange collection of artefacts under her bed – with dark and horrible Orton Hall. She can't picture her ever having lived there. 'Perhaps she left in a hurry?'

Emily brings her a plate of chocolate digestives before heading back to the front of the shop to deal with a customer. Though she desperately wants to, Kate doesn't dare open the letter in her pocket. She doesn't want to risk Emily coming back and seeing it. It feels private, somehow. Secret.

At half past three, after they've closed up for the day, Emily offers her a lift home.

'You shouldn't be carrying heavy things, you know,' she says. 'Not now, in your condition.'

Kate looks down at her stomach, swaddled in layers of wool. She eases herself into an old coat of Violet's, pulls a velvet green beret over her head.

'I'll be fine,' she says. 'Anyway, I want to see the snow.'

It's funny, now, to think of her early walks into the village, back when she'd first arrived at Crows Beck. How she'd flinched at the rustle of leaves, startled by a sparrow. Now, her amble home is something to look forward to; something to savour. She loves noticing the little seasonal changes of the landscape – how now, in winter, the trees reach bare and graceful towards the sky; the hedgerows are jewelled red with rowan berries.

She hoists the box onto her hip and pushes open the door, leaving behind the musty warmth of the bookshop. Outside, she inhales the wintry air, savouring its crispness. The cold prickles her cheeks, and she grins at the sight of the village: the buildings half hidden under great lips of snow; windows glowing orange. Someone has strung Christmas lights from the street-lamps, and as the sun sets pink in the sky, they twinkle into life.

For the first time in years, she has been looking forward to Christmas – her daughter is due a few days before. With only weeks to go, she can feel her body preparing for the birth: her breasts have swelled, and she's begun to notice streaks of golden fluid on the inside of her bra. Colostrum, Dr Collins calls it.

Even her senses seem to have sharpened: sometimes, she thinks she can hear the most incredible sounds: the *click* of a beetle's antennae on the ground; the whirr of a moth's wings. A bird clamping its beak around a worm. It's strange, how she feels attuned to things happening at such a great distance, and yet all the while her child's heartbeat thrums in her ears.

But now, as she walks home, the countryside is still and silent, muffled by snow. It is *so* still, in a way that unsettles her: she has the sense that the land, and the creatures in it, are waiting for something. As she strides on, the only sounds are her own footsteps crunching in the snow, and the rustle of the letter in her pocket. The letter. Something about it doesn't feel right. Foreboding creeps across her skin, setting the hairs on end.

When she does get home, she is almost afraid to look at it. She takes her time lighting the fire, boiling water for her tea, chopping vegetables for the stew that she'll prepare later.

Finally, everything is done. She can no longer put it off.

She sits down at the kitchen table and unfurls the piece of paper.

The note is very yellow, almost translucent in places. Lined, as though it was torn from a school exercise book. There is no date.

Dear Father, Graham, Nanny Metcalfe, Mrs Kirkby and Miss Poole,

I am very sorry about what I have done, especially to whomever it was who found me.

Father, I know that you think taking one's own life to be a mortal sin, and that you will be shocked – and perhaps ashamed – by what I have done. But please understand that I truly felt I had no other choice after what happened.

I know you all – Father especially – think very highly of my cousin, Frederick Ayres. But please believe me when I tell you that he is not the man you think he is. I know he seems charming and chivalrous – like a knight from a fairy tale, with his dark hair and green eyes. But something has happened – something terrible and wrong. I do not quite have the words for it; just that I am plagued by memories of it, night and day. Perhaps it is my fault; perhaps I should have done something to prevent it, though I do not know what. In any case, I cannot see how I can continue in this fashion.

Graham, I am sorry that I was not a better sister to you. Nanny Metcalfe, I am sorry if I have been a difficult charge.

Mrs Kirkby, I am sorry about the time I said your roast beef
tasted like a shoe. Miss Poole, I am sorry for all the times I
made fun of your singing voice.

My best wishes to you all, and my deepest apologies once
again,

Violet

PS. If it isn't too much trouble, I should like to be buried
under the beech tree in the garden. Perhaps you could also ask
Dinsdale to plant some flowers above my grave. Something
bright and colourful that will attract bees and other insects.
Any flowers will do, so long as they aren't primroses.

Kate reads the letter again.

I am plagued by memories of it.

She shuts her eyes, touches her arm, where the skin is
smooth and pink. Sometimes, Kate would wake in the night
to Simon's insistent mouth on her neck; to the feel of him
inside her. As if she had forfeited the rights to her own body
the day they'd met.

She understands, she thinks, what happened to Aunt Violet.

Obviously, she hadn't gone through with the suicide
attempt – somehow, Violet had left home and found the
strength to live the academic, adventurous life that awaited
her. To break free from her past.

Kate wonders if Violet ever told anyone, in the end. She
knows what it's like, wanting to tell: to no longer be alone
with the awful, secret knowledge, poisoning your cells like
a disease. Wanting to speak but being choked into silence by
the shame of it.

As she rereads Violet's words, something else leaps out at
her.

His green eyes.

She thinks back to her visit to Orton Hall, to meeting the
old viscount. He had green eyes, too. Her spine tingles with

revulsion at the memory – his fetid, animal stink; the yellow curls of his nails.

Fingers shaking, she unlocks her phone and taps *Frederick Ayres* into Google.

The first result is an article from the local paper, dated five years ago.

FLY INFESTATION BUGS VISCOUNT

Local exterminators have struggled to remove thousands of mayflies from Orton Hall, the seat of the Viscount Kendall.

According to residents in nearby Crows Beck, the infestation has plagued the Hall for decades, worsening in recent years.

'Every pest control company in the valley has had a go,' said a source. 'Insecticides, LED traps, the works. But they won't budge.'

Mayflies are most common in the summer, when the females can lay up to three thousand eggs. The insects normally frequent aquatic environments and rarely infest dwellings.

Lord Frederick Ayres, the Tenth Viscount Kendall, has lived in Orton Hall since succeeding his uncle to the title in the 1940s. He served as an officer in the Eighth Army in World War II and saw action in North Africa.

Viscount Kendall has not been seen in public for some years and could not be reached for comment.

Her stomach drops.

There's a photograph with the article. A young man in military uniform, handsome features blurred by time. But she can see him there – just – in the firm line of the jaw, the deep-set eyes. It is the same stooped, haunted man she met at the Hall.

Frederick is the viscount.

What kind of father would disinherit his children in favour of a man who had *raped* one of them? Surely he couldn't have known. For a moment, Kate allows herself to consider a worse possibility: that Violet had told her father about the rape, and that he simply . . . hadn't believed her.

Outside, an owl hoots mournfully. Kate feels a surge of sadness for her great-aunt, this woman she can barely remember. They'd had more in common than she realised.

She goes to the sink for a glass of water, gulping it down as if it can flush away her memories. She stays there for a moment, looking out at the snowy garden, flaming with sunset. Violet's garden.

Despite everything that happened to her, her great-aunt had built an independent life for herself. She may have never married and had a family of her own, but she had her cottage, her garden. Her career.

Now Kate, too, has built her own life.

And she won't let anyone take it away from her.

34

ALTHA

Grace and I stood looking at each other for a long time before she spoke. It was the first time she had looked at me directly in seven years. Since we were thirteen, I had only ever seen her from afar: in church, or shopping on market day. She had always passed her eyes over me as if I were not there.

'Will you not invite me in?' she asked.

'Prithee, wait,' I said, before shutting the door. Hurrying, I herded the goat into the garden, my mother's warning ringing in my ears.

When this was done, I opened the door and moved aside to let Grace through. I noticed she walked slowly, as if she were a much older woman. She sat heavily at the table. She kept her cloak on, even though it was soaked from the gale outside.

'Would you care for some food?' I asked.

She nodded, so I cut a slice of bread for her, and some cheese, and sat down opposite her. As she ate, her cap shifted, and I saw a dark shadow on her cheek. I thought perhaps it was cast by the flicker of the candle on the table. Still she did not say anything until she finished eating.

'I heard about your mother,' she said. 'Now we are both orphans.'

'You have your father,' I said.

'My father', she said, 'hasn't looked at me properly since I was thirteen years old, though I kept house for him and brought up my brothers and sisters until I left home.'

'Well, you have your husband.'

She laughed. It was a dry sound, like the crackling of flames. She did not laugh like this before, when we were children, I remember thinking. She'd had a sweet laugh then, sweeter than the hymns we sang in church, sweeter even than birdsong.

'You will have to tell me what it's like, sometime,' I said. 'Being a wife.'

'I haven't come here for idle talk,' she said sharply. 'I'm here on business. To purchase something from you.'

One small white hand went to the pocket of her kirtle, and I heard the clink of coins.

'Oh,' I said. My face flushed, and a tide of pain rose in my throat. I had been stupid to think she had wanted things to be as they were before, after all these years. After everything that had happened.

'I am with child,' she said, turning her head away. Her voice was very quiet; her face hidden by the cap.

'What joyful tidings,' I said. I remembered how much she had spoken of wanting to grow up and have a babe of her own when we were children. When I was very young, I had told her, horrified, of Daniel Kirkby's birth: his mother grunting and glistening all over with sweat, the child sliding out of her in a rush of slime and blood. Grace, who had seen her brothers and sisters born, laughed at my ignorance. 'That is just the way of things,' she had said. 'You'll learn yourself one day.'

There had been rumours of a pregnancy around the village

in the months after she married, and when I saw her in church, I had noticed a swell beneath her dress, a plumpness to her face. But no child ever came. I did not know if she had lost the baby, or if there had never been one. Either way, she must be very happy now, I thought, to be so blessed.

She did not say anything for a moment. When she spoke again, I was sure I must have misheard her.

'I need something', she said slowly, as if she were reluctant for the words to leave her mouth, 'that will make it go away.'

'Go away? Vomiting, you mean? I can see to that. I can make a tonic with balm, to settle the stomach—'

'You misunderstand me,' she said. 'I meant the child. I need . . . I need something to make the child go away.'

Her words hung heavy in the air. Neither of us spoke for a moment. I heard the pop and hiss of the fire, the drum of rain on the roof. These sounds swelled in my ears, as if they could take away what she had said.

'Has the baby quickened?' I asked.

'Yes.'

'Grace,' I said. 'Are you quite sure? What you are asking of me . . . it is a sin. And a crime. If anyone were to discover it . . .'

'It will die anyway.' She said this as coolly as if she were commenting on the yield of the harvest or the turn of the weather. 'You would be doing it a kindness.'

'Grace,' I said. 'Even if I knew how . . .'

'You must know,' she said. 'Your mother would have known. Look through her things. There's certain to have been a village girl or two who came to her for help after some indiscretion or other. Besides . . .' She paused. 'She was good at taking life, wasn't she?'

The memory of that terrible night swam before me. Anna, still and lifeless while Grace sobbed.

'Grace. Your mother would have died anyway, had we not

come. She was too ill by then . . . the fever was so strong. And the leeches . . .'

Her head turned sharply back towards me. In the candle-light, her eyes were bright – with tears or fury, I did not know.

'I do not wish to speak of it,' she said. 'Just tell me if you can help me or not. If you ever loved me as your friend . . . then you will do this thing for me. And you will ask me no more questions.'

All the moisture had gone from my mouth. I felt giddy, as though the room had lurched to one side and taken me with it.

'I will try,' I said softly. 'But I cannot promise that it will work.'

'Aye, then. I will return in one week. Will that give you enough time?'

'Yes.'

She rose from the table. 'I must be going. I have left John asleep. He does not normally wake until dawn, after so much ale. But I cannot risk him rousing to see that I am gone.'

I myself slept a poor night after she left. I thought for a long time, wondering what I had agreed to. All for the love of someone who – and I knew in my heart that this was true – still blamed me for her mother's death. Still hated me.

How it pained me, to hear that hate in her voice. My mind ran over her speech, remembering the coldness of it, and my eyes burned with tears. As children, we had learned each other before we could speak. I had once known the meaning of her raised brow, the curve of her mouth, as though they were words in a book. Now she was a stranger.

The following morning was calm and sunny, and, as I listened to the robins sing, I wondered if I hadn't dreamed up Grace's visit. Then I went into the other room and I saw the second mug and plate and knew it had been real. Grace really had come. She really had asked this terrible thing of me. She wanted me to atone for one wrong by committing another.

I would look through my mother's papers as she had suggested, I decided. If there was no recipe for the kind of draught that Grace wanted, then I could tell her that I could not do it, did not know how.

I opened the bureau that had been my grandmother's – the handle inscribed with a W, much finer than anything else we owned. She had been given it by the First Viscount Kendall for nursing his son through milk fever. It was where my mother and I stored all our notes and recipes, our cures and remedies, for relieving ailments and suffering. My mother always kept the drawers locked and wore the key around her neck. She gave it to me when she died, bade me do the same.

'To save things getting into the wrong hands,' she said.

I rifled through handwritten recipes for all manner of salves and tinctures: elderflower for fever, belladonna for gout, agrimony for back pain and headache. And then I saw it, in my mother's fine hand.

For bringing on the menses
Crush together three handfuls tansy petals
Steep in water for five days before administration

My heart sank. I had no excuse, now.

I could not be sure that it would work if the baby had quickened. Perhaps I could strengthen the dose of tansy, I thought. Just slightly, so that it would still be safe.

I caught myself. Did I even want it to work? Why would Grace want to harm an innocent babe, which had not yet had its chance at life?

I remembered her eyes, glittering and hard with fury and pain. 'You would be doing it a kindness,' she had said.

Perhaps I was too quick to judge. I had never felt a child

grow in my womb, only to lose it in childbed. I remembered the Merrywether woman I had attended to and the small, dead coil of flesh she had laboured over for hours. Had given her life for.

What if Grace carried the baby to term and bringing it forth killed her? What if Grace were to die for the sake of a child that would never open its eyes, never take its first breath?

I couldn't lose her. She may still hate me, blame me. But it didn't change the love I felt for my friend then, and always would. I had to keep her safe.

I waited until nightfall to gather the tight yellow buds of the tansy from the garden. It was still a time when villagers came to my door frequently enough in the daylight, to seek treatment for some complaint or other. I did not want anyone to know what I was doing.

I liked being in the garden. It was where I felt my mother's presence most strongly: in the furred leaves of the plants she had tended; the strong, tall sycamore she had loved; the creatures that rustled in the undergrowth. I felt as if she were still there, watching over me. I wondered what my mother would make of Grace's visit.

I knew my mother had felt a great deal of guilt over Anna Metcalfe's death. She never liked to speak of it afterwards. I could see that the end of my friendship with Grace pained her. She was afraid to leave me, friendless and alone in the world, I think. As I write this and think of everything that has happened, I know she was right to be afraid.

When I had got enough tansy, I went inside and crushed it with our old mortar and pestle. I added the water and put the mixture in a covered bowl to steep. I hid it in the attic in case I had visitors over the next five days.

Its scent was so strong – like fouled mint – that I could still smell it when I laid my head on my pallet for sleep.

35

VIOLET

Her mother. This house belonged to her mother. Violet touched her necklace, tracing the *W* engraved on the pendant.

The Weywards. Her mother's family, she could be sure of it now.

Violet looked around the dingy room for some record of them. There was barely anything to suggest it had ever been lived in at all. She sat down at the creaky kitchen table, which was covered with a thick patina of dust. She wiped some away with her finger and coughed. Underneath, the wood was scored and gouged, as if someone had taken a knife to it. The roof was leaking, and the far wall of the kitchen shone with rain. She was cold and it was dark. There was no clock anywhere in the house, and the small square of violet sky visible through the filmy window gave no clue as to the time.

She looked at the provisions that Father had left. Tinned peas, corned beef hash, sardines. One of the eggs still had a soft curl of feather clinging to it. The eggs made her think of *spermatophore* and she pushed them to one side, stomach queasy. She ate some peas, cold from the tin. She struggled to light an ancient-looking candle with one of the matches Father had left behind, flinching at the small blue flame. She sat for a long time, watching the wax bubble and melt.

It was strange to imagine her mother living here. It was a hovel, Violet thought. Like something from a fairy tale without a happy ending. She walked over to the small door that led to the back garden and opened it, sheltering the candle flame from the wind. The garden – if it could be called that – was wild and rampant: strange-looking plants shivered in the rain. A large sycamore loomed over the house, and Violet could see nests in its upper branches, the glimmer of black feathers. Crows. She felt their eyes on her, watching. Assessing.

She shut the door, letting darkness fall. She took the candle into the next room and sat on one of the beds. It gave a great creak of protest. In the bedroom, the air was thick from dust and it moved through her lungs like treacle. She lay down on the bed and watched the candle throw shadows onto the wall. Violet felt tears well up in her eyes. She was here, in her mother's house, closer to her than she had been in years, and yet she had never felt so alone in her life. She shut her eyes and waited for sleep. When it came, it was blank and dreamless.

Violet was woken by a wave of nausea. She retched into a basin she found next to the bed. Her head pulsed with pain and her mouth was dry and sour. She needed water. The candle had long since gone out, and the room was very dark. She drew back the threadbare curtains to look outside. The windowpane seemed to have thickened from years of grime, so that the outside world was just a murk of brown. She tried to open it, but the latch had rusted shut.

She felt her way into the next room, fumbling on the kitchen table for the box of matches. She knocked one of the tins onto the floor and it rolled to the other side. Violet lit a candle and left it on the table before going outside.

The garden was red with dawn, and she could hear the chatter of thrushes and wood pigeons. The wind whispered through the leaves of the sycamore and Violet detected another layer of sound – the gurgle of the beck. She could see it from here, shining in the morning sun; the garden sloped down to it. The same beck that curved through the valley and around the fells, all the way to Orton Hall. Connecting Violet to this place – to her mother – without her even knowing.

There was no tap in the cottage, but Violet saw an old water pump outside, like the one in the kitchen garden at the Hall. The pump was green and stiff with age, and she struggled to work the handle, the way she'd seen Dinsdale do. The first drops of water that trickled out were brown, but eventually she had a clear stream flowing, which she cupped in her hands and splashed at her face. She got a bucket from inside and filled it to the brim. The bucket was very heavy and she half dragged it back indoors, sloshing water over the sides.

Here, she paused, thinking of the pails of scalding water she'd watched Penny lug up the stairs, face pink from steam. She needed to heat the water. She lit the stove with a match, before fetching a dusty pan from a hook on the wall. She would bathe, then wash the windows, try to get some light in.

Violet saw that Father hadn't left her any soap. She supposed he thought it was appropriate that she sit here in squalor. *Reflect on your sins*, he had said. She didn't want to think about her sins, about the woods, Frederick, *spermato-phore*. She wanted to scrub the house and her body until both were shiny and new.

Perhaps she could find some soap somewhere. The bigger room had very little in the way of storage; or, indeed, furniture at all: it was bare, other than the stove and the table and chair. She remembered the bureau in the other room.

Lifting the candle to it, she could see that it would have been a fine piece, once, before time and dirt had eaten away at it. Much of it was covered in grime, but the bits of wood she could see were warm and rich, the handles a heavy brass beneath the dirt. It was far nicer than the battered old table in the kitchen, almost as if it didn't belong in the house. She tried one of the drawers, but it was locked. The other, too. She frowned. She hadn't seen a key anywhere. Father had taken the front door key with him, she remembered. She had heard it turn in the lock.

In the kitchen, she stripped – taking care not to look down at her body, the places Frederick and the doctor had touched – and scrubbed herself as best she could with a wet handkerchief. Once she was dressed, she set about wiping down the table and the windows. Soon her handkerchief – a present from Miss Poole, she remembered, rather guiltily – was brown and stiff with dirt.

The rooms were a little brighter now that she had cleaned the windows. No matter what she did, she couldn't get the one in the bedroom to open, but she flung the kitchen window wide, letting in the smells and sounds of the garden. She opened a tin of beans and ate it outside, feeling the warmth of the sun on her face. The garden was loud with bees and swallows, and the occasional caw of a crow from the sycamore tree. Violet thought she heard a note of approval in the crow's voice, as though it had assessed her favourably. It made her feel a little less alone.

She could do something about the garden, she thought. She could see that it would have been neat and ordered, once: there were recognisable patches of violets, mint. It was waist-high with helleborine now, the crimson heads nodding in the breeze.

Her mother had sat in this garden, perhaps exactly where Violet was sitting now. It was obvious to Violet that her mother had been very poor – especially compared to Father. Was that why he was so secretive about her? Was he ashamed? Violet remembered what Frederick had said. That her mother had *bewitched* her father.

Bewitched. Everything she knew about witches came from books, and none of it was good. The witch who ate Hansel and Gretel, for instance. The three witches in *Macbeth*, raising the wind and the seas. But what about the witch in 'The Robber Bridegroom'? She had helped the heroine escape. Anyway, she was being ridiculous. Witches weren't real. Her mother hadn't been some sort of evil hag, brewing potions in a cauldron and zipping about on a broomstick.

Still, there had to be something of her mother's somewhere in the house. Inside, Violet tried the old bureau in the bedroom again. She hadn't noticed before, but each handle was carved with a *W*. She pulled her necklace out from under her dress and held it up against the bureau to check. No, she hadn't imagined it . . . the exact same *W* as the one carved on her mother's locket. Barely breathing, she opened the locket and put the tiny gold key into the lock. It stuck, and for a moment Violet thought it must have snapped off inside. She turned it gently again, and felt the mechanism give way with a soft click. She opened the first drawer, which was empty. The second drawer was filled with paper, old enough that it was almost transparent, the writing so faded that she could not make it out. A scrap of newsprint had been daubed with what looked like a hastily scrawled shopping list. *Flour*, it read, *kidneys, milk thistle*.

There was an invitation to a jumble sale at St Mary's, dated September 1920. A crumpled letter from the Beckside branch of the Women's Institute asking for volunteers to make socks and stockings for 'our boys abroad'. Violet looked at the date: 1916.

Something familiar caught her eye at the top of the pile.

A bundle of thick, creamy paper stood out from the other scraps and tatters. The Ayres coat of arms: a gilded osprey, suspended in flight. Father's writing paper.

They were letters, from Father to a woman named Elizabeth Weyward. *E. W.* Lizzie, he called her.

Violet's mother. It had to be. Her hands were shaking.

I have not slept this past week for thoughts of you, read one missive. It then beseeched Lizzie to *be brave, for the sake of our union*. The paper was thin with creases, as if it had been continually folded and unfolded, read and reread.

Another letter, jumbled in with the rest of the pack, stood out. It was not written in her father's elegant, Etonian script. Instead, the writing was rushed and slapdash, at one point almost veering off the page.

Ma

I am sorry it has taken so long to write but I have not been able to get out a message to you. I've had nothing to write with but today Rupert has gone out hunting – the butler Rainham, who takes pity on me, has brought me some paper and ink. He has said he will take you this note on his way to Lancaster to purchase new clothes for Rupert.

It has taken me too long but I see that you were right. I should never have left home. For some time, Rupert has not let me go outside and now I am to be locked in my room.

How I hate this room. It is small, like a cage, with walls painted yellow as tansy flowers. It makes me think of the tansy tea we used to prepare for the village women, and it pains me to think that Violet will not know the cures and treatments that have been our way for hundreds of years. When I shut my eyes, all I see is that bright yellow, reminding me of what I have forsaken. My past, and my daughter's future.

I miss her so, Ma. They will bring the babe to me so that

*he can feed, but they have not let me see Violet in days. I
hear her cries echoing through those yellow walls.*

*My only comfort was Morg, but I told her to go, Ma – this
is no life for a bird. All I have left now is one of her
feathers. Though I do not like to look at it.*

It reminds me of what I did. What Rupert made me do.

*I should have listened to you, that day we argued down
by the beck. 'He takes you for a dog that he can train to eat
from his hand,' you said.*

*I thought he loved me for myself. But you were right. To
him I am but an animal, like those he hunts and puts on
display.*

*That was another thing you told me. That if a man saw
my gifts for what they truly were, he would only use them
for his own ends. I told myself I was doing it for her, for
Violet. As you guessed, she had already quickened in my
belly, then. I began to dream of her, grown into a dark-
haired beauty, but alone and bleeding in our cottage.
Whether from sickness or injury I did not know, but it was
clear: my daughter would not survive a life of poverty such
as the one I could give her. In my terror, I told Rupert of the
dream and asked him what would become of our child. His
parents would never acknowledge her, he said. He would be
ruined if he married me, being only a second son, with no
title to smooth his path in the world. And worse – his
parents already knew. They know about the child we'd made
together that night in the woods, when only the moon saw
my fear and heard my cries. They planned to drive us – the
last Weyward women – away from Crows Beck, he said.
From our home, where our forebears have lived for centuries.*

*But, he said, I had the power to give us all a chance of
happiness. He would have his title, and my daughter would
have a life of safety, riches. Acceptance.*

I liked the idea of that. I was never strong like you, Ma.

The things the villagers said, the looks they gave us – I never could stand it. I yearned for a life free from stares and whispers.

And so I did the terrible thing he asked.

I lay in wait, hidden by gorse and heather, as dusk spread over the fells. Morg dug her claws into my shoulder. I heard them before I saw them – the whinnying of the horses, the clatter of hooves. I waited until they were close enough to the edge of the hill, where the ground cut away sharply into a ravine. When Morg took flight, I shut my eyes, opening them only when the screams had stopped, when all that remained was the twisted shape of the carriage on the rocks below, the spokes of one wheel still spinning. Something sparkled on the ground near my feet – a pocket watch, a family heirloom that Rupert had spoken of with great envy. Its face was cracked and sharp, so that when I picked it up, drops of blood welled along my finger.

I stood for a while, looking. Ignoring the horror in my heart.

I thought I was like Altha, our fearless ancestor, that our deeds linked us across time. I thought I was good and brave, made strong by her blood.

But I was wrong.

We took three lives that day, Morg and I. I told myself that they deserved it – Rupert's parents, his older brother too. That they had been cruel to the man I loved; that they would hurt you, hurt my child, without remorse. But truthfully, Ma, I didn't know them – or what they might have done – at all. Rupert has lied about so many things. I suspect now that his parents never knew of our child, never planned to drive us from our home.

I wish I had seen it before – that his words held as much truth as a fairy story. That he never loved me at all.

Sometimes I wonder if he planned this from the first. He'd been watching me, he said, even before we danced at the May Day Festival. He saw how I was special, and wanted me for his wife. I believed him, from the way he looked at me. A blaze in his eyes that I took for love.

But I am familiar with that look, now. It is the same way he looks at a gun dog or a rifle, a mere instrument to deliver his wants.

I do not ask, nor expect, forgiveness. I write this because I want you to know the truth. And I am running out of time to do so. The doctor is coming: Rupert says I am to have a new treatment. I do not know if I will survive it. Shut in this tiny room, and without even Morg's presence to sustain me, I grow weaker each day.

I take a strange comfort from this – have almost willed it. For I am become like a rifle without bullets, and useless in his schemes. I will never harm another for his sake.

Ma, I beg of you, please be there for the babe – and for Violet. Keep our legacy safe for her.

I hope she has your strength.

All my love

Lizzie

Heart pounding, Violet rifled through the rest of the pack, searching for more of her mother's handwriting. But the remaining letters were from Father, to a woman whose name she did not recognise.

1 September 1927

Dear Elinor,

Thank you for your letter to Lizzie, which I am afraid she was not well enough to receive, her health having declined significantly in recent weeks.

I have discussed your request to visit with Doctor Radcliffe. Given the marked decline in Lizzie's physical and mental state, Doctor Radcliffe does not feel a visit would be appropriate at the present time.

Elinor, your daughter has become – there is no other word for it – hysterical. She has conspired to bring that ghastly crow into the house – Morg, she calls it, ridiculous name – and speaks to it as if it is human. This is, I suppose, exactly the kind of behaviour you encouraged in her. Violet may be a lost cause. She has already begun to mimic her mother; befriending flies and spiders, for heaven's sake. But I will not have this madness infect my son. My heir.

And it is not good for Lizzie, Elinor. It is not good for Lizzie to tear around the house in such a state, engaging in such fantasies. Last week she told me she could predict the weather – or rather, that Morg, that foul bird, could. I live in, I am ashamed to say, constant dread of her.

I do fear – and Doctor Radcliffe shares my concerns – that, should she lose her remaining grip on reality, she will pose an even greater danger to herself. And to the children.

In fact – and I shudder to even relate this incident to you – the housekeeper came upon her attempting to climb out of her window, which a feckless maid had neglected to lock. Most horrifyingly, she was carrying the baby. She put the life of my son – my heir, Elinor – in danger.

Fortunately, Doctor Radcliffe was able to come at once. Given the recent developments, he has suggested a treatment that may help: hysterectomy, removal of the womb. It may seem an extreme course of action, but the doctor is of the view that it is warranted in such rare circumstances, when the state of the sexual organs begins to pollute the mind.

It is my fervent hope that Doctor Radcliffe's treatment will be effective in returning Lizzie's sanity. I shall keep you abreast of developments.

Yours sincerely,
Rupert Ayres, Ninth Viscount Kendall

10 September 1927

Elinor,

Your unannounced visit yesterday was most irregular.

I regret that Rainham was unable to admit you to the Hall, but I was tied up dealing with some urgent correspondence relating to the estate.

As I think Rainham explained to you, Lizzie is currently preparing for treatment. You need have no concerns for her wellbeing: Doctor Radcliffe and his small team of highly trained attendants have installed themselves at the Hall in readiness for the surgery.

Doctor Radcliffe has the utmost confidence that the treatment will work. We must allow the good doctor to do his work in peace.

In the meantime I ask that you refrain from engaging in further correspondence. I will let you know when there is news.

Yours

Rupert Ayres, Ninth Viscount Kendall

25 September 1927

Dear Elinor,

It is with sincere regret that I write to inform you of Elizabeth's death.

She departed this earthly realm in the early hours of this morning. Doctor Radcliffe believes that a weakened heart was the culprit, no doubt exacerbated by the strain of her recent delusions.

While I am sure that Doctor Radcliffe used his best endeavours to save her, I gather that by the time it became clear that something was amiss, it was too late.

I have made arrangements for her to be interred in the Ayres family mausoleum at St Mary's church next Tuesday.

I trust that will be satisfactory.

Yours,

Rupert Ayres, Ninth Viscount Kendall

30 September 1927

Elinor,

    Given your display on Tuesday, I think it best that you have no further relationship with the children. It is my priority that they recover as quickly as possible from this regrettable episode. As such I think it best that they are not subjected to discussion of Elizabeth; Doctor Radcliffe's view is that this would do more harm than good.

    And as for your absurd request to take Elizabeth's remains to your slum of a cottage for burial – I can't imagine that you ever thought I could agree to such a thing. Elizabeth was my wife and it is thus appropriate that she be interred in the Ayres family plot.

    However, I will do as you ask and give Violet the necklace you are so concerned with – I can make arrangements for Rainham to collect it next week. I may need to revisit this decision, should you attempt to contact me again.

    Yours,

    Rupert Ayres, Ninth Viscount Kendall

Violet's cheeks were wet with tears.

Now she knew the truth. Her mother had not – as she'd been led to believe – died giving birth to Graham. She had died because a doctor – the same doctor who had slid his cold fingers inside Violet – had *mutilated* her. Killed her.

She reread Lizzie's letter, tracing the loops and curves of her mother's handwriting. At first, she didn't understand the section about the carriage, but then she remembered. Her grandparents and an uncle had died, not long before her parents' marriage.

Coach accident, it was. Very sudden.

All that remained was the twisted shape of the carriage.

Had her mother somehow been responsible? The letter made no reference to anything that might be used to engineer an accident – Violet pictured a trap hidden in the gorse, something to make the horses spook. But Lizzie had written only of Morg.

In any case, it was Father who was to blame. Who had – her stomach turned at the thought – wished for his own family members to die. She thought of the broken pocket watch she'd found in Father's desk. She wondered if it had belonged to Edward – that was the name of the uncle who had been killed, she remembered. The eldest of the three Ayres sons. That must have been why Father wanted him out of the way. With his parents and older brother deceased, he would have been free to inherit the title of viscount, and Orton Hall.

His greatest conquest of all.

Her mother must have been the only person who knew of his guilt. And so he had locked her away – pretended she was mad – to cover up what he had done.

She hadn't even been allowed to see her own mother, Violet's grandmother. What had become of Elinor? Violet supposed she must have died, which would explain why Father owned the cottage. But where were their things – Elinor's, and Lizzie's? If not for the contents of the bureau, one might think they had never existed in the first place.

The last sentence of her mother's letter came back to her.

Keep our legacy safe.

What had she meant by 'legacy'?

Blinking away her tears, she rifled through the remaining sheafs of paper in the second drawer, sending dust sparkling into the air. At the bottom of the drawer was a thick book, clumsily bound in calfskin and mottled with age. Her heart skipped a beat. The parchment was worn, barely readable. She had to squint to make out the writing: the hand was tight and cramped, the ink faded. She held it up to her candle to get a better look. There was a name . . . Altha: the ancestor her mother had spoken of in her letter.

Her fingers traced the first line.

Ten days they'd held me there. Ten days, with only the stink of my own flesh for company . . .

36

KATE

Kate is sitting on the floor in the bedroom when her phone rings.

She has been making a mobile for the baby, using treasures she's collected on her walks around the area. An oak leaf of translucent amber; the shiny whorl of a snail's abandoned shell. The white-speckled crow's feather she found in the mug on the kitchen windowsill when she first arrived. All of these things she threads onto fishing wire attached to a frame made of twigs, tied together with green ribbon.

Her phone is in the kitchen, and she's been sitting for so long that her foot has fallen asleep. She stumbles down the corridor. By the time she reaches the other room, she's missed the call, but the ringing starts up again, the vibrations harsh against the wooden table.

'Hi, Mum,' she answers.

'Darling. How are you?'

'Good – I'm just finishing up the mobile, the one I was telling you about the other day.'

'It sounds beautiful. How are you getting on with it all? Have you got everything you need?'

The cottage is crammed with baby paraphernalia: the kitchen table hidden under piles of tiny vests and muslin squares, soft as gossamer. Emily has given her a Moses crib and a car seat; donated by a niece.

'I think so. Everything but a buggy.'

She sighs. She's looked everywhere for one online, but even the most basic model costs hundreds of pounds. And she can't find a second-hand one advertised nearby: not even Emily's niece has been able to help, having sold hers years ago.

Perhaps she should buy one of those slings, strap the baby to her front. Maybe she could even make one. At least that way she'll be able to take her out for walks. Show her the beck, now frozen under a sheen of ice. The trees with their white coats of snow.

'You know, I've been thinking,' her mother is saying. 'Perhaps I could buy you one. As a sort of early Christmas present.'

'Mum. You don't have to do that. You're already spending so much money on flights . . .'

Her mother is coming in two weeks, so that she can be with Kate for the birth. It will be the first time they have seen each other in years.

'But I want to. Please, let me.'

'I don't want you going to any hassle.'

'Well, how about I just transfer you some money? And then you can pick one yourself.'

'Are you sure?'

'Positive.'

'Thanks, Mum.'

'I love you, Kate.'

She blinks away the sting of tears. When did they last say this to each other? Not since Kate was a teenager. It was her fault: she never said it back. She couldn't bear the weight of it, this love she didn't deserve. But now the words are there, familiar shapes in her mouth.

'I love you too, Mum.'

The buggy she picks is green, with a segmented hood that reminds her of a caterpillar. She smiles at the thought of her daughter nestled inside. Though part of her wishes she could stay for longer, warm and safe in her womb. Sharing everything, even the blood that beats in their veins. And yet, she can't wait to hold her in her arms, breathe her scent, stroke her tiny fingers.

She cradles her stomach with one hand as she orders the buggy. Taps in her address, the number of her new debit card. Her email address, for the receipt.

She smiles when the purchase is complete. The kettle is singing, and she is slow as she moves towards it, her body curving under the weight of her stomach.

As she sips her tea, she looks out of the window, watching the crows in the sycamore tree. Their dark, liquid movements against the white snow.

Her mug slips from her hands, smashes onto the floor.

The email.

She'd used her old email address. The one linked to her iPhone.

Simon has her iPhone. He's going to see it.

She scrabbles for the Motorola, blood roaring. Her fingers shake as she opens a new browser, brings up Gmail.

Please God, no.

The page won't load. She refreshes it, again and again.

Finally, it loads. There's the confirmation email – it's got her address, her new phone number, everything. Even a graphic of a smiling baby.

She deletes it. Stands for a moment, a chill spreading through her veins.

If he's seen this . . . then he knows about the baby.

And he knows where to find her.

Leaning over the kitchen sink, she splashes water onto her face. The icy shock of it calms her.

How long did the email sit in her inbox – three minutes? It's – what – Tuesday, 2 p.m. The middle of the workday. He won't have seen it. She's caught it in time.

It's OK. He's doesn't know where she is.

She looks down.

'Don't worry,' she says to her stomach. 'I won't let him anywhere near you.'

Outside, there's that same, unsettling stillness from the previous night. She doesn't like the look of the clouds – the way they hang low and grey in the sky. There is something ominous about it.

She sweats under her layers as she heaves herself into the car. The seat is as far back as it can go, her hands barely reaching the steering wheel.

Her heart races as she turns onto the A66, passing the snow-blanketed fields. In the distance, the peaks of the mountains spark silver.

She takes a deep breath, tries to calm herself. She is safe. The baby is safe.

For now, she just needs to focus on driving.

She's going to see Frederick at his nursing home in Beckside. Really, she's not sure what she expects: he barely made any sense last time she saw him, all those months ago at Orton Hall. Guilt twinges in her stomach at the memory. She should have told someone – those dead insects everywhere, the room he'd been living in with its animal scent . . . and Frederick himself. She shudders at the memory of those eyes. At their emptiness. And yet. She can't quite bring herself to pity him.

Violet's words come back to her.

I am plagued by memories of it.

She has an image of him barricaded in that festering study while insects swarm outside, undulating through the corridors of the Hall like one great, glistening snake.

And the strange thing he said to her, just before she left.

She had released me at last.

There had been thousands and thousands of the things, according to the newspaper article. *The insects normally frequent aquatic environments and rarely infest dwellings.* This wasn't some natural phenomenon.

A plague for a plague.

Kate thinks she knows what happened. But she needs to be sure.

The nursing home – Ivy Gate – doesn't exactly live up to its name. The imposing iron gate is devoid of all greenery. Even from a distance, the buildings have an institutional look – something about the slate grey stone, the narrowness of the windows.

'Ivy Gate,' a curt voice answers the intercom at the entrance.

'Hello,' she says. 'I'm . . . I'm here to see a relative – Frederick Ayres?'

'Better be quick about it,' says the voice, with an impatient sigh. 'Visiting hours are coming to a close.'

She is directed to the common room – or, according to a sign on the door, the 'Scafell Room' – which is decorated in insipid peach; landscapes on the walls the only nod to its alpine name. Kate's stomach turns at the smell – a combination of cooking oil, bleach and, faintly, urine. Frederick is in the corner, huddled in a wheelchair far away from the other residents. As she approaches, she realises that he is asleep: his head lolls to one side, eyeballs flickering beneath almost translucent lids.

For a moment, she wonders if she should just leave, come back some other time. But, she knows, there may not be another time – the baby will be here soon, passing into the world just as Frederick is fading out of it.

This could be her only chance to get some answers.

She lowers herself into the chair next to his, leans forward.

'Hello?' she says softly. 'Frederick?'

Slowly, his eyes open. At first, they look clouded, unfocused, but then they widen in horror. She touches the lapel of her jacket, remembering his previous reaction to the bee brooch – but it's not there, it's in her pocket. Then she realises. He's looking at her necklace. Aunt Violet's necklace.

He arches back in her chair and – Kate's heart stops – screams.

'Get away!' he shrieks, spittle flying towards her. 'You're supposed to be gone!'

An orderly comes running – young, cheeks bright with acne, peach scrubs loose on his thin frame.

'There, there, Freddie, old mate,' he says. 'Let's take you back to your room.' He glares at Kate as he steers Frederick's wheelchair into the corridor.

'What'd you do, to upset him like that?' The orderly throws over his shoulder.

'I – nothing,' she says, still stunned by Frederick's outburst.

'Hold on, are you that woman he's always talking about? Valerie, or something?'

'Violet?'

'That's right. Look, I don't know what happened between you two, but he's not stopped going on about you since he got here. What are you, his granddaughter?'

'No, I—'

'So you're not even family. Honestly, miss, I think you should go. It's Saturday. Visiting hours end at 4 p.m. anyway.'

Kate can hear the orderly reassuring Frederick as he is wheeled away.

'You're all right, mate. Just a little scare.'

'But it was her.' She hears him take a great, shuddering breath. 'She's the one who sent them. The one who sent the insects.'

Fresh snow begins to fall as Kate drives home from Ivy Gate.

She's so distracted that she stalls the car twice. Luckily, there's barely any traffic in the valley. Both times, before she manages to get the car started again, panic snakes its way up through her body, gaining intensity as it passes through her stomach, her heart, her throat.

He thinks Violet was responsible for the infestation.

She remembers something else he said, when she went to Orton Hall. That the insects had died last August.

Just like Violet.

It is snowing harder now, the air so thick with it that she can barely see the road. The radio sputters with static, and she turns up the sound to catch the weather forecast. 'Heavy snowfall . . .' a man is saying. 'Disruption while travelling . . .' The signal is lost.

In her gut, panic blooms. She shouldn't have come. What if she's put the baby in danger?

She is driving past the woods, the trees sugared with ice. The woods. Where she'd felt such unease, before her unsettling visit to Orton Hall. Fear bubbles in her chest, the steering wheel suddenly slick under her hands. She remembers the claustrophobia of those tightly packed trees, the way they'd blocked out the light.

Kate forces herself to look straight ahead, at the reflective lines of the road curving ahead of her, away from the wood, disappearing into a haze of white. The wind roars. She needs to turn the fog lights on so that she can see better, but in her terror, she can't remember how. Her fingers slip and fumble on the wheel and the dashboard, and she takes her eyes off the road briefly. There. She's found the button. She lifts her eyes back to the road and the twin beams illuminate the remains of an animal – matted, bloodied fur; pale limbs – strewn across the road. The blood impossibly bright against the snow.

She screams. She loses control of the wheel. The car careens forward, and the noise of the trees scraping against the roof and smacking the windshield is deafening.

Everything goes white.

Kate's heart pounds in her chest. It takes her a moment to realise that she has crashed into the woods, that the front seat of the car is littered with ice, with glass from the windscreen.

The wind howls through the jagged edges of the windscreen. Kate shivers. She is so cold.

Oh God. *The baby.*

She places her hands over her stomach, willing her child to show her some sign of life.

Please. Kick. Let me know you're OK.

But there is nothing.

She needs to get help. Wincing at a bolt of pain in her shoulder, she twists to reach for her phone on the passenger seat. *Please God, don't let it be broken.*

She exhales with relief when she sees that the screen is intact. Relief turns to horror when, unlocking it, she sees only one bar of reception: it flickers for a moment, then disappears.

Shit.

She thinks she's about 5 miles from the cottage: the road loops around the fells in long, lazy circles, adding extra distance. The direct route, across the fells, is shorter. Two miles, no more, she thinks.

At this hour, while the light dims in the sky, the woods seem so black and thick that it feels as if the car has been swallowed up by a beast and has come to rest in its ribcage. She imagines the dark stretch of trees, a spine running across the land.

She could wait by the side of the road, see if someone drives past. Then she remembers how quiet it is here, how she hasn't seen a single other car for the entire journey back from Ivy Gate. And no one is going to take to the roads in a blizzard. She could be waiting till morning. It's already so cold in the car with the broken windscreen. People die of exposure in situations like this, don't they?

She doesn't have a choice. If she wants to get home before night falls, she'll have to walk.

She pushes the car door open, scraping against branches, gasping as the cold hits her.

Snowflakes sting her face as she makes her way back to the road, stumbling over icy tree roots and clogs of mud. The tarmac is dusted white. There is the body of the animal – it is a hare, she sees now – splayed out and flattened. She can't take the road, not unless she wants to risk sharing its fate.

She turns back to the woods, the leaves hissing with the wind.

There's only one way home.

37

ALTHA

When five days had passed, I collected the mixture from the attic and strained it. As I bottled it, I saw that it was a clear amber colour, like the waters of the beck.

Two nights later, Grace came, as she had said she would. I remember it was a clear night, and the moon hung bright in the sky. This time, Grace wore a shawl wound tight around her neck and chin, so that only her eyes were visible, flashing beneath her cap.

She would not come in.

'Are you quite well?' I asked, for she was a strange sight, with her face half covered like a bandit.

'Yes,' she said, her voice muffled by the shawl. 'Do you have the tincture?'

'It will be painful,' I said as I gave it to her. 'It will bring on cramps and blood. And with the blood, the beginnings of the babe. Will you tell John it is a miscarriage?'

'I will burn the remains. John cannot know,' she said. 'How soon will it take effect?'

'In a matter of hours, I should think,' I said. 'But I cannot be sure.'

'Thank you. I will take it tomorrow night, while he is at the alehouse. His sleep is restless tonight – I must be getting back quickly.'

She turned to go.

'Will you – will you let me know that you are well?' I asked. 'That it has worked?'

'I will try to come another night and tell you.'

She walked away quickly, taking care to open the gate so that it did not creak, although there was no one around for miles.

I passed the next days and nights in a state of distraction. In the evenings, I flinched at the slightest of sounds, then lay restless on my pallet until the night sky paled with dawn.

On the Wednesday, Mary Dinsdale, the baker's wife, came to see me about a cut on her hand.

'Have you heard the news from the village?' she asked, as I dressed the wound with honey.

My heart jolted. I was sure she was going to tell me that Grace had died, but it was just that the Merrywether widower was engaged to be married.

The following night, there was a knock on my door.

It was Grace. This time, her face was uncovered – she wasn't even wearing her cap – and when I raised my candle, I flinched at the sight of it. The skin around her right eye was swollen pink and shiny, her bottom lip bruised and torn. There was a smear of blood on her chin, and bright flecks of it on her collar. I noticed faint yellow marks on her neck.

I led her inside and she sat slowly at the table. I put a pot of water on the fire and gathered some rags, so that I could clean the cut on her lip and soothe the swelling of her eye. When the water had warmed, I combined it with ground cloves and sage for a poultice. Once this was ready I knelt next to her and applied it to her wounds, as gently as I could.

'Grace. What has happened?' I said quietly.

'I took the draught last night,' she said, her eyes on the floor. 'As soon as he had set off for the alehouse. Some nights, when he drinks, he comes home early and falls asleep by the kitchen fire. Other times, he is out much later, and when he comes home he is . . . without his senses.

'It would have been easier if he had come home early and fallen asleep until morning. I could have stayed up in the bedchamber and, when it was over, burned my shift. I have two others so perhaps he would not have noticed. I would have just needed to take care not to bloody the bedclothes.

'But he didn't come home. Not for hours. The pain was so much worse than I thought it would be, so early. You should have warned me. It felt as if the babe was gripping at me from the inside, fighting the draught . . . so much pain caused by such a small thing. When it came out, it didn't even look like a baby at all, or anything living that I have ever seen. Just a mass of flesh, like something one might buy from the butcher . . .' She was crying now.

'I was getting ready to throw it on the fire when he returned. I thought that maybe he would be too drunk to know what he was looking at. But he was not. I told him that I had lost it – I had hidden the tincture bottle – and he was angry. As I knew he would be. He hit me, as you can see. Though compared to the other times, he was almost merciful.'

She laughed that dry, crackling laugh again, but her eyes shone with tears.

'Grace,' I said. 'Do you mean to say that he has – he has been even rougher with you than this?'

'Oh, yes,' she said. 'After I laboured – twice – and gave him a blue corpse instead of a bonny, bouncing son.'

I was silent. She looked up and saw the shock in my face.

'I made sure no one knew I was pregnant, the second time,' she said. 'I tightened my stays over the bump and, when I got bigger, took care to see as few people as I could. In case it happened again. Then – afterwards – Doctor Smythson was sworn to secrecy. John didn't want anyone to know that his wife had a poison womb.'

'I am so sorry, Grace. I wish you had come to me. Perhaps I could have helped.'

She laughed again.

'There's no helping it,' she said. 'Doctor Smythson says he cannot find the reason. But it makes sense to me – God could not mean for a living child to be brought into the world by such an ugly act.'

She looked away, staring into the fire.

'That is why I came to you,' she said. 'I thought that if it happened again – if this baby were dead like the others – he might kill me.'

I didn't know what to say. I looked at her as she watched the fire. Without her cap, I could see that her hair, which had been bright as poppies when we were young, had darkened into a deep auburn.

'I am sorry about the baby,' she said softly. 'It was innocent. I tried not to let it get to that stage. Each night, after he – after he has been in me, I wait until he has fallen asleep and take care to wash away his seed. But it was not enough.'

'It is not your fault,' I said. I knew the words sounded hollow. Really, I did not know how to bring her comfort. I had never lain with a man. In church, the rector said that the physical union between a husband and wife was sacred and holy. There was nothing sacred about what Grace had described.

'I do not want to talk anymore,' she said. 'I am tired. May I sleep here?'

'Of course,' I said, reaching over to take her hand in mine. She flinched at my touch and her grasp was limp, defeated.

We lay curled together on my pallet like kittens. On the

pillow, my dark hair mingled with her reddish strands. I could tell from the rhythm of her breathing that she was close to sleep. I drank in the smell of her – milk and tallow – as if I could keep it with me always.

I remembered, then, a sun-warmed day from childhood. We had been very small, so small that we were not allowed to wander far alone. My mother had been watching us, but we crept out of the garden when her back was turned, and followed the beck all the way to a green meadow, bright and soft with wildflowers. Weary from play, we had curled up together on the grass. There, with the bees droning gently and the air sweet with pollen, we had fallen asleep in each other's arms.

I thought of the bruises on my friend's skin and tears wet my cheeks.

'Grace,' I whispered. 'There could be another way.'

I wasn't sure that she heard what I said next, but I felt her hand reach for mine in the darkness.

When I woke the next morning, she was gone.

38

VIOLET

Violet was roused by the sound of footsteps. She had stayed up until dawn reading Altha Weyward's manuscript. The candle had burned right down, leaving a moon of wax on the floor. She felt as if something had shifted inside her. As if she had been told something about herself that she had always known. One by one, memories fell into place, revealing their true form. The day of the bees. The *click* of Goldie's pincers in her ear. The way she had felt the first time she had touched Morg's feather.

Her legacy.

Father was in the kitchen, bearing provisions and a tight expression. Violet felt as if she were seeing him clearly for the first time in her life.

The treasured picture of her parents' wedding day – their faces shining with love, the air bright with flower petals – dissolved.

He had never loved her mother. Not properly.

Deep down, Violet had known this all along. She'd only let herself be fooled by the fact that he'd held on to those things of her mother's – the feather and the handkerchief – since her death.

But she had been wrong. They weren't treasured mementoes of a beloved wife much mourned. They were trophies. Like the tusk, the ibex head . . . even Percy the peacock.

Her mother had been little better than a fox, to be discarded after the hunt, broken and bloodied.

She remembered the look on her father's face the day of the bees, when his cane split her palm in two. At the time she had thought it was fury. But now she knew better. It was fear. All along, he'd recognised that she was her mother's daughter, had known what she was capable of. That was why he had hidden her away, forbidden her from learning about Elizabeth and Elinor. About who she really was.

And as for Father himself?

He was a murderer.

Violet watched him as he lined new tins up on the table. It was a warm day, and his forehead was pearled with sweat. The blood vessel on his cheek had burst into a red spider's web. He spoke and Violet watched his jowls tremble.

'Frederick has sent a telegram,' he said. 'He has agreed to marry you. He has been granted a week of leave in September. We'll have the wedding breakfast at the Hall. You'll be able to stay for a while, afterwards. The engagement will be announced in *The Times* next week.'

Violet said nothing. The sight of him was making her ill. He was her only surviving parent, but she would have been happy never to see him again for as long as she lived.

Thankfully, after delivering the news, Father didn't linger. He left without saying goodbye. She closed her eyes in relief at the sound of the key turning in the lock.

Now she could think.

She pictured a life with Frederick. The memory of the

woods – the crushed primrose flower, the searing pain – came back to her.

I trust you enjoyed yourself?

She wouldn't – *couldn't* – marry him. Perhaps she wouldn't have to, she thought desperately. Perhaps he would die in the war. But Violet had the awful feeling that he'd survive, like a cockroach clinging to the underside of a rock. Meanwhile, his spore would continue to grow inside her. The thought of his flesh mingled with her own made her want to retch. And then, once it – the child, though she refused to think of it in those terms – had slithered out of her and into the world, Frederick would come to claim them both.

What would become of her then? She thought of her mother, who had married the man who swooned over her dark eyes and blood-red lips. Who had ended up alone in a locked room, scratching her name into a wall so that there would be some evidence that she had existed, before suffering a gruesome, painful death.

Violet would not let that happen to her.

The child was the only reason for Frederick to marry her, surely. *That* was his obligation and interest, the rope that tied them together. A noose, shackling her from the inside.

Violet saw things clearly now. She had to cut the rope.

The manuscript. *Bringing on the menses.* Menses. The same strange word that Doctor Radcliffe had used for her monthly blood.

Outside, the garden shimmered with heat. She waded through the helleborine, its flowers leaving crimson smears on her dress. The air hummed with insects, the sun catching on the wings of a damselfly. Violet smiled, remembering the words from her mother's letter.

Walls painted yellow as tansy flowers.

It was as if she was reaching out to her from beyond the grave, guiding her.

She found the plant under the sycamore: bobbing with yellow flowers, each one comprised of tiny buds clustered together like a beetle's eggs.

It had worked for Grace. There was no reason why it wouldn't work for her, too.

39

KATE

Kate draws her hood over her head as she steps into the woods. Here, the wind is quieter; the close-knit trees arching around to protect her from the elements.

But still she shivers, panting with fear – her breath a white cloud in front of her.

The silence is unnerving. She can hear nothing but the blizzard. Suddenly, she longs for the sight of an owl, or a robin – even the flutter of a moth. Anything but this white, deadened world.

Snowflakes swirl around her, landing in icy bursts on her exposed skin. She wishes she had some gloves. Instead, she draws the sleeves of her jumper down over her hands, winds her scarf around her nose and mouth. Her eyes water from the cold.

There is a crack in one of her boots – an old pair of Aunt Violet's that she's been meaning to get resoled – and now the snow seeps in, drenching her foot.

She pushes through the trees, all the while forcing herself not to think about the baby, about the stillness in her womb. She has to get to the village. She has to get help.

After a while, the trees all begin to look the same, with their branches quivering under matching lips of snow. She is no longer sure which is the right direction. A ladder of pink fungus creeps up a tree trunk in a way that looks horribly familiar, and she is seized by the fear that she has passed it before.

Is she walking in circles? Awful images flood her mind: her body, curled on the forest floor, barely visible under its shroud of snow. Her child frozen inside her, tiny bones calcifying in her womb. She stumbles over a tree root and cries out, her voice dying in the wind.

Something answers.

At first she thinks she must be dreaming, like a lost traveller hallucinating a mirage in the desert.

Then she hears it again. A bird, calling.

It's real.

She looks up, breathing hard as she scans the canopy of trees. Something shimmers. A liquid eye. Blue-black feathers, dusted white.

A crow.

Panic flickers, but fades.

Something else is there, closer than ever, on the other side of her fear. That strange warmth she felt in Aunt Violet's garden, when the insects rose from the earth. She pushes through her panic, breaches the wall to find the light, the spark she holds inside.

It reaches her veins, hums in her blood. Her nerves – in her ear canals, in the pads of her fingers, even the surface of her tongue – pulse and glow.

The knowledge comes from deep within her, some hidden place she has long buried.

If she wants to live, she has to follow the crow.

After a while, she sees a greyness ahead of her, feels wind on her face. The woods are almost like a tunnel, she thinks. A tunnel of trees. She is coming to the end of it.

Up ahead, there is a gap in the trunks. Beyond it, she can see the rise and slope of the fell, like the haunches of an enormous animal, furred pale with snow. Crouched and waiting.

She has done it. She has made it through the woods.

On the fell, she feels so exposed that she almost wishes for the claustrophobia of the woods. The wind whips her face and takes the sound from her ears. Her lips and nose sting with the cold.

The crow is still there. Flying above her in blue-black loops. She can barely hear its guttural call above the rush of the wind in her ears.

At the crest of the hill, she can see the orange glimmer of the village below. Coming down the fell is easier: she is sheltered from the wind, now. Her hands and face feel raw, and a blister throbs on one heel. But the snow is gentle on her face. And she is almost back at the cottage. Almost home.

She looks up. The clouds have parted to reveal a smattering of stars, bright in the dusk. She watches the crow and feels no fear – instead, she is struck by its beauty as it glides away, the light grey on its feathers.

She has been afraid of crows since the day of her father's death. Since she saw the velvet flash of wings, dark in the summer sky.

Since the day she became a monster.

But she *isn't* a monster, and never was. She was a child – just nine years old – with nothing in her heart but love and wonder. For the birds that made arrows in the sky, for the pink coils of earthworms in the soil, for the bees that hummed through the summer. Her throat aches as she reaches into her pocket, fingers closing around the bee brooch. She holds it up to the night and it is as radiant as the stars. Almost as if it had never been damaged at all.

She remembers the strength in her father's hands, pushing

her to safety. The last time he ever touched her. He died for her, the same way she would die for her child. Hot tears stream down her cheeks. She isn't sure who they are for – the little girl who watched her father die, or the woman who spent twenty long years blaming herself for his death.

'It wasn't my fault,' she says out loud, acknowledging the truth of it for the first time. 'It was an accident.'

The crow wheels right, disappearing into the distance, one final cry echoing.

'The baby's fine,' says Dr Collins later, her open features creasing into a smile. She is crouched by Kate's stomach, listening intently to her stethoscope.

'Are you sure?' asks Kate. She hasn't felt her daughter move since the car accident, since stumbling into the GP surgery, shivering from cold. The awful image rears up again – her child frozen in the womb, tiny fingers curled closed.

'Here, have a listen,' says the doctor, passing her the stethoscope.

There it is, the thrum of her child's heartbeat. Relief floods her body; tears burn behind her eyes.

'Like I said before,' says Dr Collins, 'this one's a fighter.'

'Are you sure you'll be OK until your mother gets here?' Emily is loitering in the doorway of the cottage. Her husband Mike, waiting in the car, beeps the horn.

It is a bright day; the snow-topped hedges sparkle in the sun. Kate watches as a waxwing forages for rowan berries, its crest quivering. It chitters as it is joined by its mate. Starlings sweep overhead, making shapes in the sky.

'Positive. Thanks so much for everything.' Emily has stocked the fridge with all the food Kate could possibly need – microwaveable meals, bread, milk. She's brought nappies, and a blow-up mattress for Kate's mother to sleep on. She and her husband even arranged for her car to be towed to a garage in Beckside. Kate doesn't know how to thank them enough.

'All right, well you just let me know as soon as anything happens! Soon as there's even the hint of a contraction, I want to know about it!' Emily gets into her car and waves goodbye, and Kate feels a pang of sadness for her friend, as she remembers what Emily said to her on Bonfire Night.

I had a baby, once.

She still can't quite believe that she – they – escaped the accident unscathed. Each day since, she's braced herself for crisis: for pain in her gut, blooms of blood on her underwear. But everything has been fine: the baby is moving again, wriggling and fluttering inside her. In the evenings, Kate watches the surface of her stomach ripple, marvelling at a tiny foot protruding here, a little hand there.

That she will soon hold her child in her arms feels nothing short of miraculous. Kate wonders what colour her eyes will be, after they've changed from new-born blue. What she'll smell like.

Her mother's flight leaves tomorrow. Once she arrives, she'll get the train from London, then hire a car so that they'll be able to get to the hospital, when the baby comes.

She only has one more day to herself. As she drifts around the cottage, aimlessly touching surfaces, picking things up and putting them down again, she wonders what her mother will make of it. Of the framed sketches of insects; the centipede preserved behind glass. Of the corner of the bedroom she's prepared for the baby; the second-hand cot, draped with Violet's old shawls for blankets. The handmade mobile, twirling with leaves and feathers, the glittering bee brooch now the centrepiece.

And of Kate herself – her cropped hair; the strange outfits she pulls together from her great-aunt's wardrobe. Today she has thrown the beaded cape around her shoulders – the twinkling of its beads reminds her of the time she met Aunt Violet. It helps her feel ready to bring her daughter into the world. Ready to protect her, at all costs. She will be strong, just like Violet was.

You remind me of her so much, Emily had said. *You have her spirit.*

Kate touches the *W* pendant around her neck. She thinks of the insects that rose from the soil of Aunt Violet's garden. The birds that have flocked to the cottage since her arrival, as if to greet her. Even now, she can hear the hoarse cries of crows from the sycamore, where they throng its snow-covered branches, darkest jet against white. She thinks of her experience in the woods. That humming feeling in her blood; the crow that led her home.

She thinks, also, of the things she's heard about Violet: of her fearlessness; her love of insects and other creatures. The infestation at Orton Hall.

Mother of beetles.

And of Altha Weyward, tried for witchcraft. Kate still doesn't know what became of her – whether she was executed; where she was buried. But she's been leaving sprigs of mistletoe and ivy by the cross under the sycamore tree. Just in case.

In the evening, Kate is heating one of Emily's meals – home-made tomato soup – when the phone rings. She rushes to get it – thinking it's her mother, maybe, or Emily. Or someone from the doctor's surgery, calling to check up on her.

'Hello?'

For a moment, Kate hears nothing – only her blood ringing in her ears. Then, that voice. The one she wishes she could forget.

'I've found you.'

Simon.

40

ALTHA

Grace did not come to the cottage again. I saw her only from a distance, at church, where her husband sat close to her, afterwards holding her arm tight as if he had her on a yoke. Her face was empty under her cap, and if she felt my eyes on her, she did not look up. At least I knew she was alive.

Winter softened into spring, and I counted the days to May Day Eve, when I thought I might have a chance to speak to Grace.

When my mother was alive, we kept our own May Day Eve custom rather than attending the village bonfire. We spent the last days of April gathering moss from the banks of the beck and making a soft, green bed on our doorstep, for the faeries to dance on. Then we lit our own small bonfire and burned offerings of bread and cheese to bless the fields.

When I was a child, I asked my mother why we could not attend the celebrations in the village, where I knew there was music, dancing and feasting around a towering bonfire on the green.

'May Day Eve is a pagan festival,' she said. 'It is un-Christian.'

'But everyone else from the village attends,' I said. 'And they are all Christian, are they not?'

'They do not need to be careful like we do,' she said.

'Why do we need to be careful?' I asked.

'We are not like the others.'

Since my mother's death, I had kept up our tradition. But this was to be the first big village festival since the end of winter, and I wondered if Grace would be there. I needed to know if she was safe and well.

I could smell the smoke from the bonfire as I set off from the cottage. I could see it, too, an orange glow in the distance. When I got to the green, the villagers were dancing in rings around the flame, which threw sparks high into the air with each offering. The night was loud with song and the hiss of burning wood.

The heady smell of ale hung in the air, and many of the villagers looked drunk, their eyes sliding over me as I approached. I looked for Grace but couldn't see her, or her husband. Adam Bainbridge, the butcher's son, grabbed my hands and pulled me into the fray. Around and around we went, until everything became a blur of orange and black. I was beginning to melt into it, to enjoy the crush and heat of other bodies around mine, the feeling of being a part of something bigger than myself.

And then I saw her. A girl, standing alone on the green, shadows dancing over her body. Dressed only in a shift, thighs black with blood. In the dark I could not make out her face, nor the colour of her hair, but it was Grace – I was sure of it.

I pushed through the ring of bodies to reach her.

'Grace?' I called.

I was too late. She was gone.

I turned back to the dancing villagers. None of them had seen her, I could tell.

I felt my eyes water, whether from the smoke or tears I did not know. I wanted to go home. I set off towards the cottage when I heard footsteps behind me. I turned to see it was Adam Bainbridge, who had danced with me around the bonfire.

'Where are you going?' he asked.

'Home,' I said. 'I am not much one for festivals. Good night.'

'Not all of us believe it, Altha,' he said softly. 'You do not need to hide yourself away.'

'Believe what?' I asked.

'What they say about you and your mother.'

Shame crept up my throat, and I hurried away. I felt relieved as I turned from the light of the bonfire, as the darkness cloaked me from the eyes of the villagers. As I walked on, I listened to the night sounds – the hoot of an owl, the scratching of mice and voles – and felt my breathing slow. I could see well enough – it was a full moon, like it had been the night that Grace had stayed at the cottage.

Grace. She had not really been there, at the bonfire, I knew.

'Sight is a funny thing,' my mother used to say. 'Sometimes it shows us what is before our eyes. But sometimes it shows us what has already happened, or will yet come to pass.'

I barely slept all night, and I rose and dressed as soon as the sky lightened. I made my way to the Milburn farm, and by the time I got there, dawn was breaking over the valley, turning the hills a soft pink.

I kept my distance, lingering under the oak trees on the boundary of the farm – the same place where my mother had released her pet crow, all those years before – so that I would not be seen. I could see the farmhouse now, but not well: there was a slight slope to the earth which hid some of it away. I needed to be higher.

I bunched my skirts around my waist and began to climb the largest oak – a great, twisted thing that stretched high into the sky as though seeking God. I hadn't climbed a tree since I was a child with Grace, but my hands and feet remembered how to find holds in the curves and knots of the branches. I climbed so high that I could see the sleek forms of crows in the branches, then went no further. I wondered if one of them was the same bird that my mother had cast out. I searched their dark feathers for the sign but could not see it.

Now, I could see the farmhouse well, and the cow byre next to it. I watched John leave the farmhouse and open the byre, so that the cows spilled out onto the field. I counted a score of them, far more than any other farm in the area, as far as I knew. No doubt some had been Metcalfe cows, and had come with Grace as her dowry. I wondered if John would ever beat one of his cows the way he beat his wife.

After a while, I saw Grace come out from the farmhouse, carrying a pail of water and laundry. I felt relief course through me. She was alive. I watched her squat on the ground and scrub the laundry, and, when she was done, hang it on the rope that stretched between the farmhouse and the byre. The white small-clothes shone gold in the early sun. I wondered if she had been washing blood from them.

I saw John cross the field to approach her. She turned her head to him and then looked away, and there was something in the set of her body that made me think of a dog waiting for a kick from its master. I saw him speak to her and they went inside together, she with her head bowed.

I remained for a while, in the tree, watching the farm-house, but neither of them came out again. The day was growing warmer and brighter. I climbed down, in case someone from the village happened to be passing and looked up to see me.

As I walked home, I wondered what my vision at the bonfire had meant. There had been so much blood, the darkness an open maw between her legs. Had Grace been pregnant again, and miscarried? Or was she pregnant still? I remembered what she had said to me: 'If this baby were dead like the others, he might kill me.'

May became June, and the days lengthened. The sun lit up the sky for hours, so that I slept and woke in daylight. While I went about my daily tasks, and when I laid my head to rest at night, I thought of Grace. She and John still came to church, and after the sermon, while John spoke to the other villagers, she kept her eyes on the ground. I wondered what she was thinking, if she was well.

I couldn't send a message, for Grace did not know her letters and would not be able to read it. I had thought about walking to the Milburn farm again – to do what, exactly, I did not know – but I was too worried about being seen, now that the nights were so brief. I dared not ask the villagers, who came to my door seeking fixes for hay fever and midge bites, what news they had of John Milburn's wife. The rift between us was well known in Crows Beck. It would raise many an eyebrow for me to ask after her now. They might guess that she had sought my help. I did not dare give her husband another reason to hurt her.

Her husband. I had not known it was possible to hate another person so much. My mother had taught me that each person deserves love, but I will not deny that I would have happily seen Grace a widow, even then.

I remembered with shame how I had thought Grace and John looked well together on their wedding day. How little I understood of anything then.

I had thought that I knew a great deal of people, just because I knew how to dress their wounds and cool their fevers. But I knew nothing of what went on between a husband and wife, the act that made a woman swell with child. I knew nothing of men, other than what my mother had told me. I was always shocked, as a girl, when a man came and sought my mother's treatment. By his size, his deep voice, his meaty hands. The smell that hung about him. Sweat and power.

The leaves darkened and began to fall. A chill returned to the air. One day, I had gone to the market square for meat and bread, when I saw a woman stooped over a table of pig hearts, a red curl escaping from her cap. Grace.

I could not approach her there, in the village square, in front of everyone. I hung back as she had Adam Bainbridge wrap up two pig hearts in cloth, then put them in a woven bag that she slung from her shoulder. I myself bought some bread, watching her from the corner of my eye. Then I followed her, a few paces behind, as she set off down the road to Milburn Farm. The trees either side of the road looked stark without their leaves, which glistened red underfoot, wet from weeks of rain. I watched as Grace drew her woollen shawl more tightly around her shoulders.

I was beginning to wonder if she could not hear my footsteps behind her, for she did not turn around. But once we could see the Milburn farmhouse ahead through the trees, she turned.

'Why are you following me?' she asked. More of her red hair had escaped from her cap, and beneath it her face was pale as milk.

'I have not seen you, other than from a distance, for six moons,' I said. 'I saw you in the village square and . . . I wanted to make sure that you are well. There is no one else on the road, you can speak freely.'

At my last words she laughed, but her eyes were blank.

'I am well,' she said.

'Are you – have there been . . .'

'I have not been with child again, if that is what you want to know. Not for John's lack of trying.'

Her eyes darkened. I took a step closer, to see if there were bruises on her face, like before.

'You will not see any marks on me,' she said, as if she had read my thoughts. 'Since the last time . . . Mary Dinsdale asked about my lip, after church. Now he takes care to spare my face.'

'Have you thought any more on what I said that night?' I asked. She was silent for a while. When she spoke, she looked not at me but up at the sky.

'A man of John's age and health does not just fall down and die, Altha,' she said. 'Doctor Smythson will know poison when he sees it. Hemlock, nightshade – they will know you had a part in it. There's no one else in the village who understands plants the way you do. They will hang you. They will hang us both. I do not much care whether I live or die, but I cannot have another death on my conscience. Not even yours.'

With these last words, she turned to leave.

'Wait,' I said. 'Please. I cannot bear to know that you are suffering . . . I could think of something, a way that we would not be discovered . . .'

'I shall speak no more of it,' she called over her shoulder. 'Go home, Altha. And stay away from me.'

I did not go home right away, as she had asked. I watched as her small frame disappeared into the trees. Some time later, a plume of smoke rose from the Milburn farmhouse. I shivered. The day was growing colder, and icy drops of rain began to fall on my face and neck. I walked on, until I reached the oak tree I had climbed to watch the farmhouse. I would not climb it today. The crows sat like watchmen in the upper branches of the tree, and their sharp cries of pain could have been my own.

41

VIOLET

Five days. Violet worried that she would lose track of the times the sun dipped in the sky and rose again. Here, in the cottage, time followed different rules. There was no gong for dinner, no Miss Poole demanding she conjugate ten French verbs in as many minutes. She spent most of her days in the garden, listening to the birds and the insects, until the sun glowed red on the leaves of the plants.

She could almost imagine that she was already free.

Almost.

At night, she slept with Morg's feather gripped tight in her hand, dreaming of her mother.

Her mother. *Elizabeth Weyward*. She who had given Violet her middle name. Her legacy. She whispered the name out loud, as if it were a spell. It made her feel strong, steeled her for what she had to do next.

On the fifth day, the wind roared and sucked at the cottage, bending the branches of the sycamore so that the leaves looked like they were dancing.

Violet strained the mixture in the kitchen. She used two empty tins to separate the golden liquid from the sodden petals with their smell of rot. She waited until she was in bed to drink it. It was strong and acrid, stinging the back of her throat. Her eyes watered. She lay down and listened to the wind shake the walls of the cottage, waiting for the pain to come.

Gradually, she felt a pulling inside her. It started out like the cramps that came with her monthly curse, dull and pulsing, but soon grew stronger. It was as though there was something inside her, tugging and contorting her innards into strange shapes. Violet tried to find a rhythm to it, to breathe through it as though she were sailing a boat through a churning sea, but there was none. The pain was overwhelming now. The window rattled, and Violet heard the crack of a branch hitting the roof. There was a rushing inside her, a breaking free, and then a great flood.

She marvelled that such a bright colour could come from her own body. It was like magic, she thought. The blood was still coming: her legs were slick with it. She shut her eyes, reached the crest of the wave. Then she fell.

42

KATE

Her heart thuds in her chest, fluttering like a trapped moth.

He can't have found her. It isn't possible. Unless—

The email.

Her phone lights up with messages, one after the other.

I'll see you soon.

Very soon.

For a while, she is still: a black hole yawns inside her, swallowing her ability to move, to think . . . then she feels the baby kick.

Everything becomes hyperreal: the sun setting on the snow outside, staining the garden red; the screams of the crows in the sycamore. Her blood, rushing through her veins. All of her senses engaged, heightened.

Quickly, she draws the curtains, bolts the doors, frantically trying to think what to do next. Curtains and locks won't be much use, she knows. Simon will just break a window. If only she had the car. Without it, she's trapped – an insect, quivering and exposed in a spider's web.

She can call the police; call Emily. Ask if she can come

and get her. But she might not make it in time . . . it's
Sunday, meaning Emily's at home, at her farm an hour's
drive away . . .

The attic. She'll need to hide. She presses a hand to her
forehead as she tries to work out what to take with her. She
grabs a bottle of water and some fruit and shoves them into
her handbag. Her phone, too, so she can call the police.
Candles and matches, so she doesn't run the phone battery
down using it as a light.

She unlocks the back door again to get the ladder, from
where it leans against the back of the house, covered in snow.
She tries to lift it, sweat breaking out at her temples as she
staggers under its weight.

She heaves the ladder onto its side, dragging it into the
house. It is heavy and cobwebbed; a spider trembles on one
rusted rung. Grunting, she positions it under the trapdoor
and climbs up as quickly as she can, her palms slipping on
the rungs.

Once she's at the top, she stares into the dark abyss of the
attic. The trapdoor is so small – she hasn't been up here for
months. Will she even fit, with her pregnant belly?

Doubt twinges in her gut. She has to try. There's nowhere
else she can hide.

At first, she tries to climb into the attic the same way she
did before, but her arms aren't strong enough to lift her
swollen body through the gap. She shifts position, tries
climbing in backwards. The ladder rattles beneath her, and
for a moment she fears it will clatter to the floor. She heaves
herself in, gasping at a sharp pain in the palm of her hand.

She's cut herself. But she's done it, she's inside the attic.

Kate's heart begins to slow again. But then: the crunch of
car tyres on gravel outside. She freezes, heart galloping, hands
growing slippery with blood and sweat. There's a knock on
the door.

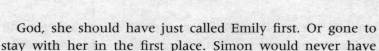

God, she should have just called Emily first. Or gone to stay with her in the first place. Simon would never have found her there.

'Kate?' At the sound of his voice, her heart drops into her stomach. 'I know you're in there. I just want to talk. Please, let me in.' The doorknob rattles, and she hears the creak of old wood as Simon throws his weight against the front door.

The door. She forgot to lock the back door after getting the ladder.

She has to stay hidden. But – fuck, the ladder. He'll see it as soon as he gets in, smack bang in the hallway, like an arrow pointing up to her hiding spot. Why didn't she think of this? Idiot. The panic fizzes in her chest, threatening to overwhelm her. She closes her eyes and forces herself to breathe in and out, slowly . . .

Think. Think. She opens her eyes. He's knocking again, harder this time, punctuated by the thud of his bodyweight against the door. She'll have to pull the ladder up inside the attic. It's the only option. She switches on the torch of her phone. The old bureau is behind her. She hooks one leg around it to anchor herself, praying that Simon won't hear, then shifts onto her side, before lowering her upper body through the trapdoor.

The blood rushes to her head, pounding like the sea. She grabs the ladder and pulls, wincing at the pain in her hand. *Come on, Kate. Come on.* Half the ladder is inside the attic now. Thank God there's so much room in here. She scoots as far back into the attic as she can, tugging hard on the ladder. She can hear Simon pacing outside, occasionally pausing. She imagines him peering through the windows, looking for her.

Kate wonders how many seconds she has until he makes his way to the back of the house and tries the door. Five;

ten if she's lucky. Her arms burn, and there's a scraping sound as she finally pulls the rest of the ladder inside. She yanks the trapdoor shut just in time to hear the back door swing open.

43

VIOLET

Violet was in the beech tree, looking down at the valley. Far below, the beck glinted like a golden thread. She could see the wood, a bruise on the land. Then air rushed at her. She was flying – away, far away.

The dream faded, and Violet swam up to consciousness. Outside, the wind had died down to a low whistle. The blankets were sodden with blood.

I began to dream of her, grown into a dark-haired beauty, but alone and bleeding in our cottage.

This was the fate her mother had foreseen. The fate her mother had done everything – had laid down her life – to alter. All in vain.

The candle was still burning, the flame quivering blue. Violet was cold, so very cold.

She lifted the candle and pushed back the covers.

It had worked.

There was nothing of Frederick inside her anymore. She was free.

It took her a long time to stand up. Her legs felt weak, and the room kept slipping in and out of focus. She was so tired. Perhaps she should lie back down and sleep, she thought. Close her eyes and return to the beech tree, feel the sun and wind on her face. But the *thing*, the thing that had come from Frederick – she had to get rid of it.

She felt her way into the other room, gripping the cool stone of the wall. She needed water, food. Her fingers shook as she cupped water from the bucket and drank. It took an age to open one of the tins of Spam. Her hand slipped and the metal sliced into her palm, the blood welling up in bright drops. Her head buzzed and she sat down at the table heavily. The blood on her nightdress was beginning to crust and darken into brown peaks and swirls, like a map.

The Spam gleamed pale and wet in the tin. It made her think of the spore. She pushed it away. The wind had picked up again and she sat for a while, listening. The wind had a peculiar high pitch to it, almost like a human voice. *Violet*, it seemed to say. *Violet*.

44

KATE

Kate puts her hand to her mouth, tasting blood.

Below her, the floorboards creak as Simon stalks through the cottage.

'Kate?' he calls. 'I know you're in here. Come on, Kate, you can't hide from me.'

She can hear him opening cupboards then slamming them shut again. There is the crash of porcelain on wood from the kitchen. He swears loudly.

She listens to the click of the back door opening. He's looking for her in the garden again. Kate takes the opportunity to light some candles, fingers trembling. The shapes of the attic emerge under the orange glow of the guttering flames. The bureau. The shelves, with their glass jars of insects. Being surrounded by Aunt Violet's things makes her feel a little bit stronger.

She needs the police. She pulls her phone from her pocket and dials 999, listening for the sound of him coming back into the house. The reception in the attic is patchy and the connection drops out after the first ring.

Swearing under her breath, she tries again.

'Emergency, which service do you require?'

She opens her mouth to speak. The back door clicks again.

'Hello? Which service do you require?'

The footsteps are in the hallway now. They stop. She hangs up the phone. There is no sound other than the beat of her heart in her ears. Kate thinks he must be directly beneath her. She is gulping at the air now, her breathing fast and ragged. What if he can hear it?

He must be looking at the trapdoor. Wondering what it leads to. Wondering if it leads to her. Tears sting her eyes as she remembers all the times he's hurt her. She touches the scar on her arm. All those years she's lost. Six years of cowering from him, of letting him tell her she is stupid, incompetent. Worthless. The fear is replaced by a hot bolt of fury.

He's not going to hurt her again. He's not. She won't let him.

And she won't let him anywhere *near* her child.

The footsteps start again. She hears him walk into the sitting room. There's a faint creak as he settles onto the sofa. She can picture him, staring at the window, waiting for her to come home.

Kate shifts position, slowly and carefully. She looks at her phone: the reception bar flickers. She needs to get help – she should have dialled 999 as soon as she saw those messages, but her mind was too blurred by panic, by the need to hide. And now it's too late for her to call. He'll hear her, and discover her hiding spot.

She wipes her bloodied hand on her trousers, then types out a quick text to Emily.

Please can you call police. Abusive ex-boyfriend at cottage. Hiding in attic.

Kate holds her breath.

Message failed to send.

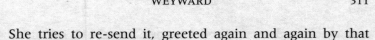

She tries to re-send it, greeted again and again by that cold, impersonal sentence.

She's on her own.

There must be something in the attic she can use to defend herself. Something she can use as a weapon. If only she'd thought to grab the fire poker from the sitting room.

She lifts one of the candles and looks around, searching for a crowbar, a hockey stick . . . anything.

The candlelight passes over the bureau, catching on its golden handles.

She sees something that she didn't notice before.

She crawls to the bureau, as slowly and quietly as she can, sucking in her breath.

There is a *W* carved onto the handle of the locked drawer.

She pulls the necklace out from under her shirt, slips it off. The engravings match.

Kate runs her fingers over the pendant. There is a tiny bump at the bottom of the pendant, barely visible. She presses it, holding her breath. Nothing happens.

She presses it again.

This time, the pendant springs open with a snap. Not a pendant after all. A locket. Inside is a rolled piece of paper. She lifts it out carefully, revealing the small golden key.

The paper looks white and fresh, as if it has been placed there recently. She unrolls it, heart thumping in her chest.

The handwriting has changed: become more refined, elegant, but still she recognises the spidery loops from the note she found in the Brothers Grimm book.

Aunt Violet.

I hope she can help you as she helped me. That is all it says. No reference to who the mysterious 'she' might be. But as she carefully turns the key in the lock, Kate thinks that she knows already.

She eases the drawer out, little by little, terrified that it will creak and alert Simon to her presence. She doesn't breathe until the drawer is open enough for her to see inside.

A book.

She lifts it out of the drawer, inhaling the scent of age and must. As she holds the book in her hands, she hears the first drops of rain fall on the roof.

The leather cover is worn and soft. It looks old. Centuries old.

She opens it. The paper – it isn't paper, she sees now, but parchment – is delicate. Diaphanous, like an insect's wings.

The writing is faded and cramped, so that at first it is illegible. She holds the candle closer, watches the words form. Her heart beats faster as she reads the first line.

'Ten days they'd held me there . . .'

45

ALTHA

I have not written this last day. Yesterday, I came to my parchment and ink, but the words could not come.

Last night, I dreamed of my mother, her words as she lay on her deathbed. Then, I dreamed that I was back in the dungeon at Lancaster, the shadow of death hanging over me. When I woke safe in my bed to the morning birdsong, I nearly cried with relief. Then I wrapped myself in my shawl and sat down to write.

To tell the story, as it really happened, I must put things down on this page that my mother would not have wanted me to. Things that she told me were not to be spoken of, with anyone, or they would risk our exposure. I must speak of the promise I made, and how I broke it.

I have decided that I will lock these papers away and see to it that they are not read until I have left this earth and joined my mother in the next life. Perhaps I will leave them to my daughter. I like the thought of that: a long line of Weyward women, stretching after me. For the first child born to a Weyward is always female, my mother told me. That is why she only had me, just as her mother only had her. There are enough men in the world already, she used to say.

I was fourteen, still weak from my first blood, when she told me what it really meant to be a Weyward. It was autumn, a twelvemonth since the couple had come in the middle of the night, since my mother had cast out her crow. Even longer since that last, precious summer with Grace.

My mother and I had been walking in the woods at dusk, gathering mushrooms, when we came across a rabbit in a trap. Its poor body was torn and bloodied, but it was still alive, the eyes flickering with pain. I knelt down, muddying the dress that my mother had laundered only the previous day, and brushed my little fingers against its flank. Its fur felt wet, the heartbeat faint and slow under its skin. I could feel that it feared death, but also welcomed it. The end to suffering. The natural way of things.

My mother looked about her, scanning the dark shapes of the trees as if to be sure we were alone. Then, she crouched next to me and put her hand over mine.

'Be at peace,' she said. I felt the heartbeat fade beneath our fingers, watched the light flicker from the eyes. The rabbit was gone, freed from this world. It had nothing to fear of traps and hunters now.

We walked home in silence. Already then, she was weakening: her back, which had always been straight, was curving inwards, her long plait of hair was dry as grass. I took her arm and rested it on my shoulders, so that I might support her weight.

When we were home, and night was falling over our garden outside, she sat me at the table while the stew warmed on the fire. I have set down the words she then spoke to me as best as I can recall them, though the memory grows dimmer with each passing year.

She said that there was something I needed to learn, now

that I had passed into womanhood. But I must not speak of it to anyone.

I had nodded, hungry at the thought of sharing a secret with my mother. At the thought of understanding at last the pull I felt inside me, the golden thread that seemed to connect me to the spiders that climbed the walls of our cottage, the moths and damselflies that fluttered in the garden. To the crows that my mother had raised for as long as I could remember, the gleam of their eyes in the dark chasing away my childhood nightmares.

I had nature in my heart, she said. Like she did, and her mother before her. There was something about us – the Weyward women – that bonded us more tightly with the natural world. We can feel it, she said, the same way we feel rage, sorrow or joy. The animals, the birds, the plants – they let us in, recognising us as one of their own. That is why roots and leaves yield so easily under our fingers, to form tonics that bring comfort and healing. That is why animals welcome our embrace. Why the crows – the ones who carry the sign – watch over us and do our bidding, why their touch brings our abilities into sharpest relief. Our ancestors – the women who walked these paths before us, before there were words for who they were – did not lie in the barren soil of the churchyard, encased in rotting wood. Instead, the Weyward bones rested in the woods, in the fells, where our flesh fed plants and flowers, where trees wrapped their roots around our skeletons. We did not need stonemasons to carve our names into rock as proof we had existed.

All we needed was to be returned to the wild.

This wildness inside gives us our name. It was men who marked us so, in the time when language was but a shoot curling from the earth. Weyward, they called us, when we would not submit, would not bend to their will. But we learned to wear the name with pride.

For it has always been a gift, she said. Until now.

She told me of other women, across the land – like those the couple from Clitheroe had spoken of, the Devices and the Whittles – who had died for having such gifts. Or for simply being suspected of having them. The Weyward women had lived safely in Crows Beck these last hundred years, and in that time had healed its people. We had brought them into the world and held their hands as they left it. We could use our ability to heal without attracting too much suspicion. The people were grateful for this gift.

But our other gift – the bond we have with all creatures – is far more dangerous, she told me. Women had perished – in flames, or at the rope – for keeping close company with animals, whom jealous men labelled 'familiars'. This was why she had to banish her crow, the bird that had shared our home for so many years. Her voice cracked as she spoke of it.

And so she made me promise: I was not to use this gift, this wildness inside. I could use my healing skills to put food in my belly, but I must stay away from living creatures, from moths and spiders and crows. Doing otherwise would risk my life.

Perhaps one day, she said, there would be a safer time. When women could walk the earth, shining bright with power, and yet live. But until then I should keep my gift hidden, move through only the darkest corners of the world, like a beetle through soil.

And if I did this, I may survive. Long enough to carry on the line, to take a man's seed from him and no more. Not his name, nor his love, which could put me at risk of discovery.

I had not known, then, what she meant by seed: I had thought a seed was something to be put in the ground, rather than inside a woman. I imagined the next Weyward girl, who would one day grow inside me, blooming into life.

When my mother lay dying three years later, on that awful night when our few candles were no match for the darkness that stole into the room, she reminded me of my promise with her last breath.

I had heeded her words for so long. But after speaking to Grace that day after the market, I felt the first desire to disobey them. The first desire to break my promise.

46

VIOLET

'Violet!' said the voice again. It really did sound like a human voice. Violet wondered if she were hallucinating: surely it was dangerous to lose so much blood. There was a tapping sound. She looked up. She saw – or at least, she thought she saw – a face at the window. Pale and moonlike, with a shock of ginger hair.

She opened the back door, and Graham was silhouetted against the garden. Behind him the helleborine rippled in the wind, a dark red sea.

'Christ,' Graham was saying. He was looking down at her nightgown, at the black stain that bloomed between her legs. Violet wanted to scuttle away from him and hide, as if she were an animal in its death throes. Graham kept talking but she had a hard time understanding the words. She could see his mouth moving and knew that sounds were coming out of it, but they seemed to float away before she could catch them, like the downy husk of a dandelion.

Graham was inside the cottage.

'For the love of God, Violet,' he said. 'Sit down.'

He picked up a candle from the table and walked towards the bedroom, his face grim in the flickering light.

'Don't,' she said weakly, but it was too late.

'Jesus Christ,' she heard him say again.

There was a rustling sound, and Graham reappeared, holding the bundle of bloodied sheets away from him. His white face looked guilty, as though he were carrying something dead. He *was* carrying something dead, Violet remembered.

'I don't want to look at it,' she said.

'We'll have to bury it,' said Graham. He stood for a moment, watching her. 'I found your note,' he said. 'I was in your room, looking for my biology book. It was poking out of that book of fairy tales you used to love.'

'The Brothers Grimm,' she said softly.

Graham nodded. 'Then Father told me that you and Frederick were engaged. After reading about . . . after I read the note, I knew that you didn't want to marry him. I was going to visit you in Windermere – in the sanatorium – to check if you were all right. But then I heard Father on the telephone in his study last night . . . he was talking to Doctor Radcliffe about you. Then . . . he gave him this address, so this afternoon I told Father I was going for a walk . . . and I came here instead.'

He looked around as he spoke, taking in the dim, low-ceilinged room. 'God knows what this place is,' he said.

Violet said nothing, but there was a twist of dread in her stomach. Father speaking to Doctor Radcliffe . . . giving him this address . . . she knew that wasn't good, but she couldn't think why it was so bad, exactly. Her brain felt thick, slug-like, the same way it had felt that afternoon in the woods with Frederick, after all that brandy. Before he—

'What happened to the baby, Violet?' Graham's voice was

low. 'Did you take something? Something to make the baby go away?'

'*Bring on the menses,*' Violet said.

'Violet, are you listening to me? You have to tell me if you took something. Doctor Radcliffe is coming here, today. He's meeting Father here. They could arrive any minute. If you did take something . . . you need to tell me. We've got to get rid of the evidence. It's a crime, Violet. They could put you away for life.'

The dread in her stomach again.

'Tansy petals,' she said. 'Steep in water for five days before administration . . .'

'Right,' said Graham. He put the bundled bedsheets down on the floor and went back into the bedroom. The door burst open and the wind roared through it, unfurling the bundle to reveal a gleam of pale flesh. Violet was gripped by the awful fear that the spore would reanimate and slither up inside her again. She couldn't bear it. She turned around to face the wall.

Graham returned, holding the tin that she'd prepared the tansy mixture in. She could smell it, dank and cloying. He took the tin and the bundle outside. Violet heard the first hiss of rain on the roof, and watched it trickle down from the hole in the ceiling. She wanted to get up, to stand in the garden and let the rain wash her clean, but she was too tired to move. Her head lolled forward onto her chest. Darkness lapped at her.

When Graham came back inside, his hair was wet and mud was splattered across his clothes.

'I've buried it,' he said. 'The child.' He brushed the dirt from his hands as he spoke, not looking at her.

'Thank you,' she said, though she wished he wouldn't refer to it as a 'child'. He nodded.

He brought her a pan of water and a rag, along with a fresh nightgown from the suitcase in the bedroom.

'I'll let you clean yourself up,' he said, walking out of the room. 'Call me when you're decent.'

I've buried the child.

Violet wondered if she would ever be decent again.

She wobbled to her feet and took off her soiled night-gown. The blood had glued it to her legs so that removing it felt like peeling away a layer of skin. Her vision slid and she gripped the back of the chair. She dabbed at her thighs with the rag and watched the blood run in watery rivulets down her legs, staining the floor. Outside, under the sound of the wind shearing through the trees, she thought she heard a crow squawk. Then, the sputter of an engine. A car.

'Violet,' Graham called. 'Quick. Get dressed. They're here.'

47

KATE

Kate has been in the attic for hours.

There have been moments of silence, when she has allowed herself to wonder if Simon has given up waiting for her and left. But then: the menacingly slow progress of his footsteps down the corridor. Of course he hasn't given up. He is never going to let her go. Never going to let *them* go.

These are the worst moments, when the fear recedes only to close its cold fist around her heart again. But as Kate turns the fragile pages of Altha's manuscript, as she reads a story that is centuries old but echoes her own life so closely, rage unfurls inside her.

The rain still falls, drumming loud on the roof, like a battle call. She has finished reading the manuscript. She knows the truth. About Altha Weyward. About Aunt Violet, too. About herself; and her child.

The truth. She can feel it spreading molten through her body, hardening her bones.

This wildness inside gives us our name.

All those years of feeling different. Separate. Now she knows why.

The rain grows heavier. There is something not quite right about the sound – rather than the rhythmic patter of water, it is erratic and heavy. *Plop. Plop. Plop.* As though hundreds of solid objects are landing on the roof. There's a scraping noise, too. At first, Kate thinks it is the wind, a tree branch scraping the tiles. She focuses. Not scraping, *scrabbling.* Claws. The flapping of wings. Kate can feel them there, a frenzied, swelling mass. Birds.

Of course. The crow has been there, ever since she arrived. In the fireplace. Watching from the hedgerow, the sycamore tree. The same crow led her through the woods after the accident. The crow that carries the sign.

She is no longer afraid. Not of the birds and not of Simon.

She thinks of all the times he has hurt her, has used her unwilling flesh as if it were there for his pleasure. Has made her feel small and worthless.

But she isn't.

Her blood glows warm; her nerve endings tingle. In the dark, her vision becomes clearer, sharper; sounds feel as if they are coming from inside her very skull.

The birds on the roof begin to chirrup and squawk. Kate imagines their bodies covering the house in one undulating, feathered mass.

She thanks them, welcomes them. Puts her hand on her stomach.

I am ready. We *are ready.*

Simon cries out downstairs and she knows that he has seen them too.

It is now, she knows. Now or never.

She opens the trapdoor.

48

ALTHA

I was busy, those last months of 1618. As the leaves turned red, so too did the sky, for a great comet appeared, chasing the stars like a streak of blood. My mother had often read the stars, and I wondered what she would say if she could see the red sky, if it would have told her what was coming.

Autumn gave way to winter, and the village was struck by fever. It seemed half of the villagers sent for the physician, and the other half – the ones who had not the coin to offer up their flesh to leeches – sent for me. In each fever-bright face – the eyes glassy with pain, the spots of fire in the cheeks – I saw Anna Metcalfe. I saw my mother.

A mistake could cost my life.

And so I stayed up working half the nights, either cooling a patient's brow at their bedside or toiling in the cottage, preparing tonics and tinctures for the next day. My fingers smelled always of feverfew, as though it had seeped into the fabric of my skin from so much chopping and crushing. Each night I was so exhausted that I fell asleep as soon as I laid my head on the pallet. I did not even dream.

Neither Grace nor her husband fell ill, as far as I knew,

but if they had, they would have sent for Doctor Smythson. They both attended church each Sunday, and though the pews were near empty that winter, with so many ill, I kept my distance and sat as far behind as I could. During the sermon I let Reverend Goode's voice fade to a low hum, the words running into each other, and watched Grace's red curls quiver as she bent her head in prayer.

I wondered, then, if Grace still kept the old ways, like her father. If she prayed to Mary for deliverance. Though I doubted the Virgin – who had been spared the feel of a man's flesh on hers – could deliver Grace from her husband.

She looked the same as always. The face white and distant, the head bowed. No marks on her that I could see, but I remembered what she had said. That he was taking care not to harm her face. I could not bear to think what lay under her shift. I remembered my vision, at the bonfire on May Day Eve. The blood.

The fever that gripped the village burned itself out by Advent, and though snow lay thick as cream on the ground, the church was full on Christmas morning. The villagers sat in the pews, with the ice on their hats and cloaks making them look like floured loaves. In my usual spot at the back, I craned my neck to see Grace. But she was not sitting next to John. I scanned the pews. She was not there at all.

All through Reverend Goode's sermon, I wondered why she had not come. Had she caught the fever? After the service, John stood with the Dinsdales, and threw his head back and laughed at something Stephen Dinsdale said. He did not have the worried look of a man whose wife was ill, I thought. But perhaps that was to be expected. After all, from what I knew, Grace's value to him was in her ability to bear him a child, and in this she had failed thus far. Perhaps he would be quite happy for her to wither away and die, giving him an excuse to marry a woman who could give him a son to carry on the Milburn name.

I stood as close as I dared in the churchyard, in case John said something that hinted at Grace's condition. But I heard nothing: the villagers were merry with the promise of the festivities to come, and the churchyard was loud with chatter. After a time, people trailed off, bundling themselves more tightly in their cloaks and hats, wishing each other a happy Christmas. I felt sad, thinking of the feasts and laughter they would enjoy with their families, while I sat alone in my cottage. I watched as John turned to go and heard Mary Dinsdale ask that he pass on her best wishes to his wife.

'Thank you,' he said. 'No doubt she'll be on her feet by the morrow. Well, she'll have to be, seeing as the cows need milking.' He laughed, a harsh, cranking sound like the jaws of a plough, and bid them merry Christmas.

I walked home through white fields, under trees as bare as bones. I thought on John's words, and the winter wind numbed my face and chilled my heart.

The next morning, I woke to such silence that I wondered if I had lost my hearing. Looking out of the window, I saw that snow had fallen so heavily in the night that the whole world was muffled by it. No birds had sung that morning and the sun, though weak and grey, was already high in the sky.

I hoped that the villagers would remain tucked up and warm inside their houses, perhaps still sleeping off the previous night's merriment. I hoped that no one would see me as I set off into that still, white world.

As I walked through the snow, my feet cold in my boots and my hands raw in my gloves, my stomach twisted with fear. Whatever he had done to her, I thought, it must have been very grave if she was not fit to be seen in public on Christmas Day.

When I first came upon the Milburn farm, I thought that I was lost, or that it had vanished. Then, I heard the cows mooing in the byre, complaining of the cold, and I realised that a great lip of snow covered the roof of the farmhouse. I tried to climb the oak tree to get a better view, but my hands and feet could not find purchase, the trunk was so slick with ice. Then, I saw the dark figure of a man make his way from the white mound of the farmhouse. Even from a distance, there was no mistaking his long, flowing robes and the leather case he carried in his hand.

Doctor Smythson.

I spent the last days of December rising before the sun, when the valley was thick with darkness and silence. As the sky greyed around the edges, I made my way to Milburn Farm, where I climbed the oak and sat high in its branches. I might have been another of the crows, who welcomed me silently with their glittering eyes. One of them settled next to me, its feathers brushing my cloak. Together we watched the farmhouse.

I watched candlelight flicker orange through the shutters. I watched the back door open as John left the farmhouse and walked to the byre to milk the cows. I heard their low protest as his rough fingers pinched at their udders, and the fear grew in me. Milking had been Grace's job. John took the cows to the fields, which were dark and swollen with melted snow. Some days, the Kirkby lad came. I did not see Grace. The winter sky grew light, and then pink became icy blue. Still she did not leave the farmhouse: not to wash the clothes, not to fetch water from the well or make her way to the market.

Five days passed thus. Then, as the sixth day dawned, I

watched as the back door opened and Grace emerged in John's stead. I saw her make her way to the byre for the milking, moving slowly, her body curved over itself with pain. I saw her stagger, and then sink to her knees and retch. I pressed my hand to my mouth as I saw the door open again. John came out, walking quickly towards his wife, who knelt in the frozen mud.

In spite of all I knew of the man, some innocent part of me expected him to offer his wife some kindness, to take her hand in his and tenderly raise her to her feet. Instead, I saw him tear off her cap and twist his fingers into her hair. In the dull light, her curls were the colour of old blood. John pulled her to her feet by her hair, and her sharp cry of pain sent a shiver through the morning. Around me, the crows shifted uneasily on the branches.

Tears froze on my cheeks as I watched him haul her into the byre, as if she were no better than a piece of waste. It had been one thing to hear her speak of his rough treatment of her. It was quite another to see it. Fury flowed through my blood like fire.

The next morning, New Year's Eve, Adam Bainbridge delivered me a gift for the new year. He had wrapped a small piece of gammon in a cloth.

'There's something else,' he said, after I thanked him. 'I stopped by the Milburn farm first this morning, to deliver my gift. John Milburn has long kept us in veal, you see, and my father bid me to take a token of our gratitude this new year.' He paused, as though the act had made him uncomfortable. He knows, I thought. He knows how John treats her.

'John was in the field, so it was Mistress Milburn who answered the door. Grace. She asked if I planned to give any other gifts that day. I said I was taking a gift to you, next,

for the care you showed my grandfather when he passed this
year. She bid me give you this.'

He pressed a bundle of cloth into my hands. I didn't dare
open it in front of Adam, and pretended the gift was a surprise
– as far as the villagers knew, Grace had not uttered a kind
word to me in public for seven years.

He looked at me for a moment, as if he had wanted to ask
me a question but thought better of it.

'Well, happy New Year, Altha,' he said. 'Blessings be upon
you.'

He touched his cap and left.

I watched him disappear down the path, then went inside.
Once I had shut the door behind me, I unwrapped the bundle.
It was a fragrant, golden orb – an orange, I realised. I had
only ever heard them spoken of, the fruit is so rare and
precious. An expensive gift. The smell of it was sharp in my
nostrils, mingled with another, woodier scent. Clove. I pulled
at the clove; it was rough against my fingers. I saw that it
had not been secured with a simple piece of twig, but a figure
fashioned from twigs and twine. It was crude and looked
hastily made, but I could see what she had intended it to be.
The figure of a woman, with a curl of twine around her
waist. A baby.

Grace was pregnant again. And she was asking for my
help.

That night, I dreamed again of my mother, as she had been
on her deathbed. Her features were waxen, and the pale lips
barely moved as she spoke.

'Altha,' she said. 'Remember your promise . . . you cannot
break your promise . . . it is not safe. You must keep your
gift hidden . . .'

I woke with a jolt and the dream fell away. I pushed my
mother's face from my mind. A sound had woken me, I

realised. I heard it again. A cry that throbbed in the quiet.
A crow. I looked outside. Night was only just beginning to
lift from the valley. It was time.

I dressed quickly. In the looking glass, my hair shone bright
as feathers. With my black cloak fastened around my shoulders, I looked as dark and powerful as if I were a crow myself.

49

VIOLET

The key turned in the lock. Violet pulled her nightdress on hurriedly, dizzy from the effort. She sat back down. The darkness was there still, at the edges of her vision. Perhaps it would be easiest to give into it, she thought. To let it take her away, before Father and Doctor Radcliffe did.

The creak of the front door, and then the wind roared into the cottage. She heard Father's voice, raised above the storm.

'Graham? What are *you* doing here?'

'Father – I can explain—'

'Where is the girl?' She recognised Doctor Radcliffe's voice, cold and clinical.

They were in the room, the rain glittering on their overcoats. Violet looked down at the floor, stained pink with her blood.

'She's lost the baby,' Graham said quietly.

Father didn't ask him how he knew about the baby. Violet felt his eyes on her and looked up. There was no concern, no tenderness in his gaze. His mouth curled in disgust.

'I'll need to examine her,' said Doctor Radcliffe. 'Take her to the bedroom and have her lie down.'

Graham slung Violet's arm around his shoulders and lifted her to her feet. Neither Father nor Doctor Radcliffe made any effort to help. Violet closed her eyes, and imagined she was in the beech tree, feeling the summer breeze on her face. In the bedroom, the small window flared bright and the air crackled with electricity. A thunderclap. God moving his furniture, Nanny Metcalfe used to say. Nanny Metcalfe. She would be ashamed, Violet knew. God, too, perhaps. She had committed a sin.

After she lay down, Doctor Radcliffe asked Graham and Father to turn around, before lifting the skirt of her night-dress. His nostrils flared at the smell of blood. It hung in the air, sweet and metallic. Looking down, Violet saw that her thighs were ringed red, like the inside of a tree trunk. She suddenly felt very old, as if she'd lived a hundred years instead of sixteen.

'Can you explain what happened?' Doctor Radcliffe asked. It was the first time either he or Father had addressed her directly.

'I felt a cramping, this morning,' she said. 'Like I get with my monthly curse, but stronger . . .'

'I found her as it was starting,' Graham interjected, still staring at the wall. 'She began losing blood not long after I arrived. And then, with the blood . . . it . . .'

'The baby,' said Doctor Radcliffe.

'Yes, the baby . . . the baby came out . . . there was so much blood . . .' Graham retched, and Violet knew that he too was thinking of that mottled twist of flesh. The spore, the rot.

Violet felt tears sting her eyes, blurring her vision so that Doctor Radcliffe's face swam before her.

'Is that what happened?' he asked her. 'You did not do anything to bring about this miscarriage? You didn't take anything?'

'No, I didn't,' Violet said softly, the tears wet on her cheeks. The darkness was there again, and she rolled towards it. Fragments of conversation drifted towards her as she fell, the air rushing at her.

'Lost a lot of blood,' Doctor Radcliffe was saying. 'A week of bed rest, at least. Plenty of fluids, too.'

'Can you be sure, Doctor?' Father asked. 'Can you be sure she didn't bring it on herself?'

'No,' Doctor Radcliffe said. 'We have only her word for that. And the boy's.'

She was flying now, the wind singing on her skin. She slept.

Graham was there when she woke up, sitting on the bed opposite, watching her. Everything was quiet and still. The candle had burned down to the wick. She could hear a fly outside, buzzing past the window.

'They've gone,' Graham said, seeing that she was awake. 'They left last night. You've been asleep since. Father said I could stay with you. He had to keep up appearances in front of Doctor Radcliffe, I suppose.'

Violet sat up. Her body felt hollow and light.

'They'll be back in a week, to see how you've recovered. Father's writing to Frederick. I expect the wedding's off.'

The feeling of lightness again. She heard a redstart sing and smiled. It was a beautiful sound.

'I don't think Father believed us,' said Graham.

Violet nodded. 'It doesn't matter,' she said. 'As long as Doctor Radcliffe did.'

'I suppose you're right,' he said. 'Father would hardly go to the police of his own accord. The scandal.'

They were quiet for a moment. Violet watched a thin ray of sun dance on the wall.

'Do you know what this place is, Violet?'

'Yes. It was our mother's house,' she said. 'Her name was Elizabeth. Elizabeth Weyward.'

Graham was quiet. It took Violet a moment to realise that he was crying, his hunched shoulders shaking, his face hidden in his hands. She hadn't seen him cry since before he left for boarding school, years ago.

'Graham?'

'I thought . . .' He took a deep, steadying breath. 'I thought you were going to die, too. Just like she did. Our – our mother.'

They had never spoken of her before.

'That's why you hate me, isn't it?' Graham lifted his face from his hands as he spoke. His pale skin was mottled with tears. 'Because I – because I killed her.'

'What do you mean?'

'She died having me.'

'She didn't.'

'Don't, Violet. I know. Father told me years ago.'

'He lied,' she said. And then she told him the truth – about what Father and Doctor Radcliffe had done to their mother. About the grandmother who had tried to reach them, the grandmother they had never known.

'So you mustn't think it's your fault anymore,' she said, afterwards. 'And you mustn't think I hate you. You're my brother. We're family.'

She touched her necklace as she spoke. The locket was warm against her fingers. She felt stronger, knowing that the key was safe inside. She considered telling him the rest: about Altha's manuscript, locked away in the drawer. After all, the Weywards were Graham's family too.

But Graham was – or would soon become – a man. A good man, but a man all the same. It wouldn't be right, she knew.

'How did you know to use the – what was it?'

'Tansy.' She paused. 'Just something I read somewhere,' she said.

Graham stayed with her for a week. He helped her mend the latch on the window of her bedroom, so that she could breathe clean air every night. Together they scrubbed her blood from the floor of the kitchen, until the wood glowed rich and brown. The cottage looked good as new.

There was a carrot plant in the garden, tangled up with the helleborine – though the carrots were misshapen and pale, unlike any she had seen before. There was rhubarb, too: she pulled the stems delicately from the soil, careful not to disturb the worms that lived nearby.

They ate the carrots with the eggs Father had brought. They no longer turned her stomach, now that the spore was gone.

Graham found a rusted axe in the attic. He chopped the branches that had been felled by the storm into firewood.

'To keep you warm in winter,' he said. They both knew she would never return to Orton Hall. Not after everything that had happened.

Graham used some of the wood to fashion a small cross and drove it into the soil where he had buried the spore, down by the beck. Violet thought about asking him to take it down, but she didn't.

Father came back, with Doctor Radcliffe.

'She seems to have recovered well,' Doctor Radcliffe said to Father. 'You can have her brought home, if you wish.'

Doctor Radcliffe left, and it was just Father, Graham and Violet in the cottage. They were silent as they listened to the sputter of Doctor Radcliffe's car engine.

'I am sure you understand', Father began, looking past Violet at the wall, 'that I cannot allow you back into my house after what you have done. I have arranged for you to be taken to a finishing school in Scotland. You will stay there for two years, and after that I will decide what is to be done with you.'

Violet heard Graham clear his throat.

'No,' she said, before her brother could open his mouth to speak. 'That won't be acceptable, I'm afraid, Father.'

His jowls slackened with shock. He looked as if she had slapped him.

'I beg your pardon?'

'I won't be going to Scotland. In fact, I won't be going anywhere. I'm staying right here.' As she spoke, Violet became aware of a strange simmering sensation, as though electricity was humming beneath her skin. Images flashed in her mind – a crow cutting through the air, wings glittering with snow; the spokes of a wheel spinning. Briefly, she closed her eyes, focusing on the feeling until she could almost see it, glinting gold inside her.

'That is not for you to decide,' said Father. The window was open, and a bee flitted about the room, wings a silver blur. It flew near Father's cheek and he jerked away from it.

'It's been decided.' She stood up straight, her dark eyes boring into Father's watery ones. He blinked. The bee hovered about his face, dancing away from his hands, and she saw sweat break out on his nose. Soon it was joined by another, and then another and another, until it seemed like Father – shouting and swearing – had been engulfed in a cloud of tawny, glistening bodies.

'I think it would be best if you left now, Father,' said Violet softly. 'After all, as you said, I'm my mother's daughter.'

'Graham?' Violet smiled at the note of panic in Father's voice.

'I'm staying, too,' said Graham, folding his arms across his chest.

Violet heard Father's shallow, rasping breaths. Several of the bees were dangerously close to his mouth now.

'The front door key, please, Father,' she said. It landed on the wooden floor with a dull clank.

'Thank you,' she called, as Father, pursued by the bees, slammed the door behind him.

Violet held out her hand, and a lone bee came to rest on her palm.

'You're not afraid, are you?' she asked, turning to Graham. 'They won't hurt you this time.'

'I know,' said Graham.

He put his arm around her. They stood still for a moment, listening to the car rumble away.

50

KATE

In the corridor, Kate can hear what sounds like hailstones hitting the windows. But they are not hailstones, she sees, looking through the doorway at her bedroom window; they are *beaks*.

Outside, illuminated by the moon, are hundreds of birds. She sees the gunmetal sheen of a crow's feathers, the yellow glare of an owl. A robin's red breast. Their bodies writhe and flutter against the glass. Snow falls around them, drifting to the ground. Their cries echo in her ears. They are here, she knows, because of her.

The door to the sitting room is slightly ajar. Simon is yelling frantically. He can't hear her as she approaches, cloaked by the sound of the birds.

She pushes open the door. Simon is standing in the centre of the room, facing the window. The poker quivers in one white-knuckled hand. She is still for a moment, watching the muscles of his back tense beneath the fine wool of his sweater. The skin on the nape of his neck is goose-pimpled with fear.

Birds clamour at the window. Kate can see cracks begin

to form in the glass, glinting silver like the thread of a spider's web. There's a scratching sound coming from the chimney.

'Simon,' she says. He doesn't hear her.

'Simon,' she says again, louder this time, trying to keep the fear from her voice.

His blond hair flashes as he turns around.

Her heart knocks in her chest. The handsome features are sharp with anger, the lips snarling away from the teeth. The shock on his face at the first sight of her. How different she must look to him, she thinks, with her huge belly and cropped hair, Aunt Violet's beaded cape around her shoulders. Then his eyes narrow, glittering with rage.

'*You*,' he hisses.

Kate takes a gulp of air as he moves towards her. She tries to shift her body away from him, back to the doorway, but he is too quick.

He shoves her into the wall, so hard that plaster dust drifts into the air like the snow outside.

'You thought you could leave?' he shouts, spittle landing on her face. 'You thought you could leave *with my child*?'

The poker clatters to the floor, and then his hand is around her neck, squeezing, crushing, like a vice.

Horror settles into her stomach, cold and hard.

Thoughts spark and die in her brain. The colours in the room look brighter, even as her vision grows hazy at the edges. She sees the flecks of gold in his blue irises. The whites of his eyes, with their red tracing of veins. His breath is hot and sour in her face.

So this is it, she thinks, as her lungs burn from lack of oxygen. The end. Even if he lets her live – for the sake of the child, he might – it will not be a life, but a cell. She thinks, suddenly, of the jail in the village: the cold grey stone, darkness closing over her.

He is saying something now, but she can barely hear him above the tapping on the windows and the scrabbling on the roof.

He says it again, louder and closer, tightening his grip on her throat. Aunt Violet's necklace is digging into her neck.

'You are nothing', he says, the words tolling in her skull, 'without me.'

The panic is rising. Except it isn't panic, Kate knows now. It never was. The feeling of something trying to get out. Rage, hot and bright in her chest. Not panic. Power.

No. She is not nothing.

She is a Weyward. And she carries another Weyward inside her. She gathers herself together, every cell blazing, and thinks: *Now.*

The window breaks, a waterfall of sharp sounds. The room grows dark with feathered bodies, shooting through the broken window, the fireplace.

Beaks, claws and eyes flashing. Feathers brushing her skin. Simon yells, his hand loosening on her throat.

She sucks in the air, falling onto her knees, one hand cradling her stomach. Something touches her foot, and she sees a dark tide of spiders spreading across the floor. Birds continue to stream through the window. Insects, too: the azure flicker of damselflies, moths with orange eyes on their wings. Tiny, gossamer mayflies. Bees in a ferocious golden swarm.

She feels something sharp on her shoulder, its claws digging into her flesh. She looks up at blue-black feathers, streaked with white. A crow. The same crow that has watched over her since she arrived. Tears fill her eyes, and she knows in that moment that she is not alone in the cottage. Altha is there, in the spiders that dance across the floor. Violet is there, in the mayflies that glisten and undulate like some great silver snake. And all the other Weyward women, from the first of the line, are there too.

They have always been with her, and always will be.

Simon is curled on the floor, screaming. She can barely see him for the birds, swarming and pecking, their wings quivering; the insects forming patterns on his skin. His face is covered by the tawny wings of a sparrowhawk; a flock of starlings have landed on his chest, their crowns shimmering purple. A brown fieldfare nips at his ear, a spider circles his throat.

Feathers swirl in the air – small and white, gold and tapered. Opaline black.

She lifts her arm – the pink scar catching the light – and the creatures draw back. Dark drops splatter on the floor.

Simon's hands, criss-crossed with red gashes, are pressed against his eyes. Slowly, he removes them, and she sees the pink flesh, oozing blood, where the left eye should be. He cowers as she stands tall above him, the crow on her shoulder.

'Get out,' she says.

The creatures leave after Simon.

Kate's hair moves in the wind created by their wings. The insects first, then the birds. As if by agreement.

She looks at the floor. It is strewn with glass, feathers and snow, glittering like jewels. It is the most beautiful thing she has ever seen.

Only the crow remains. It loiters on the windowsill, head cocked to one side. Unsure of whether to leave her.

There is the growl of an engine outside; the slamming of car doors.

The doorbell rings, then the door shakes with frantic knocking.

'Police, open up!'

'Kate? Are you in there?' She hears the fear in Emily's voice. Emily. Kate smiles. Her friend.

'We're going to force the door,' says the police officer. 'Stand back!'

The crow turns to her one last time. Kate watches as it takes flight, rising above the moon into the night sky. Free.

51

ALTHA

For a moment, I forgot where I was when I opened my eyes this morning. I had to pinch myself, to make sure that I was safe, that the dungeon and the courtroom really do lie in the past, along with that cold winter morning where ice glittered on the trees.

But the sun shone, bright as gold, through my window. I could smell spring on the air: the garden is crowded with daffodils and bluebells now. Even as I write, lambs are being born wet and bewildered, nuzzling at their mothers to get back to that dark, warm place where nothing can hurt them.

Sometimes, I remember that day so clearly that I think it is happening now, that all my life is happening at once and all I can do to take refuge from it is crawl under the bedclothes and sob. I am like a lamb, wishing for a warm place where nothing can hurt me. Wishing for my mother.

My mother. I hope she would have understood. Perhaps it would have been better to be guilty in their eyes, to have swung from the rope even, so long as I could be innocent in hers.

I do not want to write what happened next, but I must.

I moved quickly through that frozen morning. The sky was already pink through the trees, so I had to hurry. I felt something pulse in me, but I do not think it was fear. I could see my breath before me, could feel frost falling into my hair from the trees above, but I did not feel cold. I thought of what I had seen John do to Grace and the blood grew hot in my veins, warming me.

When I reached the oak tree, I saw that great skirts of ice hung from its branches and its trunk had hardened with frost. It would be slippery, I thought, preparing myself for struggle. But my feet found purchase easily, almost as if the tree were helping me up, and before I knew it, I was perched up high with the crows, their wings frosted with ice crystals. And then I saw it. My mother's crow. It carried the sign – the tracing of white across its feathers, as though it had been stroked by magic fingers. The same marks that my mother said had appeared on the first crow, when it was touched by the first of our line, before the words to describe either existed.

Tears pricked my eyes and I was certain, then, that what I planned to do was right. The crow came to rest on my shoulder, its scaly claws sharp through my cloak.

Together we watched the farm. I felt the coolness of its beak against my ear and I knew that it understood what I was asking of it.

The fields were green and white with snow. A dark spiral of smoke rose from the chimney into the sky. I watched as the door opened and John came out. As he walked to the byre, a small figure moved in his shadow and I realised it was Daniel Kirkby. I had forgotten that he worked at the farm some mornings. I would have a witness, now. But in that moment, knowing not what lay ahead, I did not care. I did not care if the whole world saw me do what I was going to do next.

John opened the byre and the cows came out. They were

already agitated; they did not like the cramped fug of the byre, but nor did they like the feel of the winter air, sharp on their flanks. I watched their tails swing and their shoulders ripple, hide gleaming in the morning sun.

It was time.

The crow took flight, wings slicing through the air. I could feel the frozen wood of the oak tree beneath me, but I could also feel the wind singing through the crow's feathers as it dived down into the field. I saw the eyes of the cows grow white and wide, I saw the fear collecting in froth at their nostrils. Their hooves stamped the frozen ground as the crow flew near, looping around and around with sharp beak and claws, stoking them as one would a fire.

I saw it up close: the new sweat that froze on a flank, the white roll of an eye, John's face as death bore down on him. And I saw it from afar: the cows a golden stampede, the body crumpling beneath them. The fields: green, white and red.

Then it was over. The morning quiet returned, and I could hear Daniel Kirkby panting in shock, and the soft gurgle of John's blood into the snow. The crow had returned to its friends in the branches, barely pausing to look at me. I climbed down the tree quickly, in time to hear the creak of the farm-house door and then Grace screaming.

I ran towards the sound, my boots slipping on the frosted grass, and as I got closer I could smell the body. The sweet meaty stink of blood, of guts and other inside things: things that were not meant to be exposed to the world. Half of the face was gone, disappeared into a red maw. I threw my cloak over it to spare Grace the sight. As I neared the farmhouse, I saw her sink to her knees screaming, again and again. The Kirkby boy stood off to the side, his fists pressed to his eyes as if he wanted to scrub away what they had seen.

I told the Kirkby boy to fetch the doctor and he ran in the

direction of the village. I went to Grace. Her breath was sour and I saw that she had vomited down the front of her dress. I brushed a brown smear of it from her cheek and pulled her to me.

'It's over,' I said, leading her inside. 'He's gone.'

She shook as she sat at the kitchen table, and her skin had a grey tinge to it. I fixed her a tisane, to calm her. The fire had gone out and the water took an age to boil in the pot. Once the bubbles rose to the surface I put my face over the steam, breathing it in as if it could cleanse me of my sins.

I made the drink and sat down with her at the table. She did not touch the cup. Her eyes stared ahead as if she were still in the field, looking at his body. I reached my hand across the table towards her, and left it there. After a time, she put her hand on mine. The sleeve of her dress fell back and I saw the bruises on her wrist, as purple as summer fruit.

We sat like that until Daniel Kirkby returned with Doctor Smythson: her clammy hand on my cool one.

So I have set it down, as I promised to. The truth. I will let whoever reads this when I am gone decide whether I am innocent or guilty. Whether what I did was murder, or justice. Until then, I will lock these words away in the bureau, and keep the key around my neck. To save them falling into the wrong hands.

Yesterday, Adam Bainbridge came to the cottage, bearing a leg of mutton wrapped in muslin. I led him inside, where I asked him to give me something else. Not his name, nor his love. I remembered my mother's lesson, in this respect, at least.

He was gentle, but I was afraid. As my body opened to take his seed, I shut my eyes and thought of Grace. Of the hot hand that had gripped mine as we ran over the fells, that last innocent summer. Of the way her red hair had spread across my pallet, of her milk and tallow scent. Of the relief that shone out of her face when I was acquitted.

When it was over, I lay curled on my side, wondering if it had taken, if a child flowered inside me already. I would name her for my friend, I decided. For my love.

I have not seen Grace since the trial. I do not know how she fares and I do not know when I will see her again. Perhaps, one day, it will be safe for her to visit me. Safe for me to take her in my arms and stroke her pretty hair, breathe in her precious smell.

Until then, all I can do is imagine her. Looking out at the same blue sky I see through my window now. Feeling the breeze on her neck and tasting the sweet air. Free.

Free as the crows that made their home in the sycamore tree, waiting for my return. The marked one eats out of my hand, now, the way she did for my mother, once.

My mother. I think she would understand what I have done. What I had to do. Perhaps she would even be proud. Proud that I am her daughter.

I am proud, too. Much as I shy away from it, the hard truth in my heart is that I am proud of what I have done.

And so I will not flee, I have decided. Not even if the villagers come, seeking justice. They cannot make me leave my home.

They do not frighten me.

After all, I am a Weyward, and wild inside.

52

VIOLET

Graham stayed until September, when he went back to Harrow. Father had written to say that he would pay for the remainder of Graham's schooling, but after that he was on his own. The letter didn't mention Violet. It was as if Father had decided that she had never existed.

'I'm not sure about leaving you here,' Graham said before he set off on the long walk to the bus station. There had been frost that morning, sparkling on the sycamore tree. The first sign of winter's approach. 'Will you be all right, all by yourself?'

'I'll be grand,' said Violet. She planned to spend the day in the garden, sowing seeds she had been given by the village greengrocer. She had thought about asking Graham to cut down the helleborine but in the end she decided to leave it. It was a good source of pollen for the bees, she thought. There seemed to be even more insects in the garden than ever, now: their constant thrum lulled her to sleep each night, an arthropod lullaby.

'See you at Christmas,' Graham waved as he set off down the lane. 'I'll bring you some new books!'

As she shut the front door, she wondered whether anyone had found the biology textbook she had hidden under her bed back at Orton Hall, along with the bloodied clothes from the woods.

She still dreamed about Frederick. The dull weight of him on top of her, squeezing out her breath. All of that blood, seeping out of her.

She would wake up and stare at the ceiling, a line from Altha's manuscript echoing in her head.

The first child born to a Weyward is always female.

She had killed her daughter. The next Weyward girl. Violet knew, then, that she would never have her own baby. She would never teach her daughter about insects, birds and flowers. About what it meant to be a Weyward.

'But you weren't supposed to be born yet,' she would whisper into the darkness, thinking of the tiny curl of bones buried under the sycamore tree. 'You were meant to come later, when I was ready.'

It was all because of Frederick, and what he did to her. What he made her do. That sun-spangled afternoon in the woods, the trees circling above. Blood, staining her thighs pink.

He had taken away her choice. Her future.

For that, she would never forgive him.

The problem was that she wasn't sure she could forgive herself, either.

Another letter arrived in November. Addressed to Violet, this time. According to the back of the envelope, it had been sent from Orton Hall. She didn't recognise the handwriting.

Violet's heart thudded as she unfolded the letter and saw the name at the bottom. It was from Frederick.

He was on bereavement leave, he wrote. Father was dead. A heart attack while hunting. Before his death, he had declared that neither Graham nor Violet were his biological children. Father had managed to produce documents – no doubt falsified – demonstrating that he was in Southern Rhodesia at the time of Graham's conception. Violet, he said, had been conceived before her parents' marriage, and so could not be proved to be his daughter.

Gripping the letter in her hands, she wished that it were indeed true – that none of Father's blood ran through her veins, that her cells weren't ghosts of his own. Tears blurred her vision, and the rest of the letter swam before her eyes.

Father had left everything to Frederick, who was now the Tenth Viscount Kendall. Enclosed with the letter was a deed, transferring Weyward Cottage into Violet's name. At this, her tears gave way to fury. She was tempted, for a moment, to throw the letter in the fire.

Did Frederick really think a piece of paper could make up for what he did to her?

And anyway, Weyward Cottage wasn't his to *give*. It was Violet's, and always had been – before she even knew it existed. Frederick couldn't lay claim to the land any more than Father had.

In the days after the letter, sadness stole like a shadow into the cottage. But Violet wasn't mourning Father – how could she, after what he had done? It was her mother and grandmother that she longed for. She hadn't known either of them, not really, and yet she felt their loss as keenly as a missing limb. For she had managed to confirm her suspicion: Elinor had died. Cancer, the villagers said. Only four years ago. She had lain alone on her deathbed, the grandchildren she'd never met just a few miles away.

Graham visited at Christmas, and they said goodbye to their mother and grandmother together. Back in the summer, Violet had dried a bouquet of lavender, and it was this that they placed on the Ayres family mausoleum, a spot of brightness in the snow. Violet hated to think of her mother encased in that cold stone. Even worse was the thought of her grand-mother, buried in an unmarked pauper's grave.

She preferred to think of Lizzie and Elinor in the garden that they had loved. In the fells, the beck.

She preferred not to think of Father at all.

'Frederick has offered me an allowance until I finish univer-sity,' Graham said later. 'I'm not going to take it, though. My form master thinks I could get a scholarship. Law at Oxford or Cambridge. Durham, maybe. It'd be nice to stay up north. Besides, I don't want his money.'

'It's not really Frederick's money though, is it?' said Violet. 'It's—' She couldn't bring herself to say her father's name. 'It should be yours.'

'All the same.' There was a crackling sound as Graham put another log on the fire. It was snowing outside. In the moon-light, the drifting flakes looked like falling stars. The garden was still and muffled; the insects quiet. Violet knew that some insects hibernated in winter – *diapause*, it was called.

Last week, she had crouched next to the wooden cross and looked at the beck, which glittered with a thin layer of ice. Underneath the surface, she knew, thousands of tiny, glowing spheres clung to twigs and pebbles. Mayfly eggs. Frozen until the warmer months, when they would continue to grow, cells splitting and changing into nymphs and then, when they were ready, rising up into an undulating, breeding swarm.

It had given her an idea.

The next night had been a full moon. She'd climbed the sycamore tree in the garden, the moonlight silver on the branches, until she could see for miles all around. In the dis-tance, she could just make out the fells, crouched below the star-studded sky. Beyond, she knew, was Orton Hall. Frederick. She closed her eyes and pictured him sleeping in Father's bedchamber. Then, she focused as hard as she could, until her whole body pulsed with energy. There it was again, that gold glint. It had always been there, she now realised, shimmering under her skin, brightening every cell of her body. She just hadn't known how to use it.

In the summer, it would begin. She pictured the Hall, her father's things – his precious furniture, scarred and black with rot, the globe on his desk eaten away. The air shimmering with insects, in a swarm that grew and grew each year, until there was no escaping it.

And Frederick. Trapped there alone.

He would never forget what he had done.

'Oh! Almost forgot. Presents,' Graham was saying, unbuckling his school rucksack. 'All the way from Harrow library.'

'Did you steal these?' she asked, as he handed her two heavy books: a great tome on insects, and another on botany.

'They haven't been borrowed since before the war,' he said. 'No one is going to miss them. Trust me.'

'Thank you,' she said. They sat in silence for a moment, listening to the logs spitting on the fire.

'Have you thought any more about what you might do?' Graham asked. A couple of the villagers had paid her to help with their farm animals. One of them kept bees, and was aghast when she insisted on tending to the hive without a beekeeping suit. So far, she'd been able to make enough to keep herself in bread and milk. Winter would be difficult, though. The greengrocer was looking for a shop girl. She'd thought about applying. Her dreams of becoming an entomologist seemed very distant indeed.

'A little,' she said, fingering the cover of the book on insects. *From Arthropods to Arachnids*, it was called.

'Don't worry,' said Graham. 'Once I'm a rich lawyer, I'll pay for you to learn all about your blasted bugs. Promise.'

Violet laughed.

'In the meantime, I'll put the kettle on,' she said. She went over to light the stove, pausing to look out of the small window. A crow was watching her from the sycamore, the moon lighting on the white feathers in its coat. It made her think of Morg.

She smiled.

Somehow, she felt certain that everything would be all right.

53

KATE

Kate looks out at the garden while she waits for her mother to arrive.

The winter sun gilds the branches of the sycamore tree. The tree is like its own village, Kate is learning. Home to robins, finches, blackbirds and redwings.

And, of course, the crows – a comforting presence, with their familiar dark capes. The one with the speckled feathers often comes to the window to accept some titbit from the kitchen. At those moments, when she feels the glossy beak nudge against her palm, Kate has the overwhelming feeling that she is exactly where she is supposed to be.

The sycamore hosts insects, too, although many of them have burrowed away from the cold, sheltering in the ridged cracks of the sycamore's trunk, the warm soil beneath its roots.

She is still for a moment, listening. It is strange, to think she's spent all her life cringing away from nature. From who she really is. It is as if she had been in hiding – like the insects – dormant and docile, until she came to Weyward Cottage.

There could be others like her, in need of waking.

She told me of other women, across the land, Altha had written. *The Devices and the Whittles.*

Perhaps one day, after the baby is born, Kate will find them. She will go south, to Pendle Hill, where the land curves up to meet the sky. Where women were ripped from their homes, centuries ago. Perhaps something has survived, in the dark, hidden places where men dare not look. But for now, she is grateful – for her mother, for Emily.

And for Violet.

Snowflakes are falling onto the little wooden cross underneath the sycamore. She isn't sure what is buried there, though she has a suspicion the grave is more recent than she originally thought.

She thinks of Altha's friend, Grace. And of Violet's note. *I hope she can help you as she helped me.* Some secrets, she's decided, can stay just that – secret.

Kate feels the locket under her shirt, warm against her skin. The key is safe inside, along with a small curl of a feather that she retrieved from the floor that night, spangled with broken glass.

The police arrested Simon in London, charging him with assault. There is to be a hearing next year, at the courthouse in Lancaster. The police have warned her that even if he's found guilty, Simon could be out in two years. Sooner, probably, with good behaviour. She is working on a victim personal statement for the trial, though she dislikes that label. She is not a victim, but a survivor.

'Are you worried he'll come back here? When he gets out?' Emily asked her.

Kate had thought of how he looked that night, clutching his ruined face while feathers swirled in the air. Powerless, once she had robbed him of his only weapon: her fear.

'No,' she had told Emily. 'He can't hurt me anymore.'

*

Tyres crunch on snow. Then, the soft chime of the doorbell.

Her mother is smaller than she remembers: there are creases around her eyes and her hair is threaded with silver. She is wearing a striped beanie Kate gave her one Christmas years ago, when she was a teenager. Along with her luggage she holds a bouquet of pink roses, crisp from the airport.

There is a moment when neither of them speak. Her eyes go to the wreath of bruises at Kate's throat; the dome of her stomach.

Together, they begin to cry.

Two days later. The first, searing clench of her womb.

'I can't do this,' she gasps, curled on her side. 'I can't.'

'Yes,' says her mother, as she calls for an ambulance. 'You can.'

And then, she is doing it. Her muscles tensing, her blood surging.

There is the warm flood of her waters breaking, then the contractions – bright waves of pain. She has the feeling, as she crouches on her hands and knees in Aunt Violet's kitchen, that the animal part of her brain has taken over.

Her daughter moves quickly through her body, ready to leave the dark sea of the womb behind. Ready to feel sunlight, to hear birdsong. As she slips in and out of lucidity, her body humming with pain and power, Kate thinks of these things, and more, that she will show her daughter. The crows that call from the sycamore tree. The insects that skim the surface of the beck. The world and all its wild ways.

The next Weyward girl is born on Aunt Violet's floor, the same floor that sparkled with snow and feathers and broken glass, in a rush of blood and mucus.

She smells of the earth, of damp leaves and rich clods of soil, of rain, of the beck's iron tang.

Kate cries as she touches the tiny fingers, the silky strands of hair. The glowing curve of her cheek. The dark blue of her eyes. The cottage is loud with her cries. With life.

Kate names her Violet.

Violet Altha.

EPILOGUE

August 2018

Violet switched off the television in her bedroom. She'd been watching a David Attenborough programme on the BBC. A rerun. *Life in the Undergrowth*, it was called. This episode had been about insect mating rituals. Not her favourite topic, really. The act always seemed quite brutal, even in the insect world. She decided to read, instead. She still had a stack of *New Scientist* magazines sitting on her bedside table, gathering dust.

First, she really had to open the window, get some air in. The cottage was absolutely boiling in hot weather – and yet Graham had still been on at her to get the windows double-glazed. Fat chance of *that*. She could already barely hear a damn thing when they were shut.

Poor Graham. He'd been dead for nearly twenty years now. Heart attack, like their father. She supposed all those long hours of writing affidavits in an airless, high-rise office hadn't helped. She was always telling him he needed more nature in his life.

She remembered the bee brooch – gold, the wings set with crystals – he had given her before she went off to university to take her first degree in biology. She had been nervous, fearing that, at the age of twenty-six, she'd be too different to fit in with the other students.

But, as Graham said when he handed her the brooch in its pretty green box, perhaps being different wasn't such a bad thing after all. Perhaps it was something to be proud of.

At first, the prospect of being away from Weyward Cottage terrified her: she'd taken a room in a ladies' boarding house run by a formidable woman by the name of Basset ('Her bite's even worse than her bark,' the residents used to joke) who charged her thirty shillings a week for a damp room with an unreliable tap. She would lie awake in her rickety single bed, listening to the pipes groan in the wall, and clasp the brooch tight in her hand, imagining she was in her garden, watching bees dance through the helleborine.

Later, she took the brooch with her everywhere. This way, no matter where she was – in Botswana, tracking the Transvaal thick-tailed scorpion, or in the Khao Sok rainforest in Thailand studying Atlas moths – she was never far from home.

She opened the window, a task that seemed to take an inordinately long time. Afterwards, Violet's arms shook from the effort. They really were quite pathetic, now. She still got a shock, sometimes, when she looked in the mirror. With her thin, weedy limbs and her stooped back, she rather resembled a praying mantis.

She heaved herself back into bed. She looked for her reading glasses, which she normally left perched on top of the tower of reading material on her bedside table. They weren't there. Damn. The girl from the council must have moved them. It was ridiculous, really – Violet didn't need some stranger in her house, fetching her cups of tea and wanting to tidy up. Last week, she'd asked if she might help 'Mrs Ayres' out by cleaning out the attic.

'Absolutely *not*,' Violet had barked, touching the necklace under her shirt.

No reading tonight, then. Well, that was all right. She might just look out of the window. It was half past nine, but the sun was only just beginning to sink in the sky, turning the clouds rosy. She could hear the birds, singing at the top of the sycamore. The insects, too: crickets, bumblebees. They made her think of Kate, Graham's granddaughter. Her great-niece.

She remembered the first time she saw Kate, at Graham's funeral. Violet had been so consumed by grief that she was barely aware of Graham's son and his wife, their little daughter. She'd have been about six, then. A tiny thing, with watchful eyes under her mop of dark hair. There was something familiar about her; the coltish legs, the sharp angles of her face. The prim white socks streaked with mud, the leaf quivering in her hair.

Even then she didn't see it.

Violet had long accepted that the Weyward line would end with her death. The only daughter she would ever have – or the feeble beginnings of her – lay buried under the sycamore tree. Frederick was paying for what he had done – she felt a dark flush of delight every time she thought of him at Orton Hall, besieged by mayflies – but she couldn't change what really mattered. The line that had continued for centuries, flowing as surely as the gold waters of the beck, was coming to an end. And there was nothing Violet could do about it.

But after the wake, Graham's son, Henry, and his wife had come to Violet's for tea. Henry was so like Graham: even the way he leaned forward as he listened to her, face furrowed with concentration. He enjoyed her story about travelling to India in the 1960s, to undertake a field study of Asian giant hornets (she still held the record for the only person who had held one without being stung).

She'd rather forgotten about the child, who was playing outside, until she heard her murmuring through the window.

'There you go,' the girl was saying. 'See, told you I wouldn't bite.'

Who on earth was she talking to? Violet opened the window and poked her head out. Kate was sitting cross-legged in the garden, looking down at something she was holding in her hand. A bumblebee.

Violet felt tears spring to her eyes, a lightness in her chest. She had been wrong, for all these years. Later, when neither Henry nor his wife were looking, she had unpinned the bee brooch from her kaftan and pressed it into the girl's hand.

'Our little secret,' she'd said, staring into the wide, dark eyes that matched her own.

Violet liked to think that one day, it would lead Kate back to the cottage. To who she really was.

After everyone left and the cottage was quiet again, Violet sat by her window, gazing out at her garden. Joy twisted into pain as she thought of the young girl she had been when she had first arrived here: motherless and afraid, thighs bright with blood. She looked at the cross under the sycamore tree, now crooked with age.

She let it go. The guilt that had grown, like a weed around her heart.

Two years after Graham's death, Violet had woken from a terrifying nightmare. Her heart drummed in her chest and her skin was filmed with sweat. She clutched desperately at the dream, but only fragments remained: the red streak of a car approaching her nephew and his daughter, a scream tearing the air. A man, tall and lion-haired, eyes slitted with rage.

A man who wanted to hurt Kate.

The old words, traced by her fingers countless times, hummed in her blood.

Sight is a funny thing. Sometimes it shows us what is before our eyes. But sometimes it shows us what has already happened, or will yet come to pass.

It was as if Altha was speaking to her across centuries. Telling her that Kate was in danger.

It was 2 a.m. – dawn just a hint of silver at the horizon – but Violet got up and dressed immediately. She drove through the morning, all the way down to London, accompanied by one of the crows – the one that carried the sign – flying ahead like a lodestar.

She reached East Finchley, where her nephew and his family lived, just before 8 a.m. No one answered the door when she rang the bell.

Violet got back in the car, for the first time wondering if it hadn't been a little mad, tearing across the country like this. But then she thought of the cross under the sycamore. She had already lost her daughter. Kate was her second chance – she couldn't let anything happen to her.

Where were they? It was a Thursday. Of course – on the way to school.

She parked near the house and sent the crow ahead, to be her eyes and ears in the sky. Her heart thudded with relief when the bird found her nephew and his little girl a few streets away, approaching a zebra crossing. But then she saw a car turning onto the street and ice brushed her spine.

It was the same red car from her dream.

Henry and Kate were already crossing the road. The car was getting closer.

Violet had to do something.

She closed her eyes, focusing on the gold glint she'd discovered inside herself, all those years ago.

As the crow called to her great-niece, Violet felt its cry in every beat of her heart, in every cell. Her only hope was that Kate did, too. She had to pull her away from that car, from the cruel-faced man she was certain was inside.

At first it seemed like it would work. The girl stopped and turned, gazing at the trees overhanging the road. But the car wasn't slowing down.

Get off the road. Hurry!

The crow took flight, and Violet saw Henry run back to his daughter. She saw him shout, then shove Kate out of the way. Rubber sang on metal as the driver hit the brakes.

But it was too late.

The sun lit on Henry's face for one brief moment, before his body crumpled underneath the car. The trees and the road swam together, a blur of green, white and red.

After the peal of the sirens had died away, Violet started the engine and drove back to Cumbria. For the whole journey back, the accident played itself across her vision, again and again. Henry, risking his life to keep his daughter safe.

He was a good man, not like Violet's own father.

Even if Violet hadn't been there, he would have done anything to defend his child. He would have kept her away from the cruel-faced man. But Violet had never imagined such a possibility, that a father could be capable of such love.

So she interfered, and in trying to save Kate, had instead put Henry in harm's way.

And now he was dead.

A strange, animal keening filled her ears. It took her a moment to realise that it was the sound of her own weeping.

*

Violet didn't go to Henry's funeral. How could she face his wife and daughter, after what she had done?

The years rolled on, and it was easier not to put pen to paper, not to pick up the phone. Violet comforted herself by picturing her great-niece growing up. She imagined the skinny child maturing into a young woman, with the dark hair and glittering eyes of her forebears. A strong young woman, Violet told herself, in spite of her loss – reaching for life the way a plant reaches for the sun.

She'll be eleven now, starting secondary school.

Eighteen. Headed to university. Science, perhaps, like me. Or English, if she likes to read.

She still dreamed of the cruel-faced man, the driver of the car. Perhaps, she told herself, she really *had* spared the girl a fate worse than the loss of her father. Perhaps she *had* been right to intervene.

Henry had loved his daughter. Maybe he'd have understood what Violet had done.

Recently, Violet had had the disturbing realisation that she was old. In fact – both her parents having died relatively young – she was the oldest person she'd ever known. (Apart, of course, from Frederick. He really was like a cockroach clinging to the underside of a rock.) Her skin and muscles seemed to be loosening from her bones, preparing to abandon ship. Before falling asleep each night, in that strange half-light between waking and dreaming, she had begun to wonder if she would still be there come morning.

Like a once bright fire burning to embers, her life was coming to an end.

She was running out of time to see her great-niece.

She'd hired a private investigator to track Kate down. He'd found an address, and Violet had been so thrilled that she'd braved the long drive down to London the next day. It was raining, and as the countryside passed in a green blur, her heart ached at the thought of a similar journey made so many years before.

But this would be different. A happy occasion.

She imagined embracing her great-niece, admiring the life she'd created. (A brilliant career, a beautiful home – filled with plants and animals, perhaps children, a kind man to share her bed. Two crickets, singing in harmony.) Sunshine broke through the clouds, making crystals of the raindrops on her windscreen. She touched the locket under her shirt and her heart swelled.

But her excitement faltered as she pulled up outside Kate's address. A block of flats.

Later, Violet would pinpoint this as the moment she knew something was very wrong. How could Kate be happy in this soot-stained place, the air warm with rubbish and exhaust? There wasn't a single note of birdsong, a single blade of grass.

But she hobbled carefully out of the car, forcing a smile.

A happy occasion.

'Hello – is Kate here?' There was something familiar about the man who answered the door. He wore an expensive-looking bathrobe, and Violet flushed at the realisation that she'd interrupted her great-niece on a Sunday. Was this man her husband, boyfriend? She looked at him more closely. His hair was a tawny sort of gold, rather like a lion's pelt. His narrowed eyes were faintly pink, as if he'd had too much to drink the previous evening.

'No. There's no Kate living here,' he said, though the set of his mouth told Violet he was lying. There was something cold in his voice. It made her think of Frederick.

She began to apologise, flustered – but he shut the door before she could get the words out.

Later, in the car, Violet realised why he looked familiar.

He was the cruel-faced man from her dream long ago, with the golden hair and livid eyes.

The world fell away as she realised.

She'd glimpsed *two* events from Kate's future, not one – the car accident that killed her father and then, many years later, the meeting of this man. The man who wanted to – perhaps already had – hurt her.

Just like her mother before her, Violet had thought she could change the course of the future as easily as tearing out the pages of a book. She'd thought she could save her great-niece.

She'd been wrong.

She hadn't saved Kate from anything.

But Violet was determined to make things right, while she still had breath in her body.

The day after her trip to London, she made an appointment to see a solicitor. It was past time she made a will.

At the solicitor's office, she remembered the bee brooch she had given to Kate when she was small. Perhaps Kate had lost it; perhaps she didn't even remember Violet – the eccentric old woman she'd met only once. The woman who had disappeared from her life, all those years ago.

But now Violet could make amends. She would give Kate her legacy.

She would give her a new life. Away from him.

'When the time comes,' she instructed her solicitor. 'Make sure you speak to my great-niece directly.'

The light was fading outside. She squinted at her watch: it was half past ten already. Who knew where the last hour had gone. Time was funny like that, Violet thought. Speeding up and slowing down at the strangest of moments. Sometimes, she had the odd sensation that her whole life was happening at once.

Violet took off her necklace and put it on the bedside table. She rolled over onto her side, facing the window. The sun was disappearing behind the sycamore tree now, turning the garden red and gold. She closed her eyes and listened to the chatter of the crows. She was so tired. Darkness pulled at her, gentle as a lover.

She felt something brush her hand and opened her eyes. It was a damselfly, its wings fiery with the sunset. How pretty.

Her eyelids drooped. But something was tugging at her, keeping her awake.

Sighing, she sat up in bed. Reaching over to the bedside table, she tore a piece of paper out from her notebook. She hesitated for a while, thinking of what to write. Best keep it simple, she thought. To the point.

She scrawled the sentence down quickly, then rolled up the paper and put it inside the locket of her necklace.

She stowed the necklace safely in her jewellery box. Just in case.

The connections between and among women are the most feared, the most problematic, and the most potentially transforming force on the planet.

Adrienne Rich

Acknowledgements

When I was seventeen, finishing my final year of high school, my English teacher took me aside. 'Whatever you do', she said, eyes bright with passion, 'promise me you'll keep writing.'

Mrs Halliday, I've kept my promise. Thank you so much for nurturing my love of stories. I've taken the liberty of naming one of my characters in your honour. I hope you don't mind.

Felicity Blunt, my brilliant agent: your email changed my life. Thank you for making this a better novel, and for making me a better writer. Much gratitude to everyone else at Curtis Brown – particularly foreign rights marvels, Jake Smith-Bosanquet and Tanja Goossens. Thank you also to Sarah Harvey and Caoimhe White. Many thanks also to Rosie Pierce for her endless support and patience.

Alexandra Machinist, my US agent – I'll never forget that incredible phone call in March 2021. Thank you so much for your support.

Carla Josephson and Sarah Cantin: I couldn't have wished for better editors. I so treasure our working relationship, and the magic you've worked on this novel. It has been an absolute joy.

Thank you to everyone at Borough Press and St. Martin's. I have been privileged to have such incredible teams on both sides of the pond. So many talented people have worked so hard on *Weyward*. At Borough Press, a huge thank you to my lovely publicist, Amber Ivatt, and to Sarah Shea, Maddy Marshall, Izzy Coburn, Sarah Munro and Alice Gomer in sales and marketing. Thank you to Claire Ward for the stunning UK jacket design. Thank you also to Andrew Davis for the incredible proof design and book trailer. In production, thank you to Charles Light and Sophie Waeland.

At St Martin's, I'm particularly grateful to Jennifer Enderlin, Liza Senz, Anne Marie Tallberg, Drue VanDuker and Sallie Lotz. Thank you also to my incredible marketing and publicity team: Katie Bassel, Marissa Sangiacomo, Kejana Ayala. Thank you to Tom Thompson and Kim Ludlam for the beautiful ARC design and graphics. In production, thank you to Lizz Blaise, Kiffin Steurer, Lena Shekhter and Jen Edwards. Thank you so much to Michael Storrings for my gorgeous US jacket design.

I'm also very grateful to my excellent copy-editors, Amber Burlinson and Lani Meyer.

I'm hugely grateful to everyone at Curtis Brown Creative, but especially Suzannah Dunn, my incredible tutor; Anna Davis; Jennifer Kerslake; Jack Hadley and Katie Smart. And, of course, my lovely fellow students – thank you for your wonderful feedback and support.

Thank you to Krishan Coupland, whose encouraging comments on a very early draft of this novel inspired me to keep going.

I've been lucky in that I've been surrounded by those who believed in me from a very young age. My parents and step-parents – thank you for investing countless hours into my love of reading and writing.

My Mum, Jo. You inspire me every day with your strength and resilience. I'm a feminist because of you. Thank you so much for supporting me every step of the way. And, of course, for reading (and discussing) this novel so many times. I don't know what I'd do without you.

Brian, I couldn't imagine a more supportive stepfather. Thanks for all your help and encouragement over the years.

My Dad, Nigel – thanks for instilling me with your strong sense of justice, and with your determination. And of course, thank you for reading this book!

Otilie, my stepmother (and another early reader!). Thank you for all your support, and for introducing me to some of the novels that inspired this one – including, particularly, *The Blind Assassin* and *Alias Grace* by Margaret Atwood.

My sister, Katie – you have always been my rock. Thank you for getting me through the bad times. The next one's for you.

My brothers. Oliver – thank you so much for reading this novel. I can't wait to see what you do with your own love of writing. Adrian – thank you for your faith in me, and for always making me laugh.

My grandparents, Barry and Carmel. Your book-filled home is my sanctuary. Grandpa, thank you for your sharp wit (and your red pen). I'm thrilled to be following in your footsteps. Nana, thank you for your brilliant stories and your constant encouragement.

My grandparents, John and Barbara – I wish you could have read this book.

My step-grandmother, Emöke. You've always inspired me so much. Thank you.

To Mike and Mary – I can't ever thank you enough for welcoming me into your beautiful home in Cumbria, where the first draft of this novel was written. Thank you for sheltering me during a pandemic and comforting me when I was so far from my family in Australia.

Ed – the first reader of this novel. I couldn't have written a single word without your love and support.

Clare, Michael and Alex – thank you for the runs together, the wine and the laughter.

My wonderful friends. I feel fortunate to know you all. But I must make special mention of Gemma Doswell and Ally Wilkes, brilliant writers themselves. Thank you for your incredible feedback – and your patience during a few panic attacks!

There was a time in my life when the writing of this novel – or indeed of any novel – seemed very much in doubt. I owe huge thanks to the medical staff who treated me after my stroke in 2017. To the doctors and nurses of the Moorfields Eye Hospital, Royal London Hospital, University College Hospital London and St Bart's Hospital: you have my endless admiration and gratitude.